"Mistaken Identity"

By Molly Gambiza

For Jennifer Hunt

Thanks for your
interest!

Molly Gambiza

www.mollygambiza.co.uk

First published in Great Britain as a softback original in 2005

This softback edition published in 2014

Copyright © Molly Gambiza 2005

The moral right of this author has been asserted.

All rights reserved.

All characters and events in this book, other than those clearly in the public domain, are fictitious and any resemblance to real persons, living or dead, is purely coincidental.

No part of this publication may be reproduced, stored in a retrieval system, or transmitted, in any form or by any means, without the prior permission in writing of the publisher, nor be otherwise circulated in any form of binding or cover other than that in which it is published and without a similar condition including this condition being imposed on the subsequent purchaser.

Typeset in Sabon LT Std and BlackJack

Editing, design and publishing by UK Book Publishing

UK Book Publishing is a trading name of Consilience Media

www.ukbookpublishing.com

ISBN: 978-1-910223-01-7

About the Author

Molly Gambiza was born in Uganda. She now lives in the UK with her husband and their two sons.

Her passion for books is what inspired her to put her own thoughts in writing to share with others readers.

True colours was her first novel.

Dedication

I dedicate this book to the three important men in my life: *my husband* and *our two sons.*

Acknowledgement:

I thank my family for their encouragement, support and understanding. Writing requires time, silence and concentration. I get all that from my family. Thank you.

My Editor Ruth Lunn, thank you for giving my manuscript a makeover.

Chapter One

As Denise sat on her window sill, she scanned her mother's compound. People were busy preparing a gazebo for her marriage ceremony. Her eyes rested on her uncle.

She blinked back the tears. How dare he! A marriage to someone she hates?

It will never work, she told herself.

If it weren't for her uncle, she wouldn't be in this situation. He'd gone ahead and accepted a marriage on her behalf as if she'd no mind of her own. How dare he force her to marry this man against her will?

The thought of marriage and what went with it made her hair stand out.

Marriage? She groaned. How was she going to spend the rest of her life looking at the man she hated and had no feelings for?

He was rich, no doubt about it. But money was nothing in a marriage without love. Love binds a marriage together.

She heard someone laughing. The voice rang a bell in her head. She squinted her eyes. Oh no! It was her Aunt Meredith. She was here to teach her about the requirements of a good marriage. She was a good aunt. She fought her case right from the start. "Richard! Leave the girl alone. Let her fall in love naturally," she had told her brother.

"Fall in love? This man is an answer to our problems. I am in charge of these children. Don't you dare interfere, Meredith," he thundered.

Denise sighed. She wasn't interested in what her aunt had to say. She left the window sill and dived under her bedcovers.

A few minutes later came a knock on her door.

Denise ignored the knock and bit into her pillow. She let her tears flow. She wasn't ready for this marriage. Her dreams had been shuttered.

What for?

"Listen, Denise," her uncle had said. "Your dowry will look after your poor family. Think about that, child. Your brothers need a good education. Have you thought about that, Denise?"

"But Uncle Richard, I don't love Desmond," she had cried out.

"That's rubbish! What is love if your marriage to Desmond will put a meal on the table and knowledge into your brothers' heads?

"I have already accepted him in this family and the dowry has come at the right time. I will invest it for the boys. I don't trust your mother. She will squander it on new clothes and hairstyles."

A loud knock cut through her thoughts.

"Denise, open this door. It's Aunt Meredith. We need to talk women stuff."

Denise ignored her but the knock made her more furious than ever. She was secretly relieved when the knocking stopped. She heard Annabella talking to her aunt.

"I think she is in the shower. Why don't you wait in the lounge? Why, I've prepared your favourite drink, aunt."

Meredith gathered her niece on her bosom. "You know how to reach my heart, Annabella," she said as she sipped on gin and tonic.

"Make yourself comfortable, I'll be right back." She smiled at her aunt.

CHAPTER ONE

The house was crawling with guests. Annabella bumped into another group.

"Annabella! There you are. Where can we find something to eat?"

She ignored them without even glancing in their direction. "First things first," she thought as she knocked on her sister's bedroom door.

"Denise, please open for me. I have something for you."

Denise sighed as she opened the door. She looked at her sister who handed her two parcels. "What is it?"

"One way to find out Denise – open them."

Denise opened the bigger package first. She glared at her sister. "I can't honestly wear this. It will encourage him. I don't want his talons near me. Take them back. I hope you have a receipt."

Annabella glared back. "So you would rather wear those-tent like knickers mother buys us? Only the other day I gave birth to a sanitary towel on a zebra crossing. I almost died there on the spot when this git blared his horn and said, 'well-done girl'! About time someone put traffic lights on this crossing. Where is amber and green? I could wait here forever.

"I was about to lift my skirt for a stinging insult when this woman stopped me. 'Don't even try, young lady. I recommend tampons. They give you all the confidence.' I told her I was still a virgin. She said to me, 'God bless your innocent soul then,' as she pushed some cash in my hands. 'Nothing holds better than "Always ultra with wings".' And she was gone. I never had a chance to thank her or ask her name. I used the money to buy more decent lingerie for you. But I don't know why I bothered."

Denise reached for her twin sister's hand. "I am sorry. I will wear them but not for Desmond." She hugged her sister.

"You poor soul!"

She opened the second package.

She looked at her sister with tears in her eyes. "It's beautiful! A

3

jigsaw pendant! Wow! Annabella! Thank you sis. I'll treasure it."

Annabella smiled at her sister. "You are my sister and best friend. You deserve it. I've the other part. When put together, it's one heart."

"Oh Annabella!" she cried.

"Don't cry, sis. You will be ok."

Denise glared at her. "Would you be ok if you were marrying someone you are not in love with? A man who will look at you twenty-four hours a day and still know why you married him in the first place? Oh Annabella. I can't bear it."

"I am sorry Denise. I know what you are going through. I am 'hurting too'." She dare not look into her sister's eyes. She gulped. "If... it doesn't work, come home, all right?"

Denise stuffed her fists in her mouth and sobbed.

"Shh shh, you will make yourself ill if you carry on crying like this."

Denise wiped her eyes. She needed time to think this marriage through. It was her life after all.

"I need to be on my own, Annabella. I'd like you to do me a favour. Look after mother and our little brothers. I will be ok."

Annabella's throat tightened. She burst out. "I will miss you, sis. You are my only friend."

"Nothing has changed. You are still my sister and friend. I will miss you though. Now, go and keep Aunt Meredith entertained. I don't want to see her yet..."

"Don't worry. I topped her up with her favourite drink." She giggled.

The sisters hugged. "Desmond loves you. Don't forget that."

"I know but let's not talk about Desmond. I feel tired." She yawned.

Annabella got the message. "I'll keep the guests away from your room."

Denise nodded. "Thank you and take care of yourself."

CHAPTER ONE

"You still have three days, sis. We shall talk, right?"

"You are right."

As soon as the door shut behind Annabella, Denise reached for her handbag. She needed fresh air, she decided. She opened her door slightly. She looked left and right. She could hear her mother talking to Aunt Meredith. Where was her uncle now? She better not bump into him or other guests who have travelled a long distance for her wedding.

She escaped through the back door. She didn't bother to look back. She would be back before they missed her.

She waved down a minibus. She jumped on without asking how much to her destination.

She'd been fully occupied with her thoughts, she forgot herself completely. She was brought back to the present when the conductor asked for her fare.

She looked at him. She looked around her. She'd no idea where she was.

"Where is this place?" she asked with fear in her voice.

"This is Masaka."

"What? What the hell are you talking about?" She calculated in her head. "That's eighty kilometres."

"That's right and this is our last stop."

She bit her bottom lip. "How much?" she asked, knowing she didn't have enough money to pay.

"It's 3000 shillings, Madam."

Her nostrils flared. "That's daylight robbery. I don't have all that money. You will have to take me back so I can get your money."

"Don't play games with me, young lady. Just pay up."

The minibus was now overcrowded by marketers, selling this and that, poking roast meat in passengers' faces and armpits, singing kikumi kikumi. One woman screamed out when she discovered she was only holding her handbag strap. "Where is the

5

rest of my handbag? Please!" she sobbed. All the attention was diverted to the screaming woman.

That's when Denise escaped without paying. She dare not look back, she thought as her heart raced. She held on to her own handbag. All she had was 2000 shillings.

"This will take me back but not quite, I will walk the rest of my journey," she said as she waved for another minibus. She didn't want to make the same mistake. She told the conductor when she needed to get off.

"That's 2000 shillings, Madam."

She paid straight away. She knew she would have to walk twenty miles to get back home. What made her forget herself was the devil himself...or it was some kind of warning.

When it was time to get off the minibus, her heart raced. It was dark already. She kissed her pendant. "I love you, sis."

She walked briskly hoping there were no wild animals around.

She had just covered about five miles when, without a warning, right next to her was this car.

The driver was telling her to jump in.

Denise's heart raced. "Over my dead body!" She knew what game he was playing. "A lift? That's easy access to my virginity. Stupid fool!" She gathered her long skirt and ran. She dare not look back but she wanted to be sure she wasn't being followed. She looked back. To her horror, the man was running after her. "Jesus of Nazareth! Help me!" she wheezed. She fell several times and picked herself up but she dare not give up. Now she was running in the wrong direction, in the middle of a forest. Her foot twisted, she lost her balance and fell. She picked herself up. Her handbag went flying. She ignored it. She had no time to retrieve it. She was now frightened. She crawled into a thick bush not bothering what could be sheltering in there. She feared her breathing would give her away. She held her breath but kept her eyes open. She heard footsteps pass her hiding place. She dare not move. Her ankle was hurting like crazy. She heard the footsteps again coming towards her. Now she was sure that this man was a murderer or a rapist. For a start, he was now moving like a thief. He wasn't calling out for her, reassuring her that she would come to no harm.

She heard him swear.

"Bitch! Women!"

She could see him clearly through the leaves. He was only a few feet away from her. She held on to her breath but it was torture. The beating of her heart was another case. She kept still.

The man looked around and finally left but kept on looking back searching with his eyes.

Denise kept her ears open hoping to hear the car engine.

It was at least ten minutes later when she heard a loud scream.

'What...the hell...is that?' Then she heard a man's voice calling for help. Whoever it was, was in agony. She could hear animal noises.

She didn't care about the pain in her twisted ankle.

She just ran. But wherever she turned, she couldn't see civilisation. The only light was the moonlight. It guided her. She was glad for that but the thought of being savaged by wild animals made her shiver with fear. She was so frightened. She wanted her family back. She wanted to marry Desmond, the man she was not in love with.

"Oh Desmond! I will be a good wife to you," she sobbed. She was now out of the forest but had no idea where she was. She dare not give up. She must carry on. She was in agony. She sent a little prayer to her maker to give her directions and protection.

Louise sobbed in her handkerchief. "Annabella? When did you last see her?"

"Louise! The girl has already told you. I blame you for this, Louise. You spoil these children," her brother in law accused.

"What do you mean, Richard? Go on: tell me how I spoil them. You of all people shouldn't be surprised why she has gone missing. She hates Desmond and he knows it. I know he is responsible for Denise's disappearance. He kidnapped her and married her against her will."

"You talk rubbish, woman. Why would he kidnap her? The wedding is only three days away."

"He knows she would change her mind at the last minute. What does he do? Marry her against her will. This kind of marriage is very common and you know it."

"You can't be serious, Louise. Desmond would never do a thing like that."

"He would," Annabella retorted.

Richard looked at his niece. "Get me my car keys. I will find out myself."

"Why don't you call him here?" Louise suggested.

"You are right."

Desmond took the call in his study. "Is it important? I have a house full of guests. I can't just leave them alone." His house was fully packed with guests and caterers all getting things ready for the wedding.

"It's important," Richard informed him.

"I will be there," he said with a tired voice.

Desmond arrived at his in-law's residence. He was taken aback by Louise's distraught face.

Richard didn't waste time. He demanded to know why he married Denise in such a hurry.

"What exactly are you talking about?" Then it clicked. "Are you playing jokes with me?" He was badly insulted. "I am not responsible." He looked at his mother in law to be. "Are you sure she is not hiding just to avoid this marriage?"

"I know she doesn't love me." He took a deep breath. "I will contact a local newspaper, radio television. I would like her recent photograph." He looked at his mother in law to be. "Believe me, I don't know where Denise is."

Louise bit her lower lip. She reached to her mantelpiece. She handed him Denise's photograph.

He looked at her straight in the eye. He could see accusation in her eyes. "I am not responsible but I will help you find your daughter."

He turned to Richard. "I guess the wedding is over. You know what my next step is. You are all frauds," he hissed under his breath. He left without a backward glance.

Richard shivered. Desmond wants his dowry back, he thought.

He looked at his sister in law. "Is he still your number one suspect?"

"I don't know what else to think. It's all your fault. Denise didn't want this marriage."

"You know why I arranged this marriage."

"Well, we will have to cope without his dowry. You have to return his dowry," she told him.

His next sentence sent her into a coma.

Annabella ran for her mother. "Mother!" She slapped her face.

"She is in shock," Richard said as he poured brandy down her throat.

Louise choked. She looked at her brother in law with hatred. "Get out of my house. Your brother would turn in his grave if he were to see what you have done to his children. You arranged my daughter's marriage to satisfy your greed and hobby?"

All the guests who had been out searching for Denise joined in.

"What the hell is going on?" Meredith demanded. "What was that I heard?"

Annabella filled her in.

Meredith's nostrils flared! "What do you mean you lost it on solitaire? Did you think for one minute that the diamond card would turn into diamonds?"

"We all have faults, Meredith. You of all people should know better. How many times have you been married? Ha! Don't tell me it's not your fault. A wagging tongue like that is enough to turn a man into a monk."

Meredith swallowed her anger. "I will describe my exes for you. My first husband was an alcoholic and impotent."

"I am not surprised," he snorted. "A mouth like that is enough to switch a man off."

Annabella pushed her brothers out of the room. "Not good for your ears."

Eric looked at his brother. "Nicholas! What is impotent?"

"Shut up, Eric! Go to your room."

"Uncle Marcus, impotent," Eric chanted as he climbed the stairs to his room.

Meredith's bust heaved. "I was still a virgin when I married my second husband who turned out worse. He was a gambler like you. He gambled all my clothes except the ones I stood in. The third one cheated on me. I can't stomach a cheating husband."

"My dear brother, you will have to pay back the dowry. You can't have your cake and eat it."

"We don't even have the cake. Denise is missing. She could be dead or... I don't know what else to think," Annabella cried.

Meredith soothed her niece. "Don't cry. We will find her. Let's check all her admirers, right."

Annabella handed her a list.

"Phew! She is popular," Meredith said as she jotted down the address of the next suspect.

Chapter Two

Denise smiled through her tears. She could see some buildings and lights in the distance. Her foot was giving her agony. She tried to remove her shoe but failed. She decided to ignore the pain and walked on.

Abraham Muganzi liked jogging. At five o'clock in the morning, his alarm clock went off. He turned it off and stretched his muscles. Yes, a good run would soothe him, he thought. His two dogs were making a racket outside. What could be the matter? Where were his clothes? He spotted his pants on the lamp shade, his shirt on the door handle; he picked his trousers from the stair. He knew where to find his shoes. It's high time he found someone to clean this place, he thought.

His dogs were barking mad and he could hear someone screaming and calling out for help.

Intruders? He thought as he took two stairs at a time and tripped over his own mess that he never got round to cleaning. "My dogs will teach you a lesson. This is a private property," he said as he released the chain on his front door. To his horror, his dogs were tearing someone to pieces. Shit! "Stop!"

They wagged their tails and licked their master.

He looked at the girl. "Who are you and what are you doing

on my property at this time of the day?"

Don't... hurt... me. I... need help, please," she sobbed.

Abraham didn't know how to handle this girl. She was...a complete mess and her clothes were like shredded paper.

"Hold...on. I will get a blanket." He was gone and back in seconds.

"Now what? I guess I will have to carry you," he said as he gathered her in his arms. She wasn't heavy. He thanked God for that.

"I am sorry about my dogs." He deposited her on a rug that was covered in dog hairs.

Denise wrinkled her nose. The house stank like a sewer.

"I will make you a hot drink. You need it."

Denise found her voice. Her mama's warning came to her mind. "Never accept tea from strangers. They use their thumb to squeeze the teabag or spike it and you will never know what hit you until it's too late." She shook her head. I am fine thank you, except my foot."

"What happened to you?" he asked as he examined her foot.

She blushed with shame. She had never exposed her legs to any man. Now to be seen by this strange man, was humiliating. "I twisted my ankle," she told him.

"I need a sharp knife to cut off my shoe."

"I think you need a doctor. That swelling..." He didn't finish the sentence. He had an idea what was making her leg swell like that.

"I will be back. Don't move. Don't panic."

She sat there massaging her foot. She was in pain. She was tired. She wanted to go back home but...the thought of marrying Desmond... She sobbed. "I am sorry. There is no turning back. I can't marry you Desmond." She sniffed. There would be hell to pay when he found out she was missing. She wondered how long it would take this strange man to fetch the doctor. She was beginning to doze off when she heard voices.

It was a local doctor.

"Let's look at that foot, shall we?"

Denise panicked.

"Don't panic, girl." He examined the swelling. "You need to go to hospital, young lady."

He looked at Abraham. "Any petrol in your truck?"

"What is the matter?" He had an idea but he wanted to be sure.

"Get the truck now and be fast about it."

Abraham hated to be ordered about but...the swelling. He hoped he was wrong, he said as he opened his garage.

"What's your name?" The doctor asked as he eased off the shoe. Her teeth chattering, "De...ni...se," she replied. She was shivering. She was cold and dizzy.

She was rushed to the nearest hospital. It wasn't just a twisted ankle but snake bite as well. Injections were coursing about her body.

Denise had no idea what was happening to her. She was in another world.

Chapter Three

Desmond's telephone was like a switchboard. He took calls one after the other, most of them a waste of time. Denise was a pampered girl. What would she be doing walking alone in the middle of the night? One caller said she spotted her near Masaka boarding a minibus. "Running away from him?" He was pissed off with her and the whole family. He still didn't believe she was missing. She was hiding somewhere. "I will get you no matter what!" he seethed.

He had no idea where to look. He loved her. She hated him. That didn't bother him at all. She would get used to him and maybe love him. He must find her before he went insane.

He stood by his window wondering what step to take next. He had told his guests not to go just in case Denise turned up. Something hit his mind. Was someone holding her for a ransom? If so, why were they not in touch?

His travel agencies were enough to bring his Denise back. A lot of people knew that he was rich and hated him for using his brain to be who he was. He had started with five hundred shillings buying and selling charcoal. When he had saved a bit, he bought himself a wheelbarrow, which he used to transport passengers' luggage from bus terminals to their destinations.

All these tasks were done during his school holidays. His

friends made jokes of him, calling him charcoal boy. He didn't mind. He knew what he wanted and was determined to get it. He never ignored his schoolwork no matter how tired he was.

One day his mother asked him what course he wanted to follow. "Tourism," he had replied with enthusiasm.

"Mother, I will do something that will rest your tired shoulders. I am doing all this for you, mother. You are the only person I love and care for and of course my little sister."

She had smiled at him. "You will swallow those words when you fall in love."

His first job after completing his course had been air ticketing. Then one day he decided to nose around his employer's private files. He wanted to know how much his employer made a year. He had been stunned by the figure. "What the hell am I doing here making my employer rich if I could run my own travel agency?" He knew how to go about it. He knew the business language. "A customer is always right."

By the time he handed in his resignation, his travel agency had been running for six months and was doing well. He stole most of his employer's customers and clients. That's one victory he never forgot.

Desmond Travel Agency prospered and he prospered with it but he lacked one thing in his life. He wanted a wife. He was not short of women but they meant nothing to him. They were just pressure relievers.

Denise was different. He fell in love with her the first time he saw her during her job interview. One minute he was firing questions at her, the next minute he was nursing his hard-on under his desk like a teenager.

She took his breath away. He had to call her back for her second interview. What interview? All he wanted was to gaze at her. When he asked for her hand in marriage, she had laughed at him. "Don't waste your time, man. I am not ready for marriage and when I am ready, it will be someone who sends sparks into my body." He had been insulted by her brutal words and he was determined to have her no matter what it took. He knew one person who would bring her down. He approached her uncle. Number one gambler.

"Why, it's ten cows, a blanket for her mother, a goat for her aunt and the girl is yours."

"Thank you father but I don't have cows. I have cash. I hope you are not offended sir."

"Offended? What a splendid idea! Cash will do fine. Welcome to the Bahiika family."

He took her out on a regular basis just to get to know her better. He knew she hated him. She was marrying him for one reason. He was a businessman. He understood. He wasn't insulted at all. That didn't put him off. He was a man in love. She needed time to get used to him. Yes, he was a patient man. It was during house viewing when she finally smiled at him.

"It's beautiful!"

"You love it?"

She'd hesitated and after a long silence, she walked to the window. "Wow! The view is breathtaking."

He stood behind her. He put his hand on her shoulder. "It's all yours, Denise. I am glad you like it."

She turned round. There was a look in her eyes he had never seen before.

He had to take his chance. He pecked her on her cheek. He was heading for the other cheek when she held his head. She kissed him full on the mouth. He was too shocked, but not for long. His hand dived into her bra. That was a mistake. She had pushed him. "I gave you an inch. You want two feet. I am sorry. I shouldn't have kissed you. Please take me home this minute."

"You can furnish the house the way you want." That was the last time he exchanged words with her.

His mother interrupted his thoughts. "Desmond, there is a woman on the phone for you. She says it's important." She looked at her son. He was hurting. She didn't know what to do to help.

Desmond picked the phone with shaking hands. And not only was he shaking, he was aroused by just thinking about Denise's kiss.

"I don't know whether this will help at all... but I saw the girl you are looking for."

"You saw her?"

"I have just said."

"Where?"

"At Masaka. I remember her correctly because I had to rescue her at some point."

"What do you mean? Was she hurt?"

"No, she didn't have enough money to pay for her journey, so I had to cut my own handbag...to save her."

Desmond was now shaking his head. "There are so many loonies about."

"Why did you have to cut your handbag?"

"What do you think? I screamed that someone had stolen my handbag and all the attention was now on me while your girl escaped. I saw her jump into another taxi heading for Kampala... I have bad news I am afraid."

Desmond's knuckles went ghostly white. "What happened?"

"Don't you listen to the news? A man is critically ill in hospital after being attacked by a leopard."

Desmond breathed in and out. The woman was mad obviously. "What does my girl have to do with this man in hospital?"

"Her handbag was found where the man was attacked. I saw the handbag on television and I recognised it straight away. It's not a cheap handbag and why she didn't have enough money in that handbag which cost more than my yearly income is beyond me."

She took a deep breath. "They are still searching the area. They haven't found her."

Desmond was now sobbing...He knew what handbag the woman was talking about. He had bought it for her. He took a deep breath. "What's your name?"

"Call me Elimila." She gave him her contact number just in case she was needed.

He held the phone for a long time until his mother offered him a brandy. She had been listening into their conversation.

"Drink this. They haven't found her. Maybe she got away. Leopards don't eat people."

"Leopards...are not... the only animals in that area. Oh God!"

"Now, don't lose hope, right? I guess you have to let her parents know."

He dialled the number but his mother cut him off. 'This is not the kind of news you give over the phone. Go to them."

"Mother, I am their main suspect, remember?"

"I know but that doesn't stop you doing the right thing. Go on," Jocelyn told her son.

"I can't. That woman insulted me badly when she accused me of kidnapping her daughter. I will phone her."

Louise held on to Denise's dress against her bosom as she sobbed.

Nicholas held on to his mother. "Please don't cry. Denise is just having a good time saying bye to her friends."

"Saying bye to her friends? Today was supposed to be her wedding day and she is still out there saying bye to her friends? Boys, what am I supposed to do?" She sobbed.

At that moment the phone rang. Eric wheezed into the phone. "Man of the house speaking. Get to the point."

"Eric, call your mother." Louise picked the phone with trembling hands. She cried out.

The boys watched their mother. "What's wrong, mother?"

Nicholas grabbed the phone. "What the hell did you tell her?"

Desmond didn't like that tone from a fourteen year old with hormone problems.

"Listen, Nicholas and listen very carefully." He told him about the news regarding Denise's handbag.

"Thanks for letting us know," he mumbled. "We are still waiting for Annabella. She has gone to Denise's friends to look for her." He hung up before Desmond could ask him who the friends were.

The two brothers comforted their mother. "Mother, you can't just collapse like that. You are our strength now that Dad is gone."

Louise nodded. "You are right. I must go and check the handbag myself. They may be wrong and I hope they are wrong."

Annabella had reached a dead end. She didn't know where else to look. She was so tired and hungry. She crossed the street on Kampala Road to buy herself a drink. As she sipped her drink, she saw two weird looking men eyeing her. They made her uncomfortable. She took her drink in gulps and left the kiosk. She headed for the taxi park. She was too busy, occupied with her thoughts, when the two men she had seen earlier in the kiosk blocked her way.

"Don't scream," they warned her. One man showed her a knife.

She panicked and screamed.

A slap landed on her face. "You sneaky fool bitch on two legs? What did I tell you?" He grabbed her hand. "Now, listen young lady, you will have to behave yourself and follow our instructions."

Annabella had no idea who the men were. She had never seen them before.

She almost jumped out of her skin when they threw a cloth

around her face as they pushed her in a van head first. She was being married against her will. The cloth on her head explained it all. Their granny had told them on numerous occasions how such marriages are conducted. She had told them to be on the look-out. Not to walk on their own when it's late.

Her nerves were now in terror. Her mother would be waiting for her. Denise was missing. What's happening to them? Who is behind all this?

She sobbed and that granted her another slap.

The driver warned his mate not to overdo it.

"You won't be paid if there is a scratch on her body. I am warning you."

"Who is paying you for this?" she demanded.

"You will find out soon. He is a dish. You will never lack anything."

The driver warned his mate to shut up. He hated what he was doing but he needed money urgently. He needed it for poll tax, and why? A man has to plant a few trees of coffee, then the poll tax shoots up. He doesn't even pick a tin full out of them. He shook his head. His wife would skew his balls if she were to find out what he has done to earn him a quarter of a million shillings. Well, she is not likely to find out. He comforted himself as he looked in his driving mirror.

Annabella searched her mind. She had no idea who was behind all this.

She fingered her pendant around her neck. "Please release me. I will pay you. I have money. Please, I beg you. My mother will be worried about me."

"Shut up! Do you know how much we have been paid for this job?" He laughed in her face. "Stop fretting and shut up. Women!"

After a long drive, her abductor opened the door. He hissed in her ear, "If you should mention the slaps I landed on your cheek, your mother is the next victim. A widow and all, needs someone to service her. Don't forget that young lady and I wish you a happy marriage."

She could hear other voices whispering; without a warning, she was lifted off her feet. She kicked and screamed but the person holding her ignored her. Not once did he tell her to shut up. Where was she? Who is he? She pleaded with him. Her abductor remained silent. She sensed they were now inside a house, doors shutting behind them, then she heard running water. Her abductor put her down. A door shut again. She removed the cloth covering her head. She took a step back.

She stared at a woman in her mid forties with a double chin.

"I am Marjorie. I am here to help you with your bath."

Annabella was confused. Was this the person who had carried her from her abductors' van?

No, the person who carried her smelt of aftershave and he had whiskers. She looked at the woman. "Who are you and why am I here?"

The woman giggled. "You don't know why you are here?"

Annabella nodded.

"It's not for me to say. I am only paid to meet your needs. The sooner you have your bath, the sooner you will find out. I am Marjorie. I am pleased to meet you." She introduced herself a second time as if the first introduction wasn't enough.

Louise let herself in the house. "Annabella? Boys?" she called out.

"Annabella is not home yet," Nicholas informed her.

Louise checked her watch. "It's well after nine o'clock." Where was she?

"Maybe she is still searching. Is it bad news?" the boys asked.

"I am not sure yet but I saw the handbag. It's Denise's. I recognised it and her handkerchief with her initials. They are still searching the area. She could be dead, eaten up."

"Stop it, mother!" Nicholas cried out. "She is not dead until we find her body. Just comfort yourself with that. All right?"

"I better let your uncle know."

"There is no need mother. It's his fault. If he hadn't arranged this marriage business, and I mean marriage business, we wouldn't be in this mess. His gambling habits have reduced us to this horrible experience. I am the man of the house. His eyes watered. I will look for my sisters. We don't want Uncle Richard's help."

Nicholas phoned the places where Annabella had been during the day. He received negative answers.

The police weren't interested. "When a girl reaches marriageable age, sudden disappearance doesn't surprise anyone," they told Nicholas.

He put the phone down. He looked at his mother.

"What did they say?"

He gave his mother a comforting look. "They will look into it," he lied to spare his mother. She was heartbroken already; there was no need telling her what the police had said.

Annabella stared at the woman. "Would you wish this kind of treatment on your own daughter?" She didn't wait for the answer. She opened the bathroom door. She cried out when she saw the person standing in front of her.

"Please, don't...I am not ready for this. I want to go home."

The old man grinned at her. "My girl! That's a compliment I will treasure for the rest of my life. I am not your intended. I am a gardener. I am here to show you where your intended is. He is waiting for you."

Annabella held on to the banister and planted her toes on the floor.

"There is no need for that. I will have to carry you. Don't mess with me girl."

She had no escape. All the doors were remote controlled. She thought the place looked familiar but she wasn't quite sure. The doors shut behind them with a click. She felt like a prisoner.

The old man had been leading the way; now he stood aside. "My journey ends here. All the best." He grinned at her.

The room was in darkness. Then the door shut behind her. She could feel someone's presence in the room. She wasn't alone. She trembled with fear. Her heart raced at a speed.

"Denise, I am glad you could make it."

Annabella recognised the voice. "Shit! What games are you playing, you bastard?" She ran her fingers around the walls looking for a light switch. She found one.

She stared at Desmond. "You got it wrong. I am not Denise. You...fool...idiot. Get me out of here, you fool."

He gave her a cold stare. "You think I don't know the difference? You may be identical twins, but I know my Denise. What I would like to know is why you had to run away from me. You thought to make a fool of me, didn't you?"

"I am not Denise," she pleaded with him.

"Denise, I am not a violent man and don't provoke me. If you should try once more, I will not be held responsible for my actions. Now, stop standing there, take a seat."

She ignored him. Her tears were now flowing down her face. She couldn't blame him for thinking she was Denise. Only family members knew the difference. Impossible to tell them apart, her aunt used to complain whenever she looked after them not knowing which one hated milk.

He gave her a weak smile. "Today was supposed to be our wedding day. You didn't turn up obviously but I am glad you turned up for our honeymoon." He reached for her. He was ready for her. "Foreplay my ass!" He was ready.

She kicked and spat and swore. He ignored all that. His mind was made up. "You are my woman now," he whispered into her ear.

"Leave me alone. I am not Denise. If you think I am lying, call my mother."

The grip lessened. He looked at her. "You want me to call your mother on our honeymoon? Denise, you need to grow up and the sooner, the better."

Annabella didn't know how to come out of this nightmare. She used to like her twin sister, but now she was her number one enemy. If she hadn't disappeared, she wouldn't be in this mess. She sobbed but that didn't stop Desmond enjoying his honeymoon. His wet kisses and groaning grated on her nerves. Was this what she would have to endure for the rest of her married life? She knew that there was no turning back. This was a forced marriage. She couldn't change what this animal had done to her. She was now used goods. What she was feeling now was something else. She felt as if she had been run over by a speeding train.

He rested on his elbow and looked at her. "It will get better when you take part in it. What was on your mind? Counting ten green bottles standing on the wall? You'd better take part next time. I can't stand a frigid woman. You are now mine, Denise. I'd better let your family know where you are. Your mother must be pretty worried. That hairdo must be out of shape." He laughed.

"Denise, you come from a confused family. I know you were not missing. You just didn't want to marry me and your family hid you and abandoned that handbag to convince me." He couldn't believe his ears when the detective he had hired informed him where Denise was. He had no choice but to marry her by force. He was not the first one to do this nor would he be the last.

Annabella found her voice. "What handbag?"

"Denise, don't play stupid with me."

"What...handbag? I know Denise had a handbag with her.

24

Please tell me. I am begging you."

"I have heard enough of your games, Denise. You are all frauds in your family. I am not ashamed to point it out. Now, you are my wife. They have my dowry. I have their daughter. It's as simple as that. One thing you should know, Denise, I love you. I have never loved another woman." And with that, he left the room.

Annabella cried until there were no tears left. She stared at nothing in particular but her mind focused on the handbag Desmond mentioned.

She looked around the room hoping to find a phone but there was no phone, only the king size bed where her virginity has been sacrificed. She wanted to die. She had nothing to live for. Her life had been destroyed by mistaken identity. She must die. Who would marry her after this? No man liked used goods. She was now used goods. What a waste of time! All this time she had been saving herself for the right man. What does she end up with? Her sister's husband... She couldn't face the outside or anyone after this humiliation. She walked to the window; they had burglar bars on them and not only that, but a fall from the window would not kill her.

She pulled out the bedside drawers hoping to find aspirins or any sharp objects. All she found was lacy knickers.

"That's your side of bed. I am glad you are getting familiar with your surroundings." He handed her a glass of orange juice.

She received it. She looked at it. She wanted to die. This was her chance.

She emptied it on his face. She waited for his hands to twist her neck. Nothing came. She waited for a blow on her head. Nothing came. She collapsed on the floor and cried.

He took a deep breath. "Denise, do you hate me this much?"

"Leave me alone, you rapist bastard!" she sobbed.

He stared at her with his mouth wide open. "Rapist? I...made love to you. I...made..." Then the realisation of what he had just done hit him. "You never consented. Jesus! You are right. I am...ashamed." He collapsed into a nearby chair. "Please... Denise, forgive me," he sobbed. "Please say something, Denise. Anything."

His mother's voice rang in his head. "Desmond? Do you think your name has been recorded yet? On the judgement day, when God opens the book in which he recorded all the names of those who followed his ways, I want your name to be the first one he calls out." He had grinned at his mother. With his innocent sixteen-year-old voice he had replied, "But mother, you must know your alphabetical order. Desmond Tumwiine comes..."

"Shut up, Desmond," she had screamed at him. "Are you not aware that God gave up his only son to die for our sins? Answering me back with that hormone-syndrome-teenager attitude is one of the sins Jesus died for. Now Desmond, what have you got to say for yourself? Our neighbour thinks you made his daughter pregnant. You forced her into sex. You must marry her at once."

"Which neighbour? I mean... I never...meant to... she provoked me, mother. She really did."

"And you thought to use your worm as a weapon to punish her?"

"But what makes her think I am responsible? The girl is well known as a leg swinger," he had replied to his mother without shame.

She had glared at him and ordered him to read from the book of Genesis to Revelation.

Desmond sighed remembering Samantha the little provocative, sneaky bitch on two legs. She asked for it. She had spread false gossip around the school calling him Mr Incompetent between the sheets even though he had never glanced in her direction.

Well, she had to be taught a lesson. As it turned out, he wasn't responsible for the pregnancy. The kid was the spitting image of their science teacher who happened to be married with three wives and Samantha became wife number four.

He looked at his fiancée/wife...she would never forgive him for this. He messed up big time. Why didn't he wait until they got used to each other?

"Denise? I...don't know what else to say apart from asking for forgiveness."

The following day Annabella met the same woman she had met the previous night.

"Your bath is ready, Mrs Tumwiine."

Annabella said nothing but the cold stare silenced the woman from uttering more nonsense. But not for long.

"Mrs Tumwiine, I have put a bit of salt in your bath. It helps. I thought to let you know in case you feel a bit of sting."

Annabella felt cheap and humiliated. This woman knows what happened to her.

"Now, don't cry. He is not bad at all. You will get used to him." She flashed her a smile. "I will tell you a little secret. I was married against my will as well."

That increased Annabella's sobs.

"You are a strong kid. I am surprised you didn't pass out. In my case I passed out and when I came round, I was expecting the bastard's child. His name is Thomas. Your guide last night. She blinked back the tears. "We have been married for thirty-five years but...I still remember..." She wiped her tears. "It's all wrong. I am on your side," she said remembering the fight she had with her husband last night.

Now Annabella was shaking and throwing up, hoping if there was a child growing inside her it would escape through her vomit.

There was knock on the door. Marjorie answered it. "She is

almost ready, Mr Tumwiine… Is everything ok?"

"Leave us alone, Marjorie and thanks."

Marjorie gave Annabella a worried look.

As soon as the door shut behind Marjorie, Desmond broke down. He saw what he needed to see to know that this girl was not Denise.

The phone call he had made to his in laws left him half man. He was ashamed. He didn't know how to repair the damage. His stupid move had hurt so many people including his mother.

"What were you thinking of, son? I thought you learnt your lesson when I told you to read from Genesis to Revelation after Samantha's incident? I am so ashamed of you, son."

Louise had screamed at him and was threatening to have his ass whipped by the law.

He had comforted himself by telling her that the law was on his side. "You have my dowry, I have your daughter."

"But the wrong daughter, you fool. Didn't she tell you the truth? Didn't she plead with you? I know my daughters. I know she pleaded with you to leave her alone."

"I thought she was lying. I am sorry."

"That's not enough. You have destroyed my daughter's future. Who is going to marry her now?"

"I will," he had replied. "I love her."

"You have no idea what love means. If you did, you would have waited to find out if she was telling the truth. Now we are where we were before. We don't know where Denise is."

"I will find her."

"Don't bother." She hung up.

Now, Desmond looked at Annabella. She was sitting in a bath tab with her arms around her trying to cover her nakedness with a look of terror in her eyes.

"Annabella, I am sorry."

She stared at him without uttering a word. The only communication between them was her fat tears.

"I ...don't know how to apologise to you. I will understand if you don't forgive me. I had no idea you were telling me the truth. I am sorry, Annabella." He touched her ear lobe. The one Louise had told him to check out. Denise was the one with pierced ears. Desmond massaged her ear. "The water is getting cold. Do you want a hand or should I call Marjorie?"

She ignored him. The fat tears told him what she was feeling.

Chapter Four

Louise looked at her brother in law for answers with hatred in her eyes.

"What... do we... do?"

"What can we do? He has to marry her. They both have no choice."

That set Louise's tears in motion. How she wanted to protest that her daughter had a choice. She knew in her heart that Annabella had to go ahead with the marriage. She was already damaged. No other man would respect her after this. She sobbed.

"Now Louise, your tears are not helping at all. We still have to look for Denise, dear," he soothed. She rested on his shoulder. For the first time she found him comforting but it didn't last long.

"Leave my mother alone!"

They turned to see Nicholas standing in the doorway.

He took a step forward. "Don't take advantage of my mother's stress," he told his uncle with a threatening look in his eyes.

"Mother, if there is anything to be done, you go through me. As I said earlier, I am the man of the house from now on. My... father left his brother in charge knowing his family would be safe but how wrong. Look at us now. Why are we in this situation? If you had left Denise alone, Annabella...Annabella...would be here where she belongs. Now, she has no choice but to marry that..."

Nicholas turned to his uncle. "I suggest you leave us alone. You have already caused enough damage."

"You are my responsibility, young boy. You better mind your language," he hissed at him.

Nicholas wasn't going to be pushed aside like that. He had to stand up to his uncle. He didn't like the look he was giving his mother. He should be ashamed of himself. He glared at him. "What have you done for us since father died? I want Denise's dowry back. It must be returned to Desmond at once.'

Richard stared at his nephew. This little puppy has got balls. He was proud of him but he dare not tell him or else he would have triple balls. He sniggered. "But he has Annabella now, you little fool."

He narrowed his eyes at him. "They may be twins, but they are two individuals. I will handle Annabella's dowry but you have to return Denise's. I am giving you one-month. Now, if you'll excuse me, my mother and I have things to discuss."

"I wonder what your father would say if he were to hear you using that tone on me." Richard couldn't believe this little puppy in nappies talking to him like that. But the kid was right. He was ashamed of what he had done. What possessed him to put that money on the gambling table was the devil himself. Nicholas wasn't the only one demanding Denise's dowry. His four wives had turned their backs on him for what he did. He couldn't even afford a hooker. A hooker? He had never paid for such services. Whenever he wanted a change of direction, he went through the right channel but now he couldn't afford wife number five. Five wagging tongues? Phew! His home was like a broadcasting centre. Gossiping and laughing as if it's a laughing competition. No wonder he finds comfort in solitaire. He married nothing but gossip mongers. He looked at his sister in law. She was meant to be mine. She was his to begin with until his brother showed his face.

Nicholas cut through his thoughts. "My father would be proud of me. He opened the front door. If you don't mind, my mother and I have things to discus."

Richard looked at his nephew. He reminded him of his brother. He was exactly like that when they were kids. Always in charge. Taking what was his. He fell in love with Louise first but no, his brother defeated him when he made her pregnant.

He cleared his voice. "You are still a child who needs discipline. I am still in charge. You still have six years before you can call yourself a man." And with that, he poured himself a drink and offered Louise one but she declined.

"I want a sober head. Denise is still out there...missing."

He drained his glass. "Now, that son of a bitch needs a lesson for running off with the wrong daughter."

"I said I would handle my family affairs from now on," Nicholas reminded him.

He ignored him as he punched in Desmond's telephone number.

His mother picked it up. "I am sorry I don't know where he is."

"Don't give me that. He can't just disappear into thin air with my daughter."

"If you must know, my son is not a child who should report to his mother for every move he makes."

"You mean you had no idea about this forced marriage he performed on my daughter?"

"Please spare me a headache. You are not in a position to criticise my son. You are sitting on ten cows, a blanket and one goat. The only thing my son owes you is an apology. He made a mistake. The girls look alike. I am sure even you cannot tell who is Denise and who is Annabella. They look the same."

She was right. They confused him most of the time but recently he identified them by the look they gave him. Denise looked at him with hatred. Annabella gave him a warning look: "Don't you dare arrange my marriage!" Those were the signs he identified them by but he wasn't going to admit it to this woman.

He cleared his voice. "You listen carefully. What your son did was wrong. Mistaken identity or not, he should not have forced her against her will. What kind of an animal is that? When your son gets in touch, tell him to do the right thing. My niece shouldn't have been reported through a stupid phone call. That's not how this kind of marriage is handled, never mind this technology. He will soon be sending me a fax next time or paying the dowry through money gram or Western Union. I expect him to report my daughter in a proper manner. Do you hear me?" He was talking to a dead phone. "Damn!"

The phone rang a few minutes later. "Leave it son, I will take it." Nicholas beat him to it.

"You have a nerve! How dare you! Thank your lucky stars we are not in the same room. I would castrate you. You bastard!"

"May... I... speak... to your uncle?"

"You are talking to the man of the house."

"Give me that phone, Nicholas," Richard ordered.

"You will be hearing from my lawyer, you son of a bitch."

Richard glared at his nephew. "That kind of attitude is not going to help your sister at all. He will take out his frustration on her. You mark my words," his uncle warned.

Chapter Five

"Wakey, wakey, rise and shine," the nurse smiled at Denise."

"How do you feel today?"

"I am thirsty." She tried to sit up but her leg was still painful.

"I will get you a drink but first, let's take your temperature."

"I want to go home." She moaned.

"Where is home?" The nurse asked as she checked her chart. They had no idea who she was except she was called Denise. The only visitor she had received for the last two weeks was this weird looking man. He was not totally weird. He only had to dress properly and remove that facial hair. The man was a complete mess.

Denise looked at the nurse. She half smiled at her. She didn't trust her enough. No one should know why she ended up with snakebite, dog's bite, malaria and a twisted ankle. She was happy she wasn't married to Desmond but she was worried about her family. She must get in touch with them but how? She could hardly move; even if she moved, she didn't have money for the call box. She would have to ask Abraham when he visited her again. He was due an hour earlier. What was keeping him? He was such a character.

"Now, you shouldn't move that leg at all. You need complete rest." She gave her a glass of water and a cocktail of tablets.

The nurse stayed until she had swallowed them all. Patients were fond of hiding medicine under their pillows then topping themselves up when they thought there was no hope.

Denise ate her lunch, which she hated. She hated hospital food especially meat that reminded her of the casualty department. Yuk! She pushed the tray away as Abraham walked in.

"Hi!"

"Hullo!" She gave him a weak smile.

He reached for the tray – waste not – he chewed on a carrot and fed her some of it. "You want to get out of here, don't you?"

She nodded.

"Then you should eat all your food."

"I am not hungry."

"It won't go to waste. My dogs will have you to thank," he said as he folded it in a newspaper and stuck it in his jacket pocket.

That sent Denise into giggles. "You are such a character. What do you do for a living?"

He scratched his bushy beard. "You don't want to know."

"I want to know as long as it's not illegal."

"I have a roof over my head. I grow some vegetables and visit patients in hospitals and end up with their leftovers. What more do I need? I bought you something to read." It was a novel by Jackie Collins.

"Oh Abraham! You shouldn't have."

"You must find this place boring. Her story will tickle you to no end. My sister loves it." He looked at her. "I wonder how you put up with these white walls?"

"Tell me about it. I can't wait to get out of here." Her eyes clouded.

"What's eating you?"

She bit her lip. "I want to phone my mother but I don…"

"Give me her number. I will give her a call if that's what you want…" He looked at her very hard in the face.

"Would you?"

"I just said." He'd been reading her story in the newspapers. The only reason he hadn't been in touch with her family was that some people are entitled to their own privacy. He put himself in her shoes. He knew why she had run away from what's-his-name in the first place. He couldn't reveal her hiding place without her knowledge. He had spoken to the man in particular. A Mr Desmond Tumwiine. "You know where she is?" he had cried out.

"Oh yes but it will cost you and I want to know why you want her so urgently."

"It's none of your business – just name your price, Sir."

"I need to think about it." He had hung up not giving the man a chance to talk him into price negotiating. After his phone call, he had driven to the hospital. One look on Denise's sleeping face told him a lot. She was vulnerable. She was still a child. She needed a friend and protection. He had made up his mind there and then that he would not reveal her hiding place until she gave him her permission. Now she had given him the go-ahead, he would let them know. She is only a child… Is she? She was about to be married.

Why did she choose to run away three days before her wedding?

She had been lucky to escape from that jungle which had left one victim in a coma. Who is he? He wanted to ask her but he had no idea how.

Her voice cut through his thoughts.

"Please let my mother know and there is one problem. I don't…want my…uncle to know where I am."

"Don't worry. I am the master of secrecy." He winked at her.

"Oh I almost forgot." He pulled two fruits out of his pocket. "They are yours."

She beamed at him as she sunk her teeth into a mango.

Nicholas took the call. Now he was in charge of incoming and outgoing calls. His mother was a nervous wreck. The ringing of the phone put her nerves on edge, so he decided he should deal with all the calls.

"I am Nicholas. If you have anything to say to my mother, say it to me."

"It's confidential. Put your mother on the phone."

"Well, you will have to phone back when my mother is in a position to talk to you."

Abraham loved the boy's guts. He took a deep breath. "It's about Denise."

"What about her?"

"I know where she is." He gave him all the details.

"Thank you, Sir. You have no idea what this means to my mother and the rest of the family."

"I have a message from Denise."

"Go on."

"Don't tell her uncle where she is."

"As if I would. Thank you, Sir."

It took Louise, Nicholas and Eric less than an hour to find St Theresa Hospital.

They found Denise's visitor leaving.

"You must be Denise's family. I am Abraham Muganzi. I am glad you are here."

Nicholas gave him a handshake. "Thank you, Sir, for helping my sister."

"It's all right! I'd better get going. She is waiting for you."

Denise gave her mother an "I am sorry" look.

"It's all right baby. I understand your reasons for..."

"I never intended to put you through all that. I meant to come back. I just forgot myself. I never meant to run away." She hugged her brothers. "Where is Annabella?"

Eric opened his mouth but Nicholas was within reach of it. He put his hand over his little brother's mouth.

Denise looked from one to the other. "Where is she?"

"Not now, Denise! You need to recover. Stop fretting. Annabella is all right..."

"She is not all right! I had dreams about her. She is not all right. Please don't spare me anything. I can handle it."

They told her.

"Bastard!" she sobbed.

"Don't use that language, Denise," her mother warned.

"Now we have found you, our Annabella should come home," Eric told his sister.

Nicholas gave his brother a cold stare.

Louise longed for the Valium she was now used to.

"I want to see my sister. I must..." she sobbed.

"I don't think that's wise," her mother said as she soothed her.

"He might marry you as well," Eric informed his sister.

Louise buried her face in her handkerchief.

Nicholas told his little brother to shut up.

Denise hugged her brother. "He wouldn't dare," she told him.

Denise's next visitor was her aunt.

"You gave us a fright young lady. What were you thinking of?"

"I have no idea, Aunt Meredith and I am sorry for being rude to you. I refused to talk to you when you came to tell me about a good marriage."

"You were too busy planning your escape. Don't think I will let you get away with it. Desmond would have been a good husband to you. He is rich. You would not lack anything."

CHAPTER FIVE

Denise was too weak to argue with her aunt. She managed one sentence.

"If I have to get married, I will marry for love. I thought you were on my side, aunt?"

"That was before I met the man himself. As for marrying for love, you will have a long wait, my girl. By the time you find someone who sings love to you, you will be beyond use.

"Now, I have come to take you home. I don't think your mother's place is the best place for you at the moment. She can hardly look after herself and later on look after three children. You really behaved like a child running off like that."

"But mother needs me."

"I have spoken to your mother. She is happy about the arrangement. As soon as you are back on your feet, there is a job for you."

Denise sat up. "What kind of job?" She had never worked in her life before.

She had completed her secretarial course all right. Her father had told her it was her future investment. She didn't have to work unless it was necessary. "In our family, men are providers." She had been delighted with the idea.

When he died, she had applied for a secretarial position which had landed her in the mess she now found herself in: she had met Desmond Tumwiine.

"Are you listening, Denise?" Her aunt's voice cut through her thoughts.

She looked at her aunt with a tired smile. "I was miles away."

"I hope you are not planning on running away. We are short of waitresses in our restaurant."

Denise opened her mouth. "Waitress? I can't see myself…" Her aunt and Uncle Eliot ran a family restaurant seven days a week. Denise wasn't prepared to join such a workaholic team. And their uniform was far too short. She had never exposed her legs before…oh, only once when Abraham rescued her from his dogs. She blushed at the thought.

"You have no choice at the moment. Your mother needs help. I am offering you a job at a good salary. You are not in a position to argue."

Denise gave a resigned sigh. "How much?"

"10000 shillings per month."

"What? What can I get out of that kind of money?"

"You have free accommodation. Free chauffeur. Free meals. What more do you need?"

"Hold on a second. Why do I need a chauffeur?"

"Wise up, my girl. Desmond hasn't given up on you. If I were you, I would watch my back. We still have his dowry. He can make you wife number two and there is nothing you can do about it. We owe him."

"You can't be serious."

"I am serious. You will not walk alone unaccompanied. We all think you made a very stupid mistake. Do you know, Annabella hasn't uttered a word since her capture? Whose fault is that?"

"I am sorry about Annabella but I am not sorry about turning down Desmond. He now knows how it feels like to be turned down. All I wanted was a job not some fucking marriage. The fool!"

"What are you talking about?"

"It's a long story and I am a bit tired." She yawned loudly.

"You have a lot to learn, my girl. Shouldn't you cover your mouth when yawning?" she asked as she helped change into clean clothes. "You have lost a great deal of weight. I will keep an eye on you from now on."

Denise managed a smile. "Thanks for the job. I will take it."

Her aunt smiled. "As if you had a choice. I will soon fix you with a rich husband. All you have to do is behave like a lady but with your history, every man will be scared of being turned

down at the last minute. Don't talk about your relationship with
Desmond to anyone." She almost told her what was waiting for
her at her home. She'd better not spoil anything.

"As if I want to be reminded. I will never forgive him for what
he did to my sister."

"Do you blame him? Only family members know the
difference. Do you know I used to baby sit you when you were
babies? It was a struggle telling the difference between you when
it came to feeding."

"I hated chicken."

"That's what I fed you on thinking you were Annabella. I
mixed up your diet until I appealed to your mother to make labels
for you."

Denise gave her aunt a worried look. "I don't know what to do
to help her. It must be hell for her."

"'It happens all the time. He will look after her. He is not
bad at all you know. I bumped into him the other day. He lost
weight."

"He must be stressed out. What he did to my sister will haunt
him for the rest of his life unless Annabella forgives him."

They arrived at her aunt's residence. She was surprised to see her
aunt's husband at home.

"Uncle Eliot! What a surprise to see you at home this time of
the day!"

"Business comes last where my niece is concerned. You need
patching up. You have lost a great deal of weight. They are all
waiting for you."

Denise took a step back. "Who?"

"Don't panic. It's only family members. One piece of advice:
don't provoke your uncle. He is pretty upset about the whole
thing."

"I am sorry."

"Don't be. I am on your side."

Denise greeted Uncle Richard. He ignored her.

"Take a seat, Denise," he thundered.

Denise looked at her mother for answers. She ignored her and sipped on her gin and tonic.

She smiled at her brothers. Eric looked tearful. Nicholas's forehead creased.

"What is the matter, Eric?"

Fat tears escaped from his big eyes. "I hate you. It's your entire fault our Annabella is not talking to any of us."

"I am sorry, Eric. You are too young to understand my reasons for running away."

"I told you to shut your trap," her uncle warned.

"Give her a chance. She is still too weak to handle such discussions," Eliot warned his brother in law. "Why did he have to gamble the dowry? Now they have to marry Denise off to pay off Desmond. The man Richard has in mind was a number one womaniser."

Richard gave his brother in law a cold stare. He cleared his voice. "Denise, we have made fresh arrangements for your future."

"I know. Aunt Meredith and Uncle Eliot offered me a job."

"And you think that's enough to pay off your mother's mortgage? Or you would rather see her homeless?"

Denise shook her head. She loved her mother so much. She would do anything to help her. She must accept what her uncle had in mind. If it was cultivating the farm at the village, she was prepared to do it. A lot of people earn their living that way. She was tired of living in town anyway.

Richard cleared his voice again. "The thing is Denise, Mr Baguma has asked for your hand in marriage regardless of your past behaviour."

Denise looked from one to the other. "Is this some kind of

joke?" she cried out. She knew the man her uncle was talking about. He was one of her so called admirers. He once pinched her nipple before she reached puberty. "The man is a waste of space," she thought aloud.

"You'd better rephrase that. This time you have no choice. Desmond wants his dowry back."

"Then you give it back. It's as simple as that."

"He doesn't have the money. He gambled some and the rest he paid his mortgage," Nicholas told his sister.

"You'd better watch your mouth, young man. I made a mistake. I will pay it back eventually but Desmond is not a patient man."

"Is he going to marry my sister for nothing?" she asked.

"Annabella's dowry is none of your business. At the moment we are dealing with your coming marriage to Mr Baguma."

Denise gave her mother a pleading look. "Mother! Is my marriage to someone I don't love the only way to overcome our poverty? How do you think I am going to feel each time he reminds me that he is my mother's bread and butter? Don't think he will not point it out when I refuse him his so called rights. I have no intention of losing myself to someone I don't love. We shall fight like cats and dogs. You mark my words.

"Mother, is this what you really want for me? Have you considered my happiness? Or does my happiness mean nothing to you?"

Louise sniffed onto her handkerchief. "It's not about me. What about your brothers?"

"What about them? My salary is enough to put a meal on the table. As for the mortgage, I will think of something. I am not marrying Baguma. If I have to marry, I will marry for love." And with that, she walked out of the room.

"Come back here!" Richard exploded. "Where do you think you are going? Running off again?"

"I need to take my medication," she lied.

As soon as the door shut behind her, Richard turned to his sister. "She takes after you. She is not a marrying type."

"Don't you dare talk to my wife in such a manner and, for that matter, in my house," Eliot fumed.

"Well, the truth has to be said. Meredith has been married three times. How she has managed to hold on to you is something I am trying to figure out."

Eliot felt like punching his brother in law but then he wasn't a violent man.

Nicholas cleared his voice. "Uncle Eliot, do you take part timers in your restaurant?"

"Why do you ask, kid?"

"I can work evenings after school and weekends and school holidays. Denise doesn't have to marry that creep."

"I need someone to clean the tables."

"I will take it. Thanks uncle."

"You shouldn't mingle into my business, Eliot. These children are my responsibility."

"I only offered them jobs. I can never take your place." How he wished to punch the bastard.

Meredith beamed at her husband. "You are such a good husband."

"Don't mention it. I would hate it if our children went through what these children have been through. I must dash. Business is calling me. Make sure Denise gets enough rest."

As soon as the door shut behind Eliot, Richard turned to his sister in law, Louise. "What do we tell Mr Baguma?"

"Did you say we? I was never part of this arrangement. I mean Mr Baguma seems like a gentleman but... I don't want to be blamed for the rest of her married life each time something goes wrong. I have reached a decision."

CHAPTER FIVE

They all looked at her.

"I am going back to the village. I will help my mother in law farm the land."

Richard laughed. "You? You wouldn't know the difference between crops and weeds."

Nicholas gave his uncle a warning look. He turned to his mother. "Let's go home. Denise and I will look after you."

Eric hugged his mother. "You can have my pocket money."

Louise smiled. She knew what she must do to keep her remaining family sane. She must return to the village. She had never done any manual work in her life but there was always a start. She missed her husband so much. She knew he was in a better place. He had suffered a lot. His illness left him an invalid for two years. She had been hurt when he asked her to help him go quickly.

She had cried out in shock. "What you are asking is too much. I can't do it," she had told her dying husband.

"If you really love me, do it. Have you thought about our children's future? Your future? My treatment is finishing all the money I saved for a rainy season. Please, I do beg you. Louise, do you love me?"

She had looked at him with tears in her eyes. "I love you. That's why I am not doing what you are asking me to do. It's wrong. I will never forgive myself. I will always live in fear, nightmares. Please don't ask me again. I will look after you until…" she had no words to say. She looked after him to the end. She had promised him that she would take care of their children even though she had no experience in anything. When Richard told him about Desmond's offer, she had been delighted knowing that at least one child would be looked after and her dowry would look after the rest of the family. Whatever made her believe that Denise would be happy with a man she didn't love was the devil himself.

Annabella's case was now another torture. She didn't know how to reach her. To comfort her. She must do what she can to save the rest of the family. It was a long road.

Chapter Six

Desmond didn't know what to do with Annabella. She refused to talk to him or acknowledge him. She was now refusing to eat her meals. That bothered him a lot. He could tolerate her silence but starvation was another matter.

He reached for her hand. "Annabella, talk to me. I said I am sorry. I will do anything to make it up to you. What do you want?"

The only answer was her tears.

He wiped them with his handkerchief. Her distress tortured him and at the same time helped him lose weight, which had been troubling him all these years. He was happy about that but how he had achieved it made him feel guilty. "Annabella, do you want to see your twin sister?"

He thought he detected a movement. "Is that a yes?"

Her tears increased.

"All right. I will fetch her for you. I will do anything, Annabella. I will make you happy if you give me a chance. You may not believe this – the truth is, I love you. Why I didn't ask for your hand in marriage in the first place is something I will never forgive myself for." He kissed her cheek and left her bedroom.

Denise sensed there was someone in her room. She hoped it

wasn't the police. They had been in and out taking statements. She was tired. She hated their endless twisted questions. Asking the same question all over again but in different styles. She had no idea who the man was. He was in a coma so they thought she would tell them who he was. They thought she was lying. Well, it serves him right. What was he doing following her in the forest? Who was in her room? It couldn't be the maid. No one comes into her room without knocking first. She pretended to be asleep.

She was expecting Abraham but Abraham wouldn't enter her bedroom without knocking. If it were Abraham, the maid would have announced him first.

She didn't like such intrusion. Her cousins were not yet back from school and besides, they wouldn't just stand there without a word. She had better face this person.

To her horror, it was Desmond. She gasped for air. "You have...lost...weight! What the hell are you doing in my room? Get out before I scream." She was now on her feet and in one hand she held an ornament. "Get out!"

Desmond put the newspaper down. "I am glad you are back on your feet but such violence doesn't suit a well brought up girl like you."

"What are you doing here and in my room for that matter?"

"Calm down." He looked her up and down. "What have you got to say for yourself? I am in this mess because of you. Did you think for one moment that I would not take care of you? Why did you run away, Denise?"

"Please leave."

"I will leave when I am ready. Answer me, girl. Why did you make a fool of me?"

She took a deep breath. "You know the answer, Desmond."

"I don't."

"If you can't figure it out yourself, I am sorry, I can't help you." She longed to ask him about her sister's health but the look

CHAPTER SIX

in Desmond's eyes silenced her.

She sat on her windowsill with her weapon in her hand.

He cleared his voice. "I need a favour from you."

"What kind of favour?"

"It's Annabella. She is...."

"What did you do to her? I was told she doesn't speak to anyone. Is that true?"

He nodded. "Maybe you can cheer her up. She hasn't uttered a word since... Now she refuses to eat. I need your help."

"What you did to my sister is something I will never forgive you for. Did you have to force yourself on her?"

"I thought she was you."

"You thought you were punishing me? No wonder she is mute. She must hate you."

"There is no need for those brute words. I need your help."

Denise shook her head. "That's one problem you will have to solve on your own. You created it, solve it. I don't trust you with my life. Get out of my room."

"Please Denise. Do this for your sister. She is losing her voice. She has to talk at some point. I need your help."

Denise looked at the man she hated and didn't trust. "There is nothing I can do to undo what you have already done to my sister. Get out. I need my sleep."

"If I have to take you by force, I will. They still have my dowry, remember?"

"You wouldn't dare. The law would be on your arse this time. Don't think you can get away with such a crime twice. The family kept quiet about Annabella because of her reputation. No man would marry her after you but I am not Annabella. I would take you to court. I am different from Annabella. I don't care about reputations. My freedom is all I care about."

"I would like you to come with me willingly. Your sister needs you."

49

"Do you think for one minute that I would trust you after your brute words?"

They were interrupted by a knock.

The maid put her head in. "There is a visitor for you. His name is Abraham."

The smile on Denise's face punctured Desmond's heart.

"Abraham? Who is Abraham?"

Denise laughed. "You really surprise me, Desmond." She looked at the maid still waiting for the answer. "Please show him into the sitting room. I will be down shortly."

She turned to Desmond. "I would like to change if you don't mind.

He remained seated.

"Suit yourself," she said as she combed her hair, applied a little make-up and a little perfume between her breasts. She left the room without a backward glance.

Desmond stared at the door through which Denise had disappeared.

"Bitch!"

Now he recognised the difference between the two sisters apart from pierced ears. Denise was wild.

He was curious about this Abraham. He'd better find out. He could hear them laughing.

He entered the sitting room. He looked from one to the other. He couldn't believe his eyes. Denise was holding a fruit basket in her hand and the dazzling smile she was giving the tramp reduced Desmond to a temper.

"Denise! What do you think you are doing inviting a tramp into your aunt's house? Have you considered what he might do?"

Abraham's jaws tightened but no one noticed since his cheeks were covered in beard.

Denise was furious. "How dare you talk to my friend in such a manner?" She turned to Abraham. "This is Desmond, he is…

never mind. He is just leaving."

"I am not leaving you with this tramp."

Abraham was dressed in denim jeans that were showing a bit of stress due to so much washing and his beard didn't help him at all. The only clean parts on his body were his white teeth and hands. Denise didn't mind him at all. He made her happy. He was the only person who had made her smile since her father's death.

"He is not a tramp. He is as good as you, if not better."

Desmond narrowed his eyes at her. "Don't you dare compare me with this Mr Nobody. Does your aunt know this person?"

"Yes, they know him."

"But he only visits when they are out," he pointed out.

"You have just done the same," she reminded him.

"Are you coming or not?"

"I told you I am not coming. It's your fault she is in that mess."

"At least I tried." He left but not before he gave Abraham a threatening look.

"I am sorry, Abraham. He is so rude."

"Who is he?" He knew all right but he wanted to hear it from her.

Denise hesitated.

"He is my brother in law. I will get you a drink. You must be thirsty."

"No thank you. I'd better get going."

"But you have just arrived?"

"At the wrong time. I interrupted your afternoon nap with..."

"Don't let Desmond spoil your visit. I love your company. Please stay. I will fix you a drink and I don't take no for an answer." She flashed him a smile and went to the kitchen.

Abraham was badly insulted but he was what he is because...

"Here is your drink. Do you prefer it with ice?"

"It's cool enough thank you. You look recovered."

"I am. I am starting work on Monday. I have been putting it

off for sometime but I have to give in for my family's sake."

"Do you have to do that job? It doesn't suit you."

"I have no choice."

"Yes you have. I will offer you a job. I have contacts."

Denise put her drink on the table. She looked at him with a smile.

"Abraham, you really surprise me sometimes. Why don't you use those contacts to find yourself a job?"

"I earn a good living on my farm. I don't like to work for other people."

"I get what you mean. I envy you."

"You can work with me on the farm. I will pay you good money."

"You know that's not possible. My aunt will never let me..."

"You mean mix with someone like me?"

"That's not what I mean."

"Do you feel ashamed when you are in my company?"

"What makes you ask such question? I love your company."

"Well, if you have finished your drink, I would love a ride with you."

He smiled. 'That's why I am here. I thought to give you a bit of fresh air."

"Hold on, I will fetch my sun hat."

The telephone rang as soon as they drove off. The maid took the call.

"What do you mean she is out?" Meredith thundered.

"This man called Abraham..."

"I know who Abraham is. Did they leave together?"

"Yes, in his pickup."

"When she comes back, tell her to give me a call." Meredith massaged her temple. What was Denise doing with that man? She didn't owe him anything. Just because he saved her life didn't give him the right to enter her house whenever he pleased. At first she thought Desmond was just putting it on until he described Abraham. I will kill this girl. She is a disgrace. She will never find a good husband if she keeps such company. The man is a waste of space. I will teach her a lesson. What made me think she would keep to her bed and rules?

Denise looked at Abraham with a questioning look in her eyes. Underpants hanging on a cooker handle shocked her.

"I am sorry about the mess," he apologised as he pushed his underpants into the corner of the kitchen. "I don't know how it got here." He winked at her.

"You like to live like this, don't you?"

"What do you mean?" he asked as he offered her well-sliced pineapples in cube style.

She looked around the house. "This is a good place. All you have to do is keep it clean."

"I lost my will power after my second divorce."

She put her fork down. "You mean you have been married twice and divorced?"

"Does my divorce surprise you?"

"Not one bit but..." She held his hand. "Divorce is a traumatic experience. I can imagine. My aunt has been through it many times."

He sighed. "I am surprised I still have my hair." He massaged his beard.

"What caused the divorce if you don't mind me asking?"

"I don't mind you asking. The thing is, they married me for different reasons and it wasn't love."

Denise bit on her lip. "How can anyone marry for something else other than love?"

"It's very simple. That's enough about myself. What about you? You haven't told me how you ended up on my doorstep."

Denise tensed. "It's a long story and a very painful one."

"Locking it up doesn't solve anything. You do trust me, don't you?"

"I do."

"Then share your problems with me."

"Where do I start?"

"The beginning is the best way."

Her eyes watered remembering the life they were reduced to after her father's illness.

She took a deep breath. "After my father died, I had to look for a job to support the family. It was during my job search that I met Desmond Tumwiine, my now brother in law. It was a clerical job. There were so many applicants. I made a stupid mistake and begged him for the job. Luckily, they called me for a second interview.

"I told him that my mother was a widow who needed my support. My brothers' school fees needed paying. Eric my little brother's bike needed repairing. Oh! I made a fool of myself and cried in his face. He offered me his handkerchief and said I could keep it. I was happy about it because I could sell it as soon as I left his office."

"Oh poor girl. Nobody told you about interviews. You don't tell the interviewer what you intend to spend your salary on. And once you have a job, you don't tell your employer how you spend your salary. The moment they find out how well you are doing, the next thing you know, the computer will be playing tricks with your wages. It's computer error, you will be told. Who controls that computer? That's what I would like to know." He grinned at her.

"I didn't know all that."

"Well, now you know. Carry on."

"I didn't get the job. The fool proposed to me."

"The bastard!" Abraham clenched his teeth.

She sighed. "I turned him down. A few days later, my uncle told me about Desmond asking for my hand in marriage. You can imagine the shock. What made matters worse, the whole family rejoiced in my good fortune. I went along with them until three days before our wedding." She then told him how she ended up on his doorstep and what had happened to her sister.

"You were lucky to escape that wild animal. The man is still in a coma. He is blind, I heard."

"I knew he was up to no good. He was too creepy. If he wanted to help me, he should have called out for me but no, he moved like a thief."

"Well, you escaped. You survived. Here we are," he grinned at her.

"I escaped with snakebite and your dog's teeth for dessert and my uncle is trying to fix me with another man."

Abraham's heart raced. "Are you going to marry this man?"

"I told him that if I had to marry, I would marry for love."

"Interesting. You will have a long wait."

"You sound like my aunt. That's what she told me."

"She is right. Look at me. Who would marry a man like me?"

"You would be surprised." She flashed him a smile.

He looked distant. "I have found someone but..."

"You are not sure," she finished for him.

"I have nothing to offer her."

"Does she love you?"

"I haven't asked her. I don't want to make a fool of myself. After my last divorce, I said no more women but how wrong. I can't live without this girl. I am afraid to ask her in case..."

"You don't ask, you don't find out. Thanks for the pineapple. It was delicious. I must get going. My aunt will be home soon."

"I will drop you off. There is plenty of time."

He looked at her. "Help me out."

"How?"

"Do you think I should tell this girl about my feelings?"

"As I said: you don't ask, you don't find out. I will give you one piece of advice. Invite her over and don't make an effort to make this place look fetching. If she can't take you as you are, then you are better off without her. The last thing you want is a third divorce."

He looked into her eyes. He smiled revealing his white teeth. "She... is here."

"What do you mean...she is here?" She moistened her lips.

"Do you want me to spell out for you?"

She fell into his arms. "Oh Abraham, why didn't you make yourself clear in the first place?"

"I was afraid of making an ass of myself."

"I...am...flattered. Honestly."

"When did you find out your feelings for me?" he asked.

"When you ate my carrots at the hospital. We looked like a couple sharing a meal together. It felt so good. I felt something inside me." She wasn't going to tell him that her body becomes a live wire by just looking at him.

"When did you know?" she asked him.

"When I carried you in my arms from my brute dogs."

They were now kissing and tearing at each other's clothes.

"Abraham, don't. You are confusing our friendship."

"I am sorry," he said as he let go.

They looked at each other without a word. After a long silence, they talked at the same time.

"What do we do?"

Meredith checked her driveway a hundred times. There was no Denise and Abraham. She moved from one foot to another. The phone rang. It was her husband. "Is she back?"

"She is not back yet... I don't know what else to do."

"She will be back. Don't worry."

"I am worried. That tramp might hurt her. The thought of what he might do to her is making me dizzy."

"Find a seat, dear. Stop fretting. Denise will come to no harm."

"Oh Eliot. I will kill her."

"You don't mean it, dear."

"Please come home. The waiting is making me miserable."

"I will be home in half an hour."

He was, and there was no Denise.

"Denise, I will look after you. You will never lack anything."

"You talk nonsense Abraham. Why should you be the one to look after me? We will look after each other. I know my family will make a racket but it's you I love."

"Let them make a racket. I have a surprise for them. I have enough dowry."

She looked at him in surprise.

"Did you think for one minute that I would marry you for nothing? I would like you to talk to your family so that when I come to ask for your hand in marriage, they already know what I am talking about."

"I will talk to my aunt. If she throws a temper, we will marry without their consent."

"If your love for me is strong, they will give their consent. The ball is in your court."

"After I have spoken to your family, I would like you to meet my family. They already know you."

"I can't wait to meet them."

Meredith was fuming. "What the hell possessed you to go out without my permission?"

Abraham apologised, "I am sorry. It's all my fault. I thought she needed fresh air."

"She gets enough fresh air all right," she snapped at him. "I don't want to see you here again. You are a bad influence. She will never find a good husband if she hangs about with the likes of you. My niece has better things to do than hang out with you. She doesn't owe you anything. You saved her life. If you want to be paid for it, name the price or get out of my sight."

Denise's anger got out of control. "You can't do that, Aunt Meredith. I intend to see Abraham whenever..."

The slap from her aunt silenced her.

Abraham was helpless. One wrong move, he would pay heavily. He reached out for the one person. "I am sorry, Denise. It's my fault. I shouldn't have taken you out without your aunt's permission. Are you hurt?"

She shook her head.

"Leave her alone!" Meredith thundered.

"You have no right beating her like this." He looked at Denise. "I am sorry."

"I am not sorry for accepting to be your wife," she replied.

There was a long silence. Meredith's nostrils flared. She was lost for words.

She took a deep breath. "Denise, go to your room. As for you, Mr Nobody, I don't want to see you here again. If I should see your face around here, I will have you arrested. Do you hear me?"

"Meredith, is that really necessary? The guy is harmless."

"Eliot, the guy has asked my niece to marry him."

Eliot laughed. "You are joking, Meredith. You have been fixing men on the kid's shoulders but this...is a bit farfetched."

Abraham felt like running away from all this but his love for Denise held him down and kept his temper under control. He looked from one to the other. "I love your niece. I will look after her. She will not lack anything."

Meredith wrinkled her nose. "You can hardly look after yourself and later on look after my niece. Denise, I told you to go to your room."

She held on to Abraham's hand. She looked at him straight in the eyes, "Nothing has changed," she told him. She let go of his hand. "Drive carefully," she said and left the room.

Abraham bowed to Meredith and Eliot. "I will see you in the near future."

As soon as they heard his car engine cry out, Meredith collapsed on her husband's lap. "What do we do with her?"

"We have to watch her twenty-four hours," he told her. "What a day! The man is a dreamer."

"And my niece is a fool. She doesn't know what's good for her."

Chapter Seven

Denise turned the door handle in her bedroom. To her horror, it was locked. What the hell is the meaning of this? She knew her Aunt and Uncle Eliot were at work. Who has the key? How would she go to the toilet?

She was being punished for falling in love for the first time. She banged on the door. Nobody came. The maid and the cook must have been given orders not to open the door.

She cried herself to sleep. The next time she opened her eyes, there was bread and a glass of milk on a tray. In a corner, there was a bucket. She let her tears flow. She was now being treated like a prisoner. She pushed the tray aside. Did her mother know what was happening to her? Was she part of this torture? She didn't think so. Her mother was now staying in the servants' quarters while she rented the big house to pay off the mortgage. It had been Nicholas's idea. Denise was so pleased with her brother's sense of duty. The servants' quarters were too small but at least they were managing somehow.

She sat in her room staring at nothing in particular. She needed a bath badly but that was out of the question. There was not a single newspaper to read.

She knew what she had to do if she should get a chance to get out of this hole.

Much later on in the evening, she heard a key in her door. She stared at the door. Her aunt stood in the doorway.

Denise looked aside.

"Why didn't you eat your lunch?"

Denise ignored her.

"Get ready, we are going to see Annabella. I received a phone call from Desmond. He needs your help."

"I am not going with you. There is nothing to stop the bastard marrying me against my will."

"Denise, I just don't have time for that nonsense. Just get ready. If I have to drag you there, I will. Annabella is under stress. You may be able to help her."

"I don't see how. I can't undo what Desmond has already done to her. Do you believe for one minute that she is still innocent?"

"Are we having a debate on Annabella's virginity or what? Just get ready. She needs our help."

"Why did you lock me up?"

"You mean you haven't grasped it? I don't want you to see that tramp."

"I love him."

"Don't give me a migraine, Denise. I had a long day."

Denise sighed. She took a quick shower. She was almost falling on her feet. She was hungry, she realised.

The drive to Desmond's residence took them half an hour.

Desmond let them in the sitting room. "I am so grateful, Aunt Meredith," he said, ignoring Denise.

He offered them soft drinks. Denise refused. "No thank you. I am not thirsty."

"Denise!" Her aunt gave her a threatening look.

"I am not thirsty."

Desmond looked hurt. He cleared his voice. "Go to your sister. Her room is at the end of the corridor on your right."

Denise opened the door. Her eyes rested on her twin sister. The shock made her take a step back. "Annabella!" she muttered.

What...has...he done to you? You are all bones. Oh Annabella!" She ran to her sister. She wasn't prepared for what came next.

Annabella slapped her.

Denise was so shocked. She could hardly move or fend off the blows she was receiving on her head.

Denise finally found her voice. "Annabella, stop it. Tell me what's eating you."

Another blow landed on her face.

Desmond and Meredith were now alerted by the noise. They separated the twins. "What is the meaning of this?" their aunt cried out.

Meredith was so shocked by Annabella. "What have you done to her?" she accused Desmond.

"She doesn't want to eat."

"I am taking her home."

"And...what...are... you going to do with me? Look... for... a rich husband for me?"

Annabella found her voice at last. She mimicked her uncle's voice.

"It's ten cows for my niece." She snorted.

Meredith looked at her niece. If this weren't a serious case, she would have laughed. She got her uncle's snorting habits right. "Jesus!"

"Sir, two cows is my last offer. The girl has been tampered with," Annabella went on.

"But you will get interest out of her. She will give you ten daughters and that's a hundred cows for their dowry.

"Ten cows, and the girl is yours." More snorting.

Annabella glared at her aunt. "Well?"

Meredith was shocked. She looked from one twin to the other.

CHAPTER SEVEN

One would think it was Denise uttering those words. "That was Denise's style. I was never part of this...Annabella."

"She is talking," Desmond sobbed.

Annabella pointed at her sister, "As... for... you, I don't want to see you again. I am in this miserable so called marriage because of you. Wherever I look, there is Denise's evidence." She opened the wardrobe and pulled out some gowns. "Now you are here, you can take them with you." She opened the drawers, out came lacy knickers and bras. She threw them at her sister.

Desmond was shocked. But not for long. He now understood why Annabella hadn't been talking. He had forgotten to remove what he had bought for Denise. He had thought that since they had the same figure, Annabella would make use of them. Now he understood why she wore a housecoat seven days a week and if he wasn't mistaken, she was pregnant.

The thought of having a child made him love Annabella more. He wanted to reach her but the thought of being rejected... If he had known it was Anabella, he would have been gentle. He was so angry with Denise. Taking her by force was part of her punishment and reminding her who was in charge. He took a deep breath.

"Annabella, I am so sorry. I will make changes for you. We can move if that's what you want. I will buy you diamonds. You name anything you want."

Denise undid the pendant on her neck. She threw it at her sister.

"You can have it. You need a complete heart more than I do. We used to share one heart, now it's all yours." And with that, she left the room.

Annabella looked at the pendant. She joined it together with hers. It made a complete heart, but the pain in her heart still lingered. She held on to Denise's pendant and let her tears flow.

"Go to her," Meredith told him.

Desmond was frightened. "She might go into a coma. How do I bring her back?" he cried. "I don't know what else to do."

"Get rid of Denise's wardrobe and everything that you had bought for her. Make a fresh start. If that doesn't work, she will have to go to a mental hospital. If I were you, I would pay her dowry. That's not for me to say but you came to me for help. I am telling you what might be bothering Annabella."

That sent Annabella into more sobs.

Desmond gathered Annabella into his arms. He was surprised when she didn't protest. She held on to him with all her life. Desmond knew what to do next. He gave Meredith a thank you nod.

Meredith left the room. To her horror, there was no Denise.

Chapter Eight

The pounding on the door aroused Abraham from his nap. A few minutes later he was staring at Denise. "What happened to you?"

"Please let me in. I will explain."

Abraham looked at Denise carefully. "Did your aunt do this to you?"

"Partly." She told him how she was locked up and later on beaten by her sister. "She doesn't want to see me. I saw hatred etched into her eyes. We have always been close. It hurts me so much. What am I going to do?" she sobbed.

"Don't read too much into her actions. She is distressed. She needs help. She needs to release her stress."

"So I became her punch bag-stress reliever?"

"Don't think too much about it, she will come round. I must fix you something to eat."

Denise wondered whether she should prepare it herself but she was too tired, hungry and weak. She rested her head on the couch. She fell asleep. The next thing she heard was Abraham waking her up.

"Your lasagne is ready."

She sat up. "What is it?"

"It's an Italian meal. It will give you strength."

She took a bite. It tasted so good. "You are a man of

surprises." She grinned at him.

The atmosphere in the room was so comforting. "Abraham, this reminds me of the time I fell in love with you."

He smiled. "Finish your meal. I have to take you home."

"Do I have to go?"

"Yes, I come from a Christian family. They will never accept a marriage that hasn't been blessed in church."

"But you heard what aunt said. They will never accept you in my family."

"I know."

"We have to do something."

"Like what?"

She pushed her plate aside. She was now behaving like a wanton woman.

Abraham had no control of his feelings for Denise. As they kissed, something kept on telling him that it was wrong. But he wanted this girl. "Are you sure?"

"I am sure but I have no idea of what to do apart from kissing," she giggled.

Abraham was beyond hearing. He forgot that this was someone's daughter and innocent for that matter. He remembered one important thing.

This was new to her. She didn't know whether she was doing the right thing but the moans from Abraham told her something. She hoped he wasn't pretending to make her feel good. She focused on the future. The life with Abraham is all that matters now. She was his. She was now a woman and soon she would be Abraham's wife and God willing, a child would be born out of their love.

She slept in his arms.

He watched her as she slept. He smiled at her innocence. She has no idea. But he loved her all the same. He must give his family a call. At last, he punched the air. He hoped that she would forgive him when she found out the real truth about him. He kissed her cheek and went to his room to fetch a blanket. He was halfway, when he heard a knock.

It was Meredith. "I know you are in there."

Abraham took a deep breath. He woke Denise. "Shh be quiet. It's your aunt."

"Shit! How did she find out your address? What do I do?"

"Hide in the cleaning cupboard. I will let her in."

"You've got to be joking. The cleaning cupboard? I will faint."

"There is no time for this, Denise. You are still under their care. Do as I say."

To her surprise, the place was clean. The cleaning brushes had never been used. That explained the mess in the house. "What's the point of buying all these cleaning materials if they are not going to be used?"

She heard her aunt's voice.

"Where is my niece?"

"Please come in." Abraham invited her in.

"Is she here?"

"What makes you think she is here?"

"She ran away."

"Why? Have you been beating her again?"

"Don't play games with me. Is she here or is she not?"

"I haven't seen Denise since yesterday. That doesn't mean I have given up hope on her. I love her. I will marry her as soon as I am ready."

"You have a cheek. Well, you have no one to marry. She has run off, God knows with whom. That girl is a disgrace. If you think that my niece loves you, you don't know Denise. She plays such games with every man."

Meredith tried all she could to put Abraham off Denise. What she said next almost made Denise jump out of the cleaning cupboard and confront her aunt.

"Young man, take this from me. Leave Denise alone. She is not the marrying type. Has she told you she had an abortion at sixteen? Well don't say I haven't warned you."

"Have you finished?" Abraham asked.

"I am going – and that rubbish tip?" She spat. She joined Eliot who had been waiting in the car. He was fuming.

"Meredith, did you have to say such horrible lies?"

"It's the only way to keep that tramp away from my niece."

"He is a tramp. Do you think he cares about reputation?"

"Please Eliot. I need your support not criticism."

"Abraham, where are we going?"

"I am taking you home. We will get there before them. Trust my pickup." He was doing over 70 miles per hour. He dropped Denise at her aunt's gate and did a u-turn. "I will be in touch," he told her before he sped off.

Denise went straight to her room and waited for her aunt. Then she saw her diary on the bed. That explains how her aunt found Abraham's address. She heard footsteps on the stairs. She didn't have to wait long.

"Why did you run off like that? Where have you been? I have been looking for you everywhere."

Denise sat up. She looked at her aunt with a tired look. "I don't feel that good. I have a headache."

"Headache or not, you are going to work tomorrow. And if you think I will let you out of my sight, then you need some screws in your brain adjusted. You better come down. Supper is ready.

"Your behaviour has spoiled a good meal. It's now stone cold. I might lose my marriage over this."

Denise sighed. Her aunt exaggerates so much. Eliot never complains. She ran a comb in her hair. She washed her face. She hoped she didn't give away her discovery. She could still feel

Abraham's touch but she was puzzled about one thing. There was no blood. Not a single drop. Why? What is the problem? Her aunt would know. She was tempted to ask her. She hid a smile behind her hand.

She joined the rest of the family in the dining room. She greeted her uncle.

He nodded in reply.

"We thought you had been kidnapped like your sister Annabella," her cousin Lydia said with a giggle.

"Sister Denise, is it true you want to marry that tramp?" Dan asked with concern in his voice.

"That's enough children," their father warned. "Denise is not marrying the tramp and as you can see, she hasn't been kidnapped. Let us pray."

Denise had no idea what she was eating. Her mind was far away. Not quite faraway. She was remembering Abraham's lovemaking. She couldn't wait to be in his arms again.

"Stop toying with your food, Denise," her aunt chided.

"I am not hungry."

"You are hungry. You refused to have your lunch."

"I didn't feel like eating dry bread and milk and using a bucket like a prisoner."

"Shut up Denise! We are eating."

"I am sorry."

"You have deteriorated since my brother passed away. Your mother spoils you. Well, she has no chance this time. I will turn you into a proper well-disciplined girl. Now, be a good girl and pour some coffee for us."

Denise sighed. She spilled some coffee on her aunt's white tablecloth. Her mind was elsewhere. She was having her third orgasm.

"Denise, that's not the way to hold a teapot. You have a lot to learn, my girl."

"You are starting work tomorrow. Don't let me down. Remember, the customer is always right. If I were you, I would wipe off that look on your face. I expect you to smile at my customers. Be polite at all times. If there is anything you don't understand, ask me."

The cousins gave her a sorry look.

Desmond cleared his voice. "Do you want any dessert?"

Annabella shook her head. "I am full up, thank you." She had no choice but to stay with Desmond. She was spoilt and pregnant. Who would marry her after this?

Marjorie cleared the table. "Sir, what should I tell your mother when she calls?"

"Tell her nothing." His housekeeper was one gossip courier for his mother.

"But she…"

"Marjorie, read my lips. Tell her nothing." He turned to Annabella. "We'd better get going then. It's a long distance."

Annabella didn't really care as long as she was out of this house. The house that gave her nightmares. The house that was bought for Denise. All decorated in Denise's colours and he expected her to wear Denise's clothes.

"What a bastard!"

She looked at him. How she wished to punch his face! She pulled her housecoat closer, the only clothing she accepted. He said it belonged to his sister Amanda. Whether he was lying or not, she had to wear it or else… She wondered what had happened to her own clothes.

"I want my clothes," she told him.

He took a deep breath. "I told Marjorie to get rid of them."

Her nostrils flared.

"How dare you! That dress…cost my mum a fortune."

"Let's get going, shall we?" He gave her his hand. She refused

CHAPTER EIGHT

to take it.

She took her seat in the passenger seat still in her housecoat.

"Fasten your seatbelt. Our journey should take us about seven hours."

She didn't care. She did care later on when they left the main road after a long drive. She had been sleeping; now the bumpy road woke her. All she could see was a small path in the middle of a jungle and the only light apart from the headlights was the moonlight.

"Where are we?"

"We are at Nyabuhikye. We should be there soon."

"I don't like this place," she moaned.

"From what I have gathered about you, you don't like anything, but trust me, you will like this place. It's my birthplace. Whenever I want to clear my head, that's where I come."

"What have I got to do with it?"

"Annabella, I thought to introduce you to this place. You will love it."

She looked aside. She knew he was right. She was now his. She was damaged. He might just as well deal with his damages.

After another long drive accompanied by a bumpy dance, they arrived at his birthplace.

"Here we are. This village is called Mbogo."

Annabella looked around her.

"Where is the house?"

"You are looking at it."

She squinted her eyes. She sighed. "It's in the middle of a forest and it's falling apart."

"You are right; it hasn't been in use for almost a decade."

She shivered. She pulled her housecoat closer to her bosom. "This is another nightmare."

"It's not. Just hang about, I will check it out." He was gone for more than an hour.

"I don't like this place. It looks spooky to me."

"Are you coming, or not?"

She tiptoed behind him. She was wearing only house slippers. She could be walking on a bed of snakes.

The place made her hair stand out. It got even worse when they got inside. The place was all mouldy and the walls were all cracks. "The ceiling must have come after the foundation," she told him.

"It's always the case." He told her.

"I mean, the ceiling is stronger than the foundation. We will be buried alive if we are not careful."

"I am glad we have an architect in the family. You are not just a pretty face. I will show you around. This is the sitting room as you can see. This is Amanda's room. You can sleep in here if you want. The one next to it is mine. The one in the far end is mother's. She will show it to you herself."

He looked at her. "Anything else?"

"I want to go back."

"That's one wish I will not grant. We are staying here for one month while I look for another house since you don't like the one we have at the moment. Another thing is, I want you to figure out what you really want. I have already figured out what I want but the decision is yours. I want you to know me. If you think I am not worth spending the rest of your life with, I will release you."

Her nose flared.

"You think I am a prisoner. You brought me here...in this hellhole...to make up...my mind whether I love you? That's where you are wrong, Mr. I will never utter those words." She closed her eyes. "Oh God! I never thought..." She opened her eyes to direct another missile at him but the hurt in his eyes silenced her. She must not go too far. She might find herself under the floorboards.

He turned on his heels. He paused in his doorway.

"Goodnight."

Annabella watched the door through which he disappeared, then she looked at Amanda's door. She made a choice on where she should sleep.

Denise moaned in her sleep. She was having a nightmare. "Annabella, Annabella," she cried out. "Run faster, Annabella. Don't look back." She watched in horror as her sister fell and her attacker raised a knife.

"Please don't…"

Denise woke up with a start. She rubbed her eyes. She sighed, "Thank God it's a dream."

Annabella lay quietly gazing into the darkness, her mind in the present and the future. She was too young to be a mother and later on a wife. She wasn't ready for responsibilities. What kind of life will this child have? She could never love this child. The child she never planned. This child was the result of rape! She tried to starve herself hoping she would miscarry but nothing worked. She felt guilty about it. After all, the child is innocent. She was sorry. She must do what she could to regain her strength hence keeping the child healthy. She was too frightened to close her eyes.

She wasn't even sure whether Desmond checked the bed thoroughly. She lit a candle and checked everywhere and winced each time the wax fell on her hand as she bent to check under the bed. It looked safe, that's what she thought.

Desmond turned and tossed. He didn't know he could love a woman like the way he loved Annabella. Why did he propose to Denise? The girl is wild. He now understood why her uncle had been happy to agree to the marriage without even checking his background. He wanted to get rid of Denise, the rude twin. He was sad he'd met Annabella in horrible circumstances. He must do what he can to win her approval. He will not rush her. His love for her is enough to sustain a marriage if there is one.

Annabella's bust heaved. She was lost for words. She tried to speak but nothing came out. She looked at the man standing in front of her bed.

Her eyes darted to the door; it was shut and the bolt was in. How the hell did he get in? She did bolt the door before she went to bed. She looked at the man standing in front of her. She finally found her voice. "Hi...!" she said with a trembling voice.

He smiled at her and left. Annabella blinked. She looked at the door through which the man had disappeared. The bolt was still on. She passed out.

The next time she woke, it was light outside. The sun was shining. Her eyes darted around the room. She didn't want to be in this room a minute longer. She removed the bolt and ran to Desmond's room.

"Shit!" The room was empty. "Where is he?"

She must get out of the house. As she was passing her room, she saw a note by her bedroom door.

"I hope you slept well. I have gone to the shops to get some supplies.

Don't open the doors. Wild animals roam around. I will see you soon.

D.T. XXX"

Annabella read the note a second time. How long had she been alone in this house? When did he go? When will he be back? She wanted to go to the toilet. She didn't think there was a toilet in the house. This was a village. Civilisation was still a long way away. What must she do?"

Who gives a damn about wild animals? She wasn't going to wet herself.

CHAPTER EIGHT

She opened the front door. The sun hit her eyes. She squinted looking for an outside latrine. She spotted it. It was as bad as the house. A wooden plank almost let go. What kind of toilet is this? Snakes must be hiding between those planks. She was really pressed, the hole in the middle of the toilet looked like a beacon but the thought of her arse being struck by a snake made her squat in the grass with her eyes moving round and round like a chameleon looking out for wild animals.

She had no choice but to go back inside. She paused in the doorway. Should she wait for Desmond outside?

The thought of being eaten by a wild animal made her shut the door. She rested her back on it. She could hear some noises. Is he back?

"Desmond?" she called out. No, the car is not outside. He is not back.

The doors bang and shut. There in front of her, stood the same man she saw last night She must be brave or she will die of a heart attack. "What's...your... name?"

He smiled at her and puffed on his pipe.

"What... do... you want? Leave... me... alone." She shivered as the wind blew the curtains even though the windows were shut. When she looked at the spot where the man had been standing, there was a fire burning but the man wasn't there. 'She must be hallucinating. What's happening to her mind? She felt dizzy. There was nothing to hold on to. She sat down and waited for the man she hated.

She didn't know how long she had been sitting there when she heard the car noise. She took a deep breath. She closed her eyes. Thank God he is back. When she opened her eyes, the fire was gone. She ran her fingers on the spot, not a single ash or any evidence that there had been a fire in the room.

She gave Desmond a weak smile.

He returned a warm smile. "Did you sleep well?"

Her nose twitched. She wanted to tell him about the ghost but she knew he would just brush her off saying she was just dreaming. She decided to keep the ghost a secret. He was harmless after all. The question is: 'Who was he? Why was he still hanging loose on Earth? Could he be Desmond's father?'

"I slept badly. We must leave. This place is…out of date. Sanitary conditions are bad. I almost fell into the toilet."

"You went outside? Didn't you read my note?"

"What should I have done? Huh! Wet myself? We must leave at once. The thought of falling into that toilet. Why are you doing this to me? This kind of life is not for me even in hard times. This is Denise's kind of life."

Denise liked village life. She enjoyed visiting their grandmother and especially cooking on an open fire and roasting nuts at the same time. Well, she was not going to lower herself to Denise's level. They must leave at once.

Desmond's voice cut her thoughts short. "It's not that deep and it hasn't been used for a long time." He smiled at her.

"I am not in the mood for jokes…" She paused, her eyes resting on a young girl.

"Who is she?"

"Her name is Agasha. She is our cook. Come in, Agasha."

The girl put the shopping down. She smiled at Annabella.

"Agandi?" she greeted her.

Annabella didn't answer. She sank in a nearby chair. She was too drained out.

"We shall have to use mother's sitting room as a kitchen. I bought paraffin stoves so they won't create any smoke."

Annabella watched Desmond put the paraffin stoves on the spot where the fire had been burning earlier. She forgot to breathe; after a while, she gasped for air.

"I …don't…feel that good.'"

Desmond was on her side feeling her temperature with his

hand.

"Go and have a lie down. I will show Agasha what to do."

She shook her head. "I will be fine. I am just thirsty." She didn't want to be in that room alone with a ghost, friendly or not.

Chapter Nine

Louise looked at the man sitting in front of her.

"Do I know you?"

"We have never met but my brother..."

"What about your brother?"

"He is in love with your daughter Denise. I am acting as a go-between."

"Well, Denise hasn't mentioned anyone to me. I will have to talk to her first."

"Your daughter has already accepted my brother."

"I haven't!" Louise shot back. "This generation!"

Mworozi looked at the lady of the house. "Is there any problem? My brother loves your daughter."

"I am sure he does otherwise you wouldn't be here but I have to speak to my daughter first."

"How long will it take?"

She glared at him. "Don't rush me, young man. I didn't carry her for nine months, babyhood, puberty, menstrual tensions and then to be told to hurry up. What is the world coming to?"

"I am sorry. I will call back. Thanks for your time."

Mworozi's next destination was the M&E restaurant. He spotted Denise all right. He envied his brother. Abraham had really landed on his feet this time.

He pretended to be checking the menu. He tried to get Denise's attention but her aunt was all over the restaurant. Abraham had warned him about her. How right!

"May I help you, Sir?" a young waitress about Denise's age asked.

"Yes please." He ordered roast chicken and salad. It took him almost an hour to finish his meal. Denise was constantly monitored. Meredith's eyes darted here and there always settling on her niece.

He had to create a diversion. He must give her a note from Abraham.

She was balancing a tray on her hand when he collided with her.

"I am...so... sorry! I do apologise." As he bent to retrieve the broken plates and carrots, you name it, he pushed a note in her hand.

Denise stood there paralysed.

Meredith apologised. "She is new. I am sorry, Sir."

"It's my fault. I bumped into her. I must pay for the damage."

"Nonsense. Your suit is soiled. Please send us the bill for dry cleaning. We do apologise."

Mworozi beamed at Denise and left the restaurant.

"I am sorry, aunt. The man bumped into me. The blind fool!"

"Denise, you are forgetting one thing. A customer is always correct."

"Well, it won't happen again. I am sorry."

"Good. I am glad you are learning."

Denise couldn't wait for her break. What break? She wasn't allowed to go out for fresh air. She took her breaks in the staff dining room. She would read her note in the toilet. But who was this man? She was puzzled.

It was four hours later when she finally found time to go to the toilet.

Dear Denise,

I am doing what I can.

My brother has been to see your mother. I hope she doesn't turn out like the rest of the family.

One thing you should never forget is my love for you. Keep fit.

I love you. We will be together soon.

Love Abraham xxx

Denise read the note a second time. She pushed it in her bra next to her heart. She must treasure it. This was her first time to see his handwriting. She was still upset because things didn't turn out as she had planned. She hated the day she saw her monthly periods. "Was there anything wrong with her or did Abraham have a problem? Suppose she was barren? He had been married before and no kids to show for it. Well, she must let him know. This is a problem they must discuss. He did mention how much he loves children. If she is the one with a problem, she will have to let him go... Oh Abraham! We have to try again. She smiled at herself in the mirror.

As soon as she went back to the dining room, she found a message from her mother. She smiled.

"If you think I will let you go alone, you are mistaken," her aunt reminded her. "I am coming with you."

As it turned out, Meredith let Denise go alone but with her driver.

"Don't let her out of your sight," she told the driver.

"Yes, Madam." He felt sorry for the young girl. She hardly gets fresh air. Well, he was doing his job.

Denise turned to the driver. "Take a left here. It's twenty minutes' drive. We will be back before my aunt says 'where is my driver?'"

CHAPTER NINE

"Oh no, girl! I will lose my job."

"Are you going to tell her?"

"But…"

"Do as I say." She pushed a few shillings into his hands. You could do with deodorant, she thought.

He took a deep breath as he took directions from Denise.

"Here we are. I won't be long."

He gave her a warning look. "If you were my daughter, I would advise a rubber relationship."

"What?"

"Nothing."

Denise knocked and knocked. There was no reply. She left a note for him.

"He is not there," she told the driver.

"Thank God for that."

"What is that supposed to mean?"

"My mouth is sealed," he giggled like a schoolboy.

Denise felt a shiver run through her body when she saw the conditions in which her mother had been reduced to. Her mother now slept in the servant's quarters. She slept in one room with Nicholas and Eric while the other room was used as a kitchen.

The big house was now rented out to help with the mortgage. Her eyes rested on the swimming pool, the orchard, and the river that ran through their land. The place looked well maintained. If this place was hers, she would sell it and buy a smaller place. She was hurt that her mother had to live like this but she was happy for turning Desmond down. Oh! Desmond would have solved all this.

"How are you, mother?"

"I am well as you can see." She was baking cakes for selling. She supplied a few restaurants in town including the M&E restaurant.

"Those cakes look delicious, mother."

"Help yourself. How have you been, Denise?"

She bit into her cake. After a long silence, she answered her mother with tears in her eyes. "I miss you, mother. I miss my family. I miss how we used to be before father..." She couldn't go on.

"I miss those times as well," she replied to her daughter.

"Now, you must have an idea why you are here."

Denise shook her head.

"Some guy asking for your hand in marriage has approached me today soon after the go-between had been. Do you know this man very well?"

"A lot of men have been asking for my hand in marriage long before I reached puberty. I don't know who approached you."

"The one who saved your life."

"Oh, it's Abraham!" A smile lit her face. She blushed. Her blood reached boiling point.

Louise looked at her daughter in astonishment. The smile on her daughter's face made her heart beat at a funny speed.

She has been there. She knew what it was like to fall in love with someone the family doesn't approve of. Her family had been disappointed when she fell in love with a bank clerk. Her father, a District Commissioner, had hit the roof. "You will not marry a lousy bank clerk. Has he told you how much he earns? Don't answer. I know he hasn't. They earn peanuts. You will never be able to live in luxury like you are used to. What more can you I tell you, my daughter? You will not marry that man. I forbid you."

Louise had cried herself to sleep but not before she came up with a plan.

Two months later, her mother was bending over her. Asking her when she last had her curse.

"I... don't know."

"You don't know? Answer me, child."

Louise had confessed the whole thing.

Her mother had been shocked. "Don't you have a caring soul in your body? This will kill your father. His reputation will be destroyed by your carelessness."

"I am sorry, mother."

"Well you have made your bed. You must lie in it. I will inform your father."

Her father's reaction shocked her. "You must get rid of it. I will not let you marry a Mr Nobody."

"But father, there are such things as promotions. He is not going to remain a bank clerk all his life."

"Your reasoning is causing me a migraine. Do as I say. Get rid of it. I am sending you abroad. Your aunt will be happy to help you. I am so ashamed of you, Louise." Then he had attacked his wife.

"Where were you when all this was going on? Tell me, woman." His slap made a dent on his wife's cheek. Her mother had received the beatings without complaint like a typical obedient African wife. That was before women's rights came into existence.

Louise made a decision. She married the man they hated. They lived in a bed-sit for four months. Then, before the twins were born, they moved into a two-bedroom house. The place was big with a huge compound with different types of trees and fruits. She made a little money by teaching women how to read and write. Her husband's income and her income put together made a huge difference. Richard, her husband's brother, visited regularly with a live chicken or wild meat, which came in handy. Louise knew his reasons for the visits. She ignored his intentions. She loved her husband. She could never cheat on him, no matter how hard life was. Richard had been the first one to flirt with her but when she met his brother, she knew whom she wanted to spend the rest of her life with. She loved her husband. She supported him in everything he put his hooks in. He followed numerous courses and by the time Eric was crawling, he was the head of investments. All of a sudden, the two-bedroom house became too small. They applied for a mortgage, hence the five-bedroom house and fifty acres of land she was now renting out to pay off the mortgage.

He had saved quite a lot for a rainy day but his illness dried up every shilling they had saved. There was no cure for him. The cancer had spread and destroyed his lungs. Her eyes smarted with tears as she remembered how he begged her for a release. She had been shocked by his request. "I can never do that. It's cruel." She had monitored all his medications. Not once did she leave medicines lying about. She could read his mind all right. His last words to her tore at her heart as she promised him that she would look after the children.

They would be safe and cared for. Has she? Where is Annabella? Why is Denise staying with Meredith? Why is Nicholas working at the age of fourteen? Why is Eric so miserable he can't even ride his bike because it has got a puncture and I can't afford to repair it? It gets worse in this small bedroom-sitting room where she has to tell her two sons to face the other way while she dresses. "Oh Isaac! I have let you down."

Denise looked at her mother through her tears. "Oh mother please, you will make yourself ill. Why are you crying? You don't want me to marry Abraham? Please tell me you approve."

Louise hugged her daughter and then let go. She looked into her daughter's eyes.

"You have my blessing."

"Oh mother! Abraham and I will look after you in your old age. I am not sure about the present. He is not well off but I intend to make use of his fertile land. We will look after you, mother."

"Don't worry about me, child. My cakes business is doing well. The mortgage will be paid off in no time. Things will go back to normal."

"Are you going to tell Uncle Richard about Abraham?"

"He is your uncle. I will tell him but Nicholas and I will handle everything."

"He will hit the roof."

"I know. We shall cross that bridge when we get to it. Now, let's talk about you. Are you happy at your aunt's place?"

Denise took a deep breath. She decided to spare her mother more pain. If she knew that Meredith beat her and treated her like a prisoner, she would go mental. "I am happy mother but I would like to come back and help you with housework."

Louise looked around her. There were two beds. Hers and one for the boys.

"I guess we could share my bed. It is big enough."

"Oh mother! Thank you. I know Aunt Meredith won't like it."

"Don't worry, child. I know how to handle her. She is a good aunt. Don't forget that. They offered Nicholas a job but he turned it down."

"Why did he turn it down? I was looking forward to working with him."

"I didn't like the idea of him wiping tables. I didn't want that on his curriculum vitae. Wiping tables is not a good start. As if God heard my cry for help, someone left an application form on my doorstep for Nicholas."

"What does he do?"

"He is a messenger for J& Sons solicitors. He delivers documents to their clients and helps with filing and making teas."

"That's a good start but when does he find time for schoolwork?"

"I make sure he does his homework before I turn off the lights."

"I am a bit puzzled. Who left the application forms for him?" Denise asked.

"I have no idea."

"Have you been to his work place?"

"Oh yes. I went with him for his interview. It's a big firm. It's on Kampala Road, opposite the main post office. They have a good reputation. The best lawyers in Uganda.

"Now, make yourself a drink. I will tell your driver to shoot off."

"I need to collect my clothes."

"Your aunt will send them."

"Oh no! She will miss out a few things." She didn't want her aunt to see her diary. She would be shocked to know that her niece was no longer innocent.

"Then I will come with you."

"Would you, mother? Thank you."

"But I must talk to your aunt first."

"Of course."

Meredith threw a temper. "But what was the reason? What has she been telling you?"

"I want my children around me, especially Denise now that she will be leaving me for good."

"What do you mean?"

"I have given her my blessing. She is to marry Abraham."

There was a long silence.

"Are...you...out of your mind, Louise?"

"My mind is quite clear. I have just remembered the promise I made to your brother before he died."

"Surely you didn't promise him to sacrifice his daughter's happiness."

"Meredith, is Denise happy?"

The question made Meredith answer with a question.

"What has Denise been telling you?"

"She doesn't have to tell me anything but your driver in my driveway tells me a lot. Tell me Meredith, are you being generous to your niece or do you want to protect her from the person she loves?"

"He is Mr Nobody. You have to undo your blessing."

"That will not do. My parents called your brother Mr Nobody and that didn't stop me marrying him."

"You mean having yourself knocked up?"

"I would like you to rephrase that." Her nostrils flared.

"I am sorry, Louise. I am trying to protect my niece. I love her dearly. I want her to have a better life.

"You have never seen poverty. Where women use their undergarments as bedcovers at night and it gets worse when you don't have to ask a woman when she gave birth. You only have to look at the yellow dry shit on her dress then you know there is another mouth to feed.

"Do you really want Denise to be like those women?"

"I know you mean well but some women choose to live like that. With all this sunshine and free water, what stops them washing shit off their clothes?"

"Louise, I thought hardship has taught you a thing or two. Where do they get soap from?"

"How much is a bar of soap?" Louise shot back. 'They only have to sell a kilo of beans and that's enough for soap. You know I taught women how to read and write. I didn't just end there; I taught them hygiene and survival. I can assure you. I am speaking from experience.

"Denise will be taught what needs to be done in order to survive. I will give her guidance. I won't change my mind about her marriage to Abraham if that's what she wants."

"I guess I won't be getting my goat." She hung up with a bang.

Louise held the phone for a long time. Her brother in law and his sister were number one gamblers. "They want to gamble with my children's lives. Well, Isaac, I must do what I can to keep my promise."

She smiled at her daughter.

"I wish you a happy marriage. Whenever you need help, come to me."

"Thank you, mother."

Chapter Ten

Desmond put the shopping in the house. To his surprise he saw Annabella preparing lunch with little success.

"What are you doing?"

"What does it look like?"

"Why are you cooking? Where is Agasha?"

There was a silence. She covered her cooking and sat back on her heels.

"If I were you, I would not cover spaghetti. It will boil over."

She looked at him accusingly as if to say: do you think I have just started cooking today?

"I have added a little olive oil. It won't boil over," she replied. She took a deep breath. "Agasha resigned."

"Resigned? Why? Have you been treating her badly? We pay her good money."

"She said there is a man in the house."

He laughed.

"Did she think I was a woman when I employed her?"

"She says there is a ghost in the house. She has been seeing a ghost since she came. She put up with him because she wanted money badly but..."

Annabella bit her lip. She smiled at Desmond. "She said that, this morning, the ghost told her to leave or he would beat her senseless."

Desmond was trying not to laugh but to see Annabella laughing for the first time made him lose himself. He laughed himself silly. "I must...talk to her family and reassure them that there is no ghost."

"Just pay her but don't bother explaining yourself because she is telling the truth."

Desmond narrowed his eyes at her.

"Have you seen him?"

She nodded.

"And you never said anything?"

"I actually enjoy his company."

"What is that supposed to mean?"

"It means, he is harmless and he hasn't told me to pack my bags. Who is he?"

"I don't know. I haven't seen him," he lied. His presence was what made his mother move to the city. She couldn't stand the torture of being watched by her dead husband all night. How wrong she had been. He followed her to town. He scared every man she tried to date. She got rid of him when she turned to Jesus Christ. From the time she accepted Jesus as her saviour, she ignored all the men that tried to date her or marry her. He was happy about her decision. He hated other men taking over his father's place. His father haunted him as well. He chased every girl he dated. They ran out crying with their clothes back to front.

"Desmond, I asked you a question. Don't tell me you haven't seen him or heard doors banging and closing."

"Well, you tell me about him then I will figure out who he is."

"He smokes a pipe. He wears a tweed jacket and corduroy trousers. He is handsome if you ask me."

Desmond frowned. "Annabella, there is a photo album in Amanda's room. You have been looking at photo albums of my family.

CHAPTER TEN

"Yes, the man you saw in the album is my father. He met his death during hunting. They said it was an accident. His mate's spear went though his heart." His mind switched back. The same mate who wanted to jump into bed with his mother, he thought sadly. The git! Bastard git! He looked at Annabella. "I was eight and Amanda six. I still remember the incident as if it happened only yesterday. Annabella, to put your mind at rest, this house is not haunted."

"Desmond, I am sorry about your father's death but don't insult my intelligence. I know the difference between a ghost and a photograph."

She ignored the look in his eyes. She dished out her cooking.

He poked his food with a fork. "Annabella, we must return to town."

She looked at him in surprise.

"We still have two full weeks. Your own words, remember?"

"I can't stand this kind of food. I have never eaten spaghetti and fish." He pushed his plate forward.

She did the same.

"I don't like it either."

"Then why did you cook it? You wasted that fish. It would have been good with roast potatoes."

"Where is the oven?"

"You roast them in hot ash."

"You have to look for another cook. I am not cooking on an open fire. I have never cooked on an open fire."

"That's why we are going back to town. In fact, my work has been neglected while I sit here waiting for you to tell me what must be done about our relationship. I could wait for eternity and you won't give a damn shit. You are a very spoilt brat. What is your decision?"

She stared at him with her mouth open. How dare he talk to her like this! Has he forgotten he is the one who destroyed her

91

future? She was miserable because of him. She was now wondering whether she has an incontinence problem. Every kick in her belly, she runs for the toilet. Her body has been disfigured for his stupid mistake and now he stands there and insults her calling her a spoilt brat? Well, let's put his love to the test. Her nose twitched. There was a bit of sweat now settling on top of her nose.

Desmond recognised it as a temper sign.

He waited for an eruption.

It came with a blow. He wasn't prepared for it. It shocked him.

"Don't you dare call me a brat! I am in this mess because of your stupid mistake. You thought I was Denise. I believe you, but did you have...to... If you call that sex or lovemaking, I don't want to go through that experience ever." She sobbed remembering the incident. Now she was carrying his child. She was trapped. Who would marry her after this? She sniffed in her handkerchief. "I have a surprise for you. I am not going back to town," she told him. "Your child will be born in this house."

He recovered from the shock. He digested her words.

"A slap on your face would teach you a thing or two but I am not a wife beater."

"A wife beater? Since when did we get married?"

"Now you are prepared to stay in this house, that makes you my wife by right.

"Well, I have a surprise for you – or maybe it's not a surprise at all. Men do leave their wives at home while they go to the city to earn a little money to support their family. I am leaving. I will be back when I am ready."

Annabella stared at him in horror but pride stopped her from begging him to take her or stay. She didn't want to stay in a place like this alone. She was only testing his love for her. Well she got the answer. There was no need going with him back to Kampala. She would be miserable knowing his heart was still bleeding for Denise. She held on to her pride and watched Desmond going to and fro packing his clothes.

The next thing she heard was the car engine crying. She stood by the window and watched the car disappear.

She collapsed in a nearby chair and sobbed. She was alone in this haunted place. She looked around hoping to catch the ghost's presence but it was all-quiet. Suppose he didn't come back in time? Who would help her with the birth of his child? She wiped her eyes. Well, crying was not going to help the situation. She cleared the dishes. She tidied up around her. Then something hit her mind. Who was going to get her shopping, fetching water? Desmond met all those tasks. The place was in the middle of a jungle. She was stranded. Her pride was the reason.

Desmond finished his call with a smile on his face. What men do for love? He shook his head. He whistled all the way to his car. He was tired but his journey had been worth it.

Annabella cried with joy as she watched the car headlights in a distance. She held her breath. Suppose it's not Desmond? She stood by the window and waited with anticipation. The house was in darkness – so if it's not Desmond, she would be ready for whoever. She reached for a panga, which Desmond had been using to clear the yard. She was ready for a killing.

To her relief, it *was* Desmond. She put her weapon away. She wiped her tears and composed herself. She took a seat in her usual chair and waited for him. Her composure will tell him that she is not scared one bit. It was a complete lie. She had been praying for his return but her pride was now back in action.

Desmond dropped his shopping bag on a couch.

"Hi?"

"Did you forget something?"

He was taken aback by the question. The girl was too headstrong. Was she putting it on, or was she serious?

"I was meant to come back. In case you haven't been to my room, my packed bag is still in there."

She gave him a questioning look. Is he telling the truth? Well, she never went to his room. In actual fact, she hasn't been to his room since they arrived.

He took a seat next to her.

"I have good news and bad news. What do you want to hear first?"

"I guess good news. I can't stand bad news."

He smiled at her.

"The good news is your dowry has been paid."

She looked away.

"And, our house is ready. It's waiting for the lady of the house to put in the furniture of her choice."

She gave him a weak smile.

"If you think this is good news, I don't know what the bad news is."

"Denise is marrying the tramp I told you about."

"I am not surprised. Denise likes a gypsy life. They will be on the move twenty-four hours. Oh that's what she likes. I am not one bit surprised. When is the wedding?"

He winked at her.

"If you think I will let that tramp be the first proper son in law in the family, then you don't know Desmond Tumwiine." And with that, he produced a small package. "It's yours. Open it."

She did. She looked at it.

"What is the meaning of this ring?"

"It means, we are engaged and next week we are getting married."

"You got it wrong Mr. I haven't said yes."

He rubbed his temple.

"Annabella, do you want to turn me down like your sister? Tell me the truth. What is so revolting about me?"

CHAPTER TEN

The question took her by surprise.

"Why, you are handsome now that you have lost weight. What makes you think there is something wrong with you? I am the one with a problem. It's wrong to marry you knowing I... don't love you."

She looked down. She couldn't look him in the face. It was too much for her to endure...

"I have enough love to sustain us. I will make you happy. Our child will have both parents. What do you say about that?"

She took a deep breath.

"Give me time to think..."

"I am glad you are thinking about it."

He ran his fingers in her hair. He looked at his fingers; he smiled remembering the women he had dated. They had different hairstyles and smells. His pillow explained everything about them. At one time he asked one girl why she didn't wash her hair.

"Oh Desmond, you know nothing about hair. These are extensions. They lose their texture if washed regularly."

"How long do you keep your hair like this before you move on to another style?"

"It lasts four months plus," she had replied without shame.

He promised himself not to date her again. He didn't have to tell her – the family ghost made her wear her dress front to back.

He looked at Annabella. She was enjoying his touch; if not she would have pushed his hand away. He smelt his fingers; he smelt Head and Shoulders shampoo.

"You do take good care of your hair, Annabella."

She pushed him away. She knew what he was up to. In his dreams, she thought as she stood up. "I will get supper ready."

He gave her a questioning look. "Don't tell me it's fish and spaghetti," he groaned. "Not again. Honestly." He had never eaten spaghetti with fish. He felt sick at the thought of repeating her cooking.

"No, I was sick all afternoon. I will make something simple. Beef stew and rice."

He made himself comfortable as he watched her prepare what she called a simple meal. He hid his face behind a newspaper each time the cooking oil dropped on her hand. He was useless when it came to cooking. He waited for her simple meal that took her three hours to prepare. This meal would have taken his mother an hour or less.

He was surprised when it tasted better than Marjorie's, his housekeeper. Marjorie's cooking was too fatty and his doctor had warned him about fatty foods.

Annabella surprised him again when she told him to put the ring on her finger. He wept with joy when she slept in the crook of his arms.

Annabella lay quietly listening to Desmond's heartbeat. She was marrying him for different reasons. The major one was security. She needed security. She had never worked in her life. When their father passed away, it was Denise who applied for jobs and ended up with Desmond now breathing on her neck. It's a very strange world. He was a caring and loving person but the circumstances in which they met would always haunt her. If he had approached her in a proper manner after Denise's disappearance, maybe...she would have considered his offer. But now...she would always remember her lost innocence.

"Annabella, I am glad you accepted to be my wife. You will never want for anything. I promise you that. I guess you have an idea what a marriage involves."

She stiffened in his arms. She sighed.

"How can I fail to know Desmond? I am carrying your child."

"Our child, Annabella," he reminded her.

"The child I didn't take part in creating."

"Annabella, are you saying our marriage will be just a front?"

"Time will tell. Please don't push me."

Chapter Eleven

Abraham frowned at his brother. "Did you read this note?"

"What makes you think I did?" He sniggered.

"Well, the look on your face tells me you know something."

Mworozi grinned at his brother. "I couldn't resist it. I am sorry. I do not blame you for..."

Abraham put up his hand. I don't want to discuss my private matters with you. This note was private. You shouldn't have read it."

"Then she should have put it in a private and confidential envelope if she didn't want other people to know her carry on with you."

"She is a good girl. Don't criticise her. If there is one person you want to criticise, it's me. I should have known better. I am glad I took precautions."

"And she didn't know?"

"Mworozi, I will change to another go-between if you don't behave yourself. Now, shouldn't you be going?"

Mworozi patted his brother on the back. "A good shave would do you good. You are a disgrace, Abraham. I am glad Mother hasn't seen what her golden boy has been up to."

"Well, she is not going to see me, is she? And please, don't tell her about these conditions. It will break her heart."

"She does ask about you."

"What do you tell her?"

"What you want her to know. Father thinks you are crazy."

Abraham took a deep breath. "Please hurry things up. I don't want that girl snatched away from me."

"You said she loves you."

"How deep is her love?" Abraham thought aloud.

Mworozi grinned. "I will find out for you."

Abraham glared at his brother. "Don't you dare seduce my girl. We love each other. You don't need to..."

"Calm down. I have no intention of seducing your girl," he lied. That's what he intended to do. His brother has been hurt twice. Both women behaved the same way as if they were cut from the same cloth. He must find out Denise's behaviour before his brother gets serious.

He arrived at M&E Restaurant with a bunch of flowers.

"Excuse me, Madam. Could you please pass on these flowers to... oh dear, I don't know her name."

Meredith pulled her forehead. "You don't know her name and yet you bought flowers for her?"

"It's an apology."

Meredith smiled. "Why? I remember you. You must be after my niece. She is called... Denise! Denise?" Meredith called out. "There is a gentleman here for you."

She turned to Mworozi. "What are you up to?"

Mworozi grinned at her. He was saved from answering when Denise appeared.

He smiled at her. "I hope you like roses."

Denise bit her lip. She looked at her aunt for answers.

Meredith busied herself with the phone. She wasn't phoning anyone. She just hoped that her niece would see sense this time and fall for this gentleman. The way he was dressed explained everything. He had class.

Denise gave Mworozi a weak smile. "You shouldn't have. I am

not into flowers but my mother will love them." She gave him a cold stare.

Meredith banged the phone down. "Denise! Apologise this minute." She fanned herself with her hand.

Denise looked from one to the other. "I am extremely busy. If you'll excuse me, I have duties to see to."

"Oh no, young lady. You are not going anywhere until you have apologised to this gentleman." The people in the restaurant were now watching with their mouths open, their food forgotten.

Eliot calmed his wife down. "I will handle her. Just calm down, dear. You will give yourself an injury."

Eliot turned to Mworozi and Denise. "I have a private lounge where you can both sit and sort out whatever is going on. There is no need for a scene, Denise. The gentleman only bought you flowers."

"But I am spoken for. I don't accept gifts from another man. It's against my mother's teachings."

Meredith banged the table.

"Spoken for? You mean that tramp?"

Eliot's stare silenced his wife.

Mworozi gritted his teeth. He disguised his temper, but he was burning inside. He smiled at Eliot. "Where is that private lounge you mentioned, Sir?"

"Follow me."

Once seated, he asked Mworozi what drink he wanted.

"If you have a little brandy please."

"Denise?"

"I am fine, uncle. Thank you. I don't see what the fuss is all about really." She sighed as she moved from one foot to another. "Idiot! Buying me flowers in order to get to my bloomers. It's written all over his face."

As soon as the door closed behind Eliot, Mworozi pushed a note into Denise's hand.

"It's from Abraham. I am sorry I didn't introduce myself the first time we met. I am Albert Mworozi, Abraham's elder brother."

Denise gasped! "Why did you make me look like an idiot? You should have told me."

"I am sorry. I am the man who went to see your mother on my brother's behalf."

"You are a go-between, is that right? Are these flowers from Abraham?"

The door opened. Eliot put the drink on the table. He looked from one to the other. He frowned at Denise. He left without a word.

Mworozi sipped on his drink. After a long silence, he replied to her, "No, the flowers are from me. You know very well that my brother can't afford flowers."

"I know and that doesn't change a damn thing. I love him the way he is."

She looked at him. "Have you ever been in love?"

He took a sip of his brandy. He nodded. "I am in love with you."

She stood up. "If you don't mind, my break is over and thanks for the flowers. My mother will love them. One other thing, please tell Abraham that I now live with my mother. I need to speak to him. Bye."

Mworozi took his drink in gulps. He grinned at the walls around him. "Phew! I do envy you, brother. I would move heaven and earth to have a faithful woman like her." His brother would be happy to hear this but he would spare him what Meredith had called him. It hurt him so much to hear someone call his brother a tramp.

He said bye to Eliot and Meredith and thanked them for their hospitality.

"I will be in touch," he told them.

"You would be a fool not to," Meredith replied with a smile.

Denise read her note from Abraham.

Dear Denise,
 I am sorry things didn't turn out as you expected. I didn't want to be called Mr Irresponsible. Do you think I like to be called Mr Nobody? Listen Darling, I took care of everything. There is nothing wrong with us. The right time is all we need. We shouldn't be long. I am almost ready.
 Remember, I love you.
 Yours always, Abraham.

Denise blushed. How the hell did he manage to do that without her knowing? She was so stupid when it came to such matters. She hoped she would not look stupid next time. She pushed the note in her bra.

When she got back to the dining room, her aunt was waiting for her.

"What have you got to say, young lady?"

"I have nothing to say. I don't like men pushing me about or fluttering their bushy eyebrows at me. I know what I want and do me a favour, aunt – please don't call Abraham a tramp. He is not a tramp. If you'll excuse me, I have tables to clear." She left without a backward glance.

Meredith looked at her husband for answers.

"The best thing to do is leave her alone. She will remember you when the going gets tough."

"I care for her, Eliot."

"I know and your interference makes her determined."

Denise knew they were talking about her. She hated quarrelling with her aunt. She went to her and apologised. "I am sorry, aunt. I have already made up my mind. Abraham and I will look after you in your old age." She gave her a weak smile.

"You mean the other way round? Get on with your work, Denise. I don't want more scenes in my restaurant."

When Denise got home that evening, she found her uncle and her mother having a shouting match.

"What do you mean, woman? Are you out of your mind?"

"I am not touching Annabella's dowry until I am sure she is happy in her marriage. If she is not, I want her back."

"Look at you, Louise. Do you like this kind of life? Annabella's dowry is enough to pay off the mortgage."

Her nostrils flared! "You should have thought about that before you lost Denise's dowry on solitaire and paying off your mortgage. How selfish can one get? Your brother would turn in his grave if he were to see what you have done to his family."

"Woman! How many times do I have to say I am sorry? I made a mistake." He gave Denise a pleading look. "Do you want your mother to suffer like this?"

"I am not suffering, Richard. Leave Denise alone!"

Denise excused herself. "I will be in the kitchen if you need me."

She joined her brothers who were doing their homework.

Nicholas looked up. "Hi?"

"Hi?"

Eric bit his lip. "Denise, I am sorry Annabella didn't invite you to her wedding."

"It's all right Eric. If that makes her happy, then I will be happy to remain behind. You will tell me how she is, won't you Eric?"

"Sure I will."

That night Denise lay awake wondering how long it would take Abraham to put the dowry together. She had plans for that land. If he did hurry things up, they would miss the rains and then what would they feed on? She had done gardening with her grandmother before. It was not a joke but she was now determined to do it.

Louise knew her daughter was wide awake. Whatever was keeping her awake, couldn't be that good. She could hear the boys snoring. God bless them. They fell asleep as soon as their heads hit the pillows. Her mind was in turmoil. Her brother in law's nagging gave her grief. She gave him and Meredith their share from Annabella's dowry. She doesn't owe them anything. They must leave her alone to run her home in peace. She gazed into the darkness remembering her husband, his last words to her before he joined his maker and the promise she made. She has been pondering on his last words lately. What did he mean exactly? She didn't want to raise her hopes for nothing but something kept nagging on her mind and he was regularly in her dreams. Before he left this world, he had held her hand and said safe three times. She had nodded at him saying she would make sure their children would never want for anything and would be safe. But the look he gave her had confused her. What did he mean by safe? What was behind that look in his eyes? She must talk to someone or else she would go mental. "Denise, are you awake?"

"I am. I can't sleep. I don't know why," she lied. She was missing Abraham.

"I need to ask you something. The kitchen is the best place. We shouldn't wake the boys with girly talk."

Louise told her daughter what's been bothering her.

"I guess he was telling you that he would be safe. I mean, no more pain. He was in such pain, remember? Oh mother! You did all you could to relieve him of the pain but...the painkillers wore out quickly and he would ask for more. I know what you did for father. I admire your devotion. She sighed. I...overheard...he wanted you to give him a quick release."

Louise stared at her daughter. "Where...did...you get that information from?"

"I said I overheard. I was not supposed to be eavesdropping but there I was with my ears glued to the wall."

Louise held her hand. She looked into her daughter's eyes. She shook her head. "I couldn't do it. I tried many times, but I changed my mind at the last minute." She burst into tears. "I couldn't do it or allow him do it to himself. I constantly monitored him."

"You are very brave mother. I love you."

She held her daughter. The warmth from her gave her comfort.

"Denise, let's go back to that issue. What else do you think he meant? I am not sure, darling."

"Hold on a second, maybe he meant a safe as in bank. Father was the head of investment. He must have invested in a lot of things.

"He did. We sold all our shares to get him proper medications. There is nothing left."

"Mother, go to your bank and find out or else you will never rest."

She looked at her daughter. "That's what I have been thinking but if he did have a safe in the bank, I would have known about it. We never had secrets."

"Mother, find out from your bank, right?"

"I hate to make a fool of myself."

"I will come with you. It's worth trying. Maybe you should talk to Annabella. She was his favourite, following him everywhere including his work place."

"He loved you all, Denise. It's you who wanted to hang around home playing with our neighbour's kids climbing trees."

"I know. I am sorry for doubting his love for me. I will come with you. There is no point torturing your mind wondering what it is he meant. When you get to the bank tell them you have come to get something from father's safety box. Don't give them a clue that you are not sure whether there is a safe or not."

Louise smiled at her daughter. "I wish I had courage like yours. I will be shaking before they ask me my late husband's names."

"I will be there to hold your hand. Don't fear."

The following day, they went to their bank.

They were told they have to make an appointment for that kind of service and they have to bring with them authorisation papers, identity card with photo and a marriage certificate.

Louise looked at her daughter. "What the hell does he mean by authorisation papers?"

"I guess he means father's death certificate."

"Oh! I see. Does that mean there is something? Why would he be asking for all these if there was nothing?"

"I don't know, mother. You will find out in three days' time."

Chapter Twelve

Louise gritted her teeth. She was running late for her cakes delivery. Who could be phoning her this time of the day? She was tempted to ignore it. She answered the phone. There was no one there. She was about to put it back when she heard someone sigh on the other end. "Who is it?" There was no answer. "If you don't answer me, I will hang up. I hate time wasters."

She was about to hang up when the sobs hit Louise's eardrum. "Who is it? Are you in pain?"

"Oh mother! I miss you."

Louise gasped for air! "Annabella…my baby! Are you all right?"

Annabella sniffed. "I am fine, mother. I am just…emotional, miss you terribly."

Louise sat down. "Now listen baby. How are you?"

Annabella took a deep breath. "I am well…apart from… the pains I get now and again. Mother, I am pregnant."

There was a long pregnant pause. "How many months?" She braved the question.

"Five months," she replied with a tired voice.

Louise did her calculations. Fat tears dropping on her cheeks. "Annabella, all I can say is, I am sorry for sending you out to look for your sister. If I had done it myself, this would not have happened."

"Mother, it would have happened. Our house was on surveillance twenty-four hours; even when you told him that Denise was missing, he didn't believe you. He thought Denise changed her mind about the marriage and was hiding in the house. Don't go on blaming yourself. What is done is done."

"Annabella, you don't have to marry him if you are not happy."

There was a long pause. "Desmond is sorry for what he did and I know the incident haunts him. I have forgiven him. I am marrying him the day after tomorrow. I will respect him and be faithful to him but love is..."

"I understand, Annabella. Does he treat you well?"

"Oh! He does in a big way. The only problem is I am lonely. He is at work all day. I have no one to talk to all day."

Louise felt relieved. At least she looks forward to his homecoming.

"Mother, I was wondering if Eric could stay with us for a few days a week, months, whatever suits you both."

"I will have to ask Eric. What does Desmond say about this?"

"He is the one who told me to invite him over. He knows I am lonely." She wasn't going to tell her mother that she had sacked all the workers. She sacked them for good reasons. Marjorie's cooking was a danger to everyone's health and she controlled the home as if she owned it. Her relatives were all over the house. Her grandchildren playing hide and seek all over the place. There was no order at all. Desmond did nothing about it. And another thing, Marjorie knew how she'd ended up in Desmond's bedroom. Her husband, a gardener, got the sack as well. He was the one who led her to Desmond's bedroom. The gatekeeper got the sack. He was the one who'd kidnapped her. The fool who did food deliveries for them got his matching orders as well. He was one of the kidnappers. The one who'd slapped her and threatened her with a knife if she didn't shut up.

Their voices as they threatened her with a knife is one thing she will never forget.

Her mother's voice cut through her thoughts. "Annabella, I know you and Denise are not on good terms. How long is this silence going to take?"

"Time will tell," she answered.

Louise wasn't going to push her. She had been through a lot. They will come round in their own time.

"Mother, Aunt Meredith told me that you now live in the servant's quarters. Why?"

"Your aunt does really interfere."

"She cares, mother."

"I know but there is a mortgage to sort out."

"I thought my dowry would help."

"Oh no, baby. It doesn't work that way. You are not marrying Desmond so I could live in comfort. Your happiness is important to me, Annabella. You only have to say, 'mum, I don't want to marry this man', I will return every shilling except the bit I gave to your uncle and the goat your aunt received."

Annabella snorted. "No wonder she is on good terms with Desmond."

"Well, two goats so far," Louise replied.

"Mother, I thought to give you a call. I miss you. I don't know when I will see you."

"Well, that can be arranged. Have you been to hospital for check-ups?"

Annabella sighed. "The hospital comes to me. That's how Desmond operates.

"Mother, to put your mind at rest, I am happy. He treats me well and please talk to Eric. I will call again. I need to know so I can prepare his room and toys."

"I will tell him to give you a call when he comes back from

school. Keep well and remember: I am your mother, your best friend."

"Thanks, mother." They both hang up.

Annabella remained in her room staring at the walls until the doorbell brought her mind back to the present. She was expecting a cook and a cleaner from an agency Desmond had recommended.

She peeped through the curtains. It was a man in his mid twenties by his looks. "Who is he?" Well, she wasn't going to let a strange man in the house. He could be a rapist, a thief – you name it.

She ignored the doorbell. She checked again, now there was a woman talking to him. The woman rang the bell.

Well, she will have to ask who they are.

They told her, but kept a bit of information from her.

"I think there is a misunderstanding Mr..."

"Call me Lucas."

"Well, Lucas, you will have to hang about while I confirm this with... I will be a minute," she told them.

Now to pass through Desmond travel switchboard was another case especially when Desmond is in the middle of a meeting. She hoped he was not.

"I am sorry, Desmond is not available," she was told.

"Well, you will have to make him available, won't you? Tell him it's Annabella and it's urgent."

"He is in a meeting. He can't be interrupted."

"I am telling you to interrupt him. I don't have the patience. Can't you use your own initiative woman? What's your name?"

"My name doesn't matter. I am doing my job. I have other calls to deal with."

"You won't have a job left once I talk to Desmond about your lack of communication skills. Now, do what I asked you to do. This call is urgent."

The receptionist took a deep breath. "What's your name again?"

"I will make sure you lose your job. I told you my name not long ago. Tell him, it's Annabella. His fiancée."

"I am... sorry... Madam. Hold the line please. I will connect you." She gasped for air at the end.

"Oh Desmond! I need your private line. I can't stand that woman on the switchboard. Getting through her is like passing a needle into an elephant skin."

"She is a good receptionist. She is doing her job. What's up?"

"It's the agency you recommended. They sent us a man to do the cooking and the woman to do the cleaning and gardening.

"Annabella, if you don't like the idea of being served by a man, you don't have to employ them."

"Well, the woman can stay but the man has to go."

"Annabella, they are a couple, man and wife. I made sure of that. They will work as a team. It's part of discipline. He doesn't have to dash off whenever he wants his sweetheart."

"You should have explained everything to me. I don't like strange men in the house. I hate men." She said that for good measure."

"I hope I am not one of them, Annabella."

She ignored him. "What do I do?"

"Give them three months' trial. If my weight balloons up, they will have to go."

"You are right. I will give them a chance and please tell that woman on the switchboard to learn a few things on communication skills. Every call is important."

"I will tell her. Have you eaten anything?"

"The new cook will fix me lunch," she giggled and hung up.

Her giggles left Desmond's nerves on edge. If he is good looking, I am the one to do the sacking this time. When he phoned the agency, he told them what age group he wanted.

He went back to his meeting. His mind was at his home wondering what Annabella and her new cook were up to. Why did she giggle? I will find out and soon. He felt relieved when the meeting got to an end. He usually takes his clients to M&E restaurant for lunch but today his secretary will handle them. He was having lunch with Annabella and the new cook. The thought of what they might be up to put a bitter taste in his mouth.

Annabella showed Lucas and his wife Vanessa where the servant's quarters were. "If you happen to have visitors, we must be told about them in plenty of time. This is a private property and I love my privacy." Annabella loved this place. It was a lovely house with a swimming pool overlooking Lake Victoria.

"You will have your privacy, Madam," Vanessa replied.

"Good." She turned to Lucas. "In my house, the only rooms you are allowed in are the kitchen and pantry."

"I wouldn't dream of interfering with your privacy, Madam. Your lunch will be ready shortly." He bowed.

She gave him a cold stare. "You don't have to bow for me. All I am in interested in is competence in your duties."

She took a walk in her compound. She was fully occupied with the surroundings so she didn't hear Desmond's car until he tapped her on the shoulder.

"Desmond! You gave me a fright."

"I can see you are miles away."

"I was thinking. Why are you home early?"

"Don't you want me here? Am I interrupting something?"

"Oh no. I am happy to see you. Maybe I could do with a second opinion about the couple."

"Where are they?"

"Lucas, that's his name, is in the kitchen I suppose. I told him to prepare lunch. There is nothing defrosted. He will have to use his skills. If the food is not on the table in half an hour's time, he knows the way out.

"The woman is called Vanessa. She is plain. I am happy about that," she said without thinking.

He grinned at her.

"What have I said?"

"Nothing. Is the man plain as well?"

"Desmond, in my books, every man is plain... I will fix you a drink. What do you want?"

He smiled. "I will fix it. I want to look at this plain cook."

He did and he felt himself go small. He didn't like Lucas, married or not.

Annabella knew something was bothering Desmond but she had no idea what it was. "Are you ok?"

"Why do you ask?" he snapped at her.

"You look feverish and pale and..."

Vanessa interrupted her. "Excuse me, Madam. Lucas says lunch is ready. Do you eat in the dining room?"

"Where else?" Desmond barked at her.

"There is a problem, Sir. My husband is only allowed in the kitchen and the pantry."

Annabella laughed. "She is right. I told him those are the only places he should go to." She smiled at the woman. "Tell him the dining is fine."

"Thank you, Madam." She walked off.

Desmond turned to Annabella. "Next time you will be telling him the bedroom is fine. He will push inch by inch like an Egyptian camel until I am out of the bed."

She frowned at him. "I have never heard of that saying."

He gritted his teeth.

She understood his behaviour. He must be crazy to think that she would let her cook in her drawers.

She gave him her hand. "Let's go. The food is getting cold."

The lunch turned out superb. It was dumplings with well-fried fish and peas. "What do you think, Desmond?"

"About what?" he asked without interest.

"The food. What else?"

"Oh! At least it's not swimming in olive oil and the salt is what my doctor recommended."

"Does that mean he has passed his test?"

"Annabella! It's just one simple meal. Yes, his cooking is good and I hope that's all he is good at," he snapped at her.

She sighed. "We should look for another cook if you are not happy with Lucas. I am not that stupid. I know what's eating you."

"Let's not argue about this, all right? Just tell what's-her-name to pack for us. I meant to tell you. We are going away after our wedding. I suggest you pack some books to read. I will be busy with meetings.

"Thanks for the lunch...and...you will be ok, won't you?"

"Trust me. I will be fine."

How he longed to hear her say that he is the only man she loves.

Chapter Thirteen

Jocelyn beamed at her son. "I am finally happy," she told Desmond. "Now that you have buried your sins, you can have your holy communion. What possessed you to take a short cut to her heart? Never do that again. You know what I mean. You should know how to control your anger, Desmond."

"Mother, I am now a new person. I am that ashamed of what I did. I am sorry. Please let's not talk about it. This is my wedding day."

"But that doesn't excuse your behaviour, Desmond."

"She has forgiven me."

"Does she love you?"

Desmond sighed. "That's not for me to say. You will have to ask her."

"I don't have to ask her. You have just given me the answer. Give her time. Treat her like a woman. Treat her well. Don't give her a reason to doubt your love for her. God bless you and safe trip."

"Thank you, mother."

Desmond could see Annabella talking to his sister Amanda. He hoped they would get on. She was a good sister. He got on very well with her.

Annabella smiled at her sister in law. "I am glad you could make it."

"I wanted to come but Mother is a very religious person. She said we should wait until Desmond did the right thing, I am glad you agreed to marry him. I know my brother. I can read him like a book. He adores you. Do you love him?"

"Mrs..."

"Please call me Amanda."

"I need time. I will respect him and be faithful to him. Who knows what may come next? Time will tell."

"Welcome to our family. If you need a friend, you know where I am. I would like you to meet my family. I have two boys aged four and ten. They have been asking about you. My husband Edward is away on a business trip. You will see him when he comes back. He works for Desmond Travel Agency."

"I would love to meet your family. Thank you for coming."

They hugged.

"Everything ok dear?"

Annabella coloured. He had never called her dear. "What is this? The beginning of seduction?" Her hair stood out. "I am fine," she replied.

"We'd better get going. The check-in is in an hour's time."

"I haven't said bye to your mother."

Desmond closed his eyes. "Annabella, Mother would be pleased if you called her mother. "Your Mother" sounds a bit too harsh."

"I am sorry. I will call her mother if it pleases you."

Louise listened to her boys' arguments and Eric was making a fool of himself as usual but she enjoyed their argument especially when Nicholas behaved like a child instead of playing the man of the house.

Their arguments put her stress on hold for a bit.

"Mother, please tell this git that Annabella's child can never be his brother or sister."

Louise busied herself with her baking.

"Nicholas, I am not that stupid," Eric told him.

"Well, your ignorance has gone too far this time."

"At least I don't say I will marry my mother when I grow up."

Nicholas rolled his eyes at his little brother. "I was only four when I said those words. Look at you at seven: you still think Annabella's baby is your brother or sister."

"I am almost eight, you fool."

"Then act your age."

"I don't like you, Nicholas."

"Oh yes you do, baby," Louise replied.

Chapter Fourteen

Denise and her mother held their breaths as they waited for the bank manger. They had been told to take a seat and he would be with them shortly. Louise checked the clock on the wall. They had been waiting for half an hour. She had cakes to deliver and Eric's dental appointment. She was running out of time as it was and it might turn out that they had wasted their time coming here. If there were anything, she would have known about it. They never kept secrets from each other.

"I am sorry to keep you waiting," the manager's voice cut through her thoughts. He put a manila envelope on the desk. It was in Isaac's handwriting and addressed to Louise. "That's all there is. Take your time." He excused himself.

Louise looked at her daughter. "What do you think this is? I am so scared, Denise."

"Well, you don't open it, you don't find out. I will open it for you."

"Please do. I can't do it." She was shaking.

Denise opened it. Out popped a piece of paper.

Louise moved closer. "What is it?"

"It's a life insurance policy."

"And?"

Denise's smile slit her cheeks. "Mother, you should have

claimed after father's death."

"But I had no idea." She was shocked. Why did her husband keep such details to himself? What about the insurance company? Why was she never contacted when they didn't get their monthly payment?

"Mother, the insurance company knew when they missed their premium. They thought to get away with it. I will make sure they pay every shilling and compensation. The stress they caused you. Crooks!" She soothed her mother. "I will kill them with my bare hands."

"Denise, calm down. I need time to digest this."

"Mother, there is no time to waste. You need a good lawyer to handle this for you."

"But it costs money."

"Mother, this is money." She waved the piece of paper in her face. She hugged her mother. "Oh Mother! I am proud of my father."

Louise dabbed at her eyes. She looked at her daughter. "I am giving my tenants a week's notice. I am sick and tired of sharing a room with my boys telling them to face the other way while I change. I miss my swimming as well."

The bank manager put his head in. "Is everything all right?"

"Yes…" Louise gulped. "Thank…you; we'd better get going."

He gave them a form to sign.

Once outside, Louise took a deep breath. "What next?"

"Why don't we try J& Sons solicitors? Nicholas thinks they are excellent."

"What does he know? He is only their messenger." Louise laughed.

"Well, do you have anyone in particular?"

"You think J& Sons will handle it?"

"If they can't, they will tell you straight away."

Denise looked around her searching for a taxi.

"Don't even think about it, Denise. We can walk it."

"Oh no, mother. You are a lady. Taxi!" she called out.

Louise wished she could share her daughter's excitement. She missed Isaac terribly. He was her husband, friend and anchor. She dabbed at her eyes.

"You will be all right mother," she comforted her.

Louise looked at her daughter. "I am lucky to have a daughter like you."

Abraham watched Denise and her mother leave J& Sons solicitors. "What the hell is going on? Mworozi, what do you think?"

"Abraham, I am your 'go-between', not mind reader. If you are really bothered, why don't you ask her?"

"Mworozi, I can smell disaster."

"I can smell it too. Why you haven't told her is beyond me. She loves you already. I think she deserves the truth."

"I can't do it yet. I have been hurt before."

"But she is different. She loves you regardless…"

"Mworozi, please find out why she has been visiting J& Sons solicitors."

"Oh no, brother. That's your job. Invite her for a meal. Get her talking. A glass of wine will loosen her tongue."

"I have a very tight schedule and I don't think she drinks."

"You will soon lose her if you think your schedules are more important."

"It's all for her, Mworozi. I love her."

"Then do the damn right thing and tell her the truth."

"Oh no. I have come this far. I can't tell her the truth yet. I might lose her. She would want to know why I didn't tell her in the first place."

"When do you intend to tell her?"

"After the wedding," he replied.

Mworozi looked at his brother. He shook his head.
"You better find yourself another go-between. You are an embarrassment, Abraham. Tell her or I am out."

"You don't mean it."

"I do."

Abraham took a deep breath. "I suppose I better shave."

"You can do more than shaving. Take her to a cinema."

Abraham gave him a piercing look. "Don't push me, Mworozi. We both know why I haven't told her."

"She is different from your other wives."

"My ex-wives," he corrected.

Chapter Fifteen

Denise took a step back. She gasped for air. "Abraham...You look different. What...the hell is..."

He grinned at her.

"It's not funny you know. You almost gave me a heart attack."

"Do you like my new look?"

She sighed. "Abraham, you don't have to be what you are not."

His heart raced. "What...exactly do you mean?"

"I love you the way you are. You don't have to sacrifice your savings to impress me. That haircut must have cost you a fortune. That would have gone towards house furnishings, and cultivating our land."

Abraham laughed. "We are running late, Denise. Our table is booked for eight o'clock. We have twenty minutes."

"I won't be long. I need to powder my nose."

Meredith watched her niece's fiancé with wonder. "What a transformation!"

"But rubbing his arse in someone else's suit. He borrowed that suit, definitely." She wrinkled her nose. Is he going to borrow clothes each time he wants to impress Denise?

Denise said bye to her aunt. "Abraham is taking me to the grill. I would have preferred your restaurant, aunt, but Abraham is..."

x

"You mean he can't afford it?"

"I will see you tomorrow, aunt and thanks for letting me off early."

"Don't make it a habit, Denise. We are short staffed at the moment."

"We need to talk. We need privacy. We are going home."

Denise tensed. "You mean you lied? My aunt knows you are taking me to the grill and that's where we are going. Got it? It's not as if I am hungry but we stick to our original arrangements, all right?"

Abraham ignored her and continued to drive.

"Abraham! Stop the car now."

He pulled up on the side of the road. "What's wrong with you? Are you having second thoughts?"

She was furious. "No, Abraham. I am not what you think. I lost my innocence to you for a reason. You know why. Now my family have accepted you. I don't have to play loose with you. I am not a loose girl."

"Denise, you got my signals wrong. I am sorry. We need to talk. Just to talk. I love you. I wouldn't force you to do something against your will.

"Trust me, Denise. You will come to no harm. I guess we can talk in here but I left my stove on."

She looked at him. "What possessed you to do that? That's a fire hazard."

She gave him a weak smile. "Ok, but no funny business, right?"

"Right," he replied with a smile. He was happy he hasn't lost her. He would die if he did. He must tell her everything but...

They arrived in time to save the kidney and mushroom pies he had left in the oven baking.

"Never do this again. It's a fire hazard," she scolded him as she dished out.

He took a bottle of wine out of the fridge.

"I prefer orange juice please."

"It's only wine, Denise. One little drop won't kill you."

"I don't drink."

"In that case I will have orange juice as well."

"That's a good idea since you will be driving me back."

Denise didn't know what to make of Abraham. There were so many changes around the house. It was tidy and she could smell a bit of air freshener. He looked more handsome without his bushy beard.

As if Abraham read her thoughts. "I am sorry I frightened you. My brother has been breathing on my neck to make changes around here."

"Don't go beyond your budget to impress anyone."

He cleared his voice. "I happened to be in town today. I saw you coming out of J& and Sons solicitors. Are you looking for a job?"

She put her cutlery down. "Were you spying on me?"

He gulped his orange juice. His Adam apple danced. "Oh no. I was just passing."

"I was helping mother with a little business that needs sorting out. Unfortunately we didn't have an appointment. We made one." She wasn't going to tell him what it was about.

"So...it's nothing to do with you?"

"Abraham! Spit it out."

He looked at her. His eyes lingered on her bosom. "I don't want you to go in there. I... don't want to lose you."

She laughed. "The place didn't look like a maze to me. I know how to get out of a maze."

"It's what is in that maze that bothers me. I know the guys who work there. I don't get on with them for some reasons... I have been in there or I used to..."

"My brother Nicholas works there. He is a messenger. He tells me they treat him well."

"It's a different story for women. Promise me you will not go back to that place. I just don't get on with the guys in there. Once they know you are my girl, that's it."

"Abraham, we are not married yet. I will go anywhere I want. I love your pies." She put another helping on his plate and her plate. "What is it you want to talk about?"

"We have already."

She stared at him. "You mean you called me here to talk about J& Sons solicitors?"

"And to see you. I miss you Denise."

"I miss you too. The ball is in your court, Abraham."

"Yes, of course. Now my father is back from his holiday, we should be discussing the dowry soon."

She took a deep breath. "How long will it take?"

"I guess not long. I was hoping for a Christmas wedding. What do you think?"

"Abraham! We are in August. I will miss the rainy season and we haven't even cleared the land."

Abraham looked at his immaculate hands. "Denise, have you ever done any manual work?"

"There is always a start."

"I will look after you, Denise. I will find a job. I have a few interviews to attend. We may be lucky. I want you to give up your job once we are married. I don't want to give your aunt a reason to criticise me."

But...she wanted to tell him that her salary helps her mother. No, she better keep it to herself. If the insurance company pay what they owe her mother, she would never work again.

He reached for her hand.

"I'd better take you home."

"Thanks for the meal, Abraham." She pecked him on the

cheek.

"I am not your brother," he chided her. He showed her how couples kiss. They were both breathless. "I'd better take you home before I ruin my chances."

"You'd better," she warned him.

Chapter Sixteen

Annabella watched Desmond as he changed into a suit getting ready for a night out. She hated London weather. Why did he have to choose this place for their honeymoon? "What honeymoon?" she asked herself remembering Desmond's temper. She didn't feel like going out and not only that, he snapped at her at every opportunity. He wanted sex or making love. Whoever came up with such an idea? Making love? Drilling would have been a better name for such act. She wasn't ready for his drilling sessions. She had no idea what real love making felt like. The thought put her nerves on edge. She found herself putting her thighs together. She winced remembering the incident.

He looked at her. "Are you ok? You are shivering."

"I wish I didn't have to go out this evening. I am exhausted."

"You are right. We don't have to go out. An early night will do us good."

"Oh no! Don't stay in. I will be fine. Honestly, I will be fine."

"What kind of honeymoon is this?" he hissed at her. "You are neglecting your duties, Annabella." He was fed up with her neglect.

"What do you expect, Desmond? I am five months pregnant. I can hardly see my toes and later on…" She sighed. She didn't want to get into details about positions.

"Annabella, we are married. You'd better break the barrier between us. We haven't exercised our marital rights. Don't expect me to look for amusement elsewhere or put wife number two on top of you."

She fumed. "Do you see me as an amusement for you? I am insulted."

"Now, Annabella, you are making a fool of yourself. You are my wife. I have feelings for you and the sooner we exercise our rights to each other, the better. I am a man, Annabella."

"You think I don't know that? What have I let myself into?" she cried out.

"I don't bite." The girl has a temper just like her sister.

She was struggling with a zip on her dress. "Damn it," she swore under her breath.

"I can give you a hand."

"No thank you. I have a hook somewhere. It was here this morning. Did you see it?"

Of course he knew where it was. What's the point of having a zipper hook if he could do it? "I haven't seen it, dear," he lied. It was in the dustbin next to her dressing table. He hoped she would not check the dustbin.

"I said I will help you and I will. There! What about that? Now, relax, we are having a Jacuzzi since you don't want to go out. You see, this is one moment you have to make memorable. Don't spoil it, Annabella. Relax and enjoy yourself."

Her nostrils flared. "I don't know why you need my consent this time. You never asked for my consent when you took my virginity."

"I thought you forgave me? What must I do to make you see that I am sorry?"

"Please! Leave me alone. I want to be left alone."

A tear dropped on his face. She hadn't forgiven him. He thought she had. What must he do to make her realise that he is sorry? "I will book into another room. Goodnight, Annabella."

Chapter Seventeen

Meredith fanned herself. It was too hot and not only that, Denise's in-laws-to-be shocked her. "Richard? What do you think of this?"

"I am not sure I heard him all right. My hearing is not what it used to be."

"I heard him the first time, she told him. He is paying twelve cows for Denise's dowry and a goat for me. Who would have thought?"

"He has his father to thank," Richard replied.

"Why does he live like a tramp?" she asked.

"Search me. Anyway, there is one in every family."

I guess the old man will look after them."

Denise's father in law's voice rang out. "I will forgive you for such insult."

"Your daughter is a remarkable girl. For you to suggest we pay just one cow for her dowry is degrading. I know what she is worth. The twelve cows I have offered are just a thank you to her parents for bringing her up properly and it's a custom that's been going on for a long time. Denise is worth more than that. I would love to say more but this is not the time or the place for me. We thank you for your hospitality. We shall be in touch with the wedding preparations."

Mworozi hung behind to speak to Denise. "What do you think of my family?"

"Abraham is full of surprises," she replied. "Tell him that."

"Is that all?"

"Thank you for supporting him. Once we are married, I will look after him. He is capable of standing on his two feet. Why you aid him is something I don't understand."

"We are a family. We look out for each other." He promised to be in touch soon.

Denise joined her aunt who looked distant. "Are you all right aunt?" she enquired.

"Denise! You startled me. Why do you walk like a thief?"

"I am sorry, I didn't mean to scare you. I am happy you could make it, aunt. This time, I need your advice."

Eliot beamed at her.

"You still have a few months dear. I will teach you how to handle a marriage. One thing you must work on is your temper. You have such temper, Denise." Her aunt waved her finger at her.

Denise went to bed as soon as her aunt and her uncle left. She lay in her old bedroom thinking hard. Now the mortgage has been paid off by father's life insurance. Things were almost back to normal. She wished her sister would get in touch. She missed her dearly. Her eyes misted. Annabella! Please forgive me. Desmond was never meant for me. What gave her comfort was Eric's reports about Annabella's life. She was leading a lady's life. The life she was used to before father passed away. Marrying Desmond must have been a blessing in disguise. That's one thought she would keep to herself.

She loved Abraham no matter what. His family is better off but that doesn't change a damn thing. She had plans for that land. She was still young and not short of energy. Now her mother and her brothers are provided for, she must concentrate on her own life and Abraham.

On her nineteenth birthday, Abraham took Denise to a cinema to watch the film 'Gone with the wind'.

"Abraham, you are an angel in disguise. You have no idea of how many times I have asked Mother to buy us tickets."

Abraham beamed at her. "This is not the only present I have for you; there is more!" Her skin tingled.

"Yup! Just bring that finger."

"Oh Abraham, it's beautiful!" She was now dabbing at her eyes. She didn't care who was looking; she kissed him.

"Ssh, the show is starting. We shall celebrate our engagement later."

Denise looked at her eternity ring. She beamed at him. "I am yours forever."

"I know. That's why I got you an eternity ring." They held hands throughout the show.

The show was almost half way through when Abraham pushed his elbow into her side. "That woman over there looks like you and I recognise that man."

Denise followed Abraham's finger. She gasped. "It's Annabella," she said aloud.

At that moment Annabella turned. Their eyes locked. Annabella bit her lower lip. She spoke to Desmond. Desmond turned. He gave them a cold stare.

"Should I go to her?" Denise asked.

"I don't think it's a good idea. We don't need a second show. Just relax and enjoy the rest of the show."

It was difficult for Denise to relax with her twin sister sitting a few yards from her. Denise was happy about one thing. Annabella looked well and Desmond's arm on her shoulder told her something.

"We both like 'Gone with the wind'," she told Abraham.

"You are twins. I hope they haven't booked a table at the same restaurant."

"I would like to talk to her."

"She will talk to you when she is ready and besides, I want your full attention."

"We used to be close, Abraham."

"She will come round. Give her time."

"I would want her to be my maid of honour."

"That's wishful thinking but don't let me stop you. You don't ask, you don't find out."

The show was over. "I will have to bring you back. You didn't enjoy the last bit."

She sighed. "I will try my luck. I can't just walk away. I want to wish her happy birthday."

Desmond whispered to Annabella. "I will bring you back, obviously you didn't see the end. Your sister spoiled this evening."

"Thanks to my sister. I thought you said her man was a tramp?"

"He is. This one must be her lover. When I say a tramp, I just mean that."

Denise and Abraham waited for Annabella and Desmond at the exit.

"There is only one way out," she told Abraham. They didn't have to wait long.

The sisters faced each other.

"Happy birthday, Annabella."

Annabella looked at Desmond for answers.

Desmond stared at Denise. He gave her a weak smile. "Your tramp is not with you today?"

Abraham's jaws tightened.

Denise sighed. She turned to her sister. "Annabella, this is Abraham my fiancé."

Abraham smiled at her. "Nice to meet you, Annabella. Happy birthday."

"Thank you," Annabella muttered under her breath.

There was confusion on Desmond's face. This is the tramp. His smile identified him. His even white teeth identified him. What a transformation! He whistled.

Denise looked at her sister straight in the face. She dare not look at her bulging tummy. "Annabella, I am sorry. Are... you ok? I would like you to be my maid of honour. I miss you, Annabella," she blurted out.

"Annabella, we are running late," Desmond told her.

Annabella took Desmond's hand. She smiled at Abraham. "Nice to meet you, Sir." She walked away.

"She will come round," Abraham comforted.

"She will never come round because...there...is no one to encourage her. Desmond doesn't help at all. He controls her. He hates me. He will do anything to keep us apart."

Annabella sighed. "Desmond, you told me he is a tramp."

"He... was, he is... believe me. You ask your aunt if you think I am lying to you. Now, eat your meal. Don't let Denise spoil your evening." He was still in shock. How did the tramp manage to transform himself? He was speechless.

They were at the Speke Hotel. Annabella's eyes kept on checking the main door.

"Annabella, she is not coming here. Enjoy your evening. After their meal, they went home. Annabella was quiet. That bothered Desmond a lot. He knew where her mind was. She had forgiven him all right but her mind still wondered. The sooner she forgave her sister, the better.

"Annabella, do you want anything hot to drink?"

She checked the time. It was well after eleven o'clock. She knew what Desmond would do if she said yes. Lucas would be woken up to heat up milk for her. Just one simple task. She felt sorry for him sometimes. He was paid to do the job but being woken up at such an hour to heat up a glass of milk. She looked at Desmond. "I am blotted. Let's go to bed."

While in bed he told her to consider Denise's invitation.

"I don't think... I don't know, Desmond. I need time to think."

"I am glad you are thinking about it. I don't know what I would do if I fell out with Amanda. We look out for each other. We have been very close since we were young."

"I admire your relationship. She has taken me under her wing as well."

"I am glad you get on. She is a good sister."

She smiled at him. She opened her bedside drawer. She took out a velvet box.

"What's that?"

"It's Denise's pendant. I...bought it for her as a wedding gift."

Desmond smiled. "I am glad you don't mind going to her wedding."

She stared at him. "I haven't said I am going."

"Then why buy her a gift?"

She took a deep breath. "I gave her this pendant on the day she disappeared."

"I don't get you. How come it's in your possession?"

"The time we fought each other. She gave it to me saying I needed a full heart to recover from what I was going through." She fingered the one around her neck.

Desmond noticed they were the same.

"They make one complete heart when put together," she told him.

"How touching," he grinned at her.

"I want her to have it back but I am not sorry for beating her up. I am...I need time but she must have her pendant back. Please post it for me."

"Oh no, Annabella. You will have to do it yourself. I would like you to forget the past. Put the past behind you. We are happy together, aren't we?"

She took a long time before she nodded.

He longed to hear her say that she loves him. She respected him, cared for him and got on very well with his family. He was happy about that. "Give her time," Amanda had said to him. "Don't forget you are the one who wronged her. What a stupid move, Desmond."

Well, he will keep quiet about Denise. If she doesn't want to make up, it's her choice. Women! He pulled one in the crook of his arms. The beating of her heart comforted him. "Annabella, happy birthday and good night."

Denise looked at Abraham curiously. He was changing by the minute. She didn't like the change. The man she fell in love with was disappearing before her eyes. What happened to his torn denims? His bushy beard? Why try to pretend to be what you are not? She felt very uncomfortable about the changes in Abraham's lifestyle. She hoped he was not a bank robber. Oh shit! That would give her aunt a chance to point out that she told me so.

"What did I tell you, Denise?" Her uncle would celebrate big time. She felt a bit uncomfortable. "Abraham?"

"Yes, my love?"

That's new again, she noticed. 'My love'?

She fidgeted with her cutlery. She felt hot under her armpits. "Well, one thing I have noticed about you is that you love foreign dishes," she blurted out anything that came out of her mouth. She tucked into her favourite dishes, cooked bananas and curry goat with half cooked spinach.

"You are very observant, dear. I am sure you have noticed that my family are different from me." He took a deep breath. "My father is better off. He employed anybody from different races. Our first cook was Italian."

"Is that why you like lasagne?" she asked him.

"Yes. When she left to get married, my mother found Omunyankole cook from the village. Her cooking was a disaster from day one. She liked boiled foods and emptied the whole of Lake Victoria in it. To get to the meat in our plates, we had to swim our fingers in the soup then the soup would run along our arms up to our armpits. We complained and she got the sack.

"Then we had an Indian cook. His dishes made one's mouth water during preparations. To be honest with you, mother and father are the only people that enjoy our traditional dishes."

"I don't know how to cook such foreign foods, Abraham. You will have to put up with my dishes."

"I will, as long as you don't empty Lake Victoria in it."

She laughed and made people turn in their direction.

They had their dessert. This time Denise tried Abraham's choice. Chocolate ice cream decorated with strawberries, peanuts and sliced bananas. "Wow! I get what you mean."

"You like it?"

"I love it. I could go for second helping but for the time. Mother must be worried sick."

"It's only half eleven. We told her we would be home before midnight."

"It's almost midnight. I don't want her to worry. She has been through a lot, that woman."

He signalled to the waiter for the bill.

When the bill came, Denise was nearly sick there and then.

"Abraham, why didn't you stop me from ordering this and that? You will never be able to pay it."

"Relax, Denise," he said as he paid. She almost hit him on the head with an ashtray when he left a huge tip.

She rested her head on his shoulder as they drove to her mother's place. "Thanks for the evening, Abraham."

"I am glad you enjoyed yourself." He kissed her on the lips before he got out to open the door for her.

"Happy birthday."

She grinned at him. She was in heaven.

Chapter Eighteen

Denise tiptoed to her room. She didn't want to wake her mother. The last thing she wanted was her mother noticing her blushing. She could still feel Abraham's lips on hers. He was still the same man inside never mind the cool suits and expensive meals. She was changing into her nightgown when her mother walked in.

"I was worried."

"I am sorry, Mother."

"It's late...Denise. I told you what time you should be home."

"Oh! I am sorry. We... saw... Annabella...Annabella..." she stammered. "She was with Desmond."

"Where was she?"

"At the cinema."

"Well, you both like 'Gone with the Wind'. How is she?"

"Grown up. She looks well."

Louise searched her daughter's eyes to see any mischief. She didn't detect any. Then she saw a ring on her finger. Her eyes lingered there.

"We are...engaged. We got...engaged."

"Oh! In our day, we never bothered with such things. You will look after yourself, won't you?"

"I will."

"Denise, how much do you know about Abraham?"

"I only know what he has told me which is not quite a lot but I love him, Mum."

Louise looked at her daughter.

'Mum'? When Denise calls her Mum, then she was up to something. "I do not doubt you. I want you to be careful. I don't want you to get hurt."

"Mother, is something troubling you?"

Louise looked at her daughter. "I don't know. I may be wrong but he is not what he seems."

Denise sat up. "You think he has another woman?"

Louise laughed. "That never crossed my mind. What I mean, he likes to disguise himself. Whatever the reason." She held her daughter's hand. "I may be wrong. But be careful. Good night, Denise. I will see you in the morning."

Denise didn't sleep at all. Her mother's words kept her awake. She was right. Abraham was a different person now. Not the person he was a few months ago. Did he rob a bank to put her dowry together and change his appearance? He was a changed man. The only thing that kept her going was her love for him. He may look transformed, but he was still the same man she fell in love with. She hoped he was not involved in illegal things.

She finally fell asleep thinking about him. She was woken up by a knock on her door. It was Nicholas holding roses. He grinned at her.

"You have a secret lover."

Denise wiped her eyes. "Who from?"

"How many lovers do you have? What is your Abraham going to say if he finds out you have a lover? Ms Hot Pants?"

"Get out, Nicholas! Aren't you late for school?"

"I am going. Don't bite me."

As soon as the door shut behind Nicholas, Denise searched for a note. Surely there is a note somewhere. The roses smelt good. They were so many. She started counting them. There in the middle popped a note. She grinned. *'I am thinking of you. A.'*

Her bosom heaved. She wondered what her mother would say about her flowers.

She wanted to leave them in her rooms but her mother would not like it. She had told them many times not to put flowers in their room because they take all the air.

She put them in the dining room instead. Her mother was already there reading a newspaper. Now she led the life she used to lead when father was alive. Reading newspapers, shopping and visiting beauticians. At least she was not bored.

Louise turned to her with a questioning look.

"Abraham sent them."

"Oh!" That's all she said. She pretended to read but her mind was in turmoil. Abraham was up to no good. One minute he was a tramp, and the next minute he was rolling in designer suits. Buying roses. What next? Hand cuffs?

Denise prepared for work and on her way out she picked one rose and tucked it around her ear.

Louise shook her head. She knew the difference between Annabella and Denise even though they were identical. Denise was too wild. That bothered her a lot. She takes after her Aunt Meredith.

Chapter Ninteen

Desmond paced the room. He was lost for words. What must he do to relieve the pain his wife was going through. Annabella had been in labour for five hours. He didn't understand such things. He wished conceiving and giving birth took the same time. He was sorry he caused her such pains. He was sweating. He noticed he was wearing pyjamas and house slippers. "Shit!" When she woke him complaining of backache, he had known what the back ache meant. He had driven here in less than twenty minutes. It was now morning. He'd better rush home and change but what if she needed him? He took a deep breath. "Think, Desmond," he told himself. He asked the receptionist if he could use the phone. "I will pay. Add it to my bill."

She told him where the phone was. "Try to be brief. It's a busy line."

He phoned Lucas, his cook.

"Get me a change of clothes, will you?"

"Sir...I am not allowed in your rooms."

"Well, I am asking you." He told him what to bring.

"I will be there, Sir."

Lucas looked at his wife. He grinned at her.

"What's so funny?"

"Please pour me a vodka. I will tell you later." He told her, "I will keep him waiting. It serves him right."

"You could get sacked for this."

"Do you think I care? I have had enough of him. He thinks I am interested in his wife."

"Are you?"

"Don't be silly, Vanessa. You know I am not."

"I hope you mean that. Lucas, please take his clothes. He must be checking his watch now." At that moment the phone rang.

"Tell him I have already left."

When Lucas finally arrived at the hospital, Desmond was in a different mood. The bundle in his arms made him forget that he was indecently dressed. He only told Lucas where to put the bag. He dismissed him immediately without a thank you.

Annabella had no idea what the baby was. She was too exhausted. The midwife did tell her but she couldn't remember. She wasn't interested.

As if Desmond read her mind, he said: "We have a son, Annabella. Do you want to name him?"

She shook her head. "You name him," she told him as she faced the wall.

Desmond looked at the bundle in his arms and then at Annabella.

Tears coursed down his face. He was hurt. He has accepted her rejection but for his son to go through what he was going through was too much for him to take in.

Their marriage was a front. Her lovemaking was very predictable. He knew what was going to happen next. He wished she didn't pretend. Now, to turn her back on their baby. He choked on his tears.

Annabella looked at him. "Why are you crying? Don't you like him? I thought you said you wanted a son. An heir, as you put it. Well, there he is. Your prayers have been answered. I want to catch my breath. Leave me alone."

"He... is... Adrian Tumwiine and I think he needs a feed."
She sighed. "I didn't have time to pack the feeding bottles."

Desmond stared at his wife. "Why do you need the bloody feeding bottles? Are your tits not enough?"

Annabella stared at him with her mouth open. "I think you better keep your voice down especially when you don't know how to talk." She thanked God for having a private ward. She would have been embarrassed.

"Well, you better sit up and feed him. I have had enough of you, Annabella. I have done my best for you. I have apologised to you God knows how many times. A man can take so much. If you think I will not kick your arse, then you don't know Desmond Tumwiine. Sit up!" he thundered. "You should be grateful I saved you from poverty. I am not going to tiptoe with you now. I have been very patient with you. Don't think I won't slap you. Now, get up and feed him."

The baby in his arms started crying at the same time as Annabella.

They both broke down. "I am sorry, Annabella. I just lost it. Forgive me."

She looked at him with tears in her eyes.

"Desmond, what is there to forgive? What wrong have you done? You said what was on your mind, now you feel relieved. All of a sudden you want forgiveness? There is nothing to forgive. Give him to me. I... will feed him." She choked on her tears.

She wiped her tears. "I want to go home. For a few days. I miss mother. I need her help."

Desmond stared at her. It was the first time she had asked for Louise.

"Are you sure?"

She nodded.

"That can be arranged. I am sorry. I didn't mean all those words."

Louise checked her watch a second time. "Where are they? Has she changed her mind?" She was happy that her daughter had agreed to come home.

"Mother, sit still," Denise told her. "Desmond phoned only ten minutes ago and there is a lot of traffic on weekends."

They arrived a few minutes later.

Louise showed them into the sitting room.

"How are you, Mother?" Desmond greeted his mother in law.

"I am well, thank you." She wasn't going to give him a royal welcome and a red carpet. She has not forgiven him but to make matters easier for her daughter, she smiled at him. "I am a grandmother," she said as she received her grandson.

She looked at Annabella. "How are you, baby?"

Annabella smiled at her mother. "I am afraid you have to drop that nickname. I am tired. I need to sleep."

"Your room is ready. Denise, take your sister."

The sisters looked at each other. "Hi Annabella?"

Annabella ignored her twin sister. She turned to Vanessa. "Please bring my luggage. I will find my way to my room. I haven't forgotten where it is."

Denise looked at her mother for answers. She was too busy with her grandson to notice Denise's hurt.

She escaped to the kitchen to prepare drinks.

After tea, Desmond said bye and thanked his mother in law for her help.

"Please call me if there is anything...no matter what time."

Louise cleared her voice. "We don't need a working girl. We can manage."

"You will find Vanessa very helpful. Annabella needs complete rest." He wasn't going to tell her that his wife hadn't lifted her fingers since they have been married. He was to blame. He spoilt her. He owed her big time.

As soon as Desmond left, Louise went to Annabella's room. "Annabella, are you asleep?"

Annabella turned round. She smiled at her mother. "I am glad he is gone. He is too possessive. I can hardly breathe on my own."

"Men are like that. As long as he is not violent. Is he?"

She shook her head.

Louise cleared her voice. She didn't know how to start. She didn't want to say anything that might send her daughter into silence. She had been through a lot. She had better keep Desmond out of this conversation. If Annabella has something to tell her, she would. She wished her daughters would go back to how they used to be. "Good, now Annabella, it's time you put the past behind you," she blurted out. "You and Denise need to sort out this silence business once and for all. I know you don't hate her. Do you?"

"That's where you are wrong, Mother. I hate her big time. I am in this mess because of her. Look at me dripping all over my blouse and I am only nineteen."

"You can control that by feeding him. He must be hungry. When did you last feed him?" The look on her daughter's face told her that she was saying the wrong words.

"I am sorry, Annabella but he is hungry. He was whimpering."

Annabella sighed. She reached for her baby. She planted a nipple in his ears, missing his searching mouth.

Louise was on her feet. "Annabella! You should look at him when feeding him. That's the only way he will recognise you. The recognition is what binds you together."

"Do you think I want to be reminded how I got him?"

"Now Annabella! This child is innocent. I am ashamed of you, Annabella. Please don't let him feel your hatred. He didn't take part in the making."

"That's why I will never forgive my sister for running away from her marriage. This baby should have been hers. I don't want

144

him. Take him to Denise." She sobbed.

Louise took a deep breath. "Then we'd better look for someone to look after him. There are so many women who would do anything to have a child to care for. I will have to talk to Desmond and hear what he says."

Annabella was now alarmed. "Please don't mention this to him."

Louise's nose flared. "I will not stand by and watch you abuse this innocent child. I will not have it, Annabella. It's either you feed him and care for him, or we arrange for adoption. You have a choice and I can guess what Desmond will say about this. Whatever made Denise change her mind at the last minute is the devil himself."

"His possessiveness would make your head spin if you lived with him," Annabella sniggered.

"Let's not argue about my son in law. Let's talk about you. I haven't spent his dowry. If you are not happy, I will be happy to have you here."

Annabella looked at her. "Does that make me your innocent girl? I will never be the same again. No matter how much I try to forget." Her eyes misted. "I have forgiven him for what he did, but..."

"Go on," Louise wanted to hear more. It's time she let go.

"He said he thought I was Denise. Ok, suppose it was Denise, why would he want to marry her against her will?

"I begged him, Mother. Denise and I have different voices. How could he get that wrong?"

"He was used to seeing you both. You and Denise swapped places whenever he came here visiting. Am I right?"

"Because Denise asked me to stand in for her. She didn't want to miss her camping trip."

"That wasn't the only time, Annabella and you know it. Now, see what it has landed you in. You shouldn't have agreed to such games."

"Are you saying it's my fault he married me against my will?"

"Annabella, let's not have a shouting match. You are frightening the baby. Change him to another breast and don't forget to rub his back after feeding. Don't stop rubbing his back until he burps. I must get lunch ready. I will prepare your favourite. Cod fish in parsley sauce with roast potatoes and half fried green beans. What do you think?"

Annabella gave her mother a weak smile followed by thanks.

Chapter Twenty

Denise couldn't stand her sister's silence any longer. She decided to give Abraham a surprise visit. She was hurt by Annabella's rejection. She missed her. She missed their little games, the games they played on outsiders swapping places. The only part she hated was when they got into trouble. Aunt Meredith had no time for such games. They each got their punishment. "Listen kids, I don't know who emptied this porridge between my chair cushions. When you are given food, you eat it."

"I don't like porridge," Annabella would sob.

"So it's you who emptied it under my chair cushions?"

Denise helped. "The cushions are a bit hard to shift."

"I know, she is the strong one. Now, what about more porridge? This time, I will watch you eat it up. And Annabella! Don't hide boiled eggs in your shoes. Denise, remove the toast hidden in your pillow. What's wrong with you kids?"

"We don't like eggs and porridge," they choroused.

"That's enough. You will eat what you are given. No wonder your mother needs a rest. You are a bunch of trouble full of mischief. Now, what do you say?"

"We are sorry, Aunt Meredith," they choroused. But that didn't stop them hiding cabbage in their dress pockets during mealtimes.

Denise smiled. Those were happy times. Oh Annabella! Please

give me a chance to say sorry, she thought to herself. She got out of the taxi. Abraham's pickup was in the driveway. There was another car packed behind it.

Whose is it?

"Should I wait, Madam?" The taxi driver asked.

"Yes please. I won't be long." Her heart raced. Who is it? The door was open and she could hear voices. He wasn't alone. He was with another woman. Her laughter grated on her heart. She gasped for air. She took a deep breath. Oh God!

They were in the kitchen and she could smell fried meat.

Who is cooking in Abraham's kitchen? She paused behind the door.

"Abraham? I don't know what games you are playing."

"If you don't tell her, I will. This can't go on."

"Drop it, Jessica. I don't want pressure, especially now in the middle of..."

He paused. "What was that?"

"What was what?"

"I thought I heard something." He left the kitchen to investigate.

He came back looking red in the face.

"Abraham! What is it?"

"It's Denise. I don't know what she heard or how long she has been here."

Denise was choking on her tears. How could he? The bastard! She trusted him, loved him. Why didn't he tell her he had another woman? Well, this is it then. No marriage. She sobbed. The whole family will be happy at least. They never liked him. How right. Sneaky lying bastard!

She went to her bedroom. She could hear her mother in the kitchen talking to Annabella's house girl. She opened her bedroom door quietly and put the bolt home. She wanted to be alone and she would be alone for a long time. She would never trust another man. She was happy the dowry hadn't arrived yet. He can use that to marry Jessica. The thought of another woman capturing Abraham's heart hurt her so much. She wasn't a sharing type. She could not share a husband with another woman. She removed her engagement ring. There was no point holding on to it. She would post it to him or give it to his brother.

How could he?

She sobbed. She was tired. She wanted to sleep hoping that when she woke up, it would all seem like a dream. But it wasn't a dream. Abraham had another woman. She was cooking for him, something he had not allowed her to do.

There was a knock on her door. "Denise, lunch is ready."

"I am not hungry, Mother."

"Nonsense! You haven't eaten. Hurry up. It's getting cold."

"I am not hungry, Mother."

Louise turned the door knob. It was locked. "My goodness child! Open this door. I told you many times not to lock your bedroom doors in case of emergency. Suppose the house was on fire how would I get to you? Open this door."

Denise removed the bolt.

Louise stared at her daughter. "You have been crying. What's the matter?"

"I have a headache."

"It must be terrible, for you to cry like that."

Fat tears coursed down her cheeks.

"Have you taken anything for it?"

Denise shook her head. "It will go. All I need is some sleep. I am not hungry, Mother. I don't think I can take in anything."

Louise looked at her daughter. "Are you sure it's a headache? You have never cried like this before." Louise was worried. It was more than a headache and for her to refuse food... She searched her daughter's face. "Denise, when did you last have your curse?"

Denise looked aside. She didn't want to look at her mother. She was no longer innocent and that pained her. She had let Abraham make love to her.

Now she was spoilt. She was no longer her mother's innocent girl. Why did she do it? She did it for love. She didn't want to lose him. She had thought if she became pregnant, Abraham would be accepted in her family. What a stupid move. They called him Mr Nobody. She had stood by him. She choked on her stress.

"Denise, I asked you a question."

"I am not pregnant, Mother."

Louise gave a sigh of relief. "Whatever is bothering you Denise is worth sharing."

She sniffed. "It's hard mother. I can't."

"You can't what?"

"The marriage is off."

Louise looked at her daughter with her mouth wide open. "I am not surprised at all. You don't suit each other and you are not the marrying type. You dumped Desmond at the last minute, remember?"

"I didn't dump him on purpose. I just got lost in the jungle."

"What made you wander off? You never liked him. Now this Abraham. I am glad we haven't received his dowry. Now, you know what type of person you are, I suggest you don't play with people's feelings again.

"I have a lot on my plate Denise. I can't cope with your problems."

"It's not my fault," she cried out. "I... caught... him... with another woman. She was in his kitchen cooking and they said something about telling me. I didn't want to hear more. I ran out."

Louise was shocked. "What the hell possessed you to go to his place? Don't you know it's not proper for a decent girl to visit a man on her own?"

"Just as well I did otherwise I would not have known what a snake Abraham is."

Louise smiled. "Well, I must admit. I am happy this relationship has reached its end. The man was beginning to worry me. One minute he is a tramp and another minute he is rolling in designer suits. Don't cry for him, Denise. All I can say is good riddance. Now, come and eat your lunch."

At that moment the doorbell went off. "I will find out," said Louise.

She looked at Abraham,

"What do you want?"

"I need to speak to Denise."

"Denise is not in. You will have to call again and I am not sure whether she wants to speak to you."

"She got it wrong. I must see her. I need to explain to her. Please let her know... Don't worry. I will leave a note for her."

He scribbled a few words and was gone.

Louise looked at the note; without reading it, she put it in the dustbin.

"What does he want?" Denise asked.

"He wants to explain."

"I don't want to hear his explanations."

"Good, now, eat your lunch and forget him. You are young and don't repeat this mistake, Denise."

Annabella snorted. "She is good at hurting others."

"This time it's not her fault. And the sooner you two get on, the better."

Abraham waited for Denise to reply to his note but nothing came. It was on the third day when he finally found the courage to face her.

He must explain himself. He found a few cars parked in the

driveway. He wanted privacy with Denise. It was time to come clean. The thought of losing her made his heart race at a speed. He couldn't afford to lose her. He rang the bell.

It was Desmond who opened the door.

Abraham took a step back. He looked around him. "I didn't know you live here?"

"I am visiting my wife. What do you want?"

"I am here for Denise."

"She doesn't want to see you." He had been told and he was happy about her decision.

Abraham fumed. Who does he think he is? He put his foot in the doorway. "Try to stop me." The two men looked at each other without a word.

"This is your mother-in-law-to-be's house. You'd better have a bit of respect."

"I will apologise to her but not before I speak to Denise. Now, get out of my way."

The two men entered the sitting room where the family were gathered. Louise had invited the whole family to celebrate the birth of her first grandchild.

Denise took a deep breath. "What do you want?"

"I came to explain."

"My niece has nothing to say to you," Richard told him.

"I told you, Denise. He wasn't good for you," Meredith put in. "I am happy the marriage is off."

Abraham cleared his voice. "I would like to speak to you, Denise. I will explain. I had my reasons for not telling you the truth about me. I didn't want to lose you."

"You lied to me, Abraham. You have another woman. I thought it's me you love," she wailed.

Desmond rolled his eyes heavenwards.

Louise wished for Valium.

Richard reached for his gin and tonic.

Annabella felt thrilled. I am glad it's not working. You will be lonely for the rest of your life, she thought to herself. There will be no one to look after her in her old age except auxiliary nurses who will slap her black arse for every nonsense she comes up with. She gave her sister a weak smile.

Meredith smiled at her niece. "I was right about him," she almost whistled.

Abraham was shocked. "What woman?"

"Don't play games with me. I know her name. She is called Jessica."

The smile on Abraham's face sent Denise into tears.

"Oh my God! Jessica is my sister. She has been dying to meet you."

"You... are... lying. I don't believe you. I heard everything."

"Yes, you heard everything and you got the wrong end of the stick. You should have stayed instead of running off like that.

"She was telling me to be honest with you or else she would tell you."

"I am glad she has found sense and dumped you. You were not honest with her, were you?" Meredith demanded.

"For a reason."

"Which is?"

He looked at Denise. "I would like to speak to you in private."

"I think you'd better leave. You have upset everyone here," said Desmond. He was fuming. This is the fool Denise has fallen for. What was she thinking of? The man is a crook. He didn't trust him one bit. How could he change his appearance within such short time? He must be a bank robber or cattle rustler.

Abraham had had enough of Desmond's mouthful. The sooner he puts him in his right place, the better. He moved closer to him and looked him in the face. "Mr Tumwiine, you are not in a position to criticise my motives. Rape is a very serious crime," he hissed at him.

Annabella heard him all right. She choked on her tears. "Stop it both of you. I can't take it."

The two men gave each other threatening looks.

"You are lucky she didn't press charges." He pointed a finger at him. "Don't you dare criticise my motives. I will explain everything to Denise. I don't know why I waited this long.

"Denise, I am sorry. I need to talk to you."

Richard cleared his voice. "Whatever you want to say to my niece, the whole family should hear it and decide for her. She is too young to decide for herself."

"I am not too young. I just don't like to be lied to. I loved you, Abraham. I wanted to share my life with you."

"Denise, you are using the past tense."

She sobbed. "I am not sure anymore."

He bit his lip. He looked at her hard in the eyes. "Denise, I love you and always will." And with that, he left the room.

Denise stared at the swinging door. She was on her feet.

"Where do you think you are going?" her uncle demanded.

"I want to hear what he wants to say. I must." She sobbed and ran out of the room. She caught up with him in the yard. "Abraham, don't go. I still love you. I want you to be honest with me. I can handle anything as long as there is no other woman involved. Please don't go."

He looked at her. He ached for her. He wanted to take her in his arms. Make love to her there and then... She was everything he ever wanted in a woman. Tears stung his eyes. He blinked to keep them at bay. "Denise, it's high time you have a mind of your own. Your family control your brain. Denise, do you want to hear what I have to say because you are curious?"

"I love you, Abraham. It hurt me so much when I saw the other woman preparing meals in our kitchen. You have never let me prepare you a meal. Now to see another woman doing that, how do you think I felt? Abraham, I am not a sharing type, all right?"

"Denise, that's not our kitchen. The place belongs to a client. He lives abroad. Our firm looks after it."

Denise stared at him. "What are you saying?"

"Let's sit down. It's a long story." They sat on the grass. He held her hand. "What I am saying is, I am or I am part of J& Sons solicitors. We own the firm. Mother and Jessica run their own business. They do general counselling especially marriages. When the counselling fails, they recommend good lawyers. We are the lawyers."

She stared at him. "Oh...my God! No wonder you were upset when you found out I had been to J& Sons solicitors."

"You are right. We are solicitors. We handle divorces, wills and probate, conveyancing and domestic violence. We deal with all sorts of problems."

"But why all the secrecy?"

"Good question, my dear. My two marriages failed for one reason. My two ex-wives were money lovers. They were interested in my position and bank book. They were not ashamed to point it out to me.

"My father thought I was a fool. How could I be cheated twice? I said to him, father, next time it will be different. I took a vacation to recover and our client's property looked like a haven to me. I didn't bother to employ domestic help. I just wanted to be alone. Then you appeared. I fell in love with you. I knew what I had to do. It was a gamble and I have never gambled in my life. I changed my appearance. It wasn't easy, believe me. I am used to luxury. I said to myself, if she doesn't show any interest, then she is not for me. I longed for someone who would love me for what I am but not what I own. Every visit at the hospital was a torture. I looked for love signs from you, you revealed nothing. I said to myself, next time maybe.

"Then I started seeing signs. I held my breath and waited for more signs. Denise, I respect you for what you did. You fell in love with me regardless of what I am worth. I want to spend the rest of my life with you and I would like you to meet my family. Jessica is my sister. She is the same age as you. I think you will get on. She is such a sweet girl."

"Abraham, it's all right. You don't have to explain yourself to me anymore. You had your reasons for not telling me. You must have realised by now that money doesn't mean anything to me. I turned down a tycoon. Desmond is a... You can see my sister looks like a princess covered in diamonds. I don't envy her. Not one bit.

"What I would like to know, is it you who offered Nicholas the job?"

"Yes, I wanted to help. I hear he is good. We haven't met. I have been very discreet."

She took a deep breath. "Where do we go from here?"

"We must be married soon. I don't want to lose you."

She smiled at him. "You won't lose me. Abraham, you must hate my family for treating you badly."

He looked into her eyes and smiled at her. "Your mother accepted me. As for your uncle and aunt, I had to control my anger. Your uncle is as good as your father and your aunt is a good client. My father handled her three divorces." He smiled. "I wouldn't want to lose such a good customer." He wondered why she didn't recognise him when he came here to discuss the dowry.

She laughed at his joke. "Abraham, you have lost her. Their marriage seems to be going strong. Let's tell the whole family."

Chapter Twenty-One

Richard moved the window curtain to see what was going on in the garden. "I don't believe this," he fumed. "She has forgiven him by the look on her face. Louise, I am taking Denise home. She must be protected. You and my sister have failed to tame this girl. She will bring shame on this family. You mark my words. The man is a crook."

"Shh, they are coming," Louise warned.

Denise and Abraham entered the sitting room. There was silence. All the eyes in the sitting room stared at them.

Abraham cleared his voice. "I must apologise to you all for raising my voice in your home. I deserve to be fined."

Richard looked at him. "The best you can do is leave my niece alone. She deserves a better life."

"I will give your niece a better life. I love her. I will do anything for her."

"You mean rob a bank to keep her in comfort?" Meredith's nostrils flared.

Denise sensed another attack on Abraham. She must stop them before they humiliate themselves. She can't afford to lose Abraham.

She was shaking and angry. "Abraham will give me a better life. Aunt Meredith, do you know J& Sons solicitors?"

"Yes. Why do you ask?"

"Do you know them well?

"As a matter of fact they handled my three broken marriages. They are excellent lawyers."

Denise gave her aunt a weak smile. "You are looking at one."

"I need a drink."

"Why all the secrecy?" Richard demanded.

He told them about his previous marriages. Why they didn't work. "Your daughter fell in love with me regardless of who I am. I will always respect her for that."

"What I would like to know is why Nicholas hasn't said anything to me," said Louise.

At that moment Nicholas walked in. He grinned at everyone. "What's going on?"

"Nicholas? Do you know this man?" his uncle asked.

"I don't know what's going on." He looked from one to the other. "Have you all suffered amnesia? I will jog your memory. This man is Denise's fiancé. Isn't he?" he asked his sister.

"Have you ever seen him at J& Sons solicitors?" Richard asked.

"I am sorry I can't help you. Confidentiality is one of the company rules. I will not break that rule. Whatever problem you have, you will have to contact J & Sons solicitors."

"It's all right, Nicholas. You can tell them if you have seen me there, which I doubt very much. I am always discreet."

He stared at him with his mouth open. "You mean...you finally revealed yourself?"

Abraham nodded.

"So you knew him all along and you never said a word?" They all accused Nicholas at the same time.

"I had to. He is my boss and not only that, I wanted to see the shock on my sister's face when she sees where he lives." He looked at Abraham. "I have been there to deliver your papers, Sir."

"Please don't call me Sir. I prefer Abraham."

Richard stood up and poured himself a good measure of brandy. He took a sip and looked at his niece. "You have x-ray vision, my girl." He beamed at her. "You have landed on your feet. You will look after me in my old age. Cheers!"

Her nose twitched. "An apology would be appropriate. You all called him Mr Nobody," she accused.

"Denise, they had your best interest at heart," Abraham told her.

The doorbell interrupted the argument.

Nicholas answered it and a few minutes later, two women walked in.

"We are here for Mrs Tumwiine."

Annabella beamed at them. She was happy to escape.

Richard stared at the departing backs. "Who are they?" he asked his sister in law.

"Search me," she replied.

"They are beauticians," Desmond replied. "Annabella wants manicure and hair wash."

Richard refilled his glass. He stared at his son in law. "Doesn't she know how to cut her own nails or wash her own hair?"

"Beauticians have to earn a living somehow." He gave his father in law a weak smile.

Abraham excused himself. "I'd better get going. You will hear from my family soon."

"You can't go just yet. Lunch is almost served," Louise told him.

"I will have lunch some other time, Mother."

"I don't take no for an answer. Forget all the misunderstandings. We love Denise. We wanted the best for her but at the end of the day it's what she wants that matters."

He beamed at her. "I will stay for lunch if it's ok with everyone."

"It's ok with everyone," she answered for them.

The lunch was superb. "Your mother is a good cook," Abraham told Denise.

"You can say that again," Denise said as she added more on her plate. "I will tell her you enjoyed her cooking."

Desmond dished for Annabella and she was protesting that it was too much.

"He is in love with her," Abraham observed. He looked at the two sisters. Yes, they are identical but he could never get them wrong. He was happy the way things turned out. Where would he be if Denise had married Desmond?

He smiled at Annabella. "Motherhood suits you, Mrs Tumwiine."

She narrowed her eyes at him.

Desmond gave Abraham a cold stare. "Some comments are better left alone."

"Please accept my apology, Mrs Tumwiine."

"Please call me Annabella."

"There is nothing wrong with Mrs Tumwiine," Desmond told her.

Abraham decided to defuse the argument. He fed Denise from his fork.

"Abraham, what are you trying to remind me?" She giggled.

"The time you fell in love with me, dear."

She giggled like a little girl.

Annabella gave her sister a cold stare. "I don't know what mother would say if she were to see this."

"She was in love once. She would know what I am going through."

Annabella put her napkin on the table and excused herself.

Desmond gave Denise an accusing look. He excused himself as well.

Denise beamed at Abraham. "Anything we did?"

"They don't like me. But I am glad they are gone. Now, I want you to meet my family."

"Mother will never let me."

"I will take you to the cinema this evening."

"To watch what?"

"You are going to see my family. There is no cinema."

"Abraham! I can't lie to Mother."

"The sooner you have a mind of your own, the better. I will pick you up at seven o'clock"

He thanked his mother in law to be for the meal and told her that he would be back to take Denise to the cinema. He didn't give her a chance to say anything. He said bye and he was gone.

"Phew! He is controlling you, Louise," Richard told her."

"Nonsense. I was once like them. He is a gentleman. I accepted him right from the start. It was only recently that I began to doubt him. I am glad my daughter doesn't have to rely on any of us for her keep. He will look after her as he promised."

Meredith cleared her voice. "Well, well, well, I don't know how to apologise to him. I called him all sorts of names. That's one thing he is not likely to forget."

"Nor am I," Denise replied. "But I need your guidance this time. I won't run away this time." She fell on her aunt's bosom. As she predicted, her aunt massaged her hair.

"Shh, Desmond will hear you," Eric told his sister.

"Who cares?" Denise asked.

"He will marry you before Abraham does," Eric told her.

"No. I won't. I love Annabella."

"Whoops!" Eric ran out of the room.

Chapter Twenty-Two

Denise looked at Abraham with a questioning look in her eyes.

"The gates are remote controlled. Don't say much. Act normal. We are on CCTV right now."

She took a deep breath. "I don't like this, Abraham. I like your farm."

"I told you, it's not our place."

"I keep forgetting."

"Don't pretend to be what you are not. You are fine the way you are."

"Abraham, you have been pretending to be what you are not since we met."

"That's in the past. Let's not think about it."

She undid her seatbelt.

He was out in seconds and opening her door. A middle-aged man greeted them.

"Good evening, Ezra," Abraham greeted him and handed him the car keys.

Denise watched the man sit in the driver's seat and drive to the garage.

She turned to Abraham. "Couldn't you do it yourself?"

"He is paid to do it."

"Your immaculate hands explain everything. I am afraid I am

going to embarrass you," she told him.

"As long as you act normal, everything will be fine."

Before Abraham could ring the doorbell, it swung open.

Denise had to blink to take in what she was seeing.

The girl smiled at Denise. "I am Jessica, pleased to meet you. Please come in. We are all dying to know you. We are a bit eccentric. Please try to be patient with us." She beamed at her.

Abraham beamed at his sister. She was an excellent hostess.

They found the whole family in the lounge.

Denise wished for the floor to swallow her. She had never seen such luxury. She remained standing and waited to be told where to sit.

She is doing fine, Abraham thought.

"Abraham, don't keep your wife on her feet."

Abraham beamed at his grandmother. "We are not married yet but it won't be long now that you have blessed us."

He showed Denise where to sit.

She sat down and waited for introductions. She couldn't just greet anyone not knowing who they are. The last thing she wants is to give her father in law to be a bear hug and say "Long time no see, man". She was a nervous wreck.

Abraham started with his grandmother. "This is our grandmother. The anchor of this house."

Denise stood up, knelt in front of her. She stretched out her hand.

The old lady greeted her with a hug.

Next one was her father in law to be. She had seen him when he came to discuss the dowry but seeing him in his house looking like a king made her nervous.

He shook her hand. "I have been to Kimberly and came back empty handed and yet you live around the corner." He beamed at her. "You are the diamond we have been looking for! Welcome to the family."

She didn't know what to say to that but a 'thank you' would have been appropriate. She was speechless! She gave him her dazzling smile and moved on.

Abraham smiled. "Father, I can see you've been reading Wilbur Smith novels."

Denise moved on to her mother in law to be. She gave her a warm smile. "I am pleased to meet you, Mother."

Margaret's eyes stung with tears. Abraham was right. She is dazzling and has good manners. Abraham's ex wives called her by her name. She found such behaviour insulting. A daughter in law should never mention her mother in law and father in law's names unless they have been told to do so.

Denise moved on to Mworozi, Abraham's brother. "Hi!" he said.

Nadine scolded her husband. "What kind of greeting is that?" She greeted Denise in her own language, the language she wouldn't swap for anything. She loved her language and was proud of it.

Denise was fluent in the Luganda language. She didn't have any problems with Nadine. Her warm smile told her they could become friends. Yes, she would need her guidance. How to run such a home remained a mystery to her.

She greeted everyone and went back to her seat.

"Abraham, now I have seen your wife, I can rest in peace."

"Granny, stop talking like that. You are not going anywhere."

"I will if you don't hurry this marriage." She looked at Denise. "Now you are here, I need another opinion."

"Oh Granny, not now," Jessica told her.

"Well, I have to know whether my dress is suitable for the wedding."

"Mother, let the girl take her breath. She has just arrived," Jerome told his mother. She was getting old and confused sometimes. It worried him a lot. She has been an anchor to this family for such a long time. He loved her so much and what helped, Margaret his wife had never interfered with their relationship. He was happy to have such an understanding wife.

Denise smiled at her. "I would love to see your dress, Granny. When you are ready, let me know."

Mworozi gave her a smile. "I am glad your family let you come."

"They sent their greetings," she lied.

Abraham beamed at her.

Jessica served cold soft drinks. "You are what I imagined. Abraham talks a lot about you."

"Does he?"

"He does and I want us to be friends. They say sisters in law never get on but what the hell! Let's enter the Guinness Book of Records."

Denise found Abraham's family very warm. She was no longer nervous.

She thanked them for the drink and proceeded to clear the glasses.

Her mother in law to be smiled at her. "I can see you have been brought up properly. Let the girls clear them."

Two girls with pink and white uniform cleared the glasses and announced that supper was ready.

They entered a huge dining room with two dining tables. The adults sat on one side and the children with their helpers sat on the other.

Two little girls waved at her. "We didn't have a chance to say hi. I am Melanie and this is Angela, my little sister."

Angela poked her sister in the rib. "I can speak for myself, thank you very much." She smiled at Denise. "I am Angela. I am eight years old. How do you do?"

Denise smiled at them. "I am Denise, how do you do?"

"I know you are Uncle Abraham's wife," Angela announced.

"She is his fiancée, you silly little girl. What did Daddy say about you putting your brain into gear before you open your mouth? Huh!"

"I am not silly. That's what Uncle Abraham said. I am not deaf if you must know," she pouted.

"I am pleased to meet you, girls."

"We are pleased too," they chorused.

Mworozi apologised on their behalf. "We never interfere with them when they are arguing. We want them to take over when we retire.

"We are all mouth in this house. They take after my side. My wife is very quiet."

Denise didn't know what to say to that. She nodded her head.

The granny led the prayer. It was quick, to the point. It made sense.

The table was covered with Banyankole traditional dishes and foreign dishes.

Denise tried both dishes. She had to pull her tummy in to keep herself going.

Whoever made the seating arrangements must have done it on purpose. Abraham sat on her right and opposite her was her in laws firing questions at her.

"Abraham hasn't told us how you met," her mother in law to be said.

"Let the girl eat," her husband told her.

Denise could see he was pretending. He was interested as well.

"It's a long story, Mother," she told her.

"A romantic one," Mworozi put in. "Abraham doesn't stop talking about it."

Abraham gave his brother a cold stare.

"Go on, cheer us up," their granny said.

She told her story and at the same time ate her meal. If there is one thing her mother taught her, it was table manners.

"So you just fell in love with him like that after eating your carrots at the hospital?" Margaret was fascinated.

She smiled. "I hate carrots. Yes, I fell in love with his after-shave. Actually it's his aftershave that woke me from the coma. I am very grateful." She smiled at Abraham who looked tickled by her story.

They all laughed. "What after-shave?" Mworozi asked. "My brother smelt and looked like a tramp."

"That's not what his fiancée thinks," his granny told him. "If I told you how I fell in love with your grandfather, I don't know what you would think."

"Go on Granny, we want to hear it," they chorused.

"Well, there is no harm, is there? It's a long time ago. Your grandfather and I grew up together. We were neighbours. We did everything together including stealing our neighbour's sugarcanes and fruits. We got caught once and the fool tied us to a tree. He told us that he would be back in the morning to release us. You should have seen the panic in my eyes. Your grandfather remained cool. I thought he was crazy. As soon as the man left, your grandfather grinned at me. 'The fool didn't search us.'

"'Well, just as well. I have a few fruits inside my dress,' I told him.

"'At least we have supper,' he grinned at me. I was mad at him for making such jokes.

"He told me to move my legs closer.

"'Are you crazy?' I asked him.

"'Well, you have no choice. There will be lions roaming about in a minute.'

"I moved my tied legs closer to him."

Jerome wasn't paying attention to his mother's tales. He had heard that story a hundred times.

"He worked on my ropes with his toes until the rope became

loose. He grinned at me. Then he told me to do the same with his using my toes. I did, and it took me almost an hour to untie him. Then with his free legs, he worked on my arms and within minutes I was loose and I was crying with joy, without realising, I was hugging him. I forgot he wanted to be released as well.

"His arms were still tied to a tree. I was too overwhelmed. I fell in love with him there and then. I never looked back or at anyone. When he died, I was twenty-two.

"I remained single because I could not let another man take your grandfather's place. The thought of another man staring into my eyes never entered my mind." She was dabbing at her eyes.

"Granny, did you manage to untie him?" Jessica asked.

"Yes, after I had kissed him, silly. Please pass me the spinach."

"How old were you, Granny?"

"Jessica, leave your granny alone," her mother scolded.

"I was ten dear and intelligent enough to know what love means and stupid enough to tell my mother that I wanted to get married."

"Oh granny! How could you?" Jessica laughed.

"We married at sixteen. You are getting late, dear."

Jessica blushed. "Please pass me the mushroom sauce."

Denise enjoyed herself.

When the meal was over, they went back to the lounge. Jessica offered to give Denise a tour.

"You should have done that before the meal," her father told her.

They moved from one room to another. Jessica's room was all white.

"You can guess why it's white. It's my own idea. My mother thinks I am crazy advertising myself like this. I can't wait to change it. I haven't met anyone yet. The only men I have met who are interested in me are J& Sons' clients. Please, give me a break!

They are either divorced, or wife beaters and drug dealers. They are filthy rich, mind you but no. My happiness is important."

Denise didn't know what to say. She envied her. What made her lose herself? She had been upset with her family for refusing to accept Abraham as a son in law. She had thought a baby would make them think twice before they call him Mr Nobody. As it turned out, Abraham had taken care of everything. She looked around the room. Everything was spotless white.

"This is a beautiful room. How do you keep it clean?"

"I don't. I have a cleaner. Don't get me wrong. I know how to run a home. Mother made sure of that but I don't have the time at the end of the day."

The last room she was shown was Abraham's. Denise had to laugh. "Why does it look like yours? He has been married twice."

"He furnished it white for you. For his virgin bride. Mother was ever so pleased. She comes from a Christian family."

Denise didn't know what to say to this lovely girl. She will talk to Abraham about this lie. She wasn't a virgin, for goodness sake. Why lie?

She realised Abraham was a number one liar. What else hadn't he told her?

"What do you think, dear?" Jerome asked his wife.

"What do I think? She will shine this home. She is such a gentle creature with good manners. She will make a good wife."

"Yes, she will make a good wife and hostess," Jerome told his wife. "His ex-wives embarrassed me most of the time."

"You mean laughing without control?" Margaret laughed.

"That's putting it lightly, dear. They laughed like hyenas," he told his wife.

Mworozi's wife was ok but shy. Margaret never bothered her where entertaining was concerned. Nadine knew how to run a home, all right. She knew how to choose the right menu but mingling with guests – she kept a distance. Margaret wondered whether it was Mworozi's idea to keep Nadine hidden. She knew her son was number one jealous man. He beat her once. She had been shocked by her son's behaviour. Mworozi, J& Sons solicitors have a good reputation. "Violence in homes is one of the problems we deal with, right? Now tell me, how are you going to handle such cases knowing you are a wife beater yourself? Don't destroy what your father has worked so hard for. If you have a problem, see a marriage counsellor but don't fight your wife."

He had apologised and promised not to do it again. He went on to explain why he beat her.

She silenced him. "I don't want to know." Margaret saw a change in Nadine. She no longer had bugs under her eyes. She wished she could cure her shyness. A smile lit her face. Denise will do. She is one sharp intelligent girl. Denise thanked everybody for their hospitality.

"We hope to see you soon," they told her.

She blushed a little.

They had just left the residence when Denise asked Abraham what game he was playing by furnishing their bedroom white.

He grinned at her. "Don't you like it?"

"But it's a lie and you know it. Lost innocence is one thing you cannot lie about. What possessed you?"

He touched her earlobe. "Denise, you have a lot to learn. There are other ways of making love to a woman without..." he looked at her. "Do you need to hear more?"

She looked at him with her mouth open. "Are you saying you didn't? You mean...it was just the tip...of...your...Mr?" She giggled.

He grinned at her. He was aroused. He felt something stir in the lower region. He'd better control himself before he embarrassed himself. "Did... you... see any trace of blood?"

CHAPTER TWENTY-TWO

"I kept wondering why there wasn't any."

"Now you know. I love you Denise, I wanted you to wait for the right moment."

"I could kill you, you know." She was secretly relieved.

"You mean for saving you?" He grinned at her. As they turned into her driveway, Desmond was driving out.

They exchanged weak greetings. "I am sure you enjoyed 'Gone with the Wind'. He didn't wait for their reply. They were puzzled by the way he said it.

She looked at Abraham. "What was that?"

"Search me but he knows something we don't know. You did tell your mother that I was taking you out to watch 'Gone with the wind' a second time."

"I did."

"Then don't look puzzled. She must have told him."

"I hate lying to her. I enjoyed 'Gone with the Wind'. I can't wait to see it again."

They both laughed.

They could see the lights were on in the living room. "Are you coming in?"

"No, and thanks for meeting my family. They like you."

"I like them too."

She let herself in. The look on her mother's face made her blood reach a boiling point. She was now sweating. Annabella was nursing her baby, looking cool as a cucumber. Denise could see she was pleased with whatever was going on.

"Denise? Sit down!" her mother ordered.

"Are you ok, Mother?"

"Ok? My daughter lies to me and you ask me whether I am ok?

"Where have you been? Don't you dare lie to me, Denise. I will twist your neck."

There was no point lying. "I am sorry, Mother. Who told

you?" she couldn't help herself asking.

"Denise, I told you to be honest with me."

"I am sorry, Mother and please don't blame Abraham. Yes, he wanted me to meet his family but lying to you was my idea. It won't happen again. I am sorry."

Denise's behaviour brought back memories from a long time ago. What Denise was doing wasn't new to her. She was doing exactly what she had done with Isaac. They had made love at every opportunity.

She hoped her daughter wasn't pregnant. She'd better check her sanitary towels again.

She hasn't checked them for a month. She had started counting her sanitary towels when she learnt about Abraham and how fascinated her daughter was.

She looked at her daughter. "Abraham's grandmother phoned."

Denise gasped for air.

"She said you left without choosing her dress. She wants your opinion. She is sending her driver to pick you up tomorrow morning at ten o'clock and to be on the safe side, she gave me the car registration number."

Annabella could see her mother was softening up. "Mother, are you going to let her get away with it?"

"What am I supposed to do? Beat her up? She said she is sorry."

"A few minutes ago you were threatening to wring her neck. I can't believe I am hearing this." She moved her baby to the other breast.

"Denise is a number one liar. She doesn't care how other people feel about her behaviour. She runs around like a wanton woman. Look at her. Does she look innocent to you, Mother? I know my sister. We are twins.

"I am...in this...position because of her." Her lip trembled.

Denise was fuming. She has had enough of her sister's tongue. "Annabella, why don't you say it's a blessing in disguise? Look at you, looking like a princess. You love him but you don't want to admit it. We used to swap places, remember? You used to meet him on my behalf. What did you say about his kissing? His wandering fingers looking for your bra strap and your breast. Go on! Tell us all. We are waiting."

The sisters glared at each other.

Louise was shocked. Her girls have fooled a lot of people for fun. She never thought they would go that far. No wonder Desmond couldn't tell the difference. He was used to them both. She wished for her Valium.

Annabella looked at her twin sister with hatred. This was supposed to be their own secret. Now, their mother knows she kissed or was kissed. "Damn it Denise. I was doing it for you."

"You were doing it for yourself. You loved every second of it."

The sisters stared at each other without a word.

It was Annabella who broke the silence. "I didn't wish to be raped. I was out there looking for you. I didn't leave any stone unturned. I was almost out of my mind. I had no idea where else to look for you and then out of nowhere, a knife was on my throat, threatening me, warning me not to make any noise. They beat me. Once again I was warned that if I should tell Desmond about it, they would kidnap my mother and marry her against her will."

Louise gasped. "The fools. I could have their arse whipped for such threats."

Annabella sobbed. "I didn't utter a word after that until I came face to face with Desmond. I pleaded with him. He was beyond listening. I can't say more. This baby is the result. Each time I look at him, my mind goes back to that night. I have tried to love him but I can't.

"It's hard. I have forgiven Desmond. He didn't know it was me he was raping. I received your punishment, Denise. Don't stand there and ask me whether I find Desmond breathtaking."

Louise watched them in amazement! "What is this?" she asked no one in particular.

Annabella ignored her. She reached for the phone. It rang for a long time.

"Desmond, come and pick me up. I will be ready in thirty minutes." She hung up. She picked up her baby and left the room.

Denise looked at her mother for answers.

"I don't know how to handle this. I wish your father were still around."

"I will go to her. I must apologise."

"Don't even try unless you want a black eye," her mother warned.

Chapter Twenty-Three

Denise sat on her sister's empty bed. She hugged her pillow. She smelt Annabella's scent. It was heart-breaking. She has lost her forever. There is no turning back. She let her tears flow.

She went to her room taking Annabella's pillow with her. Sleep didn't come easily and when it came, all her dreams were about her sister before Desmond came on the scene. It was comforting. She slept all the way through the night. When she woke up, she phoned her aunt.

"What do you mean, you are not coming in today? I am short-staffed, Denise. You have to come."

"I am sorry, Aunt. I have an important engagement today. I will be in tomorrow. I promise."

Meredith took a deep breath. "You are a very difficult child, Denise."

"Oh Aunt! I am sorry. I will make it up to you."

"Well, whatever the engagement is, it must be an important one."

"I am meeting Abraham's Granny. A second time," she added.

"I'd better go. See you tomorrow." She hung up. When she turned, her mother was standing in the doorway. "Did you sleep well, Mother?"

She nodded. "Denise, I want you to give up your job. I have

enough money to support your brothers and myself. Thanks to your father's life insurance."

"Are you sure, Mother?"

"Denise, now you don't have to cultivate the land for survival, I don't see why you should carry on working for peanuts." She handed her an envelope.

Denise stared at her mother. "What is it?"

"You need to change your wardrobe. You need decent dresses. Look at you with four breasts. Your bras are too small."

Denise checked herself. Her mother was right about four breasts. Where the hell do you get a bra that holds them in one go? She thought to herself.

"I used to change your wardrobe regularly, remember?"

"But things have changed, Mother."

"No arguments, Denise. Change your wardrobe."

Annabella greeted her mother in law. "How are you, Mother?"

"I am well. I am glad you have been looked after well and my grandson has put on a great deal of weight."

Desmond watched the two women he loves. He was happy Annabella was back. He was sick and tired of visiting his mother in law's house. He felt he was intruding on his mother in law's privacy.

Louise was a good mother, no doubt about it.

Jocelyn smiled at her grandson. "Adrian is a beautiful name."

Annabella put her coffee down. "No, Mother! His name is Timothy."

Jocelyn looked at her daughter in law. She was shaking. "Where...did...you hear that name?"

"His name is Adrian." Desmond confirmed.

"I am his mother. I will call him Timothy. He is used to it already."

Jocelyn looked at Annabella. "Has your father in law's ghost visited you?"

Annabella stared at her mother in law. She gave her a weak smile. "I am glad it's not my imagination," she said to no one in particular. She looked at Desmond. "The man I told you about when we were at the village came in my dream again. I saw him leaning on Timothy's coat. He called him Timothy. When I opened my eyes, the man was gone. I haven't seen him since."

Jocelyn took a deep breath. She looked at them both. "Your father and I had an argument about this name when you were born. He wanted you called Timothy. I said Timothy was a mouthful."

Annabella almost told her mother in law that Desmond was a mouthful.

She sighed. "We didn't talk to each other for some time. Well, that's in the past. I will not argue with you children. Timothy will have to do even though it's a mouthful."

"You can call him Tim," Desmond told his mother.

"His name is Timothy. I will not have his name shortened," Annabella fumed.

She looked at her mother in law. "I am sorry for raising my voice. I am very sorry."

Desmond raised his glass of orange juice. "To Timothy." He smiled at both women. He actually liked the name but he wasn't going to admit it to anyone.

Jocelyn smiled at her grandson. "You look like your grandfather. No wonder he wants you called Timothy. I hope you don't become a hunter."

Annabella could see her mother in law was struggling with grief. She must have loved him so much.

She turned to Annabella. "I would like to see him regularly."

"No problem. We have all the time in the world."

Desmond cleared his voice. "You don't have all the time in the world, Annabella. You will be working with me."

Both women stared at him.

His mother found her voice. "Have you run out of workers?"

"No, I want her to know our business inside out."

Annabella had never worked in her life. She had taken a secretarial course. She could speak several languages. Her father's words came back to her. "Annabella, you never know what these languages may mean to you in future. As for your secretarial course, you would make a good secretary." She knew that most of Desmond's clients were foreigners. Desmond had been impressed with her when she came to his rescue during dinner. Desmond had tried his best to impress his French client with a fake French accent. "Do you want ze wine, monsieur?" he had asked. She had taken over immediately not wanting him to make an ass of himself. Desmond had looked at her with admiration.

When their client had left, he asked her what it was they were talking about. She had no reason to lie to him. "He said you are a lucky man to have a beautiful wife."

She had seen jealousy in his eyes. What kind of man wouldn't feel jealous after witnessing his wife's hands kissed by another man?

She reassured Desmond that the kiss didn't trigger anything. The following day he bought her a diamond necklace with matching earrings.

She had refused the earrings. "My ears are not pierced."

"Then it's time you had them done." He made an appointment for her to have her ears pierced.

Yes, she would want to help him now and again but working with him permanently was out of the question. She looked at Desmond; working with him would drive her mad. He was too possessive. She had an idea why he wanted her to work. The man was insecure. He didn't want her out of his sight.

"Timothy needs me," she told him.

"I know. There is a nursery at work. I made it especially for him." He hated what he was doing to her but his son needed him. Annabella must be supervised. He hated the idea of another woman looking after his son. He knew his wife had Vanessa in mind to look after Timothy while she runs around Kampala visiting every designer shop. He will not let his son suck those damn plastic bottles.

He refilled her cup with more tea. "Timothy needs it." He winked at her.

Jocelyn cleared her voice. "Annabella has hardly recovered. She needs time to recover."

"She is not going to be running the marathon, Mother. All I want is to show her how our business is run."

"You will have to wait until she has recovered. Desmond, you can't be that cruel."

He gave his mother a weak smile. "Annabella has already recovered. There is not one shop she hasn't visited since she gave birth."

"Desmond, I hate arguments. I will work with you if that's what you want."

"I am doing this for you, Annabella. We don't know what the future holds."

She sighed. "If you let me restore the village, at least we would have something to fall back on."

Jocelyn looked at them. "What are you talking about?"

"It's Annabella who is madly in love with your village, Mother. She doesn't stop talking about it."

"I will be doing it for our son. He has to know his roots."

"Good point child, but I don't see how you can restore that place. Why do you think I gave up on it?"

Annabella looked at her mother in law. "I need your permission, Mother. I will restore it for your grandson."

Jocelyn laughed. "What a tricky position you have put me in." She smiled at them. "You both have my permission to restore the village. I have no energy left to run it."

"Mother, that's a tricky answer. You know Desmond will never let me."

"You need to talk about it, dear. I better get going." She wasn't in a position to take sides. She loved them both. They must sort it out themselves.

"Don't forget to bring my grandson to visit me."

When their mother left, Annabella continued with her argument.

"Annabella, I don't have time for your fantasies. The village is beyond repair."

"I will restore it. I have Mother's permission."

"You don't have mine. Let's not talk more about it." He smiled at her. "I am glad you are back. I missed you."

"Well, I am back and soon we will be breathing on each other's necks."

"That's not what I had in mind."

"I know what you have in mind. What I mean is, I don't want to work full time. I need time to take Timothy out now and again. I love shopping and it's time I have my own…" She hesitated.

"Go on."

"Money," she told him.

"I give you enough money, Annabella."

"I would feel comfortable if you didn't record every shilling."

"I am a businessman, Annabella."

"I hate it when you check my receipts."

He stood up. "Get ready. We are running late. This is for your own good, Annabella. If something were to happen to me, how would you cope? The sooner you learn how to run Desmond Travel Agency, the better. I am relying on you, Annabella."

"Don't… talk… like that Desmond." He was right. She remembered what her mother went through after their father died. At least she knew a thing or two about survival. She swallowed hard. "I will work with you, Desmond."

Chapter Twenty-Four

Denise held her breath as she waited for Jessica's answer.

"Denise, I would love to but what about my duties? I am expected to supervise the wedding reception. I will be needed everywhere."

"I am desperate, Jessica. My sister has let me down at the last minute. She claims she has no figure left since the birth of her child." That was all a lie. Annabella hasn't spoken to her since she stormed out in the middle of the night after their shouting match.

She missed her especially now. She had wanted her to be her maid of honour, her friend and a sister she had always been until Desmond came along.

"Denise, what you are asking is too much. Don't you think it will look strange? I mean, I am your sister in law."

"Nonsense! I would like you to be my maid of honour."

"I have to speak to my parents first. I know Abraham doesn't mind as long as he gets his bride. He has been acting nervous lately. God knows why. One would think he has never... Oh shit! What am I saying? I beg your pardon."

Denise didn't wish to be reminded of Abraham's ex-wives. She decided to push her point. "I am relying on you, Jessica. I need an answer soon."

Meredith watched the two girls with gratitude. These days Abraham's family have become her regular customers. She has Denise to thank. She still didn't know what to say to Abraham. She had treated him badly. She was ashamed of her behaviour. Well, she had her niece's interest at heart. Who would want her niece to be married to a tramp? She comforted herself.

Denise asked for the bill.

Jessica beat her to it. "Abraham would have a fit if he found out that you paid for your meal."

"You paid for the swimming," she protested.

"I know and don't forget we have the fashion show to attend tomorrow evening at eight o'clock. I will pick you up at half seven." She liked the idea of being Denise's maid of honour. She would have to speak to her mother.

Denise thanked her aunt for the meal. "I can't keep away from your cooking, Aunt Meredith."

Meredith beamed at her. "I am glad you enjoyed your meal. I hope to see you soon. Keep them coming, my girl."

Denise shook her head. "You never change, Aunt."

Denise got home only to find her mother having a heated argument with Annabella on the phone. "Annabella, just because you are married doesn't mean I can't give you a good smack on your backside. This silence nonsense has to stop. Do you hear me?"

"Mother, I don't know why you get worked up on Denise's behalf. Has she put you to it? I am not coming and that's final."

Louise sighed. "I wonder what your father would say to this if he were around."

Annabella's nostrils flared. "We wouldn't be in this mess to begin with. This is the time when I badly miss him," she sobbed.

"No matter what you say, I am not coming. I will visit you once she is gone. I don't want to see Denise ever."

CHAPTER TWENTY-FOUR

"Annabella, if you don't come to Denise's marriage ceremony, just know you are no longer my daughter. I mean every word. You have forgiven Desmond. Why can't you do the same for your sister?"

"None of you have an idea how it is like to...be ...married against...their will."

Louise turned to Denise with her mouth open. "She hung up on me. What do I do?"

"Mother, leave her. I asked Jessica if she could be my maid of honour. She has to ask her parents first if it's ok."

Louise had nothing to say to that. The two girls got on very well. She was pleased about that. "She is such a gentle girl," she said.

"Yes, I am happy to have her as a friend. I don't see her as a sister in law. I wish I had made friends when I was growing up."

"You had Annabella. I did encourage you to have other friends but you wouldn't. As we speak, Annabella is as lonely as you are."

"I know she is not coming to my wedding." She took a deep breath. "Mother, do me a favour. Please don't shut her out of your life. You didn't mean those words. We all need you and you need us."

"I will miss you, Denise. I hope your marriage turns out like mine. I had a happy marriage. We did quarrel all right, but we made up before the sun set. That was our rule. We had to make up before the sun set. If we argued in the night, we made up before sunrise. Look at me, Denise – all this stress on my face came after your father's death."

"I hope you will be all right...Mother. I mean, you are still young." She swallowed hard.

Louise touched her daughter's hand. "I know what you are getting at. I am not interested. Eric and Nicholas will take care of me in my old age."

"If you should change your mind later, you have my blessing. I don't want you to be lonely. Where is Eric now?"

"Where else? Bike riding."

The telephone interrupted their girly talk.

Louise picked it up hoping it was Annabella phoning to apologise. It was Jessica. Louise handed over the phone.

"Denise, I will do it."

"Oh Jessica! That's wonderful news. Thank you so much. You have what it takes. You will look glamorous."

"You can guess why Granny didn't mind. She said it's high time they noticed me. I feel like pulling out but I hate to let you down."

"Thanks. You have made my day."

"What are friends for?"

Denise's throat tightened with emotion. "Indeed...what are friends for?"

The following day, Denise and Jessica went to the fashion show. The evening was a successful one. Denise beamed at her sister in law.

"Things are moving fast. We have a dress rehearsal tomorrow. They agreed to fit us in at short notice."

"How many bridesmaids do you need?" Jessica asked.

"Well, I am not sure. What do you think?"

"This is your day, Denise."

"But I need your opinion."

"Ok, if it was my wedding, I wouldn't like to be over-crowded. I guess a pageboy and his partner would do well."

"Just two?" Her mind went to Eric and Lydia, Aunt Meredith's daughter.

"You asked for my opinion."

"It's a good idea but my little cousin will never talk to me if I don't include her. She is Aunt Meredith's daughter. She is eight."

"I see what you mean. My nieces would never forgive me either."

Both girls burst out laughing remembering Angela and Melanie.

"Well, let's give them a chance to show off."

When they got out, Abraham was waiting for them. "Was it a good show?"

"Yes, just what we had hoped for. We have a dress rehearsal tomorrow," Jessica told him and excused herself.

As soon as she drove off, Denise turned to him. "Did you two plan this? I wasn't expecting to see you until the marriage ceremony."

"Oh no! I was just passing and my sister is a very sensible girl. She knows when she is not wanted. Let's go. I need to talk to you."

"Are you hungry?"

"Not really. Mother was expecting us. She is not going to like this change of plan."

"I am sorry I interrupted your plans."

"What is it you want to say to me?"

"We can talk about it over a meal."

He took her to his favourite restaurant. "Denise, you haven't told me where we should go for our honeymoon."

"As I said to you, it doesn't matter where we go. We can even stay home."

"Oh please, don't let Granny hear you say that. That's exactly what she has been telling me. She wants us to have a traditional honeymoon."

Denise looked at him. "What is that?"

"Please! You don't want to know."

"I am interested."

"Ok, we stay at home, that's what she wants."

"What's wrong with that?"

"Everything. I want to have a private honeymoon, ok? I don't want their enquiring looks."

She laughed. "Abraham, I find that romantic. Do you have any alternative? Surely you don't want to upset Granny."

"It's not her wedding, all right."

"Now you sound like Eric. You know she cares. She wants to make sure we are ok."

"That's the whole point. She said…"

"Go on," she told him.

"She said, a marriage started in hotel rooms doesn't last. She was referring to my previous marriages."

"Oh! I see."

"Now you see why I am stressed out."

"There is no need for stress. We can stay for a few days and then shoot off for dessert."

He looked at her with a wicked smile. "What a brilliant idea! Ok, where do we go?"

"You choose."

"We choose." He produced a pen and a piece of paper. "You name any place. I will do the same."

"You remind me of Annabella. This is one game we enjoyed most and the funny thing is, we always came up with the same answer." She chose one place and waited for him to write his down.

She wasn't sure what he would think of her coming up with such a wild idea. "How romantic!" She gave him a hundred watt smile. It was a fantasy she wanted fulfilled and the man to fulfil it is right here in front of her. Her skin tingled.

As it turned out, they both chose the same place.

He grinned at her. "My granny won't approve, so don't breathe a word, even to Jessica."

Chapter Twenty-Five

Denise sat on her bedroom windowsill. She could see people working like crazy preparing a gazebo for her marriage ceremony. Her bosom heaved. A smile slit her cheeks and then it disappeared.

Her mind went back to the time she had run away three days before her wedding to Desmond. It was the time she didn't wish to remember. The time that had brought darkness into her twin sister's heart. The time she wished to bury but couldn't bury and forget.

She missed her so much. She didn't feel whole at all. She felt as if part of her was missing. She missed her twin sister. Fat tears escaped her. She let it run along her cheeks. There was a loud knock.

"Come in," she said without enquiring who it was. It was her aunt. She gave her a lukewarm smile.

Her aunt's voice grated on her nerves. "Oh Denise, you are still here. Thank God! We better keep a close watch on you. I have stationed a few security guards on every exit." She giggled. "The last thing we want is you doing another runner."

Denise closed her eyes to keep her tears at bay. It was no use.

Meredith looked at her niece with affection. "Oh poor baby! Come to Aunt Meredith. A marriage is not the end of the world you know and it's not a bed of roses either," her aunt told her in a singsong voice.

That increased her sobs.

"Denise, you will make your eyes sore. Listen, I don't have much to teach you. I will tell you one thing I did which I still regret."

Denise waited for her aunt's confession. Her aunt could say anything regardless of who the listener was.

"It's about my first marriage. I cried as you are doing now. Why? I was frightened of what lay ahead of me. I lost a great deal of weight. Your grandparents almost cancelled the wedding thinking I was ill. I wasn't ill. I was frightened of my husband."

She held Denise's hand. "Look at me, Denise. He turned out impotent. The poor man! We slept back to back all the time.

"I knew there was a problem but I kept it to myself. He was my husband. I respected him. I was determined to keep quiet about the whole thing but my mother in law pounced on to me big time. To her, I was responsible for her son's drinking habits and lack of heir. She called me barren, frigid, you name it. I almost jumped out of my skin when my husband joined in. 'Oh yes! My mother is right. We have been married for months now. What have you got to show for it? I will marry another woman.'

"I said to him: 'while you are shopping for wife number two, don't forget to include an aphrodisiac on your shopping list'. Did I get away with it? He gave me ten-fingers tattoo on my face. I wanted a divorce. He refused. I took him to court. He sounded so pathetic when he said I was the one with a problem. I am cold as fish. When it was my turn to talk, I said ladies and gentlemen, I don't have much to say. All I need is a couch and a few witnesses, my mother in law included." She looked at her niece. "Those few words gave me freedom. Don't suffer in silence, ok?

"Denise, I know it's all right to worry but why start so early? A marriage is not a bed of roses. I must remind you."

CHAPTER TWENTY-FIVE

How she wished to tell her aunt that she wasn't worried about Abraham and Abraham wasn't impotent for that matter. She couldn't wait to lie in his arms. She was crying for her sister.

"Now, cheer up. You and I have a lot to talk about. What I am going to say to you doesn't leave this room. You don't pass it on to someone who is not married yet. They should wait for their turn to be told what has to be told about marriage especially in the bedroom. Do you understand?"

She nodded. That's all she could do. She didn't trust her voice.

Meredith talked to her for half an hour. "Do you have any questions?"

She nodded. "How do I keep the marriage ticking?"

"A marriage is like a flower, Denise. If you don't water it, it wilts."

"Shit! He has to wilt at some point," she said.

"The swearing has to stop, Denise. You get me?"

"I am sorry."

"This is what you have to do." That lasted another half an hour. "Don't pass on what I have told you to your friend Jessica. She should wait for her turn."

How would she start anyway? Denise thought to herself.

"Thanks, Aunt. I will miss you." And she meant it.

"I will miss you too but hey! Don't forget to bring your clan to my restaurant. I have exotic dishes. You should try them."

"You never change, Aunt."

Meredith beamed at her niece.

As soon as Meredith left Denise's room, Jessica walked in. "You look red in the face. Has your aunt been?"

"I am... not..."

Jessica raised her hand. "You don't have to tell me. I know already. Granny told me everything just in case I take a short cut. By the time she was through with me, I was in tears. I recommend cold water on your face. You don't want puffy eyes on your wedding day, do you?"

"It's not until tomorrow."

"I know, today is another ceremony. It's as good as the wedding. About a million eyes will be staring at you saying what got into her head, marrying a man like him?"

"Oh please, Jessica. There is nothing wrong with Abraham. Actually I like the Abraham I fell in love with."

"A tramp, you mean? The man was a disgrace. I told him many times to change his appearance, or I would tell you everything. At first, our parents had no idea what he was on about until he explained his reasons."

"Well, that's the Abraham I love. I don't love the Abraham in suits. I love his torn denim jeans."

"Now, you are talking nonsense. I have just picked up his suits from the dry cleaners. I left them getting ready. We should be doing the same. If you have some crying to do, do it now before I apply the make-up. The film crew should be here in a minute. Whatever you do, don't cry. It will ruin your make-up."

"I don't like the idea of being filmed."

"Well, that's Abraham's idea. 'I want my children to see this day' – his own words."

Denise opened her mouth. "He is counting chickens before the eggs are hatched. Damn him!"

Jessica hid a smile behind her hand.

The film crew asked a few questions which Denise answered with confidence.

Jessica was impressed. "You are so confident. I can't believe you are the same person who looked red in the face after your aunt's lecture."

"I am a nervous wreck. If you must know," she told her maid of honour.

The marriage ceremony went on as planned, without tears from Denise until her twin sister turned up with her husband. What made people gasp was the outfit Annabella was wearing. It was the same as Denise's.

There was a long silence.

Annabella took a step back after noticing her sister's outfit. "How the hell did she copy my..." She had chosen her gown with care. It never occurred to her that Denise would be spying on her. She must have spied on her. Sneaky bitch! I will kill her for this.

"Ssh. Don't make a scene, dear. You both have the same taste. Alicia designers is the best in town. Did you expect her to go to Shauriyako market? Let's take a seat."

"Oh no! I am going back home to change."

"Oh no! You are not." He manoeuvred her forward.

She gave a resignation sigh. "It's your fault entirely. I didn't want to come. Well, now I am here, I'd better make the best of it. I have a message for her as a matter of fact."

"I am glad we are here. But don't make a scene. I hate your tantrums, Annabella. Waiter? Could you please get us mineral water? Thank you." He knew how to handle her all right. At first he had tiptoed with her not wanting to set her off. Well, she can ruin her make-up if she wants. He looked from one twin to the other. He was lost. No one could blame him for his error. Yes, he had paid a huge price for his mistake but it was worth it. He loved Annabella, he wouldn't swap her for anything. How the hell did they come up with the same gowns and the same hairstyle? He'd better mark them before they confuse him a second time.

Annabella was wearing pearls. Real pearls. He looked at Denise's neck. Damn! She is wearing pearls too. How he wished to twist her neck for making a fool of him and everyone. How dare she run off three days before their wedding. Maybe it was a blessing in disguise. His eyes travelled to Abraham. I don't envy you. Good luck to you, he thought to himself.

Denise fidgeted in her seat.

"Are you ok?" Jessica enquired.

"I am fine. What I don't understand is what game my sister is playing at turning up in our outfit."

"She doesn't look out of shape to me. She has a perfect figure, like yours. How did you manage to resemble each other like this? And you don't look as if you get on at all. There is something you haven't told me, Denise."

"I know. It's a long story."

"I guess it can wait."

Abraham wasn't lost. He knew the difference between them. It's something he found out himself and he wasn't going to reveal it to anyone just in case they tried to play tricks on him.

"Wow! What have we got here?" Richard boomed. He was acting as their father. Nicholas was too young to conduct this kind of ceremony. He looked at his nephew, a carbon copy of his father. The smile on his nephew's face told him something. "Let's see how you can tell the difference."

He cleared his voice. "Now, girls, don't play games with me. I am too old for such games." He blinked. He could never tell the difference between the two if he lived a million years. He knew how they used to swap places for the sake of fooling him. As long as they remain in their seats, he won't hand over the wrong girl.

He'd better make it quick and get over with it. He was about to call for Denise to come forward when Annabella stood up and hugged her sister. She had a message for her. "I only came for one reason. I want Desmond forgiven for what he did. We look the same, Denise. Anyone can make the mistake he did. Now, I have done what I came here for. I don't want to see your face again." She flashed her a smile to confuse those watching them.

Denise smiled at her. "I am glad you came, Annabella. I have a message for you too. I don't want to see your face again. Timothy must be wondering where his cow is." She flashed her a smile followed by a hug to confuse the fight between them. "One word of advice, don't let Mother know about this. She will go mental. We both love her. Enjoy your miserable marriage, Annabella."

Annabella stared at her sister. This was not what she had expected. She had expected Denise to beg her. But now... She went back to her seat with tears threatening her eyelids.

"Are you ok, dear?" asked Desmond.

"I am developing a headache. I want to go home."

"We have just arrived. Mother won't be pleased."

She groaned and settled back in her seat.

The sisters stared at each other. It was Denise who broke down.

"You will ruin your make-up," Jessica dabbed at her eyes with no success.

Fat tears coursed down Denise's cheeks.

All the guests were touched. "In this day and age, it's very rare to see a girl crying her eyes out during a marriage ceremony," one woman whispered to her friend.

"There is one in a million. It means she looked after herself well. She is afraid of what is waiting for her. What I mean, she hasn't tasted him. God bless her."

Louise beamed at her daughters. She nodded at Annabella. "Thank you," she mouthed the words.

Annabella gave her mother a cosmetic smile.

Denise composed herself. This is her day. She mustn't let her sister spoil it.

Richard called his niece to come forward.

Denise and Jessica walked to where Richard and Louise stood.

Abraham and his best man joined them.

Richard cleared his voice. "I hope you are Denise. The last thing I need is handing over the wrong girl."

"She is the one," Abraham replied to him.

Richard gave him a cold stare. How the hell does he know the difference?"

When the ceremony was over, Denise and Jessica went back into the house.

The two girls changed out of their gowns. "Now, tell me what this is all about. It's better you get it off your chest. The last thing we want is your make-up running during your wedding ceremony."

Denise sighed. "What is there to say? My sister hates me."

"Why?" Jessica asked.

She told her. "And do you know why it hurts so much? She doesn't love Desmond. What kind of marriage is that? I want her to be happy. And… I told her to go back to her miserable marriage."

Jessica took Denise's hand. "Listen, actions speak louder than words. This is the first time I have met the couple. She loves him but she doesn't want to admit it."

"How can you say that? She married him for her reputation. She hates him."

"That's what you have been made to believe. Listen Denise, in my work, observation is very important. If they were to come to Mother for marriage counselling and behave the way they have been behaving a while ago, my mother would tell them to go home and stop wasting their time and money.

"The way she looks at him. She touches him without planning it. She linked her hands with his more than twice."

"I noticed that. I heard a few women laughing about it. One said, 'look at them holding hands. The only time my husband's hands connect with mine is when we are throwing punches at each other. I gave him a black eye the other night.' They giggled their heads off."

"Denise, don't let your sister spoil your day. This is the day you never forget, right? Don't let your sister spoil it. She loves her husband big time."

Annabella made some excuses. She wanted to go home fast. She wanted to talk to Desmond. It was important she speak to him.

"But I thought you were spending a night here," Louise told her.

"We will be at church tomorrow," she told her mother.

"I am glad you made up with your sister."

"Yes, we had to. Life is too short, Mother."

Louise beamed at her. "Thank you, Annabella."

"How is the headache?" Desmond asked his wife as he helped her out of her gown.

She looked at him as if he was mad. "What headache?"

"You mean…you lied just to get away?" He was furious. "I was enjoying myself if you must know."

"I am sorry. I…need…a word with you. I…can't go on, Desmond. I just can't." She sobbed.

He stared at her. She was in distress. Whatever it was, it's not good. He could smell trouble. She was good at losing her temper with him. She was a good mother to their son, a perfect PR to Desmond Travel Agency. She poked her nose in everything for a good cause. He was impressed with the way she handled everyone and everything at Desmond Travel Agency. She was a perfect hostess. Her smooth talk gained them new clients. Only once was he upset with her at work. He had been shocked when she promoted his personal secretary to assistant manager and took her place instead. "Why did you do a thing like that?" He had been furious.

"Desmond, only I should breathe on your neck." She had flashed him a smile. "Your coffee should be with you shortly, Mr Desmond Tumwiine. Your first meeting is at 9:30." She had grinned at him. She was forever on his tail, which gave him hope that one day she would declare her love for him. Now, he had an idea what it was she wanted to talk about. He knew that Timothy would be his only child. She swallowed contraceptive pills like crazy. She hated their lovemaking. She pretended all the time. She was a damn fraud in bed, releasing counterfeit orgasms. Did she think for one minute that he wouldn't know the difference? Oh! He knew. He lived in hope though. But now she wants to tell him that it's over.

"Desmond, are you listening?"

He blinked. "What?"

"I said, keep an eye on Timothy while I prepare something to eat. I didn't enjoy that food, to be honest with you. I never enjoy party foods or funeral foods. Oh! I am ravenous! I shouldn't be long."

She was gone before he could tell her off for dismissing the cook for the evening. He looked at his watch; the simple meal would take three hours.

"That's Annabella. One lazy cook." He wanted to know what it was she wanted to talk about. He hated suspense. Damn her! He looked at his sleeping son. I will fight for you. She will not separate us. You are my son. The heir. Do you hear me?

Annabella had no idea what to prepare. Lucas hadn't defrosted anything. Well, he didn't know they would need supper after all.

She sighed. What do I do here? She opened a deep freezer; her eyes rested on lamb chops.

"They will take forever. Does it really matter? We have all night." She bunged the chops in the microwave to defrost.

Her next step was an easy one. She marinated the lamb chops in lamb seasoning. She cooked it in the pressure cooker for five minutes. Then she put the chops on the grill to brown. She hated white looking meat. Her meat had to be brown and succulent. She chopped some tomatoes, carrots and cucumbers. "This will do with a bottle of wine." She was in the mood for wine. She needed courage to say what she wants to say to Desmond. She wished she had strong wine. Well, Chardonnay isn't bad, she decided. Her food preparation took less than an hour.

Desmond was flipping through television channels when Annabella walked in with a tray.

"That was quick. Are you sure it's cooked?"

"We have a doctor on call twenty-four hours and besides, we are insured." She gave him a cold stare. "I can never do right," she complained.

"You know I hate eating in the lounge," Desmond reminded her.

"Just this once," she begged him.

His heart beat. They were having their last supper, he thought to himself. "Listen Annabella, I need to know what it is you want to say to me before we eat. I can't wait any longer."

"The food will get cold. Please don't spoil my cooking."

They ate in silence. After a long while, he complimented her on her cooking.

"You know I am useless when it comes to cooking. This time I used a cookbook."

Now the eating was over, his heart raced at a speed. She was bloody taking her time. Why can't she leave the washing to Lucas?

A few minutes later, she put her head in the doorway. "I am having a shower. I shouldn't be long. Please check on Timothy. He is fond of pulling blankets over his face."

She was gone before he could tell her to do it herself.

She took a quick shower. She was shaking. She didn't know how to handle such a case. She was in agony. But she must do it and it had to be tonight.

She sat next to Desmond. She twisted her wedding ring like crazy.

She took a deep breath. "I don't know how to begin."

"I won't let you go, Annabella. Just forget it."

MISTAKEN IDENTITY

She gave him a questioning look.

"Well?"

"Well what?"

"Annabella. Get on with it, damn you!"

She gave him this crazy look. "Desmond, I... want... to make love... to you for the first time." She swallowed. "I am sorry. I shocked you."

He gave her a vacant look. He was speechless. Not only was he speechless, nothing stirred in the lower region. Viagra popped into his head. She froze his feeling for her with one sentence. The sentence he has been waiting for all this time. He blinked. "Annabella, I...have never been proposed to by a woman. You have taken me by surprise." He reached for his wine.

She stopped him. "I want you sober. I want you to hear me out. Don't give me that look. I am not going to jump on you. That's not my style," she scolded him.

He winced at her brute words. He knew their origin.

"I am sorry. I didn't mean it like they way you think.

"I have a confession. I never thought I would reveal this to you. Denise knew about it. She was part of this game. She is the one who started it because she hated you."

Desmond had no idea what she was on about. He didn't really mind whatever it was. At least she wasn't leaving him.

"Desmond, I am the one who chose Denise's house. We viewed it together."

Desmond reached for his wine. He was happy when she didn't stop him. He gulped it down. He was remembering the kiss she gave him. He had been shocked by her change. Her kiss had given him hope. As it turned out, he had kissed the wrong twin.

"Why?"

"Are you asking me why? That kiss I gave you meant a lot to me. I felt bad about it because I felt like a thief. Denise and I swapped places whenever it suited us. I loved you. You killed that love when you raped me. If you had listened to me when I pleaded with you, the two of us could have worked something out. I hated you for what you did to me.

"Well, they say time heals. I want us to be a normal family. I don't want to live in the past."

He reached for her hand. "So... do... I. No wonder I couldn't tell you apart."

"Now you know the truth, what are you going to do about it?"

"I am sorry for what I did to you." He looked into her eyes. "I am so grateful you have forgiven me."

She looked at him. "Well?"

"Your wish has been granted. You may go ahead."

She was tearing him apart before he finished the sentence. "I hope I am doing the right thing," she moaned.

"You are doing perfect. Oh! You missed a button here." He winked at her.

She was like a racing machine. He didn't want to tell her that. But he had to remind her about his zip. "Mind my pubic hair."

She giggled. "Why do you think Gillette razors were invented?" This was real Annabella. The woman he loved. Her moans and orgasms were not counterfeit this time. He wondered how long she would go on for. He had to hold on for her But it was impossible to hold on any longer. After what seemed like eternity, he released himself silly.

They were both panting and exhausted. She looked at him with a lazy smile. "I shocked you."

He beamed at her. "I misjudged you."

Within minutes, Annabella was fast asleep. That's when Desmond knew that what had just taken place wasn't a fake. Annabella scrubbed herself after their lovemaking. But here she is digesting every inch of him. He grinned at her sleeping face.

At long last, he kissed her cheek and went to check on their son.

Chapter Twenty-Six

Louise moved from one foot to another. "Where are they?"

"Mother, it doesn't matter. We can't wait for them. We are running late as it is." Denise knew her sister wasn't coming. She was actually pleased that she hadn't showed up. The last thing she needed was Annabella spoiling her day. This is her day, no one is going to spoil it for her. She had said all those hurtful words so she could keep away. She hoped Annabella read between the lines.

"I have a feeling something is not right," Louise told her daughter.

"Maybe Timothy is not well. If they happen to turn up, they know where the church is."

Denise hugged her mother. She shed a few tears. "I will be in touch. Muyenga is only a stone's throw away."

Louise's eyes smarted with tears. "Denise, when you need a mother, friend, you know where I am."

Abraham checked his watch. "What's keeping them? Has she run off?"

His heart raced. The thought of being jilted put his manhood on edge.

"Stop fretting. They will be here shortly," his best man told him.

Abraham was beginning to develop a headache when the wedding march put a smile on his face. "They are here!" He breathed.

Denise looked sensational in her wedding gown. Her throat tightened with emotion. Her brother Nicholas looked handsome in his three-piece suit. She held on to his hand. He was acting as her father. He took his role seriously and beautifully. She was proud of him. Her eyes rested on Abraham. A smile slit her cheeks. She wondered whether he was as nervous as she was.

Nicholas stared at Abraham straight in the face. "She is very special. We haven't spent your dowry. Not one cent. One foot wrong, you will have your dowry back."

"I will look after her with my life. She is my life. What do you take me for?" He smiled at his brother in law.

"A good marriage is all I wish you," he told them. He took his seat next to his mother.

The wedding ceremony went on smoothly.

A few minutes later, Abraham grinned at his bride. "You look sensational Mrs Muganzi."

"Phew! We have made it." She breathed.

Desmond opened his eyes. He checked the bedside clock. He blinked. He couldn't believe what he was seeing. "This can't be true. It was after twelve o'clock in the afternoon. Annabella! We are late for the wedding. Hurry up."

She opened one eye. "Whose wedding?" She reached for him.

The wedding reception took place at a restaurant Abraham's father had hired for the occasion. It was a beautiful reception. Good food, good music, good service. It was beautifully done.

Jerome planned it that way. He didn't want his residence invaded and besides, it would be too much work for everyone. He liked his privacy.

He only invited family members to his residence to welcome Abraham's wife. He wished them happiness and hoped this time his son's marriage would last forever. He gave a speech and thanked everyone for coming.

Denise was so sad to see her brothers looking lost and lonely. "You look after Mother, right?"

"It means I won't be going back to our Annabella. I don't want Mother to be lonely," Eric informed his sister.

"Does that mean you won't visit me?"

"I guess Nicholas will look after Mother while I do my monthly visits. But I hate to leave Mother alone."

Denise could see he was in distress.

"Ok, I will visit you. What about that?"

"That's cool." His face lit up.

Nicholas wanted a private word with his sister.

"I have a message from Mother. She got a message from Desmond. I didn't want to tell you before the wedding reception in case it spoilt your lunch."

She didn't want to hear her sister's excuse, but she was curious though.

"Annabella is in hospital. She had a miscarriage. Whatever that means."

Denise didn't know what to say to that. "I am sorry", seemed the right words but the words refused to leave her mouth. "Timothy is only six months," she blurted out.

Nicholas fidgeted. "Listen, I thought to let you know." He was gone. He didn't want to know about his sister's sex life. How she became pregnant in the first place. He was curious though. He would ask Aunt Meredith. She is one person who spoke freely regardless of who the listener was. He couldn't wait to try it himself. His eyes rested on Jessica. She was only four years older than him. She was pretty and had a cute backside and nice legs. He whistled as he jumped into their waiting taxi.

Denise tried to hide her distress when she found another reception at their residence. She was too tired. She was feeling guilty for upsetting Annabella in the first place. She had called her a cow. Did she cause her to lose her baby? The question is, was Annabella really pregnant? She may be lying trying to make her feel bad on her wedding day. "Well, she is not going to succeed."

"They won't keep you long," Abraham told his wife. "It's just a formality. All these are our grandparents, uncles, aunties and cousins from the rural area. They came especially for us."

As Abraham predicted, it was a short reception. A few people greeted Denise one by one and introduced themselves. A few remained seated.

Denise asked her husband whether she should go to them.

"No, those are grandparents, aunties, and uncles. You will greet them in the morning."

"And I don't call them by their names," she told him.

"You are learning, dear. Never call them by their names. It's lack of respect if you should find yourself calling them by their names. Do you know, I didn't know my grandmother's names until recently? My mother is one careful woman. She respects all her in laws. You will find out.

"If you need guidance in those areas, Mother is the right person. You will be told that in the morning."

Denise didn't know whether to be pleased or frightened when she was finally shown to her bedroom.

"Your bath is ready," Jessica informed her sister in law.

"Thanks, Jessica. You have been a great help from the day we met. It's time you took a rest as well. I can run my bath."

"Nonsense! That's my job to run it for you while you are still in hibernation, which is going to last one month according to

Abraham. He will tell you the rest. I am lucky we don't live in the village where I have to fetch water and carry it on my head. Now, I must let you get on with it. If you need me, use the white telephone over there. All the extension numbers are there.

"Ignore the red telephone. That's Abraham's business line. It's a twenty-four hour line. You will get used to it."

Denise sighed. All this was new to her. "Thanks," she said once again.

She decided to do a tour of their suite before her bath. She remembered the last time she had seen this room. It was still the same white room. But she was curious to know what was behind closed doors. The last time she was here Jessica showed her the bedroom and the lounge only. She opened one door that led her to the balcony.

The view was magnificent. The place looked spotlessly clean. Her face lit up when she entered a library or study, whatever it was called. She could never get bored with all those books about.

"I have married a bookworm."

Denise turned to see Abraham grinning at her.

"You...startled...me, Abraham." She held on to her racing heart.

"Our bath is getting cold."

"My bath is getting cold," she corrected him.

"You must be tired. I will show you where the bathroom is."

Denise was taken aback when she saw the size of the bathroom with two baths both filled up.

"That's yours and this is mine," he told her.

Denise stared at him. "But...it's in the same room. We can't possibly have a bath in the same room."

He laughed. "Denise, we are married," he said as he helped her out of her housecoat.

Denise felt too naked. He had seen her before but she had not removed her clothes. Just a little ride up. She blushed with shame.

Part of her body had been covered. Now to stand here with her sulking nipples staring at Abraham was too much for her to bear. She dived into her bath and covered herself with bath bubbles.

Abraham took his bloody time to remove his clothes. Just to take off a tie took forever.

"You act like a sloth," she told him and busied herself with a bathing sponge. Her eyes wondered to her husband's nude body now and again. She blushed at the thought of being caught spying.

When he had folded the last item, he grinned at her. "Are you enjoying your bath?"

"I will enjoy my bath when you stop staring at me like that. Please get in your bath. Suppose someone walks in here?" she asked.

"It's a private suite. They know the rules. Let me. I will wash your back."

Denise closed her eyes. "You have magic hands," she thought aloud.

"You bet," he said in a husky voice.

She opened her eyes wide when a gurgling noise aroused her. It was coming from the next bath. "It's your water. The stopper is not well placed."

He grinned at her as he showed her the stopper in his hands.

"You did it." Before she could say more he was lowering himself in her bath tub. "I don't know what game my sister was playing filling up two bath tubs. I like her innocence though. Now it's your turn to rub my back."

"I am flattered!" She looked around. "Does the CCTV cover this area?"

He reassured her they were safe.

By the time the bath was over, Denise was no longer shy.

Later on in their marital bed, she discovered how it feels to lose one's innocence. How could she have got it wrong the first time Abraham played with her? She felt so embarrassed by her ignorance. The first time had been a simple seduction. She had waited the whole month expecting to have morning sickness only to discover it wasn't the case.

"Are you ok?"

She could only nod. She didn't trust her voice. She could see he was in the mood for conversation or, was it a conversation? His face told her something. She winced at the thought. How can he lie there with no guilt on his face? Well, he has been married before. She answered her question.

He gathered her in the crook of his arms. "The night is still young." His words made her skin tingle.

She must say something, she told herself. "You are right," she replied.

Chapter Twenty-Seven

Abraham and his wife arrived at their destination. She looked around, stretched her eyes. She couldn't see any civilisation. They were in the middle of nowhere but she didn't mind. She loved this kind of life. She loved camping. She had always loved camping. She remembered at one point she had to ask Annabella to go out with Desmond while she went camping with a church group.

She watched Abraham fixing their tent. When he was done, he fixed an electric wire around it. "No animal will get to us. Why don't you make a fire while I go fishing?"

She looked at him as if he was mad. "Oh no! I am coming with you."

"I won't be long. There is so much fish in that water. Mworozi and I have been here before. It's quite safe."

She refused to stay behind. Electric wire or not, she wasn't going to let him leave her alone.

Jerome was furious with Abraham. "Why didn't he leave their hotel details?"

"I guess they want their privacy," his wife told him.

"But I must speak to him."

"I don't think you have a chance, Father," Jessica said as she took her seat. "I am starving. Granny, please bless this food."

"I can tell you know where Abraham and his wife are. Why don't you put your father out of his misery?" He was handling Abraham's cases until they came back but there were certain things they needed to discuss." Granny gave her a knowing look.

Jessica put some receipts in front of her father.

Jerome looked at them. "It's just a damn receipt. It doesn't mean anything." He adjusted his glasses. "Damn him! How could he do such thing?"

"What?" The rest of the family chorused.

"They have gone camping," he hissed. They could be anywhere. What was he thinking taking someone's daughter into the wild? Hasn't he got any sense in his head?

"They are in it together," Jessica informed them.

"You knew and you never said a word?" her father accused.

"I didn't know it was camping. What I know is that they picked the place for their honeymoon at random and came up with the same answer. That's what Abraham said to me and the whole thing amused him. He couldn't stop talking about it saying he'd finally found his soul mate. I have never seen a chatterbox in my life before. I had to tell him to calm down. When I saw the receipt, I knew. Why would he buy an electric wire and a tent? The word is camping. That's the place they chose for their honeymoon."

"They are young, they are in love, they are wild, leave them alone Jerome," his mother told him and blessed the food.

Mworozi's mind raced. He knew where his brother and his bride were. He decided to seal his mouth. "I will help you with Abraham's cases. My schedule is not that tight at the moment," he told his father.

"What children put their parents through," Jerome mumbled. "When they are out of nappies, you think that's it but there is more agony."

Abraham and his wife sat by the fire roasting a guinea fowl for supper. It was a warm evening. The only light was their fire and the moonlight.

They had been living a gypsy life for the last three days. It was a peaceful life.

Abraham cleared his voice. "I must take you back to civilisation."

"Nonsense! I love it here. Let's stay here. Please say yes," she teased him.

"This is someone's property," he reminded her.

"I haven't seen anyone since we have been here."

"That doesn't mean the land doesn't belong to anyone. We must book into a hotel for the remaining days. We don't want the family to know about our little trip, do we?"

"You are right. We smell of fish and smoke. But I love it. This is real life."

The following day, they pulled down their tent and returned to town. They booked into a hotel. A Jacuzzi was necessary. They really needed it! They stayed for four days.

When they returned home, they found the family waiting for them.

Denise went straight to her bedroom. That was her place for the next three weeks according to her mother in law.

"You are lucky. When I married your father in law, they kept me indoors for five months. I had my needlework to keep me company. Your father in law is a workaholic. You will soon find out."

Denise smiled at her. "I am not good at needlework. But I can cook."

"I am blessed. Mworozi's wife is an excellent cook. You will get on. Nadine is good. I have no complaints."

"Now, Abraham, what the hell were you thinking of running off without leaving your hotel details?"

Abraham fidgeted in his seat.

"I thought I did, Father. It must have slipped my mind. Why, we were staying at the Lion Hotel."

Jerome removed his glasses. "Son, I was once young like you. Don't insult my intelligence."

"You mean you went camping with Mother on your honeymoon?"

"Caught you." He laughed.

"Well, there was no need hiding the issue, was there?"

"How did you find out?"

"It doesn't matter how I found out. Next time, you should let the family know your whereabouts." He touched his nose. "I never took your mother out camping. Don't mention anything."

"Oh!"

"There is no Oh! I am telling you not to mention It. Abraham, are you happy living here?"

Abraham looked at his father. He knew what he was getting at.

"Yes, we are happy. This is our home. I have discussed the whole thing with my wife. She is happy to be part of the family. We don't need to move out."

Jerome beamed at him. "That's all I wanted to talk to you about. We are one family. We behave like one family. Never forget that, right?"

"We won't. My wife is aware of how we live in this house."

"Good. That's all."

Chapter Twenty-Eight

Louise had never felt so lonely in her life before. She missed her daughters so much. Now she was left with Eric whose life revolved around his bike and Nicholas whose tantrums she was finding difficult to cope with.

She didn't know how to handle them. They were out of control, especially Nicholas. Now he had gone ahead and resigned from J& Sons solicitors. She had no idea why he'd resigned. It's not as if they really needed the money. Her little cake business was doing well and part of the insurance money put her mind at ease. He needed work experience and J& Sons was a good start for him. She sighed.

"Eric? Eric?"

"I am here, Mother, there is no need to shout."

She turned to see her son sulking in the corner. "I thought you were out in the driveway riding as usual."

"I was. I …have a little problem. My bike doesn't have brakes."

"You call that a little problem? Well at least you will keep me company for a while. I don't have money for endless repairs. It's only a week ago you took that bike to the mechanics."

"I guess I will have to ask Annabella."

"No you will not. Now, call your brother, dinner is ready."

CHAPTER TWENTY-EIGHT

"Do I have to?"

Louise smiled at him. "I know what you mean. I will call him."

Louise watched Nicholas toying with his food. It upset her so much to see him like that. She went ahead and prepared Chicken Tikka Massala with steamed rice, his favourite dish, hoping it would cheer him up. What's troubling him?

"Nick?"

He gave her a cold stare. He hated it when people shortened his name. The only person he allowed was his mother but things have changed. He wanted to be left alone. He could tell she was up to something. "Please don't call me Nick. I am Nicholas."

"You have never complained before. What's brought this on? Are you missing Denise?"

"Can I have a second helping, Mother?"

Louise beamed at her younger son. "I am glad someone likes my cooking."

Nicholas pushed it forward. "I am not hungry. Thanks Mother." He stood up.

"Sit down Nicholas! We are still eating and I want to talk to you. I have spoken to a friend of mine regarding a part time job. Apparently they are looking for someone. It's a Saturday job. It's a good opportunity if you are interested. It's a cashier job at the bank where your father worked. There is an interview of course."

"Well, you can tell your friend that I am not interested. If I need a job, I will apply for it."

Louise glared at her son. "I am very disappointed in you, Nicholas. He was trying to help you."

Nicholas stared at his mother with his mouth wide open. He gritted his teeth. "Did...you...say he? It's a he that is trying to fix me up? Oh no, Mother."

"What's got into you? The person I am talking about is

Martin."

"The Martin who used to be Father's friend, or have I got my lines wrong? Where has he been all this time when we needed help? I don't like this Martin. I don't want his help." He ran out of the room.

Louise knew what was coming next. The bedroom door slammed. She closed her eyes.

"What's got into him, Eric?"

"He wants to have sex with Jessica."

Louise opened her eyes.

"What did you say?"

"Nothing." He pushed more chicken in his mouth.

"Eric? You know what I want, don't you?"

He nodded.

"What is it?"

"The truth," Eric replied with his mouth full of chicken.

"Good."

"Will I get into trouble?"

"You don't get into trouble when you tell the truth."

He moved next to his mother and started to whisper his story.

"He is in love with Jessica."

He gulped. "I am...not sure how to say this but you want the truth, don't you?"

She nodded.

"Ok. He wants to have sex with her but he doesn't know how. He was told that the fact that he doesn't know what to do shows how immature he is. He should keep his libido locked away."

Louise wished for Valium but she wanted to hear everything without Valium in her system. She had no idea what libido means. She must check it out. But it looks like her eight-year-old son has already checked it out. He was blushing. Whatever it is, it's not good.

"Oh shit!"

Eric continued with his whispers. "He was told not to let his libido stand in the way of his studies. That's all that is bothering him, Mother. Don't pay attention to him. He is a git."

She glared at him. That was another word she wasn't sure of.

"Jesus! Help me." Louise looked at her son. She could tell that there was more. She decided not to press him.

Was it her duty to teach her boys the ways of life? She had no problems with Denise and Annabella. She must talk to Richard about it. He is their uncle after all. She sighed. "Thanks for telling me, Eric. I will apologise to Jessica."

Eric's eyes bulged. "Please don't. She doesn't know about Nicholas being in love with her."

"Eric, is there anything else I need to know?"

He nodded. "It's Aunt Meredith who gave Nicholas a telling off."

"Oh God! I should have guessed." She sniggered.

As soon as Eric left the room, Louise phoned her sister in law.

"Are you ok, Louise? You sound as if you are in pain."

"Wouldn't you be when your fifteen-year-old son falls in love at the wrong time with the wrong person?"

"So, he finally told you. Louise, Nicholas is almost sixteen. As for the wrong person, I don't know. The age difference doesn't matter when you love somebody. It doesn't matter what other people say. Why, I am six years older than Eliot and the age difference has never interfered in our marriage. Is he giving you trouble?"

"You can say that again. He hardly talks to me. Did you know he resigned from J& Sons solicitors?"

"I am not surprised. Louise, what kept you so long to teach him about life?"

"Meredith, I am his mother. Where do I start?"

"In that case I am glad I helped."

"I wouldn't have known what was going on if Eric hadn't told me."

"The little devil!" Meredith laughed. "Louise, you spoil that child. Did you know that my conversation with Nicholas was a private one? We didn't know we had company hiding behind the sofa until I heard his sobs.

"Do you know why he was crying? He thought if Nicholas was in love with Denise's sister in law, then he had to be in love with Amanda."

"Who is Amanda? Oh please!" Louise laughed for the first time.

"You mean Desmond's sister?"

"Precisely."

"I told him that Amanda was a happily married woman. I gave him a telling off. Your children are out of control, Louise. You must put your foot down. Don't let them control you."

"It's too late. I don't know what to do with Nicholas."

"You know very well what to do with him. Don't give him any pocket money. When he goes without it, he will remember J& Sons solicitors. I will have another word with him."

"Where would I be without you?"

I am doing my late brother's job, she thought to herself. What are friends for? she asked.

As soon as Louise hung up, the phone rang. "Oh Martin!"

"What did the chap say?"

She took a deep breath. "I am so ashamed, Martin. I know you were trying to help. He says he is busy with his schoolwork," she lied.

"In other words he turned down this good opportunity. It's only a few hours on Saturday. A few hours would mean a lot with his career. You said he wants to follow in his father's footsteps. I have a feeling there is something you are not telling me, Louise."

CHAPTER TWENTY-EIGHT

"Like what?"

"You tell me."

"There is nothing to tell. Thanks for your help. You have been very helpful. I haven't touched those pills," she lied. Martin was a widower. He told her that his work helped him cope with his loss. In other words, he was a workaholic. When she told him that Valium helps her cope, he had been shocked. "Please, find some activities to keep you busy. Join women's groups. Talk to other widows. Share your problems. I strongly advise you to stop taking those pills." It was too late. She was already addicted. His voice aroused her from her thoughts.

"Louise dear, I am going to be cruel to be kind to your son. Don't give him any pocket money."

She laughed. "That's what my sister in law said."

"How right! This part time job wasn't about money. I want him to have experience. Isaac was my best friend. I must do what I can to help his family."

"I am very grateful, Martin. Nicholas is going through a rough time. I will talk to him again. Thanks very much. I must dash." She hung up.

Her hands were shaking. She could never punish her son like that. He will have his pocket money. She reached for her Valium. She looked at it. Martin's words rang in her head. *"I strongly advise you to stop taking those pills. Share your problems with other widows."*

She looked at the pill again; the urge to put it in her mouth was so strong.

She must learn how to fight it. She binned the whole pack. She reached for her baking trays.

"Mother, are you baking more cakes? The ovens are full."

"Oh Eric. I forgot. Do you want me to help you with your homework?"

He gave his mother a questioning look. "Mother, we are on

half term. We can play Scrabble. How about that?"

"You are right." She beamed at him.

Louise didn't have to wait long to hear Nicholas's hypocritical voice asking for new trainers.

"Please Mother! Say yes. All my mates have these trainers. Did you know they are in fashion? I knew you would say yes. You are the best mother in the world."

Louise looked at her son. Martin's words rang in her head. "Louise, I am going to be cruel to be kind. Don't give him any pocket money. This job is not about money but experience."

Meredith's words. "Don't give him any pocket money. He will remember J& Sons Solicitors."

Louise sighed. "Nicholas, my cakes haven't been selling at all. I am in debt. I can't afford your trainers. I am sorry."

"Oh I see. I am sorry I bothered you." He ran out of the room.

She held her breath as she waited for the door to bang. It didn't.

It was a week later when he finally spoke to her.

"Is Martin's offer still open?"

Louise was taken aback. "I am…not sure. I will ask Martin."

She phoned him immediately. "You are in luck, Louise. All the applicants turned out to be useless. Isaac was good at mathematics. If Nicholas is like his father, then he stands a chance. Tell him to come for an interview."

"I don't know how to thank you, Martin."

"Don't thank me yet. He has to pass his interview. It's not easy, I can assure you."

Nicholas sat in the waiting room feeling nervous. He had never been interviewed before. At J& Sons Solicitors he kind of started work straight away.

This was different. He wanted to follow in his father's

footsteps. This is the direction he wanted. He liked banking as a career. He wanted to find his own way. He didn't want Martin's help. He hated the man. Any man that makes his mother blush is a threat. Was he really trying to help him or he was after his mother? The thought of this git staring into his mother's eyes made his heart race. I will kill him before he makes himself comfortable in my father's bed. The bastard!

"Nicholas? I am Davidson Mukasa. Please follow me." They entered a tiny office.

Mukasa handed him thirty questions. "You have thirty minutes to solve those problems."

Nicholas could feel sweat under his armpits. What made him forget his deodorant was the devil himself. He was well dressed in a suit and a tie. He looked smart but was he smart enough to solve these problems?

"When you are ready to start, tell me so I set the time."

Nicholas looked at him. Is this git staying put? He wanted his privacy so he could wipe sweat under his armpit and other awkward places. Damn him! "I am ready," he replied.

I won't let you down, Father, he thought to himself as he put his brain into gear.

It took him fifteen minutes to finish thirty questions. He looked up. "I am through, Sir."

"Are you sure?"

"I am sure Sir."

"Good." Mukasa adjusted his glasses. He marked the work. He raised his eyes to him once in a while.

Nicholas didn't know what to make of it. Why does he look at me now and again?

Mukasa cleared his voice. "You have done very well."

Nicholas looked at him. He remembered his mother's words. "You must look responsible. In a bank, they don't employ soft looking characters."

"Mathematics is one of my best subjects, Sir," he replied with a cool and controlled voice.

"Well, congratulations! Come back tomorrow at nine o'clock for induction.

"Thank you, Sir."

As soon as Nicholas left, Martin came in. "How did it go?"

Mukasa rubbed his temple. "I have a confession." He handed Nicholas' test papers to him.

"This test is for chief accountants." Martin moved from one problem to another. He looked at his colleague with a cold look. "Why?"

"Gosh! I wanted the kid to fail. He is still too young for this job," Mukasa pointed out.

"He is almost sixteen and he proved you wrong. I can't believe it – he passed them all."

"You will soon be out of a job," Mukasa warned. Martin had been chief accountant for the last five years. He was due for promotion, he thought to himself. He deserved it.

"Martin, why are you helping this kid? What's in it for you?"

"What's in it for me? Isaac was my best friend." It is true. Isaac was his best friend. When he passed away, he visited the family every day until he thought he was intruding on delicate ground. He had been there. He knew how it felt to lose a partner. In his case, it was a double blow. He lost a wife and a daughter in a road accident.

His love for his dead wife prevented him loving another woman. He has been a widower for ten years; not once had he looked at another woman. He felt ashamed when Louise contacted him about Nicholas. He was even more shocked when she told him about her hardship before she discovered Isaac's life insurance policy. He should have been there for them. Why, his house was big enough.

CHAPTER TWENTY-EIGHT

He looked at his colleague, "Mr Mukasa, thanks a lot. What about I buy you a Nile beer?"

"The grill is my favourite place after a long day's work," Mukasa replied. The two men shook hands.

Chapter Twenty-Nine

Denise never thought the time would come when she would be free to get out of her room. She was fed up to the teeth. She missed her mother. She missed fresh air.

She smiled at her sister in law. "You mean Father has finally found time off work?" When she got married, she had been told that she would stay indoors for one month. She didn't mind staying indoors. It's a custom that has been going on from one generation to another.

When one month was over, her father in law was nowhere to be seen and the family couldn't conduct the ceremony without the head of the family. He was forever moving from one case to another.

Denise missed her mother and her brothers. She hadn't seen them for three months. She missed the streets of Kampala. She wanted to be out of her confinement. The granny had been helpful with her endless jokes and stories.

There was one thing she was nervous about. She had to prepare her first meal for the family, friends and relatives. She had never prepared the required meal. Oburo. She had seen her mother make it. Not once had she tried it herself. Now she wished she had asked her mother to teach her. She will make a fool of herself.

"Jessica, I have a confession."

"Don't tell me you are having an affair."

"I wonder how. I haven't left this room."

"There is Mworozi," she giggled.

Denise laughed.

"Don't even put such ideas in your innocent head. The confession is, I don't know how to prepare Oburo."

Jessica laughed. "That's not a problem. Mother will do it."

"But according to the custom, I have to prepare it."

"Damn the custom. All the invited guests are not likely to eat it."

"But I must. I need a few lessons."

"Don't worry. We will skip it or ask Mother to prepare it. The invited guests don't have to know who prepared it."

"I feel like a fraud. In that case I 'd better research the guests' diet."

"I will help you with that. I know their eating habits."

Denise's nervousness disappeared when the guests complimented her cooking. One of her father in law's friends praised her non-stop.

"Why, this is the kind of diet my doctor recommended. You see, child, I am diabetic. I was told to eat plenty of green vegetables with next to nothing salt and oil. My good lord! Look at this chicken: it's been stripped of fat and skin."

When it was time for coffee, he cried out.

"My child, where on earth did you find skimmed milk? Abraham, I would like you to bring your wife to my ranch."

Abraham beamed at his father's friend and client. Arthur was one person who gave away cows to his friends without a second thought. Abraham knew there was one cow waiting for their collection. "I will do that. Thank you, Sir."

The next day Denise and her in laws went to visit her mother according to the custom. The rest of the family went back home except Jessica and Abraham.

Denise was very disappointed when Nicholas didn't show up for the ceremony.

"Mother, didn't Nicholas know that we were coming?"

"He is a teenager. Teenagers do what they like." Louise couldn't tell Denise about Nicholas's reasons for his absence. "I want space, Mother," he had said to her.

"But you haven't seen your sister for three months."

"I am kind of busy. Please don't push me."

Well, she had left him alone. She knew the reason. He didn't want to be near the woman he could not have sex with.

"Mother, what about Annabella? Didn't you invite them?"

"Annabella and Desmond are in France. Apparently Desmond is having French lessons." She rolled her eyes heavenwards.

"I am sure that's Annabella's idea. French was one of her best subjects. Did they have to go to France for lessons? Annabella could have done it."

"I know, she is good at it. She got high marks in French. It's your father who pushed her. He called it future investment. How right he was. I hear she is a treasure to Desmond Travel Agency. She interprets for Desmond whenever necessary. It was her idea that Desmond should learn the language so he doesn't feel left out."

"So...she doesn't hate him anymore," Denise enquired.

"Not from my point of view. You should hear her talking. It's Desmond this, Desmond did that. 'Oh! Mother did you know? We are starting a cruise boats business on Lake Victoria resort. I mean real boats with engines. You know tourists rely on those small boats. Well, Desmond and I want to make changes. Our boats will have music, refreshments, waiters and waitresses on board.'" Louise mimicked her daughter's voice. "'After that,

Desmond and I want to try buses. Those people in rural areas need transport. Did you know people travel for miles to get to the main road for transport? The thought of those people put tears in my eyes. Desmond and I want to make a difference to those poor people.'" Louise laughed. "Next time they will be talking of putting their name on wheelbarrows."

"You mean the ones in town?"

"Oh yes, they are very helpful. People don't have to carry luggage on their heads to get from place A to place B. That's how Desmond earned his school fees."

"I am glad she has finally found happiness," Denise said.

"Yes, she has. Let's talk about you. You look well Denise. They have looked after you well."

"You can say that again. They are one happy family."

Louise wished to discuss her daughter's health but she didn't know how to approach the subject. What the hell! She is my daughter.

She looked into her daughter's eyes. "You should take it easy."

Denise smiled at her mother. "I intend to do that. Abraham gave me three alternatives on how I should spend my time. I can work with him, help Mother with her counselling or stay at home."

"I can only guess what you came up with."

"I am staying home."

Abraham watched his wife and his mother in law with wonder. What the hell are they discussing with their heads together? He had never seen such closeness. He had an idea of what was being discussed. The bedroom is the most likely subject. He felt aroused at the thought of being in his wife's arms.

"Denise, is there anything you want me to know?"

Denise looked down. "I honestly don't know what you are

getting at."

"I am your mother. You don't need to hold back. I may come in handy one day. Annabella is always asking me to baby sit Timothy. Did you know she is expecting?"

"Poor Timothy," Denise replied. He is still a baby. "Doesn't she know where they sell contraceptives?"

"Let's forget Annabella. Have you been to hospital?"

Denise laughed. "Mother, I think you would have done very well if you had taken a career in journalism. I haven't been to hospital. Abraham hired a private Doctor. He comes home once in a while to make sure all is in order. Mother, everything is under control. No need to worry."

"Denise, I have never known you to be cruel. Don't you think I want to hear it from your mouth? I hate puzzles."

"I have spelt it out for you, Mother."

"Not in so many words."

Denise smiled at her mother. "Well, God willing, I will make you a grandmother in six months' time."

Louise smiled. "That's all I wanted to hear. You do look well. Keep it up."

"We had better go. Jessica must be thinking we are ignoring her."

Denise turned round. "She is enjoying herself from what I can see. It's good to see Uncle Martin again."

Louise looked at Jessica and Martin. "They were having a long conversation. Yes, your Uncle Martin has been very helpful. He is the one who recommended Nicholas to your father's former work place. In other words, he found him a job. He is a cashier."

"Mother, I still haven't figured out why Nicholas left J& Sons Solicitors."

"There is nothing to figure out. We all want changes, don't we?"

"I guess you are right. At first I thought that maybe they

treated him badly."

"You'd better put that out of your mind. You had better join the others. They must think we are ignoring them." She felt uncomfortable to see Martin in deep conversation with Jessica. She hoped it wasn't something serious. He is too old for her.

She was still wondering what it was they were discussing when a courier arrived with a bunch of flowers and another package. The two women, mother and daughter, stared at the approaching courier with greed in their eyes, but not Jessica. She continued to talk to Martin.

"I am glad you told me your story. It's good to share your problems. You know healing doesn't just come in one day. It takes time and time heals."

"You are such a comfort, dear. Your talk with me has shown me what my next step should be." He smiled at her. "How do you know how to touch the right buttons?"

"I work with my mother. She is a general counsellor." She handed him her mother's business card. She always carried her mother's cards. "We are open Monday to Friday nine-five."

"What about I buy you lunch sometime as a thank you?"

She gave him a cosmetic smile. "What a splendid idea but..." She stared at the courier in front of her. "For me?" she asked.

"Are you Jessica?"

"That's my name."

"Sign here please."

She signed with a puzzle on her face.

"I had no idea you are spoken for."

She laughed. "They are just flowers and Ferrero Rocher chocolates." She put them aside as if they didn't mean anything. She resumed her conversation with Martin. She declined the lunch offer. She had never accepted lunches from men and she wasn't going to start now with Martin, family friend or not.

"I know you are dying to read that note. I'd better join your brother and Eric."

Eric stared at his brother in law with a questioning look in his eyes. They were playing a game of Scrabble.

"Eric, there is no such word as git in the dictionary. Don't let Mother hear you say that word."

Instead of him replying, he asked Abraham a question. "Aren't you mad at your sister receiving flowers from someone? Our Nicholas gets mad when Mother receives flowers and gifts from Uncle Martin."

"Eric, there are certain things you shouldn't discuss with me. Your mother is my mother in law. Don't discuss her private life with me. It's rude."

"I am sorry."

"You should be."

"Guess what? Nicholas doesn't get mad when you send Mother gifts and flowers.

"Oh! I am glad to hear that."

"And guess what?" He looked around to make sure no one was listening but he could see Uncle Martin walking towards them. He whispered into his brother in law's ear.

Abraham looked at Eric. He must talk to his wife. This kid needs proper guidance. When he was Eric's age, he didn't know strong English words. But here is an eight-year-old kid whispering the word libido in his ear.

He felt like giving him a good smacking on his backside but then he was grateful for one thing. At least he now knows why Nicholas resigned from J& Sons Solicitors. He was secretly relieved when Martin joined them.

Jessica read the accompanied note.

My dear darling Jessica,
  Please enjoy your Ferrero Rocher. As for the flowers, I know
they will wilt in a few days' time but my love for you is an
everlasting one.
  Always yours. Brian B

Jessica read the note several times. She had no idea who Brian
was. The only people who ever tried to get involved with her were
her father's friends and Abraham's friends. As for Mworozi's
friends, they were out of order most of the time wanting to jump
into bed with her. She wondered why her brother mixed with
such people.

She must talk to Denise about this secret admirer.

Denise told her not to worry but to enjoy her flowers and
chocolates. She pushed one in her mouth. She had developed a
sweet tooth. Her doctor told her it was normal. She would go
back to her usual diet once the baby was born.

They giggled over their chocolates wondering who Brian was.

Abraham had a private word with his mother in law. "I was
wondering if you could let Eric stay with us for some time. It
must be hard bringing up two boys."

Louise laughed. "You can say that again. They control every
inch of me calling themselves men of the house.

"I would be grateful if you took Eric off my hands for a while.
I love my kids but they miss a man's voice. I sometimes think I
have failed. Eric has really gone wild. I don't know how to cope.
When he goes to Annabella he comes back worse. They spoil him.
Please, whatever you do, don't spoil him."

"He won't stand a chance of being spoiled. We are one happy
family. We follow family rules. A boarding school is not a bad
idea at all but he is still a kid. If you don't mind, I can find him a
good boarding school when he starts secondary school."

"Boarding schools are expensive. I don't think their orphan funds are enough for boarding schools, especially around here."

"Don't cross the bridge before you get to it, Mother."

"I am grateful. I better pack his suitcase."

Chapter Thirty

"Guess what?"

"Desmond, I am not good at guessing games. Please get to the point." She yawned.

"I bumped into your sister today. She was having a heated argument with shop assistants at Unique fashions."

Annabella yawned again. "Desmond, you know how to spoil a cosy night." She reached for him. "I missed you today. I can't wait to get back to work."

Desmond shook his head. He hated the lies Annabella fed her mother.

"'Oh Mother, I was with Denise today. We had lunch together. She looks divine. The marriage to that Abraham really suits her. I am glad she is happy as I am.'" Desmond sighed. "Annabella, don't you think it's time to patch up with your sister? Mother will soon find out about your lies.

"You are due anytime. She will soon realise you never had a miscarriage in the first place."

She sat up in bed. "Desmond! What a thing to say." She touched her tummy. "You are scaring the hell out of me. I will arrange a meeting if that's what you want."

"It's not what I want. It's Mother's happiness I worry about."

She wrinkled her nose. "Mother is perfectly happy." God

knows what father would say if he were to see her on the arm of his best friend, she thought to herself.

She liked Martin as a family friend but not as a stepfather. There will be hell to pay when Nicholas finds out who takes his mummy out.

"Desmond, let's go to sleep." She looked at the bedside clock. "I can't believe it – you woke me up at three o'clock to talk about my sister. Is there anything you are not telling me?"

He smiled at his wife. She was number one jealous woman. He silenced her with a slippery kiss. "Now you are getting me worked up at the wrong time."

She giggled. "I am glad I can still turn you on even in this ugly condition." She tensed. Something wasn't right. "Jesus! You'd better switch on the light. I think I have started."

"What? It's not one of your games, is it?" He was out of bed in seconds. "I will call a doctor."

"No, you drive me. It's quicker that way."

Denise woke up with a start. "What the hell is the meaning of this?"

She shook her husband out of his coma. He was tired, she knew that, but this was not the time to feel sorry for him. "Abraham!" She shook him.

He looked at her with bulging eyes.

"Oh please! Don't give me that look. Get dressed. It's too late to call the doctor; he might take too long."

His eyes closed again.

"Abraham, wake up. I am in labour!"

"You are having nightmares, dear. Go back to sleep." He groaned.

Denise stared at him. "Are you coming with me, or not?"

He sat up. "What's up?"

"Oh God! The sooner you retire, the better. Look at you. You have no idea what's going on. My water has broken."

That woke him up. He wore his shirt inside out. "You will be ok," he comforted.

She rolled her eyes. "What do you know? Men!"

A few minutes later, Abraham and Desmond were discussing parenting over a cup of coffee at a local hospital while waiting for the news of their loved ones. The two men couldn't believe that they were actually talking to each other. This distance between them had to end, they said to each other.

The two men were aroused from their conversation. "Mr Mworozi?"

Abraham found his throat dry all of a sudden. To his surprise, he found his voice. "How is my wife?"

She is all smiles. "You have a beautiful son," the doctor informed him.

Abraham moved at a speed he had never possessed before. "Oh darling. Thank you."

Denise beamed at him. "He is so sweet. We'd better call the family. They will soon be wondering why we are not down for breakfast."

"Let them wonder. I don't want anyone to spoil this moment." He rested his unshaven cheek on her cheek. "Denise, you have made me proud."

A few minutes later, Desmond was holding his baby girl.

"How do you feel?"

She gave him a wicked look. "I feel as if my inside has been scooped out."

"What a scary feeling. Darling, do you know what content means?"

She nodded.

"I am happy. I hope you are happy. I don't want you to go

through this pain again."

She gave him a wicked look. He must be mad. We shall see, she thought to herself.

"Do you want to name her?" he asked.

She shook her head.

"Let's give Mother this opportunity to name her grandchild."

She didn't mind. She loved her mother in law. They got on like mother and daughter. She was blessed.

He grinned at her. "What a good thought."

Nadine was the first one to arrive at the hospital. "My good lord! He is so beautiful. You have no idea what's going on in my mind."

"I can only guess," Denise told her. "You want a boy."

Nadine laughed. "Melanie and Angela are just as good as boys. What's missing are the balls."

"Oh Nadine! You are disintegrating my stitches."

"It's true, my dear. They don't behave like girls. I blame their father and their grandfather. They treat them like boys. The only person who puts discipline into their heads is Abraham. He is a good man. You must consider yourself lucky."

"I know."

Nadine looked at Denise. "I would like another baby," she confessed.

"What's stopping you?"

"I blame the person who invented condoms."

"Nadine, if you don't stop such talk, I will be needing more stitches.

"Oh please. I had no idea Mworozi was that selfish and stingy," Denise giggled.

"He is. Most of the time I am tempted to rush his Durex to hospital for artificial insemination. Now, don't even laugh. You will give yourself an injury."

"Nadine, I have never known you to be a comedian. You are always quiet."

"Only when I choose to be quiet. The man is so stingy. The other night he recommended a vibrator. 'I am so tired, Nadine. I think I know what will keep you quiet.'"

The two women paused in their conversation, staring at Desmond.

"What...are you doing here?" Denise found her voice.

He beamed at her. "I came to congratulate you. I have a confession. Your sister doesn't know I am here."

"You better leave."

"I brought you this." He handed her Ferrero Rocher chocolates and some flowers.

Denise stared at the chocolates. Is this Jessica's secret admirer? These are the chocolates she receives now and again with love notes. She hoped she was wrong for her sister's sake and Jessica's. She received them. "You shouldn't have."

"We are family. I came to tell you how much Annabella misses you. She is next door. If you feel up to it, pop in. I'd better get going. All the best." He was gone.

Annabella stared at her brother in law. "What a surprise!"

"I came to congratulate you." He looked at the baby. "She is pretty."

"Thank you."

"I brought you this."

She looked at him. "Are you sure you are not mistaken? I mean do you know I am Annabella?"

"I know the difference between you two. Denise has a birthmark next to her ear. Right?"

"You are very observant, Sir."

"Please don't call me Sir."

She received her gift. "Wow! Ferrero Rocher! I love them." She looked at him. "Did Desmond put you up to this? He is always spoiling me with Ferrero Rocher chocolates. You shouldn't have but all the same, thank you." She put one in her mouth.

He grinned at her. "I have a confession. Your sister doesn't know I am here. She misses you. She is next door. Pop in if you can. It's time to forget and forgive."

She gave him a warm smile. "I will think about it. Thanks for telling me."

"I am glad you are thinking about it. I better get going."

He was half way through the door when she called his name. "Abraham, how big is Denise's private ward?"

He grinned at her. "It's big enough for two lovely sisters."

Abraham and Desmond sat in the Hospital coffee bar. "We have made it," Abraham said.

"It was your idea. I am so grateful, mate," Desmond replied.

Abraham cleared his voice. "I have been meaning to arrange a reunion for them but I had no idea how. Women are difficult creatures sometimes. I want you to imagine what kind of world it would be if only women ruled it."

"It would be one gossiping and sulking planet," Desmond chuckled.

"If you go along with them, they take you along with them. Never show a woman your weak point," Abraham told him.

Desmond looked at him. "It's too late for me. I am fully exposed. Annabella knows all my weak points. I love her you see."

"You think I don't love Denise? She is my everything but I have to keep my position. She has no idea what my weak points are and I hope she doesn't bump into them."

In the private ward, the twins were cooing over each other's babies.

"Oh Denise! He looks like Abraham. Isn't that wonderful?"

"Oh! I am glad I don't have to tell Abraham that the back of his son's head resembles his."

There is another tale dishonest women use. "'Oh dear husband. Your child looks like my late uncle,'" Annabella contributed to their story. She giggled.

Annabella looked at her sister. "I am glad we have decided to put the past behind us."

"I guess it was just childish. We know better now. I would like you and Desmond to come to our home. Think about it. We are only a stone's throw away."

"We would love to have you at our home as well," Annabella replied.

They hugged. "I am glad to have you back," they said at the same time.

Chapter Thirty-One

Louise opened her eyes. "Who could be ringing me this time?" Her heart raced. She reached for the phone.

"I am sorry to wake you, Mother. I have good news for you," Desmond told her. "We have a baby girl. Mother and daughter are well."

Louise held on to the phone. If her mathematics serves her right, Annabella had a miscarriage nine months ago. How could this be?

"Is the baby all right? I mean she wasn't due for another month."

Desmond knew where the question was leading. He was trapped. "I...don't know...much about babies but she looks all right to me."

"I am glad mother and baby are well," she replied. She knew her son in law was hiding something. She knew what it was. Annabella never had a miscarriage. Desmond didn't want her to attend the wedding or the twins were still fighting wars against each other. Well, I have had enough of their fights. I will sort them out once and for all. They had taken her for a ride.

"Mother, I am saying, Denise and Annabella are in the same ward. Right now they are cooing over each other's babies. Isn't it beautiful that they should give birth at the same time?"

"They are what?"

"I said they are cooing over each other's babies. You should see the joy on their faces."

Louise's anger with her girls vanished. "I will be right there. Thanks for telling me."

She was out of her room in seconds. "Eric? Wake up."

"Oh Mother! Thisss isss the bessst part of my sleeeeeeep," he moaned.

"Eric you have to come with me. Your sisters gave birth."

He opened one eye. "What's that?"

"I said you must get up; we are going to the hospital to see your sisters. They had their babies. And do you know what? They gave birth at the same time."

"Jeeeesus! Yuk! That's grossssssssssss! I am not coming. I hate to see red babies. You can't make me. He pulled blankets over his head."

"Well, you have no choice. I can't leave you alone in the house."

"Nothing will happen to me." His heart raced. He hated small babies. They look like aliens from outer space.

Louise wished Nicholas was about. He was on a school trip and he wasn't due until that afternoon. Now, leaving Eric in the house alone is a recipe for trouble. The last thing she wanted was finding her house on fire. "Now, get up."

"Oh Mum, I will go to our neighbour."

Louise smiled. "Why didn't I think of that?"

The neighbour agreed to look after him.

As soon as Louise left, Eric found an excuse to go back to the house. "I need a change of clothes. I can't stay in my pyjamas."

Alison worked for the 'Here and There' Newspaper as a journalist. She loved her job even thought it wasn't easy to get information so easily. She was forever in disguise nosing around people's privacy. Their readers expected something new every day and she made sure they got it. For the last three days it had been a repeat. Who wants to read the same story over and over again? Now this phone call had made her day. She whistled as she changed into a nurse's uniform. She pushed her camera and Dictaphone into her handbag. She pushed her microphone into an umbrella. Phew! This is going to make headlines. She was out of the office in seconds. As she opened the front door, there was an envelope addressed to her. She opened it. What a jackpot! She whistled all the way.

About thirty minutes later, Alison was in St Peter's Hospital corridors wondering what kind of security the hospital had. Someone only had to come in dressed in a nurse's uniform and that's enough to give them access. She could be an assassin. Now she had another story to report.

She found the ward. Her heart raced. She hoped they didn't throw her out before she got her story. Not a chance. The security here was lax.

Denise stared at the nurse with a microphone poking into her face.

"Who the hell are you?"

"Mrs Muganzi, is it true you ran away three days before your wedding to Desmond Tumwiine?"

"Mrs Tumwiine, how do you feel marrying your sister's fiancé?"

"Tell me, is true that your husbands can't tell you apart?"

"Mrs Muganzi, was it love at first sight?"

"Did you know Mr Muganzi was a lawyer in disguise?"

"How does it feel to be twins?"

"Did you plan to be pregnant at the same time?"

"Did you know..."

CHAPTER THIRTY-ONE

"How does it…"

Annabella found her voice. "I have no idea what kind of a journalist you are. We haven't answered your questions. You have nothing to report or write about. Why don't you take your black ass out of here?"

"Out," the twins said at the same time.

"You haven't denied anything. Have a good day and nice talking to you."

She almost bumped into Louise.

"My good Lord! What kind of a nurse is that?"

"She is a journalist in disguise. Please find Abraham. She can't publish this garbage. He must be in the café bar."

Denise was shaking.

Abraham looked at the distraught women. They told him what had happened. "Now calm down. I will deal with everything. Now, you must have your rest. I will be right back." Abraham was a bit puzzled. Oh damn! There is no time to waste, Abraham, he told himself. He phoned the telephone operator. "Please check these numbers for me. I would like to know who phoned the 'Here and There' Newspaper within the last few hours."

"That will take time, Sir."

"Not according to technology these days. Just do it."

"I will see what I can do."

A few minutes later, Abraham had all the details. He couldn't believe it. He was too ashamed to confront the person. How could she expose Denise and Annabella's privacy? He was too shocked. He must pull himself together before it was too late. He went back to the ward.

"Abraham! Did you stop her?" they cried out.

He shook his head. He turned to his mother in law. "I need a word please."

Louise stared at her son in law. "You are wrong. I wouldn't sell

---

my own children's happiness. Do you know what this story will do to them? They will go on digging until they got to the bottom of it. You can imagine what that will do to Annabella. Married against her will. My children are my everything. Their happiness is important to me. I didn't phone those vultures.

"Desmond married my daughter against her will. Forgetting is the last thing on my mind but selling such a story to the newspaper is not my doing."

"I am so sorry, Mother. I am so ashamed. Please forgive me." He could see sincerity in her eyes. He was suddenly sweating. What a mess!

"You had a right to question me. After all it's my phone that was traced to the 'Here and There' newspaper."

"Excellent work," she told him. "If you'll excuse me, I'd better get going."

Abraham stood there feeling small. How could he make such a mistake? He phoned the newspaper and told them he was on his way. He warned them not to publish the garbage their journalist had just collected from a nine-year-old child. "If you should go ahead, I will fight you in court. Once I am through with you, you won't have a leg to stand on."

A few minutes later Abraham was talking to the editor of the newspaper.

"We give you our word we won't publish it without your clients' consent."

"I have papers here for you to sign and I need those photographs you stole from a nine-year-old child. I thought you had learnt your lesson by now. Wasn't it you who lost half a million for invading someone's privacy? My clients are ordinary people, living an ordinary life. I suggest you leave them alone or there will be hell to pay.

"You will go deeper this time if you go along with this story. None of it is true. The kid wanted quick cash. He is mentally disturbed."

"He didn't sound like a kid to me or disturbed for that matter."

Chapter Thirty-Two

As Abraham drove into the hospital car park, the 'New Vision' newspaper were driving out followed by the Daily Mail. His heart sank.

A few minutes later he was talking to Denise's doctor.

"I want my wife and baby discharged now. My wife's private ward is like a circus. What kind of security do you have here?"

"We understand your concern but your wife and baby are not ready to go home yet."

"But they are ok to be harassed by newspapers? You need to improve your security, doctor. At least that's something worth writing about."

Denise gave her husband a weak smile. "It's all right, Abraham. The 'New Vision' and the 'Daily Mail' didn't harass us like that bitch from the 'Here and There' newspaper. But, one other thing – I want to go home."

At that moment Desmond appeared. He nodded at Abraham. "Thanks mate. I am taking my wife home. Who knows who might turn up next? Did you by any chance find out who alerted the newspaper?"

"I did. I stopped the 'Here and There' Newspaper from publishing the story."

"Who phoned the newspaper in the first place?" Desmond asked.

"A family member who wanted some cash I guess."

"Family member?" they all asked at once.

"Were you surprised when the sneaky bitch didn't get your identities wrong? Only family members know the difference between you two," Abraham told the twins.

"I can only guess who that is," Desmond said with anger in his voice. "That man will do anything. I am so ashamed of his behaviour. He is number one gambler. He wouldn't give a second thought to his nieces' happiness."

"Do you mean Uncle Richard?" Annabella asked.

"Who else, my dear?"

Abraham cleared his voice. "It's not our father in law."

They all looked at him waiting.

"It's Eric."

The twins shook their heads. "It can't be true."

Louise stared at her son. "What have you got to say for yourself, Eric?"

His lip trembled. "I am sorry, Mother. I...just wanted my sisters to enter the Guinness Book of Records. The newspapers promised me that."

"Well, you have made your sisters really miserable. You have made me miserable. You deserve to be miserable too. Now, go to your room. You will not watch television or go out riding. You will not come out of that room until you digest how it feels to be miserable." She slapped him hard on the cheek. He stumbled and fell. He was so shocked. His mother had never beaten him before. This was alien to him. He stared at his mother without blinking.

Louise looked at her son. She panicked. "Eric? Oh my God! I have killed my child." He was gasping for air. "Eric, Eric, talk to me. I am sorry, Eric." She was shaking. She poured cold water on him. He came round and sobbed on his mother's bosom.

Louise took a deep breath. "Thank you, Lord!" She carried him to her room. "I am sorry, Eric. I lost my temper."

He looked at his mother with haunted eyes.

She massaged his temple. He fell asleep.

Louise sat there watching her baby's breathing. She was too frightened to leave him alone in case...in case...in case. Oh God! She cried buckets and buckets of tears. What made her lose her temper in such a manner? She could have killed him. She heard the telephone ringing. She didn't want to speak to anyone.

Annabella put the phone down. "She is not answering."

"Have a rest. We shall try later," Desmond told her.

Denise put the phone down. She looked at Abraham. "She is not answering. How did she look? Was she upset?"

"No, she looked composed. I made an ass of myself, Denise. I thought it was her who phoned the newspaper."

"Don't worry too much. Anyone could have made that mistake."

"What a mess! I haven't even named our son."

She gave him a weak smile. "Go on, I am waiting."

"His name is Jethro."

"I love it," she told him.

There was a knock on their door. "That must be Jessica."

She walked in with lunch on a tray. "Mother said you must finish it if you want your strength back."

"I am ravenous! Thanks, Jess."

She turned to her brother; "Do you want your tray here or downstairs?"

"I will eat downstairs."

As soon as Abraham left, Jessica looked at her sister in law.

"Listen Denise. I know it's not my place but I can see some tension around. What's the matter? You can talk to me as a friend, you know."

Denise took a deep breath. She poured out the whole story.

"I am so sorry. Do you mind if I check on your mother for you?"

"Would you?"

Jessica knocked a second time and waited. She could see the curtains twitching upstairs. She knocked again.

The door opened. Nicholas stood there. "What are you doing here?"

"Why are you not answering the phone? Your sister is worried sick."

"I didn't hear it ring. I am going out anyway. You can tell my sister that everything is under control."

"I need to speak to your mother."

"She is not in a position to speak to anyone. She is sleeping."

"May I come in?"

"I don't think it's a good idea."

"Nicholas! What's going on?"

"Who said there is something going on? If you'll excuse me, I have things to do."

Jessica had a feeling something was wrong. She wasn't just going to walk away. What would she tell Denise? She invited herself in. The burning smell hit her nostrils. She wrinkled her nose. "What is that smell?"

"It's nothing," Nicholas replied.

"It doesn't smell like nothing to me." She poked her head in the kitchen. She blinked. The kitchen sink was piled up to the ceiling. Jessica was looking at something strange. Louise would never let a kitchen sink pile up to this point. "Do you mind if I go to your mother's room?"

"Suit yourself."

"The kid has an attitude," she thought to herself as she went to look for Louise. She knew where the room was. She knocked. There was no answer. She knocked again. There was still no answer. She decided to let herself in. She walked towards the bed with her heart racing. She stared at the sleeping figures. She held on to her heart. "Oh! Thank God they are breathing." She sat down. She didn't want to disturb their sleep but she wanted to talk to her badly.

She must have been sitting there for half an hour when Nicholas put his head in. "What are you still doing here?"

"I am waiting for her to wake up. I want to talk to her."

"You could wait forever. Her Valium takes some time before it wears off."

Jessica stared at him. "She takes Valium?"

"You'd better go home unless you want to spend the night here. I am going out. Don't forget to shut the door behind you."

Jessica stood up. "You are not going anywhere before you clear that sink. Maybe you're the reason she takes Valium." Her voice shook. "What kind of life is this?"

He glared at her. "How dare you storm in here and take over like that. Don't talk to me in such manner. We are not responsible for Mother's addiction. You know nothing about us. Why don't you fuck off?"

She looked at him. "Have you finished?"

"Do you want some more?"

"Yes, give me a hand. When did your mother and Eric last eat?"

Nicholas blinked. Is this girl numb, or what? I have just told her to fuck off.

"Are you coming or not?"

He followed like a defeated idiot. He felt like an idiot following her orders.

Jessica washed and he dried the dishes.

"Well don't heap them on the worktop. You know where to put them," she told him. "I have two brothers, remember? I know how boys' minds operate. My mother was forever interviewing workers. If a working girl lasted a week, it was just luck. Mworozi and Abraham made their lives miserable.

"Now, Nicholas, you have to help your mother now and again. She needs a break. You have to show her that you care."

"That's what I have been trying to do all afternoon preparing something for them to eat. I am a fraud."

"You should pay attention when she is cooking."

She checked the pantry. There was enough food. She needed to prepare something simple. She didn't want to stay longer than necessary. Her family would worry.

She put nuts in the food processor and showed Nicholas what to do.

While he was doing that, she peeled some green bananas.

"I am done," he told her.

She smiled at him.

He blushed.

She didn't notice. She was looking for onions. "You can chop these onions for me."

"That's two tasks and you haven't even completed one," he complained.

"Nicholas, you are the one learning, remember?"

The meal was ready in less than an hour. "I will wake Eric and your mother. They can't go on sleeping."

Louise groaned. "Isaac!"

"It's Jessica."

Louise opened her eyes. "Jessica?"

Eric sat up in bed. He started to whimper.

Louise gathered him. "Ssssh! Don't cry. Mum is here."

Jessica cleared her voice. "Your lunch is ready."

"Lunch?"

"I showed Nicholas what to do."

Louise stared at Jessica with confusion in her eyes.

Jessica told her why she was there. "We have been worried. When you didn't answer the phone, we thought something was wrong."

"We are fine. Thanks Jessica."

After food, Jessica had a private word with Louise.

"Is that what you think?"

"It's just a guess. There had been so many changes in his life. Don't think he doesn't feel them. All these naughty things he does are just a distraction. It helps him forget. What activities does he like? What places does he like to visit?"

"To be honest with you, I haven't been myself since I lost their father. Eric loved National Parks and fishing. Isaac took them so often. I don't have the time or the heart for such visits. I can't see myself fishing." She gave Jessica a weak smile.

"You will have to try. If you want me to come along, I am free on weekends. I know how to fish. I followed my brothers around often enough to know that you put bait at the end of a fishing hook. I will ask Abraham to find maggots for us."

Louise laughed. "Is that what we have to put on the hook?"

"I am afraid so."

"What about this weekend?" Louise asked.

"I would love to come along. Now, Eric and Nicholas's problem have been kind of sorted. What about you? This is a professional conversation. Anything you tell me will not be passed on to anyone. I am trying to help you. I don't want you to destroy your life."

"What are you talking about?"

"How are you coping with these changes in your life?"

Louise twisted her wedding ring. The ring she has been trying to put aside but not been able to. Each time she tries, she feels as if she is letting Isaac down. No one can replace Isaac. She looked at the young girl in front of her. "The only time I cope is when I am sleeping. When I don't know what's happening around me."

"That's what I am worried about. Nicholas almost burnt the house down today trying to prepare you a meal. You had no idea what was happening. Do you take anything to help you sleep? I am sorry I have to ask you this question. I do care for you."

"No, I don't."

Jessica knew she was lying. Her answer was too quick. "I am glad you don't...take... anything. At the moment you are playing two roles: mother and father. You can't afford to be in a position where you don't know what's happening around you. The boys need you and you need them. You have got to help each other. You should go out often. If you need a childminder, send Eric to us. You have to have a will to fight stress. Sleeping it off doesn't help. It makes matters worse."

Louise reached for her hand. "I am glad you came. I feel totally different. Please tell Denise and Abraham that I am fine.

"I wasn't offended at all. I was ashamed."

"No need to be ashamed," Jessica told her and excused herself. "I'd better get going. I will see you this Saturday."

On her way out, she put her head in the lounge. The brothers were watching television. "See you guys."

"Thanks for popping in. I am sorry I was rude to you."

"I didn't notice." She let herself out. When she got home, she found everyone celebrating the birth of Jethro.

It was sometime later when she went to her room. On her bed, there was one rose and a note. *My Dear Jessica, You are forever in my heart. Love you always. Brian B.*

Jessica looked at the rose trying to figure out who Brian B is. She put it on her nose. The smell was intoxicating. It wasn't just the rose smell. She could smell after-shave on it. She wished to know who it was. She was falling in love with an invisible person.

She found his notes seductive.

She opened her secret box where she kept all her love notes and roses.

She closed the box. "Till next time."

The following day, Abraham bought the newspapers and headed for the amazing stories section.

Denise watched him with anticipation. "Please tell me it's all right."

"It's ok, dear. They didn't write any rubbish about you."

A few minutes later, Annabella phoned. "Did you read the newspapers? It's perfect, just the way we narrated the story.

"Yes, I read it. I am so relieved."

"Denise, 'Parenting' magazine just called. They want an interview with me. What should I do?"

"Listen to your heart. What does it say?"

"Parenting magazine is one of my best. Yes, I will tell them to come along. Desmond said it's up to me. He will be by my side."

Denise laughed. "When did he seize to be on your side? Don't forget to send me a copy." They talked for some time.

When they hung up, they were both smiling.

Denise found the running of the house very simple. She had Nadine and her mother in law to thank. Both women were such gentle creatures. They got on very well. They told her where she was going wrong. She appreciated their help.

The women of the house enjoyed sitting in the compound on weekends gossiping or reading magazines or criticising each other's hairstyles complimenting each other, or noticing a few changes among themselves, you name it. Denise had never seen such unity. She was pleased she had married Abraham. How else would she have met such family? As they sat there, Denise noticed Nadine looking pale. She wondered whether Mworozi had been fighting her secretly in their suite. Her heart raced. She hated violence. She didn't think Mworozi was a violent man but who knows what takes place behind closed doors? "Are you ok?"

She nodded. "I just feel rotten. Yam doesn't agree with me even though I love it."

Their granny chuckled and announced the diagnosis. "I looked like that when I was expecting your father in law," she told Nadine.

"I don't think I am pregnant. It's not as if I have never been pregnant before. It's yam," she told them.

Denise beamed at her. "Are you sure you didn't rush that hideous Durex thing to the hospital?"

Nadine beamed at her remembering the chat they had at the hospital when Denise gave birth. "He has been generous lately. He doesn't threaten me with vibrators anymore. But I ...don't think I am pregnant. I think I have stomach ache."

"Women! Have you forgotten I am here?" Jessica reminded them.

Her granny pointed a finger at her. "You! I don't know why you have such hard skin. You definitely don't take after your mother or me. How come you don't attract anyone's attention?"

"She has her secret admirer," Nadine volunteered.

Their granny's nose twitched. "You better watch out, girl. By the time he reveals himself, you will be too old to have children or maybe it's someone you turned down now he is playing with your mind. 'If I can't have you, no one else will.' That must be the thinking behind all those red roses and love notes to keep you occupied. By the time you open your eyes, it will be too late for marriage. Jessica, you will soon run out of children. I am warning you."

"Oh Granny! How can you say that? Women have children in their forties."

"Do you think I will be alive that time to see my great grandchildren? What's happening to this generation? In our time, when a girl reached puberty, there was nothing else for her except to get married. I give up, Jessica."

"She is still young, Mother," her daughter in law told her.

"At least I have warned her."

Jessica had no eyes for other men. She was in love with her secret admirer.

Chapter Thirty-Three

Louise knocked on the bathroom door. "You are taking ages, Nicholas."

"Oh mother! Don't do that. I will cut myself." He opened the door to reveal what he was doing.

Louise's eyes smarted with tears. Nicholas was a carbon copy of his father. He spooks her all the time. Now to look at him shaving his beard brought long time ago memories.

"I will be out of the bathroom in a minute, Mother."

"I am not bothered about that actually. I am wondering why you are not at work."

"I have a meeting with Desmond."

"A meeting?" She was surprised. "What kind of meeting?"

"It's business, Mother."

"What is it about?"

"I would rather not discuss it now. I will tell you when I come back. Please Mother. Don't look like that. I will tell you everything when I come back."

As soon as he left, Louise was on the phone talking to Annabella.

"What's all this about Nicholas having a meeting with Desmond?"

"What else did Nicholas tell you?"

"Not much. He just said he would tell me when he comes back."

"Then why are you worried? I don't know what the meeting is all about. I know they have a meeting at ten o'clock this morning.

"Annabella! You are his personal secretary. You should know what it is all about. I don't want Nicholas to abandon his career for a travel agency business, if you know what I mean."

"Honestly, Mother. You should let Nicholas choose his career. I know you want him to be like Father. But is that what he wants? To be honest with you, I have no idea what this meeting is all about. I can find out from Desmond if you don't mind holding the phone."

"Just forget it. I guess I will have to wait to be told."

Annabella sighed. "Is that all you wanted, Mother?"

"Of course not. Why don't you send the children over? I haven't seen them for ages."

"I could do with a helping hand. Their minder is down with the flu. I don't want her germs near them. I will bring them this evening."

"I could do with a bit of distraction." Louise laughed knowing what she would have to go through with Timothy's tantrum. What's new? He takes after his mother. Elizabeth was a sweet baby. She has no problem with that one.

"You will get enough from Timothy but be firm with him."

"I will try my best."

Desmond stared at his brother in law. "Nicholas, I have never heard of such a suggestion."

"I won't let you down, Sir. I am tired of being a lousy cashier. I can hardly support myself out of my salary. I would like to broaden my experience. We can call it a loan. You will be paid in full plus interest."

Desmond turned to his wife. "What do you think?"

CHAPTER THIRTY-THREE

"What do I think? I am confused as you are. Nicholas, suppose what you are suggesting doesn't work out? Who is the loser?"

"In business, you take chances. I can assure you, I won't let you down. I have thought about this and you are the only people who can sponsor me.

"It's one year I am asking for and that will enable me to go one step higher."

Desmond's mind was really racing. What has he got to lose? He has been supporting the family since he married Annabella. Now, helping Nicholas better himself will take off most of his responsibilities when he gets a better job. He is a smart kid. He deserves a second chance.

He looked at Nicholas. "Could you please give us a minute. I need to discuss this with your sister."

"Sure."

"What do we do?"

"What does your heart tell you?" she asked. This was one decision she didn't wish to make in case her brother failed.

"It's a lot of money involved. It will leave a big hole in our budget," she reminded him.

"I know but Nicholas is very intelligent. If he doesn't get distracted, he will do well. But that's a gamble one has to take. Oh damn it we are turning out like your uncle."

"I wish you didn't bring Uncle Richard into this."

"I am sorry. I can't help myself. Ok, let's sponsor him. He is family after all."

Nicholas beamed at them. "You won't regret it."

"When do you travel?"

"As soon as my papers are in order," he replied. "The college doesn't start until September. I have at least four months to prepare."

"Nicholas, you know this is a gamble we have taken," his sister reminded him.

"I know and you are very brave both of you. I will see myself out."

"How did it go?"

"What was that?"

"Oh Nicholas! I mean the interview with your brother in law."

"It went very well."

"And?"

"Why don't you sit down and I'll tell you all about it? I am joining the Institute of Bankers in England. Desmond and Annabella agreed to sponsor me."

"Hold on a second…"

"I haven't finished, Mother. The course will take one year. I am tired of being a lousy cashier. I want to be more than that. That's where the training comes in."

Louise massaged her temple. She could feel a headache developing. This was too much for her to take in. "Nicholas, you don't have to go to England to train. You can be trained here."

"Mother, it's only one year. That's all and besides, I want to see beyond Uganda."

"You have never been away from home. You will be miserable. You will miss home. What about your favourite dishes? Who will wash your clothes?

"I don't know what Desmond and Annabella were thinking of corrupting you like this. England is not a stone's throw away. Who is going to keep an eye on you?"

"Mother, I am nineteen and responsible."

Chapter Thirty-Four

Nicholas said bye to his family. He pretended not to see his mother's tears. "I will write to you often," he told her.

"We are proud of you, brother," his sisters chorused.

"Now I am the only one to look after Mother," Eric complained.

"Don't hesitate to call me if you need help," Abraham told him.

"Never forget who you are, Nicholas. Don't lose your identity. You know who you are and why you have taken such a step. Keep out of trouble," Desmond warned.

"I know and thank you, Sir."

As soon as Nicholas disappeared out of his family's view, Louise broke down.

"Mother, people are looking."

"It's your fault, Annabella. You put such ideas into his head."

"Let's go home, Mother. Nicholas will be fine. You saw him. He looked cool, not one bit frightened."

Nicholas was frightened all right. He was going to a foreign country where he didn't know anyone. He was frightened of letting Desmond and Annabella down. He was frightened of what lay ahead. He needs guidance. For the first time, he prayed to God. The God he never believed in before. I need your guidance, God!

After nine hours of travelling, Nicholas arrived at his rented accommodation. He checked the address a second time before he rang the bell. The place looked posh for a student. What was Desmond thinking of paying for this kind of accommodation? He will never be able to pay him back. He rang the bell.

A middle-aged white woman answered it.

"Yes?"

"I am Nicholas."

She beamed at him. "I am Maggie. Your brother in law phoned a few minutes ago to find out whether you had arrived. Come in please. You must be tired."

Nicholas looked around him. The place looked clean. He proceeded to take off his shoes.

"I wouldn't worry about that if I were you. None of the students take off their shoes.

"I will give you a tour of this place. This is the kitchen. I do the cooking. I serve only two meals a day. That is breakfast and dinner. Give me enough notice if you don't want any meals."

She moved on to the dining room. "This is where we all eat. I don't allow food in the bedrooms.

"This is the lounge where we all sit and fight over a television remote control. You can have your own television in your room if you can afford it. Let me know if you are interested."

Nicholas wished for the woman to hurry up. He was too tired to be bothered with all this.

They entered a long corridor with bedrooms opposite each other.

When he was finally shown to his room, he wanted to fall into a deep coma. But the woman wasn't done yet.

"No hunky panky ding dong in this room. You want a kick, do it in a hotel. I don't want my cleaners shocked by used condoms. Do you get my drift?"

By the time he was shown the bathrooms and toilets, his body was crying in agony.

"Dinner will be served at six o'clock. It's a bit early but most of the students have evening jobs so I have to serve the meals at that time. I hate to hear the microwave in the middle of the night."

Nicholas thanked her for the tour. He cleared his voice. "I would like to phone my family to let them know that I have arrived safely. May I use your phone?"

Maggie narrowed her eyes. "You will have to pay for the call."

At that moment a young man about Nicholas's age appeared. "I hear you want to make a phone call? By the way, I am James. I am from Cameroon. I phone my old lady every day. I will lend you 'Mama Africa' international phone card. There is about ten minutes on it left."

Maggie beamed at Nicholas. "There you are, you have found a friend." She gave James a cold stare. How dare he interfere with her business!

Nicholas phoned his mother first. He was brief and to the point. Louise wanted to go on forever. "Mother, this is an international call."

"Ok, I am glad you arrived safely."

The next call was to Desmond and Annabella. "Listen, Nicholas. Don't get hooked on international calls."

"I am using 'Mama Africa' international phone card. It's cheaper."

"I am glad you are learning." He laughed. "Is the accommodation up to the standard?"

"It's excellent. Thank you, Sir."

"I wish you didn't call me Sir."

"You deserve it, Sir," he replied.

Nicholas had no idea how long he had been sleeping for. He heard someone knocking on his door reminding him that dinner was ready.

When he got to the dining room, he was relieved to see different races.

He was relieved to know he would be accepted as one of the team. They introduced themselves. He found the whole thing comforting. He felt relaxed. The meal wasn't strange to him. It was roast lamb and roast potatoes with vegetables. He had no time for dessert. He wanted to go back to sleep.

The following day, he had the shock of his life when he came down for breakfast. The breakfast was English breakfast. He had never seen English breakfast before. Desmond had warned him not to eat beef. When he asked Maggie what it was, she recited it without shame. He found English breakfast so vulgar. He had no appetite for it.

When he was still at school, his friends used to tell him about their holidays in rural areas and what they got up to. One of the stories was that when a goat is killed, boys roast the goat's testicles and ate them out of the girls' sight. There is no room for girls in such ceremony. No matter how much they cry for a little bite.

Nicholas sighed as he stared at the food in front of him.

"Is everything ok?" Maggie asked.

Nicholas gave her a weak smile. "It would be ok if you didn't include pigs' willies."

There was silence in the room. You could hear a pin drop. What made matters worse, was this girl called Mina with a sausage hanging from her mouth. "I am sick." She dropped her sausage on her plate and ran out of the room.

Maggie took a deep breath and mopped sweat off her forehead.

Nicholas wondered what the fuss was all about. He had always believed in the truth. He wasn't prepared to eat something so revolting for the sake of pleasing anyone.

Maggie found her voice. "You have been extremely rude, Nicholas."

"But I don't see how. I have never eaten pigs'...dicks."

"It's not pigs'...p... Oh God! Just stay put. I will bring the packages to you."

She was back in seconds with a pack of sausages.

Nicholas read all the ingredients. He wasn't satisfied. He had another question for Maggie. "Why is it shaped in such style?"

"I am a cook not some food manufacturer. You can phone them and ask them why."

"Anything else?"

Nicholas apologised to everyone. He ate his bacon, toast and baked beans. He avoided sausages and runny eggs.

After breakfast, he took a long walk to see his surroundings. On his way home, he picked daffodils in someone's garden.

He could hear Maggie singing at the top of her voice.

"Hi!"

"Oh Nicholas! You startled me."

"I am always putting my foot wrong. These are for you. To say sorry. I was extremely rude."

Maggie smiled at the young man. "I love daffodils. Thank you. I forgave you ages ago. I hope you enjoy your stay with us."

"I will." He smiled all the way to his room remembering how he stole the daffodils from someone's garden.

Chapter Thirty-Five

Nicholas started his training which was only two days a week. What should he do with the rest of the week? He found London life extremely boring. He missed home like crazy. There is no place like home. This was a temporary arrangement. He could never spend the rest of his life in a place like this where you greet someone and all you get is a "mind your own bloody business" expression. The only place he liked was Maggie's accommodation. There was so much laughter in the house but the moment you hit the street, it was a different matter.

One evening, James came to his room. "Why do you go to bed early? Don't you find this kind of life boring?"

"I don't know anyone here and there is not much to do."

"You should consider yourself lucky. Do you know I attend college and go to work?"

"What do you do?"

He smiled at Nicholas. "My job pays the bills. It's not a job I would like to hold onto for a long time. I would go mental at some point."

"It can't be that bad." Nicholas looked at him. "What's a bad job?"

"It's not a bad job at all. It's what I have to go through that really makes me look like a maniac." He was grinning at

Nicholas. "I work for a television centre as a security officer and sometimes as a laughing plant."

Nicholas pulled his face. "What the hell is that? I mean a laughing plant."

"Nick–"

"Please call me Nicholas. I never shorten my name."

"Sorry. Ok Nicholas, not all comedians can make the audience laugh. That's where I come in."

"You mean you just laugh even though there is nothing to laugh about?"

"Yes, and before the show is half way through, the whole audience get tickled by my laughter. They want to come back for the show."

Nicholas couldn't help himself laughing. "You mean you get paid for laughing? I have never heard such tale."

James looked at him. "Do you want a job?"

"Oh no. I am not qualified for that kind of job. I have nothing to laugh about."

"You think I do? I laugh because I know at the end of the month Maggie has to be paid."

"You see, you are laughing. You would do well. I will speak to my supervisor."

"Don't even try. I would lose my job on the same day. I am so miserable. I miss home."

As it turned out, Nicholas enjoyed his job. He worked on weekends only. Not once did he bump into James. It was a big television centre with so many studios. He was glad James found him the job. The loan from his brother in law gave him sleepless nights and not only that, he wanted a secure life. He was already making plans on how to triple his savings.

The only part of the job he hated was the security job where he had to mind car parks. His finger was constantly on the gate control button.

He didn't know any celebrities. He never asked for autographs. James told him that he was silly. He should ask for autographs. It makes them feel great.

"What's the point of having someone's autograph if you don't know who they are?"

"I collect mine for my grandmother. You should hear her bragging that his grandson is George Hamilton's bodyguard. The autographs keep her on her toes all day bragging to her friends."

Nicholas wasn't interested. He liked to mind his own business.

He thought he was doing well until he ended up in a wrong studio where there was a debate going on about mad cow disease. Viewers were horrified by his behaviour. "What is there to laugh at?" someone scolded him. He wished for the floor to swallow him. The studio he wanted was right next-door. He almost died of embarrassment.

After that, they kept him out of the studios. He controlled the car parks.

He was missing his laughing job. He was beginning to wonder when they would ask him to do that job again when the supervisor approached him.

"Nicholas, how long have you been controlling this car park?"

"For the last three months and today I haven't had a break. I have been operating these gates for nine hours. As you can see, my thumb is sore."

He grinned at him. "Go to studio twenty."

Nicholas gave him a puzzled look. "Jasper Carrott show doesn't need laughing plants. His jokes tickle you to a no return point."

"Do you want to enjoy a free show or not?"

"Thanks, I love the Jasper Carrott show."

Nicholas didn't know whether it was the God he now believed in that gave him directions. He was taking a long walk after college when he passed a bank and thought to enquire within.

"We are actually looking for temporary trustworthy cashiers. Do you have some experience?" someone with glasses about the size of a satellite dish asked him.

Nicholas's heart raced. "Yes, I have been working as a part time cashier for four years in Uganda."

He was given a form to fill in. "We need two references. Your last employer and someone who has known you for the last ten years plus a police check."

"The only person who knows me very well is my mother, sir and I don't have criminal records. I will contact the local police station to check me out. I have nothing to hide."

"We need two references and your mother doesn't count."

'Uncle Martin' popped in his head. But they have no idea who Uncle Martin is. All the same, he spoke to his former boss to help him with references.

He wasn't surprised when he got the job. It was still the same title but the salary was far better. Now, he had two jobs and college to occupy him. He was determined not to let Desmond and Annabella down. He had no time for socialising. Only one thing in his life mattered. He was hungry for success.

Chapter Thirty-Six

Nicholas shivered as the February cold hit him really hard. He had never felt such cold in his life before and the buses were taking their time. He decided to walk. The walking actually warmed him up a bit but his nose was another matter. It ran non-stop. He missed Uganda where people use umbrellas to shelter from the sun. He longed for that heat.

When he got home, he found Maggie still up.

"Hi Maggie."

"Hi Nicholas. There is a message for you by the telephone."

Nicholas read the message. "Nick, please call Eric."

He didn't understand. Why should Eric be calling him? He had never called him before. He would call in the morning. There was no point waking his mother this time of the night just because a twelve-year-old boy wants to have a chat with his brother. Whatever it was it could wait. He must know by now that he is working so he needs a few shillings for his bike repairs. He went to bed still wondering why Eric phoned.

He was beginning to doze off when there was a knock on his door.

"Nicholas, call for you."

"It must be serious," he mumbled to himself as he picked up

the phone. "Eric, slow down I can't get what you mean."

"Oh Nicholas, you have to come home, something bad has happened to Mother. You have got to do something. Please tell me you are coming. You are my only hope."

"Eric, what happened to Mother?" His heart raced. It had better be something minor. He could not bear to lose another parent. Tears coursed down his cheeks.

"Nicholas, I just hope it's a nightmare so that when we open our eyes again, things will be as they have always been."

"You are talking in riddles, Eric. Get on with it. Damn it!"

"It's Uncle Martin. He asked Mother to marry him."

Nicholas gripped the phone. He didn't know what to say.

"Nicholas? Aren't you going to say something?"

"What... did... Mother say?"

"What do you think? Why do you think I am calling? I don't like the answer she gave him. He moved in today. In the guest bedroom.

"You have to do something, Nicholas. Nicholas? Nicholas? The fool hung up on me. Jesusssssssssss!" He phoned Annabella.

"Eric, why are you phoning in the middle of the night? Is everything ok?"

"I am sorry to wake you, sis. I am worried about Nicholas. I think he had a shock."

Annabella sat up. "What do you mean by that?"

"I gave him bad news about Mother and Uncle Martin."

"What about them?"

"Whoops! I thought you knew." He hung up. He didn't want to explain to Annabella. She might get a shock as well.

His next call went to Abraham's emergency phone.

"It's Eric, I need to speak to Denise."

"Eric, have you checked the time before you called this number? Why are you using my emergency line anyway?"

"This *is* an emergency. Tell Denise to phone Nicholas. I think he is not well."

"You think. You don't know for sure. May I speak to Mother?"

"She...is...not...available." He hung up.

"Damn the kid."

Denise opened her eyes. "Who was that?"

"It's Eric. He said to phone Nicholas. He didn't make any sense."

"Well, come to bed, we will phone him in the morning," she told him.

"I don't think so. I wanted to speak to Mother and he said she is not available. Does that mean Eric is on his own?"

"We better find out." At that moment the phone rang. It was Annabella.

"May I speak to Denise?"

"What's the matter, Annabella?"

"It's kind of awkward. I would like to speak to Denise about it."

"I hope it's not upsetting. Your sister is in a very delicate condition." He handed the phone to his wife. He sat there just in case he was needed.

"I don't believe you, Annabella."

"You better believe me. I have just spoken to Mother. She is cool as a cucumber about the whole thing. Not only has she agreed to marry that... She is expecting his child."

"Oh no! Does she have any idea what this means? It's an embarrassing situation. At her age, she should know better. She will have to move out of the house according to Father's will.

"That depends on Nicholas. If that's what he wants. I have been trying to phone him but I can't get through. It has an engaged tone. Eric thinks he had a shock. What do we do?" Annabella asked. She was pissed off by her mother's behaviour. She liked Uncle Martin as a family friend but now...what was mother thinking of? If it's companionship she wanted, why did she go ahead and get herself knocked up? Why does she need another child? Why is she replacing Father? Didn't she love him enough? She was sick to the stomach.

"I don't know," Denise said. Her head was spinning. She didn't mind her mother having a companion. She was lonely. She needed someone but she didn't have to put her health at risk. Why did she need another child? What happens to Eric if Nicholas should tell their mother to move out? She hoped Nicholas would ignore the condition of Father's will.

"Annabella, let's sleep it off. I will try Nicholas in the morning. It must have been a shock to him and knowing Eric, he didn't disguise anything I suppose."

"I know. Eric can be really brutal with his words. Please let me know when you finally get in touch with him."

Denise put down the phone. She sat there for a while wondering what to do next.

"Is everything ok?" Abraham asked his wife.

She shook her head. "I don't know how to say this. Let's go to bed. I am kind of tired."

He massaged her temple. "Denise, if there is something bothering you, share it with me. I may be able to help."

"Not with this kind of problem but I would like to know how Nicholas is coping with... Annabella said the phone has some kind of an engaged tone."

He didn't want to push her. He knew she would tell him in her own time but there was one thing he could do.

"Go back to bed. I will call someone to check on Nicholas." He phoned the police in the UK. He was told to call back in an hour's time.

When he did, it was something he didn't wish to share with his wife considering she was eight months pregnant.

Denise looked at him waiting for the news. What did they say?

"He is all right. He didn't put the phone back. That's why Annabella kept on getting an engaged tone."

"Abraham! You are lying to me. I can sense it. What is it?"

"Now! Go to bed. It's late."

She sat up. "I want to know what happened to Nicholas."

Abraham's eyes travelled to his wife's bulging tummy. "Denise, go to bed. Nicholas is fine. He got himself drunk. That's all."

"Nicholas doesn't drink," she told him.

"Someone must have pissed him off for him to consume five cans of lager. What happened, Denise?"

"Oh Abraham! Why do I have to tell you this? It is embarrassing if you must know." She took a deep breath. "It's Mother. Uncle Martin asked her to marry him. She agreed."

"Oh!" He didn't know what to say to all that.

"Aren't you shocked?" she demanded.

"I guess I am," he yawned. "I am knackered. Look at the time. I will be getting up soon."

"Abraham, I don't like that kind of attitude. I know you are not shocked or worried about our reputation. Well, Mr, if this doesn't shock you, I don't know what will. Our mother is pregnant." She looked at him looking for signs of shock. All she saw was a grin.

"How...? I mean... Blimey! I had no idea she..."

Denise was now crying. "What do you mean by how? What kind of silly question is that?"

"I am sorry. I am as shocked as you are. Now, stop crying. You are upsetting the little one in there."

"What...do we do?" she whimpered.

"There is nothing we can do except pray that the kid doesn't turn out like Eric."

She looked at him through her tears. "You are right."

"Ok, now go to bed or do you want something to drink?"

She shook her head. "Thanks." They went to bed but Abraham didn't sleep. He had to talk to Annabella about Nicholas's condition, the condition he refused to discuss with his wife. A miscarriage was the last thing he wanted. When he knew she was fast asleep, he crept out of the bed. He dare not use the phone in the bedroom. He used the one in the kitchen.

Desmond picked up the phone.

"Oh thank God it's you. You better break this news to Annabella and whatever you do, keep it away from Denise. She is in a very delicate condition.

"What is it? What happened? There is so much going on but I am kept in the dark. All I get is 'oh Desmond'. It's some kind of awkward."

"Yes, it is awkward." Abraham told him everything.

Yes, Nicholas had been admitted at St Thomas's Hospital. He had hit his head on the table. He is still unconscious.

"I can only guess how Eric broke the news to him. Abraham, whatever you do, don't let our mother in law know about Nicholas. She will go into labour."

"Damn! I never thought about that. I was about to phone her. What do we do about Nicholas?" Abraham asked knowing he wasn't in any position to abandon his tight schedule.

"I will have to go. I know what the kid is going through. I hated every man my mother got involved with. I breathed a breath of fresh air when she gave up." *He didn't bother to tell him that his father's ghost chased every man that tried to replace him.*

"Thanks mate and please keep me informed and safe trip."

Annabella stared at her husband. "Oh no, Desmond! I will not let you play nurse to Nicholas. If there is one person who should nurse Nicholas back to health, it's Mother. She put him in that condition, remember? He could be brain damaged. What do we do, Desmond?" She sobbed.

"But you know Mother is pregnant. Don't tell her about Nicholas' condition. She will lose her baby."

"Please tell me it's a dream."

"It's not a dream. As you can see, my dear wife, I am packing. I will be back before you miss me."

She composed herself. "I am coming with you."

"Annabella! That's out of the question. What about the children?"

"I have already worked out the arrangement. Timothy and Elizabeth will stay with Amanda, and the twins...I will ask Denise. They won't miss me considering we look the same. What do you think?"

"But we agreed not to tell Denise about this sad case. And not only that, the twins are still breast-feeding and just seven months old for that matter."

"I started them on bottles a month ago. They will not miss me. The poor mites will think Denise is their mummy. I won't tell Denise about Nicholas' condition. I will say it's a business trip."

There was no point arguing with her. He pulled down another suitcase.

Chapter Thirty-Seven

Nicholas opened his eyes. Where was he? What had happened? His head hurt like crazy. He couldn't recall what had happened.

"I am glad you are awake, Mr Attention-seeker," she snorted. "You gave us a scare."

"Annabella! What... the... hell are you doing here? And that snorting, you sound like Uncle Richard."

"Hey! Don't talk to my wife like that. How are you?"

"I feel awful. What are you doing here?"

"Desmond! I think he is brain damaged. He acts funny. What do we do?"

Nicholas listened to their conversation with concentration. He pretended to be dozing off. He now understood what had happened. His mother is pregnant. Damn Martin.

He opened his eyes. "I want to get out of here."

"You are not well enough. Your doctor will tell you when you are ready to go home," Desmond told him.

He sighed. "Where is home?"

"What do you mean, Nicholas?" Annabella panicked. "You... don't...know where home is?"

"Of course I know where home is. What do you take me for? If Mother thinks that the Martin bastard will raise bastards under my father's roof, she is mistaken. Women!"

"You can't chuck her out. It's cruel, Nicholas and what's that language you have adopted? Jeeeesus! You sound like Eric."

"How is he?"

"He is coping."

"Good. Do you mind looking after him until I come? You guys got lucky by marrying rich husbands. Eric and I have to find our own way to survive."

Desmond gave him a cold stare. "You know it's impossible to have Eric with us for longer than necessary. I will find him a good boarding school. The last thing I want is stress from my brother in law. What makes matters worse; I can't give him the good hiding he deserves."

"You would pay heavily for beating your father in law," Annabella reminded him.

"You think I don't know that? He made it clear to me that he is now in charge of the whole family. He should be treated with respect or he will have me fined heavily," he lied. The kid told him that if he should beat his sister, he would have his ass whipped. "No one beats my sister. A wife beater? It's not acceptable in my books." He had winked at him. How he wanted to twist the little devil's neck. What could he do? He gritted his teeth and then gave him a cosmetic smile.

Nicholas was now laughing. "You know Eric has been trouble since he was born but we can't just abandon him. I need your help. I want Martin off my father's property. That's my property and Eric's and soon I will be having my own family. There is no room for Martin's bastards. Why did mother have to lower herself like that? I thought she loved Father. Why does she need another man?"

Annabella sighed. "You will have to ask her and I don't wish to be around when you pose that question."

"I want my mother out of that property. That property is for my family."

Desmond and Annabella exchanged looks. "We had no idea you have gone that far," Desmond said with a yawn."

At that moment Mina and James walked in. "Nicholas! You silly idiot. What made you lose your head?" Mina asked as she kissed his cheeks. "Jeeesus! When did you last shave?"

Desmond and Annabella exchanged looks. "We'd better leave you to your..."

Nicholas introduced them as flatmates.

"We'd better get going. We see you tomorrow."

As soon as they left the hospital, Annabella asked Desmond what he thinks about Mina.

"What am I supposed to think?"

"Do you think there is something going on?"

"I don't know. I hope he is intelligent enough not to screw around. If he is not careful, we might just as well forget the loan we gave him."

"He has to pick himself up if he wants to achieve what he came here for. I am not a person who keeps quiet about such matters. I will talk to him next time we see him," said Annabella.

Chapter Thirty-Eight

Denise was having a hard time with Annabella's twins. "Oh God! What do I do here?" They both needed a change. And soon they will be crying for their bottles.

"I will give you a hand," Nadine offered. She put Jonathan in his playpen and helped Denise with one baby. "Who is this one?"

Denise was so pleased with the way things turned out for Nadine and Mworozi. Jonathan fulfilled their dreams. She was sure they were now content. They had badly wanted a boy. She wasn't surprised when they named him Jonathan. J& Sons Solicitors is behind Jonathan's name and her son Jethro. Wow!

She looked at Nadine. "That's a very difficult question. I have to check them out first to know who is who."

Isabel has a birthmark on her left foot. She checked the one she was changing. "I got her. This one is Celestina."

They changed them, fed them; once they were asleep, the two women sat down to chat.

Nadine sighed. "I am worried about Jess. She hasn't left her room for the last three days. She says she is on annual leave."

"Has she received those love letters recently? They usually change her mood," Denise asked.

"Yes, there was a courier this morning. He had a small parcel. I signed for it. It didn't look like roses. What do we do? I hate to

278

see her wasting her life on an invisible admirer. Granny may be right. The man is just playing with her mind."

"I don't know what to do for her. She doesn't confide in me anymore. She only tells me what she wants me to know. Did you know she is the one who healed Mother from Valium addiction?"

"Your little brother has a wild tongue. It was supposed to be confidential."

"Not according to Eric. He doesn't know when to keep his mouth shut."

Later on at dinner, Jessica finally left her room. Nadine and Denise exchanged looks when she entered the dining room. They exchanged more looks when they saw something glittering on her left finger.

Both women beamed at her.

"What is it? You will slit your cheeks if you are not careful."

"I am pleased for you," Denise said to her.

"Oh, you mean this?" She beamed at her.

"What's that?" her brothers asked at the same time.

"What does it look like?"

"Who is he?" her granny asked.

"Who is who?"

"Don't answer your grandmother like that," her mother scolded her."

"So, he finally revealed himself," her father said.

"Yes, through UPS courier," Melanie and Angela chorused. They gave their aunt a mischievous look.

Jessica pushed her chair back. "I am not hungry."

"You come back here at once!" her father ordered.

She sat down again. "I am sorry," she apologised to no one in particular.

"You should be. Who put that ring on your finger?" It was an expensive ring. It looked like a ruby ring encrusted with diamonds.

"No one you know."

The questions went on and on. She refused to answer any of them. It was a few hours later when she finally escaped to her room. She pulled out her secret box where she kept her love notes and roses. She put in the note that had come with the ring. The words were now etched on her mind. She didn't have to read the note a second time. *My darling Jessica, The time has come for me to express myself more clearly. Will you marry me?*

If the answer is yes, please wear my ring. If the answer is no, I will understand. I will be in touch with your father. Please give me time to organise a few things. Everything I am doing, I am doing for you. I will always love you. Brian B.

"I will wait for you," she said as she closed her secret box. A few tears escaped her. "I will wait for you, Brian." She fell asleep with a smile on her face.

Desmond and his wife arrived at the hospital only to find Nicholas had been discharged.

They arrived at his residence and found some celebration in progress.

Nicholas beamed at them. "I phoned your hotel only to be told you were out. Did you get my message?"

"We haven't been to the hotel since this morning. How do you feel?"

"I feel weak."

Annabella eyed the girl Mina sitting by Nicholas's side playing nurse. I don't like this, she thought.

"Would you like a cup of tea?" Maggie asked.

"If you have coffee please," Desmond said.

"If it's no trouble," Annabella added.

Before they left, Annabella had a private conversation with her brother.

"Who is this girl, Nicholas?"

"My dear sister. You have a poor memory. I remember introducing her to you when you came to see me at the hospital. Her name is Mina. A very good friend. They are all my friends mind you."

"You will be careful, won't you?" she asked him.

"Of course I use condoms. What do you take me for? Mina and I don't want to start a family yet..." He grinned at her. "What a nosey sister I have."

Annabella glared at her brother. "You stupid fool! Girls and studies don't mix."

He rolled his eyes. "Where did I hear this before? You sound like Aunt Meredith. I know how to take care of myself, Annabella. You didn't have to fly all the way for a minor accident unless you wanted to kill two birds with one stone. I know how you love travelling and swiping Desmond's credit cards."

"You ungrateful fool! Don't you dare forget who lifted your ass from a lousy cashier job to better yourself." Her nostrils flared.

He almost told her that he was still a cashier but thought better of it. He wanted their support until he found his feet. "I am sorry, sis. I haven't been myself since Eric's phone call."

"Nicholas, take good care of yourself. Don't lose your head each time things don't work out the way you want. I have just discovered that Mother has her own life to lead. She is lonely. You might just as well know this. She is pregnant." Annabella watched her brother's reaction and saw none.

"You will miss your flight, Annabella."

She stared at him. She sighed. "Is that all you can say?"

"What do you expect me to say? Not long ago you told me not to lose my head when things don't work out my way. I need one favour. Take care of Eric. There is no point asking Denise. They tried but Eric can't stand that house."

"He doesn't like it because they tried to put him in his right place," she shot back. "Well, I don't think I can handle him either but I will look after him during holidays. Desmond will have to find him a good boarding school. That's all we can do."

"Thanks very much for you assistance. I won't let you down. I have big plans."

"It will come to nothing if you keep on screwing around. I am warning you. We want our loan back."

"Annabella? Safe trip."

When Desmond and his wife got home, Annabella excused herself.

"I am going to pick up the kids. I won't be long."

"Take your time," he told her.

When she returned, she found a message from her husband. *"I will be home late. Don't wait up."*

She looked at the note several times. What the hell is going on? Don't wait up? Since when did he go out without telling her his movements? Damn! She kicked one of the toys.

"Mum, look at my racing car," Timothy cried out.

"Mum, my doll is talking." Elizabeth jumped up and down and before long the talking doll was on her flat nipple.

The twins were busy with their singing toys. She watched them with tears in her eyes. "You poor mites, if only you knew what I was going through." She pretended to take part in their games but her mind was elsewhere. All she could see was her husband complimenting his hooker on how hot she was in bed. The thought made her rush to the toilet to throw up.

There was a knock on the bathroom door. "Are you ok, Mrs Tumwiine?"

"I don't feel good, Vanessa. Could you please sit with the children? I need to lie down a bit."

She didn't lie down. She checked all her husband's pockets, drawers, his wardrobe, inside his shoes, his files. She turned everything upside down. There was no sign of another woman. She sat there thinking hard. She remembered him making international calls while in London and each time she asked him who it was, he said it was business.

She checked the last call. To her annoyance, the caller withheld the number.

She rushed to the nursery where Vanessa sat with the children.

"Vanessa, who was the last person to call?"

"I haven't picked up any phone today. Lucas may know. Should…I ask him?"

"No thanks. It's nothing." Her next stop was the writing pad they put next to the phone. She looked at a blank page. She could see a page where the message had been written had been ripped out. She burst into the kitchen. "Lucas, who was the last person to call and what was the message?"

He gave her a blank look. "Oh let me think." After what seemed an eternity, he looked at her again. He knew the answer would ignite her temper to no end and everyone would be on the receiving end of her temper. He decided to lie to her. "I don't know who called. The phone stopped as I was about to pick it up."

Her nostrils flared. "Lucas?"

"Yes, Madam?"

"You are fired."

"What? What…have I done wrong?"

"You should read your contract and go to the rules section. You have just lied to me. I can never trust a person who lies to me. My family's health is in your hands twenty-four hours a day. I will not risk my family's health. Out of my sight," she told him.

Lucas knew what that meant. This was a very difficult situation. Fired meant no references and no references meant no jobs. He opened his mouth to apologise, but his pride stood in his way. There was no way he was going to apologise to a woman.

He peeled off his apron. He was tempted to leave the cooker on. No, he couldn't be that cruel.

Vanessa stared at her husband.

"I said, pack your bags, we go."

"What have we done?"

"I was fired for not knowing who the caller was."

"Do you know who the caller was?"

"Yes, some woman who wanted to see Desmond urgently on a business matter. Now, try to tell that to Ms Temper, she will be wanting to know how the caller sounded like. Did she sound like someone threatening? What age group? I wasn't prepared for such investigations. I have had enough of their tongues especially from her husband who thinks I have my lines on his Mrs. They are both cut from the same branch. Enfuhi, that's what they are. What happened to the word 'trust'?"

Chapter Thirty-Nine

Annabella had no idea how she managed to bath the children, cooking, feeding, reading stories and sending them to sleep. She was now breathing through her mouth. She had no energy left. Damn Desmond and his whore. She looked at the children sleeping in her king size bed. She squeezed in next to them. If Desmond thinks he will have his ways after he has been dipping into another woman, he needs his head examined. She checked the bedside clock; it was one o'clock in the morning. The word divorce danced on her mind.

Desmond let himself in the house with a smile on his face. Yes! I have done it, he thought to himself. He was too tired to check on the children. He would take part in feeding in the morning.

He tiptoed to the bedroom. He was silent as a ghost as he looked for his bedclothes. He took off his clothes. He was on his last item when Timothy called out for his mother. "Mum, Elizabeth is taking all the blankets."

Desmond paused in his act. "What is the meaning of this, Annabella? I thought we said no children in our bed? You spoil them, Annabella."

"Well, I want my space."

She rubbed her eyes. When she saw who it was, her sleep

disappeared.

"What time do you call this?" Her nostrils flared. "Who is she?"

Desmond reached for his gown. "You'd better keep your voice down before you wake the children."

"I am awake. I want my milk," Elizabeth complained.

"No, you don't. You will wet the bed," her mother warned.

"It's for my doll."

"Jeeeeeesus! Go back to sleep, Elizabeth." Timothy gave his sister a little push with his elbow.

At that moment the doll started the crying noise. The twins sent a shrieking noise.

"I am sleeping in the spare bedroom," Desmond announced.

Annabella glared at him. "I am not surprised at all."

She put her children in order. By the time the twins fell asleep, she was again breathing through her mouth.

She didn't bother to knock on Desmond's spare bedroom. She switched on the light. "I want the truth, Desmond. Who is she?"

"Annabella, can't you see it's late? I thought with the long journey we had today, you would be in bed."

"Not before you tell me why you should... Who is she, damn it?"

He sighed. "Does it matter who she is? She will never take your place."

"So you admit it."

"How can I deny it? Go to sleep sweetheart. We have things to discuss in the morning."

"It's morning already. How long has this affair been going on?"

"Honestly Annabella, you have no idea how tired I am. I need at least a few hours' sleep." He pulled the covers aside. "Come to bed, dear. I hate to see you upset like this."

"Upset? You have no idea how I feel." She banged the

bedroom door on her way out.

He was too tired. He knew how jealous his wife was and he wasn't about to lose his sleep over such episode. He fell asleep immediately with a smile on his face.

The first thing he smelt when he got up was a burnt smell of some kind. "I will sack that idiot for his carelessness." When he got to the kitchen, a circus scene welcomed him.

"What are you doing, Annabella? Don't you know it's dangerous to let children play in the kitchen?"

"I don't have eyes at the back of my head. They should be where I can see them."

"You are doing a job for two. Where is what's his name and the childminder?"

"I sacked them. Timothy, pass me some eggs. That's a good boy. Elizabeth, that porridge is not for your doll."

Celestina was on her hip and Isabel was lying flat on her belly trying to poke her little finger into the electric socket.

"I will feed the twins. Go and have a bath. You look a mess."

"If I look a mess whose fault is it?"

"Your temper must be the reason you are doing a housekeeper's job. I saw this coming. The way you shout at them."

She pushed Celestina into his arms. She was out of the kitchen before he could ask where the feeding bottles were.

Instead of heading for the bathroom, she phoned the agency to track down Lucas and Vanessa. "I need them urgently."

"We will do what we can but they were quite upset."

"It was a misunderstanding, which I have sorted out. I will increase their pay. Please, I need them." She shouldn't have fired them. It wasn't their fault that her husband was fucking around."

They arrived some time later. To her relief, things went back to normal except one thing. She wanted to get to the bottom of her husband's affair. How long had it been going on. Has he been going from one bed to another? "Desmond, I need a word."

"I need a word too. We are going out for a ride. It's better we talk in the car where there is no one to hear our exchange."

The car eventually stopped. "Here we are and please, don't make a scene." He gave her his hand.

She refused to take it.

"Suit yourself." He sighed.

"This is where I was last night and that one in the middle is the woman," he pointed. "Does she look like a threat to you?"

Annabella's bust heaved. She swallowed hard. "I...don't... understand. It's... Oh Desmond! I am so sorry. Please say you forgive me."

"It's yours, Annabella. As you can see, I named it after you."

She breathed. "A boat! I don't know what to say."

"Don't say anything. Let's have a cruise."

"Is it safe?"

"Yes, it passed the safety test three times. It's now safe."

"It's beautiful!" she said as they cruised on Lake Victoria. "I am so ashamed, Desmond. I treated you badly last night."

"You were looking after your property."

"But that's not an excuse for my behaviour. We must trust each other."

"That's what is lacking in our marriage, dear."

"Desmond. I am so pleased with your gifts. I love you. You already know that."

"My love goes without saying. I am glad you are pleased. What about we go back home so I catch up on that sleep you spoiled?"

"You can't blame me for defending my property." They raced each other to their car.

Chapter Forty

Abraham stood at the bottom of the stairs holding his four month-old daughter Rosanna. "If your mama is not here in two minutes, we might just as well forget our adventure." She sneezed in his face covering him with milk. "What...is this?"

Denise came down with Jethro tagging on her skirt. "I am sorry to keep you waiting. I was looking for Jethro's teddy bear. Have you seen it?"

"For goodness sake! We have less than an hour to check in."

"You know he can't sleep without it. We must find it."

"He will have to sleep without it. In five hours' time he will be seeing real wildlife." They were having a two week holiday at the Victoria Falls.

They were about to drive off, when their father knocked on their car window.

"Abraham, I hope you are not taking the children to a hazard zone. They are too young for camping."

Denise blushed as she remembered their honeymoon.

"Father, I left all the details in your study in case you need to get in touch. We are running late." He told the driver to put his foot down.

"Father talks to you as if you are still a kid. Do you have to tell him everything, Abraham? He will be phoning us non-stop.

We are supposed to be having a breather, all right?"

"That's how he is. In his eyes, we are still kids."

"He overdoes it sometimes. Well, he is my father in law. I can't answer back even though I feel like having a debate with him."

"Don't even try otherwise you will miss the royal treatment you get from him."

She laughed. "Abraham, it's the other way round. I am not trying to praise myself but I do wonders with his friends. None of them go back with stomach ache."

"You are a good wife and hostess, Denise. The house is dull without you."

"Please don't say that. Nadine is excellent."

"Yes but she can hardly hold a conversation without stammering and excusing herself."

"Have you ever asked yourself why she behaves like that? I have caught Mworozi giving her signals to shut up each time she tries to contribute to a conversation. She is not a quiet woman at all. You should ask Granny. We giggle at her jokes all day."

"You are making this up. Oh, here we are." They had just a few minutes left to catch their flight.

They had a safe journey. They arrived at their hotel. Denise looked around her. "I know this place," she told Abraham.

"Have you been here before?"

"I think so or maybe I am mistaken."

As soon as they entered the reception, her memory came flooding back.

They were sat down in the reception having refreshments.

"Yes, we have been here before with Father. My father had an argument with them about a family suite. It was one room with bunk beds in one corner and our parents' bed in another corner.

"He had screamed at the manager. 'Listen, I have come here to have a relaxing holiday. How do I relax with my ten year old twins and a six-year-old boy in the same room?'

"We ended up having our own suite. Annabella had room service at every hour. When Father received the bill, he hit the roof." There was more.

"I phoned all my friends boasting about the Kingdom Hotel and the statue of David Livingstone who discovered the Victoria Falls and named it after the Queen of England."

Abraham grinned at her. "Well, Rosanna and Jethro are too young to have their own suite. They will have to share with us."

"It's a pity. We should have brought a minder." She gave him a seductive smile.

"That can be arranged."

"Oh no! I will not leave the children with a complete stranger."

They were shown to their suite.

"It's beautiful!" Denise marvelled at the view.

Abraham checked everything including fire exits. He came back with a grin on his face. "It's perfect. They have a swimming pool. Do you want a swim?"

"Do they have floats for the little ones."

"Everything and I have arranged for a guide to take us around. We have three hours to swim and relax before the tour of the Victoria Falls.

"Here is the list of activities they have. Take your pick."

She picked the ones she missed out the last time she was here. Sunset cruise was one of them, bungee jumping and white water rafting.

Abraham scanned her list. "This is daring. Forget it."

"You asked me to choose and that's what I am doing. Oh please Abraham, you are doing exactly what my parents did."

"Bungee jumping will turn you inside out."

She grinned at him. "That's what I want."

"I give up."

They had a wonderful time. Jethro never asked for his bear.

He was too tired at the end of the day.

They were due back in two days' time when they received a phone call in the middle of the night.

Abraham picked up the phone.

"Is that Mr Muganzi's suite?"

"Who wants him?"

"There is a call for Mrs Muganzi."

Abraham handed the phone to his wife.

"Who is it?"

"You will soon find out. I will check on the kids."

"Annabella, you are not making sense."

"You have to come home, Denise. It's Mother. They had to do a caesarean. She hasn't woken up since. She might die. We must be there...to hold her hand." She was now sobbing.

Denise asked the question she didn't wish to ask. The reason her mother was in that condition. "The baby?" she asked.

"She is a healthy baby. I phoned Nicholas. He hung up on me. Eric is throwing abuse at Uncle Martin. Denise, you have to come home."

Denise took a deep breath. She didn't wish to bother Abraham with this. This was her problem alone. She would deal with it alone but she didn't know how. She had insisted on this holiday so he could put work stress aside for a bit. Now to tell him about his mother in law, no, she will not say anything to him. "Annabella, hold Mother's hand for me. Tell her she is going to be all right. I love her. You tell her that. I will come as soon as possible."

Her eyes smarted with tears. She must be brave. "Annabella, I will see you when I see you." She hung up.

"Is everything all right?" Abraham asked.

She gave him a cosmetic smile. "Perfect. Annabella wanted to know whether I covered all the activities we missed out on when we were last here."

"Denise! Why are you lying to me? It shows on your face. You are crying. What is it?"

"I am fine. It's long time ago memories that triggered my feelings. I miss Father," she burst out. She hoped that would keep his curiosity away. But she was wrong.

"Denise, whatever it is, share it with me. Is there anyone else?" He has dealt with divorce cases where couples go on holiday and one of them ends up staying behind, abandoning what they have both worked so hard for.

"Abraham! How can you say that? How can you doubt my love for you? We better sleep. It's late."

"Not until you tell me what's bothering you." He cuddled her. "Go on. I will handle it."

Her sobs reached his heart. "He joined in. Why don't you tell me, Denise? It can't be your father you are remembering." He stood up.

"Where...are you going?"

"I am phoning your sister. She holds the answers."

"Please wait. Don't phone. It's Mother...she is...she might die. She is in hospital." Now she had opened up, she told him everything and why she didn't want him to know.

"Denise, family comes first. I have rested enough. We must get on the next flight."

Annabella sat with Martin in the waiting area. She wanted to talk to him alone just in case her mother was listening which was wishful thinking.

"Uncle Martin, you are taking this very hard and Eric is not helping at all. I just want you to know that I am not blaming you for mother's condition and you shouldn't blame yourself either. These things happen, right?"

"I blame myself. She did this for me. She called this baby a gift for me, knowing I didn't have kids of my own. I told her that her health was important. I was happy with what I had. I love her, you see. One thing you must know, I didn't marry your mother so I could step into your father's shoes. I know my limits."

"I know. We have behaved badly towards you. I am sure you were not surprised when we didn't show up to your wedding."

"It hurt your mother so much. She recovered somehow."

"I am here now and she can't hear my apology. I phoned Denise; she is on her way. As for Nicholas, I don't know what else to do. He hung up on me."

"Well at least he knows and I am the cause of all this. He will never forgive me if…"

"There is no if. She is going to be ok. Don't lose faith."

"I am glad you are here, Annabella. Did I tell you that your mother and I went to see Nicholas?"

"She shook her head."

"When? What happened?"

"I regretted arranging their meeting in the first place. I invited him to lunch and told him I had business to discuss with him. When he arrived he had a girl with him on his arm. The moment he saw his mother, he wanted to run back to his taxi but the girl took matters in her own hands and controlled the embarrassing situation. 'I am Mina, I am pleased to meet you all. Nicholas talks a lot about you. Nicholas dear, what a surprise! Oh I love surprises Nicholas.' She beamed at us.

"Nicholas managed to exchange a few polite words with his mother but the moment the girl went to powder her nose, he attacked us.

"'I am glad we have this chance to talk. I am getting married soon. I want to refurbish the house. You can move out quickly or you will be dealing with my lawyer.'

"Your mother had no time to answer because at that moment the girl came back. Your brother behaved in a manner I have never seen in my life before in Banyankole custom. He kissed his fiancée there in front of his mother without shame. If it was a polite kiss, fine."

"I can imagine what kiss that is," Annabella murmured. "The idiot!"

"After the revolting kiss, he looked at his mother. 'Now you know why I want my house, don't you?' He excused himself and left."

Annabella was shocked. "Is that why you moved out?"

"We had no choice. I never wanted to be in your father's house in the first place. I only stayed for Louise and Eric. I didn't want to uproot them. I have a place of my own."

"He might have been fooling Mother. Where is the marriage he was on about?"

"Marriage or no marriage, it worked. He rents it out and the money goes to Eric's account from what I gather. I am glad he is looking out for his brother."

"What about his mother? She is lying there wondering where her children are. Uncle Martin, you better be strong. Why don't you go and have some sleep? I will stay with her."

He bit his lip. "I can't. I must be there when she wakes up."

Annabella hugged him. "I am glad you have faith."

Denise arrived a few hours later. She held her mother's hand. "I am so sorry, Mother. I should have been there for you from the moment you made the decision to move on. Please forgive me," she sobbed.

Louise smiled at her daughter. She nodded. She had no strength left. She didn't know what had happened to her voice. Her body ached. Her head hurt. Her inside was another matter. She looked at her children. She saw love, joy and fear in their eyes. She wished she could reassure them that she will pull through. She longed to see Nicholas. She knew it was wishful thinking. She would not wash her hands of him. She still loved him no matter what. As for Martin, she was pleased she'd married him in the first place.

He was one caring person; of course he could never reach Isaac's standards. Her love for Isaac was still strong but she couldn't lead a lonely life while she held on to her dead husband's love. She needed a friend, a companion, someone to turn to. She wished she could love him but that would be asking too much.

The relationship they had together was enough for her. She hoped it was enough for Martin. She knew how much he loves children. She knew what was missing in his life. He warned her about it saying he was happy the way things were. She knew he was concerned about her health but she wanted to give him this gift. She almost lost her life. If she went now, at least she had fulfilled Martin's dream. She knew he had that dream.

"Mother, we'd better let you rest. We will be back in the morning."

When morning came, it wasn't Martin or her other three children who sat by her bedside. She bit her lip and let her tears flow. She found her voice.

"You came?"

"I had no choice. I had time to talk to Father when he was still alive. He left this world knowing how much we loved him. If... if...you...

"Oh Mother! I am glad you pulled through. I am sorry. I hope that's enough. If you don't forgive me, I will understand."

"Nicholas, one thing you must know is that I still love your father. I love Martin in a different way. No one can take your father's place. If I turn round and tell Martin that I love him, I will be lying to myself."

"Don't tire yourself. I wish you a quick recovery. I am here for a week. I would like to treat you to pork ribs in barbecue sauce." He grinned at her.

Louise smiled. "You cheeky monkey! You know how much I

love pork ribs in barbecue sauce."

"Well, you'd better get a rest and recover soon." He looked at his mother. He had come here to make peace with her. If he didn't look in that cot by her bedside, she would take it differently. New babies frightened him but what the hell! He stood up. "May I?"

Louise smiled at him. "Nicholas, you hate new babies but you can look."

He felt so relieved. He didn't bother to hide his relief. He bent over the cot. "She is sleeping." He thanked God for that. He didn't want Martin's seed staring at him. He would never like the man. He was here for his mother. For her forgiveness. He was happy his mother had pulled through. He wished to tell her to take care next time but he found such a topic out of the question. Another baby would kill her. He will talk to Annabella. Oh no! Not that one. She is a breeding machine. She loves new babies. Denise must know how such things are controlled. His mother cut in his thoughts.

"Yes, she loves her sleep."

"I better not wake her then." He tiptoed away from the cot. He wanted to get out of the ward very fast.

"You'd better have a rest, Mother. I will see you later."

He decided to walk to town. He wanted to feel the sunshine on his face. He missed such weather. He felt like hugging everyone he came across. Their laughing faces told him a thing or two. This was home. The place he misses so much. It won't be long, he comforted himself. There is no place like home. He didn't know how long he had been walking when he collided with a pedestrian and scattered her shopping bag. "I...am...so...sorry. How clumsy I am. I do apologise." He picked up her fruits. "I was miles away." He looked at her. "Do I know you?"

"Of course you know me. When did you arrive?"

He stared at the girl. "Jessica! It's you. Oh shit! I hope you don't tell my sister about this incident."

"What is there to stop me? Wow! You look different. What have they been feeding you on?"

"I hope that's a good compliment."

She smiled at him. "You look well."

"Thank you." He looked at the mango he was still holding. "Why don't we dump this shopping bag and I will buy you lunch?"

He was supposed to be seeing his lawyer but what's the hell!

"I would love that." They went to the grill on Kampala Road. "I recommend pork ribs in barbecue sauce."

She laughed. "That's your mother's favourite."

"I know. I promised her that when she comes out of the hospital."

"She gave us a fright."

"At her age, it was expected," he replied.

"You talk as if she is a century old."

"Why should a woman with grandchildren find herself in such circumstances?"

"Oh Nicholas, please tell me about London." She decided to change the subject.

"Nothing to tell really. There is no place like home."

"What are you still doing there then? I thought your course is finished."

"I am still tying a few loose ends."

"I hear you are engaged to an Indian girl."

He laughed and threw his head back. "That is my sister Annabella. Letting her gob run wild. She is a friend. A good friend."

"I am glad to see you, Nicholas, but I must go. My lunch break is over."

"I am taking Eric out tomorrow. What are you doing tomorrow? We could do with company or Mr what's his name

298

will teach me a lesson for taking his girl out."

Jessica looked at her engagement ring glittering on her finger. She looked at him. Is this the same little fifteen-year-old boy with pimples on his face who danced with her at Denise's wedding? What a turn of the century! She almost whistled. "I do food shopping on weekends," she told him. "As for Mr what's his name, I am not married to him yet and it's not as if I am going to be sleeping with you, Nicholas."

He fidgeted on his feet. "Well, I...have...to be...careful. Are you shopping all day? I was wondering if we could have a cruise on the Annabella boat. I hear they run a first class cruise boat business."

"I fear boats," she told him.

"I am sure they have life jackets. I will pick you at one o'clock tomorrow. I recommend casual wear. We don't want stilettos on a boat."

She looked at her stiletto. "I guess trainers will have to do."

"Thanks Jessica." He escorted her to her work place and then did a u-turn. He wanted to see his lawyer urgently. His mind was still filled with the picture of Jessica. The girl who captured his heart when he was fifteen years old. He laughed at the way Meredith had talked to him. That woman can talk. Why did he make a fool of himself like that? If he had waited, he would have known without involving other people like Eric who happened to be eavesdropping. That kid!

Chapter Forty-One

Nicholas was almost falling on his feet. He was tired. He looked at some magazines without interest as he waited for Mr Baker, his lawyer.

"Mr Bahiika?"

He turned round. "Mr Baker, how do you do, Sir?"

"I am well, thank you. My secretary tells me you don't have an appointment."

"That's right, Sir. I arrived this morning and I need to see you on an urgent matter. I am only here for a few days. I am sorry to disturb you."

"I can slot you in. Please come through."

Nicholas took his seat.

"What can I do for you? I hope you are not having problems with your tenants."

"Oh no! This is a different matter altogether. I need accommodation."

Mr Baker stared at him behind his huge glasses.

"I am interested in a certain property. It's been in the paper for sometime. I want to buy it. I was wondering if you could arrange a loan with the bank for me."

"I see. How big is the property?"

"It's eighty rooms."

Mr Baker took off his glasses. "Have I heard you correctly?"

Nicholas opened his briefcase and pulled out the newspaper. "I am interested in this hotel."

Mr Baker read all the details about the property. He knew the property all right. When he got to the asking price, he whistled. "That's a lot of money."

"I know. I am relying on you. I badly want this place. I will change it completely. I intend to knock down a few walls and reduce the rooms to fifty. I mean real family suites, conference rooms for hire, gift shop, Forex Bureau, a pharmacy. With a hotel like that, one needs a pharmacy nearby for emergencies and it's not as if I will not be following health and safety rules. But one has to be on the lookout for emergencies."

Mr Baker mopped his forehead. "I can see you have already thought a great deal about this venture. I am afraid the asking price is out of our reach. It's a non-starter. I don't even wish to try."

"Mr Baker, I have been working since I was fourteen. I am still working. I have saved quite a few shillings and I can use my house as collateral."

"I see, you want to sacrifice your family home for this ramshackle. I know this place. It leaks and has drainage problems and a few cracks here and there."

"I would like you to arrange a survey for me before we head for the loan. Please find out if it's titled. I am interested. There is nothing a good architect can't fix. We do have good architects in this country."

"You have a determined mind. I have to remind you that the bank will need the necessary papers."

"I know. I have them with me." He pulled out his pay slips and bank statements for the last six months and his address.

Mr Baker looked at his bank statement. He looked at Nicholas. "There is not much balance here."

Nicholas grinned at him. "I know. I have been working for banks a long time to understand that they don't like to lend money to those who don't know how to spend it. They like to lend money to those who get into debts and come out of it unaided." He looked at his lawyer. "I only withdrew that money for the record. "It is safe somewhere. I have a huge balance plus the house; I should be able to get the loan. I would like to be in business with you but if you are not prepared to help, I will try elsewhere." He gathered his papers.

"Hold on a second." He held out his hand. "I will do my best."

"Thank you, Sir. I am here for a few days. If you could please start as soon as possible, I would be grateful. Thank you for your time."

Nicholas's next stop was the property he was interested in. He liked the location. He stood there admiring it. "All it needs is a few touches here and there." He was in love with it. He must have it. He went inside and asked for the manager.

A man in his late fifties gave him a tour. He almost hugged every wall. What fascinated him most was the penthouse. He had an idea why it was on sale. Their maintenance was poor. The only place that looked well maintained was the reception. "What a rip off guests get! The moment they see a clean reception, they think their sleeping quarters and kitchen are the same." Nicholas grinned from ear to ear. He knew what name it would trade on: 'THE GOLDEN TOWER HOTEL' All the letters will be illuminated. It will be seen from miles around. He was in love with the Golden Tower Hotel. He liked the sound of it.

"Do you like it?" the manager asked.

"No. The asking price is too much. Didn't you do any survey on this place before you put a price on it? The place needs so many repairs. For you to price it like this is a dream which will not come true."

CHAPTER FORTY-ONE

"What's your offer?"

Nicholas hated haggling. What the hell! He mentioned half the price.

"You have got to be joking?"

"I never joke with business. There is so much work to be done here. People's safety is important that's why I am not prepared to buy this run down place. I will need a lot of money to put it back on its feet." He pointed at one corner with cracks. "Do you see what I mean? And that's not the only damage."

The old man sighed. "That needs a little cement fed into those cracks and a bit of paint and Bob is your uncle."

Nicholas looked at the man. "Have a good day, Sir."

"Sir? What about we go lower two million?"

Nicholas's nose twitched. Did he hear him right? He almost smiled but this was business. He went on haggling until he got to the price he had in mind in the first place. "I will take it."

"Thank you, Sir. I will inform my boss."

Chapter Forty-Two

"Denise, you will never believe who knocked my mangoes on the street."

Denise grinned at her sister in law. She wondered why she was in a good mood today. She has been moody for the last few days. Well, she is always moody whenever she hears from her Brian. Her mysterious man.

"Who knocked your mangoes? They must hurt. Do you need a rub?"

"Oh Denise, you are twisting my words. My breasts are ok. I don't need a rub thanks very much. Anyway, it was Nicholas who bumped into me and my mother's mangoes went scattering all over the place putting the traffic at a standstill."

"I did wonder when I didn't have my fruits today," her mother joined in.

"He was miles away. He apologised to me non-stop."

"That's Nicholas. You wouldn't get any apology from Eric. He would tell you to visit an optician for an eye test."

"He is taking Eric out tomorrow on the Annabella boat. He asked me to accompany them. He is such a gentleman."

"I hope you said no." Abraham gave his sister a warning look.

"Abraham, why should I say a thing like that? I accepted. I want to try those boats. I have been hearing a lot about them."

"We need an extra hand here. Nadine could do with an extra hand."

"I will help," Denise offered.

"No, I forgot to tell you. We are going somewhere," Abraham informed his wife.

"Abraham, you have some kind of disease. It's only an outing for goodness sake! I can read between the lines all right," Jessica said and stormed out of the room.

"What's your disease?" Denise asked her husband.

He took a deep breath. "It's nothing. I just don't want her to run off like that leaving Nadine to cope with housework on weekends when she is supposed to be having a breather." *He was only protecting his sister. She has no idea about Nicholas and his fantasies when he was fifteen. Suppose his fantasies about Jessica are still alive and kicking?*

"Where are we going?" Denise asked.

"It's a surprise."

"I don't think I wish to go anywhere with Mother in hospital and all. I am seeing her again this evening. You will have to go alone."

"He doesn't have a disease. He is just looking out for his sister," their mother said.

"Oh Mother! Not Nicholas." Denise laughed. When she looked at her husband, his face told her something different.

"If you must know, your brother had a crush on Jessica when he was a kid," Abraham informed them. "My sister is so innocent. She doesn't know his intentions."

"How do you know? Did Nicholas tell you?"

"Eric told me. Don't ask me to repeat how he put it. Why do you think I brought him here in the first place? I wanted to put some discipline in his head."

"You believed that little fool?" Denise cried out.

"He knows more than we know. He is not a fool, believe me."

"You can't believe what comes out of that mouth."

"I don't believe what Eric says half the time."

"It is an innocent trip. Don't spoil it for them. Who hasn't been in love with Jessica? Your friends worship her."

"They are very respectable compared to that fool who sends her idiotic love notes."

"How can you say that? We don't know what he looks like.

"Hold on a second, maybe it's Eric," Denise giggled. I'd better phone Eric. I haven't spoken to him for a long time and I want to hear about this crush business."

She reached for the phone. "Aunt Meredith, hi? I am looking for Eric."

"At least you can say hi."

"I did."

"Here he is. You might cheer him up. He is driving me mad."

"Eric, why don't you visit us? You haven't been here for a while. Please say yes."

"I am not married to your husband. The man has rules the size of this universe. I just can't cope, all right? I like to chill out with friends not to be locked indoors behaving like a member of the jury. What can I do for you, sis?"

Denise looked for the words but found none.

"Has the cat cut your tongue?"

She sighed. "Eric, I just phoned to say hi. I hear Nicholas is taking you out tomorrow. Enjoy the cruise."

"If you must know, he cancelled it at the last minute. One minute he is telling me how he misses me and wants to make it up to me and the next he tells me the boat cruise is off. He says he has some important engagement. I don't really care. You have all deserted me. You can piss off." He hung up.

"The fool hung up on me."

"You hardly said a word," her husband told her.

"He never gave me a chance. I will go to bed. I don't feel that good."

"Where is Eric?" Jessica asked as she put on her seat belt.

"He didn't want to come. He behaves like a twenty one year old! 'I am kind of busy,' he told me at the last minute. That's Eric for you."

He grinned at her.

They cruised for an hour. Jessica was impressed by the service on board. "I had no idea it was like this," she said as the waiter took her order.

"This is first class," Nicholas informed her as he reduced the volume on the hi-fi. "When my sister sinks her teeth into something, that's it. I feel sorry for my brother in law. This boat business was her idea."

"They look like a lovely couple. He worships her," she told him.

"My sister overdoes it. She doesn't know when she has gone too far."

"I don't think he minds being pushed. He must know that it's not a good idea keeping eggs in one basket."

"I guess you are right but that doesn't excuse my sister's wild tongue."

Jessica noticed they were drifting further and further. "Shouldn't we be going back?"

"We are heading for Desmond's residence. They are expecting us. It's about a mile further down. Our captain knows where to drop us."

"Wow! I hear their mansion faces Lake Victoria."

"We should be there soon," he told her.

Annabella offered them cool drinks.

"What about champagne to toast Mother's health?" Desmond

suggested as he called Lucas to bring the chilled bottle.

The men took their drinks outside and left the women to gossip. "You have a lovely place here, Annabella."

"Well, I don't know about that but thanks. I have been telling Desmond to put a guesthouse here for tourists but he is against the idea. He says he doesn't want his privacy invaded."

"He may be right. Your kids feel safe here. I don't think you would feel safe with strangers roaming the place."

"Yes, that's why I haven't pushed him hard. I am thinking of the children."

Lucas refilled their glasses and left.

Jessica looked at Annabella. She laughed.

"What? You fancy him?"

"What does Desmond say about that hunk? Doesn't he feel you know... What is the word... Threatened?"

"You know men. You have to reassure them every day. It makes one tired," Annabella said with a giggle.

"I don't know men but I can imagine. Imagine working alongside that hunk."

"Don't bother about him. He is married to my childminder."

"That woman?"

"Yes, that very one."

"Love is blind, honestly. What is he doing with that dry thing?" Jessica asked.

They laughed their heads off.

"Search me."

The men joined them. "What's amusing you?" Desmond asked his wife as he refilled their glasses.

"Just this and that."

As soon as Nicholas and Jessica left, they became the topic. "Your brother is besotted with that girl."

"Did he say that?"

"Oh no! I just noticed. His eyes follow her everywhere. The poor girl has no clue that this is not the same boy she used to take out fishing with Eric and Mother. If she is not careful, she will become his target. I can bet my wife on this." He laughed at his own joke.

"You know Nicholas and women. I wonder what happened to Mina," Annabella sighed.

"Didn't I tell you not to get worked up? Boys do go through such crush stages. They are very dangerous stages."

Nicholas and Jessica went straight to hospital to see Louise.

She beamed at them. "I miss those fishing trips we used to have."

"You'd better get well soon then," Jessica told her. She lifted the baby out of her cot. "She is beautiful. Nicholas, look how pretty she is."

"Yes, she is pretty." He fidgeted in his seat. Now she has spoilt his mood. He didn't want to see Martin's handwork.

"What's her name?" Jessica asked.

"Ampumwize Kimberley," Louise said with love in her voice.

"It's a beautiful name. Please don't let anyone call her Kim. I hate it when people shorten my name. I keep reminding them that my name is Jessica not Jess."

Nicholas smiled at her. "I got the message." He turned to his mother. "I am glad you are getting out of this place. I will see you before I return."

"Where are you staying? I was wondering if you could stay with us. We have enough rooms," Louise told him knowing what the answer was.

Nicholas gave her a weak smile. "I am fine where I am. Thank you."

He dropped Jessica off and went to his bed and breakfast. It was clean. It was comfortable and above all, it was cheap. He had to be careful with money if he wanted his venture to succeed.

"How was your boat cruise? I hope Eric didn't give you an earache."

Jessica smiled at Denise weakly. Nicholas's kiss was still lingering on her lips. What the hell! "He was a perfect gentleman," her lies left her mouth smoothly. She told them how they had spent the day.

"I am glad you are in one piece," Abraham commented and excused himself.

As soon as he left the room, Jessica confessed to her sister in law that Eric didn't want to go boat cruising. "I lied because you know how Abraham is. One would think he was my father. I don't know how you put up with him." She yawned. I'd better get my beauty sleep. Good night, Denise."

"I love your brother," Denise replied. "He is a perfect gentleman."

"I was only kidding. He is a perfect brother."

Chapter Forty-Three

Martin and his family drove home in silence. "You are quiet, dear."

"I am miles away. I am glad I am out of that place. I can't stand hospitals."

"I am on leave for two months," he told her.

"Martin, that's wonderful." She meant it.

"Louise, you don't know how much I appreciate what you have given me. Please don't take more risks." His throat tightened. He blinked back the tears.

"The doctor took care of that department. We don't have to worry."

"I will treasure you, Louise." He took a deep breath. "I almost lost you."

"Well, I am here, aren't I? Cheer up!" She wished to have her family back, even a few visits.

She missed her children dearly. She was no longer angry with Nicholas for kicking her out of his house. She knew the contents of the will all right. She wasn't that stupid to let another man indulge in what Isaac left for his children. The house was Nicholas's and Eric's. She could stay there as long she didn't remarry. What about loneliness? She did the right thing in marrying Martin. They will keep each other company. He will never take Isaac's place.

"Here we are, my dear." He helped her out of the car. He carried his baby in one hand and the other hand held his wife's hand.

Louise entered her home, the home she now loved. It was comfortable with so much space inside and outside. "Yes, Ampumwize will run wild." She paused in her steps. She looked at her husband. A smile slit her cheeks. She stared at her children one by one. "You...came?"

"We had to," Nicholas replied. "We want to see where you live. It's a beautiful place, I must admit. We had a tour with your housekeeper."

"I love my old place," Eric replied sharply.

"I am happy you are home, Mother," the twins chorused.

Denise scolded her sister for not choosing her own words.

"You know we sometimes speak at the same time," Annabella told her.

Louise was so happy to see her family again. It took the birth of her baby to have her family back. "I am so pleased," she told them.

When Nicholas went back to his bed and breakfast, he found a message from his lawyer. He gave him a call straight away.

"I am glad you returned my call," Mr Baker said and got to the point. "The loan has been approved."

"Thank you, sir."

"You have your family home to thank. You have to work hard to save that house and the land around it. It would be a shame to lose such a beautiful home. It's the land and the river that got their attention. They were not ashamed to point out how many houses they could put on that land if you failed to pay off your loan.

"You'd better play your cards right or you will lose that

beautiful land."

"I know. Let's get the ball rolling. And Sir, this business is private and confidential. No family member or anyone else should know about it."

"I understand you are still sitting on your brother in law's loan."

"How... did... you find out?"

"Nosing around is my business. Why don't we meet at the Empire Hotel and talk business over a glass of wine?"

"Perfect idea."

After the meeting with his lawyer, Nicholas lay down on his bed thinking hard on how to raise money so quickly to pay off the loan. The Golden Tower Hotel will take a year to bring into good order. The way he wants. There was enough money for that. Thanks to his family house. He knew the risk he had taken using his house as collateral. He must do something to raise money quickly. What? An idea came to him and he hoped it would work.

The following day he jumped into his hired car and headed for his grandmother's village, the village he loathed. He hated village life but this time, he would have to pretend to like it.

After a few hours' driving, he arrived at Rutooma.

His granny stared at him. "Isaac?"

Nicholas beamed at her. "It's Nicholas. I am happy to see you, Granny."

She laughed revealing a set of dentures. "Nicholas! That's a joke. What brings you here? You hate village life. When were you last here?"

"I have been away. Now I am back . How are you?"

"As you can see, I am still alive. Come inside, I was about to dish out."

Nicholas wrinkled his nose. He took a seat and watched his granny heap something on his plate. He had no idea what it was. He'd better not take chances. "What is this?"

"What does it look like? It's enkuru. You scrape it from a cow's hide. It's mixed with ghee. Don't you eat ghee?"

"It's my favourite but this…"

"Your father grew up eating this food. Let us pray."

Nicholas forced the food into his mouth. His mind was on business. He must save his family home. What made him take such risk? He knew the answer. He was hungry for success. His grandmother's voice aroused him from his thoughts.

"There is no sauce on your plate, Nicholas. Give me your plate; I add more."

Nicholas beamed at her. "I am full up. Thank you."

"Now, Nicholas, what brings you here? You see, I don't get surprised when Meredith visits. She only comes here to collect fresh foods for her restaurant. As for Richard, I haven't seen him for ages."

Nicholas cleared his voice. "I am here to look at Father's land."

She looked at him curiously.

"I need money urgently."

"You have wasted your time, Nicholas. Isaac's land is not for sale. Didn't you read his will? It's for your sisters. Who knows what the future holds for them?"

"I know. I want to farm it."

She laughed. "You?"

"Yes. Me. I want to raise money very quickly. I want to get married. All I need are workers with a good manager."

She looked at him very hard. "The land is very fertile. If you put your mind to it, you will have your wife in two years' time."

"That long?"

"Then you have to work harder. I suggest you hire a tractor to clear it for you and then we will take it from there."

"Oh Granny. I am glad you are part of the venture."

"Don't push your luck, Nicholas. I am too old for such

excitements. But I will help whenever I can."

They took a walk together. She showed him the land. "Don't go beyond this border. That's your Uncle Richard's. I want you to keep out of it."

"But he is not using it. It's not as if I am putting a permanent structure on his land. I will borrow his land for a certain period. He hardly visits so he won't know about our venture." He beamed at her. "It's our little secret."

"You are a crook, Nicholas but I can see your reasoning and anyway, the land needs clearing."

They returned to the house to discuss business.

Nicholas was surprised at his grandmother's sharp ideas. She was too sharp for her age. He loved her more for that. This time, he didn't pretend to like his grandmother's village. His success lay in a hundred acres of land. He felt ashamed for not keeping in touch with his granny. Denise is the only person who likes village life. Well, he must change his ways.

"Now, Nicholas, you have to grow crops, which are in demand, and on top of that, you can keep chickens and supply the whole country."

They agreed on fresh vegetables, corn, nuts, and chickens.

"Granny, I am leaving you in charge. You know the locals, so please find good workers for me. I have to return to England. I will be back soon. He gave her his details and the money to start with. Don't let anyone know you have this money."

She touched his cheek. "I may be old, but I am not stupid. You will have your wife, Nicholas. Who is she?"

He reached in his back pocket and pulled out his wallet. He pulled out a worn out photograph. "Here she is."

The old lady looked at it. She smiled. "She very pretty," she said as she read the date on it. "It's almost torn. You must look at it every day. You remind me of your father's and your mother's photo.

"Yes, I look at it every day."

Nicholas returned to England and from the airport straight to work.

The following day the bank manager approached him to ask if he would be interested in extra hours for a few days.

"It is a good opportunity, Nicholas and besides, you have what it takes. I have seen you over the months. You have customer service experience. The whole team is pleased with you."

"What do I have to do, Sir?"

"It's a balance transfer promotion. We don't want our customers to drift away so we are offering them low interest for seven months. You have what it takes, Nicholas. You have a mouth and experience. Try it and see how it goes."

Nicholas gave him a weak smile. He knew what he was talking about. He would be getting a headache at the end of it all; an earache from irate customers. "I have never done this before," he told him.

"You will be trained on that. It's simple, believe me."

Nicholas didn't find it simple. What helped, he didn't have to face the customers he was dealing with. Thanks to British Telecom. His first customer was a woman with a hoarse voice. Her kid picked up the phone.

Nicholas introduced himself. He could hear the kid calling the mother. "Mum, it's the Credit Card Company."

"Kevin, what did I say about man eating sharks? Hey! Tell them I am not in."

"But you are in, Mum and the man says it's a promotion."

The woman picked up the phone. "What's that I hear about a promotion?"

"Mrs Andrews, I know you are one of our valued customers who have been selected for this promotion offer. We are doing a balance transfer at a very low interest rate. The promotion is for seven months. Do you have other credit cards you would like to clear?"

The woman wheezed. "I have so many of them. I will never clear them in a million years. Their interest rate is driving me bonkers. I talk in my sleep; I talk to myself on the street. I am bonkers. I know whom to blame. Why I agreed to this stupid scheme, I have no idea. They have such convincing ideas. 'Mrs Andrews, a credit card is a lifesaver'," she mimicked. "I can tell you Mr, it's life destroying."

Nicholas could feel a headache developing.

"Mrs Andrews, why don't you take this promotion opportunity we are offering you? You pay so much percentage every month."

"Mr? I don't understand percentages. Why don't you talk in pounds?"

Nicholas massaged his temple. He mentioned the figure in pounds.

"Now you are talking business, Mr. I would like your offer."

"Mrs Andrews, could you please confirm your date of birth and your password?"

"What is this? Some kind of census?"

"It's for security reasons, Mrs Andrews. I have to make sure I am dealing with the right person."

"Hold on a second Mr what's your name. How do I know you are not some crook wanting to get my credit card details so you can book yourself a holiday?"

"Mrs Andrews, you haven't given me your credit card number. You can walk away and miss this opportunity or trust me. It would be a shame to miss such good opportunity."

She gave a sigh. "I guess I will have to trust you. I must remind you that fraud is a serious crime." She gave him the information he needed.

"Your transfer will take seven days. Thanks for your time, Mrs Andrews."

Nicholas was pleased when the promotion business reached an end.

He had no time for socialising. He had two jobs and worked seven days a week. He was forever tired. What soothed him was the thought of the woman he wanted to marry.

The family will have the shock of their life when they find out his intentions. They will never agree to his choice of woman. His granny approved. He was pleased to have her on his side.

The architects were doing an excellent job on the Golden Tower Hotel. No one had a clue of who the owner was. He couldn't wait to see their faces when they found out. He went to bed feeling worn out. Tomorrow is another day. He switched off his bedside light but not his thoughts.

It was later on in the year when he received a phone call from his grandmother.

"Nicholas! I am glad I finally got in touch with you."

"Oh Granny! How are you?"

"I am still breathing. What I don't understand is why you never left your bankbook with me."

"How is the farming?"

"Why do you think I am asking for your bankbook? I have been burying your money in the ground. I will soon forget where the hole is and if I put it in my own bankbook, Richard will take over when I kick the bucket."

"Granny, I don't find that funny. Nothing is going to happen to you. As for the money you keep in the ground, it will never earn interest in an underground bank guarded by ants and termites. I will ask Eric to bring the book."

"Not Eric! You'd better send him with some paracetamol. I am too old to play games with him. But all the same, I love him. Please send him. I could do with a bit of news about everyone. I call him gossip courier."

CHAPTER FORTY-THREE

"I know what you mean. I hear he wants to do journalism."

"What's that?"

Nicholas explained as best as he could.

"I get what you mean. He has what it takes. He has a mouth."

She told Nicholas how well his farming was doing. "Lorries and pick-ups park on your farm to pick fresh foods. You have a good manager. He is talking of a pay rise."

"I am so pleased, Granny. I don't know how to thank you. If the pay rise will keep the farm ticking, please increase the manager's pay."

"Nicholas, your uncle hasn't been. His land has produced more than ten pickups of fruits and vegetables; you will have your wife soon."

Nicholas laughed. "I am blessed to have a granny like you. If I weren't engaged already, I would marry you!" How he used to hate such jokes when he was young!

"You cheeky monkey! We are already married."

Chapter Forty-Four

Desmond checked the time on his office clock. What? He shook his head. Midnight? How did the time go? He now understood why most married men volunteer to do overtime. The work place is the only place where they find peace. How long had it been since Annabella kicked him out of their marital bed? He missed her. He missed her temper, her laughter, her closeness. What did he do wrong? He did it for her. He had to do something to save her. Now there is no point crying over split milk. What he did was irreversible. There was no way of turning the clock back except to pray and wait for his wife's anger to cool down. She had been boiling for the last three months. How long could he put up with loneliness?

He switched off the lights, turned the burglar alarm on and went home. The home where he found no peace.

He arrived home to find the house in darkness except his wife's room. He could see the light under her door. He stood there for a long time thinking of his bedroom. The bedroom he hated. He sighed. This punishment has gone too far this time. He headed for his wife's bedroom. At the door, he proceeded to knock and changed his mind. Why should I knock on my own door? He opened the door.

Annabella put her novel down. She looked at him. Her nostrils flared. "What's wrong with knocking?"

"It's also my room. I don't have to knock. I have come to close the distance between us."

Her bust heaved. "The distance you created when you decided to treat yourself to a vasectomy without my knowledge. I am your wife. Didn't it cross your mind that I should know about this hideous operation?"

"I did it for you. Your health is important to me. I didn't marry you so you could breed yourself to death. I want a wife not some breeding machine."

She opened her mouth. Nothing came out. She sighed. She took a deep breath. "Desmond, I was beginning to see your reason for having that operation but now I am not sure anymore. But I am sure about one thing. I want a divorce."

He looked at her in a stunned silence. He couldn't find the words. They stared at each other. After a long silence, he finally found his voice.

"Your wish is granted. I will contact my lawyer first thing in the morning."

She stared at him not believing what she was hearing. She sat there stunned into silence. Her heart stopped for a minute. She found her breath. "What? Just like that?"

"That's what you want Annabella. I have no strength left to be having battles with you."

She stood up and looked him in the eyes. "Who is she?"

"Who is who?"

"Don't play games with me. I know there is a woman in your life."

"You haven't been doing your homework properly. There is no other woman."

"Don't lie to me, Desmond. Don't think for one minute that I didn't suspect your midnight movements. I am having dinner with a client. I am your personal secretary. I know all your appointments."

"That's the trouble, isn't it?"

"Who is she? I want to know who will be taking care of our children when they come to visit you wherever you are going. I am not getting out of this house. It never crossed your mind when you put this house in my name." She gave him a weak smile.

"I can see you have already worked out everything. I can tell you that there is no other woman."

She opened her drawer and pulled out something. "What is this?"

He looked at it. His heart raced at a speed. "What the hell were you doing in my bedroom?"

"Desmond, how long has this been going on?"

"I haven't slept with anyone. Damn it, Annabella."

"How do you explain this then?" She empted the packet of condoms. A few are missing, Desmond. How...many...times have you gone behind my back?" She sobbed. "How could you?"

"You got it all wrong. I haven't cheated on you. She turned me down." There was no point denying his attempt to bed the prettiest girl in town.

He put his hand inside his blazer pocket, out popped the two missing condoms.

She felt disgusted. "You intended to have her all night?

"Who is she? I must know who she is. I don't believe you for one minute that you haven't slept with her. This packet could be your tenth packet."

"Oh thanks very much for the compliment. I am glad I still have some life in me. I need a drink."

"Desmond! I want to know. I deserve the truth."

"Annabella. I told you she turned me down. She doesn't date. She recommended marriage counselling. Here is the card she gave me."

Annabella read the card. "Jessica? How could you? Not...long

ago you were telling me Nicholas adored her. Now you want to
bed her. Is it some kind of competition?"

"Your brother is wasting his time daydreaming. She loves
someone else. I didn't catch his name."

"You were angry of course. I can visualise the two condoms
burning your pocket."

They looked at each other hard in the eyes. "Where do we go
from here?" she asked.

Desmond was saved from answering by the ringing of the
phone.

"Aren't you a lucky woman having midnight phone calls? How
many times have you been having midnight phone calls?"

"Desmond, it's you who started all this and now you are
behaving like a wronged husband."

"You'd better pick up your bloody phone before it wakes the
children."

She picked up the phone.

"Mum, I can't sleep."

"Timothy!" Does your nanny know you are making midnight
phone calls?"

"She is kind of passed out. Isabel and Celestina made her tired.
I can hear her snoring. I want to come home."

"Timothy, go back to bed. I will pick you up in the morning,
all right?"

"I am scared." He sobbed.

"What's the matter, baby?"

"I can't stand it. My friend Allan has a dad who is not his
dad. I don't like it. He beats him badly. I am not having another
daddy." He sobbed.

Annabella wished for the floor to swallow her. "Timothy!
What a thing to say."

"It's true. His dad left. His mum got him another daddy.
Mum, are you getting us another daddy?"

"What makes you ask such a question?"

"You quarrel all the time. I don't like it. I don't want a new daddy. That's what Allan said to me. He...said that...you will get me a new daddy if you keep on quarrelling with my daddy."

Her eyes smarted with tears. "Your friend got it wrong and you shouldn't be telling him what goes on in this house. Your daddy and I have things to sort out. We...don't quarrel." She looked at Desmond. She wished he could leave the room.

"Is Daddy not leaving us?"

Annabella sighed. "Timothy, go back to bed. I will talk to you when I pick you up."

"I want my daddy," he sobbed.

"Well, you can have him. Here he is." She handed her husband the phone and left the room. She needed a strong drink. She poured herself a brandy. She was about to put away the bottle when he appeared in the doorway. "Make a double for me. The marriage counselling I have just received from my eight-year-old son has left my throat dry. I had no idea they were spending the night at my mother's place. Why didn't you say?"

"I wanted to talk to you in private. What did he say?"

"He asked me whether I am going to get him a new mum. He doesn't like a new mum. His friend Harriet has a new mum. She beats her all the time."

Annabella wrinkled her nose. "I don't know who has been feeding him such nonsense. I will wring their necks when I find out. No wonder he has been restless. Poor mite!"

"We can't ignore his reasoning." He winked at her. "We better go back to where we were before...all this happened." He drained his glass. "I am falling on my feet. I am shattered."

He kissed her gently on the lips. "Goodnight, my treasure. We don't want to upset our son, do we?"

Annabella sat down thinking hard on what step she must take. Did she still love him or will she be staying for the sake of her children?

She sighed. She never thought a marriage was so hard to maintain. It had to be watered like flowers. Damn it! She walked lazily to her room. She wasn't surprised when she found her husband on his side of the bed lying there in erotica style.

"I guess we have to keep on watering this marriage for it to survive," she said as she joined him.

"I will be right behind you. I am sorry for all the trouble I caused you. I love you, Annabella."

"There is no point mentioning the operation. We can't turn back the clock. As for cheating on me, I am insulted. Do I look revolting to you and you have to shoot off to another woman and the woman happens to be Denise's sister in law, my mother's therapist who made her drop Valium addiction? She is family and a friend. How could you?"

"I never slept with her."

"In your mind you did. Damn it!"

"I think you are going too far with this. Please don't approach Jessica about it. She put me in my right place. I am so ashamed. I don't know where I will put my eyes when we visit them."

She sighed. "Suppose you meet someone who is not strong like Jessica?"

"Don't give me a reason, Annabella," he said as he entwined his leg with hers.

His live body made her tense. His erection dug into her thigh. She closed her eyes. "Desmond, I am not in the mood."

"I haven't done a thing. Good night, dear, tomorrow is another day."

Chapter Forty-Five

"This tray business has gone too far. How long has she been ill? A week? Two weeks?" Jerome asked his family. "Not long ago I saw a hairdresser leaving her room."

"Melanie, tell your aunt to come down for lunch. How can a simple cough keep her in her room for a week? I haven't even heard her coughing."

The whole family ignored him and tucked into their food.

"Has she been to hospital?" he asked.

"Jerome! Leave the girl alone," his mother said. "She is moping about something. I can't put my finger on it. She is not that ill for hospital treatment." She knew what was ailing her granddaughter. She decided to keep her mouth shut. She had listened into the phone call she'd received a week ago. Her secret admirer wanted to meet her for the first time. She knew where the meeting would take place.

She hoped Jessica would be ok.

"Well, she better come down and eat lunch with the rest of the family," Jerome pointed out.

At that moment Jessica walked in looking stunning in her three-piece suit and a hairstyle that makes heads turn. Her nails were painted in light pink to match her suit. "Hi!" she said to no one in particular.

Jerome looked at his daughter. "I hear you are ill."

"I haven't been feeling well, Father. I feel better now. I am going to town to do a bit of shopping."

The brothers looked at each other. "She is lying," they whispered to each other.

Denise excused herself and followed Jessica to the gate. "Where are you going, Jessica? You look different. I mean for someone who has been ill to look so glamorous. Please tell me. We are friends, aren't we?"

She beamed at her sister in law. "It's time!"

"I don't understand."

"I am meeting Brian B at Lake Victoria tourist resort. If you want to come with me, be my guest – as long as Abraham doesn't come with you."

"How will you recognise your Brian? The place is so big and crowded." Denise asked.

"He told me what he would be wearing. A pair of denim jeans and a white T-shirt. I am scared, Denise. I hope it's not Desmond."

"Desmond? What has he got to do with this?"

"He wanted to bed me a few weeks ago. I gave him a piece of my mind."

"What a cheating bastard! Why didn't you tell me?"

"What would you have done? Please don't mention this to Annabella."

"I will come with you," she said.

Jessica shook her head. "I don't want my brothers to spoil this meeting. The moment you come with me, Abraham will want to know where exactly you are heading for. I will be fine, I guess. I will tell you all about it if I come back."

"Why are you using if? You will come back. There are so many people about. If he tries to be funny, run for it."

Jessica looked at her sandals. "That's why I am wearing

sandals."

As soon as Jessica's taxi drove out of the gate, Denise and Abraham jumped in their car. "I don't know why I am doing this, Denise. I like my Sunday nap, the only time I have to catch up with my wife."

"Abraham, you are rattling like an old woman. Watch that marketer. She will cross the road in a second."

"Damn! Doesn't she know where to cross?"

"It's a free country, Abraham."

"I don't see Jessica's car anymore."

"Don't worry. I know the meeting place," she told him.

Jessica got out of the taxi. She noticed she was shaking. She wanted to run back but curiosity got the better of her and her love for Brian B, the man she had never met except through his love notes which had made her wait for nine years. Was the waiting worth it? One way to find out. She could see a man of Brian's description standing twenty yards away. He was facing away towards the Lake Victoria. He looked tall, muscular, nice haircut, good posture, and nice butt. What needed looking at is his face. If the face was as good as the behind, then the waiting had been worth it. She wished Denise were with her. She felt so lonely and scared.

Abraham and Denise took their cover. "He doesn't look threatening," said Denise.

"Don't judge a book by its cover, Denise. It's what is in that confused mind that bothers me. I have never come across such foolishness where a girl waits for nine years for someone they have no clue about. My sister is a fool. She is not getting younger. At least we warned her."

Jessica took a deep breath. "Brian?"

CHAPTER FORTY-FIVE

"Jessica?" The man answered but didn't turn.

Jessica had no choice but to face him. She stood there in stunned silence. Her heart stopped for a minute. "Jesus of Nazareth!" she cried out. "It's you." She read the writings on his T-shirt: "WILL YOU MARRY ME, JESSICA?"

"I am sorry I shocked you." He handed her one red rose. "There is more where this came from."

"I am gobsmacked," she told him.

"What do you say?"

"I...need time."

"I can wait. While we are waiting for your answer, why don't we cruise around? I have a lot to tell you. I booked the boat for three hours. What do you say?"

She nodded. She had no words to say to him. She wanted to weep on his chest and ask him why he took such a long time to reveal himself.

The man dismissed the waiter. "We don't want anyone on board except the captain." He opened a bottle of champagne.

They sipped their champagne not saying a word obviously gathering their thoughts.

After a while, Jessica cleared her voice. "Yes."

He beamed at her. "I will cherish you all my life, Jessica."

Abraham and his wife checked their watches now and again. "Where are they? They have been gone two hours now."

Then they saw the boat returning. To their horror, there were no passengers.

"What the hell!" Abraham cried out and ran to the captain. "Where are the passengers you took two hours ago?"

The captain gave him a wicked smile. "They are in heaven, sir. I have never seen such..."

Abraham grabbed the man by his collar. "I will make you shit if you don't tell me..."

"Abraham, violence will not tell us anything," Denise scolded him.

He dropped the man. "Where are they?"

"Why, they took the walk on the wild side to cool off the champagne. I have never seen such romance in my life. I have something to teach my wife tonight."

"I asked you a question. Where did you drop them?"

"The couple were heading for Entebbe airport."

Abraham dragged his wife behind him. "Hurry up, Denise. I will kill the bastard."

The captain laughed at their disappearing backs. "Wrong direction, Sir. That will teach you a lesson not to mess with the Annabella captain."

Abraham and his wife ran to the help desk at Entebbe Airport. "Could you please call this person to come forward?"

The announcement was made three times; no one by that name came forward.

"We are wasting our time here," Denise told him. "We must phone home. The whole family must be pretty worried."

Abraham phoned home and told them what had happened.

"I am calling the police," his father said and hung up.

The family looked at him willing him to say something. His tears told them what they feared.

He sat there for a long time feeling numb.

Margaret sat by his feet. "Jerome? What happened?"

He told her.

"Should I call the police?"

He shook his head. "Give me the phone, dear." He looked at his family. "Do any of you know Desmond's telephone number?"

Melanie was the first one to volunteer.

Jerome looked at her curiously. "How do you know their number?"

Don't play lawyer with me. This is a matter of life and death. Who cares how I got the number? She almost told her grandfather. "I got it from Timothy the last time he was here. We look after them from time after time so it's necessary to know their home number in case of emergency. Do you need anything else, grandpa?"

"Leave us alone."

"This is Jerome of J& Sons solicitors; may I speak to Mr Tumwiine?"

"Oh! My husband is not in. May I help you?"

"I suppose you can. One of your boats was hired out to a Mr Brian B. Could you please give me his full details?"

"Is there any problem, Sir?"

"Yes, my daughter is missing."

Annabella felt as if she had been scalded with hot water. Desmond was supposed to be replenishing the canteen on the boat. Did he lie to her? Is the affair still going on? "Oh God!" she moaned.

"Please Mrs Tumwiine, I need the details urgently."

"Of course, give me a few minutes to check the computer."

Annabella looked at the list. She couldn't find the name mentioned.

"Excuse me, Sir. There is no one by that name. Do you know when the boat was hired and what type of boat?"

"The boat is The Annabella."

"That is my boat. A family boat. We don't hire it out to anyone except for special occasions. Please give me a second to check another file."

She looked at the file. She blinked. "Jesus of Nazareth! I am coming over, Sir."

"Who is it? My daughter is in danger."

"Your daughter is not in danger. She...knows...the person very well. I am coming over. Oh God!" She hung up.

The whole family stared at Jerome? "Well?" Margaret asked.

"Your daughter knows her secret admirer. What a waste of my afternoon. I am going to bed."

At that moment Abraham and Denise walked in. "Any news?"

"Yes, your sister knows how to look after herself."

"If I went missing no one would raise an eyebrow," Angela complained.

"Why is that my pie?" her father asked.

"Now, I finally got your attention. I need a netball kit."

Nobody paid attention to her request because at that moment, Jessica walked in with a smile almost splitting her cheeks.

Chapter Forty-Six

"What have you got to say for yourself?" Jerome asked his daughter.

Jessica looked at their worried faces. "Has someone died?"

"Sit down, Jessica," her father thundered. "We have been worried about you. You lied saying you were going to town to do shopping."

"That's not the hairstyle you left home with," Mworozi put in.

She gave him a cold stare. "You have a crude mind brother. I might just as well tell you. Mr Brian B has asked me to marry him." She looked at them to see any effect on their faces. She saw none.

"I accepted. He is coming here this evening to meet you all." She smiled.

No one said anything.

"I thought you wanted me off the shelf?"

"Who is he?" her father asked.

"I would rather not say. You will see him this evening."

"Hoy! Hold on a second. You almost ran me over."

"You!" Annabella pointed a finger at her husband. "We need to talk."

Jessica checked the menu a second time. "It will do," she told the cook.

In the passage, she bumped into Denise. "Hi!"

"Who is he?"

"You will know him in good time. I am going to lie down for a bit. I need to gather my thoughts." She winked at her sister in law.

At seven o'clock, the bell on the gate rang. "I will get it." Jessica reached for a remote control. She was nervous again. She fanned herself with her hand. She watched her family's anticipation. You will have to like him, she thought to herself.

"I am glad you could make it. Please come in."

He was now dressed in a suit and a tie. He looked handsome and fetching. Well-groomed is the word to use, Jessica thought as she ushered him into the sitting room.

The family gasped at the same time.

Jessica held his hand. "Nicholas, please meet my family. My family, this is Nicholas. He asked me to marry him. I agreed."

Denise looked at her brother. "Is this some kind of joke?"

Jerome cleared his voice. "Young man, you have wasted your time. I will not let my daughter marry my former lousy messenger, the person who deserted his family especially his own mother. My daughter is used to having family around her. Are you looking for a mother in my daughter?"

Jessica cried out. "That's insulting. Please rephrase that, Father."

Jerome ignored his daughter's hurt. He addressed Nicholas who by now was seething with anger. How he wished to punch the daylight out of this man but his love for Jessica stopped him in his track.

"I will not allow my daughter to be married to someone who kicked his own mother out of her home. The home she worked so hard to create."

"Jerome, you are going too far. Would you have put up with a stepfather if I had remarried? I will not hear you talk like that, Jerome." His mother scolded him. "You can hold on to your daughter for different reasons. The boy was protecting what was rightly his. Please take a seat, Nicholas."

Nicholas looked at the woman he loves so much disappearing before his eyes. He couldn't bear it any longer. All this working and waiting has been for nothing.

He bowed his head. "Good evening to you all. I will see myself out."

"Nicholas! You can't listen to all that. You can't. I love you."

He looked at her. "Jessica, listen to your heart. What does it say? Bye Jessica."

She felt too numb to move.

"Please sit down, Jessica," Denise told her and reached for her hand.

Jerome gave his daughter in law a cold stare. "You! You knew all along that your brother was wasting my daughter's life and you never said a word."

"I...didn't..." Denise had no words.

"I thought you were different from my son's ex wives."

"I... It's not..."

"I should have known what kind of person you are."

"I am..."

"Do you know what your silence has done to my daughter?"

Denise was now crying openly. What hurt most, her husband said nothing.

"Your silence has turned my daughter into a spinster. She will never marry at this age."

"Denise didn't know a thing," Jessica stood up for her sister in law.

"You! You don't know the meaning of marriage. Well, let's see what those love notes will do to you in your lonely time."

Denise stood up without excusing herself. She took two stairs at a time.

She could hardly see through her tears. She must get out of this house and fast. She started piling her clothes into the suitcase.

"What do you think you are doing?" Abraham reached for her.

"Don't touch me Abraham. I will not stay married to a man who can't stand up for his wife. I saw accusation in everyone's eyes including yours. I had no idea about Nicholas's intentions. I swear on my father's grave," she sobbed.

"I am so sorry, Denise. We have never challenged Father when he is in a raging mood. He is upset. We all are."

"Well, your father mentioned ex-wives, now he can add another one on top. Three ex-wives. How does that sound?"

"Do you love me, Denise?"

"Don't ask me such a question, Abraham. Get out of my way."

"Denise, if you really care for me, don't go away. I am sorry. I was so shocked. If you want me to go downstairs and knock my father down in order to save my marriage, I swear, I will do it."

She looked at his face covered in tears. She bit her lip. She took a step towards him. Before she could reach him, there was a knock on the door.

"Aunt Denise, you have to hurry up. It's Jethro. He is throwing up," Melanie's voice rang out.

Abraham and Denise looked at their pale son. "What's the matter, darling?"

He choked on his tears. "My...tummy...hurts," he sobbed.

"Angela, you were in charge of the children today. What did he eat?" Abraham asked his niece.

Angela recited all the foods Jethro had consumed including the cheese he was allergic to.

Abraham looked at his niece. "You gave him cheese? You know he doesn't eat cheese."

"He cried for it. It was a tiny bit. What's the big deal?"

A thundering slap silenced her.

"Abraham, don't beat her again. We have to take him to hospital."

Melanie grinned at her sister. "Did you have to risk that thundering slap?"

"At least Aunt Denise forgot her packing. It worked for Aunt Annabella, remember? I love Aunt Denise. I don't want her to go."

"It worked for Aunt Annabella because Timothy is a good actor. I don't think Jethro will keep his mouth shut knowing his cartoons are on soon."

"Just pray they don't find out or else you will get more thundering slaps. Don't forget that Rosanna was in hearing range. Just pray that she didn't hear you. Let me see to your cheek."

"I am fine, thank you very much."

"I am trying to help, don't bite me."

"How is Aunt Jess?" Angela asked.

"She is crying her eyes out. I would cry if I were in her shoes. He is a hunk. Well polished and he speaks well."

"Shut up Melanie! You will set off Grandpa if he should hear you talking like that."

Abraham and Denise sat by their son's bedside.

The tests showed nothing. "We are keeping him in overnight for observation," the doctor told them.

Jethro looked pale and convincing. He closed his eyes and kept his ears open.

"I am still going, Abraham. You can't stop me."

Abraham took a deep breath, "So, the word love has been replaced by the word divorce?"

"I haven't mentioned divorce."

"That's where it's leading, or have I got it wrong?"

The sobbing sound stopped them going any further. "My tummy hurts."

Both parents held his hand. "The doctor said you would be ok. Promise me you will not eat cheese again," his father said with a soothing voice.

"I...I...want to go home," he sobbed.

"The doctor wants to give you another check up in the morning."

"I... I...didn't eat cheese. I want to go home. My cartoons," he sobbed.

"Jethro, don't cry baby. There will be more cartoons tomorrow," Denise soothed.

He got out of the bed and sat on his mother's lap. "I want to go home now."

"Not now Jethro, the doctor has to keep an eye on you." Abraham put his hand on his son's forehead. "I can feel a bit of temperature developing."

"I am fine," he pouted. "It's all Angela's fault now I have to miss my cartoons."

"Yes, she shouldn't have given you cheese."

"She didn't. I am not ill. I want to go home." He recited what had happened and why.

Abraham looked at his wife. "Angela!" He laughed. "She takes after her grandmother. Mother is an expert when it comes to marriage counselling. I guess we have to take this chap home before he misses his cartoons."

They arrived home only to find the house in silence.

The only person who spoke was Jerome. "Denise, my child, I owe you an apology."

"Accepted. If you don't mind, I need to lie down." She excused herself.

CHAPTER FORTY-SIX

"Denise, your sister in law's ran away," he said.

Denise looked at her father in law in the face with a cold look. "I didn't help her pack. Excuse me." She swept out of the room.

Abraham followed her with Jethro in his arms. He passed Angela in the passage who grinned at him.

"I owe you an apology, kid."

"Well, it doesn't come cheap. I need a new netball kit."

He grinned at her. "Consider it done."

Chapter Forty-Seven

Nicholas stared at Jessica. He felt paralysed. He wanted to reach for her. Hold her in his arms. But his legs failed to move forward. He was lost for words. In her hand, she held a wooden box.

"Nicholas? I listened to my heart." She waited for him to say something, but nothing came.

They stared at each other. After what seemed an eternity, Nicholas held out his arms. She walked into them and sobbed herself silly. "I am sorry about my father. He didn't mean to insult you like that. He was too upset because he thought I had been kidnapped."

"Let's not talk about your father. I am happy you are here. I love you Jessica. As I told you earlier, Mina is a friend. She is an actress. At the time Annabella and Mother met her, she was still practising her acting.

"You don't know what it meant to her when she realised that Mother and Annabella had believed that she was engaged to me. She is now a first class actress. It was all acting. Nothing else. You are the only girl I love."

Her cheeks flushed but her dark skin saved her ass. "I believe you. I love you too, Nicholas. You are my friend. I fell in love with your love notes – except for one love note."

"I know. I am sorry."

"I will carry your luggage."

She handed him the wooden box containing her love notes. They got into the lift to their penthouse. The only person on site was a security guard.

"This is our place," he told her.

"Nicholas! It's beautiful!" The whole place was decorated in white.

"Do you like the colour?"

"It's beautiful! Just like my room at home."

"Yes, I did it for my bride. I will show you the rest of the hotel when you have rested. We are opening it in a week's time. I want you by my side as my wife when we open for business."

"I am touched. But it's short notice."

"We must make the necessary arrangement quickly," he told her.

"What about the parents?"

"We are adults. I will not be insulted a second time, so forget about blessings. I know one person who is dying to meet you. She will bless us. We are going to see my granny in the morning.

"Make yourself at home; I will make a few phone calls regarding your wardrobe. You need a change of clothes." He eyed her three-piece suit. "It suits you." He smiled at her.

He phoned a few shops. They wanted to know the size.

Jessica took over the ordering. She told them the size and style.

An hour later, there was a knock on their door.

It was Eric. "I hope I am not interrupting anything," he grinned at his brother.

"What are you doing here?"

"You phoned me. I am here."

"I didn't mean you should come here. There is such thing as phones. Don't you know how to use a phone?"

"Please let me in. I have some news. The whole town is buzzing with your actions you two. I am happy for you."

Jessica smiled at him. "Please come in. Nicholas and I wanted a few things sorted out."

Eric took his seat.

Nicholas opened the wooden box containing Jessica's love notes. "What have you got to say for yourself, Eric?"

"I did it to help you brother, especially when I thought she was drifting. I had to do something."

"You mean using crude words? Eric, I almost lost her for your careless words. My words had meaning in them. But you, you used crude language. You must apologise to her at once."

"That was a joke. I do apologise."

Jessica smiled at him remembering one love note she had received which left her in tears. 'Sweet cherry lips, I love you I can't wait to hold you in my arms. Nice butt by the way!' Jessica held Eric's hand. "Mr? You can never get a girl's attention if you use such language. I do forgive you."

"Thanks Jess…Jessica."

"You are learning."

There was another knock. It was Jessica's shopping.

"It's getting late, Eric. You'd better go home."

"Welcome to the Bahiika family," he told Jessica and excused himself.

She grinned at him.

They started their journey early in the morning. They hoped to be back in town the same day. "It is a long drive," he told Jessica.

"I don't mind," she reassured him.

They arrived at the village to find their granny busy with the workers on the farm. "Nicholas! Help me with these tomatoes. The pick up will be here in a minute."

"Granny, please meet Jessica, my fiancée."

"She is beautiful! I wish you a happy life, kids. I'd better prepare you a nice brew. But I've run out of tea leaves." She picked a few herbs called 'Enyabarashana'.

"Oh no! Not that. I will run to the shop, Granny.

Jessica stayed with Nicholas's grandmother. She found her entertaining just like her own granny.

She gave her a tour of the farm. "Nicholas did all this for you. I have never seen a more determined child in my life."

Jessica was taken aback by the amount of food growing on the farm.

They stayed for a few hours. They invited the granny to the wedding even though they had no clue when it would take place.

"I don't mind coming at all. I haven't seen Meredith for some time. I will stay with her."

"I will send Eric to pick you up in three days' time."

They arrived in town only to discover the newspapers splashed with the news of their actions. 'A millionaire's daughter runs off with her father's messenger.' 'A former employee who now owns The Golden Tower Hotel...' They went on to describe Nicholas and Jessica's lives.

"I can't believe this." Jessica collapsed on the sofa. "Who told them about our lives? I lead a private life. I like a private life."

"You don't have to look far, dear. Eric works for the 'Here and There' newspaper on a regular basis as a messenger. He thinks that in the process of time, he will be made an editor. He is studying towards that. He must have sold them this story. Who else would know about my work in the UK and this place? The only people who know about The Golden Tower Hotel are my lawyer and Eric."

She touched his arm. "Nicholas, I am pleased you look out for him."

"I have to. No matter how naughty he is, at the end of the day, he is my only brother."

Eric phoned them to reassure them that he did it for publicity purposes. "Nicholas, The Golden Tower Hotel is opening in a few days' time. I thought a bit of advertising was necessary. I am sorry if you felt harassed. Is Jessica all right?"

"Stressed out, thanks to you."

"I am sorry."

"Well, if you should try this again without consulting me first, I will buy you out."

Eric thought of his share. "I promise, brother. I won't open family secrets again. I am always getting into trouble."

"You don't know your limits. Eric, find a good suit. I want you to give away Jessica. We are getting married on The Annabella boat. Desmond agreed to be my best man."

"Nicholas! What a brilliant idea. You don't know what a little publicity..."

"Eric, I said no more publicity. This is a private wedding. I don't want anyone spoiling this day. The old man may even turn up to snatch his daughter before she says 'I do'. I couldn't bear it, Eric. Keep it quiet. Ok?"

"All right. I know. I heard some gossips saying you can never marry Jessica according to the custom. That's bullshit, isn't it?"

"I would like to see someone try to stop me. I love Jessica. She loves me. We are not related. What is there to stop us getting married? It's all right for his son to marry my sister but it's not all right for me to marry his daughter? He needs his head checked out. Eric? Keep your mouth shut."

"My lips are sealed." He hung up and whistled. "Dream on brother."

He dialled his work place.

Chapter Forty-Eight

Jerome and his family had no escape. The phone rang non-stop and the reporters lined up at their gate wanting to know his comment about his daughter's forthcoming marriage to his former employee who owns one of the best hotels in Uganda. "What do you say about his achievement?"

Jerome had nothing to say. He refused to read newspapers or watch television. He left that to his grandchildren who were tickled by their aunt's behaviour. None of his children had ever defied him. How could she embarrass him in such a manner? How he wished he could lock himself up.

"Jerome, sulking will not bring Jessica back. The food is getting cold," his wife said with worry in her voice. She was hurt as well but there was no one to comfort her. It had always been her duty to solve family problems. Now, she had no idea how to bring her husband back to reality. "Jessica is no longer a child, dear. Let her go."

"She is already gone, Margaret. All our teaching amounted to nothing."

Margaret sighed. "Our daughter is not bothered about our happiness. You saw her earlier on television taking over the interview and advertising their hotel free of charge."

Margaret had been impressed by her daughter's confidence.

Jessica had looked at the reporter in the eye. "Mr reporter, are you married?" she asked as she arranged flowers in one of the suites.

"Yes, why?"

"Do you love your wife?" she asked as she checked the beverages in the fridge."

"Very much, where is this leading? I am supposed to be interviewing you."

"Mr reporter, then you know what love means. Love has no border. Nicholas is my father's former employee. He worked as a messenger, so what? We all start with one," she said as she used a remote control to open the curtains and show off a beautiful swimming pool with grass thatched gazebos around it. The interview went on and on from one floor to another until the reporter started breathing through his mouth. Then she led him to the restaurant area where Nicholas was. He kissed her on the mouth without shame. Then she offered the reporter a cold drink. Margaret had switched off the television only to be scolded by Melanie. "Oh Granny! This is hilarious! We were enjoying that. Imagine our aunt taking over the interview. Wow! That kiss!" She giggled ignoring her grandmother's distress.

Abraham and Denise argued in their bedroom. "Abraham, Nicholas is my brother. I have to attend his wedding. As for Jessica, she was there for me when I needed a maid of honour. She dropped everything in order to be with me. I won't let her down. I am going out with Annabella to help her with her wedding gown."

"In that case I won't stop you. What is this? Some kind of swapping? They can't marry and you know it."

"Please Abraham! It's all right for you to marry me but it's not all right for my brother to marry your sister. Wise up man!"

There was a knock on their door.

CHAPTER FORTY-EIGHT

It was Mworozi and Nadine. "What are you two fighting about? We could hear you from our quarters."

"My wife and I are going out to buy a present for Jessica," Mworozi announced.

Denise looked at her husband. "Well?"

"Abraham, she is our sister. We are invited. I am not missing the opening of The Golden Tower Hotel. I booked a honeymoon suite."

Nadine's cheeks lit up. "They need our support," she said.

"Abraham, have you made your reservation?" his brother asked.

"Don't be silly Mworozi. I am not attending the wedding to begin with."

"But you can support your brother in law. Well? Think about it. Nadine, let's go."

Denise stared at their disappearing backs. "At least someone is talking sense. The honeymoon suite is tempting. You should see the place, Abraham. I don't know how he managed to achieve so much within a very short time. Why did he keep it a secret?"

"You will have to ask him. As for my sister, she is so selfish. Father is really hurt. He loved her so much, you know being the only girl."

"One would think that my brother is a cannibal or a vampire. He adores her." She gave him a seductive kiss to lighten his mood. She could feel his anger melting away replaced by moans. "I got you." She smiled as she worked on him until he looked threatening like a live wire.

"We'd better make a reservation. The honeymoon suite is tempting. Only to support your brother if it pleases you."

"Only to support Jessica and Nicholas. They need our support," she told him.

Annabella checked 'The Annabella' a second time. "It's perfect,

Desmond.

"My brother is a romantic fool. What is he thinking of exchanging his vows on a boat?"

"You heard his reply when you said the house of God was the best place to exchange marriage vows.

"He said to you, 'Why do people kneel in front of their beds when they want to connect with God? Imagine rushing to church each time you want to pray. Annabella, God is in every place. This is where I want to be married'."

She eyed their children enjoying themselves. "We'd better keep this lot under control. Oh there comes the groom and the Bahiika clan including the Reverend who married our parents. Nicholas has really done it. You are forgetting your duties, Desmond. You should be next to him, telling him where he doesn't understand."

"He is perfectly ok. Aunt Meredith taught him when he was fifteen. That aunt of yours is something else. I couldn't believe it when Nicholas told me."

"That's Aunt Meredith for you. She is very helpful in most cases," she replied.

Nicholas's family took their seats. Louise looked smashing in a Banyankole traditional dress. She looked young for her age. Her hairstyle was something to look at with envy. One could only guess what had happened with her greyish hair. Thanks to Dark and Lovely hair dye. Martin must have been waiting for this day. His suit was a perfect style. Their daughter Kimberley sat between them holding onto both parents.

Meredith beamed at everyone. "This is a romantic wedding, Eliot. I feel like marrying you a second time."

"Why don't you?" He grinned at her.

Nicholas's grandmother beamed at her family. "Your father would have been proud of you, Nicholas."

Nicholas looked up in the sky. "He is watching us."

Another car came, out popped Abraham and his brother with

his wife Nadine all dressed up in Baganda traditional dress. They took their seats. Abraham smiled at Annabella. "I didn't know your boat was this big and stylish."

"Thank you. Desmond and I do our best. Why don't you have a cruise of your life? We operate seven days a week. If you hire it for special occasions, we need a week's notice to meet your requirements."

"You have a business head, Annabella. You are even looking for business at your brother's wedding. Wait until I tell Denise," he grinned at her.

Annabella grinned back. She was glad they had come. She could see tension around them but they will melt in time.

Another car arrived. It was Jessica looking stunning in her white wedding gown and Eric in a full suit looking mature until he opened his mouth. Denise, Melanie and Angela looked smashing in their outfits.

Jessica held Eric's hand and walked to her waiting man.

It broke Abraham's heart to see Eric doing the job he should have done.

Half way through, Eric looked at Mworozi and Abraham with a questioning look. "May I?" He mouthed the words.

"It's all right Eric." The two brother's stood up at the same time.

"Mworozi, give her away," Abraham told him.

Mworozi matched his sister to Nicholas.

Jessica tried to control her tears but it was too late. She hugged her brother. "Thank you, Mworozi."

The marriage went on as planned. Nicholas breathed out when the Reverend pronounced them husband and wife.

Eric smiled as he watched the camera crews doing their job. Nicholas will kill me for this, he thought to himself.

Nicholas kissed his bride. "I will carry you to our waiting car."

They were not surprised when reporters pushed microphones in their faces. "Let them, it's a free world and besides, they have to earn a living somehow," Nicholas said to his wife who looked troubled. She wasn't bothered about the microphones in her face. She was worried about her parents. They will never forgive me but this is my life, she comforted herself.

They arrived at The Golden Tower Hotel to find a queue of guests booking in.

"We are almost full," the manager told Nicholas.

"I am pleased, Mr Musoke. Excellent work."

The wedding reception took place in the restaurant area.

"Nicholas dear, where on earth did you get experienced architects to transform this place? It's changed completely," his aunt commented.

"I am glad you like it, Aunt Meredith. I have you to thank. The encouraging words you said to me when I was fifteen remained with me during my struggle to build myself. I never drifted from your teachings."

"I would have been disappointed, Nicholas," she laughed with pride in her voice.

Nicholas gave a speech thanking everyone including his father in law who gave him his first job. "It was my first job that opened my eyes." He thanked Martin who made him follow into his father's footsteps. "Thank you, Uncle Martin. I owe you big time." *He was talking business, nothing else. Martin's love story is none of his business as far as he is concerned. One person he could not avoid was his stepsister. Well, he will have to love her since Jessica is fascinated with her.*

"Your father in law had no clue when he opened your eyes," one man shouted out. "Isn't she beautiful?" There was laughter and joy.

Nicholas thanked his grandmother. "Thank you grandma.

CHAPTER FORTY-EIGHT

You and I have a lot to discuss."

"I bet!" his uncle mumbled. "You two are crooks. Using my land to better yourselves." He took a swig on his vodka. He smiled at his nephew. "I am proud of you Nicholas. Cheers!"

Louise's speech was a simple one. She stood up. "I don't know why I have to stand up. What else is there to say when two families become one? Nicholas and Jessica, I wish you a happy marriage." She sat down.

"Thanks, Mother." He beamed at her. "I love you," he mouthed the words.

She only had to divorce Martin, she would have her home back, he thought to himself.

She gave him a hundred watt smile. She mouthed the same words: "I love you."

The party came to an end. Nicholas almost cried when he saw all his relatives picking keys for their suites.

"We are here to support you," they told him. He blinked away the tears when Jessica's family did the same. "We have our own suite," Melanie and Angela boasted.

"Get easy on room service, girls or you will burn holes in my wallet," their father told them.

"That's wishful thinking, dear. I heard Melanie talking of Jacuzzi and champagne," his wife told him.

Denise and Annabella helped their sister in law out of her wedding dress.

"We are not far away if you need something." They gave her their room numbers.

She looked at them. "You are spending the night here?"

"Yes. In your honeymoon suites. Desmond is tickled by the idea. I'd better go before he sends a police search."

Jessica and Denise laughed as soon as Annabella left the room. "She is a live wire." They giggled.

"Denise, what did I tell you on your marriage ceremony regarding Annabella and her husband? She led you to believe that she hated her husband."

"I know. They adore each other. But sometimes Annabella goes too far with her temper."

Jessica said nothing about that. Her mind switched back to her family. She was sorry she had hurt them so badly. She hoped they would forgive her for her actions. She was happy she was now married to the man she had waited nine years for. If Nicholas had approached her with a marriage proposal when he was fifteen, would she have taken him seriously? The answer is no. She would have told him to grow up. Now at twenty-four, he was a man in every sense. She was pleased with what he had achieved through hard work.

Denise aroused her from her thoughts.

"Jessica, I have a message from Granny. She was with you spiritually."

"She is not angry with me?"

"No. She sent you this." Denise handed her a tiny box.

Jessica opened it. "It's her favourite necklace. Oh Denise," she cried.

"Now, you will set me off. As for Mother, she said she understands. She wishes you well." She handed her an envelope. There was a cheque in both names.

Jessica looked at it. "It's Nicholas's and mine." She read the message that came with it. *It's from the bottom of my heart. I wish you happiness in your marriage. Love Mother.*

"As for Father, give him time, ok? He will come round," Denise comforted her.

"I am sorry I hurt him but I couldn't let him deny me what I have waited nine years for. I am in love with your brother, Denise. I felt something for him when he came to see Mother in hospital. I was a bit troubled because of Brian B. I felt I was cheating on him whenever my thought went to Nicholas. Nicholas's kiss lingered on my mind for quite a long time. I never thought that a kiss could affect one's feelings like that."

"You poor mite!" Denise laughed. "I better go before I go too far. Do you need anything before I go?"

She shook her head. "I have your numbers in case I... need you. Thanks very much, Denise."

A few minutes later, Nicholas joined his bride. He still couldn't believe that Jessica was now his wife. She was still the same girl he fell in love with nine years ago. The age difference didn't bother him at all. He had been hurt when his father in law pointed it out but now he was glad they had taken the step they did. He had no idea of how he would have lived without Jessica the girl he loves dearly. He will have to apologise to his in laws of course. There will be a heavy fine for his actions. "Whatever the price, she is worth it." He felt himself stir in the lower region. His heart raced at a speed. "Are...you...ok, my golden girl?" He handed her red roses.

"Nicholas! You spoil me. The smell is so intoxicating." She inhaled. "I am in heaven!"

He grinned at her.

Her eyes travelled around his body. She got the message. She gave him her hand.

"I will cherish you forever," he kissed her tenderly.

"I will be a good wife to you, Nicholas. I love you." Her bust heaved.

"I know." He blocked his mind to the outside world. The only thing that mattered now was the woman in his arms. His wife. It was after some time when he heard her voice calling him. Oh God! He loved her so much. It hurts.

"Nicholas? Are you asleep?"

He reached for her. "I haven't slept a wink in case someone kidnaps you." He tenderly kissed her.

She responded with eagerness. "I enjoyed Mother's speech. It was short and to the point."

"I know what you mean. What else is there to say when two families become one? I have my sister to thank. I wouldn't have met you if she hadn't met your brother. I am glad she jilted Desmond."

"I will make you happy, Nicholas. As for my father, I don't know what to do. I know he is hurt. I am sorry. I have my life to lead." He will come round, she comforted herself. She reached for Nicholas. "I love you."

"I don't doubt you for one bit." He reached for her. They slept in each other's arms. The only sound in the room was the beating of their hearts.

Jerome reached for his wife. "This is hard for me to say but we have to accept Nicholas. We can't undo what they have already done."

"I am glad you have forgiven them. There is nothing we can do except to welcome them in our hearts. This generation! One thing we must remember, our daughter wasn't getting any younger."

"You are right. Let's sleep."

"Desmond, do you sometimes have lingering feelings towards Denise? I mean she is the one you first fell in love with."

He looked at her. "Annabella, not one bit. What makes you ask such a stupid question?"

"Now, don't get worked up. I just need reassurance."

"Annabella, I never loved Denise," he lied. He loved her the first time he saw her. "You two fooled me big time whenever you swapped places to meet me but you never fooled my feelings. You have no idea of how many times I thank my maker for steering Denise into Abraham's arms three days before the wedding. You are the one I love and I swear I would die for you."

"Blessed the Virgin Mary! That's going a bit too far Desmond. I know you love me but dying for me? Please leave that for the son of God. You know, I sometimes lose my cool. It doesn't mean that I don't love you."

"You think I don't know. Your temper is nothing compared to what we have achieved together. Above all, you have given me the family I longed for. I do apologise for that little operation I had."

"Desmond, I forgave you. After all, it's not just my health, but the children need proper education. We have to be able to provide for them and thanks for restoring our village. We must never forget our roots."

"I am glad you pushed me into restoring the place. The children love it." He reached for the phone and called room service for a bottle of wine and snacks.

She smiled at him. "Desmond, there is champagne in the fridge. It goes with the room."

He smiled at her. "I still want chardonnay wine. Nicholas will get our full support. I am so proud of him. I am glad we sponsored him in the first place."

Eric sat quietly in his suite. He rubbed his eyes. Father! I wish you could see what Nicholas has achieved. You would be very proud of him but would you be proud of me? It's time I made peace with Mother. She has her own life to lead at the end of the day. He made his way to his mother's suite. He proceeded to knock and then changed his mind. Eric! Grow up! A voice in his head told him. He decided to phone her.

Louise blinked. Eric? "Are you asking me on a date?"

"No, Mother. What I mean is that the disco is being wasted by giggling teenagers. Why don't you and Uncle Martin take the floor and I will baby sit my little sister?

"Eric, I don't know what to say."

"Don't say anything. I will be there in a sec. It's high time I showed my sister how to mend bikes."

"Thank you, Eric. You have no idea what this means to me and Martin. I love you, Eric."

"I know that, Mother. I am sorry for being a pain. I love you and I miss you. See you in a sec."

Denise sat on their suite's windowsill. Her mind switched back to the time she ran away three days before her wedding to Desmond Tumwiine. She was glad she had run away in the first place. It would have been a mistake to marry someone she had no feelings for. Her eyes travelled to their bed where the moonlight shone on her husband's face. He looked relaxed and peaceful in his sleep. She smiled. I am glad I took a step in the right direction. She remembered her mother's speech. 'What is there to say when two families become one?' She looked up at the penthouse. "Jessica and Nicholas, I wish you a happy marriage." She joined her husband, the only man she loved. She lay there recalling the last nine years they had been married. She had no regrets. She fell into a peaceful sleep.

THE END

CW00552340

Also by Sara Cate

Keep
Me

Keep Me

SARA CATE

sourcebooks
casablanca

Copyright © 2025 by Sara Cate
Cover and internal design © 2025 by Sourcebooks
Cover design by Stephanie Gafron/Sourcebooks
Cover image © Stock Story/Shutterstock
Internal design by Tara Jaggers/Sourcebooks
Internal art © Chloe Friedlein

Sourcebooks and the colophon are registered trademarks of Sourcebooks.

All rights reserved. No part of this book may be reproduced in any form or by
any electronic or mechanical means including information storage and retrieval
systems—except in the case of brief quotations embodied in critical articles or
reviews—without permission in writing from its publisher, Sourcebooks.

The characters and events portrayed in this book are fictitious or
are used fictitiously. Any similarity to real persons, living or dead,
is purely coincidental and not intended by the author.

All brand names and product names used in this book are trademarks,
registered trademarks, or trade names of their respective holders.
Sourcebooks is not associated with any product or vendor in this book.

Published by Sourcebooks Casablanca, an imprint of Sourcebooks
P.O. Box 4410, Naperville, Illinois 60567–4410
(630) 961-3900
sourcebooks.com

Cataloging-in-Publication Data is on file with the Library of Congress.

The authorized representative in the EEA is Dorling Kindersley
Verlag GmbH. Arnulfstr. 124, 80636 Munich, Germany

Manufactured in the UK by Clays and distributed by
Dorling Kindersley Limited, London
001-345484-Dec/24
10 9 8 7 6 5 4 3 2 1

For my mom—if you read this, let's never, ever talk about it.

Content Warning

Keep Me is a sexually explicit romance with elements of kink and BDSM—to include exhibitionism, partner swapping, impact play, and bondage. There is no use of a condom in this story. As always, my books are works of fiction meant to serve as entertainment and should not be used for instruction, but rather, inspiration. Should you and your partner(s) choose to explore the practices in any work of fiction, please do your research first. Be safe. Have fun.

Please be aware there are also elements of parental neglect, cheating (not between main characters), alcohol abuse, death, PTSD, and agoraphobia in this story. Read with caution.

PART ONE

Sylvie

Chapter One

"YOU'VE ARRIVED AT YOUR DESTINATION," THE GPS ANNOUNCES.

"That's the one, on the left," Aaron says, looking up from the map on his phone to the large brick mansion on the hill.

"That?" I reply in shock.

"Barclay Manor. That's it," he says, staring out the window. Rain pelts against the windows of the car.

"Aaron, you said your family had a *house* in Scotland. *That* is a castle."

"Technically, it's a manor."

"Semantics," I reply, gaping through the windshield at the massive gray stone building. It looms over us like a bad omen. Aaron pulls off on the side of the road, and I turn toward him in confusion. "What are you doing? Drive up there."

"I can't," he argues. "That sign says *Private Property.*"

My jaw drops. "So what? It's not like people *actually* live here."

"That's exactly what *private residence* means, Sylvie."

"We came all this way."

"So? What would I tell them? They're not going to let me

in just because my great-great-grandfather once visited here in the summer and wrote his book on the typewriter."

"That is *exactly* what you tell them. Based on these photos, we have proof that the typewriter is in there. We came all the way to fucking Scotland to see it. Now you're telling me you're going to just drive away because of a tiny little sign?"

He turns toward me and gives me a condescending glare. "Don't talk to me like that, Sylvie. I'm not afraid."

I roll my eyes. "So at least drive up there."

He lets out a huff. "Fine. You want to go to jail in a foreign country, let's drive up there."

He's so dramatic. I don't say a word as he pulls the car up the long gravel drive, through an open gate framed by two tall brick structures on either side. The one on the right displays the words BARCLAY MANOR 1837, and the one on the left has the PRIVATE PROPERTY sign.

The driveway is long but secluded. There are dense trees on either side, and judging by the map on Aaron's phone, there's a body of water not far on the other side of the manor. As we travel up the hill toward the manor, the rain continues to pour. It's rained every damn day since we got here last week. New York isn't sunny, but at least it's better than this.

"See, there is no one up here," I say when we get closer to the house. Aaron slows the car, clearly nervous. "Go around back."

His head snaps in my direction. "What? Why?"

"Because it's probably easier to get in back there."

"Get in? No, no, no," he barks, quickly turning the car around like he's about to flip a bitch on this narrow drive.

"Aaron, will you just relax? No one lives here. There's not a car in sight. My friends and I used to sneak into our school all the time as kids, and that had much better security than this place has."

"You're going to just walk into this nearly two-hundred-year-old manor like you own the place? Are you out of your fucking mind, Sylvie?"

"If someone sees us, we pretend we don't speak English and act like tourists."

When it's clear he can't turn his car around on this road, he pulls up farther to where the road winds around the building. He goes to the back first, his knuckles white around the steering wheel.

"Look!" I say, pointing from the passenger side. "There's a door on the side."

"Yeah, and it's probably locked," he replies, coasting the car to a stop.

Just then, the door pops open. Aaron and I both gasp and duck at the same time as we watch a woman emerge. She's wearing a black miniskirt and a white shimmery blouse missing a few buttons in the front.

One step out the door, she suddenly realizes it's raining. Instead of pulling an umbrella out, she covers her head with a black jacket and gazes around the yard as if looking for something.

Then, she's jogging in the mud and rain with her shoes hanging from her fingers instead of on her feet. And she's running straight toward *us*.

"What the...?" Aaron murmurs.

She stops by his driver's window and waits as he slowly rolls it down a few inches.

"Are you my lift?" she asks with her thick Scottish accent. There is black makeup streaking down her face and her lipstick is smeared around her mouth.

If I didn't know any better, I'd assume this woman is doing the quote-unquote *walk of shame*.

"Uh...no," Aaron stammers.

Her head pops up as she stares down the drive we just came from. "Och!" she chirps, then takes off in a jog through the mud toward another car slowly crawling up toward the house.

Aaron rolls the window back up and turns toward me in astonishment.

"Can we get out of here now?"

"What?" I reply. "No. The door is totally unlocked!"

His eyes widen further. "It's someone's house, Sylvie! Did you not just see the woman walk out of there?"

"Even better," I reply as I unclip my seat belt. "I can claim I'm her friend if someone sees me. I came all this way, Aaron. I'm getting in that fucking house."

"You're unhinged," he mutters as he faces forward and stares in shock. "People tried to warn me that you're a loose cannon, but I figured that would mean you're fun and unpredictable. I didn't think they meant it in a criminal way."

"Wait, who said I was a loose cannon? Never mind. It doesn't matter."

It really doesn't matter. I can think of a handful of people off the bat who I know would say that to my boyfriend. People in our social circle define *fun and entertainment* as tearing down other people and talking shit as if they're so much better than anyone.

The only way I've figured out how to avoid that is to beat them at their own game.

They want to call me irrational, then I'll show them irrational.

With that, I smile at Aaron and snatch my phone off the center console, shoving it into my pocket before throwing the hood of my rain jacket over my head.

"Be right back," I say as I open the car door and jump into the downpour.

"Sylvie!" Aaron calls from the car, but I cut him off by slamming the door shut and sprinting toward the place we just watched the girl emerge from.

There's a moment somewhere between the car and the door when I realize that this is, in fact, a bad idea. I'm walking into someone else's home uninvited. I could just knock and ask nicely to see the library, but where's the fun in that?

This is the moment when the adrenaline kicks in. It's invigorating. Fear, anticipation, and excitement all blend into one as I reach for the door handle without a clue as to what's on the other side.

It's an antique brass doorknob on an old wooden door. The forest-green paint is chipping away at the edges, and the knob squeaks as I turn it. As expected, it opens without an issue.

Once inside, I pull the door to just an inch from latching closed. It's my idea of a quick escape plan just in case these particular Scottish homeowners are the kind that like to pull an axe on their intruders or have large wolfhounds to protect the residence.

Shit, dogs. I didn't think about that.

The house is seemingly quiet from here. I'm standing in a large entryway, although, to be technical, this is the back of the house. So maybe it's called an exit way?

The floor is all hardwood, and the walls are painted. It looks as if it was recently renovated instead of featuring the stale, dated decor I was expecting. It smells nice, as if there's incense burning somewhere or men's cologne sprayed nearby.

In front of me is a long hallway, and I take each step slowly, listening for people or voices in the house. I pull my phone out of my back pocket and pull up the camera app to have it ready. When I get a picture of that typewriter, Aaron is going to eat his words. This will be nothing more than a funny story someday.

There are closed doors on either side of the long hallway, but none of them look like the kinds of doors that would lead to a large library like the one we saw in that photo of the typewriter. So, I keep walking slowly while listening.

At the end of the hall, I step into a giant entranceway with a grand staircase that leads to the second and third floors. The height of the ceiling in this part is massive, and I'm struck silent as I stare upward at it. This place is like nothing I've ever seen.

And if it wasn't for the warm smell of spice and musk, I wouldn't believe this is a residence.

My phone buzzes in my hand, drawing my attention from the ceiling and grand staircase.

I glance down to see a text from Aaron.

Get the fuck out of there. Now, Sylvie.

I roll my eyes and swipe the message closed. He's always so paranoid. Such a rule follower. He used to be fun, but the last year with him has been painfully boring. Every day is so predictable it makes me sick. I'm going to prove to him right now how fun and spontaneous I can be. I'll snap a picture of that old typewriter that his great-great-whatever wrote some dumb old classic novel on, and that'll show him.

When I glance up again, I spot an open door on the second floor. In the room, I spot a shelf of old books. *A library.*

Pocketing my phone, I carefully tiptoe up the stairs. I don't hear a single sound in the rest of the house. If anyone is here, they're probably sleeping or in the shower or something. They'll never know I was even here.

There is a single stair that creaks as I settle my weight on it. With a wince, I freeze and wait for the sound of footsteps, but there's nothing. Quickly, I finish my climb, reaching the top and slowly creeping into the large room. The ceilings in this room are far taller than I expected. Each wall has a tall ladder attached to a slider. For a moment, I can do nothing but stare at the massive space.

As my gaze casts downward, it catches on something on the other side of the room. Resting on a large ornate wooden table is a huge vase full of flowers next to a dusty old typewriter.

"Gotcha," I whisper as I quickly tiptoe through the room. The floor in here has a thick rug that muffles my footsteps.

I slip my phone from my back pocket and open the camera app. Aiming at the typewriter, I take a multitude of shots from various angles.

"Eat your words, Aaron," I whisper.

Then, while I'm at it, I take a few shots of the library too. It's so old-fashioned looking, like something out of a fairy tale. I don't know anyone who owns this many books, and if I did, they wouldn't store them in a room like this.

There's a creak in the house, and I quickly spin around, watching the door.

Fuck.

Time to go.

With my phone clutched in my hand, I make my way toward the door I came in through. There's no sign of anyone on the second floor, so I book it for the stairs. My heart is pounding, and adrenaline is coursing through my veins. The long hallway ahead leads to the exit. Just a few more feet and I'll be outside, sprinting toward Aaron's car in the rain, laughing about how wild this was.

Reaching the bottom step, I leap to the right.

An enormous hand wraps around my arm, hauling me to a stop before I can make my escape. I let out a scream, turning around to gape at the impossibly large man scowling down at me with my arm still gripped in his fist.

"Who the fuck are you?" the man bellows in a deep Scottish brogue.

I open my mouth to respond, but nothing comes out.

"What are you doing in my house?" he continues.

"I—I" I stammer.

Get it together, Sylvie. This was your idea. Don't let this giant oaf intimidate you.

"I was looking for my friend. She was here, but now… she's not," I reply, forcing my voice to remain steady. He's still holding my arm, his fingers pinching it so tightly it's starting to hurt.

"Your friend?" he asks.

I jerk my arm, trying to pull it free, but he won't let go.

"Yeah. She told me to pick her up, but I think she already left." I wave my phone to imply the girl has called or texted me. "So, I'll just…be on my way."

His brows pinch inward skeptically.

"So, you just barge into my house uninvited?"

"Yeah, I—"

When his lazy focus turns back to me, I notice a change in his demeanor. His eyes rake up and down my body before landing on my face and leaning in a little closer.

"Go on…" he mutters in a low, teasing manner. Goose bumps develop across my arms and neck. The man looks to be older than me, maybe midthirties. With long brown hair and a thick beard, all I can really see are his bright green eyes.

"I was just looking…"

"For your friend," he says, finishing my sentence.

"Yeah."

"I don't believe you," he whispers, his face so close I feel his breath on my cheek.

I jerk on my arm, but he still won't release it. "Then, let me go," I argue.

A wicked grin tilts the corner of his mouth. "I'm just starting to wonder…" he says with a note of sarcasm in his voice, "if you're here for the same reason she was. Perhaps you can pick up where she left off."

My blood runs cold, and I feel the heavy weight of fear settle in my stomach like I've swallowed a stone. Is he really implying that I'm here to sleep with him?

"Let me go," I mutter through my teeth.

With a few steps toward the wall, he slowly corners me against it. "Wh-what are you doing?" I stammer.

"This is why you're here, isn't it?" he asks.

"No!" I shout, putting a hand on his chest and trying to shove him away. Like a brick wall, he doesn't budge. There's a hint of humor on his face, and I can't quite tell, but I think he's teasing me. Saying all of this just to scare me. It's working.

"Then, why are you in my house?" he replies. His playful smirk fades, and it's replaced with something more sinister. "Are you spying for my sister?"

I flinch. "What? No."

When his eyes trail to the phone in my hand, his brow creases. I already know what he's about to do, so when I struggle to release myself from his grip, it's futile.

"Give me this," he growls, snatching the phone from my hand.

"Stop!" I scream.

Then, I watch in horror as he tosses my phone to the floor and stomps the heel of his boot on it so hard it shatters against the hardwood.

Finally, he releases my arm, and I gape at the broken phone on the floor. "You brute!" I scream, taking a swing at him. My hand lands disappointingly against the thick muscles of his arm, clearly causing him no pain at all.

"What did you do that for?" I shout.

He points a finger in my face. "You tell my bitch of a sister that she's not getting my house, and she can stop sending her little friends to spy on me. Now, get out."

His lips curl in a sneer as he points to the door. Then, he drops his arm and walks away, leaving me to blink in disbelief.

"Hey!" I call after him. "You need to replace my phone!"

Still walking away from me toward the back of the house, he doesn't respond to my shouting.

"Asshole!" I yell again. "I'm talking to you."

He chuckles as he enters a large living room. To the right is a bar with bottles of liquor displayed on glass shelves over a marble counter.

"Bold of you to shout at me in my own home. You're lucky I haven't called the police on you yet."

"I'm serious," I say, winding a stray curl behind my ear. "You broke my phone for no reason."

"I broke it for a very good reason," he replies with a sarcastic laugh. "You probably had pictures on it that could be incriminating, and my sister would just love that."

"Incriminating?" I reply. "I took pictures of the old typewriter in the library!"

"The typewriter?" He's uncapping a bottle of something that looks like whisky when he stops and glances up at me, bewildered. "Why the hell would she want pictures of a typewriter?"

I slam my hands down in frustration. "They're not for your fucking sister. I don't even know your sister. I snuck in to find this stupid old typewriter that was apparently an heirloom in my boyfriend's family, you stupid ogre."

His eyes burn with anger as he sets the bottle down. "Let me get this straight. You walked into a stranger's home to take pictures of an old typewriter for your boyfriend?"

He glances around behind me as if Aaron is going to

appear out of thin air. I roll my eyes. "Yes, and I was on my way out when you attacked me, threatened to defile me, and then broke my phone."

"Is this how girls behave in America?" he snaps in return. "Just barging into people's houses to take a picture of something you think belongs to you?"

I scoff. "To be fair, this is hardly a house."

"It's *my* fucking house."

"It's practically a castle. Why do you even live out here?" I ask incredulously.

"To avoid having to interact with people like you," he replies.

"You're really an asshole."

He simply chuckles in response. "What is your name?" he asks, taking a step toward me.

I take a step back. "None of your business."

"Tell me your name, and I'll replace your phone," he replies, teasing me.

Chewing on my bottom lip, I stare at him with hesitation.

"Sylvie," I say, taking another step away from him as he continues to close in on me.

"Sylvie what?"

"Devereaux," I mumble.

"Sylvie Devereaux," he says, my name sounding melodic and beautiful on his tongue.

My back hits a wall, but he continues toward me. I stop breathing for a moment as I stare into his haunting green eyes.

As he leans in, I catch the scent of his cologne and feel dwarfed by his intimidating size. He must be six and a half feet tall. As he places a hand on the wall over my head, I realize what an idiot I am.

I had my chance to leave, but now I've just gotten myself cornered by someone who's already proven himself to be volatile and angry.

His fingers delicately touch my chin. As he leans in, I shudder and try to turn my face away.

"Sylvie Devereaux, get the fuck out of my house."

My chest aches for air, waiting for him to back away enough to let me breathe. When he does, he lets out a menacing laugh.

"You asshole!" I choke out as I gasp for air.

Before he can crowd me again, I turn and run toward the door. I step right over my shattered phone on the floor, turning back to pick up what's left of it before bolting out the door I came in. The rain is still going strong as I stop and glance around for Aaron's car. He's parked just near the road, and I take off in a sprint toward him.

He's giving me an impatient expression and is clearly stressed as I tear open the passenger side door and climb in.

"What the fuck, Sylvie?" he shouts.

"Just drive," I mutter breathlessly.

"You're lucky you didn't get yourself killed."

"There was no one in there," I lie. "I just dropped my phone, so I don't have your pictures."

"You're fucking unhinged," he mumbles under his breath as he drives toward the road.

My heart is still hammering in my chest. As we reach the main road, I glance back at the manor in the distance, watching it grow smaller and smaller in my rearview.

At least I made it out of there unharmed.

And I'm never going back.

Chapter Two

"You could have gone to jail," Aaron mutters. He's sitting on the bed facing away from me, his elbows on his knees.

Rolling my eyes, I drop onto the bed and pick up my laptop. "Stop being so dramatic. I'm fine."

"Are you sure no one saw you?" he asks in a panic.

I drop my hands in a huff. "I told you no one saw me. Why do you care so much?"

"I have my image to worry about, Sylvie. I'm sorry *you* don't care about anything, but I do, and if I'm going to run for office someday, I don't need a criminal record in Scotland holding me back because my impulsive and careless girlfriend thinks she can just *do* anything."

"Technically, I *can* do anything," I mutter to myself as I open my laptop.

"Not without consequences, Sylvie."

I click on the cloud drive on my laptop and immediately scan through the photos. There at the bottom of the array of pictures of the Scottish countryside and Edinburgh's Royal Mile are the photos of the dusty old typewriter I nearly sacrificed my life for.

Aaron is still droning on and on about my actions and consequences and how it's not technically my fault that my parents didn't raise me with any discipline.

Same shit, different day.

I decide not to show him the photos.

Instead, I open an internet browser. I type Barclay Manor.

Immediately, a photo pops up on a basic wiki page about the manor, the town, the family, and its history.

The auto-generated questions below list: Does someone still live at Barclay Manor?

So I click on it.

"Are you even listening to me?" he asks. I glance up from my laptop.

"My parents were incompetent. I'm not going to disagree with you," I reply noncommittally. He's absolutely right. They were incredibly incompetent as parents. It's not that they're stupid people. In fact, they are brilliant and could hold a steady conversation for hours about the contextual theory of Van Gogh through his Parisian era, but they generally sucked as a mom and dad.

They were never afraid of being so bold to explain to me that parental love was inane and subconscious, which wasn't always the warmest consolation as a child. Biologically, my mom loved me—because she had to.

Luckily for her and my father, they are both geniuses, and that talent paid for modern conveniences like full-time childcare, which made raising me nearly effortless.

"Yeah, well, you're twenty-five now, Sylvie. It's about time you start acting like it."

"Why are you being so uptight?" I reply with annoyance. "What happened to the guy who snuck backstage at the music festival with me?"

"That was three years ago, Syl. Grow up."

As he gives me a contemptuous glare, I sink into the bed, feeling the shame he's hurling at me like knives. He sulks into the bathroom, slamming the door closed, leaving me alone with my thoughts.

It feels as if we're growing in separate directions. He's so focused on his future, settling down, and growing up. He sees twenty-five as some mature magical age when we're supposed to suddenly have it all figured out. I don't feel anywhere near having it figured out.

He's on a speedboat, headed straight for dry land.

I'm floating on a breeze with no direction at all.

And for some reason, I should feel like shit about that.

I turn my attention back to the laptop. I click on the link there under the question Does someone still live at Barclay Manor? And right there on the screen is the man I saw today.

It's a handsome photo with an inscription underneath—*Killian Barclay.*

Of course, in the photo, he's dressed up. In a black jacket and green kilt, standing in front of some PR backdrop for a charity, he looks miserable and handsome at the same time. He appears a bit younger in this photo, and when I click on his name, it takes me to a screen full of photos of him.

Most are like this one—posed, strategic, flattering. But there are a couple mixed in that look more like bad paparazzi timing, drunkenly climbing into the back of an SUV. There's one where he seems like he's in the middle of a brawl at a party. And one where he's actively yelling at the cameraman taking the photo.

This guy clearly has anger issues.

Clicking on his name takes me to his Wikipedia page, and I read that he's almost thirty-seven years old. He's the oldest of four in the Barclay family and has been living in the manor since the death of his parents when he was eighteen. As for photos, there aren't many from the past ten years.

That's all the page really says about him, but judging by the lack of details, I assume he's unmarried without kids.

How strange it must be to live in that big house all alone.

I hear Aaron's muffled voice in the bathroom, and I glance up from my laptop to try and decipher what he's saying. I can't quite make it out, so I return to my internet search instead.

I find myself staring at Killian's picture again, replaying the entire interaction today. Something about it felt so off. Who was the girl who left before I walked in? A guy who lives alone in a mansion like that with probably millions and millions of dollars at his disposal would likely hire a sex worker instead of dating, right?

God, what would have happened if I hadn't gotten out of there? Would he have expected me to have sex with him?

If he wasn't such an ass, I might have. Not that I would cheat on Aaron. I just mean…if there was no Aaron, I might have let that six-foot-five rich Scottish jerk throw me around a little bit.

And what was up with the whole spying thing? Does his sister send spies in on him often? What is he hiding that would require spies?

That's weird, right?

My phone is still shattered and will probably stay that way until we find a store to replace it, but I have been dying to tell my best friend Margot about what happened today. So I pull up our text message thread on my laptop.

Hey. I miss you.
Almost got ravaged by a giant Scotsman today.
#noregrets
But don't tell Aaron. He's being a jerk about it.

I smile down at the message thread and wait for her to read

it. Checking the time, I see that it's still midday in New York, even though it's late here. So she should be up.

My best friend doesn't have a sleep routine, or any kind of routine, really. She doesn't have a job or a partner. She's the only other person I know floating on the breeze with me.

I tell Margot everything. Her mom is an actress and model who became best friends with my parents back in the 1990s. Which means they basically raised us together. Margot took after her mother and pursued modeling, and she's flawless.

When she doesn't read my messages after about five minutes, I get a little annoyed. To be honest, I'm bored. Aaron is mad at me, and this whole fucking trip was for him. Now I just want to go home.

The bathroom door opens, and he walks in, shoving his phone into his back pocket.

"Let's get some sleep," he mutters quietly. "We have an early flight tomorrow."

As he tears off his shirt, my computer pings with a message.

He's probably just worried about you.

Her message annoys me. She's not supposed to take his side. Without responding, I close my laptop and shove it on the side table. Then, I roll over with my back to Aaron.

"Who were you talking to in there?" I ask.

"You were hearing things. I wasn't talking to anyone," he replies flatly.

He switches the light off, bathing us in darkness, and I close my eyes.

The sooner I fall asleep, the sooner we wake up for the airport. And the sooner this whole trip will end.

Chapter Three

"Dear Ms. Devereaux, my name is Monica Rodriguez, and I'm calling from First Financial. Your credit card payment is ninety days past due and currently in default. We have no choice but to send your account to collections and deactivate your credit cards."

Delete.

The voicemail disappears, leaving my inbox empty. That foreboding feeling of dread settles in my stomach. The message from my bank sucks, but not as much as what I have to do now.

When I reach the barista at the counter, I order my small black coffee and scrounge in the bottom of my purse for enough loose change to cover it.

"A name for your order?" she asks.

"It's a small black coffee. Just pour it into a cup."

The girl with a septum piercing and bright purple eye shadow gives me a condescending look. "A name for your order," she repeats.

"Sylvie," I say with a huff.

Then I turn away from the counter and find a quiet corner

of the coffee shop to wait. Staring down at my brand-new phone, I pull up my contacts and hover my thumb over the button I really don't want to push.

My initial prediction was that I'd make it eighteen months with what I had in my savings account and on my credit cards when Mom and Dad told me I was cut off. Eighteen months—*if* I was conservative with my spending and didn't do anything drastic.

Like go to Scotland with my boyfriend.

And buy a new phone.

I made it four months.

"Sylvia," the miserable wench at the counter calls out, holding a small paper cup.

I roll my eyes as I approach her. "It's Sylvie," I murmur before taking the coffee.

"Sorry," she replies, her tone full of sarcasm.

When I leave the shop, turning right toward my apartment, I pull out my phone again.

I have to do this. I have to, right?

I can't just…survive without money. And getting a job right now isn't as easy as I thought it would be. The only places that are hiring are paying less than what it costs to live in the city, so what is the point?

"Fuck it," I mutter as I punch my thumb on my phone screen. It lights up with my mom's picture.

Calling Mom…

I wait as it rings, and rings, and rings.

"Hi, you've reached the voice mailbox of Torrence Devereaux. She is currently unavailable. If you are calling to commission or purchase a piece of art, please contact her assistant, Enid Hamilton, at 290-555-1004. Thank you."

Enid's voice grates on my nerves, but I stick through the greeting until it beeps.

"Hey, Mom. It's Sylvie. Your daughter. I don't know if you're still in Florence, but I'm just calling because I'm literally fucking starving. You can't just cut me off like this. I'm not sure what you expect me to do. Can't I just have, like, half of my allowance until I figure something out? You can't do this to me. Just call me back…please."

I hang up the call as I reach a crosswalk, waiting in a crowd of pedestrians as I try my dad's number. It rings and rings and rings just the same.

"Hi, you've reached the voice mailbox of Yuri Devereaux. He is currently unavailable."

"Fuck my life," I mutter to myself.

"If you are calling to commission or purchase a piece of art, please contact his assistant, Enid Hamilton, at 290-555-1004. Thank you."

Beep.

"Dad," I cry into the phone. "It's Sylvie. Please call me back. I'm just…" My voice cracks. "I'm having a really hard time lately, and I need your help. Just a little something to get me through the season. No one is hiring right now, and my credit cards are all maxed out. I'm not sure how I'll pay rent this month, and I'm scared."

My voice is thick with emotion, but my eyes are as dry as the desert. I can feel the curious attention of the nosy people around me glancing up from their phones to sneak a peek at me.

"Thank you, Daddy. I love you."

I punch the End Call button and pull up the last contact on my list. With a disgruntled sigh, I hit the phone icon next to her name. This time, she picks up after the first ring.

"Hello, Sylvie," she says without a hint of amusement in her voice.

"Hello, Enid," I mutter into the phone. "Are my parents still in Florence?"

She sighs. "They haven't been in Florence since May. What can I help you with?"

The light turns, and the crowd begins their walk across the intersection.

"I'm trying to get ahold of them."

"They're in the studio," she replies coldly.

In the studio is a phrase I've heard since the day I was born. *In the studio* could refer to a few hours or a few months. It is both literal and symbolic, a blanket statement that refers to some artistic zone my parents escape to—usually together—where they cannot be bothered, or else it would disrupt their delicate creative process.

They were often *in the studio* over my birthdays, the first day of school, a couple of Christmases, and once when I was seventeen and was in a bad car accident on the way to the Hamptons with some friends. They showed up at the hospital four days later.

The piece they were working on is now in the Guggenheim.

"That's fine. I was just checking on them. I haven't received my deposit in a couple of months, and I was getting worried. Maybe you could log into their accounts and send it over."

"Bullshit, Sylvie," Enid barks. "They cut you off four months ago. Are you really out of money already?"

My molars grind. "Fuck you, Enid. You've been sucking their teats since you graduated college."

"I do my job, Sylvie," she replies. Her voice is so fucking annoying. Nasally and posh. "You do know what a job is, don't you?"

"Oh yes, your job must be so hard," I argue. "Being at my parents' beck and call twenty-four-seven. On the yachts and at all the parties. Tell me, Enid. Are you there when they fuck each other too?"

"You're disgusting, Sylvie. No wonder they're so embarrassed by you."

My hand squeezes the phone so tightly I'm surprised it doesn't snap in half. I should relax. I can't afford another one.

"I'd rather be an embarrassment than a leech."

"Again," she snaps into the phone. "This is my job, Sylvie. You should consider getting one. Or are you still *working on your novel?*"

I can practically hear her doing air quotes around that condescending phrase, and the urge to toss my phone into the sewer, imagining it's her, is overwhelming.

"Fuck you, you ugly, uptight little twat."

With that, I punch the End Call button and let out a frustrated, growling huff. I want to scream. I want to hurl this hot coffee at anyone I can. Just once I wish I could really let go and express all of the things I'm feeling.

I bet Killian Barclay doesn't have to deal with shit like this. I bet he lets out his frustration all the time, and no one judges him for it. I wish I knew why my mind was constantly revisiting that day, but I have no idea. He burrowed himself into my subconscious.

Instead of turning right toward my apartment, where I know Aaron is waiting for me, I keep straight on 5th toward Margot's place. Unlike Aaron, she won't give me some condescending lecture about responsibility and maturity. He's never been supportive of my dreams anyway. He doesn't care if I finish my novel. He never even asks about it.

When I reach Margot's building, the doorman welcomes me with a smile. "Morning, Sylvie," he says.

I force myself to grin back at him regardless of my irritated mood. "Morning, Chuck. She's home, right?" I ask, turning back toward him once I'm in the lobby.

He nods, but there's a hint of something hesitant on his face. "She's in," he replies.

I don't bother asking him if everything is okay, but I hurry to the elevator anyway. Hopefully, that's not a sign she's on another one of her benders. Margot has a history of going off the deep end after a fashion show if she feels like it didn't go exactly the way she wanted. Or if a photo comes out that she finds less than flattering. She'll replace food with alcohol and socializing with sex for weeks on end until I scrape her off the floor and put her back together.

I can't watch her go through that again.

When the elevator lets me off on the eighteenth floor, I rush down to Margot's apartment and try the handle first. To my surprise, it's unlocked.

What the fuck is wrong with her, leaving her door unlocked in the middle of Manhattan?

Two steps into the apartment, I hear the unmistakable sound of her moaning chants. They're loud and high-pitched, and by the sound of it, she's being railed within an inch of her life.

Oh, fuck.

Before letting the door close behind me, I grab it and quietly ease myself out. My cheeks heat with embarrassment from hearing my best friend getting it on.

Stifling a giggle, I tiptoe out the door, thinking about how I'm going to give her shit about this later.

Then, my eyes catch on a pair of familiar shoes on the floor. They look exactly like Aaron's—the ones I got him for his birthday last year. This guy she's seeing has good taste.

But then my gaze lingers on the shoes, and I realize they are a little *too* familiar. Like they have the same wear marks as Aaron's. Still tied the same way he ties his, slipping them off when he gets home without undoing the knots.

I hear a familiar grunt from the bedroom.

And suddenly, it's like I'm frozen in time. Like everything is moving around me, but I'm stuck in one place.

Reality comes crashing in, and the rage I felt a few moments ago bubbles over like a pot of water set to boil for too long.

I step inside and let the door close before marching down the hall of Margot's apartment toward her room. As I reach the door, I stand there, coffee in hand, and watch as my boyfriend of three years pounds into my best friend from behind. His white ass is on display, and he's got a hand on her head, shoving it into the mattress. She's moaning loudly, and, honestly, it sounds a little fake and dramatic.

They don't even know I'm standing here watching them. I'm gawking at them for far too long, but in my defense, I'm stunned. I can't stop thinking about the fact that the last time Aaron and I fucked, we did it in missionary position, and he ground on top of me like a disgusting slug.

He slaps her ass, and she yelps in pleasure. "My dirty little girl."

My face contorts in disgust. *What the fuck?*
Am I in the right apartment?
Is this the right reality?

"God, I love you so much," he adds. "I love you so fucking much."

His voice is strained, groaning out the words as he thrusts into her. Suddenly I feel like I'm going to be sick. And I move without thinking.

I flip the plastic lid off of my coffee, watching the steam rise from the liquid. Then, I scream as I hurl it at his naked body. I watch with delight as it lands against his back, singeing his skin and making him squeal in pain.

"What the fuck!" he shouts, flailing onto the bed and rolling onto his back, his face twisted in fear.

Margot screams, quickly covering her body with a blanket and staring at me in horror.

"Sylvie?" she cries.

Aaron freezes and gapes at me as I stand in the doorway, glaring at them both with my jaw clenched tight in anger.

My eyes bore into Margot, my best friend, as she tries to catch her breath. For the first time today, my eyes brim with tears, but I don't say a word. Not to either of them.

I just turn on my heel and barrel out of her apartment.

All I can think as I reach the door, rushing past Chuck and onto the street, is that I spent my last five dollars on that coffee. And while it was worth it, I have no fucking clue what I'm going to do now.

Chapter Four

WALLOWING IN SELF-PITY DOESN'T PAY MUCH. OR ANYTHING. Whenever you hit rock bottom, people love to say, *There's nowhere to go but up*, but they don't exactly specify when that will happen. Because I've been scraping the bottom of this barrel for two weeks now, and I'm not sure how much longer I'll last.

Aaron moved out ten days ago. When he tried to come home that night with second-degree burns on his back and tears in his eyes, I threatened him with a kitchen knife. He called me a bitch, grabbed his phone charger, and left.

Margot tried to call me. She left me a seven-paragraph text message about how I've never been that great of a friend and somehow managed to pin this all on me, explaining how my never consoling her over her breakups led to her spreading her legs for my long-term boyfriend. I don't know. I didn't really read the whole thing, if I'm honest.

She did claim that they were in love and had been for a while. Maybe *she* should have gone to Scotland with him. She could have chased around his ancestor's bullshit for three weeks.

There's been a red eviction notice on my door for the past three days, but I've been ignoring that too. I'm working on a theory that if I just ignore literally everything in my life, then the universe will just work itself out.

I mean, what are they going to do? Carry me out?

I've sold enough of Aaron's shit to feed myself over the last two weeks but not enough to pay the rent. He took the really good stuff.

Lying on my couch, bored and depressed, I scroll through the pictures on my phone, deleting every single one of me and Aaron. They just feel like lies now. Why did he ever bother to look happy with me?

There's a knock at the door that I ignore.

Ignore everything.

Nothing matters anyway.

I turn my attention back to my phone, discovering a dirty video Aaron and I made over a year ago on Halloween when he filmed me sucking his dick in my Alice in Wonderland costume. He was the Mad Hatter.

I won't delete this one just yet...

"Ms. Devereaux," a woman calls through the door, and I wrinkle my brow as I stare at it. There's something familiar about the way she said my name. Melodic and enticing.

It reminds me of...

"My name is Anna Barclay. Are you home?"

Barclay?

"What the...?"

My voice trails as I climb off my sofa and walk silently toward the door. Without a sound, I squint through the peephole and see a well-dressed woman holding a manila envelope standing on my welcome mat.

"Hello, Ms. Devereaux," she croons. "I see the light through the peephole. I know you're there."

I pull my head back in a snap. "What do you want?" I ask with skepticism.

My mind is reeling, trying to figure out why this woman is here. Is this because I broke into their house? I mean...*broke in* is hardly accurate. I just walked in. Did that brutish asshole tell on me? Can I still be arrested?

"I'd like to speak to you," she says. "I believe you already met my brother."

Her brother?

So is this the sister that sends spies into his house? Maybe that's what she's looking for now? Would she pay me to spy on him again? I'd gladly do it.

Curiosity gets the better of me, and I unlatch the dead bolt and turn the brass knob on the door. As I peel it open, I stare at the woman waiting there. She's very pretty. With long brown hair and large green eyes, she looks to be in her mid to late thirties. I can see the resemblance between her and the man who nearly attacked me. She's tall too, but not as tall as him.

"What do you want?" I mumble through the gap of the doorway.

"Can I come in?" she asks.

"For what?"

"I have something to discuss with you. A...business proposal, if you will."

My brow lowers as I stare at her, glancing down at the envelope in her hands. A business proposal? She *does* want me to spy on him.

I quickly glance behind her to see that she's alone before I slowly open the door and allow her to come in. She scans my apartment, possibly noticing how immaculate it is. I might be broke, depressed, and lonely, but I keep my space clean, always.

Leading her down to the dining room, I point to the table. "Would you like some coffee?" I ask hesitantly.

"Coffee would be nice," she replies.

As she takes a seat at the table, I move into the kitchen and grab the coffeepot from the machine. "So, how did you find me?" I ask as I fill it with water.

"My brother told me your name. I saw your face on the security footage. Then, I looked you up. Read an interesting article in the *New Yorker* about you. You were listed as a potential rising star in literature. Your parents were mentioned too."

I glance down as I continue making a pot of coffee. That piece came out nearly two years ago. I was fresh out of college and had impressed enough professors to get a spot on the *ones-to-watch* list they publish every year.

It felt like a gold star at the time.

Now it feels like a festering wound.

"Are you looking for a freelance writer? I don't really do that sort of writing," I say before switching the machine on. It whirs to life as I take down two mugs from the cabinet.

"I'm sorry, but no. I'm not interested in hiring you as a writer."

Ouch.

"Then what is it?" I ask from the kitchen.

"Why don't you come sit down, and we can discuss it? It's...sensitive in nature."

My cheeks grow hot as I stare at her. Possibilities flit through my mind, but nothing sticks or makes any sense.

Pulling out a chair, I sit down and face the woman, waiting for an explanation.

"Ms. Devereaux, what I'm about to offer you is unconventional and a bit strange. I'll warn you now."

"Okay..."

She opens her manila folder. Inside is a stack of what looks like very official papers. There's even a fancy crest at the top.

"You should know a little about my family before I continue."

I don't respond as she turns the papers toward me. I stare at her inquisitively.

"I have three brothers. Killian is the eldest. Then, Declan. And Lachlan. Then me, between Killian and Declan."

"Okay…" I say again, waiting for the part where I come in.

"My brother Killian, being the eldest, is the heir to our family's estate, Barclay Manor, which you have recently visited. He chooses to live there, regardless of our family's wishes. Our parents have sadly passed away."

"Why does your family not want him there?"

Her spine straightens. "Killian is…eccentric. He's turned our family's estate into a house of debauchery and parties."

"Sounds fun," I mutter to myself. Behind me, the coffee-pot beeps, and I quickly turn away from Anna's judgmental glare. "Cream and sugar?"

"Just cream, please."

"Got it," I reply, going to the fridge for the cream. "So, Killian won't leave your family's castle," I say as I prepare our coffees. "What do you need me for?"

"That's the strange part."

As I carry over our cups, she purses her lips and waits for me to sit before speaking again.

"I'll cut to the chase, Ms. Devereaux."

"Please," I reply, setting my cup on the table.

"I'd like you to marry my brother."

Suddenly, it's as if the entire dining room of my apartment cants to one side, and my coffee cup tips over, spilling the hot contents all over my lacquered table. Anna quickly lifts her papers, to avoid the coffee staining them.

"Oh shit," I mumble, rushing to grab some paper towels from my kitchen and quickly cleaning up the mess. She waits patiently as I dab it up.

"I'm sorry...what?" I stammer, sitting down and staring at her in shock. The wadded-up paper towels are still littered all over my table.

"It's quite complicated, but the only way for my family to access the ownership of the manor is if it's transferred out of our brother's name. And the only way for it to be transferred out of his name is if he remains married for at least one year. At which point, ownership of the home would be granted to his wife."

"One year?" I stutter.

"Or until they have a child."

My eyes nearly bug out of my head.

"I don't expect you to do that," she adds.

"Oh, good," I reply sarcastically. "You just want me to marry a complete stranger for a year so you can con your brother out of his home. Okay. Well, that's good because, for a moment, I thought you were out of your mind."

She lets out a sigh. "Before you paint us as the villains, you should know that Killian's reasons for staying in the manor are not to his benefit. He did not handle the death of our parents well, and after he spent his twenties in a drug- and alcohol-induced haze, he has secluded himself in that house since. We discovered recently just how out of hand his lifestyle has gotten. We're doing this for his own good."

"Have you, and I'm just tossing out ideas here, thought to talk to him about it?"

"For seventeen years," she replies flatly.

"Seventeen years?" I snap.

"My brother needs to move on with his life. He needs a nudge."

A laugh bursts through my lips. "A nudge? You flew halfway across the world to ask a complete stranger to marry your brother, and you call that a nudge? Why on earth would I agree to this?"

"Ten million dollars."

My body freezes, and I stare at her in shock. She said that so calmly that it took me by surprise more than the actual amount.

"Of course, we would support you during the year. You'd live at Barclay with Killian. You'd be taken care of with whatever you require. There are some serious stipulations to the contract, such as you'd be required to make public appearances with Killian. Neither of you could be adulterous, or else the contract would be nullified."

"Wait, wait, wait," I say, holding my hands up. "Why would he agree to this?"

"He thinks it's a ploy to improve his reputation in order to get his family off of his back and let him keep the house."

His reputation. I know a bit about that from what I read online the day I saw him. Killian Barclay had made a name for himself as a playboy and partier.

"Why couldn't he just improve his reputation?"

"We've convinced him that if he is seen settling down, the family might be more inclined to allow him to stay in the house without a fight."

Leaning back in my chair, I cross my arms over my chest. "So…what's to stop me from just keeping the house to myself after the year of marriage, if, like you said, I will have ownership of it?"

Her lips purse. "Because there would be a very strict contract that states you will sign the deed over to my family or face a hefty fine worth more than the cost of the manor itself."

"This is some manipulative shit," I reply with a laugh.

"Like I said," she mumbles. "It's for his own good."

"Why me?" I ask, narrowing my eyes at her. "Out of everyone on this planet, why me? You don't even know me."

"I know you were bold enough to walk into our house uninvited that day," she says with a scolding expression. "I know you were raised in a wealthy environment. You're well-educated and accustomed to a certain level of comfort. And I know that your parents recently cut you off."

My head tilts in surprise. "How do you know that? That's not something you'd find in a Google search," I say skeptically.

"No, it's not," she agrees, implying that this lady is even more manipulative than I first assumed.

The dining room grows silent as we stare at each other. My mind is spinning as I let the entire thing play over and over. It's unbelievable and sort of hilarious.

"So..." she mumbles over the top of her coffee cup. "What do you think?"

I let out another laugh. "I think you're fucking bold. How many unsuspecting American girls are you bombarding with this offer?"

She takes a sip and sets down her cup. "You are the only person we're asking."

I tug my bottom lip between my teeth. "Well, I'm sorry you wasted a trip. Be sure to see the Statue of Liberty while you're here. Thanks for a good laugh and a hilarious story I'll tell someday."

"Why don't you think about it?" she asks as she stands.

"Yeah, sure," I reply with a chuckle. "I'll think about dropping my entire life here to marry a stranger in Scotland."

"Here's my card." She sets it on the table and gives me a tight smile. "Thanks for hearing me out."

I don't have anything else to say, so I stand in silence as she walks to the door. She gets to it and puts her hand on the knob before I realize something.

"What did he say?" I ask. "About me."

She stops and turns toward me with a crooked grin. "He said you were the rudest, meanest, most infuriating woman he'd ever met."

"And that made you think I'd be a good fit for this?"

"No," she replies with a shake of her head. "But he did."

With that, she opens my front door and disappears out of my apartment.

I'm left standing in silence, confused and shocked and wondering what the fuck just happened.

Chapter Five

THE ONE PERK OF HAVING SLIGHTLY FAMOUS PARENTS IS THAT sometimes I know exactly where they are going to be and when. As I stride through the lobby of their gallery uptown, I smile at one of the security guards and thank my teenage flirting skills I used years ago to get him on my good side.

And being the daughter of the artists means I don't have to have a ticket or reservation.

I just have to get past Enid.

The gallery is in a brownstone on the Upper East Side, which means there's not a lot of space for me to hide from their bitch of an assistant who will no doubt usher me out if she sees me.

Two steps into the ground floor gallery space, I spot my mother on the opposite side. She seems thinner than I remember. Almost skeletal. Her thinning red hair is styled with wide curls that rest on her bony shoulders.

She's holding a glass of wine and speaking to a group of people gathered around one of her oldest paintings.

"Of course, the style in those days never quite allowed for

introspection. Everything had to be expressed in moderation," she says in her sophisticated tone that makes my spine tense.

There is a wall between my mother and me. Not literally, of course. A real wall I could climb over. But this one is unscal-able. I don't know where she keeps her emotions, because they are not available to me. Instead of showing me love, empathy, or compassion, my mother appraises me—finding every single flaw or room for improvement.

Once upon a time, she heralded me as her greatest piece of art, but as I grew and stopped being just a pretty thing to look at, I started to feel more like the mess left over from whatever piece of art she was making. The dried paint under her nails. The watercolor stains on the table. The stench of acrylic chemicals.

I was never the masterpiece she once assumed I'd be.

And when her eyes land on my face across the gallery, it's obvious, and it feels like a gut punch.

"Excuse me," she says politely to her friends or admirers. Then, with her lips pressed in a tight line, she hurries over to me. "What are you doing here?"

My throat burns, so I clear it. "You don't return my calls."

"Well, are you calling because you want to talk to me, or are you calling because you need money?" Her voice is so low I can only make out her words by the movement of her lips.

"No, I'm not only calling for money," I reply, averting my gaze as I talk.

She crosses her arms. "Then, what is it, Sylvie?"

Just then, an angry pair of heels click against the hardwood as Enid approaches from the next room. "What are you doing here?" she whisper-shouts.

"Talking to *my* mother. I didn't realize that was a crime," I argue, throwing my hands up.

"Well, after the shit you pulled last time you were here,

Sylvie, it is technically a crime. You've been served a restraining order."

My jaw drops, and I feel the eyes of the other people in the gallery scoping toward us. "A restraining order?"

My mother sighs. "Against the *gallery*," she says, giving Enid a serious expression. "You really shouldn't be back here, Sylvie."

"That was over a year ago. I've changed."

Enid crosses her arms now. "Oh really, how have you changed?"

Avoiding the question, I glance around the building. "Where's Dad?"

"He's in the studio," my mother replies.

I let out a defeated sigh. If anyone is likely to give me a moment of pity, it's him.

"Can't we just…talk? Somewhere? Anywhere. *Alone*." I say to my mother, not bothering to glance in Enid's direction.

Her breathing is heavy, and her expression is cold. "Come on," she says without sounding the least bit welcoming.

I follow my mother up the stairs of the gallery to where I know the office is. When we reach the second floor, I spot a piece on display in the middle that makes my heart fly up to my throat.

It's an acrylic portrait on canvas that was obviously ripped to shreds before being sewn back together. The hazel eyes in the painting haunt me, and I find myself pausing to stare at it. Tears prick behind my eyes, and my mother notices me standing there, frozen in place.

"We've made the best of a bad situation," she mutters quietly before urging me into the office.

I quickly blink back the tears before they can show. Then I follow her into the office.

She closes the door behind me before crossing the room toward her desk. "Go ahead. What is it you want to tell me?"

Everything feels stuck. As if I'm still standing in front of that painting, still ripping it to shreds, still hearing her tell me how disappointing I am, still reading the inscription, still crying in the back of a cop car.

I came here to ask for money. The plan was to beg and appeal to her nonexistent nurturing side, but even I knew that was futile. So what the hell am I doing here? Why do I even bother?

She's staring at me with a harsh expression as she waits. "Sylvie…" she mutters with irritation.

I look up from the floor and stare into her eyes. "I'm getting married," I announce.

Her brows shoot upward, and she looks momentarily surprised. "It's about time," she replies, her tone a bit lighter. "You and Aaron have been together for years."

"It's not Aaron," I say, tainting his name with bitterness.

"Then who is it?" she asks, letting her brows crease.

I swallow down my nerves. I'm not committing to anything yet. I'm just telling my mother. That hardly counts.

"His name is Killian. He lives in Scotland."

My mother laughs, and the sound of it is so patronizing I double down. "He's very rich, actually. Lives in a manor."

She's smiling as if this is all a joke. "And how did you meet this…Killian?"

"While I was there last month," I reply. "We just…ran into each other and kept in touch. His sister was actually just here visiting, and we've been setting everything up. I'll be leaving soon."

She laughs again. "*You're* going to Scotland? What about Aaron?"

"He's been fucking Margot for months."

She gasps at the vulgarity of my language, but I get some pleasure from shocking her.

"Killian loves me."

God, even uttering those words out loud makes me feel like an idiot, even though I'm the only one in the room who knows it's a lie.

"When is the wedding?" she asks, and I can no longer tell if she's taking me seriously or not.

"I'm not sure, actually. But I'll be going soon, so I just wanted to let you know…" I lift my face, meeting her gaze. "I don't need anything from you. Not anymore."

The weight of the stare between us makes the air hard to breathe. I keep waiting for her to let this grudge she's holding go, but she won't. Her expression stays tight and guarded.

"Okay," she replies coldly.

I have to fight the urge to cry. "Aren't you going to…wish me well or at least come to the wedding?" My stupid, weak voice cracks.

She shifts her weight and rolls her eyes. "No, because I don't believe for a moment that you're really marrying some rich man in Scotland. Seriously, Sylvie."

My gaze darkens. "I am."

Her scoff is dramatic and hurtful. "This is just what you do, Sylvie. The moment you don't have attention, you come in here with some elaborate scheme or dramatic story. It's all so childish."

"I literally never have your attention," I argue, unable to keep the emotion from my voice now. My vision grows blurry with moisture pooling in my lashes.

"Oh, don't be so immature. Just grow up."

When I shake my head, a tear falls. "I am getting married, Mom. It's true. I'm moving to Scotland, and I'll be gone."

Looking unimpressed, she just gives me a shrug. "Fine, Sylvie. If that's what you want me to believe, then I'll believe it. Best of luck."

"That's it?" I mumble.

"What else do you want me to say after everything you've done?"

After a shuddering breath, I wipe my tears away. "That's all. Bye, Mother."

Without so much as a hug or a handshake, I turn and bolt out of her office. I pass by Enid on the main level as she's talking to the same group my mother was.

"Bye, you greasy cunt," I call out to her, pleased to hear the gasps of horror as I dash out the front door.

As I huddle against the brisk night air, I pull my cardigan around me and force myself to breathe. With each pain-riddled inhale, I feel the dam break, and my tears form. By the time I reach 57th and Park, I'm crying in earnest.

Everything hurts from that interaction with my mother, but the thing that digs the deepest is her not believing me. Why does that one part feel as if it's swallowing me whole? She doesn't care if I stay or go. She doesn't care that I never feel loved by her. She doesn't care about me at all, but the fact that she didn't believe me…that makes my breath quiver, my lip tremble, and the tears flow.

Well, I'll show her. I wasn't lying. I will marry that Scottish man, and I will move to Scotland, and I will be taken care of for the rest of my life. I don't need her anymore.

As soon as I get back to my apartment, my face is a mess with tears. I scramble through the drawer of my desk, looking for the card I left there. For a moment, I panic, thinking I might have thrown it away.

But my heart hammers in my chest when I spot the name on the glossy forest green card—*Anna Barclay*.

With a nervous gulp, I pull out my phone and dial the international number. Then I check my time and realize it's already early morning there. Maybe even too early for her to be awake.

But after two rings, she groggily answers.

"Hello?"

"Anna," I say, feeling frantic and unsettled. "This is Sylvie Devereaux."

"Hello, Ms. Devereaux," she replies in her calm and collected manner. "Have you given some thought to my offer?"

I'm doing this. I'm really fucking doing this.

"Yes," I say with confidence. "I'll do it. I'll...marry your brother."

"Very good," she replies with a squeak of excitement in her voice. "I'll have the contract drawn up and sent over today. We can arrange for a crew to put your things into storage for you, and the fees would be covered. We should be able to get the typical waiting period waived and Marriage Notice processed quickly. Would you be ready to leave in, say...a week?"

My heart is pounding so hard that I feel like I might pass out. I glance around my apartment at the various things that I have collected over the years. It's all just things that have no real meaning to me anymore. No friends to say goodbye to. No family to see me off.

The sooner I'm out of here, the better.

"Yes. Next week is perfect," I reply.

"Wonderful. I'm very excited, and I know Killian will be too."

The mention of his name makes my blood go cold. I'm going to see him again. I'm going to *marry* him.

"Thanks," I mutter.

"See you next week then," she says.

"See you next week," I echo.

When the phone line goes dead, I plop down on my couch and stare at nothing in particular.

What on earth did I just do?

Chapter Six

ANNA IS STANDING IN THE AIRPORT, WAITING FOR ME AS I WALK out of the terminal. She greets me with a smile, and I force one in return.

Somewhere between the neurotic night I agreed to this, and the moment that airplane put its wheels down on a runway in Edinburgh, I completely talked myself out of this wild scheme.

But here I am anyway. Because I want to be? No.

Because I have a point to prove? Yep.

"Ms. Devereaux," she says in a polite greeting. "How was your flight?"

"Please, call me Sylvie," I reply. Anna is probably only a few years older than me, but she talks like she's Scottish royalty, and we're all in some historical romance simulation. "It was good. Thank you," I say, hoisting my backpack higher up on my shoulder.

"I hope you were able to get some rest. We have a busy day ahead of us."

"Yeah, actually, I did." Which is true, thanks to those first-class sleeping pods they flew me in. I bet the folks back in coach are feeling a different way right now.

She starts walking briskly toward the exit. "We'll be heading straight over to the house today," she says in a straightforward, businesslike sort of way. "You can meet Killian a bit more properly now."

My stomach tightens at the mention of seeing him again.

"It's about an hour to the manor from here. We can go over some of the terms and rules in the car."

I nod as if this is completely normal business and not the most unhinged, reckless thing I've ever done.

After we get my baggage from the carousel and our driver carries it out to our car, Anna and I climb into the back seat together. She offers me some water and something to eat but doesn't waste any time before getting down to business.

"Now, I trust you've gone through the contract you signed, so none of this should come as a surprise to you."

I nod, taking a gulp of water.

"But there are some important stipulations to the agreement that I feel we should reiterate."

"Okay…" I mutter, waiting to hear them. I *did* read the contract, but contracts are contracts, and the language was superfluous enough to be confusing and vague. So I signed it.

"The term of marriage must reach one year from the date the certificates are signed in order for you to receive your payout."

"Got it," I say. Easy enough.

"After you've reached one year, you will sign the deed to Barclay Manor over to our aunt Lorna, who will handle the estate from there. Your marriage will be annulled, and you can return to America with your ten million dollars."

I force myself to swallow. She makes it sound so simple, but this part of the bargain has me feeling dizzy. I hope by the end of the year, it will be so easy to just take this man's house from him and go home as if nothing happened.

"Both you and Killian must remain faithful to each other for the duration of the twelve months in order for commitment to be considered maintained."

"Both of us?" I mutter as I pick up a piece of meat from the tray of snacks she gave me when I climbed in.

"Yes, both of you. This is important, Miss Devereaux."

"Why should I lose out on my ten million if he can't keep his dick in his pants?"

I don't bother to tell her that I failed to keep my *real* boyfriend loyal, let alone my *fake* husband.

"This is part of the rules in the trust, Sylvie. It's not something we can negotiate. If anyone is caught stepping outside of the marriage, the union is considered void, and none of the legal propagations stand."

"What kind of rule is that?" I stammer. "If a wife is loyal to her husband, but *he* cheats, she loses out on her house? Fuck that."

Anna purses her lips and gives me a stoic glare. "Life is rarely fair."

I stare out the window of the car as we drive down the busy city streets, wondering how the hell I'm supposed to keep a man like Killian faithful to me when we're not even in a real relationship.

———

The rest of the drive is more boring talk about the contract. It starts to feel hopeless by the time we reach our destination. As I approach the manor for the second time in my life, I stare at it, amazed that anyone can truly live there. It looks like something out of a historical novel, not the twenty-first century.

I know from experience that the inside isn't quite like the outside. The interior has been renovated, the kitchen opened to the sitting room. The walls aren't dark and foreboding but white and airy.

"Welcome home," Anna says with a smile as our driver opens our door.

As we step into the manor, memories come flooding back. I pick up the same cologne and spice scent I remember from the first time I was here.

But something is different this time. Unlike last time, there is a heavy beat of music playing somewhere in the house.

"What on earth?" Anna mumbles.

Then I hear the unmistakable giggle and moan of a woman upstairs. My cheeks heat and I bite my lip as I turn my attention toward Anna to gauge her reaction. I know the sounds of sex when I hear them. The last time I walked into a scenario like this, it was my boyfriend. This time it's my soon-to-be husband.

"Excuse me," Anna says to me as she stomps angrily into the house. "Killian!" she calls with fury.

I hang back in the entryway for a moment.

The girl upstairs giggles even louder.

When Anna reaches the living room, she lets out a scream. Her hand flies to her mouth, so I hurry to catch up, curious to know what has her so bothered.

As I turn the corner into the large sitting room, my jaw drops when my gaze lands on a completely naked woman scurrying to cover herself on a dark-green upholstered sofa.

"I'm so sorry, miss!" the young woman stammers as she rushes to get dressed. "My apologies."

"Killian!" Anna shrieks as she takes off toward the stairs. Her heels click loudly against each one.

I stifle a laugh, biting my bottom lip as I turn away from the naked woman and follow Killian's sister toward the stairs.

Killian's loud footsteps echo through the house as he rushes to meet his sister's rage-fueled attack. A moment later, there's a heated argument between them, and I stop in my tracks. I'm about halfway up the stairs, eager to listen to their fight but not interested enough to get involved.

"You can't just barge into my house!" Killian bellows.

"Will you *please* put some clothes on?" Anna shrieks.

"I'll do whatever the fuck I please," he replies, that deep Scottish accent bringing back memories of the day he yelled in my face. It should scare me, but it doesn't. It just activates my anger.

Heavy footsteps pound against the floor. I take a few more steps, peering over the railing to see Killian's white ass as he disappears into one of the bedrooms.

Anna turns back toward me, looking flustered. "I'm sorry about this. I told him to expect us today."

I shrug. This entire scheme is growing more futile by the second. The likelihood of me making it more than a few months is dwindling by the second.

Twelve months? Impossible.

"You realize there is no way this is going to work, right? He's not going to keep his dick in his pants, and I'm sure as hell not going to—"

Feeling his anger-laced green eyes on my face, I slant my head to see a now-dressed Killian watching me from the bedroom.

"Yes, he will," Anna mutters heatedly. "There is too much on the line."

Another young woman comes bounding out of the bedroom. Her cheeks are still flushed, and her hair is messy with knots and tangles in the back, which is a pretty good indicator of what they were just up to.

That explains all those giggles.

"Excuse me," she murmurs sweetly to Anna and me as she

scurries past us, still buttoning up the top of some sort of black shift-dress-style uniform.

Anna glares at Killian, and then she glances softly at me. "Don't worry, Sylvie. We'll be hiring a new cleaning staff."

I press my lips together. Somewhere in the distance, I hear a door closing.

Which means I'm now alone with my soon-to-be husband and his sister. Killian saunters out of the bedroom, running his fingers through his long brown hair as he pulls it into a bun at the back of his head.

"You again," he says to me.

I square my shoulders as I turn to face him. "I was invited this time," I reply.

"I'm surprised you came."

"Well, I'm just full of surprises." I cross my arms in front of my chest and glare up at him.

"We'll see about that."

His green eyes are so fierce it becomes hard to stare at them for too long. His heavy brows hang over his eyes in austere contemplation. It's almost like I start to shrink under his gaze, and it grates on my nerves to feel that way.

But I don't back down. Soon, we're in a heated staring contest, and it's Anna who finally breaks it up.

"Killian, get this mess cleaned up. I'm going to show Sylvie her room, and we'll meet downstairs for tea in thirty minutes. I expect you to be there. We have some things to go over."

The corner of Killian's mouth lifts in a crooked smile. "I look forward to it."

Without a response, I turn away from him and follow Anna down a long hallway to the left, opposite from where the giggling girl emerged. The entire time she gives me a tour, I try to shake the feeling of irritation from that short interaction with Killian.

I realize he was trying to get under my skin. He was trying to assert dominance by mocking me and making me uncomfortable. I won't give him the satisfaction.

The truth of the matter is, I want this money. I *need* this money. Which means I have to make this work one way or another. Whatever this family plans to do to Killian when all of this is over isn't any of my business. I don't care about him or the house he wants to keep.

I'm in this for *me*.

Which means over the next twelve months, I'm about to become this man's worst nightmare.

Chapter Seven

"THERE WILL BE A FULL STAFF ON HAND...ONCE WE REPLACE them," Anna says as she pours hot water into my cup. I pick up the string from the tea bag and dunk it a few times as she continues.

It's still so odd to me that she is so involved in her brother's life. He's thirty-seven. Why is she even here? My parents practically wrote me off once I turned eighteen. Pushed me right out of that nest, and I would never expect them to put this much effort into getting me to fix my life. The only effort they've ever shown is by calling their accountant to have them cease my allowance deposits. I'm sure that took a phone call. It's so endearing to think they took the time to do that for me.

"What kind of staff?" I ask as I reach for the sugar.

"You'll have a cook, someone to clean, and a driver if you need to go anywhere."

"Seriously?" I ask with a perplexed expression. "So there will just be people here all the time?"

"Not all the time," she replies. "They keep basic hours, and they don't live here. But if you need them, they're available.

There is a groundskeeper who lives in one of the houses on the property."

"Can't I just...drive myself?"

I see the corners of her jaw click as she presses her teeth together. "You can go anywhere you'd like. I'm not holding you here, but for your safety, we'd prefer if you'd use the driver."

My hand stills mid-dunk. I'm not an idiot. I know what she means by my *safety*, and it means I'll be watched. Wherever I decide to go will be everyone's knowledge. The reminder that I'll be someone's wife, regardless of how *fake* it is, makes me shudder with apprehension.

I'll be someone's property.

I mean, not literally. But suddenly, it feels like I'm living by some pretty archaic rules. I'm in a fucking manor that is staffed like it's *Downton Abbey*, and I have to live with a real-life chauffeur like I'm some sort of princess. It feels like prison bars made of gold.

Ten million dollars, Sylvie, I remind myself. I can do just about anything for one year. One year of actual luxury, and then I'll be set for life.

"Who will know it's not real? The staff?" I ask, wondering if I really need to sell this marriage all the time to everyone.

Anna places her hand on the table in front of me and leans forward. "No. No one can know the scheme. The only people who know are myself, my siblings, and our aunt. That is all. The public, the staff, and *especially* our extended family must believe that it's real."

I force down a gulp. A moment ago I figured the marriage was just a contract we had to uphold for a while, but now I have to actually convince people for a very long period of time that I'm in love with Killian Barclay. I think I might have bitten off more than I can chew.

Speaking of the devil, he bounds loudly down the stairs

and into the sitting room, where Anna and I are stationed around a small table, each with a cup of tea in front of us.

"Join us for tea," she says to her brother.

He seems freshly showered. His hair is still a little wet at the tips, and he's in clean clothes. He's wearing a pair of dark jeans, brown boots, and a white knit Henley.

Is he *trying* to impress me with those sculpted shoulders in that tight top? It's like he's showing off, and it's cheesy and gross. Killian is a chauvinist, and I *hate* chauvinists.

Without giving him much attention, I focus on my tea, lifting it to my lips for a sip.

"No, thanks," he replies as he crosses the room toward the bar against the wall. He pours himself something, and I watch his sister for her reaction. There's a flinch in her stoic, brave expression which reveals something more similar to heartache. Just a subtle flinch of pain.

Killian drops onto the sofa lazily with his drink in his hand. "So, when's the wedding?" he asks. "I need to know when to plan my stag do."

I make the mistake of glancing toward him, and he gives me a quick wink, making my blood boil, so I look away again.

The incentive to talk business makes Anna sit taller and look a good deal more in her element than a moment ago.

"There will be no stag do, Killian. And I think it's best if we do a private ceremony at the church—"

"No church," he barks, cutting her off.

"Killian…" she pleads.

"I told you. The wedding has to be here, or I'm not doing it."

Anna lets out a surrendering sigh. "Fine. We'll have the wedding here and make the official announcement to the public next week. That would be the easiest and most efficient solution."

"What do you mean *official announcement*?" I ask, tightening my grip on my teacup.

"The family puts out statements to the public through the newspaper, but more recently on social media and through our family's bulletin. Next month, the two of you should attend an event in town, so people can see you together."

I notice the way Killian grimaces.

Meanwhile, I'm too distracted by the promise of an announcement. The thought of everyone I know seeing that, especially my parents, makes me giddy with excitement.

"Wait," I say, realizing something that makes my skin crawl. "You said the staff will all have to believe we're really married. Does that mean I have to sleep in his room—"

"Och, no," Anna answers, cutting me off.

"Oh, yes," Killian says at the same time. He's wearing a cunning smile, and it's handsome and alluring, like the devil's. He could lure women to their deaths with a smile like that.

"No," Anna says again, side-eying her brother. "There are no physical requirements in this agreement." I notice the way her cheeks blush, and her fists clench on the topic.

"Unless you want to," Killian adds with a wink.

"I won't," I quip.

"Of course, in public," Anna adds, "you would need to be convincing as a couple."

I let out a sigh and grind my molars at the thought. I can do that. For a few hours, I can at least pretend that he's not a complete pigheaded asshole.

"You can handle that. Can't you, darling?"

I glance at Killian, wondering if he can read my mind.

"How hard could it be?" I reply with a forced smile.

Every time Killian and I speak to each other, I notice Anna's discomfort grows. She's clearly recognizing just how poorly he and I get along and that this might actually be a terrible idea, which for the record, I tried to warn her about.

"Killian, why don't you take Sylvie for a little walk around the garden? Spend some time getting to know each other. You two can discuss your personal terms, and I'll just wait here, looking over some paperwork."

I turn my attention to Killian on the couch and notice the way his eyes burn with skepticism. I suddenly remember how, on that day I broke into the house, he kept insisting I was a spy for his sister. What on earth does he really think she's going to do while she's here? I mean, she's already walked in on his orgy. What more could he be hiding?

"I think that's a fantastic idea," he says as he stands from the couch. His tone is dripping with sarcasm. "Come on, darling."

With a roll of my eyes, I stand from the chair and look at him, waiting for him to lead the way.

Looking miserable, he walks toward the large French doors that lead to the garden behind the house. I never saw this part when we drove up over a month ago. Plus it was raining then, so I missed the gorgeous view.

Barclay Manor sits in the middle of a sprawling country-side. The garden behind the house is expansive and mostly flat before it leads to a large body of water with rolling hills and trees in the distance.

For a girl who grew up in Manhattan, this feels epic and overwhelming. The world felt much smaller in the city. We could only see as far as the building in front of us. Even in the high-rise apartments and rooftops, it felt like my view was limited to the edge of town. Breathtaking nonetheless, the views in New York are nothing like the views here.

It makes me feel even smaller. One puny human in the grand scheme of things. Insignificant and useless.

"Come on," Killian says with a growl as he makes his way

down the stairs to the manicured garden below. "It's not raining today, so we better make the best use of it before it does."

I let out a cynical laugh. "And what exactly would be the best use of it?"

He directs an arched brow toward me. "We're supposed to be gettin' to know each other, remember?"

"Okay, so what would you like to know?" I ask.

He stops and stares down at me. "Why the fuck would you agree to this? You must really be out of your mind."

I scoff. "Why would *you* agree to it? Your sister told me you thought I was rude and mean."

"Oh, you are, darling," he says with a chuckle.

"Then why me? Why would you agree to marry me if you hate me so much?"

He steps toward me, crowding me toward the gray stone wall. His tall frame blocks the sun from my eyes, casting him in a shadow.

"Because as soon as the year is up, I don't want to have a wife anymore. As soon as my family sees that I'm a changed man, they'll leave me be, and I can stay in my house without them meddling in my business.

"So, I'd rather marry a selfish, rude, ugly, entitled cow like you so I never have to worry about hurting your feelings or wanting to make you happy. We stay our separate ways and get through the next twelve months without having to see each other much. Do we have a deal?"

My blood has never been hotter.

"Deal," I mutter through my clenched teeth.

As he turns away to continue our stroll through the yard, I add, "You do realize you can't keep fucking the staff if we're married, right?"

He huffs, letting his head hang back with an amused grin as he turns back toward me. "I'll fuck anyone I please, and you'll keep your mouth shut about it, or you'll risk us both losing what was promised to us."

"Oh, so you get to have your fun, but I don't?" I argue, stepping up to him. I don't care that he's almost twice my size or that he could bend me in half with one hand. I refuse to let this giant brute manipulate me or have his way while I'm stuck asking for a ride and being watched like a child for the next year.

"And what are you going to do about it, darling?"

"Stop calling me that," I spit.

"I'll call you whatever I want."

I take another step closer to him.

"One thing you should know about me," I say, poking him hard in the chest. "I'm stubborn, and I don't back down in a fight. And I really fucking want that money, so if you think I'm going to risk losing because you wanna get your dick wet, you're wrong. I can make your life hell if want to try to blackmail me into staying quiet."

"You really are a conniving little bitch, aren't you?" he replies, but the insult doesn't even sting.

"Yes, I am," I say with pride. "And you're right. We are going to stay our separate ways over the next year, and then we can easily split and take what's owed to us. I won't ruin it for you if you don't ruin it for me."

"Is that a threat, *wench*?"

I glower at him. "Sure is…*brute*."

Moving around him, I continue my stroll down the gravel path, waiting for the moment when he finally moves from his spot and picks up his pace behind me.

I don't feel bad that all of this is just his family tricking him out of his home. If he wants to be a rude and uncultured brute, then I won't feel bad at all.

Chapter Eight

THE WEDDING IS NOT REALLY A WEDDING. ESPECIALLY CONSIDERING I haven't spoken a word to my soon-to-be husband in two days. Not since that day on our walk when he tried to bully me into thinking he could do whatever he wanted and I had to abide.

I don't abide. Ever.

I spent most of the last two days trying to recuperate from my jet lag without much success. Last night, around three in the morning, I heard some cursing and stumbling down the hall where Killian's room is, but there were no other voices to be heard, so I didn't bother much about it.

Now, I'm standing in front of a plain white dress, trying to work up the courage to put it on. I feel so stupid for doing this. I don't have a friend or family member here. I'm going to stand up in front of some strangers and say my wedding vows to a man I can't stand and wouldn't marry even if I did like him.

Vows mean nothing. It doesn't matter if I make them. It doesn't matter if I'm not being genuine.

Vows aren't something I can spend or eat or live in. Money

is though. Money can buy me a car, one I can drive by myself wherever I want to go, preferably far away from anyone else.

Money can buy me a beautiful house in a strange city where I can start a new life.

Money can get me whatever I want, so anyone who says money can't buy happiness is probably poor and bitter.

A knock at the door pulls me from my thoughts.

"Sylvie, are you ready?" Anna calls from the other side of the bedroom door.

I heave a sigh. "Almost."

Standing up, I grab the white dress from the hanger and toss it over my head, shoving my arms into the sleeves and shifting it down around my breasts and waist. My long wild hair cascades over my shoulders, so I grab a clip from the vanity and pull it into a French twist. Tiny wisps hang over my ears and on my forehead, so I comb them back into the curls, spraying a little hairspray to keep them in place.

When I turn to face the full-length mirror, I pause at the reflection.

I'm not much for weddings. I don't believe in marriage. And I've never pictured myself in a white gown before like so many of my friends did growing up. The sight of myself in a white dress with lacy shoulders and rich, ornate fabric shouldn't really affect me, but it does.

I look like a grown-up, happy version of myself. Like this version doesn't suffer from a strained parental relationship and reckless life decisions. This version of myself did everything right. Found a nice partner, fell in love, and is moving through life's little rites of passage without fumbling at every turn.

There's another knock at the door. "Coming," I call after one last look.

When I open the door, Anna is standing there waiting.

She's in a deep-green dress that looks lovely with her warm chestnut-colored hair.

"You look beautiful," she says without even looking at my dress. I realize as we start our walk down the hall and to the car that she's likely to be the only person to tell me that today.

As I descend the stairs, I see Killian waiting by the front door. He has his back to me as he looks down at his phone. His hair is down—deep-brown locks the same color as Anna's. His come just to his shoulders.

He has on a granite-colored wool jacket and a green and orange kilt. I bite the corner of my lips as I stifle a smile. I've never seen a man in a kilt in real life, and I'm a little annoyed with myself for how intrigued and aroused I am by the sight.

The kilt stops just above his knee and was probably specially made for him since he's built like a tree. His legs are sticking out of the bottom, thick and covered in hair. Then there's the long white socks and a pair of black shiny shoes.

It's honestly not fair how handsome he looks, even from the back. But let's be honest, that kilt is doing the heavy lifting. His personality makes it very hard to find him the least bit attractive.

When he hears us coming, he turns, and our eyes meet. For a split second, he's not wearing a rueful expression. For just a hair of a moment, he looks as if he's admiring me. As if he might be the slightest bit nervous about today too. Which would be nice to know since I'm feeling nervous as hell too.

"Let's get this over with," he grunts before painting the hatred back on his face where it belongs. Then he opens the door and marches out to the makeshift altar outside in the white gazebo in the garden.

Anna gives me an apologetic expression. "I can handle him," I mumble to ease her worries.

There is a crowd of people gathered near the gazebo, including the priest in his green robes.

When we approach the small group set apart from the rest, I notice that one of the men standing there looks like a younger cleaned-up version of Killian. Another man next to him doesn't look as much like Killian, but he's wearing a scowl like Killian, so maybe there's a gene for bad attitudes after all.

Anna leads me over to them.

"Declan, Lachy, this is Sylvie."

The first one to smile and greet me is the short-haired Killian clone. "Lachy," he says as he reaches out a hand. "It's so nice to meet you." His accent is thicker than his brother's.

"Nice to meet you," I reply warmly.

Then I turn to the other brother, who gives me a curt nod. "Declan," he says flatly.

"Hi…" I stammer uncomfortably. "Nice to meet you."

"The rest are mostly aunts and uncles and a few prominent people from the town. You'll get a chance to meet them more at the reception later," Anna says. I respond with a nod.

When I feel a heavy hand rest on my shoulder, I flinch. Feeling Killian's touch and proximity is a little unsettling, but then I realize the priest is watching us, and when he sees my fiancé sidling up to my side, he smiles.

"Let's get married, then," Killian says, and I turn to see the fake smile plastered on his face. It's not very convincing to me, but the priest seems to be buying it.

"Of course," the priest mutters as he shuffles toward the center of the gazebo. Everyone takes their seats, and I walk down the aisle on Killian's arm. It all feels very messy and rushed, but as long as everyone is buying it, I don't care.

When we reach the front, I notice Lachy smiling, and I keep my eyes on him. He looks to be closer to my age and much more like the guy I'd be dating than Killian.

My hands start to shake as I turn to face Killian. The moment our eyes meet, I feel the tremble subside. He's not scowling at me or giving me some hate-filled expression. I don't feel so alone as we stare at each other. He's in this too and hates it as much as me, and something about that is comforting.

The priest recites all the traditional things he's supposed to say at a wedding, but I'm drowning it all out at the moment.

Ten million dollars, I tell myself. *Set for life.*

That's the incantation that gets me through the next few minutes. Briefly, as Killian and I stare at each other, I replay the conversation we had the other day. About avoiding each other for the next twelve months. And I wonder to myself if this would be easier if we didn't seem to despise each other so much. Would I be dreading this the same way I am now if I could see Killian as a friend? Does it even matter?

He squeezes my hand and nods his head to the priest. "What?" I mumble.

"Say, 'I do,'" Killian whispers.

"Oh, I do," I say, feeling a chill work its way down my spine.

The priest says the marriage vows before Killian replies, "I do."

"Have you the rings?" the priest asks.

I turn toward Anna, who hands us a set of gold bands. I glance down at the one in my palm. A simple gold ring for Killian.

When he reaches a hand out for me, I place mine in his, and he slips the ornate diamond ring over my finger. "With this ring, I thee wed." He spits the words out with a hint of bitterness, and I look at the priest to be sure he didn't catch that.

He smiles at me to signify that it's my turn. Still trembling, I reach for Killian's hand.

The moment he places his large hand in mine, I stare down at it. For some reason, I'm enthralled by it. It's soft against my fingers, and I find myself admiring the size difference between mine and his, letting myself explore the palm before flipping his hand over to slide the ring over his fourth finger.

I don't let go right away. Feeling his gaze on my face, I lift my eyes to his.

"Here before God, and in His name, I now pronounce you husband and wife. You may kiss your bride."

My breath hitches. *Fuck.* I forgot about this part.

Killian doesn't waver. He places a hand around my back and tugs me to his ginormous body. My spine bends as I stare up at him. I'm barely even on my feet when he cradles my head and presses his lips to mine.

It's brutal and harsh, and I squeeze my eyes closed as his rough beard scratches my face.

The kiss is over as fast as it began. The next thing I know, my feet are back on the floor, and I open my eyes to see Killian's brothers and sister staring at us with a mixture of smiles and unamused expressions. Anna claps softly, and I touch Killian's arm to steady myself.

Then, he walks back down the aisle, and I follow him, holding tight to his gray wool jacket.

Killian marches right toward the house. I'm practically dragged behind him.

"Wait! We need photos!" Anna calls.

Killian stops in his tracks and stares at his sister expectantly.

"Here, next to the gazebo," she says, pointing to the structure.

Killian grabs my arms and hauls me to stand next to the white brick. Anna gets her camera out and points it at us.

"Smile!" she calls.

When it's obvious that Killian and I aren't willing to do much more than stand next to each other without touching and refuse to smile, she heaves a sigh and gives us both a steady glare.

"Fuck it," he mutters. Then, he slings an arm behind my back. We hold hands in front and stare at the camera. When I see him grinning, I can't help but smile too.

This all feels incredibly strange and awkward, and I have to keep reminding myself this is a fake marriage and not a real wedding, so I don't have to bother being disappointed.

Chapter Nine

AFTER THE WEDDING, EVERYONE COMES BACK TO THE HOUSE. Once it's filled with guests and food and music, it feels like a different place.

I'm a feather in a hurricane, blown frivolously from one end to the other, never landing. Killian is rarely by my side, and for that, I'm grateful. Most of the day is spent being introduced to relatives and friends by Anna. They ask about my family, how I met Killian, how I like Scotland, how many babies I want to have.

Every time I get my hands on a glass of wine, I gulp it down as fast as I can, as if it will soften the blow of this god-awful, miserable day.

There are moments when families laugh together that make the absence of mine feel debilitating. Then there are moments when they are obnoxious and overbearing that make me grateful mine are not here.

It's nearly two hours after the start of the party, and I manage to slip out the back door of the house and onto the stone veranda. Once there, I scurry down the stairs to escape the eyes of anyone at the party.

I desperately need a break.

But as soon as I reach the gravel pathway below, I nearly run headfirst into the last man on earth I want to see—my husband.

"Oy," he says with a groan when he spots me interrupting his escape. His large hands engulf my arms. "Watch where you're going, wench."

"Let me go, Killian," I argue.

He releases my arms, and I step away from him, fixing my dress.

"What are you doing out here?" he asks. I pick up the scent of something smoky on his clothes.

"Getting some air," I reply, turning my back on him. "What are *you* doing out here? That's *your* family."

"Aye, but they don't like me much. That's the whole reason you're here. Make them like you, and then they'll like me." He reaches into the small leather pouch tied around his waist and pulls out a pack of cigarettes. I screw up my nose and turn away from him, wrapping my arms around myself to keep warm in the cool fall air.

"Disgusting habit," I mutter quietly as he lights up.

"Thanks for letting me know," he replies. "Since your opinion does matter so much to me."

I scoff, spinning back to face him. "How do you expect your family to like me when you clearly despise me so much?"

"Och, you'll fit right in," he replies with a sarcastic chuckle. "You're selfish and entitled, just like them."

"You are literally the rudest and most entitled person I have ever met!" I shriek.

"Well, when your family conspires against you to take your house, how kind and gracious would you be? What's your excuse?"

"Ugh!" I stomp away from him, not getting far before

my retort comes flying to the forefront of my mind, so I turn back his way. "You do realize that all you need to do to get your family off your back is take care of yourself, get your life together, and be a responsible adult? You don't need me here at all."

He chuckles around his cigarette, and I quickly look away from that siren song of a smile. "It's my fucking life. I can live it however I want. They have no rights to *my* house or my privacy. But don't worry. You won't be here long, darling. I predict you won't make it a month before you're boarding a plane back to America."

I take a slow step toward him. "Technically, it's your family's house, Killian. It's not wrong of them to want to preserve it before you burn it to the ground. And second, I will make it the year because as much as I hope your family does get that house from you, I want the money they're offering me more." By the time I finish, we're practically toe-to-toe, but I have to crane my neck to see his face.

We're in the middle of a stare-off when I hear a set of footsteps on the veranda. I don't pull away before Lachy spots us standing so close together.

"Uh-oh. What am I interrupting?" he asks with a charming smile.

"Nothing," Killian mutters as he finishes his cigarette and stubs it into the ground with his shoe. Then he storms back up the stairs without another word, and I'm left alone with his younger brother.

"Don't mind him," Lachy says with a crooked smile. There are deep dimples on both sides of his cheeks, and I never truly understood the power of good dimples until he aimed that beaming grin in my direction.

"Oh, I don't," I reply, looking off into the distance. It's nearly dusk. The sun has set, but there's just enough light left in the sky to give the world a sepia filter. Light without the sun is eerie, like we are caught in between two days.

And maybe that's what my life is right now. A mystic dusk. Not quite day and not yet night; just stuck in the middle. A yearlong dusk.

Once this whole thing is over, I'll be free. No longer living in my parents' shadows. I won't need them anymore, and it'll finally give me the peace to just be happy.

"Everything all right?"

I've nearly forgotten Lachy was standing there when he interrupts me from my thoughts. I tear my gaze away from the misty glen in the distance and turn my attention to him.

"Yeah, I'm fine," I lie.

He scrutinizes me for a moment before he speaks. "Listen, I know this whole thing is just…a farce. But you'll be around, part of the family, for the next twelve months. And I know you have your own reasons for doing it, but I just want you to know that you're really helping him more than you think."

"Helping him?" I ask, astounded.

"Yeah. It sounds strange, and I'm sure you think we're terrible for lying to him, but there's so much you don't know about Killian. He needs this."

I kick some gravel with the toe of my shoe. "It's a bit elaborate if you ask me."

Lachy laughs. "I know. But when I tell you we've tried everything, I mean it."

"Is it really that big of a deal to you that he moves out?"

Lachy's face falls. "It's not about the house. Not to us. If Anna made it sound that way, it's because Anna is pragmatic."

I raise a brow as I take a step toward him. "Then, what's it about?" I whisper.

Lachy clenches his jaw, and his eyes dart out to the horizon.

He looks a little uncomfortable with the question. "Anna really hasn't told you much, has she? I mean about Killian."

I shake my head.

"The truth is…" he mumbles quietly. "We don't think Killian has left the house in nearly ten years."

My jaw drops. Suddenly, I'm replaying every interaction I've had with him. The argument over the wedding being at the house instead of the church.

"Why wouldn't Anna tell me that?" I say, staring straight ahead, unfocused and in shock.

He shrugs in return. "Don't be mad at her for that. Like I said, she just…thinks in black and white. To her, getting the house away from Killian is the same as getting Killian out of his grief."

"From your parents' deaths?"

He gives a noncommittal shrug. "In a way, yes."

"In a way?"

Lachy laughs uncomfortably. "This conversation is too heavy for a wedding."

"I deserve to know these things. I'm about to be stuck in a house with this guy, and I don't even know him," I argue, stepping closer to Lachy.

He puts up his hands in surrender. "Hey, I don't want to overstep, but I can assure you that you're safe with Killian. He might act like a brute, but he's not really one."

I take a step back and shake my head. "Anna told me we're supposed to make a public appearance next month. How does she expect any of that to happen?"

Lachy heaves a sigh. "Wishful thinking," he replies with a tight smile.

It suddenly feels like I'm going to have to work harder than I thought for that ten million.

"Ugh." I let out a groan, suddenly remembering our

argument the other day when I ridiculed him for being able to go wherever he wanted without a driver while I was stuck here. I feel like an idiot. "Everything makes so much sense now," I mutter quietly to myself.

Not having a car for myself must be Anna's way of ensuring that I don't abandon him here. Maybe she's hoping that Killian and I can go places together or that having me with him will give him the strength to leave the house.

"Listen…" Lachy says carefully. "I don't want to tell you Killian's business, and I think there's a lot that Anna is hoping he'll tell you himself. But I do want you to understand that my brother is a good man. He's just…been through a lot. He's hurting, and there's nothing any of us can do to help anymore. But I think having you around might."

"He hates me," I reply without turning toward him.

"Killian hates everybody," he laughs. "But I don't think he really hates anyone, ye know?"

I let my eyes drift closed, and I force a few deep breaths into my lungs. Because I know exactly what Lachy is trying to say. But I also know what it's like to hate everyone. He's just sweet and naive, so he might not understand what it's like to be so filled with hate that it blooms like flowers in your bloodstream.

He might not think Killian truly hates anyone, but I think it is quite possible he does.

Because I do.

"I better get inside," he says with a nervous laugh. His footsteps crunch in the gravel as he walks toward the stairs that lead to the veranda.

"I'll be in in a minute," I reply.

When Lachy is gone, I open my eyes.

And just like that, dusk is over.

Now it is night.

Chapter Ten

MY FEET ACHE, AND THE LACE OF THIS STUPID DRESS HAS RUBBED a patch of skin under my arm raw. When everyone except for Anna and a few other stragglers have left, I escape up to my room.

My bedroom is large, the second-largest room in the house, Anna said. It has an en suite bathroom, a giant closet, and its own small balcony that overlooks the garden.

Everything in the room is dated and ornate, save for the few random modern things like the flat-screen TV mounted above the dresser and the wireless charger on the nightstand.

When I drop my phone on the charger, my arms are so tired, it lands in the wrong spot and falls to the floor in the space between the table and the bed. With an exhausted sigh, I kneel down and reach for the phone on the floor.

Just as my fingers brush the device, my gaze lands on something strange. It's a black leather strap fastened to the post.

"What the…?" My fingers touch the strap, grazing along the frayed edge, where it was clearly cut. I quickly stand up and inspect the rest of the bedposts, but they don't have the same leather strap.

Furrowing my brow, I try to imagine which of the Barclay children was likely to stay in this room with its kinky black straps. Inwardly, I laugh at the idea that little miss uptight Anna would have a wild side.

After tearing my dress off and tossing it in a pile on the floor, I go to the bathroom and run a scalding hot bath with a big fat scoop of rose-scented bath salts. As I lower my body into the tub, I let out a sigh of relief.

This isn't so bad. I can do this.

Technically, all I have to do for the year is get through each day and somehow manage to keep Killian Barclay from screwing anyone else. Knowing now that he never leaves the house, my job actually got a little easier.

It doesn't state anywhere in my contract that I also have to help turn this man's life around. It's not up to me to get him to heal from the loss of his parents or get over this fear of leaving his house. I'm not a spiritual healer. Or a therapist. Or a miracle worker.

My job is simple. Stay married to Killian for a year and get ten million bucks for it.

What am I stressing about?

"Sylvie." Anna's voice calls through the door of my bedroom.

"I'm in the bath. Don't come in," I call back in a lazy monotone drawl.

"We're just leaving. We've put Killian to bed. He...had a lot to drink today. I'll stop by tomorrow to check on things."

"Good night," I grumble back in a low call.

She hesitates. "Good night."

Her heels click against the floor as she retreats from my door. A few minutes later, I hear the front door close in the distance.

Then, the house is quiet. *So* quiet.

It's an eerie sort of silence that makes me uncomfortable. Like the silence before a scream or the blast of a bomb. I can't stand it.

It's the sound of being alone with him. Even if he is sleeping in his own room down the hall. This silence means everyone is gone. There is no buffer between us.

Snatching my phone from the counter next to the tub, I open the music app and start playing something upbeat and melodic. Only a few minutes in, I realize it doesn't fit with the moment, so I find something slower and more relaxing. When I've picked the perfect playlist, I drop the phone on the counter and let the sound echo against the walls of the giant bathroom.

I sink deeper into the tub and try to just melt into the relaxation. I wish I could turn my mind off, but I can't. I just keep going back to the events of the day. The wedding. The feel of Killian's enormous hand in mine. The fake smile he wore for the pictures. The way he stared into my eyes as we said our vows. The smell of smoke on his clothes as he stepped up so close to me.

So far, he is nothing more than a montage of moments to me. Most of them are harsh and unpleasant. Is this how the year will be? Will I ever truly know and understand him? Will I grow to like him?

No. I've never grown to like anyone, not really. I grew to like Margot once and look at how that ended.

It's best I don't try with Killian. Keep him at arm's length. Never dive too deep. Don't look too close.

I don't know how much time passes as I sit in the hot water, letting my mind drift quietly through my thoughts. Maybe six songs have gone by when I hear a crash out in the hallway.

I jolt, my eyes popping open as I sit upright and watch the door to the bathroom. I left it open, but I'm almost positive I locked my bedroom door.

Didn't I?

What if Killian breaks in? What if he thinks that now that I'm his wife, he can just barge in and take what he wants?

My heart hammers in my chest as I listen for another sound. In the distance, I hear a string of curses, mumbled and slurred. Then another loud *thunk* that sounds like furniture falling over.

The sounds are growing distant, which is a good sign.

When I don't hear anything for a while, I sit back in the bathtub and try to relax again. Maybe he fell down the stairs and cracked his head open. If he bleeds to death, do I still get my money?

Or go to jail for murder?

Yeah, definitely the latter. There's no way they wouldn't suspect me of killing him if ten mill was on the line.

"Shit," I whisper to myself. I really, really don't want to go down there. But if he is seriously hurt, that could come back on me.

"Stupid fucking Scottish asshole," I mutter to myself as I climb angrily out of the tub, water sloshing to the floor. Grabbing the towel, I wrap it around me and quickly dry off before snatching the fluffy white robe from the hook.

Just as I tighten the belt of the robe around my waist, I open my bedroom door—which was unlocked. The round glass table on the second-floor landing is covered in water, and the large ornate vase knocked over and cracked down the middle.

Fresh-cut red roses are scattered all over the table and floor. I pick one up and set it on the surface before glancing around for Killian. If I can at least get some confirmation that he's alive and not bleeding to death, I can go back to bed and lock my door this time.

"Killian," I call in a flat, unamused tone.

He doesn't answer.

I tiptoe down the stairs. Reaching the front of the house, I turn first toward the living room in search of him there, thinking he might want to watch TV down here. But it's empty. There's an unopened bottle of whisky on the floor by the bar, and one of the upholstered green chairs is tipped on its side. That must have been the sound I heard.

When I try the kitchen, I stop and stare in shock. It looks like a tornado swept through the room. Broken glass on the floor. Whisky spilled on the counter. And when I ease in further, I recognize a pattern of red drops on the floor leading to the dining room.

He's bleeding.

"Fuck," I whisper.

As I turn the corner into the dining room, I let out a shriek when I spot Killian slumped over on the floor with his back against the wall, and his legs extended out in front of him. He's in nothing more than a pair of tight black boxer briefs. His long hair hangs forward, draped over his face.

My eyes catch on the muscles of his shoulders and the patch of dark hair on his chest that leads down over his stomach and into his boxers.

Leaning against the wall with a half-empty glass of whisky in his hand, he looks passed out cold.

Standing in my bathrobe, I stare down at him for well over a minute. When I see movement in his chest and shoulders, I breathe a sigh of relief. There's still no sign of where the blood came from. He didn't step in broken glass.

Inching forward, I lift his hair enough to inspect if the blood is from a head wound. Luckily, it's not.

Lifting up his left hand, I first see the gold band on his ring finger. The sight of it feels like a bucket of ice water being poured over me.

I put that ring there. He's *my* husband.

I have a matching one on my hand now.

When I flip over his hand to inspect his palm, I find the source of the blood. There is a long clean slice over his entire hand. Blood seeps freely from the wound, pooling on the floor.

My first thought is…*Can someone bleed out from a hand wound?* Eventually, his blood would clot and stop him from dying, right?

Even with that much alcohol in his system though? Doesn't it thin the blood?

Maybe if I just elevate it? I could grab a chair from the dining table and rest his arm on it to help stop the bleeding.

This is his problem. I mean…three days ago, I wouldn't have even been here to help him.

I could have been sleeping upstairs in my room, so really I'm not at fault if I don't do anything. He chose to drink too much. He chose to be a clumsy, reckless idiot.

With a sigh, I stand up. Grabbing a chair, I pull up next to him and lift his arm so it's propped up. Blood still drips from the gash but not as steadily.

He's fine.

Turning on my heel, I tiptoe out of the dining room and back toward the stairs, watching for blood or broken glass. My conscience is clear. I helped him, and let's be honest, he's lucky I did that much after the way he's treated me.

It's clear Killian wants to be alone. And part of being alone and relying on no one is taking the risk of not having anyone around to help him when he needs it. That's on him.

He obviously doesn't want me here, so I'll pretend I'm not here.

If he bleeds out on the dining room floor, then he probably shouldn't have chosen to be so reclusive and ill-tempered.

I make it almost halfway up the stairs before I stop and squeeze the banister in my grip.

If I wake up in the morning to find him dead, then that's a whole mess I have to deal with. Not to mention, I doubt I'd see a dime of that money. Being married to him for one day is not the same as being married to him for one year.

I do *not* care about Killian Barclay. I don't.

But I do care about not going to jail and losing ten million dollars. So I spin around on the stairs and walk to the bathroom. Rifling through the cabinet, I find what I'm looking for—gauze, bandages, and antibiotic cream. After shoving them into the pockets of my robe, I grab a washcloth and run it under the warm water of the sink.

Taking them back to where I find Killian positioned exactly as I left him, I pull the chair away and kneel on the floor next to him. Placing his large hand in my lap, I feel a wave of relief when I notice that the bleeding has almost stopped.

Using the wet washcloth, I wipe away as much of the blood as I can. A lot of it has dried against his skin. His hand is heavy in my lap, and I softly stroke each finger, straightening them, just watching them curl back into a relaxed position.

Once the wound is clean, I take the gauze out of my pocket and begin wrapping it firmly around his palm. When it's covered, I use the bandages to hold it in place. I test my work by squeezing his hand to see if it will bleed through, and he stirs.

"Ugh…" he groans. His head tilts back, and he glares at me through half-closed eyes. "Not *you*."

"I'm helping you," I reply.

"Fuck you, cow." His words come out raspy and slurring.

As I finish cleaning up his hand, I feel his drunken gaze on my face, wondering if he sees the hurt in my eyes from his cruel words. I don't bother arguing with him. I could call him a brute or an asshole or a lazy drunk, but I don't.

Maybe if I don't sling back his insults, he'll see for a moment how hurtful his words are.

The next time I look up at him, his eyes are closed, and his breathing has grown loud as he sleeps.

I swallow down the sting of resentment.

After bandaging his hand, I go to the kitchen and find some towels to clean up the drops of blood on the floor. The cleaners will have to do a better job tomorrow, but I can at least wipe it up now while it's still wet and hasn't stained the hardwood.

It takes me a while to wipe up the mess around where he's still sleeping. Once I'm done with that, I get the spots he dripped from the kitchen. As I clean up the shards of broken glass on the floor, I find the culprit. The entire bottom half of the glass is still intact on the floor, and there is a ring of blood around the top. He must have been holding it when it broke.

After I find the broom, I carefully sweep up the kitchen and discard everything into the trash bin. There is a bottle of antibacterial spray in the cupboard, so I might as well use that while I'm at it. Next thing I know, I'm mopping the entire floor, moving the mop around Killian's sleeping form.

I don't even know what time it is by the time I've finished cleaning. Killian stirs again. I can hear him groaning while I'm picking up the fallen chair in the living room. When I rush over to see what's wrong with him, I nearly collide with his giant bare chest.

My hands fly up, my palms pressing against the patch of soft black hair on his chest. He scowls down at me as he sways on his feet.

"Move," he mutters in a low growl.

"Try *excuse me*," I reply with attitude.

"Fuck off."

He attempts to shove me away and stumble past me but

quickly loses his balance and goes careening into the wall, hitting it with a loud thud. His face screws up in anguish as he reaches for his shoulder.

I let out a disgruntled sigh. "Let me help you before you kill yourself."

"Don't touch me," he replies, taking another staggering step forward.

I put up my hands in surrender as anger boils in my bloodstream. "Fine!" I shout. "Take care of yourself then, Killian. Cut your whole fucking hand off next time. I don't care."

"What are you shouting about?" he groans.

"Just what a royal asshole you are."

I cross my arms over my chest. He stops in his floundering retreat and turns back toward me. "I'm an arsehole? What about you? You don't want to help me. You just want your precious money because you're a selfish little bitch."

"I just bandaged up your hand, you dick! You should be thanking me!"

"If it wasn't for you, I wouldn't even be this fucking drunk. But after I realized I married such a heinous bitch, I couldn't wait to get properly smashed."

My teeth are clenched, and my nostrils flare as I stare at him. For the first time since I arrived here, I'm starting to wonder if I can really do this. Can I get through the next year with this insufferable pig? How am I possibly going to make it that long without killing him?

"Go to bed, Killian," I mutter coldly.

He sways in his stance, staring at me angrily, and for a moment, I swear I catch a glimpse of disappointment on his face. As if he wanted me to argue back. Instead, I relented. I let him call me a heinous bitch without calling him an ignorant troll in return.

"I'm too tired from cleaning up your whole fucking mess

to argue with you right now, so please, just go to bed and leave me alone," I say in quiet surrender.

His face tenses in frustration. "Gladly."

He barely makes it to the stairs, and when I envision him tumbling down them and breaking his neck, I hurry behind him. Without a word, I lock my arm around his and pull him up the stairs.

I feel his rueful gaze on my face as I help him, but I don't look back. I don't want there to ever be a moment of weakness between us. No sliver of kindness or compassion. Not a hint of attraction.

As we reach the top of the stairs, I let Killian go and watch him as he stumbles to his room, slamming the door once he's safely inside. Once I'm alone, I take a deep breath and let my exhaustion sink in.

Today was the longest day of my life.

One down. Three hundred and sixty-four to go.

PART TWO

Killian

Chapter Eleven

MY NEW WIFE AND I HAVE RELAXED INTO A BEARABLE ROUTINE. The only time I have to look at her is at dinner, when we sit on opposite sides of the table. A time or two, I've caught her glancing up in my direction.

She has watchful hazel eyes and the world's fiercest resting bitch face. A slightly downturned mouth, big, full pouty lips, and a brow line so straight, it frames her face in a perfect scowl.

I knew from the moment she stumbled into my house that Sylvie was the perfect girl for the plan my sister was so enthusiastically orchestrating. She didn't just break into my home uninvited like some entitled brat, but she dared to challenge me at the same time.

I had never met a more infuriating and bold woman in all of my life. If I was going to let my sister win this battle and find me a bride for a whole year, then it couldn't be some dainty waif of a woman. She couldn't be polite or delicate. I didn't want to worry about hurting her feelings or being rude to her.

Sylvie is perfect.

It's been nearly a month since she arrived. I've picked up

on her routine. She starts each day with an ungodly amount of coffee. Then she goes into her room and takes the world's longest shower. After which, she watches the trashiest reality television and eats nearly everything she can get her hands on in the kitchen.

Some days she asks the driver to take her somewhere, usually insisting he pick the place based on her requests. *The best bookshop in town. The coziest coffee shop. The seediest pub.* Then she leaves for a few hours, and I'm free to roam my own house without worry.

But for some reason, I find myself spending those hours in restless anxiety. The walls start to close in. The house is *too* quiet.

I *could* go into town too. I could easily walk into a pub or head farther south and go into the city. I just don't want to. It's too crowded and noisy, and people are daft idiots. Why would I want to spend my days there when I have so much space and comfort here?

It's not that I *can't*—it's that I don't want to.

When the front door closes in the distance, I listen for the footsteps. If they are clunky boots on the hardwood, then it's Sylvie. If they are furious-sounding heels clicking, it's my sister.

A disgruntled sigh escapes at the sound of heels.

"Killian," Anna calls.

I could escape to the garden. Busy myself with the roses or tend to the bees, but she's too quick. I'm barely out of my chair when she enters.

"Oh, there you are," she says in a rigid tone.

"Here I am," I reply.

"Where is Sylvie?" She glances around the room as if my wife and I would just be sitting together like a regular couple.

"How the fuck should I know?"

Anna rolls her eyes as she proceeds farther into the sitting room, dropping her purse on the table.

"How are things going with you two?" she asks.

I shrug. "Barely see each other really."

She lets out a frustrated-sounding sigh. I briefly wonder what it might be like if my sister wasn't perpetually disappointed in me. If, for one moment, she could just see things the way I do.

"You've been married for a month now, and no one has seen you together. The honeymoon period is over. So it's time for you and Sylvie to make a public appearance."

"Fuck that," I groan, making my way to the bar for a shot.

"It's barely past noon, Killian. Must you really start drinking already?"

"What else would you like me to do, Anna?" I reply before immediately regretting it. I just gave her an opening to meddle even more.

"Help me plan this outing for you and Sylvie," she implores.

"I don't want to go on some stupid fucking outing. What is the point?"

"So people can see you together, and our aunts and uncles believe in this marriage, Killian. Take her to a rugby match. Post some photos online. That would make them happy," she says. I reply only with a deep sigh. Her heels click softly as she inches toward me. "When was the last time you went to a rugby match?" she asks delicately. "Or a football game?"

Her voice carries that worried tone that grates on my nerves. I hate that she worries over me. Especially when I'm perfectly fine here.

"I'm throwing a party," I reply.

In my periphery, I see her shaking her head. "No, Killian. No parties."

"Not that kind of party," I mutter lowly. "I'll just invite some of my old mates to stay at the house. A dinner party. Nothing too wild."

It's mostly true. My mates and I are still capable of having *normal* parties. Things might have gotten out of hand in the past, and word might have gotten around as to just how out of hand, but it doesn't have to be that way anymore.

"Your uni mates? Are you sure that's a good idea?" she asks.

I set the bottle of whisky down without pouring myself a glass. Anna wants to see I'm changing, and if that's what I have to do to keep my house, I'll do it.

"Most of them are married now with kids." I turn toward her with an air of confidence I have to constantly force with my sister. Or else she'll walk all over me. "If we're going to do this, Anna, we're going to do it my way."

She relaxes her features and lets out a sigh. "Fine."

We're interrupted by the sound of the front door closing again. That familiar echo of boots on the hardwood causes the corner of my mouth to twitch. Instead of going up the stairs toward her room, Sylvie makes her way down the long hallway to the sitting room at the end, where my sister and I are currently standing.

When she enters the room, she's gazing down at her phone with her earbuds in. When she looks up, she flinches, clearly surprised by the two of us standing here, watching her.

"Oh, hey," she says nonchalantly to Anna and me.

"I'm glad you're home. We have something to talk to you about," Anna says, taking a seat on one of the large upholstered chairs. Then she glances up at our new housekeeper, Martha. "Could we get a pot of tea, please?"

"Of course, ma'am," she replies before rushing off toward the kitchen.

Sylvie pulls out her earphones. "What's up?"

Anna gestures to one of the chairs. "Killian and I were just speaking about you two making a public appearance as husband and wife."

Her eyes dance toward me and back to my sister as she sits. "Where at?"

"Here," I reply with a low hum.

"It would be a dinner party with some of Killian's old friends. They'd likely stay the weekend. We have over sixteen guest rooms in the house."

"Fifteen," I correct her.

"Och, yes. Of course," Anna replies. "Since Sylvie has taken one, we now have fifteen available guest rooms."

"What do I need to do for this party?" Sylvie asks, glancing back at me.

"You two will need to appear as a couple. Which means you'll need to be affectionate as well as *talk* to each other."

Sylvie rolls her eyes and purses her lips. "Tell him he needs to learn his manners and stop being such a pompous asshole."

"I will as soon as you stop being an inconsiderate little cunt."

My sister gasps. "Both of you! Stop it!"

Sylvie doesn't give up that easily. "What did you call me?" she shrieks as she bursts out of her chair.

"You heard me," I reply.

"I'm here helping *you*," she cries.

I huff with a chuckle. "For how much?"

"You are such an ignorant pig!"

My lips stretch into a smile as the blood pumps faster through my veins. It's invigorating how easy it is to rile her up and get her going.

"See, we look married already," I reply with a laugh.

"I'd rather eat dirt than pretend to be married to you," Sylvie shouts. "I'm afraid I'll have to miss your little party."

Just as she starts to stomp out of the room, my sister stands. "It's part of the contract, Sylvie," she calls, stopping Sylvie in her tracks.

I watch with pleasure as her hands clench into fists. She spins around angrily. "Then tell him to stop talking to me like that!"

Anna lets out a sigh. "Killian…please."

I put up my hands in surrender. "Fine."

"You two will need to be believable as husband and wife, or none of this will work." She grabs her purse off the table.

"Where are you going?" Sylvie asks, looking terrified.

"I can't help you with this part. I suggest you two learn how to talk to each other and figure it out. This party will be the true test. If you can't convince your guests that you love each other, then this whole thing has been for nothing. And we've failed."

My sister leaves just as Martha walks into the room with a pot of tea on a tray and three mugs. I fucking hate tea. And I know Miss America over there loves coffee, but I feel bad for having the staff make it for nothing. So, I thank her as she sets it down and leaves.

Sylvie lets out a huff when she sees me preparing myself a cup. With an obstinate expression, she walks over and plops down on the chair opposite me. I pour her cup and sit back in my seat, crossing my ankle over my knee.

"Look at us being civilized," I joke as I hold the cup up to my lips.

"Your sister is right. We have a lot on the line, and we need to figure this out," she replies grumpily.

"All right, darling. What do you suggest we do?" I ask before taking a sip.

Sylvie glares at me over her cup. I love to see the fiery hatred blazing in her eyes. It makes me so grateful I chose a little firecracker like her. This whole thing would have been so boring with some acquiescent young woman.

"Surely we can just fake it in public, right?" she asks.

"Of course," I reply with a smirk.

"What are we going to say if they ask how we met?" Sylvie kicks her boots up and lays them on the coffee table. The sight of it would make my sister faint, but I find it fascinating. Much like the time she paraded through my home as if she owned it, Sylvie has this infuriating sense of entitlement. As if rules don't apply to her. As if everything around her is absurd, and she stares right into the face of the absurdity.

It makes me hate her even more.

With a smile, I shrug. "What's wrong with the real story?"

Her eyebrows bolt upward. "You want to tell your friends we met when I broke into your house?"

"Sure. Why not?"

"Because it makes me look like a criminal," she argues.

My eyes narrow. "But you are a criminal." I set my teacup down. "Besides, it's exactly what my friends would expect from me."

The moment the words leave my lips I regret them. And judging by the creeping smile on Sylvie's face, she's about to tease me about it.

"Did you just admit that I'm your type?"

"No," I reply with a growl.

"Careful, darling. You wouldn't want your wife to suspect you of catching feelings."

"Shut up." With a grimace, I avoid her gaze.

Sylvie giggles playfully, and the sound is annoyingly sweet. "We'll tell them it was love at first sight. You were head over heels the moment you saw me traipsing through your house. Most men would have tried to kill me, but not you... You were in *love*."

"That's enough, cow," I bellow.

Sylvie bites her bottom lip as she smiles at me from the opposite chair. "You know, you can't call me a cow at the party. Or bitch or cunt."

"And you can't call me a pig or a brute or an arsehole."

"Deal," she replies. "I'll just call you darling."

I screw up my face in disgust. "No."

Her lips twist, and she closes one eye in a look of contemplation. "What about...honey or baby?"

I make another expression of revulsion.

"Fine," she laughs. "What is Gaelic for *my love*?"

"Mo ghràidh," I reply in a deep rasp.

Her face falls as she stares at me. I watch as her lips part, and her eyes settle on my mouth. She attempts to repeat the phrase, stumbling over the second part with her American accent so it comes out as *mo ger-eye*.

Quickly, she sits upright and recomposes herself. "No, don't use that."

My smirk turns into a scowl. "Why not?"

"Because it's too..."

"Too what?"

"Nothing. Just say darling."

"I don't want to say *darling*," I argue.

"Why do you always have to be so difficult?"

"You're the one being difficult...mo ghràidh," I add that last part with a hint of humor.

"Ugh!" In a fit of frustration, she bursts out of her chair and stomps angrily out of the room. Just before I hear her footsteps on the stairs, she hollers back, "This is sure to be a disaster, and it will be all your fault!"

I can't help but laugh as I lean back in my chair, teacup in hand, propping my boots up on the table the same way she did.

Chapter Twelve

"BARCLAY!" I HEAR THE SOUND OF MY OLDEST MATE, LIAM McNeil, just as the front door opens. He ignores the valet at the door taking jackets, and he comes barreling toward me with a laugh.

"McNeil!" I reply with a wide grin. He throws his arms around me and pounds his fists on my back in a brutal hug.

As we pull away, he grabs my face. "I haven't seen you in months. You got uglier."

"I felt bad for taking all the ladies. Had to even the playing field for you."

He lets out a boisterous laugh. "How kind of you."

I lead my oldest and closest friend into the sitting room, where a few of our other guests are already waiting. Most of them are coupled. Friends from uni who have all grown up together. We still have the same old parties we had when we were young. They've just changed…a little.

The only truly single ones left from the old crew are McNeil and me, but he's about to learn that I have technically left him as the only stag at the party.

This is the first time my friends have visited since I stopped throwing wild parties. Nearly two years it's been since then, and already I can feel their eyes and expectations. This won't be like it was before though, or so I keep telling myself.

What I promised my sister was true. This weekend will not end up like one of those parties.

Sylvie is still up in her room, and I'm starting to get nervous that she's really not coming. Should I go up there and check on her? I'll drag her out if I have to.

The rest of my friends greet Liam with enthusiasm as my eyes keep scanning toward the staircase at the foyer, waiting for her to make her way down.

"Let me get you a drink," I tell Liam as I lead him to the bar.

"Thanks, mate," he replies. I pour two fingers of Macallan into a glass and pass it to him.

"It's good to see you again," he says with a crooked smile before lifting the drink to his lips.

"You too," I reply.

I notice out of the corner of my eye that Liam's gaze tracks carefully around the room, but he's not focusing on the people. It's almost as if he's looking for something.

"What are you looking for?" I ask with a chuckle.

"What the hell are you up to tonight? You ain't got any of that kinky shite going on, do you?"

I nearly spit out my whisky. "I told you already. I'm done with that shit."

He smiles wickedly. "That's right. You're a married man now." He shakes my shoulders, and I hold up my left hand to display the ring there. After dropping his hands from my shoulders he adds, "But being married doesn't mean you can't still be that kinky fucker we once knew."

"Jesus," I mutter. He doesn't understand that I've got my family breathing down my neck, threatening to take my house away from me. But I'm not getting into that with him. "For me it does. None of that will be happening tonight. It truly is a quiet weekend getaway."

"Fair enough," he replies, putting the glass to his lips. "But if I remember Killian Barclay, then I know a few whiskies in you will get you to do just about anything."

He lets out a hearty laugh as he slaps a hand on my back. I force a smile in return.

My head perks up at the sound of footsteps on the stairs. I don't know why my heart suddenly starts hammering in my chest. Maybe because I'm about to introduce my wife to all of my oldest friends. I've never done this before.

When Sylvie appears in the room, my jaw nearly hits the floor. In my mind, I was expecting her in her usual style. Black jacket, loose-fitting top, tight jeans, and thick black boots.

But that's not what she's wearing tonight. She's in a thin green dress, deep cut and hanging from her delicate shoulders. Judging by the thin straps and the sight of her perky nipples under the satin, she's not wearing a bra.

Suddenly, my throat is dry, and my cock gives a twitch.

And I'm glaring angrily at her.

"Fuck me," Liam whispers. "Is that…?"

As he pauses with his lips against his glass of whisky, I let out a groan.

"That's my wife," I say with a disgruntled sigh.

Liam gapes. "Holy shite."

Just then, Sylvie spots me across the room. Slowly she makes her way toward me, and I notice how miserable and nervous she looks. Her full lips are set in a delicate pout, and her normally fiery eyes are sullen and emotionless.

And it pains me that I won't be able to call her a heinous bitch all night. I'll miss the rise it gets out of her.

When she meets me at the bar, she hesitates for a moment.

She goes in for an embrace but pulls away nervously. Trying to ease her discomfort, I throw my arm around her shoulders and drag her lithe body to mine.

Sylvie is so much smaller than me. The top of her head doesn't even meet my chin. She makes me feel like a giant, and touching her even slightly has me worried I'm going to break her.

"Sylvie, darling, this is my old friend Liam McNeil. Liam, this is my wife, Sylvie."

Liam makes a dramatic show of putting his glass down and turning toward the both of us.

"Killian Barclay, you can make a better introduction than that. This is your wife," he shouts.

All of the chatter in the room dies, and just like that, all eyes are on us.

Turning Sylvie toward the rest of my friends mingling around the room, I make a proper announcement. "I know you've all seen the announcement online and in the paper. I'd like you all to meet my wife, Sylvie Barclay."

Just then, her face turns up toward mine. Perhaps it's the sound of her full name now that we're married. My friends' reactions are loud and excited, clapping and murmuring to each other.

But I'm too busy staring at her. It's not like the day of our wedding, when she was still a stranger, and there was nothing in the eye contact between us.

Now, she's staring up at me with cold, lifeless eyes. It's the insignificance in her gaze that pains me. As if she doesn't care about me at all.

I much prefer the hatred.

"Mo ghràidh," I add so softly no one can hear it but her. I throw in a smirk and a wink.

It causes her eyes to squint angrily and her hands to pinch

my sides, struggling to push me away, but I don't let her move an inch. Instead, I haul her closer and press my lips firmly against hers.

My friends whoop and holler at the show of affection. Sylvie keeps up her struggle, and it only encourages me more.

Without meaning to, I slip my tongue between her lips. She immediately stiffens, letting out the smallest whimper. Instead of pulling away or ending the kiss, I deepen it. This only makes my friends grow louder, urging me on as I scoop her tighter to my body and kiss her with heat and passion.

Our tongues tangle, and our teeth nibble, and somewhere along the way, she stops fighting and simply melts in my arms.

When we finally part, she gives me a fiery wide-eyed stare. Her angry gaze stays affixed to my face as Liam jerks me away and pats me hard on the back.

"Let's fucking celebrate," he shouts before the sound of a bottle of champagne popping jerks Sylvie out of her reverie. We're each forced a flute of bubbly into our hands, and the next thing I know, we're toasting with my friends.

But I'm in a daze. I'm too focused on her, her reaction, her attitude. Even when she fakes a smile and laughs with my friends' wives, she hides her discomfort under the surface. I want to drag it out of her.

After the first bottle is gone, I start to worry that this party is off the rails already. Just then, Martha walks into the room and announces that dinner is ready. So the party files into the dining room where the large table has been set with a modern arrangement.

The group mingles around the table, and Sylvie ends up on the end opposite me. It grates on my nerves to have her so far away. We're supposed to be proving to everyone how in love we are. It's hard to do that when I can't even reach her.

Which means it relies on our abilities to talk to and about each other, something we've failed at miserably up until now.

We don't even make it through the first course when one of the wives at the table asks, "So, how did you two meet?"

My gaze flits to Sylvie, who stares back with a challenging expression.

Here goes nothing.

"Well…would you believe this little criminal broke into my house?"

With hooded eyes, she glares at me from across the table.

"Broke into your house?" my friend Greg laughs from the opposite end.

"I did not *break* in," Sylvie replies defensively. "The door was unlocked."

"I was just out of the shower when I heard footsteps on the stairs. I come out to find a beautiful American woman standing in my foyer."

I catch the way her throat moves when she swallows.

"What were you doing?" someone asks.

"My boyfriend at the time wanted to see something inside the house but was too scared to walk in. I happened to see a woman leaving through the back, so I just…slipped in."

Holding my glass in my hand, I lean back in my chair. How have we not talked about that day since Sylvie moved in? I completely forgot about the woman who left that morning. I couldn't remember her name if I tried.

But I sense a hint of jealous pride on Sylvie's face at the mention of the girl. I like the way it looks on her.

"You just…slipped into someone's house?" Liam asks with a laugh.

"I knew from that moment I would marry her," I say proudly from the head of the table.

Sylvie rolls her eyes and shakes her head, biting back her

smile. "What he means is he knew from that moment he would trick me into marrying him."

"They trick us all into falling in love with them, don't they?" one of the women at the table says with a grin.

Sylvie stares at me. Her bright hazel eyes are all I can see. "I was definitely tricked."

Everyone laughs, and I join in. I know she's saying it all for show, and none of this is real. I know deep down she still despises me. It's fun though. I'll admit that. To see her coerced into being nice to me. She hates every second, and it brings me more pleasure than anything I've ever done. And that's saying a lot.

Chapter Thirteen

AFTER DINNER, THE PARTY MOVES TO THE BAR. WE'RE ALL sitting around the living room, and I'm too drunk already. I can tell.

It feels as if Sylvie is a moving target I can't seem to keep focused on. Every time I turn around, she's moved. One moment, she's sitting next to Greg's wife, whose name I can't remember, and then when I blink, she's outside on the veranda, staring out at the infinite darkness over the garden.

I'm sitting on the sofa next to Liam with an empty glass in my hand. He knocks my shoulder.

"That is one hell of a wife, Barclay. How the hell did you manage that?" he slurs.

I laugh and rub my brow. "Fuck if I know," I reply. I have to keep my answers vague and noncommittal. I'm too fucking drunk to answer anything specific.

"She's hot as fuck. I bet she's fire in bed. Tell me all the dirty details, please. I hear American girls are wild."

I give a chuckle, avoiding the sour taste in my stomach. "I don't kiss and tell."

"You arse," he replies with a laugh. "I haven't shagged anyone in months. I miss your parties. I'm fucking desperate. Does she have a sister?"

I smile at the ceiling without answering. Does she?

No. She's an only child. I think.

Fuck, I'm an arsehole.

The group of us are all scattered in a circle. Angus is across from me, the smartest mate in the crew. He and his wife, Claire, have been married the longest. Next to him is Greg and his wife…Emma? Then there's Nick and his longtime girlfriend, Theresa, to our right.

We started partying hard here every month a few years back. That's about the time I stopped leaving my house. Stopped doing a lot of things. As my eyes scan the group, I let myself imagine I could have ended up like them. I could have gotten married, moved to the city, and had a few kids. Lived a normal life. Instead of burying myself in the past.

They seem happy. But then again, none of them had gaping wounds of grief and regret to cure with alcohol and women.

Sylvie walks in from outside. She has her arms wrapped around herself as she shuffles toward me, taking a seat at my side, leaving a foot of space between us.

"Let's play a drinking game," Liam announces before going to the bar to retrieve a fresh bottle of wine. He sets it in the middle for us. When he notices Sylvie doesn't have a glass, he gets one and fills it for her with a wink.

My molars grind, and I don't understand why I can't just relax.

"Never have I ever…" he says. A few people around the group give a positive reaction, but I personally hate this game. It somehow only makes me drunker and feel like a piece of shite. Not to mention, if I want to keep this party under control, a drinking game is not the way to do it.

I feel the weight of Liam pouring whisky into my glass, and I force a smile toward him. "Thanks."

"Killian...why don't you start?" he says as he drops into a seat next to me.

I let out a groan. Then I glance at the woman to my left. "Never have I ever broken into someone's house."

Sylvie gives me a stern glare as she lifts her glass to her lips. The people around us break out in laughter, but no one else takes a drink.

"Your turn," I say to her as she wipes her lips.

"Never have I ever been so drunk I sliced my hand open without even knowing it."

I try not to give much of a response. I just lift my hand, revealing the still-healing scab, and take a sip of my whisky.

Sylvie stares at me for a moment, looking not quite proud but not quite apologetic either. The game goes around the circle, most of the questions staying innocent and fun. That is until it comes around to Liam.

"Never have I ever fucked two chicks at once."

"Of course you haven't," Greg teases.

Sylvie's eyes glance toward my face. This one isn't too bad. The guys here know me, so it's not like I have anything to hide. I lift my glass and take a small sip as everyone reacts with laughter and cheers.

When I bring my glass back down, I do my best not to look at Angus's wife across the room.

"Your turn, Barclay," Liam says, prodding my shoulder.

Fuck, I'm tired of games. I used to love shite like this, but now it feels targeted and dangerous.

Aren't we getting too old for this?

"Never have I ever...been cheated on."

I don't know why I say that. It's a risky and strange thing to say in this crowd, considering what happens every time we're together. But I figure it's the only one I know I can say, mostly because I've never had a real relationship to cheat on. To my surprise, quite a few people drink—including Sylvie.

Something about that irritates me.

Angus doesn't drink though. I do notice that.

Again, I force myself not to look at his wife, Claire.

When Nick's girlfriend notices Sylvie drinking, she asks, "I assume it wasn't Killian."

Sylvie shakes her head. "No. My stupid ex. Caught him fucking my best friend."

"Oh shite," someone replies.

"What did you do?" one of the women asks.

Sylvie sits up proudly. "I threw scalding hot coffee on his back. Gave him second-degree burns."

The corner of my mouth lifts in a smile.

———

After about three rounds of that game, it becomes glaringly obvious that we are not in our twenties anymore. We're all smashed. After I get up to use the restroom, I come back to find Liam sitting closer to Sylvie than I was.

He's laughing, clearly toasted. She's wearing a forced, hesitant smile that makes me want to scream.

"Sylvie," I bellow. They both turn to stare at me. "It's time for bed."

Her brows pinch inward, clearly surprised at me trying to tell her what to do. But if I drink anymore, I'll end up passed out on the floor again, and I can't leave her down here with Liam in this state.

It takes her a moment of my harsh gaze before she realizes that she can't stay down here without me. As she stands, I take her arm in mine. She glares up at me with frustration.

"We're off to bed," I tell our friends. "Everyone sleep well, and if you need anything, the staff will be here bright and early."

The crowd says good night as I practically drag Sylvie out of the room and toward the staircase.

"Let go of me," she whispers as we reach the stairs.

I let go, although I don't want to.

When we reach the second floor, she goes left, so I grab her arm again. "You're sleeping with me tonight."

She rears back and stares at me with ghastly shock. "The fuck I am," she replies in a hasty whisper.

I drag her closer until my mouth is near hers. "I'm not leaving you alone. Liam is too drunk, and he has eyes for you."

"I don't care," she replies with disgust. "I'll lock my door."

"We're supposed to be married, Sylvie. What will they think if they see you sleeping in a separate room?"

I don't know why I'm so desperate about this. I truly am worried about Liam. I've known the man a long time, and as wild as things get at our parties, I've never known him to be the kind to hurt or violate someone. But with the way he was talking about her tonight, I can't stand the thought of her and him together.

Sylvie lets out a sigh. "You're not going to give this up, are you?"

I shake my head.

"Fine." She jerks her arm out of my grasp and moves toward her room. When I grab her again, she looks back at me in shock. "I have to get some pajamas. I'm not sleeping near you naked."

The thought of her naked in my bed has my cock twitching again. It's been over a month since I've seen the least bit of action, and it has me thinking irrationally.

Sure, Sylvie is infuriating and stubborn. I may hate her personality, but her beauty remains, and my cock doesn't care much about personality.

She emerges from her room a few moments later with pajamas and a toothbrush under her arm. She closes her door behind her before following me to my room.

Once we're both inside, I close the door and lock it. Sylvie turns back to see my face after the lock clicks into place. Something about being in a locked room together makes her uncomfortable—I can tell.

"Sorry," I mutter as I unlock it.

She closes herself in the bathroom, and I hear water running and the toilet flushing as I sit on the side of the bed. I've sobered up in the past hour, but I still feel numb and reckless. Like I could say anything on my mind. I could do anything.

Normally when I'm drunk, I'm alone or with friends. Being with someone like Sylvie when I'm wasted is dangerous. It makes me want to spill my secrets, and that's a very, *very* bad idea.

The door opens, and she comes out in a pair of dark-blue satin pajamas. Her wild strawberry-blond curls are piled on top of her head and wrapped in a satin ribbon. She's wiped every ounce of makeup from her skin, leaving her cheeks spotted with freckles and her lips bare of color. I'd like to kiss them again to feel what they'd be like without the makeup covering them. Her eyes are so much rounder and brighter without the black lines and shading.

I'm staring for too long. Quickly, I stand up and rush into the bathroom. In there, I douse my face with cold water, brush my teeth, and empty my bladder. I don't own a pair of pajamas, so my only choice is to sleep in my undergarments and white T-shirt.

When I come out of the bathroom, Sylvie is already curled up on her side, facing away from the middle. I laugh to myself at the row of pillows she's placed between us. As if pillows could protect her if I wanted to touch her. Which I don't.

I climb into bed and click off the lamp on the nightstand. I roll away from her, and the room is bathed in silence. It's so quiet, I can hear her breathe. It's choppy and shallow. And I can feel a slight quiver on the bed.

My stomach aches with dread.

"Are you really so afraid of me?" I whisper.

"I'm not afraid of you," she replies defiantly. I let out a sigh before replying.

"I can feel you trembling."

Silence engulfs us again, and in the silence is the harrowing truth staring at me like a mirror held up to my face. It tells me that I'm too harsh. Too cruel. Truly a brutish monster, as she's pointed out repeatedly in the past month.

"I'm not," she argues before punching her pillow and settling back down into the mattress.

We don't say another word, but even as her breathing settles into a sleeping cadence, I stay awake. I can still feel her shaking.

Chapter Fourteen

WHEN I WAKE, SYLVIE IS GONE. HER SIDE OF THE BED STILL shows the indentation of her body and carries her soft, flowery scent.

I hear movement downstairs, but I don't stir for a while. Staring at the ceiling, I replay the events of the last twenty-four hours. This whole fake-wife arrangement is so strange. Only a month has gone by and we still have eleven to go.

What will we be like in a year? Will she still hate me? Will she hate me even more?

Can I truly go a full year without sex? Surely at some point, she and I can reach some sort of arrangement where we keep our extramarital affairs between us.

Last night I actively tried to keep her away from Liam, but what if something did happen between them? It would give me the leverage I'd need to do the same. Tit for tat. A secret between us. The contract stays in place, but we still get to have our fun.

Deep down, I hate the idea, but I know it would be better for me in the long run.

It was wrong of me to bring her to my room. The last

thing I need to do at this point is treat my wife like...my wife. I don't need her getting the wrong idea about me. When this is over, she has to leave. One year, and then I'm on my own again. Besides, I promised her we'd spend this time separately, not with me dragging her to my bed.

When I do finally get up, I hear shouting outside, so I peer out of my large window. Liam is on the vast grassy field outside, shirtless, with a rugby ball under his arm. When he sees me watching, he waves.

"Get your ugly arse out here!" he bellows.

I laugh, spotting Greg, Angus, and Nick on the field as well. They turn to see me, each of them waving. Briefly, I wonder where the women are. Should I be nervous about Sylvie being alone with them, especially Claire?

I shake the thought away. It's not even ten in the morning. I doubt they'd be sharing stories this early, anyway.

After hurriedly getting dressed, I jog down the stairs. Heading straight out the door to the field behind the house, I greet the ladies, who are all sitting around a table with cups of tea in front of them.

Except for Sylvie, who's sipping what I assume is her third cup of coffee. She glances up at me over the steaming liquid. Before jogging out to meet the guys, I hesitate.

I'm supposed to treat her like my wife, aren't I? What would a husband do in this scenario? I imagine Greg or Nick would kiss their ladies. Sylvie's eyes narrow at me over her cup as I hesitantly make my way over.

"Mornin," I mutter as I press my lips against her forehead. The other women at the table ooh and aah over the gesture, but Sylvie barely reacts. With a cold expression, she softly mumbles, "Morning."

"All right, two on two!" Liam bellows from the stairs of the veranda. "Let's go, old man."

He tosses the rugby ball at me with force, and I catch it against my stomach. It nearly knocks the wind out of me, but I keep my smile.

Before he and I rush off to the field with the other guys, I notice the way his gaze lingers on Sylvie.

My idea from earlier resurfaces.

If I could get Sylvie to sleep with Liam, it would clear my conscience for the rest of our marriage. He's a good-looking guy. Built, tall, rugged. He has more of a clean-cut look without the beard, and he makes a lot of money. I know that's important to her.

The four of us play a slow and painful match of rugby, all putting in far more effort than we have at our ages. Nick takes a hit that he almost doesn't get up from, which we all tease him about since he's the oldest by four years. The ladies come out and cheer us on a bit, taking pics and laughing at us as we fall over.

It's nothing like it used to be when we played in uni nearly fifteen years ago. But it's fun.

Not once in the past decade have I thought about what I was missing—until now.

After an hour, we are all sweaty, muddy, and starving. Angus ambushes Claire with a disgusting hug, making her squeal as he wraps his arms around her. Sylvie gives me a pointed glare.

"Don't you dare," she mutters. I laugh, wanting to hug her just to piss her off now.

I choose not to and walk beside her instead.

Liam strides beside me. "So, Sylvie. You're not taking this big Scotsman to America, are you?"

She glances up, first at me and then at him. "No," she replies, shaking her head. "I'm not going back."

"Ever?" he asks.

She gives him a shrug. "I don't have much reason to. My parents and I don't get along well, and I like it here."

"I read something about your parents," Claire says from behind us. When we all turn, she gives us a sheepish grin. "I hope you don't mind me bringing that up, but I saw it online when Killian's family made the announcement. That your parents are famous artists or something."

My gaze darts toward my wife, waiting for her reaction as the entire group meets the gray stone steps of the house. My sister mentioned something about Sylvie's parents being artists, but I never gave it a second thought. I didn't care much, and technically, I still don't. It's just curiosity.

Sylvie smiles at Claire. "It's okay. They are pretty famous in the art world. They have paintings in museums all over the globe."

"But you don't get along with them?" Angus asks.

Softly, she shakes her head. "No. They're just...fucking assholes."

This makes the group laugh, but my mouth doesn't move toward a smile.

Sylvie has been calling me an arsehole since she arrived, and I'll admit...I *am* an arsehole—to her. Are they? What could they have done to warrant that sort of reaction?

"Well, you turned out all right," Liam says with a wink. She gives him a soft smile.

That's a good sign.

"Let's get inside and get cleaned up," I reply, breaking up the moment.

Once in the house, we all scatter in different directions. I jog toward my room while the rest of them move toward the guest rooms, which are mostly on the third floor. After taking a quick shower, I step out of the bathroom and dress in a rush. My growling stomach has me hurrying. Whatever Martha made for lunch smells delicious all the way up here.

Just as I burst out of my room, I nearly knock someone

over in the hallway. It takes me a moment to register that the petite woman isn't Sylvie.

It's Claire.

My hands fly from her shoulders, where I held her to keep from bowling her over.

"I'm sorry," I stammer.

"It's okay," she replies uncomfortably.

"I didn't see you there."

"I was just…poking around," she replies. Her eyes stay on my face as I back against the wall, putting as much space between us as possible. Then I quickly scan the periphery of the hall to realize she and I are alone.

My lungs hold my breath, my gaze raking over her face.

"How are you?" she whispers.

I force myself to swallow.

"Fine," I mutter quietly.

It's clear she expects me to return the question, but I don't. I shouldn't be talking to her at all.

"Sylvie is really lovely," she says, making casual conversation.

I glance around again, wondering where my wife is at the moment.

"Where is she?" I mumble.

"She's downstairs," Claire whispers so softly I can barely hear it. "Everyone is."

My eyes lift to her face again. My feelings are so conflicted and hard to describe.

"Claire…" I start, trying to back away even more, but for some reason, she sees this as an invitation to step even closer.

"I've missed you."

I force in a deep breath. There's a part of me that's dying to tell her I don't think about her at all. And when I do, it's only when I'm drunk, and my demons show up to remind me what a liar and bad friend I am.

"What about Angus?" I murmur in question.

"I love Angus," she replies as if it's obvious. "But there will always be a part of me that…"

She reaches out and rests her fingers against my chest.

Fuck. Fuck. Fuck.

"Angus can't please me the way you do, Killian."

I can't breathe.

"I told you it was over," I reply softly. "You shouldn't be here. You're married to one of my best friends."

She takes another step closer. "I thought this was why you invited us."

"I invited you all here to meet my *wife*." If only I could just tell her the only damn reason I had this fucking party at all was to prove to the world that I'm not a fucking mess and that I have a happy marriage.

I can't even pretend I'm all right.

"Besides," I add. "I won't do that to him again—"

A creak on the stairs makes the both of us jump back. We barely do it in time before I turn to find Sylvie staring at us skeptically.

"It was good catching up with you," Claire says to me with a polite smile. Then she turns toward the stairs, passing Sylvie as she goes. "You two are such a lovely couple," she says to her before she disappears down the stairs.

I'm left alone with my wife, who is staring at me with that cold, lifeless expression she so often has. "What was that?" she asks with a scrutinizing gaze.

"Nothing," I grumble before pushing past her to go down the stairs.

She grabs my arm. "It didn't look like nothing."

Frustration builds inside me, and I turn back toward her, ready to blow with anger. I put my face in hers, muttering in a low, angry growl. "I said it was nothing."

"I don't care what it was," she replies, stepping up, her neck craned to see my face. "Just keep it in your pants so I don't lose what's owed to me."

"You think I would fuck my friend's wife?"

She tilts her head with a cynical smirk. "Of course not, Killian. As you said…that was *nothing*, right?"

"Fuck you, cow," I growl.

She shakes her head with a roll of her eyes. Blowing me off, she squeezes past and walks to her room. "You won't be fucking anyone." Then she turns toward me and gives me a fake smile. "Darling."

As she disappears into her room, I have to fight the urge to punch a hole in the wall. Instead, I head downstairs to be with my friends—the *real* people in my life.

Last night, it was kind of me to remove her from the situation and spare her from Liam's advances. Tonight, I won't be so kind.

Chapter Fifteen

THE DAY GOES BY IN A BLUR OF LAUGHTER AND CONVERSATION. My friends leave tomorrow, and already I'm feeling like a real ass for staying out of touch for so long. We reminisce about uni, catch up on each other's lives, and make plans to definitely do this again soon. Like this.

I manage to avoid Claire for the rest of the day, never even daring to look in her direction over lunch or the walk around the grounds later in the day. At the same time, I also manage to avoid Sylvie as well. When she is with our group, she keeps her distance from me, blending in nicely with the ladies so it doesn't seem strange that she and I aren't speaking or touching.

The plan tonight is to throw an old-fashioned rager. Everyone wants to get piss drunk, and I'm feeling uneasy about it. I can't let things get out of hand like they used to.

I'm the first one down for dinner, and I can't ignore the sour feeling of anxiety gnawing at my gut. Something about what happened today with Claire and Sylvie isn't quite sitting right with me.

What do I have to feel bad about though? I've called off things with Claire.

I'm certainly not going to feel bad about it now. And the last person I'm going to explain myself to is Sylvie.

To my relief, the next person downstairs for dinner is Liam. I'm standing near the bar in the parlor when he walks down and finds me deep in contemplation.

"What's on your mind?" he asks with a smile as he crosses the room.

"Not much," I reply nonchalantly.

As he pours himself a drink, he nods toward the hall. "Where's that hot wife of yours?"

I chuckle. "Still getting ready, I think."

Liam whistles with a shake of his head. "If that were *my* wife, I wouldn't let her out of my sight."

It's not the first—or even second—time this weekend my friend has commented on the beauty of my wife. This is exactly what I want, but for some reason, it bothers me.

"I couldn't control her if I tried," I reply with a smirk.

"It's not *her* I'd be worried about."

Glancing out the side of my eye, I wonder exactly what Liam is talking about. Is there another man in this house I should be worried about? What is he implying? Sure, my friends can be flirty, but none of them would truly touch my wife in my own home. Would they?

Suddenly, I see an opportunity. And I'm not proud of myself for it.

"Well, you know…" I mumble quietly. "Sylvie and I…we keep things *open*."

Liam's head pops up, and he stares at me for a moment as if he's trying to put something together. "You mean…"

I nod.

When he picks up on what I'm implying, a smile stretches across his face. "You're still a kinky fucker."

"Shhh… Keep your voice down," I mutter. Trying to keep

things casual, I smile at my old friend. "She knows what she's getting herself into this weekend. I let her do what she wants, and she lets me do what I want."

He scratches his head. "I don't understand you married guys. Doesn't that bother you? For other men to touch your woman?"

My jaw clenches, but I bury the rising hesitation. "It just means I get to remind her who she belongs to when she comes back."

Liam's eyes widen. "Good point."

I shoot back my drink, hoping the alcohol will cool the buzzing heat in my blood. I hate the way this feels, and I really shouldn't give a shite. I barely know Sylvie, let alone have any romantic feelings for her. Hopefully, she's into Liam, and this could all work out in my favor.

What happens at the house this weekend stays here.

When I look up, I spot a mess of reddish-blond curls. My eyes collide with Sylvie's. She's wearing that same cold, dead expression she always seems to wear around me.

Liam still has his back to the room and has no idea she's on the other side. "So…does that mean you wouldn't mind if I—"

I knock him with my elbow, nodding toward my wife. Liam spins to find her there, quickly putting a fake smile on his face. "Sylvie!"

Sylvie stares at us in contemplation for another minute before turning silently on her heels and walking into the dining room. I'm willing to bet my wife will be glad when this weekend is over, and she can go back to her solitary routines.

Liam and I laugh for a moment before the rest of the crowd files down the stairs. Most of us have been drinking already so the party is already rowdy as we head in for dinner. The first thing I notice is that Claire sits right next to Sylvie at the table.

I take the seat at the head again, but I can't get Sylvie to even look at me. And it's bugging the hell out of me.

The group is rowdy. As soon as we're all seated, Angus clinks his fork on his glass to make an announcement.

Standing up, he stares at me with a smile. "Thanks for inviting us, Killian. It truly is great to be back with old friends again. To you and Sylvie and your happy marriage. And to get fucking bladdered tonight."

The group erupts in raucous cheers as everyone shoots back their drinks. Even Sylvie gulps down the contents of her wineglass.

As soon as the food is served, the dinner conversation turns vulgar and inappropriate.

"Okay, be honest," Nick says as he glances at me. "You guys have fucked on this table, haven't you?"

Everyone laughs.

I look at Sylvie. She tilts her head to the side and stares at me as if waiting for my response.

"Twice," I say around a bite.

The group cheers.

Nick's girlfriend laughs. "Yeah, this is a nice sturdy table, perfect for fucking."

The ladies chuckle along.

Then it's Greg's wife's turn. "God, I miss the honeymoon period. I bet you two are still fucking like animals."

Sylvie clenches her jaw but glances at me again. I don't know what's holding me back. I could easily lie and tell stories about how raunchy our nonexistent sex is. But the words won't come.

So Sylvie chimes in. "He's the one who struggles to keep up with me." A hint of a smile tugs at the corner of her mouth, and I bite my tongue.

"It's the age," Theresa replies playfully. "Once they hit thirty-five, they lose their stamina."

"Hey!" Nick complains.

"My stamina is just fine," I reply heartily. "Tell them." I glance expectantly at Sylvie.

Everyone looks at her too.

After a moment, she shrugs. "His stamina is just fine."

"How many times a day are you two fucking? Living alone here at this manor, I bet it's like five times a day."

Sylvie's throat moves as she swallows.

"What is it now, darling?" I ask, drawing her attention. "Three times a day?"

"At least," she replies with a challenge in her expression.

"Your new wife must know everything about you, Killian," Emma says, with a drunken slur in her voice. "That you have some wild and kinky tastes."

My skin grows hot as I stare at Sylvie to gauge her reaction. There isn't much of one.

It's funny to think she knows nothing of my sex life at all, and I know nothing of hers. People around this table would be shocked to know that. They're already imagining us fucking in ten different positions in every room of this house.

"Well, does she?" Claire asks, holding her glass of wine in her delicate fingers.

I freeze as my gaze settles on her face. She wouldn't...

"Let's just say..." Sylvie says, filling the awkward silence. "Don't go snooping through drawers or under the beds."

Everyone laughs, and my head tilts as I stare at her across the table. It almost felt as if she was covering for me, and I don't understand why.

———

After dinner, the party spills into the parlor. It's darker than last night, and Liam has figured out how to work the speaker system. Music blasts through the built-ins. After the very first beat drop from some twenty-year-old song from our younger days, people start dancing.

I'm not drunk enough. I wish I was drunker. I keep going for the whisky, but something is stopping me. I can't stop watching Sylvie.

"Come on, Killian," Emma whines as she tugs on my arm. "Let's dance."

She drags me into the middle of the room.

"Dance with your husband," I reply with a lighthearted laugh.

"Boring," she drawls.

I don't really want to dance. I feel too old for this shit. It's songs from my younger days, but I don't feel like that man anymore. It's not a fun time to relive.

But I play along, letting her grind against me as another random mismatched couple starts to dance behind us.

I can already tell this will be trouble before long. Everyone is too drunk.

Wait. What the fuck am I saying? I love parties like this. I love nights that go off the rails. I want the mistakes and the sex and regrets and the fun and the reckless abandon.

Suddenly, I feel myself leaning into it. This is what I want.

Going to the bar, I crack open a new bottle and pour my glass with far too much. By the time I turn around, I notice Liam is sitting next to Sylvie. He's touching her arm.

So far, she's giving him the cold front of greetings, but when he says something to make her laugh, she tugs her bottom lip between her teeth and actually blushes.

I'm suddenly dying to know what he said.

Instead, I throw back another glass of whisky, waiting for the alcohol to numb my system.

Another song on the makeshift dance floor.

Another full glass emptied.

Then, another.

And another.

The room is starting to soften into shades of blue. It's dark and hazy, but the alcohol isn't kicking in as much as I'd like. It's like I can still see too much too clearly.

Everyone around me is obviously wasted.

I'm dancing with someone. Her fingers are under my shirt, and she's laughing. I glance over her head to see Theresa on Angus's lap, and I know in the back of my mind that image is wrong. She's Nick's girl.

Two years ago, it wouldn't have been wrong at all. This is what we did. We blurred all the lines and we fucked without abandon. We were wild and untamed.

But I've changed. This party wasn't supposed to end this way.

Where is Sylvie?

I pull away from the woman with her hands up my shirt and stumble out of the room. The hallway feels long, and I stare down it toward the staircase on the opposite end. A feeling of dread crawls up my spine.

Are Sylvie and Liam up there?

That's what I want.

But I don't.

These feelings war inside me, and no matter how hard I try, I can't seem to tear them apart.

I stumble down the hall toward the stairs just to see for myself. I make it about two steps before another pair of soft hands wrap around my waist.

Sylvie.

"Come here," she whispers softly, tugging me into a dark room. It's a storage closet, but before I can argue, she's pulling my mouth down to hers, kissing me with passion and need.

I surrender to the kiss, letting the intensity sweep me out to sea. Her lips feel so good, and I'm so focused on the fact that she's supposed to be somewhere with Liam, but she's not. She's here with me.

Fuck, that's not what I want. But I can't seem to stop it.

"God, please touch me. I need you," she whimpers into my mouth. It sounds wrong.

But I'm too drunk to stop it.

Her hand takes mine, and she drags it between her legs, shoving my fingers against the moist center of her panties. She's so wet for me, I let out a growl when I feel it.

I don't understand these feelings for Sylvie. This hate-fueled desire. This need to own her, dominate her, force her to submit, make her mine. I don't want her. I don't care about her. I just *need* her.

My cock is rock hard behind my slacks at the thought. It's never felt so full of life before, a fire blazing in my groin at the idea of fucking my headstrong, stubborn wife into submission.

Before I know what I'm doing, my finger is inside her. She's clinging to my arm, moaning and whimpering. And suddenly, I realize that this is all too easy.

Something is missing.

She's supposed to fight with me.

"I missed you so much," she mutters. "Please fuck me, Killian."

I yank my hand from under her dress. "Bloody hell," I groan as my back hits the wall, and I realize what I've done.

"Wh-what's wrong?" she murmurs.

"Claire?"

"Yes, of course. Who else would it be?" she asks, her voice cracking with emotion.

My heart fucking shatters.

"I have to go," I stammer as I tear open the door and nearly fall out of the closet and into the hallway. There are moans and cries of sex from the parlor.

Where the fuck is Sylvie?

I take one marching step toward the stairs when I hear voices from behind me. I turn to see two silhouetted figures outside through the open doors. Two bodies pressed together, practically as one.

Rage boils inside me as I inch closer to the door. The only reason I'm not barreling out there is because a part of me needs to know. Would she really let him touch her?

In the back of my mind, I remember that that's what I want, but I can't fucking remember why.

In the silhouette, I see her hands pressed against his chest. He has her crowded toward the low wall. He leans his mouth toward hers.

"I can't," she says with the cool defiance only she can pull off.

"Come on, baby. I'll make you feel so good," he murmurs.

Rage cracks inside me like dynamite. I've never felt such anger. Suddenly I can't keep the slow pace. I'm practically running. Grabbing Liam by the collar, I yank him away from Sylvie.

"What the *fuck* did you just say to my wife?"

He holds up his hands in surrender, shock on his face. "Whoa, man. I thought you said it was cool."

"She said no," I snap.

"Okay, okay," he stutters.

"Killian, stop it." Sylvia tugs on my arm. "We were just talking."

"You were not just talking, Sylvie. He was trying to fuck you."

"I can handle myself!" she snaps.

"Go upstairs," I growl in her direction.

She looks offended for a moment. "You can't tell me what to do."

With my teeth clenched, I drop Liam's collar and turn my attention toward Sylvie. I'm too filled with anger to think clearly. My hand encircles her arm, and I drag her back into the house and all the way down the long hall. She's digging in her heels the entire way, slapping my arm and screaming.

"Let go of me, you fucking brute!" she shrieks.

But I don't stop. All I can see is her letting Liam put his hands on her. Letting him take what should be mine. Making a fool of me.

When we reach the bedroom, I toss her inside and slam the door behind me, locking us both in.

She swings her arm back and lets her hand come flying across my face. I don't even feel it.

"What is wrong with you?" she screams. "Everyone was having a good time, and *you* had to ruin it! You're so fucked up, Killian!"

"You were about to let another man fuck you in *my home*," I argue, my voice so loud it's practically shaking the walls.

"Everyone is down there fucking, Killian! You think I can't tell what kind of party this is? You think I couldn't see the way you were pushing me toward him? I know what you told him, Killian! That we have an open marriage. I know deep down you were *hoping* I would fuck him because you think that would be your free ride to fuck whoever you want!"

"You're delusional!" I shout in return, meeting her level of anger.

"I'm *delusional?*" she retorts. Her eyes are wild with rage, and I don't want it to end. I love the fire in her expression when we fight. "You are so manipulative and ignorant! God, I fucking *hate* you!" Her voice is a screaming pitch now, and there's no way our guests can't hear us.

I'm still drunk, but something about her fired-up state has me wanting to touch her. Not in a sexual way, but in a desperate way. Reaching toward her, I grab her arm again and haul her toward me. She immediately puts up a fight.

"Get your hands off me!" she shrieks, trying to tear her arm from my grip.

I tighten it and lean in, sneering in her face. "You are my wife, and I will put my hands on you as much as I want." I say it only to fuel her rage. It's too easy to do.

Her nostrils flare, and her molars grind as she glares into my eyes. Deep down, she's silently wondering how much I'm truly capable of. "Touch me, and I swear you'll die in your sleep," she mutters with vitriol.

"Being dead would be preferable to being married to an ugly, selfish cow like you," I say. It's like a game. One insult is traded for another until we're both satisfied. "You mean *nothing* to me."

"Good!" she snaps. "Then I'll just go back down to Liam."

She tries to move away, but I yank her back toward me. When I do, I spot a hint of moisture in her eyes. Something I said hit a nerve.

"Over my dead body," I bellow. She swings an arm out toward me. I snatch it at the wrist before it can make contact with my face.

"That's what you want, isn't it?" she shrieks. "You want me to fuck your friend so you can be free of me. Just keep living the way you always have, Killian. So nothing has to change."

The more she screams, the more we struggle. Until the only way I can calm her is to force her to the bed, draping my body over hers. Taking her wrists in my hands, I pin them to the bed over her head.

Suddenly, with our faces only inches apart, she stops yelling, and we are caught in silence. The way her body feels under mine is visceral. I feel so large in comparison to her, but I know I'm not crushing her. She can handle my size and anything else I give to her.

Again, I notice the moisture in her eyes. When she blinks,

a tear rolls down the side of her face, disappearing into her hair. What could I have possibly said that would truly hurt her feelings?

"Why do you care so much about what I do?" she asks, her tone dripping with hatred.

"I don't," I reply.

Her vibrant eyes hold mine for a moment. We're staring at each other as our breathing returns to normal. Finally, she mumbles, "Get off me, Killian."

Carefully, I release her hands and roll away from her body.

Without another word, she stomps toward the bathroom, slamming the door behind her.

I struggle to keep from passing out as I wait for her to come out. When she does, she's wearing the same pajamas as last night. Giving me the silent treatment, she marches to her side of the bed and climbs in. With her back to me, she huffs as she punches her pillow again.

I stagger as I tear off my clothes down to my underwear. After switching off the light, I climb into bed next to my wife.

I know I should feel bad for how I handled this tonight, but I don't. Honestly, I'm still a little confused. I don't understand if things went right or things went wrong. I just know that wherever this woman is concerned, I'm often more confused than not.

PART THREE

Sylvie

Chapter Sixteen

THE FAMILIAR CLICK OF HEELS ON THE HARDWOOD PULLS ME from my book. Lounging on the chaise in the library, I turn my focus back to my current read and wait for Anna to find me. The rain is really coming down outside, and it's been doing this all week, throwing me into the worst seasonal depression I've ever felt. I haven't seen the sun in days—or is it weeks now?

"There you are," she says in a forced chipper tone as she enters the library and hovers near the door as if she's waiting for me to greet her.

"Hey," I mumble, looking back at the page I was just on. "What's up?"

"Where's Killian?" she asks.

My head slants toward her. "How the hell should I know?"

I haven't seen him in days. I know he's here in the house. I feel and hear his movements around me every day. But we don't acknowledge each other or talk. We begrudgingly cohabitate.

In fact, I don't think I've even made eye contact with him since that night two months ago when he pinned me to the bed like a territorial ape. It was that night that I knew I *really* had to keep my distance from Killian. Not because he's dangerous or cruel but because we could easily teeter into treacherous territory.

When our arguments grow particularly intense, it's hard to tell what is hate and what is passion. This thing between us is like a spreading fire, and every time we light the match, I never know where it will end. The desire to punch him and the desire to kiss him feel the same.

"How is my brother?" Anna asks as she lowers herself into an armchair.

I drop my book on the table and sit up, staring at her impatiently. "You realize he's not really my husband, right? I have no clue how he is, Anna. We don't talk. We're not even friends."

She waves me off, and I get the feeling she's trying to ignore the truth sitting right in front of her. "I know that. I just mean... has he left the house at all?"

Letting out a frustrated sigh, I scowl at her. "No. And while we're on the subject..." My tone is exasperated as I clench my hands between my knees. "Why didn't you tell me about that? He hasn't left the house in *ten years*?"

Anna puts her face in her hands. "I wasn't sure. None of us were. We had our suspicions, but how could we know?"

"What the hell happened? How could you *not* know?"

She bursts out of her seat, pacing the room. "Our parents were killed in a car accident when Killian was just eighteen. The rest of us went to live with our aunt and uncle, but Killian stayed here. He became a different person after they died. He used to be so...happy and ambitious. Then, it was like...he fell apart. He went to uni and partied all the time. Drank too much and stopped coming around."

Leaning forward, I hang on to every word, trying to ignore the gnawing feeling of regret in my stomach as I think about Killian in such pain. Alone.

"So why are you doing this now? Why are you trying to take his house away?" I ask.

Her eyes squeeze shut, and I see the pain etched in her features. "It's my aunt who really wants him out."

Anna sits down again, and I can see the discomfort in her eyes. "Two years ago, my brother Declan discovered just how out of hand Killian's parties had become. I won't go into detail, but he turned our family's house into…" Her voice trails as her cheeks begin to blush.

"Into what?" I press.

"It doesn't matter," she responds, waving the answer away. "The point is that my aunt doesn't want to see our family home treated like some sort of…sex club."

I press my lips together. I swear, every time this woman opens her mouth, I get more and more irate with what she says. What kind of family treats each other this way? How can they claim to love him so much but want to hurt him at the same time?

"It's *his* house," I argue, a touch too loudly. I slam my hand against the arm of the sofa. "Legally, it's his, right? So he can do whatever he wants with it. It's *just* a house. And so what if he doesn't leave it? It might be the only thing in his life that brings him comfort, but here you are, the people who are supposed to love him, and you're trying to take that way. Killian might actually be hurting, and you only want to hurt him more! What is wrong with you people?"

"What's going on in here?" a deep voice bellows from the doorway. Sylvie and I spin around to find Killian standing there, watching us with an expression of anger.

"Killian," she says softly as she stands up.

He ignores her and turns his eyes toward me. "Why are you yelling at my sister?"

"I—" The words get stuck on my tongue. Why *was* I just yelling at her?

"It's okay, Killian. She was just sticking up for you."

"I was not," I argue.

He snickers as he crosses his arms over his chest. My blood is still hot with anger that I don't understand.

"The holidays are coming up," Anna declares. "Auntie Lorna would really like to see you both at the Hogmanay party."

"No," Killian replies before she's even done speaking.

"What is that?" I ask.

"New Year's Eve," he replies in a disgruntled tone.

"Will you just think about it, please?" Anna implores.

His eyes find mine, and I see the warring thoughts written all over his face. This is part of the deal. It's not about just staying married for a year. It's about proving to his family that he's settled down. That he has every right to keep the house.

Of course…to *him,* that's the plan.

To everyone else, it doesn't really matter if he's settled down or doing better. It's about getting the rights out of his hands and into theirs.

"Fine," he mutters. "I'll think about it."

"Thank you," Anna replies, looking relieved.

Before Killian leaves the room, he lets his gaze rest on my face for a moment. I nearly forgot how intense his eyes could be.

"Now, stop talking about me," he says before disappearing out the door.

The room is bathed in silence as I sit on the chaise lounge with my book still on my lap. There's a lingering anger deep in my bones from my conversation with Anna.

We wait until we both hear the front door close, letting us know Killian has left the house before either one of us speaks.

"Don't you feel bad?" I whisper. "For what you're doing to him? Tricking him out of his own home with this fake marriage?"

"You wouldn't understand," she replies.

And I know that's probably a jab at my family and how little they care about me, but I'll never understand how lying to Killian about why we're doing this is their way of showing they care.

"Please, Sylvie," she mumbles softly. "Will you just try to help him? Talk him into going to that party, and I'll sweeten the deal."

My head perks up. "How much?"

"Ten thousand," she replies plainly.

"He's not going to listen to me," I argue. "He hates me."

When her eyes lift to my face, I'm surprised to find a hint of humor in her face.

"He doesn't hate you," she says. "At least not as much as you think he does."

I scoff out a laugh. "What makes you think that?"

"I see the way he looks at you. You two are more alike than you think. If he didn't like you, he wouldn't bother arguing with you. He's not afraid to hurt your feelings because he knows you can take it. He sees your strength, Sylvie. And I truly believe he will miss you when you're gone."

She picks up her purse from the table and walks toward the door. "If anyone can talk him into it, it's you," she says. And with that, she leaves.

Her words hang in the air after she's gone. I'm lost in contemplation, running through everything over and over and over as if I'm trying to pinpoint something on a map. How do I feel about this? This house. This marriage. Him.

My feelings are scattered and confusing. I've been in this house too long. I've been so deep in this for so long that I can't seem to find my way out anymore. The reward at the end doesn't glisten as brightly as it did three months ago.

———

Boredom settles in my bones like a sickness. Not for the first time in the past month, I consider picking a fight with Killian because at least it's something to do. But again, fighting with him has gotten dangerously heated. And that's a line I don't need to cross.

Fucking my husband would be a terrible idea.

I've tried working on my novel. But opening my laptop usually leads to opening a browser which leads to watching the lives of people I once knew and used to like flash by me like I'm stuck in some time travel simulation.

They're at Burning Man or at a resort in Bali. I'm wasting away in a nineteenth-century Scottish manor like I've been dropped in the middle of a Charlotte Brontë novel.

Nine months to go. I can do this.

I'm lying on the couch in the library, the fire crackling as I stare mindlessly at the hundreds of titles on the shelves around me. The words all fade together like meaningless stars in the sky.

The book I was reading grew too boring and political for me. It was supposed to be about a torrid love affair, and I wanted something salacious and dirty, but the author chose to delve into the inner workings of the Russian political climate after the war, and I gave up.

Nothing interests me now.

That is, until my eyes catch on a title that doesn't seem to fit with the others.

The Act of Submission.

I sit up and squint my eyes at the book title again. The spine is deep red, and the text is eloquent and flowery. It's between a book about beekeeping and a classic novel. Climbing from the couch, I cross the room and pull the book from the shelf. The image on the front is a pair of wrists bound together with a strip of red satin.

My eyebrows shoot upward. Quickly I check my surroundings to be sure he hasn't snuck into the room. Then I open the book.

Inside are illustrations and mostly text. The illustrations are sexual in nature without being explicit.

A man kneeling with his head bowed.

A woman staring up at another woman.

A naked woman hogtied and suspended in the air.

Does this book belong to Killian? Is he really into this? I mean, I found that leather strap on the bed frame, but that could have been anything. It could have belonged to someone else. Maybe Anna has a secret kinky side.

Suddenly my mind conjures images of Killian forcing me into submission, and everything inside me bristles. Are these the kinds of women he likes? Was Claire like this?

This is why we would never work. I could never let him have that kind of control over me. I don't want to let him think he's won something.

Then I remember his weight on me that night. My adrenaline kicking up. My heart pounding. Arousal blossoming low in my belly.

Movement out of the corner of my eye draws my attention to the window. The first thing I notice is that the rain has stopped. A glint of light cascades across the panes, and something in me delights at the prospect of sunshine.

Walking to the window, I stare out at the wet trees of the fields behind the house. Then I spot Killian walking through the grass toward the house.

His hair is down, drenched from the rain and slicked back. His white shirt is tight against his body, wet and transparent. As he marches back toward the house, I find myself watching him with curiosity.

I've never met anyone like Killian in my life. He is tasteless and stubborn and so bold it's exasperating. But he knows exactly what he wants, and he takes it without apology. He truly cares about himself and no one else.

And if I didn't hate him so much, I might actually like him.

Chapter Seventeen

I snatch my scarf from my closet and throw it around my neck. As I emerge from my room, I hear another door closing down the hall and look up to find Killian standing just two doors down.

We both pause and stare at each other for a moment. It's rare that we end up at the same place at the same time anymore, but when we do, it's always a little unsettling. His wild green eyes bore into mine for a moment.

"Where are you going?" he asks after his eyes rake down my body, noticing my winter boots.

"Into town to do some shopping," I reply.

He doesn't respond, only stares at me. So I casually add, "Wanna come?"

There's a flinch in his expression. Then he shakes his head. "Fuck no."

"What's wrong?" I ask, taking a step toward him. "Afraid of a little shopping?"

He tilts his head and gives me an unamused expression. His hair is pulled half into a bun at the back of his head, and I notice the rest falls past his shoulders. For some reason, I find myself reaching out to brush it with my fingers.

"You need a haircut," I say.

His eyes follow my fingers and then settle on my face, probably as confused as I am as to why I would *touch* it.

Naturally, he reaches out and tugs on one of my unruly curls. "So do you."

"Want to give each other haircuts?" I ask with a playful tone. *What is happening right now?*

He gives an uneasy chuckle. Even he's confused. We're standing here teasing each other in a casual conversation without slinging insults. I think finding that book yesterday has somehow morphed my perception of Killian. I'm not exactly sure how. It's almost like curiosity has overpowered the hatred.

"Okay, well...if you're sure you don't want to come..." I awkwardly head toward the stairs, and I swear I spot a hint of hesitation on his face.

For the first time in three months, I almost feel bad for leaving him here alone.

"Have fun," he mutters, leaving his back to me as I walk down the stairs toward the front door, where Peter, the driver, is waiting for me.

I carry that feeling of guilt with me during the entire drive into the city. And even as I shop, it's there. Nothing interests me. There's a street full of stores and restaurants, and along the center of the pedestrian road are stalls selling holiday things like baked goods and ornaments.

I was never much for Christmas back home. New York City makes it hard not to feel the spirit though. But this is different. There's no Rockefeller Center Christmas tree, but there is something more quaint and comforting.

After coming out of a clothing store, I stop at one of the stalls. It's handcrafted leather goods, purses, belts, and other things. My eyes catch on a very large pair of brown leather gloves. The leather is soft, and I pick them up, letting my fingers graze the surface.

I think about Killian's hands. I remember the weight of them as they rested in mine on our wedding day. And then again that night, bandaging the open gash across his palm.

Then I feel them around my arm—and around my waist.

It's a memory, but it's burnt into my mind like an iron brand. I can still remember how they felt as they pinned my hands to the bed. So much larger than mine. Capable of so much, but never used harshly against me. Even when he held me back, there was care in his strength.

"Would you like to buy those, dear?" the woman behind the booth asks.

I press my open hand to the gloves, noticing the size difference. The long fingers dwarf my tiny thin ones.

"Yes, please," I murmur as I look at her with a smile. Reaching into my purse, I pull out my wallet and hand her two bills to cover it. "Keep the change."

"Thank you," she replies sweetly. Then she offers me a bag for the gloves. "Happy Christmas, dear."

"Happy Christmas," I mutter in response.

The gloves don't replace the guilt still souring my insides. What the hell has gotten into me? Why would I feel bad for coming into town? It's not like he really wanted to come. If he wanted to, he could have said so. I literally asked.

Besides, he wouldn't want to come with *me*. I'm sure someday Killian will be able to get over his fear of leaving the house, and it will probably be to attend a rugby match with his uni friends. It certainly wouldn't be for shopping with an American girl he can't stand.

"Sylvie?" I glance up from the cobblestone ground to see a familiar woman standing near a storefront.

"Claire," I reply with hesitation.

As she smiles at me and crosses the passing crowd to hug me, I quickly try to decipher how I'm *supposed* to feel about this woman. Because my natural reaction is that I think she's a lying, cheating home-wrecker who tried to fuck my husband. But Killian is not really my husband, and that's not really my home.

Still, I hate her.

When she pulls away from our quick hug, she holds my shoulders and gives me a cheesy grin. "How are you?"

"I'm good," I reply, unable to meet her level of forced enthusiasm.

"How's Killian?" she asks, and my smile fades.

"He's fine," I mutter without emotion.

"Good." She draws out the response, clearly gauging my reaction to her speaking his name.

She has to know I don't like her. Why play these fake games? I caught her in the hallway with him. I heard the way she pulled him into the closet that night. I also know she didn't have him in there long enough for them to do anything— which means he turned her down—because of the contract, of course.

She doesn't know that though. In her mind, she must think that he loves me more, and that gives me a sense of smug pride.

"He's not with you today?" she asks, her eyes grazing the crowd.

My molars grind. "No. He stayed home." I emphasize the word *home*. Our home.

"Are you busy?" she asks. "We should grab a drink."

I don't want to grab a drink with this woman, but I do want to hear what she has to say to me. My curiosity always gets the better of me.

"That sounds great," I lie with a fake smile.

She leads the way as we walk down to a nearby pub. Once

we enter, we hang our coats and scarves on the hook next to the door. Then we find an empty table and sit across from each other. The bartender brings us each a beer, and I keep Killian's gloves at my side.

We make small talk for a while. Claire tells me about her job in restaurant management. I tell her a little about my life in New York and how I'm working on a novel—that I haven't touched in over a year.

When there's a lull in our conversation, I feel her ready to pounce on a more scandalous topic.

"So…" Claire says after taking a drink. "I heard a dirty little rumor about you and Killian."

I take a long sip of my beer, waiting for her to elaborate.

"That you two like to…share. Is that true?"

I set down my beer and press my lips together. I know exactly why she's asking me this. She's testing me to see how much power she can use against me. It takes everything in me not to explode on this woman and call her out for being the meddling bitch that she is. Instead, I reply softly.

"You know…you can't trust rumors."

She laughs. "Surely, there's some truth to that one though."

"There's not." My answer is clipped. I meet her gaze, and while her expression is playful and happy, mine is cold and ruthless.

"Okay," she says with a laugh. "I was just asking."

"I'm sure you were," I reply. "Just curious, right?"

Her brows lift and her smile fades. "Did I do something wrong?"

I take another sip, letting her sit with that question for a moment, hoping it tortures her, waiting for the answer.

Deep down, I know I shouldn't care if she did try to sleep with Killian. It's none of my business…

Except it is. Because he is legally my husband, and if she

did manage to fuck him that night, she could have cost me ten million dollars.

All of that aside…she tried to seduce *my* husband.

"You know, Claire…" I say, trying to keep my cool. "You may not be able to trust rumors, but you can trust your gut. And my gut is telling me that you tried to fuck my husband that weekend at my house."

"Sylvie—" she snaps, glancing around to see if anyone heard.

"My gut also tells me that you've fucked Killian in the past, probably when you were already married to Angus."

She leans forward, and I notice the tremble in her breath. "Stop it."

But I don't. The more I think about it, the more I'm starting to realize something. "Let me guess," I say with a tilt of my head. "Your little affair wasn't part of that kinky swinger shit you guys do at the parties?"

Her eyes half shut, which tells me I must be right.

"He told you about that?" she whispers.

"Killian is dealing with his own shit," I snap. "He doesn't need you fucking with his head even more."

Killian doesn't seem like the kind of guy who would screw his friend's wife. At least not without feeling like shit about it. Is that the prison he's locked himself in? One made of remorse and regret?

"It wasn't just my fault, you know?" she replies. "He's just as responsible as I am. I feel terrible for what I've done, and I'm paying for it with my own guilt."

That part pulls me out of my thought process. "Oh yes, so much guilt that you tried to screw him again?"

"Will you please keep your voice down?" she whispers angrily.

When I feel the curious stares from around the pub, I

shrink down and keep quiet. Normally, I wouldn't care about attracting attention, but this isn't about me. This is his business, and the more people seem to meddle in it, the more fired up I seem to get.

I take another drink of my beer, desperate to calm my nerves.

"You know…" she says, scratching the back of her neck. "You're not at all what I expected for Killian. You two are so alike; I can't imagine how you're compatible."

"We're not that alike," I argue. That comment caught me off guard. I'm nothing like Killian. He's brash, rude, and inconsiderate.

When Claire doesn't respond, I swallow and look away.

"What? You think you're so much better for him?" I ask.

"I know what he needs," she replies smugly, and my blood starts to boil again.

"Oh yeah? And what is it he needs?" I'm asking to be defiant, but I'm also a little curious.

She rests her arms on the table and leans forward. "Killian doesn't need some headstrong brat who is going to make everything difficult for him. He needs someone who puts their trust in him. Someone who will let him have control and be the dominant man he is."

My face contorts into a sneer. I would never force myself to be something I'm not just because it's what he *needs*. But the more I let her opinion settle in my mind, the more *wrong* it feels.

"You don't know him at all," I reply.

She scoffs. "And you do? You've known him for what? Three months? If you think kinky swinger parties were the extent of it, then you don't know a damn thing."

Suddenly, I feel very confident that I know Killian far better than she does, even if she has known him for ten years.

Hell, at this point, I feel like I might know him better than his own family. Maybe because he isn't afraid to be himself around me. He shows me the ugly parts—the parts he won't let anyone else see. I see when he's scared and frustrated and lonely and angry. All they see are fake smiles and rehearsed fronts.

I grab the bag, holding the leather gloves off the seat. The sudden desperation to be out of this pub and out of this city is overpowering. I just want to go home.

Standing up in a huff, I lean down toward Claire and force out everything on my mind, no matter how irrational it is.

"You don't know him, because if you did, you would know that's not what he needs at all. Killian doesn't need more control. He blames himself too much for that. What he needs is someone he can *trust*. Someone who will take away the decisions and the burden of having to make them. Someone he can truly let go with."

She lets out a sarcastic chuckle. "And you think that's you?"

I inch closer. "I know it is."

When her face flattens in anger, I resist the urge to throw the rest of her beer in her face or punch her in the nose. The old Sylvie might have done that, but I refrain. As much as I'd love to lash out at this cheater the same way I lashed out at Aaron, I don't.

Instead, I stand up tall and stare down at her.

"If you touch my husband again, I'll kill you."

Her eyes widen in surprise. And with that, I storm out of the pub, grabbing my coat and scarf on the way.

I realize as I march angrily into the now-dark city streets that threatening murder might not be a huge improvement in maturity from throwing drinks at her like a child, but it is an improvement nonetheless. And for that, I'm sort of proud.

Chapter Eighteen

My mind is still reeling from that conversation with Claire as I storm down the cobblestone street toward where Peter dropped me off. I told him to pick up me around seven, but I realize as I glance down at my watch that it's well past eight thirty now.

Stopping in front of a closed store, I pull out my phone from my purse. I quickly find Peter's contact and notice the battery is down to one tiny sliver.

Shit.

Quickly, I punch out a message to him.

I need a ride—

The screen goes black.

"Fuck!" I bark as I squeeze the buttons again, hoping it will magically come back to life. Holding my useless phone in my hands, I glance up to check my surroundings. Surely there has to be a store around here that sells chargers.

But nearly every storefront displays dark spaces and locks on the doors. I forgot nearly everything in this town closes early.

Okay, okay. I'll just walk back to where Peter dropped me off. I'm sure that's where he's waiting. So I continue down the street toward where I think I'm supposed to turn. But when I reach that street, it's definitely not like I remember. Which means I must have made a wrong turn somewhere.

Panic starts to build inside me. I'm out of cash to call a cab, not that there are any on the streets for me to hail like I did in New York City.

I'm screwed.

Stop panicking, Sylvie. You've been in worse situations.

Shoving my phone back in my pocket, I continue my walk, waiting for any of these street names to appear familiar. But the night is so dark, and nothing looks like it did five hours ago. I never should have let Claire lead me away from the area I knew. I never should have walked off with her at all.

That conversation only frustrated and confused me more than I already am. I may not like Killian like she thinks I do, but I do sympathize with him. Everyone in his life seems to know what's best for him. No wonder he's locked himself away. Not a single person in his circle has actually offered to help him. They just want to control him.

And not in the way he needs.

I know that feeling. My parents want me to be someone else entirely. Everything I do and say disappoints them. To the point where I have alienated myself from everyone because it's easier to be alone than to be less than what someone expects.

But even that gets lonely.

So lonely.

I can only imagine what that's like for him. I meant every word I said to Claire. Killian just needs a soft place to land. A person who supports him for him. All the bad parts with the good. Someone who gives him room to be himself.

Hell, maybe that's just what I need.

Because now that I think about it, I never felt that with Aaron. He never supported me without his own judgment. He was just as bad as Anna and Claire, claiming they can fix Killian.

Before I know it, I feel the moisture of tears pooling in my eyes. It must be from the panic of being lost in the city. Or the frenetic energy of that fight with Claire. But once I start crying, I can't stop. I'm wiping tear after tear from my eyes as I walk angrily through the dark city streets.

The only things that are open are bustling pubs and seedy tobacco stores. I could go in. I'd likely find someone or something to help. But I don't.

What is going back to the house going to help? I'd still be lost.

The screech of tires jerks me from my thoughts, and I let out a scream. Turning to stare into the bright lights, I back away from the black car, waiting for someone to emerge—praying it's my driver, Peter.

The door flies open, and I let out a gasp.

Killian's panicked expression has my skin tingling with goose bumps. "Where the fuck have you been?" he bellows. I've never heard him sound so angry. I take a step farther away.

"Killian?" My mind can't seem to catch up and process what I'm seeing.

"Get in the fucking car, Sylvie," he shouts in a growly command.

My expression twists in revulsion. "I'm not getting in there with you if you're going to yell at me like that."

As he slams the door and marches toward me, my eyes widen even more. "I told you to get in the fucking car, woman. You can either listen to me, or I'll toss you over my shoulder and put you in there myself." He crowds me against the building with an enraged snarl on his face. I can't help but notice the way his hands are shaking and his eyes are erratic.

"What is wrong with you?" I reply defiantly, but my tone doesn't carry the same livid heat it normally does. I'm too confused and shocked to be as angry as he is.

"For fuck's sake," he mutters as he reaches for me.

Before he can cause a scene and have the police take him to jail, I put up my hands in surrender. "Okay, okay!" I shriek. "I'll get in. Just…relax."

"Relax?" he howls at me. "You have had us worried sick. Peter came looking for you, but you didn't answer your phone, and he couldn't find you."

"I lost track of time. I'm sorry."

"Just get in the fucking car."

His chest is heaving in a panicked, shallow sort of way. I quickly move around him and rush to the passenger side, climbing in and forcing myself to relax. I didn't actually do anything wrong. I was just a little late. My phone died. It's not my fault for getting everyone worried.

As Killian climbs in next to me, I stare at him behind the wheel of the car. It's such an odd image for me. I've only ever seen him at the house. Something isn't right about him, but I can't put my finger on it.

"Are you okay?" I mumble delicately as he takes off down the cobblestone road.

His head snaps in my direction. "I'm fine," he grumbles.

He doesn't look fine.

But I don't push the subject. I still can't get over the fact that Killian is driving a car. He's not at the house. He…left.

"You're so…inconsiderate, Sylvie," he snaps.

I lift my head and give him a terse glare. "Inconsiderate? It was just an accident. I said I was sorry!"

"You had us worried sick." His hands squeeze around the steering wheel as my temper grows.

"Because I was a little late?"

"Because you don't think about anyone but yourself. Peter couldn't find you. And I don't like seeing my staff upset."

My gaze intensifies on him. None of this makes any sense.

We stay quiet for the rest of the drive. It feels as if there's a lump of something in my chest. Emotion I can't seem to swallow. Pain that won't go away. Guilt that rots inside me like a cancer.

He's angry at me because I worried him, and I can't make sense of it. I don't think I've ever felt someone's concern so intensely before. And I don't know if I like it.

When we reach the manor, I barrel out of the car, desperate to run from this feeling inside me.

He stomps after me, clearly not ready to let me go. I slam the door, but he quickly opens it and bounds inside before slamming it himself.

"Sylvie!" he roars after me. I'm halfway up the stairs when he practically chases me up them. There is a shake in my bones, and I don't know if it's adrenaline or fear or anticipation.

We are on the precipice of something big. I can feel it, and it terrifies me. Because it means I have to come out of the quiet, safe little bubble I've been living in.

I turn on my heel and shout back at him. "What do you want?"

"I want you to stop being an insolent brat!"

Stepping up another few stairs, he stops two away from me. I'm just barely as tall as him at this level.

"Why am I such a brat? Because I made you worry? That's not my fault, Killian! It's yours. I never told you to care about me."

I spin around, knowing full well what he'll do next. That familiar large hand wraps around my arm, hauling me back toward him. My hands go to his chest, but instead of pushing him away, I tighten my fists in his shirt.

We are chest to chest. I'm staring into his eyes blazing with fury as one of his hands grabs the back of my neck and brings my face close enough to brush our lips together.

"You make me so angry," he mutters.

I manage one desperate gasp before his mouth crashes against mine. The kiss isn't anything like our last two kisses. Those were performances. This is real.

Our tongues collide in a needy tangle of desire. He bites on my bottom lip, and I scratch his arm through the flannel of his shirt. The grip on the back of my neck tightens as he pulls me even closer, devouring my mouth and making me forget why I shouldn't be doing this.

I try to tell myself I don't like Killian. I *hate* him. But the argument is so weak. It fades away on a breeze in my mind while my body seems to be caught in a storm of passion.

Without breaking the kiss, he lays me on the steps and moves his mouth from my lips down to my jaw. I let out another gasp as the rough texture of his beard scratches my neck. His kisses are brutal, much like his attitude toward me.

He's not afraid of breaking me. He knows I can take it.

In a frenzy, he works off my coat and scarf. My fingers dig into his hair, dragging him closer as my legs part, allowing him space to settle between them.

The size difference between us is even more alarming in this position. My thighs are pressed as wide as they go while he grinds himself against me, and I let out a needy yelp.

I drag his mouth back up to mine and kiss him even harder. I don't want to think about anything. I just want to feel. I want to douse this fire that's been burning for so long.

He lifts himself from my body and moves his hands to the button of my jeans. Those large fingers work the zipper down, and I lift my hips, eager to shed my clothes. As soon as I feel the cool wood of the stairs on my ass, I shiver in anticipation. This is all moving way too fast. But I don't want to stop it.

My pants don't go far. They barely reach my knees before Killian moves downward and latches his mouth around my sex. I grab his hair again and let out a squeal of surprise. My arousal intensifies, exploding inside me as soon as I feel his warm mouth on my clit.

But this angle is too difficult, and I can't spread my legs for him, so he sits back up and starts tearing at my boots as if he's overcome with the need to get between my legs.

I pull at his shirt, and he takes a break from untying my laces to tear the long-sleeved flannel off. Touching his bare chest and shoulders with my hands is intoxicating. With every graze of his skin, I need more.

He finally works my boots off. Then he strips my pants off in one violent motion.

And then that's it. Just like that, I'm lying naked from the waist down on the stairs, spread bare for him like a meal on the table. It's unnerving and a little scary.

But my body is drunk on lust, so I reach for him. Without a second of hesitation, he drops to his knees a few steps below me and buries his face between my legs. Wrapping one arm around my thigh, he loudly devours me, sucking and licking every sensitive inch.

The other arm reaches up to my breast, tugging my shirt open enough to pinch the tight bud of my nipple. I suck in through my teeth, thrown off by the sensation.

My spine arches, and my lungs desperately try to suck in air, but it's useless. I'm helpless against him. I clench my fingers around the steps, and I close my eyes as I let him take my body.

I want to scream his name. I want to beg him not to stop. I want to look into his eyes as he pushes his tongue inside me, but I don't do any of it. Killian has his mouth in the most private, intimate part of me, and I'm not ready to face what this means.

I just want to come. I want to take the orgasm he gives me. And I want him to feel how much I love it.

Before I fly over the edge of pleasure, I grab the hand that's cupped around my breast, and I pull it to my mouth. I'm so caught up in the passion that I don't even know what I'm doing or why I'm doing it. I love the way his fingers feel in mine as I wrap my lips around the middle digit. Softly I suck and lick, mirroring his actions between my legs.

My climax builds so quickly that I barely have a chance to prepare myself. On a quick inhale, my body explodes in pleasure, and I bite down on his finger, hearing him howl against my sex. I only have enough air left in my lungs to groan out a feral sound of pleasure.

He tears his hand from my mouth, moving it to my throat and holding me there as I'm assaulted by wave after wave of sensation. I see stars as my body is rolled through the climax. Over and over and over again. It pulses through me for an impossibly long time until it feels like I can't take it anymore.

I collapse on the stairs when it finally ceases. He pulls his mouth away, and I can hear him gasping.

We both seem to surrender to the moment together. Neither of us speaks. Neither of us moves.

After a while, I slowly sit up. He's facing away from me, his elbows resting on his knees and his head hanging forward. My clothes are strewn over the stairs in a mess.

Part of me wants to reach for him, but that fear of facing the truth resurfaces, and I hold myself back. Instead, I quickly gather my things and quietly, without a word, tiptoe up to my room and shut the door.

Chapter Nineteen

I TOSS AND TURN ALL NIGHT. EVEN THOUGH I HAD MY RELEASE, I still feel strung tight. Everything between my legs is red and sore from the scratch of his beard. All night, I find myself touching it, exploring the sensitivity, and remembering what it felt like to have him down there.

The warmth of his mouth. The friction of his tongue.

It's all too much, like it's overloaded my system.

And one thing that keeps barraging my mind like a storm is the question of why. Why would he kiss me? Why would he touch me? Why on earth did he make me see stars on that staircase without wanting a single thing in return?

He had me feeling so guilty in the car for making him worry. And at the time I was feeling heated and defensive. Now, I'm seeing it clearer. Killian worried because he cared, and I have literally never felt such concern in my entire life.

Have his feelings for me changed?

Have mine?

Getting tangled up in our emotions is a bad idea. Killian still has no idea that being married to me will result in him losing his house. If I start feeling things for him, then I'll have to start dealing with things like guilt and responsibility. And I'd like to avoid those.

The space between us now feels so potent. Every single inch from my bed to his down the hall might as well be nothing at all. It's like I can just reach out and touch him, but I don't. The thought of tiptoeing into his room crosses my mind all night.

What would I even do? Crawl into his bed uninvited? Just climb on his dick like a cat in heat?

What we did today feels like peeking over a wall before quickly returning to our opposite sides. And I'm not going to lie. After today, I want to go back over that wall. I want more. Not just because the orgasm was great but because, for a moment, I didn't feel so alone.

But I won't. I can't. Getting physical is a bad idea if I want to keep my eyes on the prize. I need to get through this year and get my ten million so I can live the rest of my days in peace.

Don't do anything stupid, Sylvie.

It's sometime after three in the morning that I finally jump out of my bed, unable to take it anymore. I march angrily down the hall and burst into his room without a single idea of what I'm doing.

He's sleeping peacefully in his bed, lying motionless on his back. He doesn't even stir when I slam the door behind me.

I walk right up to his bed and poke him in the chest. "Hey!" I bellow.

He wakes with a start. When his eyes focus on my form standing near his bed, he lets his eyebrows fold inward with a scowl. Then he turns away from me and closes his eyes like he's going back to sleep.

"Killian!" I shriek as I shove him again.

"What do you want, wife?" he shouts.

I'm hot with anger, and I let it come flying out of my mouth. "Why did you do that?"

Turning back toward me, he holds his hands up. "Do what?"

"On the stairs," I reply, exasperated.

"What the fuck are you talking about?" he says as he sits up and rubs his eyes.

"We're not doing that, you know? We're not a real couple."

I hear myself. I sound flustered, but right now, I *feel* flustered. One moment Killian said I meant nothing to him, then he was yelling at me, and then suddenly, he was tongue fucking me. I don't know if this is what gaslighting is, but I certainly feel like I don't know my own mind anymore. He's infiltrated it with desire and passion, so I don't know where the hatred ends and lust begins.

He scrubs a hand over his face as he lets out a groan. "What on earth are you going on about? We're not doing what? It was just sex, Sylvie. Would you relax?"

"No," I snap. "Because I didn't know you and I were… doing that, and it took me by surprise, and I just want to know why. Why did you do that?"

"Why did I go down on you?" he asks, and my cheeks heat with embarrassment.

"Yes."

His expression is guarded as he stares at me through the moonlight. "Because I wanted to."

I feel unsatisfied with that answer, and I don't understand why. "Well, we're not doing this. Like I said, we're not really married."

"Yes, we are," he replies before folding his arms.

I let out a sigh of frustration. "I mean…we're not really a couple. So we're not doing the *just-sex* thing."

He scratches his beard for a moment, and I find myself

zeroing in on his fingers, remembering the way they felt in my mouth. I wonder if I left a mark from where I bit him.

"Why not?" he asks.

"What do you mean, why not?"

He shrugs. "Why can't we have a physical relationship? We are married. We have a long cold winter ahead of us with nothing better to do."

Suddenly I imagine just how fun this house *could* be if I weren't constantly secluded in the library and living room.

But no. I just went over this in my head. If I get physical with Killian, feelings will surely get muddled, and that's a bad idea.

I quickly shake the thought away. "No."

"Is that really why you came in here and woke me up? To tell me we wouldn't be doing that again?" he asks, and I hear the skepticism in his voice.

"Yes," I reply, standing my ground.

To my surprise, he responds with a low, grumbly, "Come here."

My heart rate picks up. By the time I answer him, it's too late.

"No," I murmur half-heartedly.

He lets out a growl. "Come here *now.*"

My brow furrows, and I take an angry step toward him. "You can't talk to me like that! I don't have to listen to you."

In a flash of movement, he reaches out and grabs my hand, hauling me to the bed and flipping me over his body so I'm lying next to him. Then he rolls his large body on top of me.

"Killian!" I shout.

"You're all bark and no bite, my wee wife."

"Oh, I'll bite," I reply with fuming anger.

He chuckles down at me as he holds up his right hand.

"That's right. You do. How could I forget?" As he shows me the red line across his middle finger, he uses it as an opportunity to flip me off at the same time.

Suddenly, I feel his heavy weight pressed between my legs. He's in nothing but a pair of tight boxer briefs, and I'm in a simple long T-shirt and a pair of panties. Which I'm realizing now was not wise to come to talk him in.

"You're telling me this wouldn't be nice?" he asks as he grinds his hips against my core.

By some miracle, I hold in the moan that wants to escape.

Because it does feel nice. It feels *very* fucking nice.

"No," I reply through clenched teeth.

"Don't lie, mo ghràidh."

"Don't call me that."

Ignoring my protest, he continues. "We could do this all winter. Fuck like animals all day long. With nothing better to do. You can still hate me. Call me a brute and an arsehole, and I'll call you a cow and selfish bitch. But with lots and lots of orgasms."

He grinds against me again, and I fail to hold in my reaction this time. A tiny whimper escapes, and I know I'm done for. Any argument is now weak and meaningless.

"I've been tested," he groans against my neck.

"So have I," I reply. "And I'm on the pill."

"See?" he murmurs. "There's nothing stopping us."

"I do hate you," I reply, my voice cracking on the high pitch.

The hard length of his cock slides against my clit, and I fight the urge to wrap my hand around his shaft just to feel the size of it. Based on what I sense now, it's impossibly large.

"I hate you too, darling," he replies, grinding again.

I whimper again.

Our eyes meet, and I stare into the green orbs, unable

to deny that having messy casual sex with a handsome, rich Scottish giant isn't the worst thing to happen to me. I'd be a fool to turn him down.

He keeps up the grinding, and soon, I start to notice how heated and unhinged he's getting. His breathing is growing shallow, and his lips part with desire. The stiff cock in his boxer briefs is so hard it hurts as he rubs it eagerly against my clit. But it's a good pain. A needy, visceral pain that radiates through my entire body.

"I can still taste your cunt on my lips, Sylvie. I can't stop thinking about it."

His filthy words set me on fire. Any hope of turning back now is lost.

My back arches, and my head tilts backward. "Killian."

I moan his name like a plea.

"Tell me to stop," he mutters with his lips near my throat.

"Don't stop," I reply.

Reaching down, I rest my hand on the firm surface of his ass. It feels so weird touching him but also so good. How long have I wanted to press my palm to his backside? Squeeze it. Use it as leverage to pull him closer to me.

He grinds harder, and I start to wonder if he'll settle for this dry humping or if he'll take the opportunity to slip my panties aside and enter me. I don't know which one I want at this point.

I love this *almost-sex* feeling. Having him so close but still not quite where I want him.

My mind is already lost to the sensation. I'm supposed to be stopping this, but I can't remember why. I just want more.

So I wrap my legs around his hips and hold tight to his ass to grind him harder and harder and harder to a rhythm that makes my body tighten, and my blood flow hotter through my veins.

Angling my face toward him, he quickly latches his lips to mine.

I've already committed his kiss to memory. It's so different than the ones we have to fake. His real kisses are brutal and passionate, biting and nibbling and devouring.

"I'm gonna—"

The words fall off my lips as he kisses me again. When he pulls away, I see the look of ecstasy on his face—the near-climax expression.

"Let me see it again, darling. You come so pretty."

My hips are moving fast now, tilting and grinding, trying to keep up with the momentum of his hard cock. Two thin layers of cotton are all that separate us, and it feels like we're striking a fire with them.

I let out a high-pitched squeal when the pleasure seizes my body in an earthquake of sensation. My muscles clench tight around him, and I let myself drown in the feeling. It's not as potent as the one on the stairs, but chasing it is half the fun anyway.

His movements pick up speed until I look up to find him shuddering with a look of euphoria on his face. I feel the twitch of his cock against me as he comes, and I stare down between our bodies to watch the way it soaks the inside of his boxer briefs.

We freeze in our spots, him hovering over me. Lifting my fingers, I press them against the muscular planes of his chest. Softly, I touch the chest hair and wait for him to decide this is a terrible idea.

He doesn't.

He collapses next to me, staring at the ceiling as he catches his breath.

"See?" he mumbles in a quiet drawl. "This could be fun."

Fun. Fun until he finds out he's about to lose everything because of me.

"Sure," I reply softly.

He turns, jumping out of bed and going to the bathroom. I watch him through the darkness as he disappears inside.

"Don't move," he barks at me, and I roll my eyes at his order.

"When are you going to learn you can't just boss me around?" I reply.

He laughs to himself in the bathroom before coming out in a fresh pair of boxers and climbing into the bed next to me.

"You're still here, aren't you?"

I turn on my pillow to face him. "It's warmer in here with you," I say as an excuse for why I'm still in his bed.

"Sure it is," he replies sleepily. "Good night, darling."

"I'm not your darling," I reply.

"You still hate me, right?" he asks playfully.

"Yes," I lie. I *wish* I still hated him, but I have to be honest with myself now. I can't find a single reason to keep hating him.

"Okay, good," he says with a yawn. Before long, I hear his breathing change as he falls asleep with me in his arms.

I want nothing more than to sleep, but my mind is reeling. If we do go down this path, could we keep things strictly physical? Sure, I may not hate Killian anymore, but I'm confident I could never come to love him. There are too many things about him I can't stand. He's controlling and ignorant, and most of all, I mean nothing to him. Nothing more than a warm body and a means to an end.

Yes, I believe we could keep things strictly physical.

Besides, I don't have any other choice. When Killian finds out that this marriage was just a scam to steal his house from him, then he'll *really* hate me.

As I lie here, I try to remind myself that I don't care what happens to him after this. We are not in a real relationship.

In nine months, I will be gone from this place, and he will continue to mean nothing to me.

I'll be ten million dollars richer. I'll no longer be Mrs. Barclay. And everything will be as it should be.

Chapter Twenty

I FINALLY FALL ASLEEP, AND WHEN I DO, I SLEEP SO DEEPLY that I don't think I move all night. When I peel my eyes open, I'm almost surprised to see Killian's room. What a whirlwind the past twenty-four hours have been.

I turn slowly to face him and stare at his sleeping form across the giant bed. He's lying on his back, his dark-brown hair strewn across the pillow. His beard has grown longer and thicker since I first met him.

For a while, I just lie here and stare at every raw inch of his bare skin as if I'm not normally allowed to see him like this, so I have to sneak my peek when I can. Reaching out, I delicately run my fingers over the muscles of his shoulder and down his bicep.

What is he doing out there in those fields all day that helps him keep this physique? He has the body of a man who I assume frequents the gym, but as far as I know, there's not one in the house.

My gaze cascades down, over his pecs and abs until his body disappears under the dark green sheet covering his lower half. Last night I got a taste of what he's hiding in those boxers, and I can't help but be curious about it now.

Slowly, I lift the sheet and just take a quick peek underneath. All I can see at this angle are his dark boxer briefs and his thick, hair-covered thighs. Dropping the sheet, I find myself smirking.

Killian is really not my type—beefy, broody, and vulgar in every way. So why am I so attracted to him all of a sudden?

Maybe it's because I can finally enjoy a physical relationship without the worry of whether or not the other person likes me. I *know* Killian doesn't like me. It makes things easier. Less about emotions and more about sensations.

And even if feelings *were* involved—which they're not—how do I know what Anna and her brothers are planning isn't really for Killian's benefit? So what if they're meddling? They're trying to help him, which means I'm helping him too.

So, really, my conscience is clear.

As he stirs, I'm pulled from my thoughts and watch to see if he's about to wake to find me staring at him as he sleeps. When he doesn't open his eyes, I relax into the pillow.

Suddenly, I'm thinking about his sister and his aunt again. The Hogmanay party is next week. I never answered Anna back about Killian attending, so I assume she gave up on the idea. But I haven't.

She offered me ten thousand dollars to get him out of the house, and it really can't be that hard. Now that sex is on the line, I'm sure I can think of something to entice him to go to that party.

Trailing my fingers over his chest, I let them slide down his abs. Then I delicately run a soft line just above the waistband of his boxer briefs. He stirs again but doesn't wake. Very carefully, I climb over him, straddling his waist and settling my weight on his still-soft cock.

Seriously, what am I doing?

Twenty-four hours ago, I never would have entertained the idea of sleeping with Killian. Now I'm riding him like a horse while he's still asleep. I'm touching his body as if I have any right to.

He lets out a groan without opening his eyes. Sleepily, he reaches down and grabs on to my leg, holding me in place as he grinds upward against me.

"Killian..." I whisper.

He's fighting it, keeping his eyes closed as I move slowly on top of him. I feel his cock hardening beneath me. With every passing second, I grow more and more desperate to touch it, feel it in my hand and about a dozen other places.

Being on top like this gives me a sense of power and control that I don't normally feel with him. He's so much bigger than me. But I know I could easily slip my hand into his boxer briefs right now and have him completely at my mercy.

That is until his eyes pop open, and he grabs me by the waist, flipping me until I'm on my back and he's between my legs again. I let out a scream as he does it, but the scream quickly dies as he buries his face in my neck and grinds his erection against me the same way he did last night.

I'm still sore from where his beard scratched my sensitive skin. I can feel it, but it's a delicious pain that only intensifies the pleasure.

"What a way to wake up," he groans into my neck.

His large rough hands caress my body, making my thoughts fuzzy. I was going to say something to him...wasn't I?

But then he lifts my T-shirt and kisses his way up my belly, latching his lips and teeth around the tight bud of my nipple. A breathless gasp escapes my lips as my eyes flutter closed.

What on earth was I going to say?

"Hog-a...something...party." The stuttered words slip through my lips like a plea.

Killian freezes before lifting up and staring at me in confusion. "What did you say?"

I have to recompose my thoughts. "The New Years party is next week...at your aunt's."

His expression turns to a scowl. "You're bringing that up *now*?"

"You're the one who threw me on the bed," I argue.

"Because you were riding my dick."

"Well, I think we should go," I say persistently. "To the party."

Scoffing, he climbs off of me and rolls onto his back. We lie there for a moment until he speaks again.

"Why do *you* care so much about whether I go to a stupid fucking party?" he asks, staring at the ceiling.

"Because your family seems to think you haven't left the manor in ten years." Slowly I turn my head toward him. "Is that true?" I ask softly.

"Of course not," he replies gruffly. I keep my eyes on him as he adds, "More like six."

I wince. *Six years*.

Turning on my side, I prop my head on my arm and stare at him. "Why?"

He mirrors my position and stares at me with a bemused scowl. "Why haven't I left? Because I don't want to. I don't like people. I like it *here*."

After a deep breath, I reply with a shrug. "Fair enough." I don't want to press Killian too much. That's what his sister does. That's what they all do. They push and prod and meddle and call it caring. But if he truly hasn't left the house in six years (before last night), then there must be a reason.

I genuinely wonder if any of them have thought to ask.

"So, let's prove them wrong and go to the party," I suggest.

"No."

I let out a scoff. "Come on."

When he doesn't bend, I reach out a hand and touch his chest, letting my finger drift around his pebbled nipple. "I'll sweeten the deal."

"Oh yeah? How will you do that?" he asks with a mischievous smirk.

"I'm sure you can figure it out," I reply, giving him a light shove.

He rolls onto his back. "Whatever you're thinking, you were probably going to do anyway."

As he folds his hands under his head, I let my jaw hang and shoot him an offended glare. "Don't be so cocky, brute. I never wanted you."

He smiles at me, the dimples on his cheeks barely noticeable through his beard, and I have to press my lips together to keep from smiling.

"Yeah, you did. Don't lie," he says with so much charm it makes me hate him more.

Pounding the pillow, I scurry off the bed with a huff. "Well, unless you agree to go to that party, *nothing* is happening."

"You vindictive bitch!" he calls after me, but I don't reply. I march down the hall to my room, still biting back my smile.

I'm still upstairs, getting dressed in my room, when I hear Killian's brothers and sister coming in. It's Christmas Day, which isn't normally something I celebrate much at home.

Aaron and I rarely exchanged gifts. In fact, I don't think I bought him anything for Christmas last year, but immediately my mind returns to the leather gloves sitting in my coat pocket downstairs.

I'm not an idiot. I see what's happening here.

It only took three months, but somehow, I stopped hating Killian and started feeling things that look like—

No. I won't say it. Not even to myself.

That is simply not an option. Killian and I have no future. Come September, this marriage is over. I'll have my ten million, and I will have to move on with my life.

That is the thought that has comforted me since I arrived here, but suddenly, it makes me sick to even think.

As I descend the stairs, laughter echoes from the parlor. I can clearly make out Anna's voice as well as Lachy's and Declan's.

Rounding the corner into the room, I smile at the sight of Killian and his siblings gathered on the sofas, smiling and opening presents.

When Anna sees me, her face lights up. "Happy Christmas, Sylvie!" she shouts, coming toward me with a cone-like hat and a popper.

I laugh as she places the hat on my head and pulls me in for a hug. "Merry Christmas," I reply softly.

There's a spot on the sofa next to Killian, and I take the seat, carefully glancing in his direction. His arm casually slinks around me, which only strikes me as odd after I remember that everyone in this room knows our marriage is fake. There is no reason to pretend.

"Here, Sylvie," Anna says as she drops a present in my lap.

"What is this?" I ask nervously.

"Open it," she replies.

"I…didn't realize we were exchanging gifts."

She waves me off. "Don't worry about that. Just open it."

As I peel off the paper, I feel sick with guilt. Under the wrapper is a cardboard box, and I lift the lid to find a soft cashmere scarf folded up inside.

"This is beautiful," I say, pulling it out and letting my fingers slide over the silky weave. "Thank you so much."

When my eyes meet hers, she sends me a smile. "You're welcome."

"I didn't get anyone anything."

Killian squeezes my shoulder. "It's okay. Really."

It doesn't feel okay. I feel like an ass. How was I supposed to know that this was going to be a family occasion? I don't belong here. I feel like an imposter in someone else's home. It's just that my parents never did a conventional Christmas. We did events and parties, and our gift exchanges often took place in the early hours and for never more than fifteen minutes.

"I got you something, too, but you don't need to feel bad." Killian stands from the couch and crosses the room to the tree. He takes a small box out and brings it over. My skin grows hot with anxiety as he sets it in my lap.

When I gaze up at him, our eyes meet, and I feel that same pull I felt last night.

I quickly look away. The gift in my lap is wrapped messily, which means he must have done it. He wrapped a present for me.

With a tremble in my hands, I tear off the paper. Inside is a brand-new cell phone. Blinking, I stare at him in confusion.

"I figured I'd replace the one I broke," he says with humor. I swallow down the emotion rising in my throat, remembering that day all those months ago when I watched a complete stranger shatter my phone with his boot.

"I know you have a new one already," he replies casually. "But this one has a better battery life, so it won't die on you while you're out shopping."

Lifting my eyes to his face, I meet his stare again. The rest of the room is quiet, and I can feel them watching us.

"Thank you," I whisper to him. His lip curls in a subtle smirk. "I got you something."

Jumping up from the couch, I rush over to the entryway where my winter coat is hanging. Digging into the pockets, I find the leather gloves I picked up last night. Staring at the gloves, I instantly remember how things felt *so* different between him and me just twenty-four hours ago.

I carry them into the living room and set them on his lap. "It's not much, but I saw them yesterday and…"

My voice trails as his eyes lift to my face. I don't even recognize us anymore.

He reaches into the plastic bag and pulls out the brown leather gloves. I watch nervously as he gazes down at them, a smile tugging on the corner of his mouth. "I love 'em," he says.

As he slips his large hand into the glove, I bite back the emotion that rises to the surface. My obsession with his hands only grows stronger seeing them covered in that soft leather.

"Aren't those lovely," Anna says with a smile from the other side of the room. When I look up, I see that they're all watching us.

It makes my skin crawl. Like the walls are closing in.

None of this was supposed to happen.

Suddenly, I feel a strange sense of irritation. Killian has clearly tricked me into feeling something for him I never wanted to. Or maybe it was just from being stuck in this house for so long.

I need to get out. Clear my head.

In a rush, I burst up from the couch. I go into the kitchen, forcing deep breaths into my lungs to stave the rising feeling of dread, like a rat in a cage.

Trying to force myself into a sense of normalcy, I start making coffee, but I can feel the tremble in my hands. As I'm filling the pot with water, a warm hand touches my back.

"What's wrong?"

I shrug his hand off. "Nothing."

"I said thank you for the gloves," he replies defensively.

"I know you did. I said I'm fine."

"You don't seem fine." He leans against the counter and crosses his arms. "Is this about what happened last night?"

Glancing up at his face, I pinch my eyebrows together. "Of course not. We didn't even have sex, Killian. I'm not going to get all clingy on you."

Without replying, he arches a brow at me. Feeling his gaze on my face makes me even more uncomfortable.

"Stop staring at me!" I snap before taking the water to the coffeepot.

As soon as I set it down, I let out a sigh. It's like I can suddenly hear myself, and I sound neurotic.

Holding on to the counter, I let my head hang. "I'm sorry. I don't know what's wrong with me."

He responds with a soft exhale. "It's Christmas, Sylvie. You're homesick, and I've not seen you talk to your family once since you got here."

I let out a huff and laugh. "And I likely never will."

He takes a step forward. "No one? Not even a friend?"

"My best friend was sleeping with my boyfriend, so no. Not even a friend."

"Sylvie…"

I hate the pity in his voice. I hate the attention. It makes me want to scream.

"You have us. You're not alone."

"Yes," I bark, slamming my hand on the counter. Then I turn toward him and let out all of the frustration boiling inside me. "Yes, I am, Killian. You're not my family or my friends. You're not my husband, and you know it. So can we just *stop* pretending for one second?"

His expression of sympathy morphs into contempt. "Are we pretending, Sylvie?"

I glower at him. "Of course we are. None of this is real."

When he only responds with a patronizing nod, I fight the urge to slug him. Why is he trying to push my buttons on Christmas? Why must he be so smug and difficult and handsome and likable?

Who gave him permission to stop being that ignorant prick he was when I first showed up?

"Fine, Sylvie. I'll stop pretending."

He folds his arms in front of himself and the room grows silent as we stare at each other. There's something about the way he just said that that's making me doubt the sincerity.

"You were pretending…weren't you?" I ask carefully.

He takes a long menacing step toward me. "Of course I was. You mean nothing to me, remember?"

My teeth clench as I fight the sting of those words. Feigning indifference, I scoff loudly, but he only takes another step closer. "I don't believe you," I reply.

"And I mean nothing to you, right? That's why you bought me those gloves."

Pressing my hands to his chest, I apply force as I stare up at him in shock. "You're the most insufferable asshole—"

Ignoring my onslaught of curses, he pins my body against the counter. Taking my wrists in his hands, he holds them behind my back. No matter how much I struggle to get out of his hold, I can't.

What's worse is that I stop trying. Because I love the feel of his body against mine. I love the way he quiets my anxious mind.

And I hate how much I love it.

When his face is just inches from mine, he softly whispers. "I don't know what's going through your head, but you're out of your mind if you think all of this has been pretending. Even when we're alone. You *are* my wife, Sylvie. At the end of this year, you can try to leave, and if you piss me off enough, I might let you go. But I have a feeling you won't. Because I don't mean *nothing* to you, and you know it."

I struggle against his grip. "Oh, I will leave at the end of this. And just because there's a contract in place doesn't make me your real wife."

With one quick motion, he wraps his free hand under my thigh and lifts me until my ass is on the counter and he's squeezed between my legs. I let out a gasp when I feel the hard length in his pants grinding against my clit.

Still holding my wrists together behind my back, he dives forward and kisses me hard on the lips. It's embarrassing how quickly I melt into it. A small whimper escapes as his tongue invades my mouth, and my legs wrap around his waist.

"I could fuck you right here, and you'd let me. Wouldn't you, darling?" His warm breath against my lips makes it hard to think.

"You can't just fuck me into submission every time we fight." I mumble in response.

"Can't I?"

Just as he starts to fumble with the elastic on his loose sweats, releasing my hands, we hear footsteps approaching the kitchen. When I shove against his chest this time, he relents and backs away.

"What's going on?" Anna asks as she steps into the room.

Killian keeps his back to her, likely to hide his erection, and I play innocent, crossing my legs and staying on the counter as if he and I were just having a simple conversation.

"I was just making coffee," I say, nodding to the pot.

Her eyes sparkle with the excitement of the holiday. "Lovely. Well, you two have to come back out to the parlor. We have more presents to open."

"We'll be right there," he replies in a deep grumble. She scurries out of the kitchen excitedly.

With a smile, I hop off the counter and continue making the pot of coffee I was working on.

After hitting the Start button, I turn to face him. As I look into his eyes, ignoring that potent connection I felt earlier, I realize what I have to do to get through the rest of this year.

I need to shove aside all of my feelings for Killian. He is still an ignorant, rude, brutish, moody asshole who only cares about himself.

Eyes on the prize, Sophie.

All that matters to me is that ten million dollars at the end of it. I'm certainly not going to let a handsome Scotsman with a big dick and a charming smile get in the way of that.

As I brush past him, I notice the way his scowl curls into a mischievous smirk. He snatches my arm and holds his face near mine. Our eyes meet for a moment, but instead of acknowledging that connection, I ignore it.

We stare into each other eyes like it's a challenge. Then, he gives a shake of his head, and I know he understands. We both got too close to feeling things we shouldn't. And it's best we just go back to the way things were.

"Happy Christmas, wench," he mumbles with a teasing smile.

I jerk my arm away from his hold. "Happy Christmas… brute."

And with that, I walk away, feeling as if a heavy weight has been lifted from my shoulders.

Chapter Twenty-One

LYING ON THE COUCH IN THE LIVING ROOM, WATCHING THE trashiest British reality show I can find, I hear Killian stomping down the stairs, and I glance up and feel my jaw drop as I take in his appearance.

Normally he's in boots, and they clunk loudly against the wood floors, and it sounds like we're being attacked by a giant. But this sound is different. It's lighter and softer.

I pick myself up from the couch to peer back at him as he enters the room.

He's in his green and white kilt with the same slate gray jacket he wore at our wedding. There is no way to fully prepare myself for the effect that kilt has on me.

I completely skip over confused and directly into aroused.

Then it dawns on me. I bolt further upright. "We're going to the party?" I chime excitedly.

"Get dressed before I change my mind," he mutters lowly.

I'm not even focused on the sexual favor I have to perform in order to get him to do this, but I'll worry about that later. Right now, I'm busy barreling up the stairs, thinking about which dress in my closet will work for tonight's event.

I settle on a gold velvet gown that hugs my curves. The plunging neckline is covered by a piece of netting covered in gems. My hair doesn't take long to pull into a half-up style with a clip at the back of my head. I spray my curls with something to clean up the frizz. Then I quickly apply some makeup and scurry downstairs before Killian has a chance to back out.

I'm not sure why I'm so anxious for this party. Maybe it's the promise of ten thousand dollars for getting him to go. Maybe it's the sex. Or maybe it's for the look on his family's face when he shows up and blows them all away.

When I come down the stairs, Killian is waiting.

"That was…" His eyes lift from his phone as he settles his gaze on me. "Fast."

I stop near the bottom step, struggling for something to say. "Ready?"

He swallows. "You look nice, wife."

"Not too bad yourself, brute."

I grin to myself as I sit down on the bench to put on my shoes. Moments like this always strike me as ironic, the way we can banter like a married couple and how *real* it feels, even though it's not.

As I slip on my heels, I glance up at Killian's hair. It's past his shoulders now. It looks silky smooth and well kept, but honestly…too long.

Standing up, I tug on the ends. "Can we please trim this up?"

"Now?" he asks in disbelief.

"It'll only take a minute." I grab his hand and drag him back up the stairs. "Come on."

Begrudgingly, he lets me pull him into my en suite bathroom. I pull the chair from the vanity and gesture for him to sit. A small giggle escapes when I see how massive he looks on the tiny thing. But it puts him at the right height for me.

Snatching a towel off the rack, I drape it around his

shoulders and fasten it into place with a hair clip. Then I pull open the top drawer and retrieve the scissors I use to cut off my split ends.

I feel Killian's eyes on me as I move around the bathroom. When I spray his hair with water, he winces and curses under his breath. And I'm not gentle when I comb through the long strands.

"Who has been cutting your hair?" I ask as I try to line up the ends.

He shrugs. "Random women. Sometimes the housekeepers. Sometimes me."

"Tsk, tsk, tsk," I reply.

Leaning back, I take a look at him. "How much can I take off?"

"It's hair. I don't care how much you cut. It grows back."

I screw up my lips as I think this through, trying to imagine what he'd look like without the messy mop of wild brown hair on his head.

"Okay…" I reply. Then I lean in and start chopping. He barely reacts as long chunks of hair fall off the white towel and onto the floor. It's a little nerve-racking to watch the way his signature look slowly morphs into something cleaner and simpler.

"Are you a hairdresser?" he asks as he watches me work.

"No," I reply as I style the length I left on the top. "But I've always loved styling hair."

"So, why don't you do it?"

"As a job, you mean?" I reply.

"Yeah."

I stop and look at the finished product. It's not too short but still looks fresh on him. And I think back to when I was growing up. There was never a moment when I considered this as a career path.

"I'm a writer," I reply without enthusiasm.

"I haven't seen you write a thing," he replies.

"I need to trim your beard now," I say, quickly changing the subject.

Leaning over, I get dangerously close to Killian's face as I comb through the length of it, trimming the excess as I go. His eyes stay glued on mine, but I don't dare look at him. It's too close. Too intimate.

"Who decided you were a writer? You?" he asks softly.

I force myself to swallow. But I don't answer.

"Do you light up when you write the way you're lighting up right now?"

I freeze. In my mind, the answer is immediate—no.

"It doesn't matter," I reply as I set the scissors on the counter and unclip the towel from around his shoulders.

"It doesn't?" he asks.

"No. It doesn't matter whether I'm supposed to be a writer or a hairdresser or a grumpy Scot's wife. Because no matter what I do, it will never be enough."

"Enough for who?"

"Drop it, Killian," I harp in return. Then I gesture to the mirror. "Just look at yourself. Tell me if you like it."

With a disgruntled sigh, he stands from the tiny chair and turns toward the large mirror. Pausing for a moment, he stares at his reflection with hesitation.

"You don't like it," I say, suddenly nervous about his reaction.

He angles his head back and forth to see the new look. Immediately, I notice that he appears older with a more sophisticated style. But older in a good way. There are patches of gray starting to peek out around the edges of his hairline.

"I love it," he says in a low whisper.

"Don't lie."

"I'm not lying," he says as he turns toward me. "You did a bloody good job."

I swallow again, twisting my mouth in uncertainty as I force my eyes away.

"Good. I'm glad you like it."

When I turn to walk out of the bathroom, he snatches my arm and pulls me back toward him.

With two fingers under my chin, he angles my face upward. "It does matter."

I clench my jaw and fidget impatiently, waiting for him to let me go so I no longer have to stare into his eyes. "Okay," I mutter unconvincingly. "We're gonna be late."

Relenting, he lets me go, and I march out of the room. Blinking the emotion out of my eyes, I paint a smile on my face and try to look forward to the way his siblings are going to react when they see him.

————

When we climb into the car, I start to feel Killian tense beside me. His leg is bouncing, and I can hear the clicking of his jaw as he clenches it. Peter tries to make small talk to cover up the fact that Killian is a mess of nerves.

It's glaringly obvious to me that Killian's choice not to leave his house in six years wasn't much of a choice at all. He's struggling right now. I wish there was a way to help him, but I don't know how.

Reaching my hand across the seat, I rest it on his bare knee. It doesn't do much to calm the jittery movements. He stares out the window with a scowl, so I reach over his lap and take one of his large hands in mine.

While Peter continues to chat with us about the weather and the holidays, I squeeze Killian's hand and watch as the jumping in his knees quiets.

That is, until we pull up to a large house outside the city. It's nowhere near as big as Barclay Manor, but it's still large nonetheless. There are other cars parked in the large circular drive, so Peter pulls all the way up to the door to let us out.

Killian doesn't even move until Peter opens his door.

"Have a lovely evening," he says before we both climb out.

"Thank you," I reply softly.

There is a bagpiper near the door, playing as guests arrive, although we seem to be the last to get here. It takes me off guard to see him there. I sort of assumed this would be an intimate family gathering, but judging by the size of the house and the noise coming from inside, this is a full-blown New Year's bash.

Standing at the front entrance, I wait for Killian to take the first step. But he's hesitating. So I wait beside him. After a moment of loaded silence, I turn toward him.

His face is tense, and his chest moves with slow, shallow breaths. Reaching out I take his hand again. "We don't have to go in if you don't want to."

He shakes his head. "We're going in. Just give me a second."

"Take all the time you need," I reply, giving his hand a squeeze.

His gaze cascades down to our linked hands and then up to my face. After a moment, he seems to reach a conclusion, and he turns toward the front door with purpose.

"Let's get this over with," he mutters before pulling on the handle.

We enter through a foyer first, much like something from a normal-sized home. Nothing like the mansion we live in. He takes my hand again and walks through the hallway of the family home until we reach a large living room.

The moment we step inside, the conversation immediately dies.

I glance around at the crowd, recognizing Anna first. Then I find Killian's brother, Lachy, talking to his other brother, Declan, both decked in matching kilts like Killian is in. They are all staring at us with their mouths hanging open, frozen in shock.

It's Killian's sister who approaches first. Anna hurries over to us with her arms stretched wide for a hug. I notice tears in her eyes as she throws her arms around her brother. When she finally releases him, she smiles at his new haircut.

Then, Anna hugs me, whispering a grateful "Thank you" as she does.

A sense of pride floods through me at that sentiment. I really didn't do much, and she probably doesn't want to know what I really had to offer in order to make him come, but she doesn't need to know. At least he's here.

Next, Lachy wraps me up in a hug. "It's been too long, little sister," he says with a playful tone.

"Och, leave them alone, Lach. You know what they've been up to in that big house all this time."

"Declan!" Anna snaps, scolding him with a slap on his chest. The men laugh, and I instantly glance up to see Killian's reaction. The tension in his face is gone, and he's even cracking a smile now.

The rest of Killian's family comes over and greets us. We're offered drinks and food, and we stay at each other's side the whole time. An hour easily goes by before his aunt finally comes over to greet him.

I met her briefly at the wedding, but it was clear to me then, as it is now, that she is not the biggest fan of Killian. My shoulders immediately tighten as she approaches him.

"It's about damn time, nephew," she says.

She's an elderly woman, probably in her late seventies. Like Killian, she has dark hair and pale skin. Unlike Killian, she is gaunt and thin.

"Hello, Auntie Lorna," he replies in a low, muttering voice.

"You look good," she says with a drink in her hand, letting her gaze scan his clothing. "And you brought your American wife."

My jaw tightens as I glare at her. If this is the woman pulling the strings on this whole scheme with Killian, I have a very bad feeling about it all of a sudden.

"Of course I did," Killian replies, pulling me closer. I rest a hand on his chest and stand close to him.

"What would your father say about your long absence?" she asks over the rim of her crystal glass.

"I'm sure he'd be very happy to see Killian doing so well," I reply, tapping my husband on the chest.

His aunt laughs into her wine. "You didn't know him."

"I'm sure if he was here," Killian says, breaking in, "he'd love Sylvie too."

My heart has the stupid idea of beating faster hearing him say that. But I quickly have to remind myself it's just a trick. He doesn't love me. But he's doing a great job at pretending.

"Well, he's not," Lorna replies.

I notice the way she glares at him as she says that, and it makes my nostrils flare with anger. She slowly walks away from us, and I fight the urge to throw my punch in her face.

"Oh look!" one of the younger women, who I assume is Killian's cousin, calls as she points above our heads. "Mistletoe!"

"You know what that means," Declan adds with a haughty smirk.

I glance up and see the green ball hanging over our heads. I glance at Killian and give him a playful expression. Then, he does exactly what I hoped he would do.

He scoops me up by the lower back and tips me dramatically as he plants a deep, passionate kiss on my lips. His family cheers around us, and when he finally pulls me upright, I find it harder to wipe the smile from my face.

He's starting to relax. I can tell.

When we first entered the party, Killian wasn't himself. He was too tense to be the sarcastic, snarky asshole I know.

When Killian and I move to the corner of the room with fresh drinks in our hands, I turn toward him and whisper, "Your aunt is a real cunt."

He chuckles to himself. "You're not wrong."

I glance around the room. "So, this is her house?"

"Yep."

"Does she have anything cool we can steal?" I mumble into my glass.

"Nothing I want," he replies.

"Come on," I mutter, grabbing his hand. "I'm sure we can find some trouble to get into."

No one notices as we slip out of the room. I pull him past the kitchen and up a flight of stairs. We come across an office, two bedrooms, a large bathroom, and the primary bedroom. We end up in what I assume is her bedroom, and I immediately start to snoop.

"Why does she hate you so much?" I ask as I peer at all of the jewelry on her dresser.

He shrugs as he leans against the doorframe. "She blames me for my parents' death."

My head snaps in his direction. "What? Wasn't it a car accident?"

"Yeah," he mumbles as he nods his head.

"That's terrible."

"I don't want to talk about it," he replies, looking down.

Picking up a pearl necklace, I hold it up over my dress. "What do you think?"

"She'll kill you if she catches you going through her things."

I scoff. "I'd like to see her try. After the way she spoke to you tonight, she's lucky I'm not doing worse."

"Aww," he says as he steps toward me, smiling. "You sound a little protective of me, mo ghràidh."

I give him a twisted expression. "No. I just think she's a bitch, and clearly, being a bitch to you is *my* job."

He saunters up behind me, grabbing me by the hips and grinding himself against my backside. The intimacy still takes me by surprise, but it doesn't stop the blossoming heat building in my belly.

I stand up straight as he brushes my hair away from my neck and kisses me delicately above my shoulder. Letting out a small hum, I let my eyes close as I savor the warmth of his touch.

Then I open my eyes and stare into the large mirror in front of us. My eyes devour the sight of us together. Something about it is satisfying, as if we fit so well together that I can't possibly deny it. But the longer I look at us, the more shame I feel.

So I spin toward him and push him against the wall. Before he can say a word, I grab him by the neck and drag his mouth toward mine. I kiss him with fervor, devouring his lips and tongue. He matches my passion and kisses me back with just as much.

I feel his cock beginning to stiffen against my stomach, so I reach down and stroke it through the thick fabric of his kilt.

"Wait, wait, wait," he mutters, pulling away from the kiss.

"What?" I ask breathlessly.

"I can't do it in here."

"Sure, you can," I reply, pushing him back with a smile. Then I look down at where his cock is pitching a tent. "Because you certainly can't go back down there with that."

Digging a hand in my hair, he tilts my head back as he

smiles down at me. "Then, maybe you can take care of that for me, darling."

I quickly shove away, torn between wanting to cuss at him for teasing me with that pet name and desperately wanting to *take care of that for him.*

Naturally, I side with the latter.

My hand drifts downward, sliding his kilt up until I brush the fabric of his boxer briefs.

"Well, that's disappointing. I thought you weren't supposed to wear anything under these."

He chuckles as he kisses my neck again. "It's a wee bit cold out for that. Don't you think?"

When I reach the waistband of his boxers, I gently tug it down, releasing his cock. The moment I have it in my hand, the heavy weight against my palm, I let out a mewling cry. He sucks eagerly on my neck as I stroke him, my fingers barely reaching all the way around.

"Wrap your lips around my cock, darling. I need to feel that mouth of yours."

My core lights up with desire, and I don't hesitate as he uses the hold on my hair to guide me to my knees. My head slips under his kilt as I pull down his boxers further to see his entire cock for myself. My eyes widen when I take in the size.

Long, thick, and bulging at the tip, I admire it for a moment too long. Wrapping my fingers around the base, I drag the head across the surface of my tongue. He lets out a growling moan as I do.

Closing my lips around the tip, I taste the precum leaking as I suck eagerly, licking my way around the rim. He groans again.

"Do that again, darling."

I tease the head of his cock again, flicking my tongue just under the tip. His hand finds my hair again as he guides his dick farther into my mouth. Having his impressive length on my tongue is satisfying, and I challenge myself to go deeper and deeper with each stroke. I wrap my hands around the base and fill the space my lips can't reach as I suck, feeling the way he tenses on every upstroke.

I can't get enough of his moans, so I chase them with each movement of my mouth. Arousal pools between my thighs. With my free hand, I gently cup his balls and massage them as I bob my mouth up and down on his shaft.

"Fuck me, mo ghràidh. That mouth of yours feels so good."

When I feel him nearing his climax, I ease up. I'm not ready for this to be over. I've never enjoyed a blow job in my life, but hearing Killian's praise becomes my motivation. I need more of it.

"Sylvie," he mutters in a raspy tone. "Look at me."

I pause my stroking and gaze up at him. Holding his kilt up, he stares down at me, his face frozen in pleasure. "Keep going."

Using my hands and mouth, I draw him closer to his climax again, this time gazing up at him as I do. I feel addicted to his pleasure and the intensity of his gaze, needing it more than my own. I'm moaning wildly around his dick, squeezing tight and sucking hard, knowing full well he's about to unload in my mouth at any moment.

And I want it.

"I'm almost there, darling. Don't stop."

When he finally seizes up in my hand, I wait eagerly for the salty release on my tongue. When I finally get it, I'm not disappointed. I feel it hit the back of my throat, so I quickly swallow before I risk gagging.

Killian lets out a string of curses at the sight. I wait for his climax to end before I pull my mouth away, quickly wiping the mess from my lips. And when I venture to gaze in his direction, I notice he's staring at me as if he's seen a ghost.

"What?" I say as I stand up.

He shakes his head. "Nothing."

But I notice that his hands don't leave my body for a second. He holds on to my arms, dragging me closer to him. Then, instead of kissing me, he cradles me against his chest. I don't expect it, but I also don't push him away.

I let the pounding of his heart echo against my ear, and I try to push away any nagging reminder that this isn't what people who hate each other do.

Chapter Twenty-Two

WHEN KILLIAN AND I MAKE OUR WAY BACK DOWNSTAIRS TO the party, I instantly feel the scrutinizing gaze of his aunt, but I do my best to ignore it. Instead, I grab another drink, and we walk hand in hand over to his siblings, who are standing near the large Christmas tree.

I can't explain the good mood I'm in. I'm not one for holidays. I don't generally like family gatherings. And I know in nine months, I will be gone from this country forever.

But with the music playing and the scent of something sweet and spicy in the air giving this party a cozy, warm vibe, it's impossible not to feel good.

"Our brother's not being too difficult for you, is he?" Declan asks with a stern expression. Judging by his sudden comfort in talking to me and the slight slur in his words, I'd be willing to bet that's not his first glass of whisky.

I bump Killian with my shoulder and shoot him a smile. "I can handle him."

When I turn back to the group, I notice the way they're all looking at us. It's easy to forget that these three know the truth while no one else at the party does. They wouldn't actually suspect that Killian and I are casually hooking up in the privacy of our home.

Why would they?

Well, these three and his vicious Aunt Lorna are the only ones who know.

Feeling her eyes on me again, I look over my shoulder and find her staring menacingly. It's like those eyes are the cruel reminder of what I've agreed to. These people have made me an accomplice in something vindictive and cruel.

Which I totally agreed to and knew the entire time.

When I turn back to the group again, I feel a bit more uneasy.

"Killian never was one for manners," Lachy jokes, smiling at his brother.

"My manners are just fine, thank you," Killian replies. "Besides, no one here is nearly as harsh and cutting as this one."

He looks down at me, and I fake a smile. I'm supposed to joke back, but I'm starting to feel sick.

Lies, lies, lies.

The room starts to grow uncomfortable, and I peel my arm away from Killian's.

"I have to use the restroom. I'll be right back," I mumble softly before squeezing through the party toward the hallway. I reach the bathroom without incident, but as I close myself in and stare at myself in the mirror, I feel the same scratching anxiety crawling up my spine.

Relax, Sylvie. You're not doing anything wrong.

I take three long, deep breaths and try to remind myself that this is for the best. This isn't my family. They're just trying to help him.

Those three things just keep echoing through my head, over and over. For the most part, it works. I manage to talk myself down from the panic attack threatening to set in.

But when I open the bathroom door, I'm met with those menacing eyes again, and it takes me by surprise. Lorna is waiting for me in the hall.

"Excuse me," I mumble softly before trying to squeeze past her.

"You and my nephew are getting along well," she says, stopping me in my tracks. We're alone in the hall, far enough away from the party to not be overheard.

I swallow my discomfort and turn toward her. "It's all for show. I promise you."

"It doesn't look like it's for show."

Her expression is cold and flat. It reminds me of my mother, and I tighten my hands into fists to fight the anger coursing through my veins.

I hide it by giving her a simple shrug. "Does it matter? We'll still get through the first year, and everything will go as planned."

Her eyes crease as she leans against the wall. "Will it?"

"Of course."

As she takes a step toward me, I bite back everything I want to spew at her.

"Good," she seethes. "Because if anything goes wrong, then you won't see a dime of that money."

"You don't think I'm aware of that?" I snap back.

"If I were you, I'd be more careful not to let Killian mistake your feelings for him. You are nothing more than a clause in a contract."

"What do you think I'm doing?" I reply in a heated but hushed tone. "I'm doing everything I was told to do."

She steps closer, so we are basically in each other's faces. "I see the way you look at him. I don't even want to know what filthy things you did to him upstairs. And I'm telling you now, harboring feelings for my nephew won't change a thing. You can't stop us from getting that house, and if you even think about getting in our way, you'll be going back to America worse off than when you came here."

I want to shove her. My hands itch to reach out and throw her against the wall, and I don't care how elderly she is. But one deep breath stops me.

Instead, I get in her face. With a snarl, I point a finger at her and it takes her by surprise. Her eyes are wide with fear as she gazes up at me.

"Don't you dare threaten me. I'm only here for my money, and then I'm gone, but don't forget that you need me. So you should think twice before you get in my face again."

I hear footsteps behind me, but I'm too lost in my rage to stop. There's a nagging reminder in the back of my mind that I don't want Killian to hear any of this. He can't know the truth.

"Sylvie," he mutters from the end of the hall.

Without turning my gaze away from Lorna, I continue. "You are nothing but an old hag, and you don't care about Killian at all. So if you know what's good for you, you'll leave him alone. Don't look at him. Don't talk to him. And if you even *think* about coming to Barclay Manor, just know *you'll* leave worse than when you came."

"Sylvie." Killian's voice is a harsh bark. Then I feel his warm hand around my arm, and I stand upright to find that my hands are shaking. I gaze up into Killian's eyes, and instead of a scowl of anger, he gives me a hint of a smile.

He runs his thumb along my jaw. "Come on, darling. Let's go home."

In the distance, I hear cheers and the crowd singing "Auld Lang Syne."

Shakily, I nod. I bury myself under his arm, and he pulls me out of the hallway toward the front door. We leave without even saying goodbye to his brothers and sister.

"Happy New Year!" someone shouts toward us, but we are moving too quickly toward the exit.

The next thing I know, he's covering me with his jacket and pulling me out the front door. Peter is there waiting for us, and Killian guides me into the back seat. There are fireworks lighting up the sky in red and gold, but I'm too focused on him. Once we're settled in the car, Killian tilts my face toward him again.

Gazing up into his eyes, I feel something I never felt with him before. It's a feeling without words, or if it has words, I don't have the capacity to conjure them at this moment. It feels like *mine* and *home. Safety. Comfort.*

I look at him, and it feels like I'm looking at myself.

He inches his face closer to mine, and I close the distance, finding his lips with mine. I kiss him differently this time. Not like I need something physical, but like I need something emotional. When our lips touch, it's like I'm pulling him inside me. Inside my mind and my heart.

When he pulls away, our eyes meet. A spark of something cosmic glistens between us.

A wave of panic starts to build inside me. This can't be happening. I can't feel this way for anyone, least of all him. I don't *want* to fall for Killian.

I *hate* him.

He smiles crookedly down at me, and it shakes me from my panic.

"Forget the blow job; seeing you give that old biddy a piece of your mind was the hottest thing you've done all night."

I force out a chuckle even though inside, I'm being swept away by fear. But for some reason, I find myself clinging closer to him. As if *he* could possibly protect me from falling for him.

Beneath all of that uncertainty is more anger from the altercation. I just keep replaying her words, hearing her talk about him. I've never felt so enraged in my life. More than the night I ripped up my parents' painting. More than any moment with them.

She was cruel to someone I'm supposed to despise. So why am I so mad?

Killian puts his mouth next to my ear, and when he whispers, it feels like words written in breaths. So low even Peter can't hear in the front seat.

"I need to be inside you, Sylvie. I need to make you my wife."

Goose bumps cascade across my skin as a wave of heat pummels me from the inside. Squirming in my seat, I turn toward him and find his mouth with my lips.

The kiss is all the answer he needs. *Yes. Yes. Yes.*

Chapter Twenty-Three

WE PRACTICALLY SPILL OUT OF THE CAR AS IT PULLS UP TO THE house. Killian lifts me into his arms, carrying me through the front door. When he finally sets me down, I tear his coat off my shoulders as his lips devour my face and neck.

This need for him is acute and burning. And I know he feels it too. We are tearing each other's clothes off, fumbling with buttons and zippers. We're still standing in the foyer when he yanks my dress over my head, and I pop a couple of buttons off his shirt as I claw it open.

It's a miracle we even make it up the stairs, but by the time we reach his room, our clothes are gone. He lifts me off the floor, and my legs wrap around him as he carries me inside and tosses me on the bed.

His cock is jutting straight out from his body, and the sight of it again sends a thrill of excitement and trepidation through mine. Standing over me, he grabs my legs and drags me to the edge of the bed. He reaches down and grabs a handful of my hair at the scalp.

"Let me see that pretty mouth wrapped around my cock again, darling."

Without a second thought, I sit up and take his swollen shaft in my hands. Eagerly, I put my lips around him and cover his length with saliva, sucking hard on the tip like I know he likes. His hips cant forward as he lets out a moan.

"What a wee good wife you are," he mutters, holding my head and slowly fucking my throat.

I know the *wife* bit is a role-playing thing, but also…being treated like his wife makes my body grow hot with arousal. I love the thought of being his.

Which is very unlike me. I don't want to feel like someone's property. A thing he could use to fuck and get off.

But right now…I do. I *really, really* do.

When I feel his cock swell, he yanks me off with a growl, and I watch him fight the urge to come all over my face.

I've never felt so hot in my life. There's a fire blazing under my skin.

When a drip of cum leaks from the tip of Killian's dick, I reach my tongue out and lick it off with a hum.

"Bloody hell, woman," he mutters.

I smile up at him as my hands slide up and down his legs, eager for more.

When his eyes cascade up to the headboard and back, I see a glint of mischief in his expression.

"I'm gonna tie you to my bed and have my way with you now," he says, and somehow I grow even warmer with need.

"I'm all yours," I whisper, watching the corner of his mouth lift in a lopsided smirk.

Then he picks me up under my arms and tosses me back on the bed like I weigh nothing. I let out a shriek of laughter as he crawls ominously toward me.

I squirm with anticipation as he hovers above me. "Arms up," he says in a sexy, growling command.

Immediately I obey, and he notices. "Oh…look who listens to me now."

Biting my bottom lip, I fight a smile. "Don't get too used to it."

He sinks down and presses his lips to mine in a sweet, slow kiss. When we pull apart, he stays there for a moment, frozen in place while we breathe the same air. It's a tender, intimate moment.

Slowly rising back up, he takes my right hand in his. Craning my neck, I watch as he pulls a leather strap already attached to the bedpost and winds it around my wrist. It matches the one from the bedpost of my own bed, which I found when I first moved in.

I can still remember how much I bristled at the idea of being tied up then. Now, I yearn for it.

His fingers move with expertise as he finishes the knot, keeping the loop around my wrist gentle and not too tight. When I test the hold, it doesn't budge. Then he does the other, and immediately, I'm overcome with a feeling of aroused anticipation.

Moving down my body, he peppers me with kisses, stopping at my breasts to massage and suck tenderly on each one. I let out a hum of pleasure as more moisture pools between my legs.

"Killian," I cry out in a breathy plea. "I need you."

"I'm here, mo ghràidh." His deep voice vibrates through my torso as he mutters those words against my rib cage.

It's like my lungs won't hold air as I gasp with each inch his mouth devours, lower and lower. My thighs are rubbing together in search of that delicious friction. When his beard scratches the insides of my legs, I tremble with excitement.

"Open for me, beautiful," he murmurs.

My legs part, and he doesn't waste a second before lunging his mouth toward my core, licking and nibbling fervently.

"God, I love the taste of your cunt," he says with a carnal rasp in his voice.

Hanging my head back, I let out a groan as the pleasure assaults me. When he plunges a finger inside me, growling against my clit, I nearly come undone.

"So tight." He sounds overcome with lust, and he keeps up his thrusting, dragging me to the precipice of my climax.

"Killian, please!" I shriek, my arms jerking against the holds.

"Tell me what you want, darling."

I look up from the mattress and stare down my body at where he's stationed. His lips are wet with my arousal, and it makes me feral for him.

"I want you to fuck me. Please."

He chuckles, giving me that disarming smile. "Such a filthy mouth on you."

"I'm literally begging you," I reply.

For a moment he seems to consider my request, but eventually ignores the plea and dives back in between my legs. Curling his finger inside me, he adds a second and thrusts harder. I'm strung tight, ready to detonate at any moment.

"My wife comes first," he growls between my legs. Then he wraps his lips around my clit and sucks, using his tongue to flick the sensitive bud.

And that's it. I'm done.

My orgasm nearly shatters me into tiny pieces. It's too intense. Too good. So pleasurable it hurts.

My legs are thrashing, my arms are tied down, and the sounds that are coming out of me are downright pornographic.

When I finally relax back into the mattress after what feels like a never-ending climax, the space between my legs is soaked and sensitive.

Killian doesn't waste any time. Climbing to his knees,

he positions himself between my legs and presses my thighs upward to make room for his wide hips.

I hold my breath in anticipation when I feel the warm head of his cock press against my tender opening. When the head breaches the entrance, I start to panic. The skin is pulled so tight it burns.

"Go slow," I whisper. "You're bigger than I'm used to."

With a grunt, he slides in a little deeper. My skin breaks out in goose bumps as the adrenaline and arousal mingle into a heady desire. Killian is staring down at the spot where his massive cock is disappearing inside me. He's moving slowly with delicate care not to hurt me. I don't think he's even all the way in when I feel as if I can't take another inch.

I tug against the arm restraints again. His attention snaps up to my face. "I won't hurt you, darling. You can trust me."

As our eyes meet, I feel that tug of emotion again. When did this happen? When did the man who uttered such hateful words to me become the one who holds my fear and pain in his hand, offering me safety and comfort instead?

I have no reason to trust him, but I do.

He looks back down as he eases out and thrusts back in again, a little deeper this time. "I don't know what you were so worried about," he says in a strained tone. "You're taking every inch, mo ghràidh. And you're taking me so well."

God, those words might as well be a stimulant. They buzz through my body, making everything feel so good. I wish he'd whisper them to me as he fucked me, like some secret code that unlocks the nerve endings in my body.

"Go faster," I whisper, and immediately his hips start to piston. With every thrust, he goes deeper, and I wait anxiously for the pain that never comes. Finally, he pounds fully inside me until I can feel his hips against mine, and it's a perfect fit, as if he's made to be inside me.

Pleasure blossoms down my spine from the sensation, and as he moves, filling me again and again and again, I become overwhelmed by it. It's all too much.

My eyes won't leave him, watching the look of ecstasy on his face as he fucks me, moving harder and faster as he uses my body to chase his own pleasure. He can't tear his gaze away from where our bodies are joined, and it's endearing how much he likes to watch it.

I wish I could see inside his mind. I want to know if he's feeling this all-encompassing thing that I feel. Is this still just casual sex to him? Or is he being swarmed by this feeling of something *more* the same way I am?

When he lifts his gaze to my face, our eyes meet, and that connection is back. I let out one pleading cry, and he answers the call, collapsing his body over mine and kissing my lips as he keeps up the relentless driving of his hips. His arms frame my head as his tongue tangles with mine.

My legs wrap around him, and I'm amazed at how well we fit together, even with our different sizes. Our bodies are so close it's as if we are one.

Keeping our lips together, he fucks me harder as he whispers, "I'm going to fill you up. My wife. I'm making you mine."

I wish I could wrap my arms around him. More than anything, I need my body to say what my mouth sometimes struggles to express. But with my wrists still tied, I have no other choice.

Hesitantly, I stutter. "F-fill me up, Killian. Make…me yours."

"You are mine."

With a deafening groan and a shuddering in his hips, I feel his climax tremble through us both. His cock pulses inside me, and I'm overcome with warmth. With his body still draped over mine, I swim in his nearness. I absorb his scent, his touch, his breath. Every part of him becomes a part of me.

This is so much more than sex. He has to see that.

When he finally lifts from my body, our lips touch again in a more hesitant kiss. Then, he climbs away from me and watches intently as he pulls his cock from inside me. His eyes don't leave that spot, and when I feel the cum dripping from my pussy, he quickly wipes it with his thumb.

I let out a gasp when I feel him gently pushing it back inside.

Our eyes meet again, and he shoots me a soft smile. "Well, it's official, darling," he says softly. "You're really my wife now."

Chapter Twenty-Four

"What are you reading?" Killian asks from the doorway of the parlor. I glance up from the book in my lap with a sheepish smirk.

I'm not ashamed of my curiosity. I found this book in the library months ago. But it wasn't until the night Killian tied me to his bed and claimed me as his, that I realized this might be something I'm slightly intrigued about.

Slowly I lift the book to let him read the title.

The Act of Submission

His eyebrows lift in astonishment. "Forgot I had that," he says. "Are you reading it because you're curious, or are you reading it because you want to try it?"

I let out a sigh. "I don't know. Is this what you like?" I ask.

His gaze bores into mine, the tension growing charged with every passing second.

"Sometimes," he mutters. Slowly, he walks deeper into the room, closing the distance between us, and I have to force myself to swallow. Killian carries himself with a presence that sometimes steals my breath, and I think I've spent so long pushing him away that I haven't given myself a chance to appreciate that.

"I love the trust that it requires," he adds, looking into my eyes. "I love feeling so connected to someone that they give me full control over their body."

When he reaches the chair I'm sitting in, he places his hands on either side, caging me in. I feel his presence like the heat emanating from a fire.

"Is that something you want with me?" I add.

His eyes close briefly as he replies, "Oh, absolutely, mo ghràidh."

"Well then," I smirk. "Maybe someday."

That word, *someday*, stings, but I quickly brush it off. Killian and I don't have a future full of somedays, and it's not something I like to focus on too much.

He grins back at me. "Yeah, someday."

When I turn my attention back down to my book, he stands up and goes to the bar for a drink. I'm finding it harder to focus on the words on the page since we started talking about it. After only a few months, I've noticed how much Killian has changed. He seems less drawn to recklessness and outbursts, and for a man who was introduced to me as such a partier and playboy, I'm just not seeing that anymore.

It piques my curiosity, remembering something Anna mentioned back when I first came around.

"Did something happen that made your aunt so angry?" I ask.

He chuckles. "What didn't I do to make her angry?"

"No, I mean…with the house."

"Och," he replies, turning toward me with a drink in his hand. Leaning against the bar, he takes a deep breath and stares off as if he's reminiscing about a tough memory. Then he nods toward the book in my hands. "Has a lot to do with that, actually."

"This?" I ask, lifting it from my lap.

"Aye. You know that party we had a couple months back?"

I nod. "Yeah."

"Well, I used to have a lot more of them. Sometimes with that crowd. Sometimes with others. And after a while, I got a bit of a reputation. Nearly every weekend, people would come. They'd invite their friends, and I knew it was getting out of hand.

"My house was filled with strangers, but I loved it. They weren't…regular parties, you understand?"

"I think I do," I mumble, gazing up into his eyes.

"They were out of control, but I felt free. And soon my house wasn't such a prison anymore. It was like…an escape. A place where normal people would come to let go. To express themselves. To try new things."

"What happened?" I ask, although I have some idea.

"Word got out to my family. They found out that our family home had turned into a sex club on the weekends, and they weren't happy about it."

I bite my lip as a feeling of regret washes over me. I understand now why his aunt was so angry, but at the same time, I feel so much empathy for what that must have been like for him. To feel something important to him ripped away.

"So you had to stop the parties," I add remorsefully.

He nods his head, looking melancholy.

"I'm sorry."

He gives me a shrug. "It's not your fault."

He's right. That part is not my fault, but him eventually losing this place that brings him comfort, is my fault.

"You know…someday you could open a real place like that, and it wouldn't have to be your home. I think it sounds wonderful."

I'm trying to give him hope or solace or something, but his expression isn't giving me the assurance I want.

Then, finally, he leans down and presses his lips to my forehead as he mutters, "No, I couldn't."

I glance up at him with confusion.

With a smirk, he adds, "But maybe...*we* could."

"Killian..." I start to protest his relentless argument that any of this is real, but the words die on my lips.

Setting his drink on the bar, he comes toward me again, and I feel myself burning from the inside out with that heated look in his eyes. Then he cages me in again, leaning so close, I forget how to breathe.

"I thought we settled this already," he mutters lowly. "I *am* your husband, Sylvie. You are my wife."

When he says my name like that—not *cow*, or *darling*, or mo ghràidh—it feels too real.

"I'm not—" I argue, but he quickly cuts me off with a scorching kiss. His tongue invades my mouth, and I forget what I was about to say. I can't believe I'm letting him disorient me like this. I have to get him out of my head before he costs me everything.

With a hand against his chest, I forcefully shove him away. We're both left gasping, and he's wearing a smug grin on his face as he wipes the moisture from his lips with his thumb.

"You can believe whatever you want, Killian Barclay, but just because I let you touch me doesn't make me yours. I'm nobody's wife."

As I suspected, this only makes him laugh. "You can believe whatever you want, Mrs. Barclay," he replies, accentuating the title to drive home his point. Then he picks up the book in my lap as he adds smugly, "But you are my wife, and it's only a matter of time before you truly submit."

I sit up, straightening my spine as I bring my face to his.

With a look of steely determination, I snatch the book back and toss it to the floor.

"Never," I mutter, staring into his eyes.

With a grin, he kisses me again. And when he drops to his knees and begins to tear my clothes off, I let him.

He can have my body for now, but I refuse to let my husband have my heart.

PART FOUR

Killian

Chapter Twenty-Five

THERE WAS A TIME WHEN I LOVED BEING ALONE IN MY HOUSE. I liked the quiet peace of solitude. No one to harass me or hound me with questions. No one to worry about me or tell me what's best.

Now, I find myself gravitating toward *her*.

I hear my wife's gentle footsteps everywhere I go. I hear her humming to herself down the hallways of my home. She lives here like a ghost, haunting each room with her scent and her delicate presence. The rose and lilac of her hair. The lotion she puts on her face every night. Everything about her has seeped into the crevices of this house, deep into the stones. She's even stained the upholstery and curtains.

When she came six months ago, I hated it. Now, I love it.

Sylvie is willful and stubborn. For every smile she gives me, she scowls ten times as much. I've never met someone so hardheaded and desperate to show her disdain.

I wish I could return that disdain, but somewhere in the last six months, she's grown on me. And it was long before she started climbing into my bed every night around Christmas.

It was her fire. Her passion. The way I recognized that level of heat was because I could feel it too. It was as if she spoke a language I understood.

I never intended to fall in love with my wife.

But Sylvie came to my home with a sense of loneliness that I related to. And even if she wants to deny it, somehow, we met in the middle.

I don't feel the need to fill the space in my life with parties and strangers anymore. I don't miss any of that, although if I'm being honest, I hope Sylvie and I can get to a place in our relationship where I can introduce her to that lifestyle.

She might be a stubborn hothead, but I bet she would submit to me beautifully. I'd love to make her mine, have her on her knees for me, completely at my control.

Coming in from the fields, I stand in the doorway of my home, and I listen for her. In the deep, endless quiet, I hear the faint clicking of something upstairs. So, I move toward the sound, walking quietly so I have a chance of taking her by surprise before she can put on her armor of contempt.

When I turn the corner toward the library, I pause in the doorway and watch Sylvie at the desk near the window. She's typing frantically on the old typewriter she once broke into this house to see.

Her wild honey-colored curls are piled on top of her head in a messy bun. She's wearing a long-sleeved flannel I recognize as my own, and her gray-sweatpant-covered legs are folded in front of her as she leans over the typewriter.

Honestly, I don't know how I'm supposed to resist her when she looks like this.

I clear my throat to grab her attention. The clicking stops, and she turns toward me with a gasp.

"You jerk!" she snaps. "You scared the shit out of me!"

I chuckle to myself as I enter the room. "What are you working on, mo ghràidh?"

She's stopped reacting with venom toward my terms of endearment, ones I used to use with sarcasm, but no longer do.

"I was feeling inspired so I started working on a new story," she replies, turning back to the typewriter.

"On that old thing? Don't you have a laptop?"

She shrugs. "It's oddly motivating. I think it's the clicking noise. Was it bothering you?"

I shake my head. "Not at all."

"Pity," she says flatly, and I chuckle again.

"Can I read it?" I walk up next to where she's sitting and lean against the table, crossing my boots in front of me.

"Absolutely not," she replies.

"Why not? Is it about me?" I tease.

"Maybe."

"So, it's about a dashing Scotsman with a massive cock?" I respond with a lopsided grin.

She rolls her eyes. "More like an ugly brutish drunk who can't hold his whisky."

I feign a gasp. "I'm offended. Does he at least know how to please his woman?"

She can't fight the smile this time. "He's average."

Standing from the table, I cage her in, placing my hands on either side of the desk and press my lips toward the back of her neck. "Well, I bet the heroine has never complained before." Then, I kiss her tenderly below her ear, and I revel in the way her skin breaks out in goose bumps.

I'd be lying if I said I didn't love fighting with my wife. I enjoy how easily I can push her buttons, and doing so has quickly turned into my favorite thing to do.

Right after making her moan and purr in my bed every night.

I've witnessed the pleasure of countless women in my time, but Sylvie is by far my favorite. Because she fights it. Even her own orgasms are hard-fought. It's like she prefers to suffer, as if it's programmed in her psyche. So if I have to devote every moment of my life to teaching her to indulge in her own pleasure, I'll do it.

"So, does your book require any *research*?" I ask as I deepen my kisses down her neck. I tug back the collar of the shirt she's wearing to pepper more kisses along her shoulder.

She lets out a pleased hum. "Not that kind of research."

Her words sound bothered, but her tone gives me hope. The thing I love about Sylvie is that she's always in the mood. I still laugh to myself every time I remember that morning she woke up to tell me we *wouldn't* be partaking in a physical relationship, but she has never pushed me away since.

She is quite literally addicted to my touch.

"Killian…" she whines. "I was trying…to focus."

"Then, let me clear your mind." My hand drifts around to the front of her shirt, popping open buttons as my lips continue their journey down her shoulder.

"You're not clearing it," she groans. "You're fogging it up."

I get her shirt open enough to find her bare breast inside. My hand engulfs the small mound, massaging and pinching it to hear her voice grow higher and more erratic.

"Then tell me what your book is about, and I'll leave you alone."

Her laughter vibrates through her back as I continue to kiss her. "That's blackmail, you asshole."

"Mmmm…" I hum against her skin. "Call me more names while I undress you."

"We are not—"

Her words are cut off as my hand slides down inside her joggers, quickly slipping under her knickers to find her soaked and ready for me.

"What were you going to say, darling?" I reply as my

middle finger sinks between her folds, curling to find the spot that drives her wild.

She clings to my arm as she turns her face up toward mine. "You're such a dick," she murmurs just before our lips crash together. My finger plunges inside her at a steady pace, and I find it so exquisite how she tenses up around me the faster I move.

My cock is leaking at the tip inside my trousers, and I'm growing more and more restless to free it.

While my finger is still buried deep inside her, I happen to glance up at the typewriter and catch only one small line.

He's the last person on earth I want to love, but I can't help it. I do.

A smile tugs on my lips as I turn my attention back to her. With my finger still hooked in her warm cunt, I wrap the other arm around her waist and hoist her out of the chair. Dropping her onto her feet facing the desk, I retrieve my hand from her joggers and quickly work to undo my own trousers.

It only takes a second before my cock is free, and I move fast to tear down her bottoms, aligning myself with her waiting heat.

"Grip the desk, mo ghràidh. Hold on tight."

Shoving her shoulders down to bend her over more, I watch as she white-knuckles the edge of the table just before I shove my fat cock inside her. She moves to her tiptoes and lets out a relieved squeal of pleasure.

It still takes her body a few strokes to open for me before I can work myself all the way in. Once her pussy is stretched and she can accommodate my size, I pound harder against her.

"Go ahead, darling. Call me a name now. While you're mewling like a goddamn cat in heat."

"Fuck you," she mutters, shoving her hips back against me to increase the intensity of my thrusts.

"You can do better than that," I reply with a grunt.

"I hate you, you brute."

"I know you do," I reply with a smile. "Keep going."

She responds with a high-pitched moan. "You...asshole."

"You said that one already," I tease her.

"Just shut up and fuck me," she pleads.

Looking down, I enjoy the sight of my cock disappearing inside her, but I want her to see it too. So, in a rush, I pull out and lift her up onto the table. Her bare ass rests on scattered papers, crumpling and tearing them as I rip her joggers completely off. Then, I hold up her right leg and ease myself back in.

"Look how well you take me, mo ghràidh. Like you were made for me."

Her gaze moves downward and she watches with me as I move inside her. When she turns her attention upward to my eyes, I find a hint of something warm and affectionate on her face. Her fists grip my shirt and she drags my lips to hers.

She holds tight to my body as I fuck her, and I know in this moment I could never possibly tire of this. Her body would never feel anything but perfect to me.

Her teeth bite on my lower lip as I feel her body tighten and tremble with pleasure. I groan against the pain as I start to come, pounding three more times inside her. Filling her up gives me more satisfaction than I ever expected it to. It's like I'm giving her something she can't give back. Something she can't refuse or fight. She takes every drop because deep down, she wants it too.

We pant against each other for a moment before I slowly ease out. When I see a drop of my seed dripping free, I quickly push it back in with my thumb. She never argues with that either.

Without a word, I pull her underwear and sweats back

up. She presses her lips together as I set her back in the chair the way I found her. But now her hair is falling out of its bun, her shirt is crumpled, and her cheeks are flushed. And she's wearing that postorgasm dazed expression.

"Write *that* in your book," I say as I press my lips to the top of her head.

I watch as she bites her bottom lip and fights a smile.

After tucking my cock back into my trousers and zipping them up, I leave the room and head toward the door to get back to work outside. I do so with a smile, knowing her scent is still on my skin and her ring is still on my finger.

Chapter Twenty-Six

"Supper is ready, Mr. Barclay," Martha says from the kitchen as I close the door behind me. I somehow lost track of time and didn't realize how long I had been out at the farm on the edge of the property. The groundskeeper lets me lend a hand during the planting season, and I can often get lost in time out there. With nothing but the earth under my fingers and the calming silence of the glen, I find it therapeutic.

"Thank you, Martha. Let me just get cleaned up then," I say as I tear off my coat. "Have you seen Sylvie?"

"Still upstairs in the library," she calls after me as I jog up the stairs. I don't bother tiptoeing now. Although I probably should have because when I find her in the library, she's no longer at the desk typing away. She's in a restful sleep on the lounge while the fire crackles in the fireplace. The room is warm when I walk in, but as I rest a hand on her fingers, clenched at her chest, I find them cold.

Grabbing the blanket off the back of the sofa, I delicately drape it over her, tucking her in with care. She stirs slightly from my touch but drifts back off immediately.

As I stand up, I notice the typewriter still sitting on the desk. But instead of just a few pages strewn about the surface, there's a thick stack now. Frowning, I cross the room and pick them up, reading the title at the top of the page.

Idle Hands.

Before I read any further, I turn back toward where Sylvie is sleeping. She hasn't moved an inch since I laid the blanket over her.

It would be an invasion of privacy for me to read this, but also…this is a story directly from her mind. How could I possibly resist?

Gently sitting on the chair, I tell myself I'll only read a few pages. But those first few pages fly by, and soon I'm five chapters in. It's messy and poetic, much like she is. The story doesn't resemble ours, and to my initial disappointment, the main character is not a mean Scottish drunk who lives alone in an old house.

But by chapter ten, I realize that's a very good thing because the man in this story is god-awful. He is a famous musician who is loved by many, but behind closed doors, it's revealed that the woman secretly writes his music for him. Regardless of that, he constantly dismisses her, never gives her credit, and makes her believe that she's worthless.

With every page I turn, I grow more and more frustrated, at some points worrying that *I'm* the arsehole male character who treats her like she doesn't matter. Is this how Sylvie sees me?

Do I dismiss her? Make her feel unwanted and worthless?

There's a scene when another man flirts with her right in front of the boyfriend who does *nothing*. Even when Sylvie meant nothing to me, I couldn't bear the sight of her with my friend.

Another hour goes by while I read, and my anxiety is never settled because the story is only half finished. And the heroine still hasn't left that arsehole of a musician.

Setting the unfinished book on the table, I turn toward Sylvie, who is still sleeping peacefully. How could anyone let someone so perfect and brilliant feel worthless? Was it her idiot ex-boyfriend? Or her parents, who she has such a volatile relationship with?

Why won't she just give me the chance to make up for everything they lack?

Staring at her now, I notice that her cheeks are redder than they were before although the fire has died and the room has grown cooler.

Standing up from my chair, I walk quickly toward her and rest my hand against her cheek. I'm instantly filled with dread as I realize how hot she is. It takes only a split second for me to feel incredibly useless and panicked.

I rush to the door, yelling over the banister, "Martha! Quick to the library!"

There's a frantic pounding of feet against the floor as our housekeeper and cook run up the stairs to see why I'm so desperate.

"What is it?" she asks when she reaches the second floor, panting and breathless.

"Sylvie is burning up," I reply in a frenzy.

Martha brushes past me into the library and goes straight to where Sylvie is out cold. She rests her hand against Sylvie's cheek and forehead, making her wince in her sleep.

"It's just a fever," the woman replies. "Nothing to be worried about, sir."

"What should I do?" I reply worriedly.

She lets out a clipped chuckle. "Let's get her to her bed—"

"My bed," I bark. "I mean…*our* bed." I'm a stammering mess and trying to make sense without sounding out of my mind. The housekeepers know that Sylvie keeps her own room even though she's my wife, but barely sleeps in it.

"Of course," she replies, thinking nothing of it. "Help me carry her then."

"I've got her," I say as I easily scoop Sylvie off the couch.

She immediately wakes up and stares at me with a glossy-eyed expression of confusion. "What…are you doing?" she says in a sleepy, slurred tone.

"Take her to bed, and I'll get something to bring that fever down," Martha says, leaving the room—not nearly fast enough.

"You're sick, mo ghràidh." I kiss her forehead, hating how hot her skin is against my lips.

"I'm fine," she stutters, trying in vain to climb out of my arms. She barely has the energy to lift her head.

"No, you're not," I say in a bellowing command. "You have a fever, and you need to be in bed."

When I reach my room, I realize how cold it is, feeling bad that I just took her from a warmer space. After resting her under the covers of our bed, I tuck her in again. She curls onto her side and falls back to sleep in a moment.

Then I get to work building a fire in the fireplace. I don't often have one going in here, but this will warm the room faster than the furnace.

By the time Martha returns with a tray, I have a warm blaze going. She sets the tray on the bedside table. There's a pot of tea, water, some medicine, and a thermometer.

Then, she stands up and stares at me as if she's waiting for further instructions.

"What now?" I ask in confusion.

"Take her temperature," she replies, hiding her annoyance at my stupidity. "Anything over thirty-nine-point-four degrees, and you should call an ambulance."

My eyes widen. An *ambulance*?

"But don't worry, she doesn't feel that hot. Just keep her

fever down with some aspirin. Make sure she gets lots of water and lots of rest."

"Wait, wait, wait. *I'm* supposed to take care of her?" I ask in a panic.

The look Martha gives me can only be described as astonished judgment. "Well, you *are* her husband, Mr. Barclay. Who better than you?"

"But I don't know what I'm doing," I nearly shout in return.

Her face cracks with a smile. Then she pats me on the arm. "It's a cold, sir. Just give her what she needs, and she'll be fine."

"Okay," I reply with a nervous gulp. She makes it sound so simple. *Give her what she needs.* But how the hell am I supposed to know what she needs?

"We'll be right downstairs until the end of our shift. You should really eat, sir."

"I'm fine," I reply stubbornly. I can't possibly eat like this. My stomach is in knots, and Sylvie is still burning up in my bed.

The next thing I know Martha is gone and I'm alone with my sick wife. On the bright side, the room is warm now.

I hope it's not *too* warm.

I shrug off my long-sleeve shirt and sit on the bed next to where Sylvie is sleeping. "Sylvie, I need you to wake up, darling."

"Hmm."

"I need to take your temperature."

Her mouth opens as if she's waiting. Quickly, I pick up the thermometer, press the button, and place it gently in her mouth. She closes her lips and we wait. When I hear the beep, I pull it out and read it.

Thirty-eight.

No need for the ambulance, then.

"I've got some medicine for you, mo ghràidh."

With a look of discomfort, she moves herself into a half-sitting position. I quickly shake out two pills from the bottle and place them in her mouth and hand her the water. She gulps it down before falling back down to the pillow.

When she lets out a cough, I pause and stare at her with concern. But it was just a cough, and within seconds, she's back to sleep.

Affectionately, I brush back her hair. Staring at her like this makes me feel as if my heart is suddenly outside my own body. How could she possibly understand the hold she has on me?

Sylvie is not perfect. She has flaws, but she wears them on her skin like scars. And it makes her so much more beautiful.

I have scars too, but I keep mine hidden behind humor and whisky. I stay locked away in my parents' house and I lie to myself every single day, saying I could leave if I wanted to.

For her, I could be better. I could leave this house more. I could be a real man. There's nothing I wouldn't do for her. If that's what she needs.

Give her what she needs, and she'll be fine.

I refuse to be like that man in the book.

Standing up, I tear off the rest of my clothes until I'm down to my boxers. Then, I climb under the covers next to my wife. She gravitates toward me, resting her face on my chest. It pains me to feel how hot her skin is.

But after a little while, I notice that the temperature slowly drops. By the time I drift off, she feels almost normal, so I feel as if I can rest. I know it's just the medicine and the fever will likely be back in the morning, but for now we can at least sleep.

So, I do.

Chapter Twenty-Seven

"WHERE THE FUCK DO YOU THINK YOU'RE GOING?"

When I emerge from the shower with a towel wrapped around my waist to find my wife, with her red nose and glassy eyes, putting on a pair of boots, I gape in horror.

"I need to get out of this house, Killian. I'm going out of my mind," she argues.

"You're still sick," I bark as I cross the room and steal her boot from her.

"I've been lying in this bed for three days. My fever is gone. I just have some congestion left. It's nothing."

My jaw clenches in frustration. The morning after she got her fever, she woke up with nothing but endless sneezing and coughing. I was a mess for days, trying to give her what she needed. Medicine, rest, water, food.

Normally when I get sick, I just sleep for days, but Sylvie is stubborn as hell. Over the last three days, she fought me on every decision. She hated having me dote on her and worry about her. I assume it's because she's just not used to it.

"You're not leaving, Sylvie." I keep my voice low and my tone flat.

She stands up in a huff. "Are you keeping me prisoner now?" The force she uses to yell at me sends her into a fit of coughs. She collapses back onto the bed to catch her breath.

There's a swell of pity in my stomach from seeing her struggle so much. Sylvie isn't like me. She hates feeling cooped up in the house, and I know she longs for fresh air.

"Come on," I say.

She lifts her arm from around her eyes and stares at me skeptically. "What?"

I kneel in front of her and unlace her boot enough to get it onto her foot. "You're not a prisoner here, Sylvie. You need some fresh air, but I can't let you leave alone while you're so sick. So let me help you."

She sits up and gives me a narrow-eyed expression. "Where are we going?"

After sliding her foot into the boot, I tie the laces. "Just on a walk of the grounds. We're sitting on sixty acres, you know."

Letting out a rattling exhale, she fights the urge to cough again. Then, she says in a raspy voice, "Fine."

"It's not raining for once, and I'll stay by your side the entire time."

She cocks her head to the side. "I'm not a child, Killian."

"No," I reply, tightening her laces. "But you are my wife, and it's my job to take care of you."

"It's really not," she replies weakly.

"Shut up, cow," I say, making her laugh. "Too harsh?"

She shakes her head with a soft smile. "Not at all."

Then, she puts out her hands for me, and I hoist her off the bed. I feel her forehead again for good measure, but as she said, her fever is gone, even without the medicine to keep it down.

On the entire walk along the gravel drive out to the farm, I keep Sylvie's hand in mine. It's warm enough now that we don't need gloves, although the leather ones she bought me are still tucked away in my pocket.

"We're not walking all sixty acres, are we?" she asks wearily.

"Of course not," I reply with a chuckle. "Are you feeling okay? We can head back."

She shakes her head. "No, I'm fine." Then she wraps herself around my arm, resting her head on my shoulder as we slowly walk down the path toward the farm.

"What do you do out here all day?" she asks.

With a laugh, I say, "Not much, really. The grounds crew keeps most of it up. I do like to help out where I can."

Then, she squeezes my arm. "You must do a lot. Enough to keep up this physique."

We stop, and I turn toward her. "Are you...complimenting me?"

She rolls her eyes. "Don't get used to it."

"I won't. I think I prefer the name-calling."

"Okay, good," she teases as we start walking again. "You have large muscles, but you're still stupid and ugly."

"Well, that's just a lie," I reply with a grin. "I'm incredibly handsome."

The next time I look down at her, I notice she's chewing on her lip and trying to hide the blush on her cheeks.

———

When we reach the farm, Ben, the groundskeeper, is standing outside his quaint brick house in front of the barn. I introduce him to Sylvie, and she greets him warmly, which is nice to see. She reserves her bitchiness just for me.

As Ben and I get into a conversation about the garden we've been working on, Sylvie walks away to explore the farm. When she finds the gray mare, I excuse myself from the conversation with Ben and run over toward her.

"Is it nice?" she asks before getting too close.

"She's very gentle." I grab an apple we keep in a basket near her stall and place it in Sylvie's hand. Then I hold her against my body as I ease her hand out to the animal.

"What's her name?" Sylvie asks.

"Moire," I reply, which makes Sylvie giggle.

"What's so funny?" I ask.

She shrugs, wiping her slobber-covered hand on my jacket. "Just like hearing you say that."

"Moire," I reply, drawing it out for her and giving the *R* a bit more of a roll. Then, I tug Sylvie closer and lean in to press my lips to her ear. She giggles from the tickle of my beard.

But when I try to move my mouth to hers, she shoves me away. "Don't kiss me! I'm sick."

"I don't care," I reply as I pull her back toward me. I just want her body in my hands at all times. I crave her against my body and my lips on her every second of my day.

"You're disgusting," she squeals as I hold her face and kiss her hard right on the mouth. I don't care that she's sick or that I've seen her go through an entire box of tissues in a day. If that's disgusting, so be it. She's my woman, and I'll take the bad with the good.

"In sickness and in health, remember?" I say with my lips just inches from hers.

Our eyes meet, and I see the slight panic in her gaze. She gets that way anytime I bring up our marriage, as if she's afraid of it *now*. We've been married for six months. And we have six months to go. I've not made any indication that I expect her to stay after the year, at least not *yet*.

I desperately hope she does.

Sensing her discomfort from that phrase, I quickly let her go. She averts her eyes, and I busy myself with giving Moire another snack.

As I'm petting the horse's mane, Sylvie points toward the barn. "What are those?"

Looking up, I see the boxy white structures on the other side, and my mouth twitches with a smile. "Let me show you," I say as I take her hand and lead her toward the hives. Stopping near the barn, I quickly roll up my sleeves and rinse my hands clean with the spout.

Then, I watch her expression as I pull open the box from the top and lift the frame from out of the shelter. The sound of the swarm is immediate, and Sylvie lets out a squeal as she starts to run from my side. Snatching her by the arm, I give her a stern look.

"Calm down, darling. They won't hurt you."

At that moment, a few dozen bees leave the frame and start to buzz around us both, so I quickly grasp my wife to my side, whispering into her hair. "Just relax. I've got you."

She lets out a muffled sound, and I look down to see she's buried her face in my shirt, her eyes clenched shut.

"Sylvie, look," I say as I prop the frame up on the side of the box. With one arm around her to keep her safe, I press the other to the bee-covered hive to show her how gentle they are.

She whines as she clutches tighter to me.

"There's nothing to be afraid of," I reply. "That honey you put in your tea comes from here."

"Yeah, well, I could also get it from the store."

"Where's the fun in that?" I dig my finger into some of the honeycomb at the edge of the frame, and I show her how easily it drips. My fingers are covered as I bring one to my mouth and lick it clean.

When I look down, her eyes are zeroed in on my hand, so I bring it to her lips. She inspects it for a moment before running her warm tongue along the length of my middle finger. I can't keep in the low growl that emits at the sight and sensation of her tongue against my digit.

"Bloody hell, woman," I growl, making her smile.

Just then, a bee buzzes past her head, and she panics, swatting at it with a squeal. As she starts to run, I lose grip of her, and she gets out of my hands.

"Sylvie, relax!"

But she doesn't. She flails and stumbles until she trips and falls, landing in the grass with a hard *thunk*. That forces another coughing fit, and I rush over, grabbing the worker bee that had gotten himself stuck in her wild curls. The moment my fingers close around him, he stings me, and I toss him to the ground.

When I hiss, Sylvie looks up at me with concern. Between her coughs, she manages to squeak out, "I told you they were dangerous!"

Using my teeth, I pull out the stinger and spit it into the grass. Then, I lower myself to my knees in front of my wife.

"No, mo ghràidh. They're not dangerous. You just have to know how to handle them."

She continues coughing, so I pull her up and pat her back through the spell. By the time she's done, I can hear the rasp in her breathing. The doctor said the virus will work itself out, but the cough could take longer. I wish it'd hurry. I can't stand the sound of her like this.

When she's done heaving, she takes my hand in hers, staring down at my finger. There's a red, swollen lump there already.

"Does it hurt?" she whispers.

"Nah," I say. "Not too bad."

Then she brings it to her mouth and presses her lips to the end of my index finger. "I'm sorry."

"Come on then," I reply after kissing the top of her head.

"Let's get back home and get you to bed. Enough fresh air for you today."

"Okay," she agrees.

I pull her to her feet and leave her a good distance away from the hives while I go back to replace the frame I had removed. When I'm done, I return to Sylvie and tuck her under my arm so we can walk back to the house together.

Chapter Twenty-Eight

"Is tomorrow your birthday?" Sylvie finds me kneeling in the dirt by the farm. Squinting through the sun, I stare up at her with a bad feeling in my gut.

"Yeah...why?"

"When were you gonna tell me?" she replies. "Your sister just mentioned it in a text."

I shrug. "Why would I tell you? It doesn't matter."

"Of course it does," she replies. "Anna said you always have your friends over for your birthday."

My only response is a disgruntled sigh.

It's true; I always do have my friends over for my birthday, but that's not always a good thing. The party is nothing more than a binge of sex, alcohol, and debauchery. It just doesn't interest me anymore.

If I could have anything for my birthday, it would just be a typical day at home with my wife. Or perhaps her admitting to me that she actually gives a fuck about me. I'd like that too.

"So, let's throw a party," she says with excitement.

Now that she's finally able to argue with me without setting off a fit of coughs, she takes advantage of it and argues with me ten times as much. I'd be lying if I said I didn't enjoy it.

"No," I grunt as I turn my attention back to pulling the weeds that have sprouted along the fence line.

"Come on, you miserable ogre. I *need* a party. I'm so bored."

"I'll keep you busy," I reply as I glance up at her with a wicked grin.

She rolls her eyes. "We're already screwing two times a day, Killian. My poor lady bits can't take anymore."

Out of the corner of my eye, I see Ben fumble with the tool in his hand before quickly scurrying over to the barn and out of earshot of our conversation. I let out a small chuckle.

Then I turn back toward Sylvie. "Wait… I'm not hurting you, am I?"

"No, my dear husband. You're not hurting me. Besides," she adds with a shrug. "I like a little pain."

My eyebrows nearly shoot to my hairline. *Oh, we're coming back to that.*

"How about for my birthday, we see just how much pain you like?" I ask.

"No," she barks, stomping her foot on the ground. "We can't just sit around this house alone every single day, Killian. We need human interaction. We need to celebrate. We need to have *fun*. You remember what that is, don't you?"

Sitting back on my haunches, I let out a sigh of defeat. I know at this moment that I'm not winning this argument. It's clear. When my wife puts her mind to something, there is *no* talking her out of it.

"Fine," I say with a relenting sigh. "One party. Just a few people. Nothing wild."

"Thank you," she replies with an elated bounce in her feet. Then she holds out her hand. "Give me your phone."

I don't even argue. I just pull it out of my back pocket and hand it over. "Don't go looking at my search history now."

She screws up her face in disgust. Then, without a word, I watch her type out a message.

"Who are you texting?" I ask, feeling a sense of hesitation and paranoia.

"The group chat," she says, showing me my phone screen.

"How the hell did you find that?" I reply in shock.

"It's not that hard, Killian. You don't really text that many people."

My phone starts vibrating with responses immediately. She smiles down at the screen. "They're in."

As she passes back my phone, a sense of dread rises up inside me. I'm always happy to see my friends, but I also know what comes with that. I've always been the single guy at our parties, but now I have someone else to protect. Because if any of those men think they can lay a hand on my wife, this weekend won't end well.

———

"Barclay!" Liam greets me in his usual bellowing excitement as he jogs up the drive from his car and throws his arms around me for a hug. "How the hell have you been?"

I force a pleasant expression and nod. "I've been good."

"Now that you're married, you never want to party anymore, is that it?" he asks with a laugh, slapping me on the arm.

"I guess you could say that," I reply with a wince.

"Where is that stunning wife of yours?"

My teeth grind as I stare at him, gauging his interest in Sylvie. At that very moment, I hear her light footsteps as she comes down the stairs and meets us at the door.

"There she is!" Liam shouts when he sees her.

I turn around and watch him approach her with enthusiasm, pulling her into a hug. Her eyes find mine, and she widens them briefly as if she's scolding me. She told me multiple times to be on my best behavior this weekend; I know deep down she doesn't mean to not drink too much or to use my manners. She means to avoid acting like some possessive caveman who snaps off anyone's head for the smallest thing.

I can make no promises.

McNeil and I go into the parlor for a drink while Sylvie goes to the kitchen to talk with the staff. I catch a glimpse of her as she walks away. She turns back to me for a split second, and our eyes meet. The subtle warmth in her gaze is fooling me. It's telling me she's happy here and that we make a good couple. Because right now, she *feels* like my wife.

"So," Liam adds as we grab a drink from the bar. "I know I apologized last time, but I just feel the need to do it again."

I shake my head. "Liam, it's fine."

"No, it's not. I pissed you off last time I was here, and it was wrong of me."

"I gave you the green light," I reply, but he puts up a hand to stop me.

"You clearly love your wife very much, Killian."

Forcing myself to swallow and remain stoic, I let out a heavy breath through my nose. Liam's words send a shot of regret to my chest. This marriage isn't even real, but he's right. I do love her.

Instead of arguing with him, I simply say, "You're right. I do."

Then, his face pulls into a grin. "I'm happy for you."

That guilt returns, stinging a little bit more.

An hour later, the rest of the crew starts piling in, and the drinking starts as it normally does.

Greg, Nick, and their ladies congregate on the couches in the parlor, and soon the room is filled with laughter. I stay off to the side, hanging by the bar with a drink in my hand as I watch the rest of them go on and on.

"You've been sipping that drink for a long time," Sylvie whispers after she sidles up next to me.

I glance down at my half-empty glass of whisky. "Taking it easy tonight," I reply.

Her eyebrows shoot upward, and I watch as she bites her lip as if she's fighting the urge to respond with something sarcastic and quippy. Instead, she takes the glass from my hand and shoots back the drink in one quick gulp.

She coughs and sputters after it goes down, making me laugh. "What the hell did you do that for?"

"You might be taking it easy," she replies through a strained voice. "But I'm getting drunk."

I let out a low growl. "Easy, mo ghràidh."

"Oh, relax, you big dumb oaf. What could possibly go wrong? I've got you to protect me."

I watch as she pours herself another shot, but as she moves to shoot it again, I grab her arm to stop her. "Keep your wits about you, wife."

She rolls her eyes before gulping down the next shot. "Relax, Killian."

Then, I pin her against the bar and put my mouth down by her ear. She's so much smaller than me I have to practically bend over to reach her. "I'm not a monster, you know. If you get too drunk, I won't be able to fuck your brains out later, and I plan to. So, I'll say it again…" I take the shot glass from her hand and set it on the bar. "Keep your wits about you."

I watch as she gulps nervously before meeting my eyes. Then, to my surprise, she grabs me by the back of the neck and drags me down for a kiss.

The conversation behind us dies as they notice us

practically making out by the bar. Then, of course, there is a round of whoops and whistles.

"The party is starting early!" someone shouts with excitement.

Everyone erupts with laughter as I pull away from Sylvie's kiss. She's beaming up at me as I stand upright and turn toward our friends with a smug grin.

That's when I catch sight of the couple in the doorway, and my smile instantly fades. Standing there by the entryway are Angus and Claire. He's wearing a wide expression of excitement, but she's simply scowling at me and my wife.

That's when Sylvie tightens her grip on my arm as if I'm being claimed. And I'm not going to lie, I sort of love it.

Chapter Twenty-Nine

SYLVIE IS ADORABLE WHEN SHE'S DRUNK. WELL, TECHNICALLY, I think she's just tipsy, but it's enough to have her telling hilarious stories at dinner, mostly about me and the idiotic things I've done. The group adores her. Well, all but the short-haired brunette across the table who is staring daggers at my wife.

I get the sneaking suspicion that something happened between Sylvie and Claire that I haven't been told about. When we all sat around the table, Sylvie aggressively stole the seat beside me from Claire, who already had the chair pulled out and was about to sit.

Everyone at the table noticed. Even Angus, who has been silent ever since.

Guilt pierces my chest again. It's like a blade stuck between my ribs that I can't seem to remove.

Sylvie, in her usual commanding style, completely saved the dinner from debilitating awkwardness and had everyone laughing in seconds. By the time we finished our meal, her hand was resting on my stiffening cock, and I had to fight the urge to drag her up to our room right then and there.

I've barely had anything to drink all night. We've been lingering at the table for a while now, and I can see how toasted everyone is getting. It's about *that* time—when things go from a tame dinner party with friends to something far more wicked and depraved.

My favorite part of the night if we're honest, but not tonight. Tonight, I just want to make them all go away so I can be alone with my wife.

"Wait!" Sylvie shrieks with a slur in her voice.

"Jesus, woman. What are you hollerin' about?" I ask.

"Your cake!"

"My cake?"

She jumps up from the table and scurries off into the kitchen. I can feel Claire staring at me, but I don't look in her direction.

"She's really amazing," Greg's wife, Emma, says with a warm smile.

"Yeah," I mutter to myself. "She is."

Just then the lights go out in the dining room, and a warm glow emits from the kitchen. Before I know it, I hear Sylvie crooning off-tune.

"Haaaaappy…" she starts while waiting for the rest to join in. "Birthday to you," she sings when they do.

Throughout the entire song, she's grinning at me over the candles on the giant chocolate cake, and I can't help but smile in return. By the time she sets it down in front of me, the song is over, and she's gaping at me expectantly.

Closing my eyes, I make a quick wish, and I blow the candles out. Everyone cheers, and I swallow my embarrassment.

While Sylvie cuts the cake and passes out each piece, I find myself watching her with wonder. This is somehow the same woman who threw hot coffee on her ex-boyfriend and broke into a stranger's house. She's the same woman who kissed my beesting and mended my hand when it was bleeding. Every moment I thought I had her figured out, she surprised me with more layers and beauty than I ever expected.

"We should play a game!" Sylvie exclaims, with a glass of wine in her hand.

"Not another drinking game," I mutter.

"No…" She snatches the empty wine bottle off the table and smiles at me. "You've played spin the bottle, right?"

My heated gaze turns in her direction. "Sylvie…"

The party reacts with excitement.

"I knew your wife would know how to get the party started," someone says with a giggle.

Immediately, everyone is on board, practically running from the dining room table and into the parlor. They clear a spot in the middle of the large room. Sitting right in front of the fireplace, they form a circle on the floor, and Sylvie reaches for me, gesturing for me to sit next to her.

Liam grabs another bottle of wine, and I realize how painfully sober I am.

This is a bad idea. I can feel it.

My friends and I have been kinky together in the past. These parties always lead to sex in some way or another, and I've always been open to playing along, although there is only one other person in this room I've actually fucked, and *that* wasn't part of the party.

No, *that* was something very different entirely.

But these couples have no problem with sharing all the time. It's almost as if my house is the safe space where they can fuck each other, and it doesn't mean anything.

But now that I'm married, I realize that it means a hell of a lot to me. For a guy who hangs out with a bunch of swingers, suddenly, I don't feel as if I belong here.

"Okay, so the rules are simple. If the bottle lands on you, you can choose to kiss or drink," Sylvie explains.

"Or more…" Liam adds, making everyone laugh.

When Sylvie moves to spin the bottle, I immediately grab it from the floor and pass it along to Liam, who is sitting on the other side of her. Sylvie gives me a grumpy look as if she's disappointed in me, but I don't care. I sit in frustrated silence while Liam spins.

The bottle lands on Emma. Everyone claps and cheers. Her cheeks redden immediately. Then she crooks a finger at Liam, basically implying that she'd rather have a kiss than a drink. He crawls across the floor toward her, and she grabs his face, planting a long wet kiss on his mouth. Everyone reacts with excitement, even Greg, who's laughing next to her.

When the kiss is done, Liam sits back down, and Nick is next. His bottle lands on Claire, who opts for drinking instead of kissing. After Nick, Theresa goes. The bottle spins until it lands on Angus.

"Get over here," he says to Theresa. I notice the way Claire's mouth sets in a thin angry line.

Theresa laughs as she crawls over to Angus, but instead of kissing him on his mouth, she dives down and latches her lips onto his neck, sucking on his flesh and making his eyes roll into the back of his head.

"Holy shite," he mutters after she releases him. As he touches the now red circle she left behind, he mutters a low "I'm fuckin' hard as hell after that."

We all let out a string of laughter, and I feel Sylvie nestle closer to my side. Theresa looks downright proud of herself now.

Then it's Claire's turn, and I grow tense. I watch with nervous anxiety as it spins, and when it stops pointing dangerously close to me, I panic.

"It's me," Sylvie says, cutting off my thoughts.

"It looks like it landed right between you and Killian," someone argues.

"No, it's on me," she argues. Then she glares at Claire. "So… what's it gonna be?"

"Technically, it's your choice," Claire replies flatly.

"I'm not afraid of a little kiss."

"Sylvie…" I say in warning. But she ignores me. Instead, she leans toward Claire and stares obstinately into her eyes. The tension between these two women is palpable, and I'm legitimately concerned about what my wife is about to do.

Claire leans toward Sylvie, but it's Sylvie who makes the leap. She latches her lips around Claire's, kissing her with passion and fire, and I see Claire's bottom lip pinched between Sylvie's teeth. Claire lets out a whimper but meets Sylvie's fervor with her own, pressing back against her. For ten long seconds, the two of them fight for control of the kiss while the rest of us watch with trepidation.

When they finally pull away, Sylvie's mouth is red, and Claire looks angry and defeated, as if Sylvie somehow won.

"I think it's time for another bottle," Liam says, changing the mood in the room. He immediately jumps up, grabs a bottle of wine, and walks to the wall to dim the lights. I can feel the radiating anger from Sylvie's gaze as she glares at the other woman.

She only relaxes after Claire leaves the room in a huff.

"What was that all about?" I whisper.

Sylvie shrugs. "I don't like her."

"Obviously," I joke.

"Don't act like you don't know why," she replies without looking at me.

My head tilts as I stare at her in confusion. Leaning my mouth next to her ear, I softly whisper, "Is my wee little wife jealous?"

"I don't like cheaters," she mutters, denying that she's jealous of another woman wanting me.

"You're in a room full of cheaters, darling."

"You know what I mean," she huffs.

My hand slides along her jaw, turning her face toward me. "I like to see you jealous."

She jerks away from me. "I'm not."

"Then you won't mind me kissing another person tonight?"

Her eyes turn to fire, glaring at me with rage. "You wouldn't dare."

I chuckle softly. "It's not really cheating. Just a kiss."

Reaching into the middle of the circle, I pick up the wine bottle. "My turn," I announce, stealing the attention of everyone in the circle who are all having their own flirty private conversations.

"Should we wait for Claire to come back?" Liam asks.

"She's fine," Angus replies, waving off his wife instead of looking for her.

Sylvie is still shooting daggers at me with her eyes as I give the bottle a spin. After three turns, it stops in front of Theresa, the same woman responsible for the blossoming hickey on Angus's neck.

The group lets out a collective "Ooooh."

I wink at my wife before leaning in toward Theresa and pressing a chaste kiss on her lips before sitting back in my seat.

The group lets out a collective "Awww."

Sylvie is still fuming. She picks up the bottle and spins it for herself. When it lands on Greg, my jaw clenches. We've stopped doing the drink option, apparently because she crawls defiantly toward him and grabs his face. I watch with buzzing anger as she kisses him deeply, pressing her tongue in his mouth.

"That's enough," I bellow.

Thinking it's just a joke, everyone laughs. But I haul my wife back to her seat next to me just the same. When she lands on the floor, I wipe the saliva from her mouth and give her a warning glance.

"She's been bad, Kill," Theresa murmurs. "How are you going to punish her?"

Sylvie shoots me a tense glare, but I tilt my head back and stare down at her menacingly. "I don't know, but I would like to punish her."

Across the floor, Theresa bites her lip, looking as if she's dying to see it happen. Everyone else is fidgeting, and I know they are craving to see it as much as I'm craving to do it.

I lean down toward Sylvie, teasing her with a smile.

"Go on, then, Killian," Greg says. "Show her what we get up to at our parties."

"What do you think, mo ghràidh?" I whisper. "Can I show them how tough my girl is? How well she takes it?"

"You hurt me, and I'll hurt you right back," she responds with venom.

I smile wickedly. "I'm counting on it."

Then I take her lips, kissing her hard and reclaiming her mouth as my own. After she starts melting into the kiss, I stand from the floor and drag her up with me. The rest of the group stays on the floor, mingling together in a drunken mess until Theresa is in Angus's lap and Emma is in Liam's.

But to be honest, I'm not concerned with them anymore. All I can see in my mind is Sylvie kissing Greg and Claire. Her tongue in their mouths. Their hands on her body. I'm seeing red as I toss her on the couch, kneeling on the cushions as she bends over with her ass in the air. In one swoop, I lift her dress, and she lets out a yelp of surprise.

"This, my sweet wife," I say, grabbing her ass cheeks in my hand, "is mine."

She only whimpers in response. As I knead and massage her pale, tender flesh, I hear the soft moans of those behind me. They must be enjoying the show.

"Tell me I can punish you, Sylvie. I need to hear you say it."

She lets out a tortured groan with her face pressed into the cushions of the sofa.

"Say it, wife. Yes or no?"

Lifting her head, I can see the arousal mingled with resistance in her eyes.

"Don't worry, darling. I'll let you pay me back, but I want to show you how good it feels first—to be claimed by your husband."

Her head falls back, and her spine arches as she lets out another moan. "Yes," she replies breathily.

"That's my girl," I reply with a grin.

Then, I waste no time. Peeling down her thin lace panties, I let my friends behind me take their fill of my beautiful wife's cunt, glistening and pink. When I spread her folds wide for them to see, I hear a muffled "Fuck yeah," coming from the dark side of the room.

"She tastes good too," I mutter lowly before dipping my head down and taking a long salacious lick of her wet pussy. She fidgets and moans as I do.

While I play with her, sliding a finger inside her only to pull it out and tease her arsehole, she squirms and mumbles curses into the cushions.

"All mine," I mutter with a sneer as I take another long lick. "No one else can ever touch you. Is that understood?"

She groans without a verbal response. So I rear back my hand and lick my lips before landing a hard smack on her right ass cheek. The sound that comes out of her is a mixture of surprise and enjoyment—a gasp and a whine.

"You liked that, didn't you, mo ghràidh?"

Biting her bottom lip, she nods.

I let my hand fly again, landing on the opposite cheek but not giving her time to recover before doing it two more times. She howls and mewls, the pleasure fighting for dominance inside her.

"Do you understand, Sylvie? Tell me you're all mine."

"No," she says through gritted teeth, shaking her head. A sinister smile stretches across my face.

"You need more then."

Holding her dress up, I land another harsh smack on her ass. I love the way her flesh reddens with every strike of my palm. Her moans are guttural and needy as I spank her again and again, growing more and more desperate to fuck her with every hit.

"Say it, Sylvie," I mutter darkly. "Tell me you're mine."

She continues to fight it angrily, and I love the way she struggles. She could easily tell me to stop, and I would, but deep down, I know this is what she wants.

"More," she whines, shoving her hips backward.

My hand burns with every resounding slap of her ass. Inside my trousers, my cock is straining against my zipper, leaking at the tip with the thought of sinking inside her. Sylvie's knuckles are white as she grips the back of the sofa through her pain.

Finally, on the last harsh hit, she screams, "Okay!"

I pause, breathing heavily as I wait for her to finally say what I want to hear.

"I'm yours," she cries out in a breathless whimper. "I'm yours, I'm yours, I'm yours."

Without a moment of hesitation, I tear down my zipper and pull out my aching cock. Shimmying my pants down enough, I drop onto the sofa and grab her from beside me.

"Ride my cock and show me, then."

She climbs onto my lap in a rush, straddling my hips as she

lowers herself over my shaft. This time, she doesn't give herself time to adjust to my size. She winces in pain as her soaking cunt swallows my length.

I grab her by the back of the neck and hold her face to mine. When I kiss her lips, I taste the tears and sweat on her face as she starts to bounce eagerly on my lap.

"That's my girl," I whisper, kissing her lips.

My heart swells in my chest. There is only her, only us. And I know she could have said those things because of the heat of the moment, but in my heart, I pray they're true.

My woman. My wife. My darling.

Her hands grip tightly to my neck as she grinds her hips on my dick, chasing her own pleasure and crying out loudly with every thrust. Her voice grows louder and higher in pitch the faster she goes, and I know there's no stopping the cosmic onslaught of pleasure as it barrels through her.

Then it's as if she holds me tight to pull me under with her. My cock jerks and shudders as I release my load, growling loudly with my climax.

When she finally collapses on top of me, her head rests on my shoulder, and her heart pounds against my chest.

The moans and cries of pleasure from behind her barely register at all to me. I'm so focused on her, and she's so focused on me.

Her eyes are filled with tears, and she is staring at me with astonishment, as if she's about to say something profound. I wait with bated breath for the words I so desperately want to hear.

"Killian..." she whispers.

Quickly, I brush the sweat-soaked hair out of her face.

"Yes, darling," I whisper in return.

Her lips part, the words lingering on her lips. One moment after another passes by as I wait for something, *anything*.

There is so much torment in her eyes, as if it's so hard for her to express how she really feels, and I know it's there. The hatred she once expressed is gone, but for some reason, she refuses to let me have anything else.

Instead, she closes her lips and rests her head on my shoulder again. Her breath is warm against my neck as she relaxes into my arms.

Chapter Thirty

I HEAR THE FAMILIAR *CLICK-CLICK* AGAIN FROM THE LIBRARY, and I stop in my tracks as I walk in the back door, shedding my boots from the field before quietly crossing the floor. Sylvie hasn't worked much on her novel in the past few weeks. First, she got sick. Then, we had my birthday party. And ever since then, she's been back to acting strange again.

It's as if Sylvie will only let me in one tiny bit at a time. That night of the party a couple of weeks ago, I think she realized how much we mean to each other now, and she didn't like it. I don't blame her. I didn't like it at first either.

It's such a strange feeling to fall in love with someone you don't intend to. It's like being coerced or tricked. Everything that reminded me of what it was like to despise her is gone. Wiped from my memory forever.

Slowly, I tiptoe up the stairs, mesmerized by the hypnotic sound of her fingers punching those loud keys. As I reach the library, I do the same thing I always do. I stand in the doorframe silently with my arms crossed as I watch her.

"I can see you," she calls, sounding amused while still typing away at her typewriter.

I let out a low chuckle as I step into the room. She doesn't stop what she's doing. In fact, she seems captivated by the story she's typing, and when she reaches the end of the page, she rolls it out of the old machine and loads a new one.

I could remind her again that she owns a perfectly good laptop, but she already knows that. And if this is working, then who am I to stop her?

After the fresh white page is loaded, she rolls her chair backward and stretches her arms over her head, arching her spine and revealing her back and belly. I have to force myself to focus.

It's now early May, and I'm starting to feel a sense of panic building inside me because the days of our marriage are numbered. Sylvie only has four more months here. It will take me four more months to convince her to stay. To be my wife *forever*.

"It's a beautiful day outside," I say carefully.

She looks momentarily surprised as she pops up and glances out the large window. "It actually stopped raining."

"We only have a matter of time before it starts again."

She spins toward me, tugging at the rubber band around the ponytail, letting her wild, warm locks fall around her shoulders. "What did you have in mind?"

"It's a surprise," I reply.

The corner of her mouth tilts upward, fighting a smile. "Fine. I can stand to take a break anyway. Let me get my shoes on."

When I meet Sylvie outside, I watch her expression as she pulls the back door closed and spots Moire standing near the garden wall. Sylvie's jaw drops.

"What is she doing here?" she asks with sweet surprise as she jogs down the gray stone steps toward the large animal.

"I thought you might like to go for a little ride," I say

without sounding too enthusiastic about it. I've learned that approaching Sylvie is like approaching a wild animal. Be gentle. Don't be too charismatic. She spooks easy.

"I've never ridden a horse before," she says with fright.

I reach out my hand toward her. "I've got you."

When her gaze lifts to my face, I spot a hint of something affectionate, but she quickly wipes it away. "Promise?"

"Of course," I reply. The desire to call her something special and intimate is strong, but I refrain. *Tread carefully.*

"All right," I say, pulling her toward the saddle. "Left foot first."

She slides her foot into the stirrup and leaps onto the horse's back. As I climb up behind her, she relaxes against my body with a sigh. She's more at ease with me close to her. I wish she could see that.

Sylvie leans back as we take off in a slow trot around the perimeter of the grounds. We don't say much as we go, but my wife and I have reached that point in our relationship where we are comfortable together, even in silence. We don't need to fill it with meaningless chatter. She's not like my sister or my friends' wives. Sylvie lives as if she doesn't owe anyone in the world an explanation or an apology. She doesn't belong to anyone—not even me. At least not in that way.

Sylvie is fearlessly herself. And I love that about her.

Especially when I feel as if I'm constantly battling with everyone to let me be myself—my sister, my aunt, and even my dead parents had a vision for me in their heads of what I was meant to be. I have failed time and time again. I've never truly been what anyone wished for me to be. So it's easier just to be alone. In my house, I can't feel the disappointment.

"Your property goes all the way out here?" she asks when we see the river in the distance.

"Yes."

"I had no idea it was this big," she murmurs to herself.

"This runs right out to the sea," I reply, pointing to the river ahead of us. "It makes me feel more connected to the rest of the world," I add, unsure why I need to be so open with her. My hand grips around her waist. "I sometimes come out here just to stare at the current, watch as it leaves."

She's silent for a while before carefully speaking. "Why don't you leave? You could go too, you know?"

I swallow down the discomfort building in my throat. "Where would I go? I belong here."

"You could go wherever you want, Killian. You could leave your sister and this house behind and live your own life."

My hand tightens around her. "And where will you go?"

I hear her exhale softly. "I don't know, Killian."

"Come with me, and we can go anywhere." It's foolish of me to try, but I have to. I still don't understand, after everything we've been through, why this woman still wants to hold me so far away. As if *nothing* between us is real.

"It's not that easy," she whispers.

"Yes, it is. I'm your husband. I'll take you anywhere you want to go."

"For what? For how long? What happens when this year is up?" Her voice is growing frantic, and I've come to learn the sound of Sylvie getting caught up in her emotions. I'm doing exactly what I'm not supposed to be, spooking her with talk of the future and our feelings, but I can't take it anymore. She *has* to know how I feel about her—how I feel about *us*.

"I'll have our house for good, then," I say in a pleading tone. "My aunt will be off our backs, and we can do whatever we want."

She lets out a defeated sound as she places her face in her hands. "Killian."

My jaw clenches. Is this her way of letting me down? Am I really so wrong about these feelings that she truly doesn't feel them too?

"It's all in my head, then," I reply with a frustrated grunt. "You really do feel nothing for me."

Her head lifts, and I see a tremble in her lips. "I didn't say that."

"Then, what are you saying, mo ghràidh?"

"I don't know. Why are you asking me all of this right now? Why do I have to decide?"

I feel her body shivering against me just as the clouds start to drop a heavy mist on us. Guilt assaults me for being too hard on her, too desperate to know I'm not alone in this.

"It's okay, darling," I whisper with my lips against the side of her head. "Let's just go back home."

As we make our steady walk back to the house, the rain picks up from a light drizzle to a slow fall. When we reach the farm, I quickly put Moire back in the stall and shut the door. Sylvie is standing under the roof of the barn, watching the rain. Judging by the look on her face, she's deep in contemplation and downright worried. It makes me feel like shite for bringing the whole thing up in the first place.

She has only been here for eight months. That's fast for any relationship, especially a marriage. It's ridiculous of me to be pressuring her to be married to me beyond the contract we initially set out.

But as I approach her from behind to apologize, she quickly spins toward me and grabs my face in her hands. It takes me by surprise, so I pull back to stare into her eyes.

"Fuck the house, Killian. Fuck this stupid contract. Let's just blow it all off and go away together."

My eyes widen as I stare at her in shock. "What are you talking about?"

"You said you would take me anywhere I want to go, so let's give the house back to your aunt now and go somewhere!"

My hands cover hers as I gaze into her eyes skeptically. "Sylvie, I meant on a holiday. I'm not giving my house to my aunt."

Her face morphs into an expression of defeat as her lips close, and she stares up at me with sadness.

"Fine," she whispers. "Then…just kiss me."

I stare at her in confusion. "Are you all right?"

But she doesn't answer me. Instead, she tugs my mouth down to hers and bites my bottom lip between her teeth. Latching her arms around my neck, she kisses me as if she's trying to distract me…or herself.

Her body clings to mine, and I feel her legs spreading like she wants me to lift her so she can wrap them around me. But I have the sense I'm being misled, and I'm even more confused than I was before.

What is Sylvie not telling me?

Keeping my mouth against hers, she breathes between us. "I do want to go away with you, Killian," she whispers. "I just—"

The sound of tires on gravel down the driveway stops her words before they leave her mouth. We both turn to watch a car driving slowly toward the house. It's a black sedan, expensive and private, with dark tinted windows.

"Who the hell is that?" I mutter.

"I have no idea…" Sylvie responds wearily.

We each tug our rain jackets over our heads and walk hand in hand toward the house, but I feel the hesitation in my wife's touch. Even if she doesn't know who is at the house, I get the feeling she has a specific fear of who it might be.

By the time we reach the front door of the house, whoever

it was has already been welcomed inside. Sylvie glances up at me nervously before I guide her toward the door.

"It'll be okay," I whisper comfortingly.

Then I pull open the front door just as Sylvie peeks around me and tears down the hood of her jacket.

Standing in the large entryway of my house is a couple I don't recognize. The woman is slender with a downturned mouth and long red hair, a few shades darker than Sylvie's. The man has dark curly hair and a receding hairline, leaving the top of his head bald.

Sylvie's hand squeezes mine as if she's suddenly afraid. I glance at her as she gapes in shock at the two people standing before us. I'm just about to scream at someone to tell me what's going on when she finally opens her mouth to speak.

"Mom…Dad…what are you guys doing here?"

Chapter Thirty-One

"She doesn't look very excited to see us, Tor," the man says with a hint of sarcastic humor and a nasally voice. I stare daggers at the two people standing in my home, referring to my wife as if they were the sun, just waiting for her to orbit around them.

"Of course she is," the woman replies, giving Sylvie a smug, teasing expression. "She's just surprised."

"What are you guys doing here?" Sylvie repeats as if to herself.

The woman looks at the man and then back at us. "Well… you said you'd be in Scotland, so here we are." Then, her eyes trail upward to my face. "You must be the man our daughter ran off to marry."

"He exists," the man jokes as they both laugh together. Sylvie and I stay silent.

The woman looks around as if assessing my home. "Truly remarkable design," she says, pointing to the accents and fixtures.

The man quickly jumps in. "And this rug, Torrence. Did you see this rug?"

"It must be hand knotted," Sylvie's mother replies, staring down at the floor.

The two of them go on about the rug as my gaze slides over to Sylvie. She's staring at them with an expression on her face I've never seen before. Lips parted, eyes moist, nostrils flaring. She's on the verge of tears while being frozen in place.

My heart splinters with rage, but I swallow it down. These are her parents. They might be a bit unconventional, but they are still her family, so I'll use every ounce of strength inside me to watch my tone and bite my tongue.

When I spot Martha reentering the foyer to help greet our guests, I decide it would be best to invite them in and at least try to act civilized.

I raise a hand to guide them toward the parlor. "Please, come in. Martha will make us some tea, and we…" I stammer, unpracticed in my manners. "We can get to know each other."

Sylvie's hand clasps onto my arm, her nails digging into the skin. When she turns toward me, I read the expression of hesitation on her face. *Please, no*, it says.

I pull her against me and press my lips to her forehead. "It'll be fine," I whisper.

Then I rest my hand on her back and lead her toward the parlor. Her parents fuss about the house some more, admiring the art on the walls and the architectural details around the windows. Things I've become so accustomed to over the years of my life that I hardly notice them anymore. Then again, I don't find the value in my home in its history or design. I find the value in its comfort and the fact that it's given me shelter and warmth for just over thirty-eight years.

"Well, we haven't been properly introduced," the man says as he strides toward me with a hand outstretched. There's something odd about him. He won't look me in the eye. He's much shorter than his wife, which must be where Sylvie gets her smaller size from. But although he's a small man, he carries himself much like a lapdog does, not as if he's the largest and most powerful thing in the room, but like he sits on the lap of the person who is.

"Yuri Deveraux," he says politely. I shake his hand, clenching my jaw together.

"Killian Barclay," I reply proudly.

The woman doesn't bother with introductions or handshakes. She pulls her glasses off and holds them in front of her as she studies a painting on the wall.

"Torrence, dear, come sit down," the man says as he takes a seat across from me. Sylvie has hardly uttered a word to her parents, but judging by the look on her face, she's fuming inside. She's sitting next to me like a powder keg with a very short fuse. Reaching over, I clutch her hand in mine, holding it tightly, hoping to calm her if necessary.

"Sylvie and I didn't know you two were in the country," I say calmly.

"Well, we haven't been to London in years, but we had some good friends holding an exhibit there, so we made the trip."

Sylvie's hand flinches in mine, so I squeeze tighter.

I think her father notices because his eyes dart down to our hands and up to his daughter's face. He doesn't keep his eyes on her for long, and I sense a flash of sympathy in his expression. He quickly clears his throat.

"So, how did you two meet?" he asks.

"Umm…" I stammer, glancing at her and searching for an answer.

"There was a typewriter," she mumbles lazily.

"A typewriter?" the man replies, perking up. "Sweetie, have you been writing?"

"Writing?" the woman squeaks from across the room. "What have you been writing?"

While the man sounded curious and interested, her mother's reaction is almost accusatory.

"It's nothing," Sylvie replies, pinching her forehead.

Suddenly, the story of how we met has been swept under the proverbial hand-spun rug because her parents are fully invested in the prospect of their daughter *writing*. I had no clue it was ever so significant.

"What do you mean it's nothing?" her mother replies, suddenly showing far more interest in her than the paintings. She walks over, but instead of sitting with the rest of us, she hovers over her daughter. "Have you been in contact with your professors? Perhaps they could give you a critique. What was the name of that professor at her school, Yuri? The one with the connection at the *New Yorker*?"

"Stop," Sylvie mutters, placing her face in her hands.

"She's just trying to help, sweetie," her father says to her, but it doesn't help.

Just then, Martha comes in with the tea, thankfully defusing the situation. Sylvie's mother finally sits in the seat across from her daughter, her nose poised in the air as Martha pours the tea.

"Thank you, Martha," my wife says with a smile. When the housekeeper leaves us, the conversation picks up right where it left off.

"Like your father said, Sylvie, I'm just trying to help. Getting a publisher's interest early is going to help you cut the competition down the line."

"I'm not publishing it," Sylvie replies obstinately. She stares down at her teacup as she stirs a cube of sugar into it.

"And why not?" Torrence replies with shock.

"Because I don't want to." Sylvie's tone is cutting and clipped.

The table clangs with the force of her mother slamming

her own spoon down at hearing Sylvie's response. My shoulders tighten up by my ears as I struggle to maintain my composure.

"Dear," Yuri says, holding a hand toward his wife.

"No," the woman argues. "She's doing this on purpose," she snaps at her daughter.

I clench my fists, and keep my response slow and calm. "I can assure you my wife is not doing anything to hurt you."

"No, but she does it to spite me."

Sylvie glares at her mother, a dead-faced expression covering her features. "How is me living my life and being happy to spite you?"

"Because you won't let me help you. It's as if you don't want to be successful."

"Is that really so important to you?" Sylvie argues.

"It's important to everyone, Sylvie."

My jaw clenches again. I glance sideways at my wife, watching the spark grow closer and closer to the end of the fuse.

I wonder if it's for me that she holds it back. Is it for my sake that she refuses to really let these people know how she feels about them? The Sylvie I know doesn't hold back. She lets her fire burn without care for who is in the path of her flame. But now…she's keeping it all in. And I don't like it.

When the room grows silent, it's Yuri who attempts to carry on a casual conversation. "What have you been writing, sweetie?"

Sylvie smacks down her cup. "Can we just drop it? Forget I said anything about the writing."

The man barely reacts to her outburst. But I notice the way her mother watches her. I can see the criticism perched on her lips, ready to take flight, and I stare at that woman, willing her to keep her ugly mouth shut and to think twice about saying anything critical of my wife.

Naturally, she doesn't heed my warning.

"You always were so volatile," she mutters. "Here we are, at your home to meet your new husband that you haven't told us anything about or introduced us to before today, and you really can't manage to have a decent conversation with us, can you, Sylvie? We didn't raise you like this."

"You didn't raise me at all," Sylvie snaps.

"Don't be ridiculous. You'll never truly know how much your father and I sacrificed for you."

"Did you sacrifice birthdays? Christmases? Did your mother ask *you* to pose naked for strangers when you were sixteen?" she shrieks in frustration.

My head snaps up to level an angry gaze at the two of them.

"That was for an art class, Sylvie. Please, be reasonable," the mouse of a man whines.

Sylvie ignores him. "And you didn't come here to visit me and my husband. You were *in the area* and stopped by. The reason you don't know anything about him is because you don't call me. You don't ask. You don't…care. You show up and talk about the fucking *rug* when you haven't spoken to your daughter in almost a year."

Her voice trails, and I hear the quaver in it that shatters my chest into splinters on the ground. I'm seconds away from throwing these two pieces of worthless flesh out of my house.

I stare at Sylvie's father, mentally begging him to do something. To stand up for his fucking daughter, but he doesn't. He stays silent.

For one second too long.

Sylvie sniffles through the silence as her mother stares contemplatively at her. Then, the woman shakes her head as she softly mutters, "Ever since the day you tore your own portrait to shreds, I knew you'd never be happy unless you were the center of our universe. Poor little Sylvie, always so desperate for everyone's attention. What an entitled little bitch you've turned out to be."

The small round wooden table between us suddenly flies across the room, taking the tea tray, pot, and cups with it. There's a scream of fear and a few curse words to be heard as I launch out of my chair and point an angry finger at the two sitting across from me.

"Get the *fuck* out of my house!" I bellow so loudly the art on the walls trembles from the noise.

"What on earth is wrong with you?" the woman shrieks.

"You," I shout, reaching forward to take her by the collar and yank her out of her chair. "You…are *not* welcome in our home anymore." With that, I drag her toward the door.

Somewhere behind me I hear the man nervously stutter, "Get your ha—hands off my wife."

As we reach the front door, I nearly throw the woman toward the exit. She stares at me with horror before glancing at her daughter.

"This is the kind of man you've married? Someone who resorts to violence and outbursts?"

"Why should we leave our daughter with you?" the man argues as he takes his place at his wife's side.

"Because *I* love her, you fucking twats. And I would *never* talk to her the way the pair of you do. And for your information," I add, pulling open the front door to find a deluge coming down outside. I put my finger in Sylvie's mother's face this time as I lean in. "Your child is *supposed* to be the center of your universe, you ungrateful, selfish bitch."

I toss them both into the rain. They're both so appalled by my reactions that it grates on my nerves. Has no one ever defended Sylvie around these two in her entire life? What sort of damage could a pair of incompetent, emotionally neglectful parents like these do to a person?

They're both gaping in shock on the front step of my house. Before shutting the door, I turn and see the red and gold pattern on the floor. In a fit of anger, I pick up the square rug and roll it quickly in my hands before hauling it toward the frail, frightened people standing just a few feet away.

"Here! Take the fucking rug." It lands with a thud on the ground in front of them, getting soaked by the rain. Then I slam the front door closed and force myself to steady my heavy breathing.

I hear the closing of a car door outside before I dare to leave that spot. When I make out the sound of gravel under their tires, I finally leave the front door in search of Sylvie.

To my surprise, she's no longer in the parlor or in the entryway. I nearly panic when I hear her footsteps upstairs in the library.

"Sylvie!" I shout, desperate for her reaction. I need to hear that she's okay.

A moment later, she's stomping angrily down the stairs, tears streaming down her face while wearing an expression of stubborn rage. In her arms, she's hoisting the typewriter down toward the front door.

"What are you doing?" I stammer before she clumsily tears open the door and storms through it. I watch with confusion as she sends the typewriter soaring into the rain. "Sylvie, stop!"

I grab at her arm, but she shakes it free. Running out into the rain, she stomps her boot into the typewriter over and over, sending shards of broken wood and keys flying. At one point, I just stop trying to save it. If this is what she needs, then I'll let her have it.

Finally, I walk over and take hold of her arm again. "Mo ghràidh," I whisper.

To my surprise, my wife turns toward me in anger. "Leave

me alone, Killian! You lied! You don't love me! You're not my husband. None of this is real!"

I grab her by the arms to stop her. "What are you talking about? Of course, I love you."

She struggles to shake free of my grip. "You do *now*, but the novelty will wear off. You'll get sick of me, or I'll ask too much, and then you'll get angry at me. Didn't you see the way they looked at me, Killian? How could you love someone who isn't loved by her own parents?"

My mind is reeling as I stare at her in this state. This isn't the Sylvie I know. Her eyes are wild and frantic and *scared.* I just want my wife back.

When she finally slips out of my grip from the rain on our skin, I watch in horror as she takes off in a sprint toward the trees lining the property and quickly disappears.

Chapter Thirty-Two

THE RAIN PELTS MY SKIN AS I TAKE OFF IN A SPRINT DOWN THE grassy field toward the trees. The sound of the rain muffles her footsteps, but I still see movement up ahead. With the sun setting now, the sky is growing dark, and I'm losing sight of my wife. But I won't panic. She can't go far before she'll hit the road or the river.

"Sylvie, please," I beg only a few feet behind her. "You're soaked, darling."

"Leave me alone, Killian," she shouts back as she continues marching away from our home.

"Where are you going?" I call.

"It doesn't matter."

"Yes, it does. Sylvie, please. Fuck them!"

When she doesn't respond, I pick up my speed. Only a few feet away from her, I'm finally able to get ahold of her. With a rough hand around her arm, I stop her from running any further away. Instead, I pin her against a tree, and I put my face in hers.

"Stop running from me, damn it!"

"Leave me alone, Killian!" she fights back.

"No!" I bellow close to her. "I'm your husband. I won't let you go. I will *always* be by your side. I will *always* care about you, you understand?"

Tears fall against her cheeks, blending with the drops of rain that continue to pour down on us. "You're not really—"

I quickly cut her off. "Don't you say that to me again, Sylvie Barclay. I don't care about some stupid fucking contract. I love you. With my whole fucking chest, I love you. So don't give me any of that shite about not being your real husband, because I'm right here. And I'll never fucking leave you, not like they did."

She collapses against the tree, hanging her head back as she sobs. "It hurts so much, Killian. I feel it all. I wish I could reach into my chest and tear out my heart. Sometimes, it feels like I might die of this pain, this…loneliness. I've been surrounded by people my whole life, but I always feel alone."

"You're not alone, Sylvie. Not anymore."

She sobs again. "I'm so angry all the time, Killian. And no matter what I do, no one cares."

"I care."

"I just want to scream," she cries.

"Then, scream, Sylvie. You can scream all you want at me, and I still won't leave you."

When nothing comes out, I shake her again. "So, no one else loves you. Big deal. But I'm here, mo ghràidh. And I am telling you that I will love you enough to make up for all of them. I will keep you, and you can trust me that no matter what you do, I won't let you go. Because you're *mine*, understand me?"

When her eyes finally meet mine, tear-soaked and red-rimmed, she surrenders. Throwing her arms around me, she latches herself onto my body, and I yank her off the ground, holding her against me as she cries.

For a while, she just rests in my arms, not caring that we're getting soaked by the rain. I just let her cry.

Eventually, she mumbles into my neck. "Killian…"

"Yes, darling."

"Let's go home."

With that, I lift her into my arms, cradled against my chest, and I carry her home.

———

Sylvie is shivering in my arms as we reach the house. Martha has the door open, waiting for us with a large towel. Sylvie doesn't have so much as a rain jacket on. Every inch of her is soaked to the bone, as am I, but I don't feel the chill. I just feel her trembling.

"I'll run a bath," Martha says as we enter the house.

"Thank you, Martha."

"Poor thing," she mumbles, brushing my wife's wet curls from her face. I'm not sure if she's referring to her wet and cold state or what she witnessed today in how her parents treated her.

Muddy boots and all, I rush upstairs with Sylvie in my arms. I don't care about a single rug or piece of furniture we're ruining as I carry her to our room and take her straight to the bathroom.

Martha is quick with the bath, setting out the towels and putting granules of something into the water that smells soothing. Then she scurries out, leaving me alone with my shivering wife.

I set Sylvie on the counter. Her lips are blue, and her eyes are rimmed red. Every muscle in her body is quivering, so I make quick work of removing her layers. Sweater, T-shirt, bra, trousers, underwear. The cold touch of her skin chills me to the bone, so I carry her to the bath in a rush, setting her in carefully.

Even when she's folded up and sitting in the hot water, she's still trembling. "Come in with me," she says through chattering teeth.

There's not an ounce of hesitation in my body as I tear off my clothes before stepping into the bathtub and facing my wife.

She climbs onto my lap, straddling my hips as she forms her body to me, her face in my neck.

"I've got you," I whisper into her hair.

Warm tears hit my shoulder, and I know she's crying again. "It's okay, Sylvie. Just cry, darling. I've got you."

It feels as if an hour goes by like that, with her tears streaming down my chest and shoulders. When all of her tears have dried up, we relax together in the bath. She's lying flat on top of me as I recline in the water. I finally feel warmed up, and her fingers are no longer like icicles, so she must be warmed up too.

When I can tell she is more stable, I feel comfortable to talk to her.

"What did she mean?" I whisper. "When your mother said you ripped up your portrait."

Sylvie lets out a heavy breath. "On my eighteenth birthday, they made a portrait of me. It was supposed to be a gift for me, and it won all of these awards, so they had this big party at one of the galleries to present it. The painting was even called *Our Greatest Achievement*."

"You didn't like it?" I ask.

Sylvie doesn't lift her face from my chest as she replies, "It was beautiful, but that fucking painting got a party, and I didn't. The day that was meant to celebrate me still somehow became about them, and I realized as I was sitting in the back of that room that I was just another creation of theirs. An imperfect creation. A mistake. I didn't win awards or get put on pedestals or celebrated. I was no one's masterpiece.

"So, that night, after everyone had left, I snuck back into my parents' studio, and I tore that painting to shreds. And they cried about it for days. My mother didn't speak to me for nearly a year. The thing that I had ruined was nothing more than some paint and some fabric and a rainbow of colors, but it would never be *me*. I think deep down, I just had to show them that. But they didn't get it."

I stroke her back, remembering that angry and lonely woman I found almost a year ago. I had no clue the pain she was hiding inside, just as she had no idea of mine. Our own torment blinds us from seeing the torment of others.

But now that I truly see my wife, I think I love her even more.

"You are a masterpiece, Sylvie," I whisper against her hair.

"I'm a mess."

"We're all a mess, but the trick is to find someone who thinks your mess is a masterpiece. Your parents might be blind fucking eejits, but I'm not. I know a masterpiece when I see it."

For the first time since before those monsters showed up today, I see my wife smile.

After a moment, she softly whispers, "I love you."

My heart starts to pound, and I have to force myself to breathe, but I try not to let it show. Instead, I stroke her back and let those three words wash over me.

"I love you too, Sylvie."

She squeezes her tiny body tighter against me, burrowing her face in the crook of my neck. I feel the warmth of her breath against my skin. I'll wait for the day when she can say those words to me while looking in my eyes. I can wait. For today, this is enough.

"I tried really hard not to," she murmurs, making me laugh. When she finally lifts up and looks at me, it feels like fire burning through my chest. "But you made it so hard."

"I'm sorry," I lie. Then she grabs my face and presses her lips to mine. Her soft tongue presses into my mouth, and I slide mine along the surface, feeling as if we are melting into one.

With each stroke of her tongue, my chest grows tighter, and my hands roam more around her body. My cock twitches between us as she starts grinding herself against me.

Suddenly, all I can think about are those three words being spoken between us and everything they represent.

"Killian," she murmurs against my mouth.

"Yes, mo ghràidh."

Pulling away, she holds my face as she stares into my eyes. "I'm ready."

Those two words escape her lips in a soft, breathy whisper, but the power they carry is far stronger than the way she uttered them.

"Ready for what?" I reply, although part of me already knows.

"Make me yours."

My cock aches at the realization of what she's asking. "Tell me exactly what you want," I add for clarity.

Her eyes moisten with intensity as she clings tighter to me. "Make it hurt. I trust you. I just need you to distract me from this pain. Help me let all of it out, Killian."

There's an ache in my chest to see her say those words to me. I don't want to hurt my wife, but God, I know it will be beautiful to see the way she takes that pain. My fierce, strong, incredible wife.

"Come with me," I say.

Clumsily, we climb out together, barely breaking contact and not bothering with the towels. As I hoist her naked body in my arms, she wraps her legs around my waist, and I carry her to our room.

Draping her on the bed, I take more care with her than I

usually do. I want to be a good husband for her and show her how gentle I can be while giving her exactly what she wants. That I will always keep her safe and protected.

"Do you trust me, mo ghràidh?"

Emphatically, she nods.

"Use your words, wife."

"Yes," she answers without hesitation.

Kneeling down, I trail my lips along the inside of her legs, kissing from her ankles to her knees and all the way to the apex of her thighs. She squirms restlessly, but I don't let myself get carried away.

Sitting upright, I let my fingers graze the skin of her knee. "Your safe word will be *red*, understand? If you want me to stop at any point, just say *red*, and I'll stop."

Breathing heavily, she nods. "I understand."

"That's my girl." Her expressions softens at the praise. "Now, get on your knees."

I can tell a part of Sylvie struggles with taking a command. It's not what she's used to. She's gone too long fighting alone in her life that she's never built up enough trust to allow anyone control over her, but this relief is what she needs.

To let someone else make her decisions. To let someone else carry her pain.

And I will be that for her. I will never let my wife feel alone ever again.

Obediently, she climbs from a lying position and kneels in front of me. Although I'm kneeling as well, I still tower over her, so when she gazes up at me, I pet her hair back from her face and plant a kiss on her forehead.

"Hands on the bedpost."

I watch her throat work as she swallows. Then she turns toward the head of the bed and places her hands on the wood. Climbing from the bed, I go to the bottom drawer of my dresser. There, I find the smooth paddle with a soft leather handle.

I catch her watching me as I pull it from the drawer.

"We're going to go easy tonight, Sylvie. You've been through a lot today, but you asked me to make it hurt, and I will."

I watch as goose bumps erupt along her back. She shivers in anticipation as I climb onto the bed behind her, stroking a hand softly along her bare back.

"I'm not going to strap you to the bed. But you won't let go of that headboard, understand me?"

"Yes," she murmurs.

"Grip it nice and tight, my love."

She shivers again.

Before I rear back the paddle and let it fly, I slide my hand over her ass. "Let me hear you say it one more time, Sylvie. Tell me you trust me."

Turning her attention back to me, she looks into my eyes as she says, "I trust you."

"Good. Now let me hear you scream."

The paddle lands with a deafening smack against her tender white flesh. She lets out a gasp, flying forward from the force of the hit. I watch as the blood rushes to the spot where the paddle landed, turning her right ass cheek a lovely shade of pink.

"One," I say before rubbing the spot.

Rearing back my hand, I let it fly again. This time, she lets out a yelp. Her knuckles have turned white where they're gripping the headboard.

"Two."

On the third hit, Sylvie cries out louder, and squeezes her face in anguish.

She's so strong. She won't even let me see her pain. Eventually she will.

Her expression doesn't change much through the fourth or fifth hit, but by the sixth, her sounds grow louder.

"Come on, baby. Let it out."

It feels as if I'm coaxing a wild animal from their nest. If she trusts me like she says she does, then she wouldn't be so afraid to let me hear her cry. But it's not really about me. It's about Sylvie protecting herself from others. Always keeping the most vulnerable parts of herself guarded.

The pride I feel when she lets out a wailing cry on the sixth smack of the paddle is visceral.

"That's my girl. Let it go, darling."

Her scream on the seventh brings tears to my eyes. It's not just that Sylvie is finally letting it all go; it's that she's letting *me* see it. Out of everyone in the world, I'm the one she lets in.

Her trembles turn into quakes as she pulls at the headboard through her agony.

"Say the word and I'll stop," I offer when she has to gasp through her sobs. Tears streak down her face, and I'm ready to hold her now. I want to bury myself inside her so that I become a part of her forever.

"No!" she wails. "Don't stop. I can take it."

On each following wallop, Sylvie sheds far more than I thought she could. It's as if I'm watching her come undone, letting herself *feel* and *express* far more than just pain. She's crying for the fear and loneliness and anger.

I hate that she's hurting, but seeing her work through this pain is the most beautiful thing I have ever seen.

"Two more, mo ghràidh," I say, rubbing at her backside. "You're almost there."

My cock is aching as it leaks from the tip, crying for how badly it needs her like this. Her howls and moans are making me feral, and I don't know how much longer I can wait.

Sylvie's cries turn sexy and carnal through the last two hits, and I wonder if she can feel this energy too. This is what I love about domination, feeling so close to someone that everything is aligned. Our needs. Our desires. It has always been my favorite part, but it was never like this.

Everything is different with her.

After the last smack of the paddle, I toss it on the bed and move behind Sylvie, dropping to my elbows so I can devour her from behind. Her voice turns high-pitched as I kiss and lick every inch of her.

I want her to know I cherish every inch. Every single part of her is mine to love and worship and devour. So I do. She lies on the bed in ecstasy as I kiss and lick every drop of water on her bare skin.

As I move to my knees again, nibbling and kissing my way up, I rest my aching cock on her backside. Then I pull her upright so she's resting against my chest. Gripping her chin, I turn her face toward me so I can stare into her eyes.

"I'm so proud of you," I say, pressing my lips to her jaw. "You did so well."

Her face is still tear-soaked as she smiles, absorbing the praise.

"But I need to fuck you now. I need to be inside you."

"Yes, please," she whines.

I take her mouth in a bruising kiss before I bury my hand in her hair and press her forward so she's gripping the headboard again. Aligning my aching cock with her wet core, I tug on her hips and impale her on my cock.

When she lets out a breathless cry, I moan loudly along with her. Her ass presses backward as I fuck her, finding the spot inside her that makes her scream with every thrust.

"That's it," I grunt. "Show me how good that feels."

"Yes," she replies with a whimper. "Don't stop, Killian."

"Tell me you love me again, mo ghràidh."

"I love you," she says, her stunning soft curls draped across her back as she hangs her head in ecstasy.

"Say it again," I grunt, fucking her with more force, still careful not to hurt her.

"I love you," she screams this time.

Unable to keep it in any longer, I tear Sylvie away from the headboard and roll her onto her back so I can pound her into the mattress with my thrusts. Hooking a leg under my arm, I stay right on that spot she loves, watching her expression for a sign that she's close.

"Come for me, darling," I mutter, fighting the urge to lose it myself. "Come for your husband."

"I'm almost...there," she shrieks, her voice tight and high-pitched.

Reaching between us, I press my thumb to her clit and help her ride out her climax when it hits. Her hips jerk, and her grip tightens, so I keep up my thrusts. She goes breathless, but I don't let her stop.

"One more time, Sylvie. Say it."

"I love you," she breathes, this time gazing into my eyes. It's as if she's yanking me over the edge with her, making me feel the same earth-shattering pressure she was feeling. My cock shudders and shoots inside her, filling her up more than I expected in what feels like a never-ending orgasm.

We rock together, riding out the rest of it in sync. When my body is spent, and my heart has stopped hammering, I slowly rise and look down at her. Brushing her hair out of her face, I kiss her softly again. Our kisses are unhurried now and familiar. As normal as breathing.

"Aren't you going to say it?" she whispers.

"I don't need to say it, mo ghràidh. You should just know."

"Well, I want to hear it anyway," she argues with a twist of her nose.

Caging in her face with my arms around her on the bed, I press my lips to hers as I whisper, "I love you, you stubborn little woman."

She smiles softly up at me as she runs her fingers through my hair.

"How are you feeling now?" I ask in a gentle tone.

"I feel good. And tired."

She looks exhausted, but after the night she's had, I'm not surprised. "I want you to drink some water before you fall asleep, understand?"

Naturally, she rolls her eyes. "Are you going to be bossy now?"

"When it comes to taking care of you, you bet your arse I am."

Tears glisten in her eyes, and neither of us say anything for a moment. "Thank you, Killian."

"I'm your husband. You don't have to thank me."

Very carefully, I rise from between her legs. Resting on my heels, I watch as my seed slowly leaks from its home, so with a smile and a wink in her direction, I very gently push it back in.

PART FIVE

Sylvie

Chapter Thirty-Three

"KILLIAN," I SHOUT DOWN THE LONG HALLWAY. "ARE YOU ready yet?"

"I'm comin', woman. Would you calm down?" he replies huskily as he stomps down the stairs.

"The car's ready," I say, urging him as I give him an impatient expression.

I know I shouldn't rush him. This is a big deal for him, but the thing with Killian is that if he doesn't make it a big deal, then I can't make it a big deal. So, I have to act as if this little trip to the coast is nothing out of the ordinary and a simple road trip.

It's anything but.

I know that. He knows that.

It took me weeks to talk him into this plan, and while I've been slowly easing him out of the house here and there, I know he's ready for a weekend away from the manor. It's the middle of summer now. The weather is beautiful, and I desperately need some coastline sunshine in my life.

I'm trying not to think about how there are only two more

months until the end of this contract. And since I can no longer deny that my feelings for my husband are real, I have to face the truth. He's going to lose this house.

Regardless of what happens to us when that happens, I have to protect him. Which means I need to make sure he's ready and able to leave it. I'll figure the *us* part out later.

For now, I need to get this man out of this house. And I'm running out of time to do it.

As he takes my hand in the entryway, I watch the way he swallows and hides his nerves from me.

"Ready?" I ask softly.

His eyes meet mine as he winks. "Ready."

Hand in hand, we walk out to the car parked by the front door. The house staff helps us off, and Killian drives. But I watch his face as we leave the property line, and I watch it again as we leave the county line.

He seems at ease, far more than I expected. His hands are a little tight around the steering wheel, and the muscles of his jaw keep clicking, but overall, he seems fine. There's a lazy smile on his face, his eyes hidden by his sunglasses as we travel down the long busy highways. I look over the passenger seat at my fake husband in those dark jeans and tight white T-shirt and realize just how used to him I've become.

If he truly opened himself up to it, he could get used to a regular life outside that house with me. We could go anywhere we want. Any city. Any country. That dream I had of taking my ten million and running off someplace where I owe nothing to no one could be a dream with Killian. That could be *our* dream.

I just need to make him understand he has so much more life outside of those walls. He reaches across the seat and puts an arm over my shoulder. Leaning toward him, I rest on the center console and place a kiss on his left cheek.

"Next time, I'll take you to a warmer beach. You can't go swimming in these waters. You'll freeze your cute little nipples off," he says as he reaches across and pinches the tip of my breast.

I let out a shriek as I jump backward. "I don't care about that. I'm just excited to get out of the house for a while."

His fingers squeeze tighter around the steering wheel, but I brush it off as nothing.

It's only a short drive to the house we've rented for the next two nights. It's a bed and breakfast that typically rents out at least six rooms, but Killian's reserved them all for a bit of privacy. As we pull up to the old house, I smile at the quaint and stunning sight of it on this desolate coastline.

I jump out of the car and walk immediately toward the endless dark sand glistening in the sun. The wind is strong, blowing my hair wildly in the breeze, but as I stand just on the edge where the dunes meet the drive, I breathe in the fresh air.

It smells like freedom.

"I'll get us checked in. Don't go far," he whispers, kissing me softly on the cheek.

"Okay," I reply, watching him go up the three short steps to the front door of the house.

It's been two months since we first spoke those harrowing words. The ones I tried so hard to deny and ignore. That day with my parents still replays in my mind over and over. It wasn't just that he protected me or defended me. It was the fact that Killian carved out a space for me where there hadn't been one before. Until him, I didn't know what that felt like—to be a priority in someone's life.

That night changed me in ways I don't think he fully understands. It was about so much more than the submission or the paddle. It was the way he let me be me, without expectation or criticism. He took the ugliest parts of me and loved them right along with the beautiful ones. He let me scream and cry and held me afterward like I was the most important person in his life.

I *am* the most important person in his life.

And meanwhile I've been denying how much I cared for him. Why? Because of some stupid contract? Or ten million dollars?

Yes, the past two months have been heavy with anxiety thinking about that looming deadline. And yes, I know I will have to come clean with him eventually about my part in the whole thing. But I have a plan, and that plan involves getting my husband *out of that house*.

If I can do that, I can save everything. Him, us, our future.

He just has to learn to let it go.

"All checked in," he says, landing a strike on my ass and making me jump. Then he slings an arm over my shoulder. Seeing him in such a chipper, relaxed mood settles me too.

So, with a smile, I turn toward him. "Hungry?"

"Fuckin' starvin'," he grumbles, rubbing his stomach.

We take a walk together just down the road from the house toward the center of town, where the owners promised us one of the best pubs in Scotland. We sit across from each other at an old table near the window, and each order two ales and two orders of stovies and talk like regular people.

For the first time in our long and twisted relationship, we are just two regular people. A couple of newlyweds on a honeymoon. He even reaches across the table and twirls my wedding band around my finger while he finishes his beer. It's a bit of a nervous habit for him, and I've caught him doing it before with his own ring.

I don't think he's acting *too* much more nervous than regular. He's always a little fidgety.

"What do you want to do now?" I ask.

"Go back to that big ol' house and shag like animals," he suggests while holding his beer to his lips.

"Before that," I reply with a lazy, half-drunk smile.

"Go walk on the beach, I suppose."

"Okay," I say, nodding as I grab his fingers.

The wind has died down a bit as we take a stroll along the water. It's surprisingly blue and clear, but as he promised, it's ice cold. Still, it's beautiful to be out.

"Didn't you ever go on vacation with your family as a kid?" I ask as we walk.

He shrugs. "Of course. We spent summers in Greece and Italy when I was a kid."

"Didn't you like it?" I ask.

"Not as much as being home," he replies, and I chew on the inside of my lip, uneasy with that answer.

I've never pried much into what happened to Killian's parents or why it seemed to have hit him so hard. I don't want to open up old wounds for him, but I can't help but feel as if that wound didn't heal properly. How do you fix what's broken without breaking it further?

Instead, I squeeze his hand and offer him a hint of a smile. His hair has grown out again. Not as long as it was at Christmas, but past his ears again. It's time for another cut, but I also enjoy the many variations of Killian.

In truth, I did fall recklessly in love with him. The hate I once felt never went away—it just changed. The passion is a different color now.

But loving someone is terrifying, and this feeling is nothing like it was with Aaron. If I let Killian get hurt, I'll never forgive myself. As hard as I'm trying to make things right, I feel this looming darkness up ahead reminding me that my bottom line is his best interest, and that's never happened to me before. I've only ever looked out for myself, but now, I have him.

But having him and keeping him safe aren't necessarily the same thing.

"For a woman at the beach with her incredibly handsome husband, you look awfully depressed."

He knocks on my shoulder, and I force a smile.

"I'd be less depressed if you jumped in that water," I tease back.

"With you?" he replies, grinning mischievously.

I yank my hand away. "Oh, absolutely not with me."

"We're married, darling. We do everything together. Come here. Let's go swimming."

I take off in a sprint away from him with a shriek, but I don't make it far before he scoops me up from around my waist. I'm screaming and laughing as he carries me toward the rising tide.

"Killian, stop it!" I shout hysterically.

But I know my husband better than I know anyone, and this man doesn't back down from a challenge. I've brought this one on myself.

The next thing I know, the waves are rushing toward us, soaking us from our knees down in frigid water. But he doesn't stop. He keeps on marching.

I'm caught in a fit of laughter as I cling to his body to climb out of the water. Due to his height, he's getting far wetter than I am.

"You brute!" I scream as another wave crashes into us, soaking us to the bone.

"Just think how fun it will be to get warmed up after this!" he replies with a laugh. His smile is wide and warm and genuine, and it doesn't even matter how cold the water is or how uncomfortable these wet shoes are now. That smile is worth everything.

Chapter Thirty-Four

KILLIAN IS STILL SPRAWLED OUT NAKED ON THE BED WHEN I come out of the shower.

"Ready for round two?" he remarks with a wink.

Keeping my towel around my waist, I climb onto the high bed and curl up beside him. "You'll be the death of me."

"I don't have to be rough this time," he says, gently petting my hip. Then he starts to crawl down my body, shimmying between my legs. "I can be very, very gentle."

With a smile, I run my fingers through his hair. But instead of going where I thought this would lead, he pauses and rests his chin on my lower belly. "Do you want kids someday?"

My eyes nearly pop out of my head. "Kids?"

He chuckles, making his chin bounce on my groin. "I keep forgetting how much younger you are."

"Young or not, it's a little early to start talking about kids. We're still *fake* married, remember?"

He growls at me for saying that, but at this point, I just say it to piss him off.

"We're *legally* married. And I'm not saying we should have them right *now*," he argues. "I'm just asking if you want them."

"Do you?" I run my nails through his hair again, softly scratching his scalp.

He shrugs. "I picture your belly growing big with my child, and it just does something to me. I never thought like that before."

I can't help the way that makes me feel too. My stomach actually warms as if it can feel it too. My own little piece of Killian growing inside. Creating someone that is truly *ours*. Forming our own family that makes up for all of the shit our own have done to us. We would be so much better than them.

"Is that smile a yes?" he asks, looking so hopeful it crushes me.

How could I take anything away from him, especially something that is so perfect and wonderful?

"Yeah...someday," I reply.

"I can already imagine them scampering around the manor, playing out in the garden, and going with us for rides around the grounds."

And just like that, the good feeling spoils and dies. He still thinks he gets to keep the house after our year.

"Or..." I say, testing the subject. "We could buy our own new house somewhere different. Someplace that's all ours."

His head slants. "The house is ours," he argues. "It will be ours and then our children's. I want it to be their home the same way it was mine. Do you not like it at Barclay?"

I swallow the rising dread. "Of course I do," I reply quickly to cover up the gaping wound this conversation is creating.

"Good, then we'll need to make lots of babies to fill it," he replies, peeling apart my towel to place a kiss just below my belly button. I let out a squeal as I wrap my legs around him.

"I didn't say anything about *lots*," I whine, but he's already trailing kisses down to my clit, quieting my mind and replacing my thoughts of worry with the sensation of pleasure.

———————

I wake in the middle of the night to the sound of groans. On the other side of the bed, Killian sounds as if he's having a nightmare. This is the first time it's happened, so I carefully turn toward him and rest a hand on his shoulder, hoping to ease him out of the dream.

His skin is soaked with sweat and covered in goose bumps, so I cover him with the blanket, hoping that will help.

Within a few minutes, the groaning stops, and he falls back to sleep.

So I wrap my small arms around his waist and try to hold him tight enough to keep it from happening again. It takes me a bit longer to nod back off. Worry follows me into my dreams.

When I wake up again, it's still dark. But the other side of the bed is empty.

I sit up in a panic, looking through the darkness of the unfamiliar room for him. Then I hear thrashing downstairs.

In a rush, I dive out of the bed and snatch a robe off the hook, wrapping it around me as I scurry down the stairs. "Killian?" I call for him.

When I reach the main floor of the house, I hear heavy breathing from the dining room, and I burst through the doors to find the chairs all tipped over and a bottle of whisky resting unopened on the carpet.

It takes my eyes a moment to adjust before I spot Killian sitting on the floor with his back to the wall, much like that first night ten months ago.

Please, don't let there be any blood this time.

I rush to his side, placing my hands on his shoulders to find him clammy and cold. His head is in his hands, and he's breathing like he can't take in enough air.

He's having a panic attack.

My voice shakes with fear as I call his name. "Killian, breathe. It's okay. I'm right here."

"I can't," he gasps. "I can't do this."

"It's okay," I repeat. Again and again, I stroke his back and tell him it's okay, and I don't know if it's enough.

"I can't, Sylv—I can't...do this," he stutters. Struggling with his words, he suddenly snaps, shoving the table hard until it flips on its side. His arms are shaking so bad as he buries his face in his hands again and wheezes through his tears.

"It's okay," I whisper, afraid to upset him again. This fear is paralyzing. What am I going to do if I can't get him to calm down?

"I'm going to call an ambulance," I cry, about to run for my phone.

He nearly screams. "No! No...no, no, no." His head shakes emphatically, and I kneel closer to his side.

"Okay," I say, trying to calm his fears. "I just need you to be okay, Killian, so please breathe."

"I'm trying," he replies, but this time, his voice cracks into a sob, and he starts to really lose it.

In my head, I just know that if Killian loses it, then I'm lost. He holds us together. He's our strength, our force, the thing that keeps us together. Without him, I have nothing.

I hold his face in my hands, tears spilling over my lashes as I press my forehead to his. "We can do this," I cry. "I just need you to breathe."

He tries to suck in air, but his breaths are too shallow and don't pull in anything. It's all just short gasps and choppy inhalations.

"Hold on to me, Killian. Please hold on to me. I've got you, okay? Just breathe."

His grip is weak and trembling as he attempts to hold tight to my arm. And for the next thirty minutes, we struggle for each breath. Each inhale is a chore, and I keep second-guessing myself, afraid that I've royally fucked up by not calling an ambulance, but he refused even to let me leave his side.

The only thing I have to offer is my comfort, and it's not enough. He struggles in pain, and it tears me apart to watch.

By the time I see the sunrise start to bleed into the sky out the window, he is finally through it.

He's practically deadweight, collapsed on top of me as if he doesn't have the energy even to raise a hand to my face.

"Let's get back to bed," I whisper when I feel certain the worst of it is past us.

He nods with exhaustion and lets me pull him off the floor. We stumble together up the stairs, and when we reach the room, I wipe his face clean with a warm rag and kiss his eyes as he finally drifts off to sleep.

But I don't go to sleep. I sit next to him and replay over and over and over what a terrible wife and person I am. I've dragged him out here before he was ready just because I wanted to believe he could do it. I wanted to believe that he was capable of something, and for that, I could have seriously hurt him.

I *did* hurt him.

I can't stop crying as I rest my face on my knees and stare at him, realizing just how much I love him. The thought of putting him through that again guts me to my core. Right now, the only thing I want to do is take him home and curl up with him in *our* bed.

But I know deep down what this means.

First, it means that Killian needs help far beyond a weekend away and a wife who can love the pain out of him.

Second, it means that my dream of creating a life with Killian, safe from that awful contract, no longer exists.

I cannot and will not take that house from him. Not until he's healed and ready to do that himself.

While Killian sleeps, I hatch my plan. And I worry about him, about us, and about me if this somehow doesn't work. Because now that I've come here and flipped my whole life around, I no longer care to know what my life could be like without him. I don't want that.

I want him. I want this life that I borrowed.

After picking up the mess in the dining room, I come back upstairs to find Killian lying in bed with his eyes open. I stop in the doorway and stare at him, waiting to see how he's feeling.

"I want to go home," he mutters lowly without looking at me.

"Of course," I reply, my lip quivering as I try to hide the fact that I'm barely holding it together.

Carefully, I cross the room and climb into the bed to face him. When my head hits the pillow, his eyes meet mine. The restraint I was carrying until this moment is gone.

My face crumples, and my tears fall. "I'm so sorry," I sob.

He reaches for me, dragging me against his body as he tries to quiet my cries. "Stop, Sylvie. You don't need to apologize. I just wasn't ready."

"I knew you weren't ready," I cry. "I knew it, and I tried to push you anyway. I thought you could handle it."

"Shhh…" he whispers with his lips in my hair. "You had no idea, mo ghràidh."

"Have you ever had that before?" I whisper, carefully wiping my tears as I pull away to stare into his eyes.

I see the movement of his Adam's apple as he swallows the heavy weight of emotion in his throat. "After my parents died, yes."

"I'm sorry," I whisper again.

He touches my cheek, but his face doesn't have the same animation it had yesterday. It's dull and tired, and I cry again at the memory of his smile on the beach.

"It's okay."

It's not okay, I think to myself. None of this is okay. Nothing his family is doing or what I've done is okay, but he's toughing it out. He's surviving the only way he knows how.

I just wish I could help him more, but I can't if I don't understand.

So very gently, I brush back the hair in his face. "What happened…to bring them on?"

He looks uncomfortable as he swallows again. "My parents were always really hard on me. My father was a very strict man, and he had so many expectations for me and the kind of man I was supposed to be. I always did as I was told, and I always made him proud."

"That sounds like a lot of pressure," I whisper, touching his hand.

He nods. "On the night of the car wreck, I was leaving the house to pick up Anna from my aunt's house. My parents had been out at a party. It was dark, and the roads were slick. I remember seeing their headlights and briefly wondering if that was them. They swerved toward me so fast there was nothing I could do. We collided, and they both died on impact."

I let out a gasp, gripping his arm tighter as tears pour over my lashes. "Oh my *God*, Killian."

"I found them. I didn't have a phone on me. I had to wait with them, with a concussion, until a car drove down that long empty road and found us."

I squeeze my eyes closed and let the sobs rack through me.

"That wasn't your fault. You have to know that," I reply through my cries. "Please, Killian. Tell me you know that."

His eyes are wet with dark circles around them. He looks so tired and in pain. But he does eventually nod. "I know it's not. It was an accident. My father had a lot of alcohol in his system, and the swerve marks were still on the road, but it didn't stop my family from treating me differently. As if I could have saved them. As if I wouldn't have given my own life just to see that night end any other way."

I squeeze him tighter. "Don't say that. They died, and that was terrible, but it wasn't your fault, Killian. And you didn't deserve to live your entire life with that sort of pain."

Then, his eyes focus on my face for a moment. "I thought for a while I was really getting over it. I thought I could finally move on. Having you has helped, Sylvie."

"We can get you even more help," I reply, nestling closer. "Whatever you need, we can do this together."

With one more brave swallow and nod of his head, he pulls me into his arms.

For a while, I convince myself this could work.

Deep down, I know that nothing else matters. Not really. Not the contract or the money or even the house. Eventually, everything around us will cease to exist, and while I've spent my entire life numbing the pain of being agonizingly unloved, as I hold Killian in my arms now, I realize something more profound.

The world outside this room is cosmic and too massive to comprehend.

But the world that exists between him and me is more so. The love we share is infinite.

Chapter Thirty-Five

I'VE NEVER BEEN TO ANNA'S HOME BEFORE, BUT TODAY I'M NOT going for a tour and a chat. I'm not even coming to bargain. I bang on the front door of her quaint house near town. Her heels click against the floor before she opens it and stares at me in shock on her doorstep.

I'm sure she's surprised to see me because I'm coming uninvited, but also because Killian and I are still supposed to be on our trip by the sea.

"Sylvie," she stammers. "Is Killian all right?"

I push past her, barging into her home and marching right into the sitting room at the back of the house. Much like her first visit to my apartment, I come with some astounding news for her.

"Call it off," I bark as I slam my bag down on the table.

"Call what off?" she asks, scurrying in behind me.

"The contract, Anna. That stupid fucking contract." My blood is already boiling, and I know the further we get into the conversation, the hotter I'll get.

"I don't understand…"

I slam my hand down again. "You are *killing* him!"

She puts up her hands in surrender, and I can tell by the look of fear on her face that if I fly off the handle again, I'll never get my point across. Now is not the time to be angry. Now is the time to be clear.

Taking a deep breath, I close my eyes and refocus. "Anna, you cannot take that house away from Killian. You think you're helping him, but you're not. His issues run deep, and forcing him out of that house could kill him."

"Did something happen?" There's a tremble in her voice and fear in her eyes.

"Yes, something happened. He had a fucking panic attack on the floor of that B and B in the middle of the night. It looked like he tried to drink the anxiety away but didn't make it in time. Anna, he's *not well*. And that fucking aunt of yours..."

I clench my hands into fists and try to ease my temper again. "I know what happened to your parents, Anna, and I think that awful woman is trying to punish Killian for it. And I refuse to let her get that house from him. I *refuse*."

Anna blinks, and a tear slips down her pale cheek. She quickly grabs a tissue off the table and wipes it away. Then she sits on the chair and places her face in her hands. She's struggling to maintain her composure, but at this point, I want to see her lose it. She should be screaming and crying the same way I am.

But I think this poor motherless girl fell into the wrong hands and did everything she did with the best of intentions. "But the contract is already in place, and the trust says..."

"Fuck the trust!"

"We can't, Sylvie," she argues. "The trust states that after one year of marriage, you will inherit the house and hold enough power to transfer the deed to my aunt, which *you* swore to do in that contract. And that contract is airtight," she says.

I drop into the seat across from her. "So, what if I break the contract? I just won't sign the house to her."

"Then, *you'll* owe her the ten million."

"I don't have ten million dollars!" I shriek.

"Then you should be careful what you sign," she replies coldly.

I squeeze my eyes shut and try to breathe.

After a moment, she adds in a sniffly whimper. "I don't want to hurt my brother."

Opening my eyes, I stare at her imploringly. "Then, don't let your aunt take it from him. Beg her. Do whatever you have to. Blackmail her. Threaten her."

"It won't matter," she argues. "What's done is done."

"Ugh!" I stand up in a huff and cross the room, feeling like a rat in a cage. That same rage that burned through me that night when I ripped the painting flows through me now. I want to lash out at her, at her aunt, at *everyone*.

And this isn't even my family. This isn't my home.

When I reach the window, I take a long, deep breath. And I realize what I have to do.

"So, the only way for Killian to keep his house at this point is if the marriage fails."

She sniffs, and I see her in my periphery as she looks up toward me. "Yes, technically."

"And I wouldn't be indebted to her for anything?"

Anna shakes her head. "No, but…"

Her voice trails, and I feel the needles of emotion starting to form in my throat.

"He would need to sign the divorce papers, and you know he wouldn't do that, Sylvie."

"I know he wouldn't," I reply as my eyes fill with moisture.

"So, what are you going to do?"

"What are my choices?" I ask, turning toward her and shutting down the faintest sign of weakness.

Her pale brows wrinkle as she contemplates it for a moment. "Technically, if you leave the country for more than thirty days."

"We don't have time for that," I argue. "I'd have to leave *now*. I can't just disappear on him."

"Then…you'd have to cheat on him."

I drop into the chair and let the realization wash over me. There really is no way out of this that won't end in catastrophe. I can't cheat on Killian. I *won't*. I won't even lie about it. It would devastate him.

"I'll explain it to him," I say, my voice tight with the threat of tears. "I'll tell him everything and explain that we *have* to divorce before the year is up. Then we'll be fine. He can keep his house, and we can stay together."

She nods through her tears, but I can see the uncertainty on her face. It matches mine. I'm sure deep down, she's scared of what this means for her family. To disobey her aunt. To have lied to her brother. To know that nothing can be achieved peacefully. Not really.

"He really had a panic attack?" she whispers.

I nod. "Yes, and he tried to hide it from me. Said he used to have them a lot, which explains why he never leaves."

I watch as she winces in pain, maybe from remembering what those panic attacks look like. I'm sure she's been telling herself whatever lie she needs to get through the guilt of what their parents' death did to her brother. He has put on the facade of someone being *fine* for nearly two decades. But rather than taking care of anything, they let those wounds fester instead of heal, only making it worse by throwing shame, guilt, and isolation on top of it all.

I may never understand this family, but I don't have to. I just need to make this right for him.

"Maybe I should tell him," she says, but I cut her off.

"We can tell him together."

"When?"

I take a deep breath and work through the dates in my head. The sooner, the better. It's nearly August, which means we have only a month left.

"Let's give him a week to recover from the trip. Then we'll talk to him."

She nods. "Okay."

With nothing left to say, I stand up from the chair and cross the room toward to where I dropped my purse. Just as I make my way toward the door, Anna calls, "Sylvie."

I turn toward her.

"You've been really good for him. And I had hoped you'd be enough to get him to leave the house on his own."

"He needs more than me," I reply. "He needs you too."

Her lips tremble as she nods. "You really do love him, don't you?"

Choked with emotion, I nod.

Then, to my surprise, her mouth lifts in a crooked smirk. "Then, you'll figure this out. I know you will. I have a feeling you always get what you want."

Not always, I think to myself. If I had gotten what I wanted, I never would have come here. I never would have needed ten million dollars, and I would have never married a stranger for it.

But I'm here now, and I fully intend to get what I want this time.

———

"Stop the car," I say as Peter delivers me back home. We're

halfway down the drive toward the house when I see Killian walking through the trees in the same direction.

As the car comes to a stop, I call back, "Thank you," before shutting the door and jogging over to where my husband is quietly strolling.

"I'm not disturbing you, am I?"

He greets me with a smile as he puts out his arm and welcomes me into his embrace, holding me tight to his enormous chest.

"I found a Q," he says, and I pull back to stare at him quizzically.

Then, he holds up a tiny round button with the letter *Q* in the middle. "Is that from the typewriter?" I ask.

He chuckles and then nods. As I gaze up at his face, I can still make out the sunken, tired features of his eyes and the lifelessness of his smile. The panic attack was almost twenty-four hours ago. Is it normal to still look so tired?

People don't just bounce back that quickly, Sylvie.

"What is that doing all the way out here?" I ask, taking the letter and inspecting it.

"The rain washes everything out," he says, glancing toward the river. His gaze grows unfocused as he stares into the distance. I clutch his arm and try to squeeze him tighter.

How on earth could they possibly do this to him? It's not fair. It's *cruel*.

But I'm going to make it right. I just have to keep telling myself that.

"I'm sorry our trip was ruined," he mumbles softly without looking into my eyes.

I grab his face and force his eyes down to me. "I don't care about the trip. I care about *you*."

"It's not right to keep you locked up in this house with me."

My stomach sinks as my eyebrows pinch inward. "Don't say that," I argue. "I'm not locked up. And I love it here. You know that."

"For how long, Sylvie? How long can you really stay like this? You're a lot younger than me. You have your whole life ahead of you."

"Killian, stop!" I snap, wrapping my hands around his neck and pulling him closer. "Please stop talking like that. We're going to get through this together. We'll get you the help you need, and I will be there every step of the way. So stop talking like that."

As his eyes bore into mine, I search for the same fire I saw in the man I first met. So much life, vigor, and personality. Have I ruined that? Have I put out that light?

I don't know what else to do, so I press my lips to his, hoping it will reignite the spark we had before. Before that stupid fucking trip. Before I royally fucked it all up.

On top of that attack, he's now dealing with the guilt of bringing me down with him. I can't stand it, so I try my best to make him believe that's not true.

He kisses me back, but it's weak and missing something.

"Come on," I whisper, pulling him toward the house. "Let's go inside."

I hold tight to his hand for the rest of the walk, but neither of us speaks. When we reach the house, I pull him all the way to the bedroom. I know I shouldn't, but I can't help myself. I'm desperate for him, for all the parts of him that make up the whole of this person I love. He's shattering into a million tiny pieces, and I don't know how to hold him together anymore. So I figure if we keep doing the same things we once did, he'll be himself again. And we'll be us.

I let him undress me, and then I undress him, and when I lie in our bed, using his body like my security blanket, I imagine this is what he wants too. His grip on my body is so tight, and his grunts are so loud, and I hold him the same way I did last night. I give him every part of myself he might need to make himself better, and I pray it's enough. My pleasure, my voice, my body.

When he finishes, he trembles inside me with his lips latched onto my shoulder, biting me just enough to make it hurt. Then, he kisses it better, trailing his lips to my ear, where he softly whispers, "Mo ghràidh."

And I fool myself into believing this is a step in the right direction. But then he pulls out of me and rolls to his side of the bed. I'm left there lying alone, feeling the drip of his seed between my legs, and he does nothing to stop it.

Chapter Thirty-Six

WHEN I WAKE UP THE NEXT MORNING, HIS SIDE OF THE BED IS empty again. Just like last time, I sit up in a panic.

"Killian!" I shout as I burst out of our bed and bolt toward the door. It's morning, and the sky is bright, but as I run from the room, I barely even notice that something is amiss in our room. In nothing but a pair of panties and one of his shirts, I scramble down the stairs, desperate to hear his voice.

Instead, I hear Anna's. And my heart drops.

My footsteps hurry down the rest of the stairs, but when I hit the landing, I nearly trip over the two large suitcases sitting at the bottom. *My* suitcases.

"What the…?"

Dread swarms like bees in my belly as I walk slowly into the parlor. When my eyes find Anna sitting on the chair, tears streaking her face, I know exactly what's happened.

"Anna, no…" I whisper at the sight of her.

"I'm sorry, Sylvie. The guilt was eating me alive. I had to tell him."

"Everything?" I whisper. And when she nods, it's like a punch to the gut.

Then I hear his familiar stomping. Turning, I spot my husband coming toward me, but his eyes don't meet mine. "Killian," I say, pleading as he brushes past me.

"By now, you've realized I know everything," he mutters darkly. There's a slur to his voice, and my heart shatters at the sound.

"Don't do this," I beg.

"I have to," he replies.

"No, you don't," I argue. "We can work this out together."

"I won't lose my house. You have to leave," he murmurs, reaching for his drink on the bar. I sprint toward him, grabbing the glass from his hand.

"Stop it!" I scream before flinging it across the room.

Anna screams and covers her head from the shards of broken glass. Then, I look into his eyes and point my finger as I shoot my accusations.

"Stop it, Killian. Yes, it's true that my part of the plan was to have your house taken away from you, but I'm not going to let that happen now. And you can't be mad at me for that. We barely knew each other then."

"But what about now?" he bellows.

"I was just at her house yesterday, Killian," I shout, pointing to his sister. "You know I was doing everything in my power to fix this!"

"I know you were doing everything in your power to get your money."

"You nasty brute," I snarl in his face. "You know that's not true. You *know* how much I love you. You think I wanted this?" I cry. He turns away from me, marching from the room in anger. "You think I wanted to fall in love with you?" I continue.

"You think I wanted to fall in love with *you*?" he replies in frustration. "It's better this way, Sylvie. Sign the papers, go back to America, let me keep my house, and I don't have to worry about keeping you locked up in this old place for the rest of your life."

"That's what this is about, then. You think you're sparing me from your sadness. In sickness and in health, remember?"

He ignores me, refusing to look me in the eyes as I watch the pain hit him again.

I wish I could hit him with this rage that's rolling through my veins. I hate what he's saying. I hate it all. He's taking away my choice. Where is the part where I get to decide to stay? To be with him forever? Where can I choose us?

He grabs my bags, and I quickly tear them from his grip. "Killian, stop it! I'm not leaving. We can figure out another way."

Shaking his head, he still refuses to look into my eyes. "This solves everything, Sylvie. If you truly want me to keep my house, then walk away."

"Don't ask me to do that," I cry.

"You were going to go anyway, weren't you? So, just go."

A tear rolls over my cheek. "What happened to being your *real* wife? Is this really so easy for you? To just write it all off like it never happened so that you can have your fucking house?"

Finally, for the first time, he looks into my eyes. And the sadness I see in them makes it hard to breathe. "What do you want me to do, Sylvie? Everyone I love is trying to hurt me. Nothing I do is ever right, and even if I did keep you, I'd only drag you down with me. And I refuse to do that. So, I think it's best you just go."

"You don't mean that," I reply tearfully.

He leans forward, and my palms itch to reach for him. "It's the first time in my life I've ever been truly sure."

With that, he turns away and storms out the front door, leaving me to fall apart alone.

———

None of this feels real. I pack the rest of my clothes. I gather my things. I wait for him to walk back through that door, but he never does.

How can I seriously consider this? Just leaving like nothing happened?

But I have to. Because if I don't, then he will suffer.

So, with shaking hands, I do it all. Even in the library, I gather everything I've left up here. But when I spot the novel I typed on the old typewriter still sitting on the table, I leave it. I hope he finds it. I meant what I told my parents—I will never publish that story, and I don't want to.

It was for him anyway. The main character was never me; it was him.

I set the story where the typewriter used to be, and I walk out of the room.

Peter said we have to leave for the airport in an hour, but I'm all packed, and I can't stand to keep walking around this quiet house, emptying it of pieces of me. When I reach Killian's room, I crawl into the bed and hug the pillows, sobbing into them and praying he changes his mind.

When I hear his footsteps on the stairs, I perk my head up and watch for him. He enters the doorway, and I see the red spots on his face and the puffy bags under his eyes. Where does he go to cry when he's alone? The thought nearly slices me open.

"Please don't do this," I beg him one more time.

"I've set you up with an account to help take care of you until you can get back on your feet. It's not ten million, but it should help."

I squeeze my eyes closed as more tears leak through my lashes. "I don't want anything from you, Killian. Truly, I don't."

"I know," he mumbles quietly. "But this is the right thing to do, Sylvie."

"I know," I whimper.

"You should publish that novel," he says, stepping closer. "It's good. And don't go near your parents. They're not good for you. Maybe start fresh."

"I can't," I sob. "Killian, I can't."

He crosses the room, not daring to get too close to where I'm curled up in his bed. "Yes, you can. You can do anything, Sylvie. You once broke into this house. You moved across the world to marry a complete stranger. You turned my entire world upside down, mo ghràidh. You can do just about anything."

I'm soaking his pillow with my tears as my body shudders through the sobs until my bones are sore and my muscles ache. "Are you sure you're going to be okay?" I whimper.

He swallows, clenches his jaw, and nods. "I promise."

Part of me wants to ask if I can contact him. If I can come back after the thirty days is up, and the contract is voided. I need to take some sort of promise with me so that I'll have a line back to Barclay Manor, but deep down, I know he won't give that to me. That's the point. We're supposed to do this on our own.

No matter how much it hurts to think about it.

There's a honk in the distance, and I squeeze my eyes shut again. Maybe if I just lie in this bed, they won't make me leave. They'll have to carry me out if they want me to go.

"Come on, Sylvie. We can do this."

When I finally peel myself off the bed and stand in front of him, I drink in my last look. The last moment when I will see him as my husband. The last time I will see him as his wife.

After I've had my fill, I move toward the door. But first, he scoops me into his arms and holds me tight against him. Even as I wrap my hands around him, I feel half gone.

"I'm gonna miss you, my wee little wife," he whispers in my hair.

"Please take care of yourself, you brute," I reply.

But when I finally tear myself away, I don't look back. I can't. If I look into his eyes again, I'll never leave. And right now, he desperately needs me to.

Chapter Thirty-Seven

KILLIAN AND I GOT MARRIED LAST YEAR ON SEPTEMBER 18. The divorce papers showed up just shy of one year later, on the twelfth. They were hand delivered by a notary who had to watch me sign them while I sobbed into the sleeve of my sweater.

And just like that, it was over.

I found a furnished short-term rental in Manhattan, but I spend every night tossing and turning because I forgot how loud it is here. I miss the quiet of the country, the creaks of that old house, and the sound of his footsteps when he would come in from the fields.

I miss his voice, the deep, rasping texture of it when he'd growl into my ear. I miss the feel of his enormous hands in mine. The safety, the comfort, the familiarity.

Almost immediately after leaving Barclay Manor, the loneliness crept in. I've typed so many messages to him just to delete them later. If this is what missing someone feels like, I wish I had never fallen in love with him at all.

Killian wasn't just my husband for a brief, strange period.

He was the first person I ever truly cared about. The first person who loved me for me. The first person it hurt to say goodbye to.

Walking down the streets in New York, I try to imagine that it was all just a dream, but then I swear I hear him call my name in the distance or the buzz of a bee, and I'm transported right back to where it all started.

If I could tell him anything right now, I'd tell him that I'm trying. I moved some of my things out of storage. I've started working on a new novel. I even made a friend in my building who tells me way too much information every time we strike up a conversation, but he makes me laugh, and someday, I imagine I might tell him about the bougie swinger parties I used to go to with my fake husband in Scotland.

But not yet. Maybe someday I will.

For now, I try to get through each sunrise and each sunset. I bring my laptop to the coffee shop and I watch the people walk by while trying to piece together some sort of story that sounds half as fascinating as ours.

I imagine he's over my shoulder reading it like he did that day. In my imagination, the couples always start as enemies, more at war with themselves than each other. But then they eventually realize that the only people willing to fight with them are the ones who care about them.

Or at least that's how this new one is going.

"Sylvie?"

I glance up from my laptop at the sound of a familiar voice. It takes my eyes a moment to recognize the woman glaring at me from a seat near me. Her hair is much shorter, in a pixie cut, and the scowl she often wore when I saw her has relaxed into a soft frown.

"Enid?" I question, trying to remember the last time I spoke to my parents' right-hand woman.

"I thought you lived in Scotland with your mean husband," she says in a bitter tone.

In the past, I might have reacted in anger, but now I only laugh. "No, not anymore."

"Oh," she replies, swallowing her discomfort. "I'm sorry about that."

I shrug. "Thanks."

"Do your parents know you're back?"

My spine stiffens. Rather than have a conversation with this woman from the next table, I decide to join her at hers. For a woman I *still* despise, this feels like a very mature step for me.

"No," I reply. "Please, don't tell them."

She scoffs. "Oh, I don't work for them anymore."

My jaw drops. "What?"

"They fired me back in July."

I knit my brow as I recount the last time I saw them. They never said anything about firing Enid, and she's been with them for years.

"Artists," she says with an eye roll. "So temperamental."

"Did it have to do with me?" I ask, which immediately makes me feel like an idiot. Of course, it doesn't. Nothing in my parents' life ever has to do with me.

"Yes," she says plainly. Staring right into my eyes, she says, "I told them what a self-serving, entitled, talentless brat you are."

We stare at each other before a chuckle bubbles from my lips, spilling out into a full laugh. Tears fill my eyes, and I can't seem to stop myself.

She doesn't laugh with me, but she doesn't look as mean and miserable as she usually does either. Who knows, maybe Enid got laid this year and it made her loosen up a little.

When my laughter finally dies down, I wipe my tears and let out a heavy sigh.

"I thought you'd like to hear that," she says softly.

"I did. It's probably the most they're ever going to stick up for me, but it's nice."

She nods. "You're probably right. Just remember, it's not you. It's them."

"Oh, you're on my side now?" I reply with a laugh.

She shrugs. "They don't sign my paychecks anymore. And I started to feel as if they never really *saw* me anyway."

"I know how that feels," I reply, staring down at the coffee cup in my hands. "Well, thank you for telling me that."

"You're welcome."

I'm about to stand up to return to my table when she asks, "Is it true your husband threw a *rug* at them?"

This time, we both break out into laughter just before I tell her the whole story.

———

Most nights, I don't sleep much. I've been home now for over a month and a half, and I still blame jet lag for the reason I'm wide awake at 3 a.m. Part of me wonders if it's because I know somewhere he's awake too. When he's active, I can't rest. We are that in tune now.

With time, I'm sure it will wear off, but so far I can't get through a single night without crying myself to sleep.

On this particular night, I wake up at three in the morning with a new text message. I bolt upright as I stare at the screen.

Killian: I like the ending.

The sight of his name makes my chest seize up, and my cheeks grow hot. Just four words, and I feel whole again.

It takes me a moment before I realize he is referring to my story.

I quickly type out my reply.

Me: Thank you.
Killian: You should publish it.
Me: I wrote it for you.
Killian: I love it.
Me: I'm glad.

We're silent for a moment, both of us probably unsure where to go from here. What do we say to each other now? My fingers are aching to type out *I miss you. I love you. Please let me come home.*

But he responds first.

Killian: How are you?
Me: I can't sleep.
Me: How are you?
Killian: I'm trying.

My chest aches, and I choke down a sob. Deep down, I keep asking myself this one burning question. If Killian thinks he's sparing me from a life spent in that house, what is left to motivate him to get out? Won't he just fall back into his own ways? Why can't I help him?

Killian: I need to hear your voice.

I dial his number so fast my fingers hurt. As the call rings, I chew on the inside of my lip, waiting to hear his voice.

"What time is it there?" he asks in a growly whisper.

My skin erupts in goose bumps at the sound. His voice seeps into my pores like warm honey.

"Three thirty," I reply.

"It's half past eight here."

"You're up early."

"Couldn't sleep," he mutters.

"Me neither."

"Do you feel different?" he asks. "Being home."

"What do you mean?"

He clears his throat. "I mean, do you feel like you belong there?"

I shake my head. "No. I don't know where I belong."

I belong with you, I want to say, but I hold myself back. Putting too much pressure on him isn't what I want to do either. I can still see the gaunt look in his eyes that day after the beach. I can't do that to him again. I can't be as bad as the others.

If letting Killian Barclay go is what I have to do for his own good, I'll do it.

"Do you feel different? Now that I'm gone."

He clears his throat. "The house feels smaller. I don't like how quiet it is without your footsteps in the hall."

I swallow the pain climbing up my throat. *Don't push, Sylvie.*

"How did your aunt react?" I ask.

He lets out a breath of laughter. "She lost her mind, but Anna spoke to her. The house is mine, and she can't take it away."

"Good," I reply, and I mean it. Nothing pleases me more than hearing him say that. "It's all over, then," I add. The contract, the marriage, the whole thing.

"Aye," he replies. "It's over."

"What will you do now?" I ask.

He doesn't reply, and I hear the struggle in his heavy breath. I'm waiting, hoping, praying that he'll say something that might possibly involve me.

"I need more time, mo ghràidh. And I can't ask that from you."

I blow out a silent, quivering breath as I stare down at my bed, letting a tear fall directly from my eyes to the pillow. "I'll give you whatever you need, Killian. If you tell me you need my help, I'll help you. If you tell me to wait, I'll wait. That was the vow we took, remember? It might be over, but I still believe in those words we swore. I'll do whatever you need because that's what wives do."

He lets out an exhale that sounds hopeful.

"Oh, darling," he replies. "Sylvie, I don't want you to wait."

My heart shatters. I didn't know heartbreak could hurt so much, but it's true. It's agony.

I physically bow over in my bed from the pain, holding in a silent cry as he devastates me with his words.

"I need to do this on my own, love," he continues. "And I'm afraid it might take forever. So, if you want to make me a vow, then promise me that you won't put your life on hold for me. You're not coming back to Barclay Manor, and we are not married. Tell me you understand."

The phone line is silent as I cry into my pillow.

"Please, Sylvie. I need to hear you say it."

He must hear the wet sounds of my next inhale because he makes a sympathetic sound.

"I'm sorry," he whispers.

After a moment, I work up the courage to give him what he wants. "I understand. I won't wait for you, but I will be here to help you. No matter what, I will always want to help you."

"That's good enough then," he replies softly. "Then, right now, I want you to get some sleep."

"I don't want to hang up," I cry.

"Then, keep the phone on your pillow. I'll be here until you fall asleep."

Wiping my tears, I do as he said. I lie on the bed, resting my phone face up on the pillow. Staring at his name on the screen, I let the sound of his breath on the other line lull me off to sleep.

It's the first restful sleep I've had in weeks, and the entire time, I dream of gentle bees and typewriter keys scattered in the grass.

Chapter Thirty-Eight

Dear Sylvie,

Today marks two months since you left. And I've been seein' this therapist now for over a month. She suggested I write a letter to everyone who I need to express something to. And although she said I don't need to really send them, I decided that I wanted to send yours.

There are some things I need to say to you.

When you showed up at my house, I was stuck. I spent nearly two decades of my life lost and grieving, but then you came along. You were stubborn and rude, but you weren't afraid to tell me what I needed to hear. Out of everyone, you were the only person who could pull me out.

I'm sorry that you had to spend a year with me when I was at my worst, but I think we were both a mess. And I want you to know that I'm not angry about the lies you told in that arrangement. I think part of me knew the entire time that the real plan was to take my house from me.

Maybe deep down that's what I wanted.

But then I fell in love with you and everything I wanted changed. I wanted you to stay. I wanted to be happy for you. I wanted a normal life.

But we were never a normal couple. Or a real couple.

The love was real though, wasn't it?

I'm sorry this letter is such a bloody mess. Clearly, you're the writer.

What I really want to say is that I'm sorry we didn't have a chance to be real. But that day you left, I knew you were different than the woman who showed up in my house the year before. You changed, Sylvie. I think somewhere in our marriage, you forgave yourself for not being perfect and loved yourself anyway.

Maybe you just needed to watch someone fall in love with you to see it.

I'm glad it was me.

Thank you for the best year of my life. I hope when you get married for real, your real husband won't be afraid to fight with you because you are never more beautiful than when you stick up for yourself. Don't lose that.

Your brute,
Killian

KILLIAN'S LETTER IS FOLDED UP IN MY PURSE. I RECEIVED IT A couple of months ago, and since then, I've heard nothing. I've gotten comfortable with the silence, like learning to live with a nagging pain that won't go away.

He told me not to wait, and I'm not. I even downloaded a dating app recently, although I didn't swipe right on anyone, or even upload my photo. But I figure it's a baby step.

I'm doing exactly what he asked of me. And yet, I still miss him so much it hurts.

I'm not holding on to hope that Killian and I will ever get back together. I'm not.

But I'm also not ready to walk away from that year of my life like it didn't mean anything. Enid says I'm just dating myself now, and I think she's right. I am my own rebound.

So when my phone rings in the coffee shop as I'm typing on my laptop, and I see his name on the screen, I freeze.

It's been so long since I heard his voice. At the prospect of hearing it again, I nearly fumble my cell phone out of my grip as I struggle to hit the Answer button.

"Hello?" I stammer.

"Sylvie," he responds. There's a hint of panic in his tone. I jump from my seat and rush out the front door so I don't have to carry out this conversation in a quiet room with strangers.

"What's wrong?" I ask as fear courses its way down my spine.

"I just need you to talk to me," he says through the phone line.

"I'm here," I answer without hesitation. "Where are you? What's going on?"

"I'm going for a drive."

To anyone else, those words would be simple enough, but for Killian, they have me pausing in my tracks. "Where are you driving?"

"Just into town. Not far. My therapist suggested I do this."

"And you're alone?" I ask.

"Aye."

It dawns on me in this moment that he's doing something difficult, and he needs me. He's asking me for help, and the feeling sends a bolt of excitement through my body.

I know he needs me to stay calm, so I let out a relaxed sigh. "What would you like to talk about?" I ask casually.

"I don't know. Anything. I just need your voice."

He lets out a deep breath through the phone as I pause on the sidewalk, listening for the sound of his car starting.

"I'm here," I say. "It's just a small drive, right? You've got this."

"I'm fine," he tells himself.

"Exactly," I reassure him. "You're perfectly safe."

"I know I'm safe," he argues. "I'm sitting on the bloody drive in front of the house. Are *you* safe?"

A chuckle bubbles out of my chest. "I'm standing in front of a coffee shop in broad daylight. I'm fine."

"Keep telling me that," he grumbles, and I bite my lip with a smile. "It helps me for some reason."

"I'm freezing my ass off, but I'm still fine," I say through the phone line.

I hear the crunch of tires on gravel. "Do you need a better coat?" he asks, his voice tense.

"No," I reply. "It's January in New York. It's fucking cold."

"It's cold here too," he replies.

"How far are you going?" I ask.

"To town and back."

"You can do that," I said. "You did it before, remember? That night you picked me up in the city."

He chuckles. "I was so bloody mad at you."

I laugh in return. "I know you were."

He's quiet for a moment before he responds. "I wish you were in the car with me now."

I let out a sigh. "Me too."

Don't start hoping, Sylvie. Don't get your heart broken again.

I mean, who am I kidding? If he asked me to be there, I'd be on that plane in a heartbeat. But that's not what he needs right now. He needs to do this part on his own. He needs to hear my voice and know that I'm here, but also know that he can do it without me.

"Talk to me," he says in a grumbling tone.

God, I've missed that.

"Um…I'm publishing my book," I say.

"Good," he replies immediately.

"Well, not publishing it, exactly. More like…just printing it. For myself."

"Can I have one too?" he asks, and I bite my bottom lip as a smile stretches across my face.

"Of course."

"Do you have a new boyfriend?" The question catches me off guard. I freeze in my spot as my mouth falls open. Is this really what he wants to talk about while he's trying to calm down?

"God, no," I spit back.

"Why not?" he asks.

"Because the only man who's spoken to me since I got home was a guy at the coffee shop who tried to hit on me by offering me advice on writing my novel."

"You told him to fuck off, I hope."

"I told him I wasn't interested," I reply with a smile.

"I miss the days when you threw your coffees at men like him," he replies.

Still chewing my lip, I pace around the space in front of the coffee shop. The wind is starting to pick up, and my nose is like an icicle, but I'm not going inside. It's easier to focus on him out here. As if being outside brings me closer to him.

"How's the drive going?" I ask.

"Good. Your voice helps. Keep talking."

I let out a sigh. "Why don't you try it without my voice for a while? Just keep me on the line. You know what to do if your attacks come back."

My eyes sting as I wait for him to respond.

Finally, he mumbles, "Just because I can do it without you doesn't mean I want to."

A tight smile stretches across my face as my eyes fill with moisture. "It only matters to me that you're doing it."

"I'm doing it."

For the rest of the drive, he goes in silence. I go back into the coffee shop, and I stare out the window as I listen to his breathing on the other end of the line.

With every drive and every trip and every day that passes, I know he's finding peace inside that he hasn't had in far too long. Even if I never make it back to Scotland or to Barclay Manor or to him, at least I can rest knowing he's found that.

On a warm day in late March, I'm walking back to my apartment when I spot a package on the front steps, and I nearly sprint down the street when I see it lying there. Just a simple brown cardboard package that doesn't look very exciting, but I know exactly what is inside.

Squealing as I pick it up, I do a little hopping dance outside the front door before I unlock the door and run inside with excitement. I quickly pull out my phone, dialing Killian's number, and putting it on speakerphone before setting it on the table.

He picks up immediately.

"Hello?"

"It came!" I shriek, making him laugh.

"For fuck's sake, woman. My eardrums are bleeding. What came?"

"My book! I had it printed and it just showed up."

"Oh, Sylvie," he responds softly. "That's incredible. I'm so bloody proud of you."

Killian and I have hardly spoken since he called me two months ago, asking for me to talk to him while he drove. Since then, I've tried my hardest to not pick up the phone or reach out. But these brief conversations feel like getting to know him for the first time.

Ironically, I think I'm even more in love with him now, and I can't even say it.

"I'm opening it." Grabbing the box cutter off the counter, I quickly slice open the package.

"Careful not to cut too deep. You'll slice the pages."

"I'm careful," I argue.

As the box slides open, I freeze. Ever so slowly, I pull out the paperback book from within. As I lay it in my hands, feeling the weight of all the words inside, tears begin to spring to my eyes.

"It's perfect," I whisper.

"Describe it for me."

"The cover is simple and beautiful. It's green, and the title is in gold. Simple cursive letters."

"And your name is on it?"

With a smile, I trace my name across the bottom: *Sylvie Devereaux.*

"Yes."

"That's your book, mo ghràidh. You wrote that."

A tear slips over my cheek as I flip through the pages, remembering the exact place in the library where I was sitting when I wrote it. It feels as if I'm being transported back in time to my favorite place in the entire world.

Technically, this copy I'm holding is the only one in existence. And, other than the one I promised Killian, it will remain the only one. He begged me to publish it, but I had to make him understand that I never intended to do that. Writing was my passion, but it was never the thing I wanted to squeeze dry. I didn't want to treat my passion the same way my parents treated me. I would just love it and cherish it and celebrate it for exactly what it is.

Holding it to my chest, I do exactly that.

"Feels good, doesn't it?" he mumbles into the phone.

"So good."

"I'm really fucking proud of you, Sylvie."

My eyes squeeze shut as I breathe in those words, letting them fill all the tiny crevices inside me where I need them.

When I hear someone shouting in the background, followed by the honk of a horn in the distance, my eyes open.

"Where are you?" I ask.

"London," he groans.

My blood runs cold. I've missed so much. Why is he in London? Who is he with? But I don't pry. It's not my business. He told me not to wait, so I'm not.

After a few minutes, he fills the silence anyway.

"Anna and I are just here on a short weekend holiday. It was her idea. After our last talk, I've been doing more drives. More outings. And now, this is my first trip away from home."

Pride swells inside me.

"That's amazing, Killian. I'm proud of you," I reply.

"I was grumpy, but your call made me feel better. Thinking about you holding that book makes me feel better. Sign my copy before you send it."

"I'm not signing anything," I reply haughtily.

"Yes, you are, you stubborn brat. You wrote that book in my home. I want a copy, and I want you to sign it. Then I'm going to put it in my library, and someday, a hundred years from now, a stubborn American girl will break in just to see the great masterpiece of Sylvie Devereaux."

"And get conned into marrying a giant Scottish grump," I add, making him laugh.

"Yeah, that's how the story goes."

I drop into a kitchen chair, fixating on the book on the table. Deep down, I fight the urge to admit to Killian that missing him and being so far from him is harder than I think I can handle. I want to tell him that I still love him, and no matter how many times he tells me not to wait, I will. I can't help it. I'll love him until the day I die.

"Sylvie…" he whispers.

"Yes?" I feel as if he's about to say something big. Tugging my bottom lip between my teeth, I wait, praying it's going to be something I want to hear.

"You're still waiting for me, aren't you?"

I swallow, frozen as I stare straight ahead. I could lie. I could tell him that I've moved on and maybe that would be better for him in the end, but I can't bring myself to do it.

"I will always wait for you."

"I—"

I wince at the sound of Anna's voice in the background, interrupting him. The miles between us feel so vast at moments like these.

"I have to go," he replies. "And Sylvie?"

"Yeah?" I reply softly.

"I'm really proud of you for writing that book."

"Thank you," I mumble just as the phone line goes dead.

Chapter Thirty-Nine

KILLIAN MADE SURE I DON'T NEED TO MAKE ENDS MEET FINAN-cially, but I still have a shit ton of boredom to stave off and time to kill. So, for fun, I sometimes help Enid out with her new gallery. I dragged my feet about it for the longest time because I couldn't stand to even be around art, but she finally wore me down and talked me into helping, to at least get out of the house.

Besides, Enid's place isn't anything like my parents' gallery. It has a younger, fresher vibe. Fewer pretentious ass-sniffers and more expressive realism from modern artists. She actually sells a lot of reprints at prices real people can afford, making it all so much more accessible, and I like that. It's something my parents never bothered to do.

On the weekends, I come in and help answer phones or do other menial stuff she doesn't care for anymore. And as much as Enid drives me nuts with her uptight attitude and crass sarcasm, she's started dating a woman named Nikki from England, who I adore. So most days, it's just me and Nikki sitting up front, making conversation and cracking jokes while Enid does all the work in the back.

By this point, Enid and Nikki know everything about Killian—then and now. They find our story both bizarre and romantic, and I can't say I disagree.

"We still talk from time to time," I say as I unpack a box of paper bags and tuck them under the cash register.

"You're not thinking of seeing other people, are you?" Nikki asks.

"Fuck no," I reply. "If anything, I'm just going to board a plane and march right up to his doorstep and say *enough*."

"Why don't you?" she asks. "Go over there and whip your tits out. That'll do the trick."

With a sad smile, I let out a sigh. "Because he needs me to be supportive, and I am. I do support him and everything he's doing. It's incredible, but…" My eyes trail downward, and I clench my jaw.

"You miss him."

Solemnly, I nod.

"You can't wait forever, Sylvie. At some point, you're gonna have to move on."

Despondently, I nod. "I know."

The door chimes as someone comes in, and Nikki greets them casually. "Welcome in."

My eyes lift to the door, expecting it to be another customer, but I'm struck silent when I see the person standing there, staring at me in surprise.

"Mom?" I mutter as I stand up.

"Sylvie?" she says at the same time. "What are you doing here? I didn't know you were back from Scotland."

I close my mouth and square my shoulders. I won't fall silent like I did the last time I saw her. "I've been back since August."

"August?"

Immediately, I recognize how my mother puts me on

the defensive, whipping questions around on me. So before answering her, I turn toward Nikki. "Handle this customer, please. I'll be in the back."

"Ummm…" Nikki stammers, but I don't wait for her response.

"Goodbye, Mom. Enjoy the gallery." I spin on my feet and march toward the back of the room.

"Sylvie, wait!" my mother calls.

"I don't have to talk to you," I reply. "In fact, I *choose not to*."

She follows me past the front desk and around the corner to the back of the building. "Sylvie, please. Just wait. Give me a second."

"No," I argue. My blood pressure is rising with every moment. I've been preparing myself for this instance and I just keep repeating the same thing to myself over and over again. *Don't engage. Don't engage. Don't engage.*

"Can't I at least apologize?" she cries.

Out of the corner of my eye, I see Enid standing frozen near the service entrance, but I brush right past her.

"No," I call back to my mother.

Even when I reach the alleyway, I just keep on walking. I have no clue where I'm going, but I can't turn back. I can't get into a conversation with my mother.

"Sylvie, I'm begging you."

I hear the sadness in her voice, but it only makes me angrier. Stopping in my tracks, I spin toward my mother and point a finger in her face. "No! You don't get to be sad now. Not when every conversation we've ever had has made me feel like complete shit."

Tears fill her eyes as she reaches for me, but I quickly wave her off. "No! I'm not engaging. I have to protect *my* peace, which means I can't talk to you."

"Okay, then don't talk!" she shouts. "Just listen."

I let out a frustrated scream because *listening* to her is even worse. It's the last thing I want to do. But now I'm out of places to run. I've hit a fence line, blocking me in.

So I freeze at the end of the alley and let her catch up. I'm waiting for the inevitable, *You don't try hard enough, Sylvie.* Or *I'm just trying to help you, Sylvie.*

What comes out of her mouth is nothing close to what I expect.

"Your father and I were terrible parents!" she shouts. "We are still terrible parents. I wish I knew how to even try to fix it, Sylvie, but I don't. You didn't deserve us, and if I could go back in time and give you to people who would have raised you better, I would."

I shake my head, keeping my back to her as I try to force my brain to block out the hurtful things she's said to me. But even I know that's impossible.

I don't respond as she continues. "There was never anything wrong with you, Sylvie. I'm sorry if I ever made you feel that way, and I'm sure it's too late for apologies now, but I have to try at least. And we might have been terrible fucking parents, but look at you!"

"What about me?" I shout, turning around to find my mother with tears streaming down her face, her hair windblown and sweat-soaked. She's a mess.

"You turned out to be the most resilient, insightful, brilliant person I've ever met."

A wrinkle forms between my eyes as I scrutinize her. What is she getting at? What is the catch? Where is the *but* of that statement?

She just raises her hands and lets them fall at her sides. "That's it. That's all I want to say—just that I'm sorry. And...I'm proud of you."

Still panting from the chase, she lets her shoulders slump with a look of defeat on her face. Then, she turns away from me and walks back toward the gallery.

I let her go without another word. At the moment, I don't quite know what to say. I'm not ready for hugging it out and handing out forgiveness, but I do feel a sense of relief wash over me. It's like I don't feel the same heavy cloud weighing over me anymore. That whole your-parents-hate-you-and-you're-a-disappointment fog has started to clear.

Still standing in the alleyway with an expression of disbelief on my face, I pull out my phone and dial Killian's number. It rings and rings and rings, going to voicemail. And I realize that's to be expected now, especially now that he's probably doing things like going to rugby matches with his friends and spending hours away from the house. And that is *great*, but it's hard not to feel a little disappointed too.

It's like he's moving in the right direction, but that direction is away from me.

———

When I get back to the gallery, I have to tell Nikki and Enid everything about the bizarre interaction with my mom.

Enid is shocked, and Nikki is a slut for good gossip and drama, so she eats the entire story up, wanting all the juicy details. When Enid realizes Nikki doesn't know the full story about how they came to our house in Scotland and the way Killian escorted them out, she has to tell that part of the story herself.

We're all laughing together when I feel my phone buzz in my back pocket. A sense of relief washes over me as I assume it's Killian. Pulling it out, my face falls when I see that it's not him.

It's his sister.

Quickly, I swipe open the call and step away to give Anna my full attention. Immediately, I hear her panic.

"Sylvie!" she shrieks in tears. "He needs you, Sylvie. You have to come *now*."

My eyes widen with fear as something cold and heavy lands in the pit of my stomach. "Anna, where is he? What happened?"

Already I'm moving. I don't even say a word to the girls as I burst out the front door, walking toward my apartment. I'm just a few blocks from my place.

"He's gone," she wails into the phone.

"What do you mean he's gone?"

"He's *not here*!" Her voice is frantic and screaming. "My aunt called me this morning to tell me that Killian had just dropped off the deed for the house to her, and then he was gone. No explanation. No warning. I'm scared, Sylvie. What if he's gone somewhere to hurt himself? What if we drove him to do it? He was doing so well."

My hands are shaking now with fear, and I know she's being hysterical. I know Killian would never do that. Don't I?

I haven't seen him face-to-face in months. What if he's lied to me? He's made me believe he was fine before.

And he didn't answer my call today.

"I'm coming, Anna," I say because it's the only thing I can manage at the moment. I'm sprinting now, just a few blocks from my street. I'll pack my bag in less than five minutes and be at the airport within an hour. I could be in Scotland by morning, and we will find him. He has to be all right.

"Please, Sylvie. You're the only person I knew to call. He talks about you so much still, so I knew you would help us. He needs you."

"I'm coming," I say again. Nothing could stop me. I've never moved with so much purpose in my entire life. I've never felt something so true and real. There are no doubts or questions. If my husband needs me, I will be there—every single time.

"Anna, I'm almost home. Let me try to call him again. I'll let you know when I get a flight at the airport."

"Please hurry," she sobs.

"I'm hurrying." With that, I hang up the phone.

I have to cross one more intersection before I'm on my street. The light takes forever to turn, and all the while, I'm running through possibilities in my head. Maybe he's on a bender with his friends somewhere, drunk out of his mind. Or he met someone and stayed at her place. Or he decided to leave us all behind and took off like a thief in the night.

Or the very real possibility…he had an attack somewhere, and I wasn't there to help ground him. And he got hurt or worse.

Finally, the light turns, and we cross. I sprint to the next street, making the last turn as his phone's voicemail picks up again.

"Damn it!" I snap as I shove my phone back into my pocket. Then, I look up from the street and stop dead in my tracks.

My chest is heaving for air, and I'm staring down the long street with my building halfway down. There, on *my* stoop, is a large dark-haired man sitting on the steps as if he were waiting for me. I continue walking toward the apartment, not wanting to let my heart get away with my head.

But the closer he comes into focus, the more hope I allow myself to feel.

Then he sees me coming. In one quick movement, he stands, and I gasp as goose bumps cover my skin. My heart might as well fall out of my chest and down to the cement. My hand covers my mouth as I walk toward him.

I'm begging my mind not to play tricks on me. I need to know it's him before I let myself believe it. And when he smiles, that same smile I saw on the beach, I break out in a full sprint. My shoes click against the pavement as my legs carry me the rest of the way, anticipating the moment when I have my arms around him again.

And when I finally get there, I launch myself against him so hard I nearly knock him off his feet.

Chapter Forty

KILLIAN'S BODY IS LARGE AND WARM IN MY ARMS, AND HEARING his breath in my ear feels like home. My arms are clutched tight around his neck as his huge arms engulf me, pinning me in place against him.

He's here. He's in my arms.

Questions are swirling in my mind, but I brush every single one of them aside because he is *here*.

"Hello, darling," he whispers into my neck.

"What are you doing here?" I reply.

After a moment, he finally sets me down, but I refuse to let him go. My hands stay glued to him.

"I came as fast as I could," he replies, brushing a wild curl from my face.

"I don't understand. Your sister said you gave the papers for the house to your aunt. Why?"

"Sylvie, you traveled across the world for me, and I kept you secluded in that house for nine long months. I knew that if I was going to make things right, then it was my turn to come to you.

"And when you told me last month that you were waiting for me, I knew what I had to do."

My face stretches into a smile as I take in the sight of his face again. Warm green eyes, chin-length brown hair, strong brows, and full lips. It's him, and he's standing on the street in front of my apartment in New York City. None of this makes any sense in my brain, but I love it all the same.

"So this is what you were working for," I say as everything suddenly clicks into place. Rather than bringing me back to Scotland, he wanted to come to me. He just had to wait until he was ready.

"Thank you for waiting," he says, lowering his forehead to touch mine.

My eyes close, and my heart swells. Reaching for his hands, I grip them in mine, sliding my small fingers between his thick ones. And I never want to move from this spot.

But then my phone rings in my back pocket again.

"Oh shit, Anna," I say, quickly grabbing it and seeing her name on the screen. When I slide the call to answer, I can hear her panic again.

"Sylvie?" she cries.

"Anna, he's here."

She falls silent. "What?"

"He's standing right in front of me," I say, staring into his soft, content eyes.

"He's *what*?"

I let out a chuckle.

"In New York?" she shrieks.

"Yes, in New York. And he's okay."

"I'm going to kill him," she replies as I bite my lip to stifle my laugh.

"Tell her I was just trying to be spontaneous," he says, but when she hears him say that, she only launches into a fit of curses.

"He said he's sorry," I tell her. "And that he'll call you later."

She's still going on as I hit the End Call button, and the phone goes silent. Killian pulls me back into his arms, and I suddenly feel very desperate to have more of him. I want *all* of him.

But I don't want to be too eager. I still don't quite know what state he's in and how much he's struggling. He's hidden it well from me before, and if I push him too hard again, I'll never forgive myself.

"Want to come inside?" I ask.

I notice the tension in his jaw as he nods and picks up his bag from the sidewalk. A slight crease in his brow has me concerned as I gently pull him up to the front door, unlocking it before welcoming him inside.

He looks ginormous in my apartment, which isn't small by any means. But I'm used to seeing him in a house with thirty-foot ceilings on sixty acres.

He drops his bag by the door and follows me into the kitchen, admiring my apartment and all the personal touches I've added over the months.

"Are you hungry?" I ask as I reach the kitchen counter, placing my back against it and suddenly feeling oddly uncomfortable. We've never had to do this before. Killian and I have always collided like two stars. We never had to do this awkward dance of defining exactly what we are. Are we just friends? Or are we still the same couple we were before?

He doesn't sit at the table like I expect him to. Instead, he stands in the middle of the room, staring at me keenly with his hands stuffed into his back pockets.

"No," he replies flatly.

"Thirsty?" I ask, swallowing as my mouth goes dry.

He shakes his head.

My body is buzzing, and I think if I don't get to touch

him soon, I might actually explode. But I *need* to know he's all right first.

"What do you need?" I ask cautiously. "Whatever it is…"

He hesitates for a moment, standing there looking almost nervous as his gaze rakes over my body. My eyes stayed glued on his, wishing I could tell him with just my eyes that he can have everything. He doesn't even need to ask. I am all his, and everything I own is his. In my heart, he is still my husband.

I'm not sure if that's what I conveyed in one single look, but suddenly he's crossing the room toward me, and in two long strides, I'm in his arms again. Pinning my body between the counter and his tall frame, he holds my face in his hands as he stares down at me.

"What I need?" he growls.

Without another word, he crashes his mouth against mine. Our lips tangle and slide in unison, licking and nibbling on each other until we're practically fused. His kiss feels like crawling back into my own bed after months away. It feels like finding the one other soul on this planet that matches mine. It feels like home.

My hands ache to touch him, and I roam his body, remembering every muscle, every ridge, every valley of his hard, sculpted frame.

"I just need *you*, mo ghràidh," he murmurs against my mouth. Wrapping his hands under my thighs, he hoists me onto the counter, and my legs open easily for him. His mouth trails from my lips and down my neck. He pops a button off my blouse, tearing my shirt open to get his lips on my breasts.

I let out a loud whimper when his tongue finds the pink bud of my nipple. "I needed *this*," he growls against my flesh. My hand digs into his hair as I pull him closer. But his fingers don't stop. More buttons go flying as he tears my shirt clean open, shimmying it down my arms and unclasping my bra until I'm topless on my kitchen counter for him. His coarse beard scratches my skin, but I welcome the pain. I need more of it.

When his fingers start fumbling with the button of my pants, a thrill of excitement courses through me. It doesn't take him long until they're undone, and he's working them down my legs, pulling my panties with them. My pants are barely off my ankles when Killian drops to his knees and presses his face between my legs.

"This," he growls against my sex. "I've been dreaming about the taste of your cunt for eight months. *This* is what I needed."

I let out a shriek of pleasure as he licks at me ravenously and sucks on my clit. My back arches, and my head hangs as I'm suddenly reminded of what pleasure feels like.

He touches my pussy like he's missed it, spreading my folds and sinking his long thick fingers inside me. My body winds up quickly, and it only takes a few thrusts for me to lose control. Fireworks explode inside me, radiating pleasure in pulsing waves behind my closed eyelids.

"Fuck me," I cry out, suddenly desperate for him.

Standing in a rush, he kisses me, letting me taste my own arousal on his tongue. His shirt falls to the floor before he starts on his pants. While he works them down, I touch his chest, kissing the spot above his heart and running my fingers through the patches of hair.

When his cock springs free, I forget how to breathe all over again. His size takes me by surprise again, and I reach for him, eager to wrap my fingers around his length. A satisfied groan vibrates from his chest as I do. Lazily, I stroke his shaft, savoring the way it drags reactions from his body. Moans, expressions, trembles.

A drop of cum leaks from the tip of his cock, so I wipe it

with my thumb and bring it to my lips, humming when the flavor touches my tongue. At the sight, he turns feral.

With a grunt, he grabs my hips and yanks me to the edge of the counter.

"Watch it with me," he orders with a husky rasp in his voice. As he lines up his cock, I reach one hand for his chest and the other for his jaw, holding him tight as he slowly works his way inside me.

He hooks one arm under my leg for more access as he slowly drives in deeper, stretching me until I have him all. Pleasure, relief, and elation flow through my body, making me dizzy. Our foreheads touch as we stare down at the place we are joined, and it's perfect.

Pulling out ever so slightly, he eases back in. I can feel his restraint crumbling. Pulling him closer for a kiss, I bite his bottom lip, making him howl and thrust his hips harder. He digs a hand in my hair and jerks my head back, smiling wickedly at me as he picks up his speed, fucking me with such force he has to hold me in place.

I smile up at him as our bodies smack together in an echoing cadence of pleasure. It's all so perfect that I don't know if I've ever been happier in my life.

"What a wee dirty wife you are," he grunts, staring down at me with smug pride.

"*Your* dirty wife," I reply with a sly grin.

"You love your husband's cock, don't you?"

My hold on him tightens, and the pleasure starts to crescendo again. "Yes," I cry out. "I love my husband's cock."

He pounds harder, dragging me off the counter entirely. I'm barely hanging on as he fucks me, tossing me around like his rag doll. Another orgasm detonates inside me, and I let out a scream, clutching my legs around him tighter.

He lets out a guttural roar as his own climax rolls over

him. His cock shudders inside me as I wrap my arms around his neck, holding tight to him as we ride out these waves of pleasure together.

Finally, once his cock is spent, he rests me back on the counter and peppers kisses all over my chest and neck, and face.

"I love you," he whispers with each one, and I swear I could die of happiness right here.

All this time, I was afraid Killian would move on without me, or that I was the one dragging him down. Instead, I managed to guide him out of the hell he had been living in. And I didn't even know it.

"I love you," I whisper in return.

"I mean it, Sylvie," he says, lifting his eyes to my face. "I'm here, and I'm all yours. For as long or as much as you want me."

A smile stretches across my face as I pull his lips to mine. "I want you forever, Killian."

"Good," he mumbles into the kiss.

When he finally eases out of me, I can already feel the warm cum sliding out of me. With a wicked grin, he leans down and pushes it back in. I bite my bottom lip as I watch him.

"Then you keep this," he mumbles before pressing a kiss to my inner thigh. "Forever."

Chapter Forty-One

KILLIAN IS OUTSTRETCHED ON MY BED, NAKED ON HIS stomach, and I can't seem to stop staring at him. He's really here. It feels impossible but incredible at the same time.

"Stop watching me sleep. It's creepy," he mumbles into the pillow.

"Get over it," I reply.

"Were you really that surprised?" he asks, sounding half asleep.

"Yes," I say emphatically. "It's been so long I was starting to assume you were just trying to figure out a nice way to get rid of me."

He groans as he hooks an arm around my waist and tugs me nearer to him. "You're still my wife, Sylvie. I'm not just going to *get rid of you*."

"Technically…" I start, about to point out the fact that we are neither real nor fake married anymore.

"Don't say it," he groans. "We will be fixing that as soon as I recover from this bloody jet lag."

"What?" I snap, staring at him in shock. "Getting married?"

"Yes," he mumbles.

I let out a gasp as I try to move away. "You're not even going to ask me first?"

"I don't need to ask you," he complains.

"Why not?" I shriek.

"Because I know what you'll say. What the fuck is the point of asking?"

"To be romantic!" I try to climb off the bed, but he doesn't let me get far. Holding me around my waist, he pins me down to the bed, shifting his weight on top of me. I let out a howl of laughter as I struggle to get away, but he's too strong.

"Since when are you and I romantic, wench?" Putting his face in the crook of my neck, he growls, making me yelp as goose bumps erupt all over my skin.

"Fine. I'll marry you again, but you have to stop calling me names like *cow* and *wench*," I say with a moan as his growls turn into kisses.

"No deal," he replies curtly.

My arms wrap around him as I smile. Then I find my mind going back to the house as it so often does. "So…" I start. "Did you really give the house to your aunt?"

"Yes," he says on an exhale.

"And you're okay with that?"

"It's just a house. If it means that much to her, she can have it."

"Where will you live?" I ask, although I already know the answer.

"With my wife, of course," he replies, nuzzling closer to my body.

With his face buried in the pillow and his hair strewn in a mess around him, I stare at him and try to find the differences from the man I knew at the manor. But I don't see anything. It's just him in a different setting.

He does seem at ease now. And not the same sort of *at ease* I thought I saw before when I tried to tell myself he was fine. Now, he seems free.

"How are you feeling?" I ask, brushing his hair out of his face to plant a kiss to his bearded cheek.

"I'm fine," he groans.

"And you won't lie to me?" I ask, biting my lip. "If you're not fine, you'll tell me?"

He lets out a sigh and rolls onto his back. "Yes, mo ghràidh. If I start to feel anything, I'll tell ye. But I promise, I didn't make this trip until I was sure I could do it without worrying you."

A tight smile pulls at my lips as I set my cheek on his chest and wrap my arms around his midsection.

"I'm proud of you," I whisper, feeling him kiss the top of my head.

"Thank you," he replies softly.

———

I wake up early the next morning, and Killian is already sitting up in the bed next to me.

"How long have you been up?" I ask groggily.

In nothing but his tight boxer briefs, he holds up the green book in his hands, and it takes me a moment to recognize it as my own. "Long enough to read this again. My cell phone doesn't seem to work here."

"I can't believe you're reading that again. I own other books, you know?"

He shrugs. "This is my favorite."

I smile to myself as he continues to read. Then he looks down at me as he adds, "Do you have anything new?"

"It's not done yet."

"Are you going to publish this one?" he asks, stroking my hair.

"Nope."

With a smirk, he leans down and kisses my temple. Thinking about writing makes me think of my mom and the weird encounter yesterday. "My mom came and saw me yesterday," I say, making him tense immediately.

"Did she stop by to compliment your furniture?" he asks sarcastically.

I chuckle into my pillow, remembering her obsession with the rug in Killian's house. "No. She came by Enid's gallery. I don't think she was expecting to see me. But she sure had a lot to say."

"Oh yeah?" He's on guard and skeptical as he waits for my response.

"Yeah, she told me what a terrible mother she was and what a good person I turned out to be."

He lets out a laugh and then scrutinizes my reaction. "Wait, you're serious?"

I nod. "It surprised me too."

He sits back and shrugs his shoulders. "It must have been the rug that knocked some sense into her."

"It might have," I laugh.

His eyes rake over me again before he drops the book on the end table and lays his body over my back, grabbing my hands and putting them above my head as he grinds into me from behind.

I let out a sultry moan as he groans into my ear. "This is one way to wake up," I say with a squeak as he kisses his way along the back of my neck.

His cock grows incredibly fast in his boxers as he continues rubbing against my ass. Before I know it, he's pulling my hips up, positioning himself between my legs, and thrusting himself inside me.

"Eventually, I'll learn to take my time with you again," he

grunts as he slams into me again. "But right now, I need you too much."

As his hand slides up my throat, a wicked smile stretches across my face. "You won't find me complaining," I moan.

It takes most of the day to get us out of bed. Every time we try, we end up screwing instead. When we do finally get hungry enough, we manage to get showered and out the door.

As we walk together down the street, I keep his hand in mine, squeezing his fingers and clutching to his arm like he might float away on a breeze. I love showing him New York the same way he showed me his property. Especially since it's spring and New York is beautiful in the spring.

We end up taking a longer walk than we intended. To neither of our surprise, we find ourselves at the City Clerk's office.

As we're waiting in line, he turns to me and whispers, "Are you sure you don't want a big wedding?"

I rest my head on his arm. "I'm sure. We already had a wedding."

"It was bloody awful. We hated each other."

The woman in front of us turns and gives us a quizzical look.

"I know," I reply to him quietly. "But that's just part of our story. I don't want to replace it."

He shrugs. "If you insist."

When the clerk informs us that there is a twenty-four hour mandatory waiting period, Killian slips her a disarming smile and begs in his thick Scottish accent.

"You see," he says. "We've already been married, for almost a year. Far more than twenty-four hours, and I came a very long way to make her my wife again. You wouldn't make a desperate, lovesick Scotsman wait, would you?"

To my surprise, the clerk actually falls for it. After a heavy sigh, and a little fudging up the date on our documents, she directs us to head into the office and wait with the others. We take our seat between other couples who can't possibly wait another moment until their union becomes official.

With the filled-in papers in my lap, I rest my head on his shoulder. There are no contracts this time. No ten million dollars or historic mansions. There is just us—two people who, by some slip of fate, ended up in the same place at the same time. It feels like a miracle, and I don't intend to let go this time.

"Devereaux and Barclay," the woman at the front calls.

Killian and I walk to the front together, smiling at the clerk as she reads us the same dull terms of our marriage she reads to everyone. And it might seem like the least romantic wedding in the world, but no one here knows that we've already lived these vows.

Our love has survived the trials and come out the other side stronger for it. Like most relationships, we entered ours as two people who only cared about ourselves, but as marriage tends to do, we learned to put each other first. It's no longer about him or me, but us.

"Ms. Devereaux," the clerk says to me. "Do you promise to uphold the vows of this marriage and keep this man for the rest of your life?"

"Do you, darling?" Killian murmurs with a lopsided smirk. "Do you promise to keep me?"

With a smile on my face and his hands held in mine, I gaze into his eyes as I graciously reply.

"I do."

Epilogue

One year later

"LORNA'S DEAD."

The words pull me out of a dreamless sleep, and I peek one eye open to stare at my husband just to make sure he really said that.

He has his phone in his hand, and he turns toward me with alarm in his features. Quickly I sit up.

"Wait. You're serious?"

"Dead serious."

I snicker. "Killian."

"The old hag is gone. Dec just texted me."

Leaning over, I glance at his phone, and there it is. A single text from his younger brother.

Aunt Lorna passed away in her sleep last night.

"Holy shit," I mutter. "What does this mean? For the house."

Killian shrugs. "I'm guessing she left it to Anna. She sure as hell didn't leave it to me."

"Not that you'd want it…right?" I ask, looking up into his eyes.

Killian and I have made a home here in New York. Sure, we haven't exactly set down roots yet, but we do have a nice life at the moment, enjoying this honeymoon phase we're in.

But I'd be lying if I said I haven't been thinking about what the future holds for us. I'm not even from Scotland, and I'm itching to go back. He says he's fine where we are, but if we had the opportunity to live in Barclay again, would we take it?

"Nah," he replies with a confident shake of his head. "If I go back there, I'm afraid I'd fall right back into the same old routine. Here, I finally feel alive."

Turning toward me, he gives me a charming little smirk. My love for him swells in my chest like a tiny little bomb that goes off every time he smiles at me.

"Besides, I don't need a big house to do this," he says as he drops his phone and tackles me down to the pillows. Burying his face in my neck, his thick beard scratches my skin as he kisses and nibbles the sensitive flesh.

I squeal in delight as my legs wrap around him. And then just as our laughter turns into moans, his phone rings.

"Och," he groans. "Fuck off." He flings his phone off the bed and resumes kissing his way down my neck and across my collarbone.

"I'm willing to bet my left tit it's your sister," I say as he inches his way down.

"Well, at the moment your left tit is mine," he replies with a groan, his teeth gently closing around the sensitive bud. My back arches as I dig my fingers in his hair.

But only moments after the buzzing of the phone stops, it starts back up again.

"She won't stop," I say breathlessly.

"And neither will I."

He continues to kiss his way down, but just as he reaches my belly button, the phone rings for a third time.

"Fucking cow!" he bellows as he reaches down to the floor to quiet the incessant device. With irritation in his eyes, he lies back between my legs as he hits the Answer Call button. "I've got my mouth just inches away from my wife's pussy, so you better make this good."

Letting out a laugh, I cover my mouth as I listen for Anna's response. I can't make out her words, but I can hear her shrieking at him.

"Aye. I know she's dead. Good riddance."

Anna screams at him so loud it echoes through our bedroom. Then, she continues on and Killian's demeanor changes from annoyance to intrigue.

"She what?"

Anna continues on and Killian's gaze travels up to my face.

"What is it?" I whisper.

"She left it to me?"

"Left what?" I ask.

Killian listens intently to what Anna is saying, and after a moment, he lets out a heavy sigh. "All right," he says with resignation. "I'll think about it. Thanks for the call."

After he ends the call and sets his phone down, he gazes up at me with concern. "The bitch left me the fucking house."

"Why would she do that?" I ask. "After all the trouble to take it away from you?"

He shrugs. "I don't know, my wee little wife."

Hugging my body closer, he rests his cheek on my stomach, using my body as a source of comfort. I stroke his shoulders and his hair. Feeling the tension in his muscles, the answer is immediate and easy.

Lifting his face, I force him to gaze into my eyes.

"We don't have to do anything. You don't have to go back to the house. We don't have to go anywhere. If the thought brings you any stress, we'll never return. We have everything we need right here."

His brows relax and the lines of his forehead disappear. "You're right. But what about the house? I can't let it out of the family."

"You have brothers, Killian. Let them deal with it. You've gone through enough."

Finally, with a sigh, he nods. "You're right."

"I know I'm right," I reply astutely, making him smile.

"I have everything I need right here."

Lifting up, he stares down at my naked body, pressing his lips to my belly. But instead of moving his way down like I expect him to, he picks up his phone and types out a message.

"What are you doing?" I ask, running my nails along his scalp.

"Sending a text to my brother."

"What did you say?"

The phone blares a *whooshing* sound as the text is sent. Then, Killian shows me the screen. The words in his reply have me feeling suddenly at ease.

Barclay Manor is all yours now.

"I'm proud of you," I say, tugging his mouth to mine for a kiss.

Finally, he pulls away with a wicked smirk. Then he glances down the length of my body as he says, "Now, where the fuck was I?"

I let out a giggle as he works his way down and presses his lips between my legs.

**KEEP READING FOR AN EXCERPT
OF THE FIRST BOOK IN SARA CATE'S
SALACIOUS PLAYERS' CLUB SERIES**

Prologue

"So I HAD A FISTFUL OF HER HAIR IN MY HAND, AND WE WERE both in the moment when I looked her right in the eye and said, 'Suck my cock like a good little girl.' The next thing I knew, she reared back her fist and clocked me right in the face."

"Oh shit!" Garrett curses with a grimace.

"Damn!" Hunter bellows.

Across the table, Maggie, the only woman in our group, looks horrified.

I wince, poking at the raw purple bruise growing around my eye socket.

"I don't think she liked that," Maggie adds with a light chuckle before taking a sip of her white wine.

"You think?" I burst out, grabbing my beer and holding the cold glass against my face to quell the throbbing ache pulsing around my eyeball. It hurts only half as much as my pride. The humiliation from getting my first real shiner from a pretty little brunette I had been flirting with for weeks and was beyond eager to stick my dick into being the worst of my injuries.

"I mean…I thought we were getting along great. She seemed kinky enough, and she definitely appeared into it, but I guess I was wrong. Not a fan of a little sexy degradation, apparently."

The table grows silent for a moment. My three coworkers and I have made these Thursday night happy hours at the bar a little tradition. We collectively hate the entertainment company we work for. When we took these jobs, we did it for the excitement and love of the industry. Now we meet for drinks once a week to rant about how we would run the company differently and how much better we'd do on our own. But we're all talk. None of us are ready to leave our steady positions to start new ones.

And more than occasionally, we talk about sex, each of us dishing out our dirtiest bedroom secrets like a bunch of old men sharing epic war stories. Even our modest Maggie joins in. Aside from Hunter and his long-term girlfriend, Isabel, we're all single, and we all intend to keep it that way. One of the perks of working in the entertainment industry is that we work nights, parties, and drunk soirees, which means we get laid fairly consistently, giving us ample conversation topics, so we don't have to spend *all* of our time together bitching about the company we work for.

"Fuck, man," Garrett replies with a contemplative look. "It's bullshit that there isn't a way to match people up by the kinky shit they like to do in the bedroom."

Immediately, the table breaks out in laughter. Because this is what Garrett does. He makes jokes and expects a roll of amusing reactions after every sentence that comes out of his mouth, something we've come to anticipate.

"I'm fucking serious. How nice would it be if you could

meet up with someone who likes the same twisted shit you do? You wouldn't have to hide it or be embarrassed by the kinks that get your panties wet."

"You're fucking crazy, Garrett," Hunter replies, but by the time I set my empty glass down on the table, I can't get the thought out of my head. Why don't dating apps match people by their kinks? Or better yet…what if you could hire someone to fulfill those desires?

And a safe place to indulge in them.

It dawns on me at that moment that a group of people with experience in the entertainment industry might have the right skills to pull something like this off. If only we had the guts to take the leap. It could start with a dating service for more than just booty calls and hookups—but something serious where people didn't have to feel so ashamed for what they enjoy.

It could only grow from there. An app to a service…and then someday, a real kink club.

"I am not," Garrett argues. "Who here doesn't have some freaky bedroom desires you've always wanted to do but are too afraid to ask? I mean, obviously, Emerson isn't afraid to ask."

They laugh again, and Hunter elbows me in the ribs, but I don't reply because I'm still thinking about this idea.

"Come on. I'm serious," Garrett says. "Out of all the shit you've done, what is the one thing you wish you could ask for? You know you have something. So let's hear it."

"You first," Maggie replies with a smug grin. As the only woman, and a slightly reserved one at that, Maggie has mastered the art of spinning conversations around on us, keeping the attention off of her whenever she can.

"Fine," he says.

I sort of tune them out for a minute while they each share their deepest, darkest sexual fantasies because, like Garrett predicted, everyone has one. And they're not all that weird really.

It has me thinking...if everyone at this table has their specific kink they're too afraid to talk about...then does everyone at this bar? Everyone in this town? The country? The world?

"All right, Emerson," Hunter says, nudging me in the shoulder. "Your turn."

"Oh, that's easy," Garrett cuts me off. "Didn't you hear his story? Emerson likes to degrade and get punched in the face for it."

The crowd erupts in laughter, and I join in, but I don't respond. With a smile around my glass, I take a drink, but I don't indulge any more. Because they may think degradation is my style, but that's not it at all.

The next morning, we get the call that the company we work for is going under. They're filing for bankruptcy and we're all out of a job, but before any of us can file for unemployment, we have a business plan. I head the company. Garrett handles the clients. Hunter works with the developers. And Maggie manages all of us. And it's that easy.

Salacious Players' Club is born.

Rule #1: Never put up with a douchebag boyfriend— dump that loser.

Charlie

"WHAT THE FUCK IS WRONG WITH YOU, CHARLIE?" BEAU SNAPS when he sees me pull up with my windows down. My jaw clenches as I climb out my car and slam the door behind me. I glance back at my little sister, watching from the passenger seat, and swallow down the humiliation at her hearing my stupid ex-boyfriend berate me on the front lawn of his new house. I don't even bother asking what I've done because, with him, it's always somehow my fault.

"Fuck off, Beau," I mutter through clenched teeth. "Just give me my half of the deposit so I can be on my way."

He stops in his tracks between the pickup truck and the front door of his house with a moving box in his arms. "I wish I could, but you weren't at the final walk-through with the landlord, so they sent the money to my dad. You'll have to pick it up from him."

"Your dad? What? Why?"

Beau carries the box labeled *Xbox shit* into the house and

drops it on the floor next to his TV before returning to the truck. He's renting a new place with his best friend, and it would seem he's still holding a grudge against me for breaking up with him. Beau and I dated for fifteen months, six of those we spent living in a shitty rental where we quickly learned that we actually hated each other. Apparently, we could date and sleep together casually, but being in a mature live-together relationship was a no-go.

It only took three months in the apartment for him to cheat on me—or to get caught, I should say.

"Yes, Charlie. My dad. He was listed on the lease as our cosigner, and when you weren't around to pick up the deposit, they sent it to him."

"Fuck," I mumble. "Well, I'm sorry I wasn't here, Beau, but I was busy *working*." I make sure to emphasize the word, since I've been the one carrying two jobs while he can barely hold down one for more than a month.

"Frying corn dogs at the skating rink hardly makes you the responsible one in this relationship."

"At least I could pay the bills."

"Let's not do this again," he shouts as he slams the tailgate of the truck closed. Beau doesn't have *anger* problems, per se. He's just an asshole.

"You started it."

I glance back at Sophie, watching from the car. She has a tight-lipped expression with her eyebrows pinched together. A look that clearly says she hates everything about the interaction between me and my ex.

I'll give her credit. Since the beginning, my fourteen-year-old sister has been the biggest Beau critic. Of course, back then I was starry-eyed and blinded by love. And at only fourteen, she's still immune to the sorcery of guys with sandy-brown curls, piercing blue eyes, six-foot frames, and abs for days.

"So what am I supposed to do?" I ask when Beau continues on with his unpacking while ignoring my presence.

"Well, if you want your half of the deposit, I guess you're going to have to get it from my dad."

"Can't you just get it for me?"

For some stupid reason, I feel like *I'm* the one being a pain in the ass. Beau was always like this. He just had a way of making me feel worthless and desperate for any positive attention from him, so much so that I spent more time trying to please him than actually being happy—something that became abundantly clear after we broke up. Sometimes we really can't see the forest for the trees, as they say.

"You know I don't talk to that asshole anymore."

"So you're not going to get your half of the deposit back?"

"Not worth it," he snaps. I follow him back into the house.

"Well, I can't afford to lose that money, Beau."

With a long, annoyed sigh, he spins on me and rolls his eyes. "Fine. Here." He pulls his phone from his back pocket and types something quickly with a furrow in his brow. A moment later, my phone vibrates from my purse. "That's his address. Take it up with him."

Then, he just walks away, leaving me with my jaw hanging open. "Seriously? That's it?"

"If you really wanted the money, you should have met with the landlord yesterday."

"You're an asshole," I mumble, before turning and leaving him to unpack his shit in his new place. Walking down the driveway toward the car where my sister waits with her AirPods in, I do my best to not appear as bothered as I am. But as I climb into the driver's seat and shut the door, I feel the intensity of her sympathetic eyes on me. My forehead drops to the steering wheel as I fight the urge to cry.

"Beau's a dick," she says quietly, and I laugh. Letting Sophie

cuss around me is sort of the big-sister deal. My mother has a
fit when she hears either of us swearing, so I let Soph do it
when we're alone. And in this case, I can't really argue with her.

"I know."

"At least you broke up with him."

"Yeah. Too bad I still don't have my money." Fishing my
phone out of my purse, I open the text from Beau.

"Why not?"

"Because I'm an idiot and messed up. So now I have to
go pick it up from his dad, and I'm willing to bet that asshole
didn't fall far from the asshole tree."

"So let's go get it," she replies, looking a little too pumped
to go pick up money from a complete stranger.

"I have no clue where this guy even lives. I'm not taking
you." As I click on the address in the text, it pulls up the map
app and shows a red pin on a street directly next to the ocean-
front. "That can't be right."

"What is it?" she asks, leaning over.

"It says his house is over in the Oceanview district."

"Let's goooo."

I laugh again and ruffle her short, faded blue hair. It's still
growing out from the buzz cut she gave herself last summer, so
now it hangs just below her ears.

"Nice try, little Smurf, but you have piano lessons, and
Mrs. Wilcox will have my head if you're late again."

Sophie rolls her eyes and gives me a dramatic pout as we
pull out of Beau's driveway and head across town to the high
school where Sophie gets her lessons. The entire way, I replay
every moment of the fight with Beau, his harsh tone etched
into my memory. And a feeling of dread settles in my gut as I
think about having to confront his dad.

Beau rarely spoke about his family when we were together,
and whenever I asked about them, he would just change the

subject, as if he was ashamed or embarrassed. Getting his dad to cosign for us last year was hard enough, but shortly after, there was a rift between them and Beau stopped talking to him altogether. At first, we bonded over our mutual disdain for our fathers. And if Beau's dad is anything like mine, the whole interaction is sure to be a fucking blast.

Acknowledgments

Sometimes, a couple comes along, and their story steals my heart. Killian and Sylvie will forever have a special place, and I can honestly say I had a blast writing this book.

If I tried to do this alone, it would be an unorganized, unedited, unpublished mess of a story with a scrambled timeline and constantly changing eye color. Which means I have a lot of people to thank for making it what it is now.

My editor—Rachel Gilmer, and my marketing guru, Alyssa Garcia, and the rest of the team at Sourcebooks Casablanca. Thanks for letting me, no—*encouraging me*—to be me.

My agent—Savannah Greenwell. You're never getting rid of me.

My assistant and spreadsheet mistress—Lori Alexander.

My biggest cheerleader and overall voice of reason—Amanda Anderson.

My beta readers—Jill and Adrian. Your unending support (and emojis) mean the world.

My new Scottish friends—Rebecca and Ashleigh. I loved our chats about kilts and stovies and Hogmanay. Thank you for bringing Scotland to me.

My family—Jeremy, kids, Mom, and Misty. Love you all.

And last, to every single one of my readers who continue to find space on their Kindles and shelves for a spicy Sara Cate title. Who put up with me sometimes making them cry or scream or…you know. Thanks for being here and for keeping me.

Much love,
Sara

About the Author

Sara Cate is a *USA Today* bestselling romance author who weaves complex characters, heart-wrenching stories, and forbidden romance into every page of her spicy novels. Sara's writing is as hot as a desert summer, with twists and turns that will leave you breathless. Best known for the Salacious Players' Club series, Sara strives to take risks and provide her readers with an experience that is as arousing as it is empowering. When she's not penning steamy tales, she can be found soaking up the Arizona sun, jamming to Taylor Swift, and watching Marvel movies with her family.

Website: saracatebooks.com
Facebook: saracatebooks
Instagram: @saracatebooks
TikTok: @saracatebooks